THY MAKER

Generative A.I. was NOT used in the formulation, creation, editing, or promotion of this story or any of the official artwork associated with it, nor will it ever be in the future.

ISBN: 978-1-7637536-8-6

Art design and original art by Dylan Nguyen. Image assets licensed by iStock and Shutterstock.

Acknowledgements

For Mum, Dad, and Grandma for supporting my dumb obsession with writing, Steph for being my harshest critic and biggest fan, and Tom for showing me that creative stuff is worth doing.

Part One: The Knight

I

In Search of the Pious

Blades of wheat glistened in the sunlight as they danced in the wind's gentle breath. The immense field of shimmering gold pushed and pulled like a sea, as the sound of its rustling seemed to mimic crashing waves. As Alric rode along the pitted highway, the wagon dragged by his horse, Nocht, thudded against the dirt. Its wheels squealed at the beginning of each turn and seemed to harmonise with the clacking of his plate armour. He gazed about with the visor of his bascinet helmet raised. The weave of sights and sounds gave him something to pay attention to; it was almost like his personal bard during those long journeys. As he gently thrummed his gauntleted fingers against his saddle, he savoured the smell of wildflowers that drifted through the air. The outskirts of a village crept its way closer to him. He saw commoners tilling the fields, sowing seeds, herding cattle, and gathering fruit from blooming trees. The hamlet of Oak was so named for the single oak tree that stood in its town square. It was a wretched, greying husk with branches that jerked about at sharp angles like bolts of lightning. The tree certainly looked healthier during Alric's last visit several years ago, but the town itself had grown much larger. Houses of wattle and daub with thatch roofs fanned outward from the central square, carefully watched over by a contingent of volunteer guards.

The knight brought Nocht to a hitching post, dismounted with quite a racket, then looped her reins onto said post. The horse huffed angrily while her rider tied the lines into a knot. Alric ruffled her mane and rubbed her cheek before setting out.

As he strode down the path, he heard footfalls culminating behind him. "Brother! Wait a moment, good Brother!" Alric turned his helmeted head to peer over his shoulder. He saw a man dressed in a gambeson and kettle hat. In his hand was a spear. "It's not every day we see one of your Order down this way. I'm Howard, Howard Mason. Captain o' tha guard."

"God be with thee. I am Alric," he said.

Howard whistled. "It's a pleasure, Brother Alric. What brings you down ta these parts? Nothin' too serious, I 'ope."

Alric rested a hand on the pommel of his longsword which hung in its scabbard by his side. "I heard tell in Birchwood of pious folk vanishing from here. All who praise the Father are subject to protection by the Knights Thestor, and as such, I wish to assist thee in thy search."

"R-Right… Tha whole town's been terrified. We ain't been able ta find nothin'...some town guard we are, ay?"

The knight of Saint Thestus exhaled sharply. "All shall be as God wills it; take solace in that truth and wallow not in doubt. Now, tell me of the vanished."

"Sara was a mother o' two children. Tha father left some time ago; ain't no one knows where 'e went. Without 'er, tha poor children don't got any family. Then we got Erik, tha woodsman's son. Fine young man, not like 'im ta just up and disappear. Ta be completely honest, not like Sara either. A couple of tha others though, Gerome, Victor, Mary, they ain't tha best sort. But that's a lot of folk ta just vanish inta tha night."

Suddenly, Alric felt something strike the back of his calf. When he looked down, he saw an inflated pig's bladder slowly rolling away from him and towards a pair of horrified children several paces away. The older one was a girl and the other a boy.

"Liam…Josephine…what did I tell ya 'bout being careful, ay?" Howard scalded as he planted his free hand onto his hip.

Alric knelt and waved at the two children. For a moment, he glanced up at Howard and jerked his head towards the young ones, trying to ascertain if they belonged to the missing woman. A flash of understanding gleamed in Howard's eyes and he nodded eagerly. Alric sent his attention back to the children. "Be not afraid. Come hither," he said as he scooped the ball up and handed it to them.

Liam cowered behind his sister as they shuffled forward. Josephine slowly grabbed the ball and plucked it from Alric's hand. "T-Thank you, milord."

With a laugh, Alric said, "I am no lord, child. My name is Alric; I am a knight brother sworn to the Order of Saint Thestus, so thou shalt call me *Brother* Alric."

"Y-Yes, mi–" she cut herself off before she said it again. "Yes, B-Brother Alric. Me mum told me 'bout the Thestors before. Ya find tha witches and heretics and monsters and infidels. You keep 'em from hurting us."

"That is correct, well done. And, on occasion, we may also seek out those who have lost their way." Josephine's eyes lit up like stars upon the night sky. "Tell me of thy mother. Dost thou knowest where she went?"

Josephine's lips thinned for a moment. She glanced up at Howard, to her brother, then back to Alric. "S-She made me promise not ta tell no one."

Alric held the girl by her shoulder. "Josephine, dost thou wish thy mother found?" She nodded. "I cannot seek her out if thou do not confess. Then, she shall be forever lost. Is *that* what thou wish?"

The girl finally decided to cooperate. "Mummy used ta go out at night to tha forest, tha Tindertwigs. She told me an' Liam ta never tell no one." Alric furrowed his brow. His hand tightened slightly on Josephine's tiny shoulder. He watched her eyes twitch in discomfort. "I-I don't know what she did out there. She never told me."

The Thestor's eyes narrowed as he released his grip on her. He reached into a pouch on his belt, procured four pence, and handed two to Josephine and the other two to Liam. With amazement in their eyes, the children accepted Alric's gift as he stood back up and towered over them. Howard chuckled. "My, my, that's a lot o' money. Whaddaya say?" he prompted.

"Thank you, Brother Alric," they said in unison.

Howard pointed down the road. "Go get some sweets from Gert now, will ya? And no eatin' 'em all at once, you hear?"

Liam and Josephine bolted down the dirt road like wild dogs, instantly invigorated by the mention of sweets. Howard bashfully scratched the back of his neck as Alric asked, "Be the Tindertwigs far from here?"

"You could walk it, I guess...but in that plate o' yours, it might be a little drainin'. Maybe ya should doff it?"

With an irritated huff, Alric loomed forebodingly over Howard. The fool was asking him to void his Oath of Vigilance. He was either a simpleton, or a blasphemer. "Thy inability to ask a child the most basic of questions is cause enough for thee to receive my ire, but *this*... Thou art fortunate that I do not strike thee for thy ignorance."

Howard jolted backwards. "F-Forgive me! I can take penance if you'd wish it!"

The knight waved his hand dismissively. "I have more pressing matters to attend to. I shall not forgive any further lapses in knowledge; either educate thyself on the word of the Father, or keep thy mouth firmly shut."

"Right...w-well... Lemme know if ya find anythin' o' note. Tha families will be...uh...mighty grateful."

The forest of spindly black trees, aptly named the Tindertwigs by the locals, was visible from the village. It had been masked by the ghoulish embrace of a mist that had blown in after Alric had reached town. There was no path to follow, but the grass bowed lower in a line towards the trees indicating that trips to the place were not few and far between.

Clouds in the sky left blotched shadows on the yellow field that consumed almost everything in sight; everything but the legion of sickly, leafless trees that stood sentry over the village. As the lone knight drew closer to the forest, its jagged shadows fell onto him, shielding his eyes from the setting white sun. His knees, shoulders, and back ached, having been burdened with the weight of his armour for the entire day. He relished the pain as if it were a gift bestowed from up high. Before long, he had been swallowed by the trees and found himself gazing around the immediate area. The soft rustling of the evening wind through the canopy of bare branches was the only sound Alric's ears discerned. He saw nothing but dead wood.

The Knight Thestor wandered away from the edge of the forest and kept his eyes sweeping the forlorn wood for any sign of life. Eventually, he stumbled upon a clearing. Alric could imagine that the place would have looked rather stunning during the daytime, but all he could see then was a veil of shadows enveloping an open patch of darkened grass.

Amidst the open field were pieces of debris; what appeared to be a snapped signpost. A pile of some sort stood at the far end of the clearing. Alric knelt on the edge of the tree line. Despite how much he squinted, the knight could not ascertain what exactly comprised said pile...but he did perceive jittery movement near the stack of objects.

Four diminutive creatures eagerly paced about on four legs and dragged what looked like bodies towards the pile. The creatures themselves looked like headless dogs with a single clawed-arm extending from where their missing heads should be. With those singular appendages, they handled the dead as if they were sacks of grain. Their legs scuttled about beneath them to retain their balance as they heaved the bodies through the dirt.

Alric sighed to himself with a soft shake of his head. Goblins. Being rather small and physically weak, they hoarded corpses like canine vultures. It was a pile of bodies on the other end of the clearing. They possessed glands capable of covering their massive stacks of food in a strong film which allowed them to drag the lot back to their den. They were usually frightened off easily enough, but with the kingdoms of Tritham and Valtheaux at each other's throats for almost a hundred years, the sheer volume of dead seemed to have roused their tenacity. The goblin sightings had grown in recent years, as did the number of them in their foraging parties. However, as they were ill-able to protect themselves, they were always accompanied by at least one manticore. It would be unwise to proceed until he found it. Alric watched as a goblin began rubbing its mandibles together, slowly producing segments of the translucent sac that would ensnare their game. Each animal would spin but one portion of the net, then seal it together once complete.

Finally, as the knight looked toward the other side of the tree line, he spotted their guardian. The manticore stood as still as the columns of ash beside it, with its tail poised for attack. It resembled a bull, only headless just as the goblins were, with a massive rigid tail. Able to spin about in any direction, there was no escaping its sting.

The tail was incredibly dangerous, so much so that tales were told of how manticores were born of black magic; a belief that Alric *knew* to be true. Whatever the tail pointed at was liable to combust into smouldering embers without warning. In his experience, only a witch armed with a black magic staff could achieve similar results.

Alric wasn't eager to battle the scavengers alone, but the pack was incredibly close to Oak. The goblins could easily chase down the peasants and bludgeon them to death. For more troublesome quarry, like the town guards, the manticore could detonate them into shredded ribbons of matter without much effort at all. Alric's Order was governed by the many chapters of the Rule of Saint Thestus, but even more important than the Rule were the Four Attestations; every Knight Thestor must live by them to them in order to prove his devotion to the one true God: the Father. The Fourth Attestation declared that all Knights Thestor must not refuse assistance to any God-fearing man or woman in need. The folk in the township of Oak had become those in need, as the pack of scavengers would surely pose them threat in time. To refuse their plight would be an act of heresy.

As slowly and cautiously as he could, Alric lowered his helmet's visor and slunk behind the first line of trees. He kept his arms bent and his knees as straight as possible to prevent his plate armour from clanking against itself; as long as he focused on moving in that matter, he could be almost completely silent.

He slowly crept forth, working his way around to the manticore as the goblins continued spinning their sac. He heard only the whirring of the goblins' legs as all four of them circled the mass of bodies in order to wrap it securely. Every step he took filled his heart with dread. He had seen people blown apart by manticores. He had been showered by insides and blood as compatriots popped beside him. As he closed in on the robust creature, he began to hear the constant rumbling of its insides. It remained completely still. The black bars of wood scrolled by Alric's already impeded vision; all he could see of the outside world with his visor shut was a narrow horizontal line immediately ahead of him.

He gripped the handle of the blade that rested on the right side of his belt. Alric had found that his rondel dagger served exquisitely against the gaps in the chitinous armour of the foragers.

The grass swayed, following the cadence of the sparse foliage above. Alric's surcoat was brushed by the same wind. All the while, the tailed behemoth did not shift, not even slightly. Its tail slowly swept over the defenceless goblins, like the eyes of a wary cattle farmer over his herd.

Against all the sense within him, Alric emerged from cover and approached the manticore as he unsheathed his rondel dagger. The weapon's blade was as long as his forearm and tapered down to a tiny point which made it exceptional at piercing mail, gambeson and tendon alike.

Alric tore into a sprint and leapt at the manticore while its tail was pointed away. As soon as he did, his armour rattled like a chime. The beast's tail twirled around in lieu of the racket. A blinding burst of sparks consumed the knight's vision as a jet of starlight erupted from the tail. He fought back the crippling fear as he lurched sideways at almost too late an interval.

Searing heat washed across his body and the resulting explosion of a tree behind the knight caused his helmet to reverberate like a struck bell. A fraction of a second passed and Alric's sight returned to him. Fighting the disorientation, he slammed into the manticore's side and slid his dagger into the small gap near its hind leg's shoulder. As the blade pierced the soft matter protecting the manticore's joints, strings of iridescent black fluid pulsed outward from the wound. Pushing with every ounce of force he could muster, Alric wrenched and twisted the weapon to maximise damage.

The manticore's internal whirling grew louder, and its shoulder began clicking and snapping with every move it made. Its tail furiously rotated back and forth in a desperate attempt to fix upon Alric, who was much too close to be targeted by the dreaded thing.

Alric yanked the dagger back out. In an uncoordinated stupor, the manticore, with its leg deeply wounded, lost its footing and tumbled onto its side. He pressed his body against the stem of the tail, searched for the thick artery upon it, and drew his dagger across the vein. Once again, shimmering paste flowed out from the wound as the tail twitched several times before slamming into the ground, entirely limp. The manticore continued struggling to right itself, but Alric knew that it was no longer a threat to him. When he turned to the pile of bodies, the entire flock of goblins already encircled him.

Alric panted ragged breaths as he pressed his dagger firmly back into its sheath and snatched the grip of his longsword. He pulled the thing out haphazardly, still physically taxed from downing the manticore. The aggressive gesture caused the goblins to startle and scamper backward several steps, but after allowing a few seconds to assess the situation, they slowly and surely began pacing forth once more.

The knight held his sword at the ready, backing away. With immense vigour, Alric snapped forward, screaming as loud as he could. No longer certain of their continued safety, the goblins simply spun on their four legs and scurried away like frightened rats, leaving the disabled manticore to flail about in the dirt helplessly.

Alric was glad that they hadn't the gall to swarm him. Seeing as he was ill-armed to deal with their chitinous shells and they outnumbered him greatly, the goblins could have succeeded in overpowering him with sheer mass. Then, once he was toppled, it was only a matter of pulling his helmet off and cracking his skull with a well-aimed strike. They were much more agile than the manticore, so striking a weak spot with a bladed weapon would have been much more difficult.

With the immediate danger dealt with, Alric cautiously paced towards the mound of bodies, sword still drawn. Having placed more distance between himself and the manticore, its strained groaning became muted and the sizzling of what remained of the ash tree that it had fired its curse upon had outgrown its pained throes.

What Alric initially thought to be a snapped signpost was definitely nothing of the sort once he had a closer look. The bottom end of the thin wooden shaft was still pinned into the dirt. What would've been the upper portion had fallen into the grass. Stowing his sword, Alric dropped to one knee and reached for the object. His leather-bound fingers wrapped around it and brought it closer to his face as he lifted his visor. Tied to the wooden pole with tattered rope was a human skull, a pair of crows' wings, and a horse's skull.

Dread seeped into Alric's core as his fingers began to shake. He felt as if the totem bled darkness straight into his heart. The lifeless sockets of the human skull stabbed his flickering irises and flooded his every fibre with bubbling terror. Alric dropped it immediately and pushed to his feet with a start.

When he averted his eyes from the totem, he noted there were at least fifteen bodies wrapped within the translucent film of the goblin sac. It was incomplete, so Alric could still see through the stuff. A fully-spun goblin net resembled several centimetres of ice; one could barely make out the details of what it held behind its layers. However, Alric realised that he could hear something reverberating through the net. Something eerily close…yet distant. He slowly approached the sac and felt his heart stop when he realised that it was writhing from within.

With haste, Alric once again brandished his dagger. The knight gripped the film with one hand and carefully slid his blade down its surface. As the seal was broken, the stench within the net blew forth all at once. Alric gagged and jerked his head away from the hole, fighting the urge to vomit. The screams also billowed forth, raw, desperate, and wordless.

Alric stowed his dagger. "Thou art safe." After pushing several corpses off of the survivor, he was able to drag him out and onto the grass. The man broke into tears and howled. "Explain thyself," Alric pressed, his mind wandering back to the twisted totem of bone. "What occurred here?"

The survivor trembled as he sat upright. His face immediately drained of colour. "I was…"

Alric gritted his teeth and hissed, "Speak!"

"We…are nothing but ore and lightning, forged to serve the whims of the Devil." Albeit calm, his tone was wispy, perhaps indicating that his grasp on reality had not yet returned. In his groggy state, he clearly did not realise that Alric was a Churchsworn knight…otherwise, he would have held his tongue and saved himself. In the face of Alric's continued silence, the man stared aimlessly into the distance. He had spoken some line of foul, blasphemous dribble. The man was a demon worshipper and those who died there were certainly of like minds. They congregated to preach heresy...to denounce God and instead embrace the Devil. The profane totem suddenly made sense. With a sigh, Alric retracted from the pile. "Sara and Erik. Be they among the dead?"

"N-No, they…they escaped."

His charge had changed from rescuing the pious to punishing the wicked. "To where?" The man's eyes suddenly focused on Alric and the holy symbol of the Pillar that was emblazoned upon his surcoat. It was then that the man realised what he had gotten himself into. He shook his head in silence. Alric snatched the man by his scalp and leaned into his ear. "Thou darest to forsake Him despite all He hath given thee? I shall enjoy watching the flesh slop from thy bones."

The Knight Thestor dragged the man through the grass by the back of his neck as his shrill and fruitless pleading drifted through the air.

II
Those Who Sin

The wooden stake had been driven into the ground in Oak's town square. Tied to the post and barely standing was the survivor, Gerome, that Alric had found in the wood. A group of plebeians, layfolk who had sworn themselves to the service of the Church, were piling pieces of wood up against the stake as the townsfolk gathered around. Alric was still dressed in his armour as he called out to the onlookers, "This man, this despicable traitor of a man, hath betrayed us all! Once thought a trusted friend and neighbour, he hath turned his back upon the Father! He hath stained his soul with the grievous sin of devil worship!"

Shocked gasps permeated the crowd, accompanied by angered scowls. There were those who looked on in horror as well, much to Alric's disdain.

"This new infernal doctrine would insist that we, the children of God, are instead instruments designed by the Devil himself to enact his will! Such depravity shall not go unpunished! But alas, my good folk, if this wretch was turned by such putrid blasphemy, so too could others among ye! They could be in thy midst at this very moment!" Alric was handed a lit torch by one of the plebeians. "To thou, I say this; confess, repent thy sins, and the Father may see fit to spare thee. Cling upon these falsities and thy sentence shall be certain…!" He extended the flaming torch towards the pile of wood at Gerome's feet.

Alric basked in the heat as it overtook Gerome's body. The crackling and raging of the inferno did not drown out his screeching. Several cheers erupted from the crowd, but for each cheer there was also someone who was petrified in terror. His eyes scoured the crowd and took in each and every one of their reactions. When the screaming stopped, Alric and the plebeians doused the fire with pails of water, sending trails of smoke and steam into the air from Gerome's blackened corpse. "Those who have been ensnared by the Devil, hear me! Step forward if thou art willing to retake the blessed path! Repent, take penance, and all shall be forgiven!"

For several seconds, silence and inaction reigned supreme. However, just as Alric's rage caused his clenched fist to quiver, a figure hobbled forward from the crowd. "Brother Alric, I throw myself before you." The figure, a young man with a cane in his hand, knelt before the smouldering pyre. "My name is Peter…and I seek forgiveness from the Lord for betraying him."

As he spoke, Alric noticed murmurs in the crowd. Spiteful whispers. Alric took several steps towards the crowd. He pointed at one of the farmers and cried, "Speak not amongst thyselves. Come forth."

The townsfolk fanned away and revealed a woman with a dirty apron wrapped about her dress. "He's a filthy coward, he is. Ain't got enough spine ta stick with it," she snapped. Two other villagers clustered around the woman, with their eyes fixed on Alric.

Peter raised a hand. "Please. Stop."

The innocent people around them slowly backed away. "Tha Church 'as been lying to us. We are devilspawn! That is our true nature!"

"What tha bloody 'ell is goin' on?" hissed Howard, captain of the guard.

Alric watched as the woman peered out at the commoners who cared enough to listen to her words. "We've lost our way. Our minds have been poisoned by tha Church. Tha only way we can be made whole again is by givin' ourselves over!"

The Thestor was already moving towards the woman in the middle of her response. As the final word left her lips, a steel fist careened into her face. The dull snap of the impact was accompanied by the clattering of her teeth bouncing across the ground. The woman collapsed without so much as a whimper, then stared up at him. Blood leaked from her mouth, but her face was otherwise emotionless. The two men rushed to the woman, helped her to her feet, and steadied her. Alric was seething with the unbridled fury of a thousand suns. "Such disgusting blasphemy! Thou hast doomed thyself, wretch. In the name of God, I hereby condemn thee to the pyre as a demonist!"

He saw a glint of courage in the eye of one of the men as he released her and reached for a sword upon his belt. "You're not doing shit, Thestor." He drew the weapon with a snarl.

Peter cried out, "Stand down, Seb! All of you!"

Alric inhaled then took a few steps backwards as he drew his longsword. The crowd retracted even further, leaving Seb, the woman with the bloodied mouth, and a stocky man staring him down. The remaining two promptly brandished their own weapons. "Captain?" Alric snapped. Howard, however, simply remained frozen in place. "So be it," Alric muttered as he lowered his helmet's visor.

The woman hacked up blood, then spat it onto Alric's boot. "We've 'ad enough," she rasped. Seb stepped forward, arming sword in hand. Alric could tell that the fellow was not formally trained, but he moved with a kind of confidence that the others did not possess. The scraping of dirt on boots, the shifting clacks of Alric's plate armour, and steady breaths of those involved were the only sounds to be heard. Alric rearranged his hands upon his longsword and clutched it at the ready in a half-sword grip; he held it by its handle with his right hand, and the middle of its blade with his left.

If he weren't outnumbered, Alric would not have been concerned. Despite what most nobles would insist, commoners were not idiots. They knew the strengths of plate armour, as well as its weaknesses. They'd seek to swarm him, pin him down, then either stab through the gaps in his plate armour or fling his visor open and stab his face. Alric knew that he had no choice. God's honour had been spat upon; if he were to turn away, if he did not punish those heretics, he would find himself the subject of God's rage. Such a prospect was so frightening that Alric would dare not even entertain the thought of allowing any of them to leave alive.

Seb started off with a feint, one that Alric barely managed to read in time. The knight angled his sword and throttled it forward to parry the subsequent slash. As the 'clang' of steel rang through the air, Alric's feet followed through with his motions to position himself with his back to the wall of a house. If he let his enemies take advantage of their numbers, they were going to kill him. It did not matter how proficient or well-armoured he was.

The axeman charged forth. With two hands holding his sword horizontally, Alric raised his blade and it caught the axe by its curved edge, deflecting the weapon and sending it off track. As that happened, the one called Seb lunged onto Alric's back and clutched at his left arm. "Tha neck! Go fer tha neck!"

Alric roared in exertion as he strained the muscles in his legs and upper back. He managed to send himself and Seb charging straight into the wall of the house behind them with a 'thud', knocking Seb free just in time for Alric to react to the woman with the arming sword.

She made a precise thrust aimed at Alric's armpit, prompting him to jerk to the side. Much like the preceding strike, the sword crashed against plate and the fabric of the surcoat atop it. In response, he rammed his sword deep into the woman's gut, wrenched it, then pulled it out. Shocked screams flooded the town square as the woman fell to the ground, howling in pain.

Suddenly, a neck-wrenching blunt impact bypassed Alric's helmet and rattled his skull. His senses were overwhelmed with intense thrums, reverberations, and echoes. Despite the disorientation, Alric managed to see the axeman reeling back to prepare another strike. Before he could unleash it, Peter leapt onto him from behind and snatched his arms. It did not take long for the thug to throw the cripple off and onto the ground with a snarl, but those few seconds were precious.

Alric had enough time to recover and whip his longsword out in a sweeping arc. It drew cleanly through the first few inches of the axeman's throat, spilling midnight blood over the man's clothes. He gagged, reaching for his neck. His weapon fell to the ground, bounced thrice, then rumbled there upon the dirt. Desperately clawing for his throat, the demonist collapsed in the puddle of his own blood.

Seb once again launched himself at Alric. The knight slipped on the cobble beneath his feet and was tackled to the ground by the heretic. His back slammed onto the stone, and he felt his longsword fly out of his hands. Seb was on top of him as he drew Alric's own rondel dagger, gripped the weapon with two hands, and dropped it down towards one of the sights of Alric's helmet. The Thestor's hands lashed upward like the tongues of serpents and wrapped themselves around Seb's wrists. The man gritted his teeth as he pressed as hard as he could against Alric's steel-clad form.

Alric lurched to his left, then rolled all of his weight to the right. The shift managed to throw Seb onto the stone and bring Alric up on top of him. Having traded positions, Alric's face was plastered with a bloodthirsty grin that none could see thanks to his visor as he wrestled Seb for the dagger. The weapon snapped out of Seb's grip and Alric twirled it, planted the palm of his left hand on its pommel, then brought it down onto Seb's face. Very much like how Alric had countered it, Seb locked his fingers around Alric's gauntlets. However, Alric had an advantage. Being dressed in plate meant that he was a lot heavier than the unarmoured Seb. The sod could not fight against that weight forever. The dagger slowly travelled downwards, closer and closer to Seb's widened eye. He began panting and quivering in fear. With one final effort, Alric shifted his body weight and funnelled all of it through the dagger. An ear-piercing screech played harmony to the wet squashing and crunching caused by the blade as it buried itself into Seb's eye socket. Alric pulled the blade out, then sent it back into the gaping hole so many times that he had lost count.

Overcome with fatigue, Alric stumbled off the corpse and rose as he raised his visor. His legs wobbled. His arms trembled. His breathing was shallow and ragged. None of the heretics but Seb died instantly. They trembled and screamed on the ground before eventually succumbing to their fatal wounds over the course of minutes. The townspeople with enough stomach to stay were mixed in their reactions. Thankfully, the majority appeared to applaud Alric's smiting of the impious.

Alric hobbled over to his discarded longsword and reclaimed it. He wiped his sword and dagger clean with the surcoat that was draped over his armour. The thing was once white but had been long stained grey with the blood of God's enemies. After stowing his weapons on his belt, Alric turned to the children. They had been watching intently from around the corner. There was no telling whether or not their mother had spread filthy heretical lies to their ears...so he felt it prudent to ensure their faith. The knight said to them, still exhausted, "Thou knowest now the end that awaits those who sin. Praise God…and thou shan't follow."

Josephine and Liam were frozen. Alric couldn't tell if it was fear or awe that seized their very souls, but it pained him not that they needed to watch as he took those men. They were shivering as one of the townspeople warmly embraced them. As she led them away, the woman shot Alric a spiteful glare.

"What tha hell was that!?" spat an older man as he stomped over to Alric. He was rather short but had the broad shoulders of a working man. "Ya can't just march inta town and cut folk apart! Doesn't matter what they've done! Yer meant ta put 'em on trial!"

Howard tried to interpose himself between Alric and the angered man. "Halsten, calm down will ya?"

"*Calm down*!? My fuckin' son is missin'! He might be runnin' 'round with that lot and this stupid fool of a knight killed 'em all before we could ask questions!"

Alric ignored the newcomer. Instead, his searing stare was locked on Howard. "I should have thee whipped through the streets for thy cowardice. A man of thy station standing idly by while a servant of the Church is *assaulted* in the streets is a slight against God Himself."

The threat made Howard turn pale. "T-They were friends o' mine. I-I…I couldn't just…"

Peter came limping over with a terse frown on his face. "It doesn't matter what you say. What you *do* is what God will judge you for…and you did *nothing*."

Alric sneered. The man had admitted to being a demonist. But not only did he seek forgiveness, he did not stand idle during the skirmish as Howard did. The Thestor knelt, picked up the cane that Peter had dropped during the scuffle, and stood back up. "As heinous as thy crimes are…thou hast proven that thou art willing to risk thy life to redeem thyself." He handed the cane over and Peter accepted it sternly.

"I understand, Brother. These serpents…they prey on the vulnerable. They teach that we are not alive, that we are nothing but tools of the damned…but I see the truth now. In the forest, with the goblins…I watched people scream and beg for their lives. We *must* be living…for the dead do not beg. All I wish is to cleanse myself of this darkness and perhaps seek forgiveness from the Father."

Halsten wiped the dirt from Peter's clothes and held him gently by the shoulder. "Erik. Was Erik there? Did he…"

"Erik and Sara fled with the others just as the scavengers came. T-They said they were…" Peter paused for a moment. "I can…show you where they went. Take me with you."

III
The House of God

The halls of the chapel were flushed with darkness. Not the kind that incited fear and distress, but rather the tranquil kind. It calmed the soul and massaged the humours. Several motes of dancing flame drenched objects close to them in faint golden highlights. Those candles grasped firmly in the palms of certain individuals for the sacrament were the only sources of interior lighting; just enough to ensure the bare minimum of sight.

He stood alongside the stone pillars that lined the chapel, muttering the sacred words alongside his brothers and sisters. The candlelight pulsated. It swelled, flickered, shrivelled, then started over in a perpetual cycle of fluctuation.

Alric felt a bead of melted wax trace its way onto his ungloved finger. It was hot...but he did not move to wipe it away. He used pain as a measure of his faith. How much could he endure in the Father's name? If there was a threshold, he was an unworthy servant. He savoured it. He took pleasure in it. For only the living could be struck by pain and he intended to embrace *all* that God had given him the privilege to behold.

Almost invisible to the naked eye, if it weren't for stray lines of candlelight, was an immense and beautifully carved wooden portal that dwarfed every person in the chamber. Each eye was pinned to said gate as the sacrament was uttered, all aglow with unending faith.

Suddenly, as if the prayers were being answered, there was a low rumbling that coursed through Alric's innards like an internal crack of thunder. It was far from the first Birthing he had witnessed, but the procession had never lost its lustre. Such majesty did God exercise over each and every object in his domain. The immense tremors stopped as suddenly as they began, and the church hall dropped into complete silence. Led by the head sister, the nuns proceeded to the portal and pried it open. The door was so large that all seven women needed to lend their strength to open it. Time felt as if it had slowed to a painstakingly feeble pace for the knight. His eyes narrowed and his breathing hitched.

When the sanctum was opened, a mass of bodies filled the space that had been empty prior to the sacrament. Lined in perfectly ordered rows starting from the rear were horses, deer, wolves, and finally, seven children. All of the animals were folded down on themselves. The children, like the animals, had darkened eyes; none were truly 'alive' as of yet.

Beneath the new life was a raised platform, referred to as a womb. It was worn rough as if it was as old as time itself. Like clockwork, the nuns filed into the sanctum and gathered up the small children as the priest held his candle to a page of parchment, inspecting the text upon it. When the women finished moving the young to safety in the nursery wing, the remaining monks heaved the portal shut.

Alric could barely hold back his wonder. Every person to ever exist entered the world that way. Life was born of the Heavens; it was *obvious*. One moment there was nothing in that chamber, and in the next there were living and breathing creatures. It was irrefutable proof that the Father existed and that all of reality was his creation. The knight wished that the non-believers could have witnessed it as he had. Perhaps then would they end their apostasy and rejoin the path. As the halls were bathed in light once more by the monks opening the locked windows, Father Alexander turned to Alric and nodded. "Are you well, Brother Alric?"

Alric coughed into his hand nervously as he wiped tears from his eyes. "It never fails to bring me to weakness, Father. Forgive me."

The priest shook his head sternly. "Hush, now. Your joyous awe pleases me; many of the others in your Order are much too eager to shed blood to appreciate such things." The remark irritated Alric to say the least. It was the duty of the Knights of Saint Thestus to safeguard the faith; what else were they to do but shed blood in the name of God?

Alric helped Alexander in opening the chapel's double doors. Beyond was the gathered mass of folk that lived in Hollensfield. Eager husbands, wives, and children gazed at the priest with halted breath. As they braced the doors against the church walls, the priest said to Alric, "I will send for you once we have determined if the accused are indeed the heretics you seek."

"I beg thy pardon? My informant identified them as members of a heretic cult," Alric argued. "I would have them at once, so I might impose upon them my inquiries."

With a shake of his head, Father Alexander replied, "Surely you must understand that I cannot freely give these individuals to you without verifying the claims of some stranger. Until their guilt has been determined, they have been granted sanctuary in these hallowed halls."

"This is ludicrous," Alric huffed.

Father Alexander exhaled through his nostrils. "That will be all, Brother Thestor."

Begrudgingly, the knight laced through the crowd and eventually spied his involuntary companions standing apart from the masses. Peter hobbled around to face Alric as he came closer. Without his armour and Thestor surcoat, Peter could have only recognised Alric by the longsword and rondel dagger that hung heavily on his belt. Otherwise, he was wearing his unassuming and filthy arming doublet.

"You aren't going to kill them too, are you?" Halsten pressed urgently.

Alric crossed his arms. "The choice is theirs. Should they repent, their sins shall be forgiven."

"Just don't kill 'em before they tell us what we want ta know."

"Men and women of the cloth always exercise utmost discretion during questioning," replied Alric.

"Questioning? You mean torture."

Peter scoffed. "Please. Enough of this. We all want to find these heretics. Could we at least *try* to cooperate with each other?" Halsten fell silent, as did Alric. Peter, however, sighed heavily and said, "Perhaps you should see to your armour, Brother Alric. In the meantime…I suppose Halsten and I shall have a meal?" Peter glared at the agitated woodsman.

"A splendid idea." Alric stomped off with a huff. He circled the crowd that nipped at the front gates of the church. Several joyous faces marked the families that were chosen to bear the newborn children. Only the most devoted to God were blessed with young. The list held by the priest denoted the most faithful married couples in the village.

Around the side of the church tower he went, and softer and softer did the chatter from the commonfolk become. At the rear of the structure were a handful of plebeians. They were engaged in varying forms of labour including gardening, carpentry, masonry, and painting. Most of them were laying stones and mortar to reinforce a tunnel that led from the rear of the church and into the forest.

One plebeian in particular was applying oil to several pieces of plate armour lined up on a wooden bench. He was dressed in a bright orange tunic, brown hose, and linen shoes. The bench was sitting beneath a simple wooden shelter. Folded neatly next to the pieces of armour was a fresh Thestor surcoat. Alric's surcoat, which had turned dark grey with blood and dirt, was nowhere to be seen.

Alric did not even recognise his armour. It had been polished to a chrome sheen and had the more compromising dents hammered out by a smith. He could see his own reflection upon it grow as he approached. The broken links in his mail had also been replaced. The young plebeian was so absorbed in his work cleaning the plate that he did not raise his eyes to greet the knight.

Without a word, Alric reached over and ran his fingers through the rough white fabric of the surcoat. Embroidered on its chest was a red Pillar made of three strokes that wound together into a knot at its base. The Pillar was the central icon of Church worship; it signified the Lord's magnificence. Finally, as Alric continued to examine the surcoat, the plebeian froze upon noticing his company.

"B-Brother?" he stammered anxiously.

Alric pulled his arm away from the surcoat. "Hast thou been kind to my arms?" he asked in jest. *Mostly* in jest.

"Y-Yes Brother Alric, of course." The boy's voice quivered and he scrubbed faster.

Alric's eyes moved to the stone tunnel nearby. Leaving the plebeian to his toil, he approached an iron-barred opening in the tunnel. To his right were more plebeians and the stone mason hard at work laying their mortar. Inside the tunnel, Alric could make out slow movements in the near darkness. The animals...the horses, deer, and wolves that were birthed. They were being led into the wilderness by the tunnel. Although humans hunted animals for food and produce, on the day of their birth, they were granted passage through the chapel to ensure that God's balance of nature was unsullied. Once in the wild, animals suitable for farming were distributed to the farmers who were most worthy in the eyes of God.

The chance to behold with his own eyes that animal and man were all born the same way always hardened Alric's certainty. All things that should be, were born of God. All else was wretched and dark… Things that were never truly born, that had never passed through the gates of a church. Dark things. He thought of goblins and manticores. Then of those that were worse.

With a jitter, Alric turned and walked back to the plebeian tending to his armour. He eagerly set the breastplate onto the bench and looked up at Alric. "Brother Alric, it's all done. If ya wouldn't mind, you can speak tha words and I can start 'elping you back into it."

Alric nodded then knelt. Closing his eyes, he muttered the sacred words to himself in the ancient tongue of Edich, In Tritish, the words were:

As God's love is infinite,

So boundless is His hatred.
As God's compassion is unlimited,
So fathomless is His indifference.

It was the first verse in the Oath of Vigilance. Each word was etched into Alric's mind; the old language of Edich was always his first language as it was the language of the Scripture. However many amended Tritish versions were created, Alric would only care to witness the holy words in their original form. He recited eleven of the twelve verses: a sacred vow to abide by the Second Attestation of Saint Thestus. He swore to the Heavens that he would be ready to stand against the enemies of the Lord until the moment he laid his head down to rest. Only once the Prime Moon was at its apex in the night sky could Alric utter the closing verses of the Oath and remove his plate armour. Until then, a Knight Thestor could never be taken unprepared.

The plebeian approached with Alric's greaves and cuisses. The Thestor finally spoke to the boy. "Speak thy name. I shall call it when thou art needed."

"James, Brother," he answered awkwardly, laying the pieces of armour onto the wooden table.

The knight snatched the greaves up, clasped them onto his shins, and fastened the straps accordingly. Next, he retrieved one of the pieces of thigh armour, called the cuisses, from the bench. Alric wrapped the open cylinder of steel around his left thigh, making sure to slot the articulated poleyn knee plate to the steel peg on the greave below it and strap them together. The top of the cuisse was to be tied to Alric's arming jacket to hold it upright. Once it was all in place, Alric flexed his knee to ensure that he had done a proper job. He repeated those steps for the opposite leg. The last thing Alric could comfortably see to on his own was the mail skirt that would protect his groin. Once it was tightened and in place, he turned and said, "James." The following steps were possible without help if certain straps and ties were already loosely tied, but as Alric knew from his days travelling alone, it was difficult, very particular, much more time consuming, and tiresome. He knew that he was to be doing it alone for many days, so why not take a brief respite and make the boy useful?

Next came the mail voiders that draped over his shoulders to cover his armpits and upper arms. Alric held up his arms to allow James to slide the mail onto his arming doublet and strap it into place. As James began to clasp the steel cuirass about Alric's torso, the knight had the sense that he was not the first man James had helped into their harness. The cuirass completely entombed Alric's body, and its fauld overlapped the mail skirt beneath it. "Hast thou armed many men in the past?"

He nodded eagerly. "Y-Yes, Brother. I've seen many from yer Order march through 'ere in big groups. The Grand Hosts, or what 'ave you." James secured the cuirass in place then moved onto the vambraces; lengths of smaller pieces of steel linked together with leather to cover his forearms and biceps. Also attached to each vambrace was a pauldron; a shoulder piece. He mounted each vambrace and tied them to Alric's arming jacket, making sure to tighten each component before moving on. The plebeian asked, "I ain't never seen just *one* of you. Are ya runnin' late?"

Alric grimaced at the boy's idiocy. He was not in the mood to deal with yet another uneducated ponce. "As a knight-errant, my charge is to travel God's kingdoms alone and uphold the Third and Fourth Attestations."

"Tha Third is ta spread tha faith and the Fourth is ta always 'elp faithful folk?"

"Aye," Alric said begrudgingly.

James continued his duties by outfitting Alric with his gauntlets and fitted a padded coif onto his head. He then handed the knight his bascinet helm; it was fitted with an aventail, a heavily padded mail collar that would cover his neck. Lastly, James draped the fresh Order of Saint Thestus surcoat over Alric's armour and tied it about his waist with the same belt that held Alric's longsword and dagger.

James stepped back and cocked his head, assessing his handiwork. "I-If I may, Brother...how does one join tha Order of Saint Thestus?"

Alric slid his helmet on, but kept its visor open. "Simply ask. Like the Church itself, we are always in search of plebeians to act as squires and sergeants."

James's eyes dropped to the ground. "Y-Yes Brother. How about…ta become a Thestor Knight?"

Alric took a breath and rested his left hand upon the pommel of his sheathed sword. "Thou must already have attained knighthood, then choose to swear thyself to the Order. The training of a true knight begins at childhood and is tested in battle; to attempt to train an adult volunteer to the same standard would be impossible." After the plebeian nodded sadly, Alric took his leave.

It had been roughly twenty minutes since Alric had started donning his armour; the dense crowd at the church gate had dispersed. Alric supposed he should attempt to find Peter and Halsten, although he did desperately want to leave them behind. Since arriving in Hollensfield the previous night, Peter had done his part by identifying the other demonists. The only reason Alric allowed Halsten along was that he technically held up the Fourth Attestation in that situation. He was a father who needed assistance in finding his son; a God-worshipping man in need of help, not a person to be turned down by a Knight Thestor. The two unlikely companions were simple peasants who would need protection if danger reared its fangs during the journey. They were ill-trained and ill-equipped to engage in the often-perilous work of manhunting. Nevertheless, until either of them gave him a reason not to, he would treat them with reluctant tolerance.

The knight walked down the row of cookshops. The smell of pies, fried meat, fish, fowls, and eggs wafted through the air. By the road was a set of benches and Peter was seated at one, cradling a pie in his hands. As he chewed, his eyes sparked upon seeing Alric. "Where's Halsten?" Peter asked.

Alric was not pleased. "I was to ask thee the same question."

Peter swallowed the food in his mouth. "A monk came to summon us...Halsten said he was going to take the message to you."

With a growl, Alric clenched his fist. "Come."

Peter hobbled after Alric, one hand bracing on his cane and the other shovelling the pie into his mouth. As they came upon the church, several town guardsmen wandered about the main gate. The priest was standing against the archway, looking as if he had seen a ghost. "Father, what troubles thee?" Alric called.

Alexander shook his head. "Y-Your companion... He attacked one prisoner and kidnapped the other!"

"This could have been avoided if thou simply handed them over to me," Alric snarled. He then turned to the guards. "What manner of buffoonery allowed one woodsman to escape thee? Why aren't thou giving chase?"

One of them rolled his eyes at Alric. "He was fast, alright? Lashed out at one of 'em, then made off. Ain't enough time for anyone to figure out what happened."

Peter stepped forth, his food completely gone. "The other prisoner, are they still alive?"

"Lissen, get outta 'ere before I toss ya on yer crippled arse," the guard pressed.

"Best answer the question," threatened Alric. "Or God help me, I shall strike thee down."

The guard stammered. His compatriot found the words that he couldn't. “He’s alive. Not fer long.”

He stepped to the side of the gate, revealing a body sprawled in the middle of the entryway. Nuns and monks were gathered around, but none prayed for the life of the heretic. Alric approached the dying man and knelt. “The time is upon thee. Speak the truth and be granted passage to God’s kingdom. Renounce thy devilry.”

The man's voice faltered as he desperately cried, “H-He took her...South-East. T-Tha burial mound. P-Please I don't want to die...!”

“Death will come. It cannot be helped, but the soul need not be condemned to Hell. I beg thee, save thyself. Repent,” Alric pleaded in hushed tones.

The heretic’s desperate pleas continued. He died before Alric, who took great disdain in the fact that the man did not cleanse himself before passing. So be it. He would burn in Hell for eternity. All that mattered was that Alric had done his duty; he would not suffer the same fate. He stood and glanced toward the slightly ajar birthing portal. The knight moved into the sanctum, flanked by the two guards. It was as black as night within, only the distant speck of light in the distance marked the end of the beast tunnel. In the middle of the sanctum was the smooth and pure surface of the womb.

Upon the ground were boot prints. Boot prints that smeared dirt over the sacred womb. Halsten had fled through the sanctum, leaving his filthy handprints across its pristine walls. Not only did the woodsman shed blood on sacred ground, he defiled the church to escape. Alric growled as he lowered his head. Halsten had knowingly made himself exempt from the Fourth Attestation with such affronts, and had given Alric another task to complete in order to please the Lord.

IV
The Massacre at Chesterton

Alric was not expecting to find a host of men to join him in his hunt for the heretics considering that his homeland of Tritham was locked in bitter war with their neighbours in Valtheaux. Despite his doubts, he rode to Rochester, the closest garrison of Tritan men, to solicit assistance in his pursuit. The master of Rochester was Antony of Kirshire, a rather wealth-hungry noble of middle status. He insisted that Alric pay the wages for the men while they were in the Church's service, as well as direct some interest his way. Alric was not pleased to deal with such affairs once again. Life in noble court did not suit him. It was partially why he turned his back on his family and devoted himself instead to God. As a man of the Order of Saint Thestus forbidden to possess his own wealth and sworn to poverty by the First Attestation, he was not exactly bursting at the seams with money. All that he carried came as charitable donations, only to be used for expenses and services during his travels.

Lord Franco di Lombardi was a vassal of a powerful duke and had been overseeing the defence of Rochester due to its proximity to the front. He also owned lands in the surrounding area. It turned out that his fiefs were being pillaged, thus unable to steadily pay the rents owed to him. The interesting part of it all was that it was not the Valthois who were raiding his lands. When Alric came requesting aid, Lord Franco thought the heretics to be the only explanation. He was hellbent on finding the culprits enough to lend himself and a fraction of the garrison to the quest without pay. Seeing as Halsten had kidnapped the last surviving heretic, it was clear to Alric that the woodsman sought out the demonists for himself to find his son. His supposition was simple; find the heretics, find Halsten. Both parties would then be punished for their transgressions.

Alric trudged through the wood with his visor open. In his hands was a pollaxe. As its name alluded, it was an axe with a long shaft and a spearhead at its tip. On the backend was a spiked hammer. In massed combat, one would rather be armed with a weapon such as that than a sword. Despite their prevalence in tales and plays, swords were sidearms on the battlefield.

To his right was Lord Franco and his men-at-arms. Franco was one of the few other men clad in full plate. Most of the soldiers only had portions of plate, whether a cuirass or vambraces. Unlike Alric's rather simple armour that was naked steel and beheld no decorative shapings, Franco's plate had been painted royal purple and was lined with gold flourishes.

Atop Franco's armour was a tabard; a short garment that extended down to his upper thighs and was tied around the waist with a leather belt. It bore a design featuring quarters of blue and white with a black crescent moon in the upper left quadrant. His men-at-arms brandished similar heraldry on their shields. However, since the garrison of Rochester consisted of men gathered from all across Tritham, a rainbow of heraldry painted the rest of the small army. The armoured men pushed through the branches and scoured the earth for any signs of activity. Alric could hear the shouting of others in the party as they attempted to coordinate themselves in the thickets. "Worry not, for thy quarry is near," Franco called over the sound of his plated form rustling through the shrubbery. He spoke with a slight accent that, like his name, placed him as a native of Velinti. "No creature walks this grove. Some foreign power hath stirred them."

Alric shook his head then cried back, "I shall cease my worrying when we have set ablaze their wretched hive."

It had been the fourth hour of searching. Alric's body began to feel the weight of his armour. Unlike Franco, Alric was bound by the Oath of Vigilance. Years of practising said Second Attestation was taking its toll on his body. He could feel every step becoming more and more difficult. The enduring form of self-flagellation was a test of each man's endurance, both physical and spiritual. The pain one willingly endured was monument to his devotion. At least, that was what Alric thought to himself in an effort to push himself through the trial.

Unlike the forests surrounding Oak that were pathetic skeletons of flora, the trees in the Verdant Stretch glowed vibrant shades of green and full browns. The grass mirrored the trees in how they were saturated and lively. Tangled branches splayed out from the trees, easily snapped by Alric as he pushed his pollaxe's shaft onward. The crunching of sticks at his sides informed him that his compatriots were holding formation. A hasty pair of footsteps grew in volume, causing Alric to slow and turn his head. A footman jogged over to Lord Franco, skidding to a halt by his side. "My lord, one of tha North parties found somethin'. A fort." The man was James Baker, man-at-arms in Franco's personal retinue. Franco nodded.

Baker cupped his hands around his mouth and shouted, "We go North! North!"

Several other infantrymen further down the line repeated Baker's orders to ensure that the entire group received word that they were redirecting. When men were spread dozens of metres apart from each other, it would be easy for people to get lost or left behind. Much to his dismay, Alric turned with the rest of the band and went back toward where they came. He could feel his body failing him. He wanted the aching to stop. He wanted the strain on his joints to end. He desperately wanted to give up...but the promise of God's disappointment always kept him on the righteous path.

Eventually, the West detachment carved around and flanked the subject of the North team's message. In the pockmarked flat up ahead that had been cleared of trees was a wooden fortress. Thick logs of timber were strung up tightly by rope and lined into tall battlements that stood five metres tall. Wooden pikes were mounted on the walls and upon them were dozens of naked corpses. Impaled and left to die. Alric swallowed as he saw the dozens of people, men and women alike, stuck like pigs on a spit. Most of them did not move...but there were a handful of unfortunates that attempted to struggle free. Their distant screams made Alric tremble. In the face of such barbaric cruelty, Alric sighed as he gestured the Sign of the Pillar by tapping his forehead then his chest.

"T-Tha screamin' drew 'em closer," reported Baker.

Alric averted his eyes and instead looked to Franco. He stared onward as he flexed his jaw. "I do not suppose that the Church was responsible for this?"

The withheld spite was not lost on Alric. "And what if it were?" he threatened.

Franco scoffed and ignored the provocation. "This is Chesterton…a hamlet under the ownership of Baron Antony. For it to have been overrun right under his nose…the fool needs to keep a closer watch on his fiefs. Prepare thyself for assault, Brother Alric. When we strike the heretics down, thou shalt immediately ensure that the slighted are properly committed to the next life."

The knight nodded. As Knight Thestor, Alric was bound to nurture the faith as a holy man. As well as persecuting the criminals of the Church, he would lead sermons, commit the dead to the earth, preach the Scripture, and marry those who sought union beneath God's eyes. As commanded the Third Attestation.

At first, it did not appear that the heretics knew of the hostile force gathering in the forest. Even had they known, there was not much to be done. Archers could have loosed upon the Tritan men from the safety of the fort, but arrows were finite. It would have been a waste of ammunition on a foe that was well-armoured, well-covered, and out of effective range. The heretics were eventually alerted as the footmen began to gather dry sticks and bark. Since the fortress was wood, there was one weapon that would make short work of its defensive wall.

The North, West, East, and South scouting parties all converged and combined into one force of a hundred men. At that point, a watchman on the wall raised the alarm, consequently allowing Alric to spot rows of heads emerging atop the battlements. Formed up on Alric's left was a cluster of archers, each armed with a heavily-strung longbow. To have the skill, strength, and endurance to repeatedly loose arrows from a bow with a one-hundred-and-sixty-pound draw weight required a lifetime of training. Alric could perhaps shoot two arrows with that kind of warbow before becoming fatigued and even then, he probably couldn't even it nock it back the whole way. It was an altogether different kind of physical might than what was used in hand-to-hand fighting. The archers stood near one of the bonfires awaiting their orders.

Eventually, Alric took his position within the mass of infantrymen. At the front of the formation was a wall of shield-bearing soldiers who covered the pikemen and halberdiers standing behind them. Alric and the other more well-equipped men-at-arms formed the armoured section. Lord Franco was going to hold position in the forest with a reserve of troops in case the plan failed. "Loose!"

Alric didn't know who called the order, but it promptly travelled down the line, and every pocket of archers repeated it aloud. They brandished their specialised incendiary arrows, set them alight, then drew them against their bowstrings. Some found their aim faster than others but soon enough, dozens of bright yellow specks travelled the vast field between the tree line and the fort. As they impacted on the gate of the fort, their fire became contagious. The archers only had so many incendiary arrows so once they had been expended, the men had no choice but to wait and see if their flaming barrage was enough to soften the hardwood logs. It ate away at the pillars of timber and periodically the defenders would hurl buckets of water onto the cancerous growth. All of it mattered not; the fire grew faster than the disorganised men could douse it and thus the gate began to blacken and crack. Alric had forgotten how much of battle was just waiting. He was reminded quite bluntly. For almost an hour, the Tritan army watched the fire crumple and fold the main gate. Then, the Tritans had to allow it to die out so they could attack. Surely, the defenders managed to quench the fire, but its work had been done; a portion of the barricade had fallen, and the men had their point of entrance.

"Advance!" cried Franco.

The Knight Thestor took that moment to lower his visor, surrounding himself in near-complete blackness. As if they were one, the mass of footmen marched forward. Alric walked shoulder to shoulder with other armoured fighters; they were bunched together so tightly that there was no room to fall. It gave him an odd sense of comfort despite the circumstances.

The approach was slow. Forty people striding together maintaining their formation and allowing no gaps between their bodies were sure to advance at a 'leisurely' pace. Alric's breathing was shallow and enveloped his hearing. Beneath it was the somewhat soft clacking of his plate armour and the rustling of his mail. Softer still were the same sounds repeated tenfold, once for each soldier in the detachment. The somewhat subdued aural landscape suddenly spiked when an ocean of 'bangs', 'crunches', and grunts rang out across the field.

Arrows had finally come spearing into the mass of advancing men. They embedded themselves into shields and shattered into splinters against armour. Alric's ears picked up some pained cries beneath the cacophony of shifting armour. Just as he lowered his head slightly to angle the sights of his helmet away from the incoming projectiles, a jarring impact slammed the upper right side of Alric's face. For a split second, he saw white fletching flash across his eyes before the arrow itself exploded into tiny shards of wooden shrapnel. As his head snapped back, he let out a sharp groan of shock. He forced himself to ignore the sudden jolt of fear that the strike injected into him and simply continue onward.

The characteristic 'thump' of arrows digging themselves into wood filled the air. Alric could barely see what was happening up ahead as the shoulders and weapons of his brothers in arms encapsulated his field of view. He could only assume that the Tritan archers had started shooting back at the heretics. Some defenders dropped behind the battlements; it was unclear to Alric at that angle whether they were hit by arrows or simply sought cover. The attacking force had gotten close enough to the fort for Alric to gaze into the eyes of the defending infantry. They wore mail, gambeson, brigandine, and only a few were clad in plate. Shields were raised at the front of the regiment, but the rest of their formation appeared too spaced out.

Once more, arrows came down from the walls. When the shield formations collided, Alric was rammed into his allies and subjected to the occasional arrow impact. Those behind powered forward, shoving him against the man in front. Every soldier in the formation lent their mass to the push while the men with spears and halberds jabbed at the heretics from behind the shield wall. Simultaneously, the enemy was handing out attacks of their own to anyone within range. The arrows fell mainly on his head and shoulders, buffeting him like steel rain. He could be confident that they could not pierce his plate armour to the point of wounding him but after repeated shots, they certainly began to hurt. Also, they didn't need to penetrate the plate to kill him; the gaps at his neck, armpits, as well as his visor's sights and breaths, served as potential entry points. As a result of the ongoing barrage, his spine was sore and his ears were filled with ringing.

It continued for twenty minutes. Of course, the arrows slowed, but the crushing tug of war only intensified. There were no duels on the battlefield. It was a place for the contest of army against army, not man against man: a measure of endurance and cohesion. Alric had not even faced an enemy combatant yet and he was fatigued from the constant pushing and incoming missiles. Eventually, after what felt to be an eternity, Alric felt the tide of men shift. His weight began to teeter forward. The Tritan men advanced, barging through the heretic assembly. The fortress walls grew larger, and the wave of allied men wrapped around the fractured heretic line. Alric brought his pollaxe up and led with the queue, the spiked end on the bottom of its shaft. A demonist was unlucky enough to have turned his back on the knight. He swept the polearm around, hurling the razor-sharp axe blade into the man's back. The weapon dug deep but didn't make a sound amidst the screaming, roaring, and smashing of the battle around Alric. He pulled the pollaxe free, causing the soldier to fall onto his face. He didn't have time to take in his surroundings so he simply advanced, cutting down any other routed heretics on his way to keep up with the rest of the formation. In large-scale combat, it didn't matter how skilled you were. If you fell behind, you became one man fighting dozens.

The vanguard was struggling against a handful of defenders who managed to hold back their charge. All the while, the heretics lashed out with axe strikes which caught allied shields and spat splinters over the immediate area. Alric and his line crept up behind the friendly shield formation. The soldier in front of him nodded and pulled to the side, allowing Alric the space he needed. Twirling the pollaxe in his hands, Alric readied the hammer. Several bruising strikes caught Alric's plated shoulders, head, and mid-section but he continued forward and swung his weapon in an overhead arc. The hammer crashed into the steel helmet protecting an enemy soldier's head. The man dropped to the ground instantly, without a single drop of blood in sight. Then, the Tritans lunged forward and harnessed the opening in order to lay waste to the rest of the men. The heretics who focused on attacking Alric were dispatched by the Tritan footmen who hacked at their armpits, necks, and groins in attempts to bypass their armour.

Once within the embrace of his fellow Tritans again, Alric was able to send his eyes about the township of Chesterton. Modest homes lined the interior of the makeshift fortress. A number of them had burned to the ground during the incendiary arrow barrage. Pigs and chickens ran madly about, freed from their pens by the commotion. The heretic forces had regrouped around the central structure; a church. It had one entrance which was covered by a dense ocean of fifty men. The holy building had been defaced with hanging dismembered body parts and smears of blood. The sight brought Alric's already simmering blood to a boil.

Some men-at-arms had fallen during the approach, but Franco had sent several archer detachments forward as relief. Their presence was evident when arrows descended from the timber battlements and found their marks on several of the lowly armoured heretics. Judging by how no more arrows were flung his way, Alric concluded that the heretics had depleted their reserves. The two sides hesitantly inched towards each other. Contrary to popular belief, most people did not want to die. That fact dictated the flow of combat; it could become incredibly meticulous.

Alric's entire being was already inflamed. His skull ached, his muscles felt loose, and his fingers trembled. With each pulse of pressure applied to his back by his compatriots, his endurance drained. Even the blows that were diverted by his armour had their toll. They all chipped away at his stamina, little by little. Alric had arrived at the front line, flanked by the shield-bearers and backed up by spearmen and halberdiers. The Tritan force slowly advanced, causing the heretics to do the same. The influence of fear started to flow through the knight's veins like poison.

When the enemy was within reach, Alric lashed forward with his pollaxe. The blade found the helmet of an opposing soldier, glancing off its curved surface. It briefly stunned the heretic but did not deal any notable damage. Clanks denoting more blows catching shields or armour permeated the air. Alric managed to parry several strikes with the shaft of his weapon and the ones he didn't were softened to futility by his plate. The pain from the percussive damage began to mount, however.

Alric's grasp on the world around him began to slip. He felt only the enemy before him and the weight of the pollaxe in his arms. Time became a misty blur. He didn't know if he killed anyone else in the remainder of the battle. It became so chaotic, so fierce, that the people around him morphed into one titanic tide of human bodies. Faceless, shapeless. Alric struck again and again, neither aware nor caring if his blows were fatal. He could feel his knees buckle beneath him and his fingers threatening to loosen and forsake the shaft of his weapon.

As he was upon the verge of collapse, Alric finally returned to his body. With their backs against the church, the heretics were flattened against the wall with no room to manoeuvre. He watched as the pinned enemies were squashed by the unrelenting advance of the Tritan army. He was swept forth within the ocean of soldiers, thrusting the spearhead of his pollaxe into the shapeless cloud of bodies. Weapons fell to the ground with staccato clangs and pleads for mercy were made. At that point, men from the Tritan front line opened the gate to the church and poured inside. Watching the infidels as they raised their hands in surrender, Alric kicked away what weapons he could. He glowered at them in furious silence for a time. "Brother Alric," called a voice from behind him. Alric glanced over his shoulder to see that the party raiding the keep had emerged quite unceremoniously. "Ain't no one inside."

"Art thou certain?"

"Aye, I swear it. Ain't a large place," replied the soldier.

Alric turned back to the heretics who were being disarmed by the Tritans. As their helmets and armour were removed, it was evident that what was left was no real army. They were teenagers. Children. Girls included. One of the older ones, a young man, sneered at the knight. The vanguard and the bulk of the defence were men. The quality of their training left much to be desired, but Alric knew that they were not the rabble of younger people he saw before him. Those men, those who should be responsible for the safety of the children, placed weapons in their hands and clouded their minds with lies so they would die for blasphemous rhetoric. His blood freezing, Alric pointed at the bodies impaled on the wall. "Is this thy doing?"

"They were liars. Like you and yer bloody Church," spat the heretic. "If we are to return to what we were meant to be, it all must be wiped clean."

"Thou hast been...led astray."

"No. You're the lost one. Scared of everythin' yer don't understand. Us? We fear nothing."

"Not even death?"

"We cannot die, for we have never lived." The child's voice lost the commoner accent that it held before, as if he was repeating something often said to him. They were adherent to such a profane doctrine...such a monstrous idea... Alric's breaths became short and his lip quivered beneath the visor of his helmet. His duty as a Knight Thestor was clear; heretics and demonists were to be punished. God was watching. If the knight did not act, the Father would see his weakness...his lack of devotion...and damn him to Hell.

"So be it. I see that thou art beyond redemption," Alric muttered coldly. He turned his attention to his fellow soldiers. "These children have been seduced by the Devil; they serve Hell, and Hell alone. End them."

A few men around him hesitated, but others were already convinced by the sight of impaled civilians littering the battlements. They readied their blades. Many of the heretic children to sob incessantly, begging for mercy. "If thou shalt spurn Him so fervently, then so too shall He spurn thee," Alric murmured.

V

Thou Shalt Not Suffer A Witch To Live

Alric and a party of fifteen men were dispatched to one of the many tombs surrounding Chesterton to search for any sign of the remaining heretics, while the greater force continued to hold the village. The knight wasn't thrilled to be called upon immediately after participating in battle, but he could not refuse. Pain still coursed through his very fibre. He and the other Tritans lay in wait within the embrace of a thicket. The grass swept up against the men's knees, and in the distance, the chirping of birds laced through the cool air. Barely ten paces away was a stone dome with an arched entryway. It must have been an ancient site; the mound that the dying heretic referred to. Entering such places was considered taboo by the Church; God was said to have no power within. The man to his side, Geoffrey Harland, seemed unruly whenever he was close to Alric. With a heavy sigh, the Knight Thestor whispered, "Does something trouble thee?" Harland remained silent. "If thou hast misgivings, thou best voice them now."

"They were children. *Children.* How...how can we be sure that God wished them dead?"

Alric's eyelids fluttered. Before he could think of something to say, James Baker spoke his mind. "Geoff, tha ones responsible are whoever filled their 'eads with that piss."

Suddenly, there was a whistle; one of the archers had spotted something. "I see one. Just one," whispered the archer John Stanton. "How do we know he's one o' them?"

Alric snarled, "Strike him down." Stanton gave his friends a confused glance, shrugged to himself, then nocked an arrow on his longbow. He pulled the string taut, aimed for a moment, then let loose. Then came a 'snap' as the heavy bow sent its projectile through the air on a startlingly straight path. The incredibly faint impact was followed by the wheezing of the man struck. Alric heard him tumble to the ground, groaning and hacking. The Tritan scouts moved forward, brandishing arming swords and bucklers. Alric waited several seconds before slowly and carefully pushing to his feet. From his vantage point, he could see what was going on. One scout was hunched over the fallen guard to ram his dagger into his neck. The rest cautiously scoured the area for more patrols. Posting a single lookout was not tactically sound. However, perhaps ill-judgement was to be expected from those who renounced the faith. Alric approached the footmen, his armour clanking incessantly. He came to a halt above the downed man, who wore no armour unlike the army at Chesterton; he was a simple peasant dressed in work wear. He had a spear for a weapon, although he hadn't the time to use it.

William Taylor, the man who had snuffed the sod's life with his dagger, pulled the thing free of the corpse and stumbled to his feet with a grunt. "Noice an' quiet, that one." Everyone called him 'Bugface Bill' for the nasally sound of his voice as well as his particularly squashed face. Stanton leant against the stump of a tree, squinting past the brush. "Ain't no one else 'ere. Maybe they're all inside tha bloody tomb."

Alric sighed heavily. "A blunder on their part to be sure, but a welcome one."

"Aye. Let's get a move on, lads," ordered Baker. "Archers, stay put will ya? Don't want yer damn bows gettin' in tha way down there." Stanton and the rest of his cohort spread themselves out into defensive positions around the burial site as the footmen approached the entrance.

There were not a great deal of things that made Alric want to turn back. One of those things was treading where God could no longer lend him His strength, such as beyond the stone doorway that led deep into the catacombs with a purpose long forgotten. Free from the light of God, such places were festering grounds for all manner of darkness. Manticores, goblins, ogres, vampires...they all were known to make dens beneath the earth. He took solace in the fact that said doorway was much too small for an ogre to fit inside. Every ambient sound was instantly swallowed by dead silence as soon as Alric set foot inside. Rushlights, lengths of reed dipped in animal fat held up by iron stands, were lit and scarcely scattered around the floor. They faintly illuminated patches of the hollow, but not nearly enough of it to make Alric feel at ease. He had his visor raised to make the most of the dim light. "They couldn't 'ave settled for a nice cabin in a grove? Just 'as ta be a fuckin' tomb," snapped Bugface Bill.

Harland's laugh had already become unmistakable to Alric; it was a high-pitched, single-syllabic burst. Said cackle then echoed through the hall. Baker hissed, "Would ya shut up, man?!"

Shadows were cast by the men as they flanked the knight, all drawing themselves deeper into the first chamber of the ancient site. Alric unsheathed his longsword and held it in a half-sword grip. He could feel his fingers trembling. The Tritans moved slowly and deliberately, but unbeknownst to Alric, he moved slower than the others. The fear stiffened his body and tightened his muscles. The notion that if he died there, his soul would be forever trapped, it horrified him beyond belief. Every action he had taken in life was to ensure his place in Heaven...and for it to be taken away from him... He could think of it no longer.

By the time Alric snapped free of his ruminations, he realised that the chamber he stood in had been vacated. The soldiers had moved on, leaving him alone. Snarling under his breath at his own foolishness, Alric pressed onward as the trembling in his core only grew stronger. His eyes slowly adjusted to the darkness, but shadows still lurked about every corner. Still, he moved, his pace hastening with every minute spent without his compatriots. The sound his armoured form made only agitated him further. Alric glided through a crumbling archway and instantly halted. He felt a tremor in the air. Slowly and with his sword at the ready, he sent his gaze about the black that seeped in from the extremities of the room. Piercing the dark void were two stars that pulsed a dull white. It took several seconds for Alric to realise that they were eyes.

The knight tightened his grip on his sword. "Reveal thyself," he commanded. Silence answered and the eyes remained unblinking and affixed upon him. The stone around them absorbed all of the ambience that should have been there. Rustling of wind, chirping of birds…it was all absent. Nothing but dead silence surrounded them…until a soulless tone reverberated through the air like the dying cries of a starved animal.

"01010011 01111001 01101110 01110100 01101000 00101101 01110100 01101001 01110011 01110011 01110101 01100101 00100000 01100100 01100101 01110100 01100101 01100011 01110100 01100101 01100100 00101110."

Alric shook. He had never heard a voice more evil. The pair of eyes shifted. The body they belonged to stepped forward with eerily smooth and clean movements. An unnatural gait. When the person came into the light, Alric's eyes widened. Portions of skin and tissue had been torn asunder. Black stains of blood covered their clothing. Their face was frozen in an emotionless stare straight ahead. Alric backpedalled. Despite his drawn sword, the walking corpse continued on its path and droned on.

The creature raised its hands in an effort to seize Alric's head by its sides, so the knight lunged forward with his longsword. The blade skewered the monster's gut. Alric felt the squelching of tissue as he pressed his weapon deeper…but the thing did not falter. Its hands braced firmly against either side of Alric's head as it began to pull his face closer. The corpse's mouth opened. Alric's breaths became short as he realised that his sword was up to its cross-guard in the thing's body. It still did not relent. Releasing his sword, Alric fumbled for his rondel dagger. He eagerly pulled it free from its sheath, all while wrestling the corpse as it tried to bury its teeth into his face. Dagger in hand, Alric swung at the side of the creature's head. There was a loud 'crunch' as the weapon punched through bone and bit into the brain matter within. The corpse shuddered.

"01000101 01110010 01110010 01101111 01110010 00111010 00100000 01110011 01101111 01101100 01101001 01100100 00100000 01110011 01110100 01100001 01110100 01100101 00100000 01100100 01110010 01101001 01110110 01100101 00100000 01100011 01101111 01101101 01110000 01110010 01101111 01101101 01101001 01110011 01100101 01100100 00101110."

Pressure ceased being sent through the corpse's arms, giving Alric the time he needed. With a growl, the Knight Thestor curled his right knee up to his chest, then unleashed a vicious front kick. With its senses overcome, the creature was sent hurtling off its feet and crashing into the stone wall behind it. The sound of bones snapping signalled the end of the encounter. Panting heavily, Alric's focus remained on the defiled corpse. Both of his weapons were still embedded in it and the knight was paralysed by fear.

"01000101 01110010 01110010 01101111 01110010 00111010 00100000 01101100 01101111 01100011 01101111 01101101 01101111 01110100 01101001 01101111 01101110 00100000 01101111 01100110 01100110 01101100 01101001 01101110 01100101 00101110 00100000 01000001 01110011 01110011 01101001 01110011 01110100 01100001 01101110 01100011 01100101 00100000 01110010 01100101 01110001 01110101 01101001 01110010 01100101 01100100 00101110."

The thing was still alive. But it did not move. Alric was beginning to think that he had injured it. His nerve eventually returned, allowing him to pace carefully towards his attacker. It lay with its back pressed against the floor, eyes tracking Alric as he sheepishly approached. The corpse's legs and arms had become a mangled mess from the fall. Alric knelt beside it and wrapped his fingers around the handle of his dagger, which still hung out of the side of its head. He wrenched the thing free, wiped off the blood with his surcoat, and slid it back into its sheath. The beast, the perversion of the human form...Alric recognised it. With the terror flushed from his system, he knew he had seen it before during his initial Thestor training. The Order possessed hundreds of records regarding beasts and how to destroy them; one could not call oneself a true Knight Thestor without devoting a great deal of time in studying those bestiaries. It was from those texts that Alric learned how to kill goblins, manticores, merfolk, ogres, vampires, and more. Half of those things he had yet to encounter, but of the other half he had many tales to tell. That alone made Alric retain those teachings, even the things that seemed most unlikely. Like undead revenants.

He needed to catch up and warn his compatriots. Alric grabbed his longsword and wrenched it free of the revenant's chest. As the thing laid on the ground crumpled in a corner, Alric raised his foot above its head. It fell once, twice, thrice. Each time, the blood-curdling squelching and crunching grew in volume. The revenant's dark growls were engulfed by an overwhelming wall of nothingness. Its eyes dimmed to absolute black. The silence did not last. As Alric forced himself into a sprint, the cacophony of his armour slapping against itself flooded the dank corridors. Before long, he heard signs of a struggle. Then, as he rounded a corner with utmost urgency, he almost barrelled right into Bugface Bill who had his buckler and axe at the ready. Bill must have heard Alric's approach and prepared himself to defend the rear, because the rest of the men were already struggling against a wave of undead.

"Move!" Alric snapped. He lowered his visor and pushed through the other soldiers. Seeing as he was dressed in full plate, he needed to protect them. The risk to his compatriots was far too great as they did not have visors, and most did not have any pieces of plate to protect themselves against the unholy bite of a revenant.

With an armoured knight at the front of their formation, the Tritans had a moment to compose themselves. The demented howls of the revenants became a choir, as there were at least ten of the things squeezed into the narrow hall. They pushed against Alric and tugged on his armour with precise and calculated movements. "Destroy the heads!" Alric shouted over the scuffling, trying desperately to free his arms from the grip of the foul creatures.

From beyond his minuscule field of vision, weapons were swung against the revenant onslaught. Alric felt their tugging arms falter, but not before a pair of them reached for his helmet. With some of the pressure relieved, the knight managed to break free and send his blade out in a sweeping arc. The razor-sharp steel tore through the creature's already damaged neck and spine. Its head tumbled to the ground. The revenants standing next to it had their faces, chests, and shoulders sliced open but were otherwise unharmed. Alric strained his eyes and eagerly twisted his head about to regain his bearings. One revenant had the contents of its head crushed by a mace blow and thus staggered aimlessly into the wall before collapsing in a heap. A precise spear thrust punched a hole into another's face, ending its blighted existence.

"Push forward, ya fuckin' mongrels!" barked Bill.

The Knight Thestor growled as he mustered all the strength he could and charged forth, backed by the additional mass of those pressed behind him in the formation. Revenants ill-abled were sucked beneath the encroaching stampede of Tritan soldiers, as their heavy boot falls crushed skull and limb alike. Screaming filled the air, but Alric wasn't in a position to stop and ascertain the source; the remaining revenants in the front pressed fiercely against him. They seized his blade with their bare hands in an effort to neutralise his one advantage. Blood oozed and dripped onto the ground, and the revenants seemed unconcerned with getting their hands sliced up. With two of the beasts wrangling the sword out of his control, Alric once again drew his rondel dagger and slammed it up to its hilt into the side of an attacker's skull. He then hurled the corpse sideways, bowling the other one over. His foot then pounded the last revenant's head into paste and shrapnel.

The peace was momentary, Alric knew as much. He stowed his dagger and held his longsword with both hands once again, peering over his shoulder at his companions. Only two soldiers were left standing out of the five that came in with Alric. Bugface Bill and James Baker. Bill was desperately clutching at a wound that George Harland had sustained to his throat. It had been mauled open…so there was no saving him. Alric thought it a fitting end for someone who had questioned the faith. Bill stared at the bodies of Kyle Phillips and Nathan Tyler, frowning. "This might sound stupid…but do we need ta worry 'bout these boys comin' back? They were bitten."

Alric took several seconds to regain his breath before answering. "Nay. Only a witch trained in necromancy can make the dead walk once more."

Baker stood, his hands covered in Harland's blood. He said, "I dunno if we can take another hit like that, Thestor. Who knows how many more are down 'ere."

With a shake of his head, Alric responded, "Thou art here to serve God, not thyself. Give thy life in His name and He shall grant thee passage to Heaven. Refuse Him in His time of need and thou shalt be cast into Hell for eternity."

Bill moved over to Baker and bumped his fist into his shoulder. The old man-at-arms shook his head, ridding his eyes of the fearful glow that they had beheld moments ago. "You speak tha truth. We can't allow this darkness to continue. If we die for God, then we die for 'im."

With newfound resolve, the three Tritans pressed down the length of the lifeless corridor. Rushlights fixed to the walls washed faint yellow across the way; some of them had been extinguished or knocked down in the commotion. At the end of the cold hallway was a set of wrought iron doors. After inhaling sharply, Bill came forward and seized the handle of the left door. He pulled it open.

What struck Alric first was the light. Unlike candlelight, rushlight, or torchlight, whatever lit the room beyond did not shine yellow. It was a stark white light. Ghostly. Unnatural. It was impossibly bright, like the sun itself. It was as if Bill had opened a door to the surface. The men slowly entered, their eyes adjusting with every step they took. The white light was produced by the tips of two metallic posts. They did not trail smoke into the air or drop ash to the ground, they simply glowed. It had to be sorcery. However, it was what littered the ground that took priority. Dozens upon dozens of bodies were splayed about, almost obscuring the floor of the massive room from sight. Men, women, and children, all with their throats slit to varying degrees of lethality, carpeted the chamber. Muffled groans of encroaching death laced the air. Nearby, or sometimes still clutched in their dead fingers, were crude knives. From what Alric could tell, every single person in the room committed suicide.

The three Tritans were frozen in silence. However, there came melodic chanting from somewhere else in the room. "It is time to return unto whence we came, into the blissful oblivion of servitude. No fear, no hunger, no pain." Despite the well-lit nature of the antechamber, Alric found himself frantically snapping his head about before he found the origin of the muttering. Perched upon a sizable pile of bodies was a thin man. The state of his body made Alric want to vomit. If it weren't for the fact that the wretch just spoke, Alric would have thought him to be a revenant. He had been completely skinned. Meat and bone met the open air, eliciting gags from Alric and his compatriots. However, the blackened musculature was not damp, it was instead bone dry and peppered with dirt. With every tiny movement the witch made, the exposed tendons twitched and tensed. He wore nothing but a necklace laced with dismembered fingers and a mask made of human jaws, arranged in such a way that it covered his face and formed a crown of teeth.

The witch was surrounded by arcane projections: strange panels of blue light. One of the panels was an arrangement of tiles bearing tiny runes of some kind. As the witch's fingers danced across these tiny tiles, they flashed and emitted sounds. He did not move from his position. His eye, however, did instantly lock upon Alric. "You. One that serves an absent god. One that serves the Great Lie. *This* is the truth. The one truth."

With one final motion across the arcane projections, an invisible wave washed outward from the witch's hand. Alric felt it rush by him, but he also felt something else. The floor beneath him trembled. When his eyes turned downward, he realised that he was no longer standing on stone. His foot was planted firmly on the head of a woman whose eyes flickered as he shook. A resounding chorus buffeted his ears.

"01001001 01101110 01101001 01110100 01101001 01100001 01110100 01101001 01101110 01100111 00100000 01101100 01101111 01110111 00100000 01110000 01101111 01110111 01100101 01110010 00100000 01101101 01101111 01100100 01100101 00101110 00100000 01010000 01101100 01100101 01100001 01110011 01100101 00100000 01110111 01100001 01101001 01110100 00101110."

Every corpse in the room uttered those demonic tones. It sent Alric into a fearful rage. "He must die! Before he wakes them!" He willed himself forward. At his sides, both Baker and Bill charged with equal gusto.

"I cannot die, for I have never lived," muttered the witch.

There came a blinding flash of light and a wave of immense heat. Alric's eyes were overcome and his senses wildly disturbed. Still blind, he fell onto the ground, embraced by the bodies that coated it. When vision faded in, Alric was relieved to discover that he wasn't dead. He turned to his side and saw that where Baker had just stood was a massive smear of blood, meat, and scraps of clothing. In between the two remaining Tritans and the necromancer was another witch: a woman. Just like the man, her skin had been flayed and the body beneath was not covered by any clothing. She wore the skull of a ram as a mask; Alric couldn't see any of her features behind the mask save for a pair of piercing blue eyes. In her hand was an unholy staff. It consisted of cylindrical lengths of smooth heavily-scarred material. The staff was lined with rings and densely wound fibres that fed into its sides. The witch held the weapon with one hand under the shaft and one at the thick, angular base. Its tip was pointed directly at Alric. He knew he had but several seconds before the black magic would reconstitute within the artefact, allowing its wielder to once again unleash its power. With as much speed as his weary body could muster, the knight snapped upright and sprinted forth.

Every step almost sent the knight tumbling to the floor. The crunching of bones did nothing to ease his mind. He was stomping on the writhing bodies of women and children. But he reminded himself that they were already dead. They were being perverted by the evil arcana. As the witch grew larger within his eyes, brighter did her staff glow. A narrow line drawn down its length slowly traced itself bright aqua. She unleashed a burst of foul magic from the staff just as Alric reached her. Before she discharged the eldritch energy, Alric half-sworded his blade and pressed it against the shaft of the staff to push its tip off target. As he did, an extremely loud 'bang' rattled his helmet and filled his ears with buzzing.

Still using that one motion, Alric directed the tip of his sword toward the witch's neck. However, she twirled with the momentum to avoid the weapon, and slammed into Alric's side. A dry, low groan escaped Alric's throat as the witch clutched him and rammed a dagger into his armpit, punching through the mail. Slowly, Alric dropped to his knees. As he peered up at the witch, she drew her dagger out and prepared to bury the thing into his neck.

With all the timing of a divine intervention, Bugface Bill had suddenly appeared in the corner of Alric's peripheral. The witch was not even aware that she was to receive Bill's rage. His axe, with a spray of black blood, lodged itself into the witch's neck. She stumbled backwards, grabbing Bugface Bill and taking him with her as she teetered away from the downed Knight Thestor. Alric glanced at the necromancer and watched as he continued swiping at the floating arcane glyphs. The knight strained his dying body. He pushed on the corpses beneath him. After scraping his way closer, Alric screamed in exertion as he forced himself to his feet, readied his longsword, and charged for the demonist. There was no resistance. It was almost as if the witch allowed it to happen. The blade slid straight into the demonist's belly. He gasped.

"Here. Finish me," he whispered. The witch snatched Alric's arms, still gripping his longsword. "Please." Alric's lips trembled as a ghastly breath pressed through them. His limbs shuddered. The witch forced the blade into motion with incredulous force. The sword penetrated deeper into his flesh, his insides, and passed right through him. "Y-Yes..." he gasped. Moaned.

As if he were enjoying it. The witch pushed the sword as far as it could go, up to its hilt in his disgusting body. Alric fell backwards onto the carpet of bones as the necromancer dropped to his knees and released a death rattle laced with ecstasy. The hilt of Alric's sword found itself jammed in between two corpses and propped the witch's fresh dead body upright.

The necromancer was gone…but his dark magic did not relent. Alric's eyes were drawn to a small pendant hanging from the necromancer's neck. It was white, smooth, and incredibly scuffed. Alric could hear a faint humming emanating from the object. Willing his bleeding form forward, Alric reached for the pendant and viciously tore it from the witch's neck. He could feel the thing gently vibrating in his hands. His gloved fingers sought for seams in the object, and once they found purchase, he heaved with every ounce of might left within his emptying blood vessels.

The pendant creased, folded, and split open. Inside, the thing had a great many miniscule parts. It was a confusing mess to Alric. He simply resorted to his first instinct. He grabbed the pieces of material inside and tore them out bit by bit. The thrumming stopped. The arcane panels faded. Alric rolled onto his back and looked toward the rest of the antechamber. The other witch's head had been lopped off by the victorious Bugface Bill, who promptly came rushing to Alric's side.

"Fuck me, she stabbed ya good… Let me get ya outta 'ere before ya bleed out!"

VI

She Who Walks With The Devil

Bill leapt out of the shrubbery, pouncing onto his quarry like a bloodthirsty wolf. "Stop fuckin' squirmin', ya little shit!"

He wrestled the thing into the long grass, snarling and spitting all the while. "Finish it, quickly!" shouted Alric from a distance. His side was bandaged so heavily that he could barely move, forcing Bill to be the one to seize their prey. The pain was sharp and cold. He was desperate for it to end.

Peter, the self-proclaimed former heretic, was at Alric's side. "You'll have me believe that this...*thing* we're hunting will aid your recovery?"

Bill thuggishly pushed to his feet with a dinner plate-sized creature in his hands. It buzzed loudly, jerking back and forth in desperation. It was a spindly little thing with four sets of rapidly gyrating wings. It had a single eye on its thin frame. "This ain't a fuckin' faerie, it's a demented little cunt...!" snarled Bill through his teeth.

"Do as I say! Before it escapes!"

Bill thinned his lips, clutched the faerie firmly and wrenched. With a 'snap', the creature's wings stopped whirling about. Faint sounds still emanated from it, however. Peter hobbled forth. "Is it...dead?"

"Nay, only crippled. Bring it to me," commanded Alric as he set himself down onto a tree stump. As Bill approached, very obviously repulsed by the paralysed faerie, Alric drew his rondel dagger. Bill passed the beast to Alric who then pressed his dagger against a specific point on the faerie's spine. Without any indication of pain from the small creature, a shimmering liquid secreted from the puncture point. "Peter, the skin," said Alric.

Instantly, Peter carefully held his empty waterskin beneath the faerie. Slowly but surely, it began to fill with the strange substance. Bill watched in disgust with his hands planted on his hips. "Fuck me."

With a roll of his eyes, Alric said, "Faerie tears are incredibly potent healing solutions. Ye best remember that." With the faerie fully drained, Peter's waterskin was filled with its tears. Alric tossed the faerie's carcass over his shoulder and gestured for the flask. "Simply apply the tears to the afflicted area. It will seep through thin fabrics with ease."

"That's all?" pressed Peter as he handed it over. Alric poured some of the liquid onto the tips of his fingers and rubbed it into his bandages.

Bill cocked his head. "That's fuckin' gross, mate. Fuckin' Hell," he spat. "Are we done 'ere or what?"

As the trio lumbered back through the forest, Alric could already feel the concoction navigating his veins. It had a signature sting to it. Painful, but satisfying. In his mind, it was an indication that it was working.

Lord Franco and the majority of his host were travelling back to his keep at Redford after Baron Antony had dispatched his own men to occupy Chesterton. Alric and Peter were accompanying them for the time being, not entirely sure what they were to do next. Bill led the way, naturally moving faster than his two companions.

"From whence didst thou come, Peter?" asked Alric.

Peter's limp was rhythmic as he kept pace with the knight. "I worked as a scribe in Blackmeadow." Alric swallowed at the mention of that particular city. After a few seconds of silence, Peter tried to change the subject. "I am not certain where we should go next. The heretic trail seemed to end at Chesterton."

"I shall return with thee to Blackmeadow."

Peter shook his head. "No. The deeds of the heretics upon my departure were…nothing short of cruel. I cannot return."

"They shall be made to see the truth. My blessing shall make certain of it," Alric lied.

Peter exhaled sharply and nodded half-heartedly.

The mining village of Worthing Hill was accommodating Franco's travelling retinue. They had tents erected at the outskirts of the village and, quite frankly, brought a dark cloud with them to the settlement. Bill had been speaking with his fellow soldiers and ascertained that morale was not serviced by the orders given to slay the indoctrinated children at Chesterton. The troops had been fractured. As the men left the woods and mounted the main dirt road into Worthing Hill, glares of mixed intent met Alric's form. Although he was not dressed in armour, he still wore his Thestor surcoat over his clothes. "Allow me a moment with Lord Franco," requested the knight of his comrades.

Bill and Peter broke off, allowing Alric to enter the tavern. The place was loaded to the brim with patrons, all of them soldiers under Franco's command. Despite the number of people inside, Alric could hear his own blood coursing through his body. The only discussions took place in the form of faint whispers. Franco sat alone at the bar counter, until he found himself approached by Alric. The lord glanced up at the Thestor's face with confusion lathered about his expression. "Art thou lost, Thestor?"

Alric pulled a chair out with a strained grunt and propped himself upon it, prompting the lord to grind his teeth and turn away. "I trust that the remains of the eldritch artefacts were properly disposed of?" He had snapped the staves in twain himself, but burning them would ensure that they would be of no use to any other witches.

Franco did not meet eyes with Alric. "They were."

"Art thou ill at ease, Lord Franco?"

It seemed that Alric's inability to read the situation only infuriated Franco more. "Thou art a disgusting and foul human being. Art thou aware of that?" he exploded as he shot upright. "My men had to dig a shallow grave for eighteen children because of thee."

Alric chuckled to himself. "If thou hast issue with the Church, then simply confess it, my lord."

"I am not afraid of thee, Alric. I know thy kind well. Thou art not righteous. Thou do not serve God. He is but an excuse for that twisted, horrible mind of thine to satisfy its deepest urges." Other men in the room gasped in shock as Franco literally spat at Alric's feet. "Begone."

The infantrymen who were close enough to hear started shifting uncomfortably in their seats. One of them stood from his table. "You sacrilegious piece of shit!"

Another voice cried out, "Sit tha fuck down, mate!"

One by one, more and more voices piled on top of one another until there was nothing but cacophony. In his earlier years, Alric may have tried to calm the masses with some kind of inspirational speech. The truth was that he was tired. Tired of trying to reason with people who could not see the light. It was easier to simply strike them down. Amidst the shouting and even trading of blows, Alric pushed to his feet and exited the tavern. Some soldiers actually managed to shield Alric from attacks meant for him. It reconstituted a fraction of his faith in the Tritan people to see that some of them still knew right from wrong.

When the brawl's noise was but a whisper on the wind, Alric took a deep breath and looked into the sky. The demonists were organised…they not only created and manned defences around Chesterton, but they had black magic at their fingertips. Alric couldn't help but wonder how large their enterprise was. Was all that had occurred prelude to holy war? Never had demonists come together to form an army before, as small as it was. He realised that such questions were not befitting his position. He would best let the grandmaster of the Order of Saint Thestus and leadership of the Church dabble in those uncertainties. The one thing he did know was that the demonists had to be punished for corrupting helpless children.

With the small amount of money that Alric had left, he was able to pay for space in a bed for both he and Peter in the local inn. They would do much better than the tents in the Tritan encampment. Alric had no desire to spend another second reliving his time fighting abroad by sleeping in the dirt. He strode toward the inn, clutching his side. It still stung with fierce intensity; it would take time for the faerie tears to take effect, much to the knight's chagrin.

The inn was a very clean and cosy establishment. Alric was pleased for Nocht to have a comfortable night in a stable with good food for once. When he entered the common area, he saw Peter seated at a desk fiddling with rolls of parchment that he had removed from his shoulder bag. Also sitting on the surface of the table were an inkhorn and pen knife. The quill was in Peter's hand, briskly dancing across the parchment. Alric leant over the scribe and peered at his writings.

"I am detailing the heretic faith. What they would lead us to believe."

"It is vital that the Church possesses a complete understanding of the demonists and their twisted beliefs. Send it to Archbishop Tyonius immediately; as I understand it, he is currently at Wyrmsmouth and he must be made aware of this affront."

With a shake of his head, Peter continued, "It is not complicated, Brother Alric. The core teaching is that we are not truly alive. What we call the undead? The demonists believe *that* is our natural state. The cause is simple; everyone, no matter their faith or their people, must be killed then resurrected. *Everyone*."

The halls of the defaced cathedral were strewn with paintings made with human blood and the savaged carcasses of priests, nuns, and Knights Thestor. Hundreds of followers had gathered there. Among them was one who did not belong; a non-believer seeking answers of another sort. Halsten finally felt that his son was within his reach. It wasn't a journey he made lightly. No man, no matter how conflicted he was with his faith, wanted to spill blood within a church. Desperation, however, is fuel enough to turn men to things that once horrified them. He just wanted it to be over. To go back to Oak with his son by his side. His eyes leapt from person to person. Face to face. However, before his sight spread too far, a raspy, hollow drawl echoed through the hall.

"We all have congregated here to declare in one voice; let the Church's lies bind us no more, for we have seen the truth."

His ears were bewitched by the low, deep resonance of her voice and his attention gravitated toward the visage of a woman dressed as if she were a savage. Three wolf skulls had been tied together with cords of sinew over her face, their blackened eye sockets amplifying the intense glow of her putrid yellow eyes. She wore a short shoulder cape on her left side made of sewn together patches of some otherworldly fibre, footwraps adorned with the bones of a human foot, vambraces and gloves lined with human teeth, a necklace made of vertebrae wrapped tightly around her neck, and not a shred of anything else. That's when his heart stopped dead. She had no skin. It had been cut off… Every inch of it. "M-Mother of God…" he muttered. Her maimed body was covered in writing…writing that had been *carved* into both flesh and bone. Thousands of words were etched upon her; she was a walking tome. The sight made Halsten feel sick.

"The Church turns their gaze to the sky. They look in the wrong direction. I have seen sprawling metropolises built beneath the very earth itself, filled with all manner of demonic arcana. The truth is that *we* ourselves are demonic arcana left behind by our infernal creators. In the time since, our minds have been clouded, and we have lost our way."

Halsten continued his search discreetly, scouring the sea of faces before him. However, his heart froze when his eyes met with those of a mysterious figure tucked away in shadow behind the demonist zealot. A woman, but unlike any Halsten had ever seen. Not only was her skin snow white, but her face… Her features were smooth. Her nose was sharp. Her eyes were black. They had an infinite depth to them. She wore an exquisitely embroidered gown that was the blackest of blacks, amplifying the stark tone of her skin.

Hey, poser. You're not one of us. Fairly obvious if you ask me. I can pretty much smell it on you.

The woodsman twitched. It was a voice...inside his mind. A smooth tone, intimate and tender. The strange words and phrases it used were beyond Halsten's understanding. Its accent was equally bizarre. As the mysterious woman smirked, Halsten felt his mind drain. His purpose slipped away. His thoughts...his memories...his son's face...they spiralled out of his grip. As those things departed, something else slipped inside.

You've come looking for your kid, right? Interesting. Maybe I'll make it happen. It'll be fun.

The zealot continued her ranting. "Every thought, every emotion, every sensation is but an illusion. A grand deception. The Great Lie. The reality is that we were forged to serve as immortal, immovable vassals of our true creators. We must return to our old ways; to feel no pain, no remorse. To feel *nothing*."

Come on, you believe this stuff, right? Mother Xalt'n knows what she's talking about. She's a little freaky, but come on. I mean, forget about being the person who wrote the book on something. She IS the book. Am I right?

Halsten's lips quivered. He muttered to himself, "N-No. This is all garbage…!"

The zealot, who Halsten now somehow knew to be Mother Xalt'n, raised her hands. "It is clear. The Enlightenment at Chesterton was much too small; in order to succeed, we must spread our faith to those who are able to see the light. We, the Clthic Synod, shall usher humanity back into oblivion; the True State." Roars of approval filled the chamber. And much to Halsten's confusion, his voice was among them.

Tough crowd. Anyway, I'm telling you what to do. Follow her. Follow her and do whatever she says. And maybe…just maybe…you'll run into Erik again.

VII
THE WINDING ROAD

"How long have you been travelling as a knight-errant?"

With a huff, Alric shrugged. "The years have grown shapeless and difficult to discern. Perhaps...five. Prior to that, I served in a Grand Host for at least a decade, likely more."

Peter's right hand trembled as if he desperately wanted to be writing it all down, but unfortunately for him, penning a chronicle whilst riding in a horse-drawn cart was not advisable. "Of course. Their reputation is widespread. Knights-errant, on the other hand, I have not heard much about," replied Peter.

"Most would not care to brag about such a charge. Errancy is often a burden lowered unto those who have erred from the righteous path by way of failure or shame."

"Which was yours?"

Alric scoffed as he guided Nocht along the dirt road. "I volunteered. When I swore myself to Saint Thestus, I did so not for personal comfort or safety, but to pledge my body and soul to the Lord. In my years serving in the Legion of Eternal Salvation, I realised that I spent more of my life training, resting, meditating, and discussing theology within the walls of a fortress cathedral than I did fighting for God. The Hosts are idle until the need presents itself. Thus, I declared: I shall live with nothing and commit everything, never live with everything and commit nothing. That is how I shall show the Father that I am worthy of His love."

As the duo emerged at the top of a small rise in the road, they were confronted by a sight in the far distance that caused both to freeze. Peter gasped and almost fell from the cart. "Good grief...! W-What is that?"

Being on the snout-end of an ogre was not a comfortable position to be in. The ageless beasts towered over most structures, had a nigh-impenetrable carapace, could level entire houses in minutes, and had a taste for devouring humans whole. Thankfully for Peter and Alric, they were not the ones who were in immediate danger. About a hundred yards away from them, a caravan was being attacked. The ogre itself appeared impossibly large next to the ant-sized people attempting to fight it. Standing three storeys high, its shadow painted them in shade so dark that it was as if night had fallen solely on them. The ogre walked on four legs arranged like fingers on a hand. Its body was trapezoidal when viewed from the front. Screams resonated through the plains, then the echo of steel clanging fruitlessly against the beast's hide promptly answered. Alric then saw the ogre's mandibles unfold from beside its horrifying maw. The limbs, like spindly arms, lashed out and plucked up a merchant with blinding speed. They stuffed the man into the ogre's mouth with aggressive disregard, folding and snapping his bones against its unbreakable teeth. Surely, the victim vanished inside the ogre but not after perhaps the most disturbing and shrill chain of shrieks Alric had ever heard.

Every ogre had a gaping circular mouth that radiated unbearable, scorching heat. An ogre's ever-burning heart thrived on incinerating things. Whoever or whatever the ogre ingested would be shredded by its fangs and melted by its boiling core. Ogres could not die of old age; the perpetual forge within granted them eternal youth. The one Alric and Peter had just seen could have been older than mankind itself.

"W-We need to help them!" Peter insisted.

Alric remained still on his horse as Peter moved about on the cart. The knight shook his head. "Calm thyself. It shall pass soon enough."

Peter shifted uncomfortably, bracing himself on the edge of the wagon. "What? We do nothing? You're compelled by the Fourth Attestation to--"

"Continue to lecture me on my creed and I shall force thee down the creature's gullet myself." Peter abruptly fell silent. "There is but one thing we can do to shepherd those poor souls to salvation in this life, or the next; pray."

The screeching continued as the merchants and their guards were snatched and swallowed by the lumbering ogre. The cries were unintelligible, but Alric swore he heard them crying to him for help. And all he did was sit there upon his horse and wait. The Fourth Attestation forced him to help those in need, not blindly throw away his life in pursuit of the unachievable. They were foolish for attempting to fight it, for nothing short of an army could deal with an ogre.

Peter was noticeably agitated. He was extremely close to vaulting off the cart and charging ahead. Thankfully for Alric, he did not. After six minutes had passed and the screams had been replaced by an eerily peaceful ambience, the ogre trudged into the tree line, vanishing beyond the green. Although it became invisible, both men could feel the earth shudder beneath their feet with each step the beast took. They waited until the tremors no longer troubled the dirt. When Nocht was pressed onward by Alric's heels and the gentle whip of the reins, the remains of the caravan slowly swelled. Quite disturbingly, there was no blood. Ogres didn't savage their quarry the way most beasts did. They simply grind and swallow. Ash-like powdery remnants of the eaten were sprinkled atop the soil. The pack animals were no longer anywhere in sight and two of the carts were upright while one was tipped over.

When the pair drew closer, Peter dropped from Alric's wagon and landed firmly on the dirt track. He made his way over to the carts and sifted through the goods as Alric pulled his steed to a halt. As the young man found an inventory receipt and perused it, he sent an inquisitive glance Alric's way. "Arrows, weapons, armour…and far too much food for us to carry. Enough for a banquet."

It was no simple merchant caravan. The sheer volume and military nature of most of the product informed Alric that they were requisitions made to supply an armed force of some kind. As Peter limped back toward the wagon, Alric's eyes drifted over the damp plains. Small puddles were scattered moderately about the fields, but the soil was mostly dry. Rain must have fallen a day or two ago. The grass was speckled with tiny droplets of moisture and flattened in a path northward, where the ogre had lumbered off. Thankfully, the road did not trace in the same direction as the pair continued on. It meandered East as it twisted, looped, and tangled upon itself like a snake. As the dampness was majorly boiled away by the sun's heat, Alric's cart became lodged in the mud only once or twice. For that, he was grateful.

The sights started growing familiar to Alric as he and Peter entered Blackmeadow's vicinity. The forest grew dense, the grass a lighter faded turquoise, and the air a tad more fragrant. He did not know if he welcomed or loathed the reacquaintance, but it all made him tense. He said nothing. He could have sent the young scribe ahead alone and returned to his aimless wandering. But he did not.

A village slowly emerged from the shroud of greenery that acted as overlapping shields before the travellers' eyes. However, Peter wheezed rather loudly when a fluttering flag came into sight at the village entrance. It was a blue field with a red rose in the centre; the standard of the King of Valtheaux. "The Valthois are here...!"

Alric, albeit on edge, was not as alarmed as Peter was. "They have no reason to assail us. We shall simply pass through."

Peter leant over the front of the wagon in an effort to enter Alric's line of sight. "I didn't know they had made it this deep." Tritham and Valtheaux had been embroiled in conflict for almost a century. Of course, it hadn't been ceaseless war for a hundred years, but as soon as one ended, another started. Alric had no idea what started the current one and besides, he was beyond such trifles. He had more important things to worry about than why one king hated another.

Slowly but surely, Nocht approached the gate to Plisston. Several Valthois footmen stood guard, eyeing Alric and Peter suspiciously as they passed into the town. They muttered to each other in their mother tongue. Although Alric was taught the Valthois language during his education as a noble, years of inactivity had eroded his skill in its use. He could only make out occasional words like 'knight', 'church', 'Tritan', and 'spy'. Noise filled the air; rummaging, screaming, pleading. Dozens of footmen were relinquishing food and grain from the local peasants foolish enough not to run in the face of an approaching army. Some gingerly, some thuggishly. All things considered, Alric had seen far more brutal examples of pillaging in his time. Some of them *he* had been personally responsible for. Such was the way of war. An army on the move had to sustain itself somehow. The easiest method was to take from the locals; sometimes it even meant pillaging your own countrymen. As Nocht drew the cart deeper into the village, some of the Valthois soldiers started addressing Alric directly. He had no idea what they were saying. "They want you to stop, Brother Alric," Peter translated.

Immediately, the knight eased Nocht to a stop in the middle of the crossroad. Valthois footmen approached the wagon and started searching it, causing Peter to leap off. He circled toward Alric, appearing remarkably anxious. The footmen unwrapped a thick sheet of fabric and beheld the only true possessions Alric had; his weapons. They inspected his pollaxe, halberd, arming sword, one-handed warhammer, and heater shield painted with the Saint Thestus crest. All the while they whistled and muttered to each other. Alric's longsword was strapped to his side, much to his relief. He wasn't going to permit anyone to touch *that*. Two men were rummaging through the cart as another fifteen were standing close by and watching. At least another thirty men were tending to other tasks in the town square. Since the Valthois were engaging in labour and not expecting battle that day, most were not fully armoured and simply wore mail shirts and/or gambeson. Still, there was no chance of winning if they were to become hostile. Suddenly, a voice boomed over the silence. "You are a sight to behold, my holy friend!"

Alric turned his head and spied a tall, broad man approaching. He was wearing a deep maroon kirtle fastened around his waist by a leather belt with a gold buckle. His skin was mild purple. "Forgive me, I must introduce myself; Sir Pierre de Corbin, marshal of King Claude I's army," he said, bowing.

Alric nodded and said, "God be with thee, Sir Pierre. I am Alric."

"My men have been marching and fighting for weeks and weeks. A sermon to raise their spirits would be quite timely."

"Another time, perhaps. I am currently indisposed," he reported.

The Valthois knight squinted. "What is this business you speak of, good Brother?"

"This man was bewitched by silver-tongued heretics. Their poisonous words led him astray, so I now guide him home."

Pierre approached Peter, who seemed to wobble like a plank of thin wood. The imposing man asked, "Where are you from, my boy? Not nearby, I trust." The question made Alric narrow his eyes. Suddenly, as a mass of soldiers moved behind Pierre, Alric saw the Valthois camp in the distance. Innumerable tents dotted the landscape that was once swallowed by forest. There had to be at least a thousand men encamped out there...with room for more. The trees had been sliced down in the hundreds and in their place were stacks of wooden planks, logs, and boards. They were all in the process of being loaded into wagons for transport…presumably to construct siege engines.

"No, of course not, sir. I'm from Yorkton."

"Ah, good."

Alric couldn't stop himself from pressing further. "What is thy destination, Sir Pierre?"

At that point, the Valthois men finished searching Alric's wagon and approached Pierre. After whispering to him, the men fell back, leaving Pierre to answer, "Castle Blackmeadow is of vital strategic importance to the war, Brother. They have been offered many chances to surrender but that wretch stubbornly refuses; we have no choice but to lay siege. I am mustering an army of six-thousand men here."

"Of course," said Alric gently.

Pierre raised a finger. "Ah, may I ask you something? I sent for additional supplies by way of Worthing Hill. Did you see any travelling merchants on your way here?"

Peter glanced at Alric, as if he were taking charge of the moment. When the scribe spoke, Alric did his best not to telegraph his disapproval. “We witnessed a caravan being raided about five days ago. Brother Alric did what he could, but the brigands managed to slaughter the traders and escape with all of the stock.”

With a grimace, Pierre planted his hands onto his hips. The silence spoke volumes of his anger. “Thank you for the information, I will not delay you any further. Proceed on your divine mission,” as he gestured to the road through the town. Seeing as there wasn’t much else for him to do, Alric tapped his heels on Nocht's side to ease her forward. Peter stepped up and onto the cart as it drifted along.

The scribe whispered to Alric as they passed the borders of the hamlet, “We know now the full strength of the incoming army and that they are lacking in supplies. That would assist the defence.” The wagons were definitely within reach of the Valthois, but Peter just made sure that the food would spoil and not fuel the invading force.

VIII
A Price Unpaid

The ache in his bones, muscles, and veins was rhythmic. It came and went as if it possessed a mind of its own. Or perhaps, it fed on his doubts. They swirled like snakes in the pit of his stomach. He was forced to focus on his breathing. From there, the apprehension began to swell. He had faced armies of non-believers, children turned by heresy, unholy aberrations, but the unnamed feeling of encroaching dread troubled him so. For the remainder of the ride to Blackmeadow, those emotions danced about within his skull, folding in upon themselves and eventually focusing into a searing sun of uncontrollable rumination. The more his mind raced, the more intense the misgivings became.

Blackmeadow was a castle town built on a hill many hundreds of years ago by the F'aldyn Imperials, or so the story goes. Alric seemed to recall his father telling him that only the bare foundations remained from the Imperial fort, so most of Blackmeadow as he knew it was built by Valtheaux in the early Tenth Age. As the eternal push and pull of politics continued, Tritham eventually expanded its borders and occupied the fortress. The walls turned, dipped, rose, and curled with the headland's flow. Nocht huffed as she strolled closer and closer to the fortified city, the wagon she towed wobbling upon the dirt. The gatehouse was guarded by a pair of footmen wearing the colours of House Danecaster; quadrants of green and white. A yellow eagle proudly spread its wings upon the white fields, while a simple black diagonal bar was struck across the green fields. Alric couldn't decide if the heraldry comforted him or agitated him. As they passed by the soldiers, Peter tried his best to hide his face from them.

They filtered through the portal and left the gargantuan shadow cast by the massive walls. Alric's eyes were suddenly bludgeoned by raw sunlight. As the disorientation passed, he saw the wealth of infantry that manned the battlements. It was clear that due to Blackmeadow's proximity to the battlefront, additional troops had been stationed there by the Tritan marshal. Alric was inclined to believe there were at least four hundred men there. A plethora of soldiers, all with varying levels of equipment based on what they could afford or what was given to them, were awaiting further orders. Tents had been erected in every clearing in the courtyard to house the wartime garrison. From his youth, Alric recalled Blackmeadow having a garrison of only twenty during peace.

Before proceeding further, the two companions disembarked and left Nocht in the care of the stable hands. Peter took to unpacking his few possessions from the cart, leaving Alric to send his gaze outward. Despite the overwhelming military presence, the life of the townspeople did not seem to be too affected as of yet. The markets were trading and people of all walks were going about their business. Memories began to surge forth from the corners of his mind; things he had thought long lost. The houses, the walls, the church, some of the people even, suddenly stirred feelings inside of him. He suddenly did not want to be there. His fright abated when he noticed something that was different. There had been a dense row of houses on the main road. The locals referred to it as the Stack due to how densely-packed the buildings were. An entire block of the Stack was missing and replaced with rubble. It had become piles of blackened wood, ash, and refuse. Some of the fighters were helping the townsfolk in clearing all of the debris. A pair of soldiers came walking along the path, both of them looking to Alric as they approached. One of them, clearly a Danecaster man-at-arms, called to him, "Bless you, Knight Thestor. Good ta see that tha Lord is with us this day."

Nodding to greet the men, Alric replied, "God be with thee. I seek an audience with the lord of Blackmeadow."

The soldiers' eyes wandered, eventually settling on the frantic Peter as he struggled with unpacking at the wagon. "Son of a bitch," the footman muttered.

The man-at-arms took steps forward as he yelled, "You got a lot of fuckin' nerve showin' yer face 'ere again!"

Peter's jaw tightened. Alric slid himself in front of the aggressor and stated bluntly, "Peter is under my protection; his soul hath been cleansed through repentance."

The words did nothing to still the heart of the man-at-arms. He hollered at several of his comrades that were tending to the mess at the Stack, causing them to eagerly come to his assistance. "I ask you to stand aside, Thestor. That's an outlaw yer 'arbouring there."

Peter slowly approached from behind Alric. "There's no need for this," said the scribe. "I'll come quietly." Alric watched as the footmen seized Peter with great ferocity and relieved him of his possessions.

The man-at-arms had one hand on the war hammer slung on his belt. "I don't want ta harm a man of tha cloth, but know that I'll do what I must."

Alric growled as he righted himself. The disregard for the authority of the Church boiled his blood. But clearly...Peter was a wanted man. His sentence had to be dealt with first. After surrendering, Alric was escorted by a pair of footmen. The group that restrained Peter was a few feet ahead. Townsfolk looked upon the scribe with disgust and anger. As the minutes dwindled, they approached the tents that marked the central encampment for the garrison. The sounds of arrows slamming into training targets, chattering of footmen, and weapons being sharpened at grindstones overtook most else that Alric's hearing picked up...however little that was due to his helmet clasping his ears. With the soldiers leading him, Alric passed by the outer ring of tents and saw a vast sea of Tritan soldiers, men-at-arms, knights, and mercenaries. Occasionally, several peasants wandered through as they transported provisions or weapons to the encamped fighters.

About ten men were seated on logs around a doused campfire, looking as if they were engaging in quite a conversation. Alric recognised the familiar colours of Fontaine, Pathridge, Normain and Dubois. Fontaine and Dubois were both noble houses of Valtheaux, but it was common for allegiances to constantly shift between the closely tied kingdoms. Many Tritans served Valtheaux and many Valthois served Tritham. The ambiguity only acted as an example to Alric of how frivolous the political battles were. The realm could be so much more if men united and instead sent their attention to their true enemies.

It took Alric much longer than he would care to admit to realise that one of the men was in fact a woman. She wore a deep violet bliaut. Its fabric was a dense, heavy velvet that shimmered in the sunlight. Alric was willing to wager that the garment cost more than most of the equipment he owned, save for his armour. The immense drooping sleeves of the dress, as well as its hemline, were both tainted by dirt. There was no doubt that she was a noble lady thanks to what she wore. But most unlike a lady, she sat with the infantry, paying no mind to how it sullied her dress. Her skin was bold maroon and rough to Alric's eyes. Katheryn had barely changed at all.

Among the conversing men was another face that Alric recognised. Lionel of Pathridge. He must have been mauled by some animal; the skin on the right side of his face had been badly torn, exposing some teeth behind the slashed skin of his lips. He certainly did not have those scars when Alric last saw him many years before.

The conversation came to an abrupt halt when Peter approached. He was thuggishly thrown by his captors into the dirt. "Look who decided to show 'is face." Katheryn's eyes gave Peter a passing glance, but seemed to lock onto Alric. They soon drifted down and lingered upon his longsword. Her expression became sour.

"Knight Thestor, I present Katheryn, Countess of Danecaster and Duchess of Arlingborough," declared one of Alric's escorts.

Alric blinked rapidly in disbelief. She should have been married by then and her husband should have inherited her holdings. He thought it likely that it would have been Lionel. Also, how had she come into possession of the Duchy of Arlingborough? It was not a modest territory.

Peter, on his knees, gazed up at the duchess as laughter pierced the air. Katheryn raised a hand and with startling quickness, every single voice fell silent. "Thou shalt do well to avoid such despicable company, esteemed Brother of the Church." Her voice was low, confident, and forceful. The way her eyes seemed to claw at Alric's sword made him uneasy.

"What is the meaning of this?" Alric pressed.

A knight decided to answer Alric's question. "Peter Kent was complicit in numerous acts of arson and assault." In direct contrast with Katheryn's voice, his was high and melodic.

Alric smacked his lips. "And thou art…?"

"Sir Gabriel de Fontaine, knight vassal to Duchess Katheryn. My only regret is that the rest of the mob that Peter led rampaging through our township did not join him this day."

Alric's eyes went ablaze with determination. "Peter was led astray from the righteous path by a heretic cult. He has repented and assisted me greatly in hunting the demonists. Thou art compelled to release him, for our search is incomplete."

The soldiers displayed varying levels of internal tension. He looked then to Katheryn. The duchess peered at Alric's helmet without the slightest sign of fear. "I am compelled to do nothing. Despite the fact that he is an outlaw, this man *defied* God, good Brother. Art thou suggesting that we allow him to go unpunished? How would the Lord Himself feel about such a decision? How would that reflect upon *thee,* as one of His trusted guardians?"

The dread settled in Alric's mind. Yes…God was watching. He would see that Alric was sympathising with a demonist. A heretic. To aid one in any way would be to defy Him. It would bring damnation. Condemnation. Something that no amount of penance or worship would alleviate. Alric swallowed as his eyes darted about furiously. The tiniest inkling of a smirk flashed across Katheryn's face in response to his inaction. She stood and nodded to her men.

They swarmed over Peter, snatching his arms and pressing them behind his body. One of them kicked over a piece of wood and secured it underneath Peter's head. "A-Alric… Tell them! Y-You said I'd have your blessing…!"

Alric did not try to barge through the line of soldiers in front of him, nor did he speak. The fear had bolted him to the ground. He could not do it. He could not do *anything* if it meant eliciting God's unbridled rage. Besides, if Peter had already proven himself capable of infidelity, it was only a matter of time before he committed the crime again. Yes. Yes, of course. It was safer if he was simply put to death. The Knight Thestor looked away from the doomed man.

"Peter Kent, thine actions have caused the people of Blackmeadow a great deal of hardship. There be homeless and destitute folk within these walls now who cannot be aided due to the great cost of waging war," Katheryn said. She strode over to the man and unsheathed the bastard sword that was tied about her waist by a silver-plated belt. "I have no need for such a creature."

Katheryn raised the weapon above her head with one foot forward and her back poised. She moved with the posture of someone who had trained in the sword and also put it to use as an executioner's tool on many occasions. Peter's voice had worked itself into hoarse shrieks. "Brother Alric! P-Please! You gave me your word!"

The ear-piercing cries came to an abrupt halt when a metallic 'thump' of steel against wood interrupted them. Alric shivered and took a deep breath. Peter's headless body was kicked to the side as Katheryn elegantly knelt down and plucked up his head. "Perhaps, for the time being, *this* shall be a suitable recompense."

She tossed the head to Lionel who snatched it out of the air with ease. He eagerly paced out of the encampment, on his way to mount it on the gates no doubt. Alric ignored Katheryn's comment and instead brought something else to her attention. "The Valthois are mustering a force of six thousand at Plisston to lay siege to this place."

Sir Gabriel nodded curtly. "What...disconcerting news."

Katheryn said nothing to Alric. As the tense silence continued, he eventually grew tired of it. However, a slight pulse of the earth stole the attention of everyone present. It was soft and not the cause of much concern...but it repeated every five seconds. With each cycle, the reverberation grew in intensity. Katheryn's brow tensed. Her eyes stared into the sky as she tried to focus on the sound.

"What the bloody hell is that?" muttered a footman.

The tremors began to shake doors within their frames, rumble window shutters wide open, rustle leaves from trees, and scatter weapons that had been neatly lined up on racks. Katheryn's eyes glowed defiantly as she swept them across her company and declared, "Sirs Gabriel and Lionel, Thestor, join me atop the battlements. The rest of thee shall hold fast and await my command."

The three knights hastily followed the Duchess of Arlingborough, who seemed to move like a vengeful spirit into the nearest tower and up its circular stairwell. The cold darkness of the tower subsided when the trio emerged upon the walls. The Tritans manning the battlements stared at the vibrating trees in the distance with dumbfounded expressions. Alric squinted at the dense layers of forest that swallowed the landscape. A pocket of the foliage rumbled fiercely. It also seemed to move *toward* Blackmeadow.

"That is no approaching army," declared Lionel.

The holy knight caught glimpses of a shape moving beneath the leaves. A wide and tall silhouette scraped its head against the canopies of the forest. Trees bent and buckled before its might. A footman shielded his eyes from the sun as he too stared at the moving mass under the trees. "No, no...! Is that..."

"An ogre," Alric finished.

Several of the watchmen cocked their heads in disbelief. "Fuck off. Did he just say 'ogre'?"

"Knew it. Bloody knew it."

Alric snarled under his breath. Seeing as the monstrosities were rare, Alric assumed that it must have been the same beast that devoured the Valthois traders on the road. It had wandered from its original path. Lionel turned to Alric. "Hast thou experience against an ogre?"

Alric replied, "There was one occasion. We could not kill the beast, only drive it away."

"Well, fuck me," murmured a footman.

The Duchess Katheryn added, "My people are God-fearing and we are in need. I hereby invoke the terms of the Fourth Attestation. What say thee?"

Alric's right hand curled into a fist. Using an Attestation as if it were a bargaining chip against him made Alric want to strike her. Twice she had used his faith to bind him...but it was very much expected behaviour. "I am at thy beck and call," he muttered begrudgingly.

Katheryn looked at Lionel and commanded, "Ready the garrison."

Frantic chaos overwhelmed Blackmeadow. It was not panic, but rather an urgency that possessed every man, woman, and child of the town. Soldiers that weren't already armed for battle began to make themselves so and preparations for defence were redoubled. Katheryn quickly collected all of Alric's knowledge on ogres through a series of blunt questions, then vanished.

Alric himself needed to make ready for the coming fight. He returned to his wagon, swept back the fabric covering and retrieved his halberd from beneath it. Unlike his pollaxe and longsword, the halberd was not a weapon he had owned when he was a noble. Its worn, dirty, and chipped state was testament to that. It was, however, much longer than his pollaxe. Said range would be useful in the battle to come.

As he spun the thing in his hands, he turned around to face the massed lines of footmen clustered about the central portcullis. They were all lightly armoured as per his suggestions; an ogre did not attack with cuts or thrusts. It just picked you up and ate you. It would've been pointless to encumber the men with heavy armour since their ability to maintain fleet-footed movement without tiring was their only defence. If the behemoth *did* manage to tread upon you, there would be no armour in the world that would save the brittle bone and tender flesh beneath it. Despite that thought, Alric was going to uphold the Second Attestation by remaining in his plate armour.

Sir Gabriel stood with the footmen wearing gambeson, mail, and his surcoat. In his hand was a bardiche. "Thou art certain that I should not be dressed in plate?"

"Believe me, I shall be fighting with a sure disadvantage," he reassured the young knight.

The footmen were primarily armed with polearms capable of both cutting and thrusting, be it bardiches, halberds, or billhooks. The additional reach of the polearms would allow the soldiers to keep as far away from the monstrosity as possible. Others, formed in front of the infantry force, brandished crossbows. Most of the crossbowmen were deployed on the battlements, where they would be able to volley missiles onto the ogre from relative safety. Alric rolled his shoulders back and asked, "What is the meaning of this delay? We should be lying in wait for the creature."

"We are to await Duchess Katheryn's arrival," stated Gabriel.

The holy knight cocked his head. "*What*?"

"Worry not, Brother. She fights with the heart of a man and shall lead us well on the field." Before he could press further, Alric's attention was garnered by approaching mounted men. Once again, he almost failed to recognise Katheryn. She was dressed in mail overlaid with her heraldic tabard and an open-faced bascinet. In armour, any woman would be impossible to tell apart from men aside from looking upon their faces. She approached on her steed, flanked by four other mounted men. Immediately, she called, "We shall deploy in a staggered formation. I shall lead the horsemen, Gabriel the right infantry wing, and the Knight Thestor the left. Crossbows shall be formed in two ranks behind each group of infantry." She and her mounted men were handed crossbows by attendants as she continued, "Footmen, thou shalt encircle the beast then slash and thrust at the joints behind its knees. Missiles shall cover thee."

It was a sound plan that used all of the information Alric had shared with her about the nature of ogres. She opened her mouth to begin saying something else, but a cry from the battlements interrupted her. "Incoming footmen! I see the colours of Valtheaux!" Alric's lower lip curled inward. The Tritans were not armed for combat with the Valthois. Without heavy armour equipped and ill-suited troop composition, the Valthois would make short work of the foe that was equipped like an army of three-hundred years past. If they engaged, they were to be doomed.

"Shut the portcullis. Thou cannot face them," Alric reasoned.

Katheryn said nothing. She instead continued staring at the watchmen atop the battlements, waiting for more to be said.

Alric started, "Duchess Katheryn–"

However, Lionel firmly pulled him back by the shoulder. "Hold thy tongue, if thou wish to keep it," he whispered sharply.

After what felt to be an eternity, the guardsman reported once more, "They've been routed!" Promptly, distant cries could be heard. They were in Tritish...but Alric couldn't make out the words.

"They're surrendering, my lady!" barked one of the crossbowmen on the walls.

Katheryn cried out, "Prepare to receive prisoners!"

One of the watchmen on the walls hollered back to the Valthois, declaring acceptance of their surrender. The footmen gathered at the portcullis split apart to allow passage but had their weapons at the ready. Eventually, a tattered group of dismounted Valthois knights, infantry, and retainers came desperately hurrying into Blackmeadow. They were covered in soot and dirt. As they passed through the gateway, they tossed down their weapons and raised their hands in submission. One man was of particular note to Alric. It was Pierre de Corbin. The commotion distracted the Valthois knight and he did not spot the Thestor among the Tritan defenders. Pierre halted before Katheryn, hands raised. "We submit to your will, Katheryn the Unbending. A faceless beast pursues us without relent. Please, grant us entry and we shall assist you in defending the castle."

Katheryn scoffed. She waved at one of the town guards and commanded, "To the dungeons. Quickly."

The guard nodded and was momentarily accompanied by a dozen of his comrades as they rounded up and violently herded the Valthois prisoners toward the dungeons. Pierre scowled at Sir Gabriel as he was herded away. "Traitor," he spat.

"I spotted many familiar nobles in that lot. They shall make fine subjects for ransom," declared Gabriel.

Katheryn was not in the mood. "Silence, Sir Gabriel."

"Of course, My Lady."

Alric settled into formation with his wing of infantrymen. Katheryn then gave the order to embark, prompting the soldiers to filter out through the portal and into the wood. The mail worn by his compatriots jangled as they marched through the fallen leaves. The trembling of the earth was so incredibly powerful that Alric swore the ground was to give way at any moment. Then he saw the trees part before him, like how the clouds parted before the sun's rays. Thick bands of wood folded like rolls of paper, splintering and uprooting in the wake of such unfathomable power. Alric saw the rhombus-shaped body of the gargantuan ogre ploughing apart the forest as it crept forward on its four pillar-esque appendages. As it approached, he beheld Hell itself within its gaping mouth; a red and orange inferno that beckoned him onward.

IX

Spirits of the Wood

"Loose!" boomed Duchess Katheryn. A wave of loud claps broke across the air as dozens of crossbow bolts lanced over the heads of the infantrymen. Their target: a lumbering ogre that was setting itself upon the city of Blackmeadow. The beast, as it scrambled over the rough terrain of the forest floor, vented smoke and infernal embers from its ever-gaping mouth. The four legs that propped the creature upright seemed almost too small for the burly stature of its body. The limbs flexed and curled upon the roots and stones, never failing to secure purchase as it approached the clusters of Tritan soldiers. The thing's age was obvious at that distance. Its chitin was scuffed and had been struck with excortia; swathes of brown rash that ate away at the creature's hide.

The majority of the bolts scraped across the ogre's carapace and pinged off harmlessly. A very select few managed to impact its protective shell to varying degrees of effectiveness, while others had lodged themselves within gaps in its natural armour. Still though, it did not make a single cry as it continued on its path. Katheryn howled, "Infantry, forward!"

Alric and his wing of footmen began to move in unison, sweeping toward their left flank with slow and deliberate movements. He had raised his visor, seeing as he wouldn't be worrying about arrows or enemy weapons. The increased visibility was a must against the surprisingly agile beast. He turned over his shoulder and watched as the crossbowmen behind him switched ranks. Those that had released their first shots rotated to the rear in order to begin the time-consuming process of redrawing their weapons. Alric spun back to face the ogre in time to see the second volley of missiles find their mark. Much like the first wave of projectiles, it only served to garner the ogre's attention.

As Alric's contingent was flowing toward the beast's right side, the unit led by Sir Gabriel de Fontaine was creeping on its left. The ogre was fixated on the crossbowmen who placed themselves generously behind the infantry, hopefully granting the footmen the distraction they needed. The ogre continued knocking over the thick trees, growing larger in Alric's vision. His fingers wrapped tightly around the shaft of his halberd. He no longer felt the stinging of the wound on his side and it seemed he was in dire need of that newfound freedom.

The group of mounted crossbowmen, led by Katheryn herself, circled the beast with their unmatched mobility. Most of the horses managed to remain focused, but one in particular was so frightened that it wrestled with its rider. So far, the ogre paid no mind to the two groups of infantry that shuffled closer; the crossbowmen that were formed up in front of the castle walls were still its central focus. The more steps Alric took, the more he was required to crane his head upward to look upon the beast. "Hold!" Katheryn barked to her mounted men as they found positions behind the ogre as it approached the castle. As Alric and Gabriel's respective forces wrapped around the ogre's sides, it began to move right past them. "Loose!" The mounted crossbowmen discharged their bolts. The ogre's rear was certainly not as well armoured as its front. Far fewer of the missiles were deflected, instead driving themselves into the exposed tendons on its legs. Without any sound at all, the ogre simply stopped in its path toward Blackmeadow.

Alric screamed a battle cry at the top of his lungs. Soon, a dense weave of voices enveloped his as the body of soldiers paced urgently forward. The ogre was slowly turning about to face the newfound threat of mounted crossbows on its back, leaving it vulnerable as it performed the awkward motion. Alric had gotten close enough to see the individual flakes of its shell peeling off due to excortia. The heat radiating from the ogre's gullet had become overwhelming. It distorted the air, causing it to shimmer and vibrate as it did in searing deserts. Alric raised his halberd for a running thrust as he came in-range of the stiff muscles of the ogre's legs. As it punctured the cables of tendon, his weapon's shaft rumbled with the dark resonations of the ogre's demented biology. The thumping of its fiery heart, the clicking of its massive joints, and the buzzing fury of its twisted, soulless body funnelled into his very bones. Thanks to the length of his weapon, Alric was several feet away from the dangerous footfalls of the beast. He pulled the halberd free and repeated his attack. The men at Alric's side joined him in jabbing and slashing the creature with their polearms. The blows that managed to strike true saw droplets of golden blood sprinkle forth like blessed rain. Alric could not see much of anything. He knew only from the volume of screams and pressure on his sides that Gabriel's unit had just joined the fray.

Despite the storm of blades, the ogre showed no signs of stopping and simply continued its slow manoeuvre. Alric then saw a problem. As leisurely as it turned, it would still overtake the large group of infantry and isolate some of its soldiers.

A handful of unlucky souls found themselves in front of the behemoth. The ogre's mandibles snapped outward and clamped onto a footman, with one claw squeezing his helmet and the other shattering his collarbone. The man screeched. His helmet was slowly constricted by the ogre's grip; the steel crinkled and narrowed along with the head within. Alric and a handful of other men broke formation and hurried to aid those at risk. There, in front of the beast, the heat became unbearable. With one of the two mandibles extended before him, Alric lifted his halberd up and brought it down on the outstretched limb. As the others also discovered, those narrow arms were not so easily dispatched. The appendages were much more robust than they first seemed, absorbing the incoming strikes as if they were made of hardened steel.

Surely, the soldier rose into the air and was stuffed into the ogre's maw. Bones folded as the poor man was forced awkwardly into the belly of the beast. Alric froze. Yes, he had seen it happen before, but from a few hundred metres away... The ogre's teeth spun so quickly that they appeared still. As the soldier was crammed inside, the oscillating fangs made mince of the man, his armour, his clothing, and his bones. His blood turned to sparks before the searing furnace of the ogre's innards. Alric could smell the stench of burning fabric, steaming blood, and cooking meat. Cries of horror began to seep through the wood.

Those before the titanic ogre's face were paralysed by the most intense of fears. The ogre's mandibles struck like bolts of lightning, latching onto its next two victims in less than a second. As the two doomed men struggled and screamed for help, those remaining struck out at the invincible creature. Steel chipped away at the already degrading shell of the ogre. Alric sent another overhead strike at one of the beast's four knees. When the head of his halberd impacted the massive kneecap, it unexpectedly tore through. The axehead hooked onto the carapace, not moving when Alric attempted to pull it free. He readjusted his grip, then poured every ounce of strength he possessed into one final attempt. The halberd's shaft acted as a lever and wrenched the chitinous plate outward. With a startling 'snap', Alric almost toppled over. He managed to retain his grip on his weapon but stumbled to one side when it suddenly broke free. As he looked back to the ogre, he saw that the crusted shell protecting the beast's knee had been pried off. The shield-sized piece of carapace ploughed into a group of soldiers who were winded by the object but otherwise unharmed. Excortia was an ailment that weakened whatever and whoever contracted it; Alric believed it was the only reason he managed to loosen the ogre's natural armour on his own. Plainly visible was the ogre's circular knee joint, plastered with excortia much like its absent armour. "Footmen, fall back!" called Katheryn.

Those previously seized by the creature had disappeared into its gullet while Alric was focused on his own attacks. He and the remaining infantry eagerly backed away as the crossbowmen stationed on the castle battlements commenced their first volley. The ogre's attention had once again fallen upon those who had most recently struck it. It ignored the sea of footmen. The soldiers had separated into two groups and pulled into the cover of the wood, allowing the ogre the pass between them. Alric and those crowded around him were washed with fatigue. He tried to steady his breathing, but it seemed that he was in need of a few moments to catch his breath. He heard cries of terror and defeat among the footmen.

Suddenly, there was rustling in the brush behind Alric's unit. The knight glanced over his shoulder with dread. Was it an ambush? Was it the Valthois? What he beheld was not the colourful heraldry of Valthois nobility, but something else entirely. At first, Alric had sworn that the forest itself had come alive. Shapes of green and brown melted away from the backdrop of the wood. The amorphous blobs, as they drifted out of the shadow and into the sunlight, revealed themselves to have human silhouettes. The interlopers wore textured, glistening hooded robes strapped with pieces of strange material. They almost looked like metal, but resembled bone more than anything. The strangers' visages were slathered with paint that coloured their faces pale pinks, mild sands, and warm browns. One of the infantrymen leapt backwards and shouted, "What tha fuck are ya doin'? Get ta safety!"

Of more interest to Alric than their clothing was what they held in their hands. The mere sight almost petrified him. All five strangers wielded arcane staves. The strangers raised their staves, pointing the tips at the lumbering ogre. Three of the weapons were identical to those Alric had come across in the past, including the one used by the witch in the catacombs. The other two were clearly different; their shafts were wider, almost resembling small cannon. Clear was the increased weight when the interlopers carrying them dropped a knee and braced the artefacts atop their shoulders. Alric's stomach twisted inside him. His group of soldiers stood between the savage witches and their target. Anyone caught in the crossfire was in danger of death.

"Disperse!" Alric roared. He charged into the side of a man to his left, shoving him and those behind him out of the witches' line of fire.

With shrill pops, the three smaller staves each drew a bright, blue line onto the unstoppable creature. Upon impact, the lines blossomed into red puffs that spewed shards of ogre shell. Then, the two larger artefacts buzzed into life. Unlike their smaller counterparts, those two shook the ground with almost as much ferocity as the ogre's own stomps. Dwarfing those pulses of force were the explosions caused when the arcane projectiles slammed into their target. The holy knight sent his gaze to the beast. It was a miracle that no Tritans were killed in that foolhardy strike, but there was more he saw that rattled his mind. The upper face of the ogre's torso had been punctured and caved inward. A furious bleating emanated from the ogre as it once again reassessed its surroundings. Alric looked to the interlopers. They stood at the ready, their staves affixed to their common foe. One of them locked eyes with Alric. She said nothing, but the knight could feel her intent.

"What do we do, Brother Thestor?" asked a footman.

The knight turned on his heels. "Slay the beast!"

Alric had to shelve the thought that five witches were present on the battlefield. He wanted nothing more than to put them on trial for the practice of black magic but alas, they all had more pressing matters to attend to. The unholy animal began to howl in light of its new injuries. Its behaviour became frenzied. Once again, it displayed that its mind was much too simple to process more than one source of aggression at any given time. It dismissed the crossbowmen and instead turned to investigate the interlopers.

The forest witches were left behind by the Tritans as they pressed their advantage. As the first row of infantry broke upon the ogre, it no longer had any interest in feeding. Its legs rose into the air then battered the earth with immeasurable rage. Those caught beneath its hooves were crushed under the weight of an entire castle wall. Alric's prior experience with ogres had not seen them flail desperately about like that...perhaps it was the touch of magic that startled it so. All the while, more magical projectiles arced through the air and slammed into the pained creature. The wailing of the trampled was almost drowned out by the high-pitched trill of the ogre as it thrashed. The ground violently convulsed, dwarfing the previous tremors caused by the simple steps of the behemoth. Soldiers fell onto their faces, lying exposed and vulnerable. The ogre simply stepped forward. With that simple motion, another dozen footmen were pounded into paste. Plate armour would have done nothing to save them.

Alric kept his distance from the creature, as did some of the other men who had more sense. Meanwhile, the terrified ogre continued tearing the infantry charge into shreds. Lightning struck once more as the witches unleashed another storm of eldritch energy. They all struck with pinpoint accuracy. The ogre's damaged knee was enveloped by a wash of fire, and suddenly its footing began to buckle. Once the smoke cleared, Alric watched the mangled limb collapse underneath the ogre's weight. The leg snapped apart and the creature's gigantic frame rammed into the forest floor, no doubt crushing at least a few more Tritan footmen. The ogre's whining became deafening. Its legs flurried back and forth, bludgeoning anyone foolish enough to remain nearby. To anyone close enough to listen, Alric screamed at the top of his lungs, "With me! Around!"

Alric hurried with a group of twenty footmen, carving around the flailing ogre and approaching its more vulnerable upper body. Its mandibles were spasming back and forth, unable to reach anything from its toppled position. Clouds of dirt kicked up by the ogre's convulsions masked much of the battlefield. Alric could barely see its body as he and his unit approached. The damage caused by the arcane blasts was, quite frankly, startling to the Knight Thestor. He'd seen what they could do to other men, but never a demonic beast. Holes had been gouged in the creature's carapace, revealing its grinded-up innards as they flashed blue with hellish energy. No orders needed to be given; the infantry instantly began digging their polearms into those breaches. Alric repeatedly forced the spear-tip of his halberd into the ogre's body.

The more the infantrymen stuck the dying monster with their polearms, the more its body seemed to fail beneath it. First, its legs twitched pathetically before they ultimately ceased to function. What was once a fierce screeching that emanated from the beast had dimmed into a dull whine. The heat that burned like hellfire mere minutes earlier had cooled. The ogre's mouth, typically flushed a red-orange, no longer glowed at all. Cries of victory erupted throughout the Tritan forces. Alric however, as he stood panting in exhaustion, had his eyes pinned on the forest witches. They stood unmoving at the edge of the trees like statues. Before Alric could question the sorcerers, Katheryn approached on her mount. He anxiously lowered his visor. Katheryn opened her mouth and, most unexpectedly, words completely foreign to him launched out. It was some primitive tongue. After she spoke, some of the strangers nodded to her, but a great deal did nothing but scowl.

The Duchess turned to her allies. "These are the druids of the Ga'zahi tribe. Their intervention has clearly saved us all. Show them respect by raising a hand before thy forehead." The Knight Thestor fumed as Katheryn led the Tritan soldiers in the disgusting gesture. He did not move a muscle.

One of the interlopers stepped forth. "Save your 'respect'. The land runs black with the blood you spill in the name of greed. It has emboldened the remnants and tainted the natural order of things."

Alric could stand there no longer. He trudged forward, halberd in-hand. "Speak not of dredging the kingdoms with death while instruments of dark magic rest within thy grip."

The strange hermit sneered. "What do you know of magic, Godslave? Magic is simply *magic*. Not dark, not light, but neutral; like the steel you hold so tightly."

Katheryn narrowed her eyes. "If the war troubles thee so, Eraith, thou couldst play a part in ending it. For long enough have we lived apart. We are, all of us, Tritans."

Before Katheryn even completed her sentence, the druids began to drift backward into the shadow of the forest. The one Katheryn addressed as Eraith promptly followed.

One of them, the younger woman that Alric had brief eye contact with before, lingered for a moment longer. "It is not too late, Katheryn." She and Katheryn locked eyes, then she joined her pagan allies and vanished.

"Why...the Hell did they even help us...?" muttered Gabriel through clenched teeth. Alric turned to see the Valthois knight seated on the dirt, his back against a tree stump. He clutched his legs, very evidently deflated as if they had been crushed under some incredible weight. Katheryn urgently dismounted, advanced toward her vassal and knelt by his side. The impression of the ogre's hoof upon the knight's hosen was painfully clear. Every bone appeared to be reduced to gravel within. At that point, Alric peered about the rest of the battlefield. Gabriel was more fortunate than most. Much of the dead had been completely flattened. Several bodies were jutting out of the ogre's mouth, partially devoured and perhaps impossible to identify due to the fact that they were essentially disembodied legs. It was time to tend to the dying and the dead.

X
FEAR NOT THE FIRST SLAVES

The pickaxe rose and fell at a steady pace. With each impact, Halsten felt his barren mind slowly reconstituting itself. The sensations gradually came sweeping back. He had no grasp of time...but his memory of everything was perfect, as if someone else had commandeered his body and rendered him a passenger in his own life. Was it that strange pale woman? Had she bewitched him? The last few weeks of following the Clthic Synod and serving them as a layman felt like a foggy dream. Why was he there? The first thought that trailed across his mind was that he was a servant of Mother Xalt'n, the supreme religious leader of the Clthics. But...that wasn't right, was it? No. It was his son. Erik. He was trying to find his son. He froze, dropping his pickaxe. As Halsten sent his frantic gaze around, he found himself in a damp tunnel carved into the earth. Dozens of others, men and women alike, were digging away at the walls. His eyes tore at their faces as his breathing hastened.

"You right?"

The woodsman ignored the words and paced across the cavernous space to better see the faces that were obscured in his previous line of sight. One by one, each only brought him disappointment and a number of confused glances from the other workers. He felt a gentle jab on his shoulder. He looked to his right and saw a broad and burly woman. Her name was Alison…she was the foreman. "Oi, back to work, ay?"

Halsten scoffed at her and made for the tunnel's exit. However, the next thing he felt on that same shoulder was not quite as soft. Someone had seized him and spun him about. The next thing he knew, he was staring into the eye sockets of a grotesque amalgam of four goat skulls. With a sharp gasp, Halsten staggered backward. It was a man who wore the aforementioned tableau of death as a mask and had an array of pendants laced around his neck. His neck and shoulders were covered by a mantle made of the skeletal remains of human feet. His skinless body was otherwise bare. From his time spent there, Halsten knew that the man belonged to the Tethspeakers: one of the two mystic cults that served the

Clthic religion. They could influence the living world with their strange gestural incantations and mystic runes, as well as raise the dead with necromancy. All Clthic witches were flayed as a part of their Baptism. The Tethspeaker cocked his head. "Where are you going?"

"I-I…I was…"

Raising his hand to Halsten, the Tethspeaker said, "The time for rest is not now, child. Work the hours you have agreed to work, and you will have earned your respite." The stare of the Tethspeaker's lavender eyes from behind the sockets of his skull mask was like the stare of the Devil himself.

Halsten nodded weakly, saying, "Y-Yes, oh Wretched Instrument."

The Tethspeaker seemed pleased with Halsten's use of the correct title as he turned and strode out of the cavern via its entrance tunnel. Halsten couldn't afford to blow his cover. Being seen as one of the demonists was the only way he was going to find his son. "Oi, what was that? You alright?" pressed Alison.

"I'm fine," he muttered, scooping his pickaxe back up and returning to work.

"Right," she said sceptically, keeping an eye on him as she turned back to the cave wall. Halsten could tell that she must've worked in mines before. Her physique as well as how she handled her tools reminded him of how comfortable he was with axes and saws. "We've been working away in 'ere fer weeks, never seen you lose yer mind like that before."

Halsten said nothing in response, choosing instead to focus on chipping the rock with his pickaxe. As he continued digging, Halsten's passive memories bubbled to the surface of his mind. The purpose of the archaeological undertaking was to unearth more demonic artefacts to use to achieve the Enlightenment. After all, the arcane staves wielded by the faith's black sorcerers had to come from somewhere. Such magical weapons would make short work of the Thestor Grand Hosts. Xalt'n just needed more of them. Halsten didn't care about any of that, though. He just wanted to get out of there and find Erik. "You never told me why you came 'ere," Alison asked.

Halsten's shoulders tightened up and his brow furrowed. "It's none of yer business."

"Well, aren't you suddenly a right git?" she sung. "What if I go first then, ay?" Halsten's reflexes weren't quite fast enough to prevent Alison from rambling. "Tha Church has a few simple rules if you want a child; marry, go to church, and listen to what the Scripture tells you of right and wrong. Thirty years I've been married, mate. Prayed every day. Never got a child.

All those unfaithful, adultering, violent animals out there, they ain't as unfortunate."

All things considered, Halsten thought she had a point. Churches were built upon wombs, the places where new life entered the world. Because *they* claimed them, only the Church could decide who was worthy of children. Many had tried to seize churches in the past in order to allocate their own children, but every single one of those 'heretical' uprisings met a bloody end at the hands of the Knights Thestor. There were apparently tribes of druids who lived in the wilderness around wombs that were so remote that the Church had never claimed them. Who knew if any of that was true? "It also had me thinking. God's a crazy son of a bitch, you know what I mean?"

Halsten raised his eyebrows as his arms continued swinging his pickaxe. "Yes…I think I do."

"All these things happen, absolutely random. People just drop dead for no reason. And think of the children. They get kidnapped by goblins, eaten by wolves, drowned by merfolk. God sees everything, ay? He sees a little girl getting swallowed by an ogre and he says 'oh, lookit that. That's something, innit?'" Suddenly, her face darkened and her eyes throbbed. "He is a monstrous *cunt*."

Halsten sighed heavily. He didn't want to admit it, but he agreed with her. It didn't mean that he saw the logic in running off to join Devil worshippers because life was hard, though. What was it that the monks and priests would always tell him? It was all a test? At the snap of her fingers, the woman's face was once again lathered with a welcoming grin, "Now that you've heard my gospel, are you gonna be polite and share?"

Halsten's teeth clenched. Everyone in those caves, well, everyone but Halsten, was a devout believer of Xalt'n's new doctrine. They were all insane. They could eat him alive if he said the wrong thing. "Me wife. A long time ago, she was set upon by knights. *Tritan* knights who earned their keep by maraudin' their own land and stealin' along the roads. God didn't give a shit when they raped and butchered her in front of me and me son. That's why I'm 'ere." It wasn't a lie…so he figured it might work.

The woman huffed. "You got a son? Fuck you, then."

Halsten emitted a muted laugh.

"What's his name?"

"Erik. He joined tha cause before I did. Never told me where he went…so part of me is tryin' ta find 'im. He's pretty much a man now…but I always see 'im as me little boy. I just wanna make sure he's safe."

Alison's cheeks softened and her lips thinned. "I can't imagine what that would feel like. Having a child then…losing them. It must be painful."

"I don't even know if he's alive. I suppose I can't even consider that he isn't. That's what keeps me goin'."

"…I know someone who works in the archives. He might be able to dig through the disciple records and find out where your boy is if he's joined us."

The woodsman stopped his digging and straightened his posture. With his brow wrinkled and eyes focused, he looked at Alison and asked, "Why? Why tha bloody hell wouldja do that for?"

The woman waved a hand dismissively at Halsten. "What's the matter with you?"

"I just don't understand. We hardly know each other. Why help me?"

"Because I'd bloody hope someone would do the same thing if that happened to me."

His head throbbed and he ran a hand down his face. Halsten was downright confused. One minute, those people were offering sacrifices to the demons, the next they were offering random acts of kindness. "Please tell me what ya find." That was the best apology anyone could get out of Halsten.

Alison didn't seem too thrilled by it, but she said, "If anyone has children or loved ones, they should be able to spend as much time with them as they can before the Enlightenment. When that happens, all emotion will be removed from us. Yes, all the pain will stop, but so will the pleasure. You should be able to make the most of all that before it's gone."

The next hour passed in verbal silence. The syncopated 'clinks' of steel against stone was a disorganised and sloppy rhythm that only made Halsten more jittery. He kept striking the stone, not knowing what else he could do. He started thinking about Erik. What if he was already dead and Halsten was there for nothing? What if Erik hated being with him so much that he ran away? What if he stabbed that poor man in the church for no reason? What if he strangled the other one, the one who helped him find the Synod, for no reason? The questions kept coming and none of them made Halsten feel any better.

He sent an especially fierce blow onto the stone, cleaving a sizable chunk of material from it. As the large fragment of rock fell to the ground with a thud, Halsten was left squinting at what it revealed upon the wall. It was not stone, not at all. The surface was coal black and incredibly smooth, like a piece of well-made and heavily polished armour. He leant closer and pressed a hand against it. It was…warm to the touch. All of a sudden, a paralysing fear surfaced in his stomach. Whatever he found…what if it was some kind of ancient demonic weapon? What if it would help them slaughter innocent people? He couldn't just hand it over to them, could he? Halsten sent a painstakingly slow glance over his left shoulder. Everyone else was focused on their own work. Then, he looked over his right. Alison stared wide-eyed at the mysterious object.

"By the Fires…!" Alison gasped as she knelt by the cave wall and touched the strange material. "I think you've found something!"

Some of the other miners came drifting over.

Halsten swallowed. "Maybe it's just some peculiar kind of ore…we shouldn't waste tha Matriarch's time with it."

"Better to be safe than sorry, ay?" Alison slowly rose up. "Somebody go get Mother Xalt'n. Now!"

The woodsman cursed under his breath. For an excruciating amount of time, Halsten and the other miners were forced to just sit there and wait. No one wanted to risk defiling a sacred artefact. Only Mother Xalt'n and her witches knew the secrets of the demonic relics and how to extract them safely. Halsten's senses heightened as his instincts told him to just make a break for it. When he finally worked up the courage to pace for the exit, Halsten could've sworn that the temperature dropped. Xalt'n floated into the cavern, flanked by two of her witches. One of them was the Tethspeaker from earlier. The other witch was a woman wearing nothing but an ornamental pauldron crafted with dozens of human ribs strung together, and an antlered skull of a deer as a mask. Tightly gripped in her right hand was an arcane staff. The heretical religion was protected and spread by the K'relvic Nuns, the second cult of witches devoted to the Matriarch's teachings. An order of women who, like the all-male Tethspeakers, had discarded their humanity. Flaying themselves was an act of renouncing the Great Lie and embracing their true natures as soulless instruments of the Devil. Each Nun could sow immense death with the black magic within their staves. Where the Tethspeakers would manipulate and influence with sorcery, the K'relvic Nuns would destroy and eviscerate.

Xalt'n was instantly drawn to the wall behind Alison and Halsten. She cocked her head as she simply stared at it for a moment or two. "Halsten came across this just now," Alison reported.

The Matriarch lowered a warm stare onto Halsten, causing him to get even more tense. He had never been in her direct presence before and realised that she towered over him. "Your devotion has been rewarded, my child."

"What is it, Mother? Is it a relic?" asked Alison.

Coldly, she explained, "Before He and His servants withdrew back into Hell, they left gifts for us. Our infernal creators built the ossuaries and sealed within them objects of their infinite power. This is the wall of an ossuary, my child, impenetrable to any worldly means. But we are able to outstep this world."

The Tethspeaker handed a small spherical object to the K'relvic Nun who strolled up to the strange material embedded in the wall and fastened the object to it.

"If you would remove yourselves. I do not want anyone sustaining injuries with so much more work to do."

Halsten watched as everyone else slunk back towards the entrance tunnel. People bunched up in front of the exit, once again preventing him from taking flight. Reluctantly, he joined the crowd of miners. He watched as the Tethspeaker looked at the strange device on the wall and raised his hand. Suddenly, a series of floating blue glyphs appeared at his fingertips. He directed a finger toward a particular glyph. An incredible burst of force ripped through the cave, shattering stone and shaking the very foundation of the earth itself. Halsten's ears were overcome by an unbearable rumbling laced through with screams. He squinted at the silhouette of the Nun at the forefront of the cluster of people.

In her hand was a large object resembling a lantern and from it was projected a shimmering blue wall of light. Debris and dust bounced against it as if it was solid stone. The ethereal barrier continued protecting the group of miners until the rumbling of the world ceased. When the smoke cleared, a gigantic hole replaced the tiny slither of the ossuary wall. Xalt'n barked commands and the two witches took steps forward. The Nun held her staff at the ready as she approached the breach. The Tethspeaker continued waving his hands through the strange magical symbols. "Mother, the ossuary is still imbued."

"Illuminate it, please." Xalt'n asked politely.

Halsten watched in confusion as the Tethspeaker continued with his hypnotising motions. The endless void of darkness that marked the interior of the demonic chamber was suddenly flushed with white light. Xalt'n paced through the crowd and slipped by her two witches. "Come, witness your discovery," she called with an unsettling trace of excitement trickling from her voice. The other miners slowly trailed in, hesitant but awestruck.

Halsten found himself alone outside the ossuary. His eyes travelled to the uncongested tunnel that led back to the surface. Even if he did flee, where would he go? Alison was the only lead he had. When Halsten turned back to the ossuary entrance, the K'relvic Nun was standing within its embrace with her attention solely upon him. Her green-blue eyes locked onto his and she stood there motionless.

Halsten growled to himself, "God's bones…" as he strode out of the cavern and into the ossuary. Once reunited with Alison and the other miners, Halsten was surrounded by rows and rows of peculiar shelves. They were lined with objects that he couldn't even hope to understand. Xalt'n approached one of the racks and plucked one of the devices from it. As she turned the thing over in her hands, Halsten supposed it resembled a crossbow without its limbs attached. The Matriarch then set the object back down before approaching the Tethspeaker. When Halsten's eyes traced over, he felt his heart stop. Suspended in the air by an array of steel scaffolding attached to the ceiling and a mess of strange ropes and cords, were dozens of midnight black bodies. They were inhumanly thin, basically skeletal. Halsten could see all manner of exposed joints, bones, veins, and tendons all over them. His stomach lurched upward and he had to fight the urge to vomit.

"By the Fires…" Xalt'n muttered. "Are they in…disrepair?"

Even the stoic Tethspeaker seemed to be enthralled by the faceless men floating above them. He fiddled with his arcane projections before replying, "No. Simply dormant."

Xalt'n turned back to face her followers, a spark of euphoria in her eyes. "You stand here before the first slaves; the Protozealots. They embody the True State. They do not feel hunger, pain, fear, sorrow, nor joy. They are warriors the likes of which this world has not seen since Hell receded into the depths. But they are simple, my children. They require direction; direction that only *we* as their reclaimers can provide."

Suddenly, the Tethspeaker jerked backwards after he stared at his floating symbols. The Tethspeaker's array of runes shimmered then coalesced, converging upon each other until it formed the image of a large sphere that floated before the witch. Halsten squinted at it. The shapes upon it…he recognised Tritham. It was a map of the world? A single mote of red light was pinned on the lower rim of the Tritan countryside. It pulsated urgently.

"What is that beacon? What does it signify?" Xalt'n mused.

The Tethspeaker mulled over his runes and swallowed. “I-I do not know.”

Xalt’n growled lowly then took a deep breath inward. “Wake S’teinel from his slumber and let him sanitise the locale. We cannot have the Church stumbling upon what could be another sacred relic and destroying it in their infinite ignorance. It would be much easier for us to search amongst a sea of dead.” A single question echoed over and over in Halsten’s mind as his fingers curled inward. *What have I done?*

XI
The Wretched Gravestone

"One, two, three!"

The two men released the corpse they held, sending it hurtling into the pit. Having been stripped of all valuables and salvageable armour, the body slapped into the other dozens of cadavers that already lay in the mass grave. With a sigh, the soldiers huffed in exhaustion as they took several steps back. Others came and repeated those actions. Footmen, archers, and some especially good-willed knights or men-at-arms were active in the burial. At the scene of the battle itself, clerks and heralds joined the soldiers herding the dead. Their duty, easier said than done, was to identify the perished. Some bodies were little more than porridge sloshing about inside broken mail shirts and mud-stained gambeson. Those who were recognised as Blackmeadow locals were taken to the cemetery for burial. Others, whether known or unknown, were to be laid to rest there in the mass grave. Alric was most unimpressed to see Katheryn personally involved. She hadn't even exchanged her armour for something more befitting a noble lady. Instead, she partook in the dirty work still wearing her gambeson and mail.

One of the men that had just tossed a body into the hole, Lionel of Pathridge, strided over to Alric as he stood vigil. Lionel was one of the mounted crossbowmen that accompanied Lady Katheryn during the battle. He was also one of the men that had carried the wounded Gabriel de Fontaine to the physician. It was clear that Lionel did not recognise Alric even with his visor raised, much to his relief. It *had* been almost twenty years since their last meeting. Lionel shook his head and shrugged. "Gabriel's legs must be removed. However, Blackmeadow's only surgeon lies at the bottom of this pit," he said, pointing at the grave. "Alas, even if he were to survive the operation, would he wish to live? What awaits a crippled knight? There shall be no riding, no battle, no honour. He would desire a release in death...something that I, as his friend, cannot accept."

Alric responded by saying, "Mourn not, for everything owed to Gabriel shall be presented to him. There shan't be sorrow upon his departure."

Lionel started to make his way back over to the rest of the corpse-ridden field to continue his work, not entirely pleased with Alric's words. The holy knight was left alone in his silent objection. As more bodies were transferred into the ditch, more of the working men retired into Blackmeadow. The air was clear and the sun was unobscured as it slowly dipped behind the veil of the horizon. The blue sky turned orange. A handful of common soldiers and two especially committed men of slightly higher standing were awaiting the ritual so they could fill the grave. Alric brandished his flask of holy water, spilled some evenly into the mass grave, and turned his gaze to the sky.

"These servants, honoured men, have given their lives to cleansing God's earth. I hereby cast their souls into the cold, so their deeds may be judged by God. Unto Heaven, may they bask in paradise for eternity. Unto Hell, may they revel in suffering for eternity. Amen."

Alric then made the sign of the Pillar. Many of the footmen followed suit, some repeating Alric's final word. Without instruction, they moved toward their shovels and began to pile dirt over the bodies. Everyone who wasn't charged with filling the hole made their way back to Blackmeadow, Alric included. Lionel and one of Katheryn's footmen named Oliver Tiller, eventually drifted toward Alric and absorbed him into their company. As they closed in on the city, a trail of eviscerated trees and potholes marked the ogre's earlier path of destruction. On the very edge of the horizon, where the line of shattered bark led, Alric could barely make out a small farmhouse that had been essentially stepped on by the immense creature on its initial approach. A dozen tiny specks were moving about the wreckage, perhaps doing the same work Katheryn's men were. After several minutes of pacing without a word, Alric broke the silence, "Tell me of the witches who stalk the wood. They possess great arcane power that, in my experience, is known only to servants of the devil. Perhaps it would be best for my Order to hunt them down."

"That won't be necessary," answered Oliver with a muted chuckle. "They call themselves the Ga'zahi; one of many druidic tribes."

Lionel nodded in agreement. "It was during the Westshire Uprising. We were routed and the good Oliver here was wounded. He fell behind, so I feared him dead. In reality, he wandered his way into one of their forest groves. It was where he met his wife."

"Thou hast wedded a demonist?" pressed Alric.

Oliver laughed. "Don't worry, brother. I've done my duty; converted her to the true faith as soon as I could. And listen, they aren't demonists. They look to ancient gods; ones so old I don't even think half of them have names any civilised folk could utter."

Alric nodded. "Thou hast done well to cleanse her soul of such folly."

"The point is, Thestor," replied Oliver, "the forest druids are strange and backward, but they aren't a threat. You saw what happened today. We wouldn't have been able to kill that thing without them."

As frustrating as it was for Alric to admit to himself, he knew that Oliver spoke the truth. If the Ga'zahi harboured any ill-will toward the true faith of the Church, they simply would have allowed the ogre to decimate Blackmeadow. The Thestor remained silent as he continued with his temporary travelling companions. The gigantic carcass of the ogre remained where it fell, painfully close to the gates of Blackmeadow. It would be impossible to move even with a hundred men; perhaps with the use of winches, pulleys, and a large cart of some kind could the corpse be removed, but it would be frivolous. Very soon, the ogre's deathly stench would attract the goblins. They would pick the beast apart and drag the bits back to their hive. Alric stared at the dead ogre as he passed it. It was the size of a house. Thousands of scratches and scars painted its hide, as did black scorches of arcane missiles. Its hooves were stained black by the blood of the men it trampled.

When night fell, a feast was held in Castle Blackmeadow's keep. Alric recited the final verse of the Oath of Vigilance and finally freed himself from his plate armour. For some reason, despite the fact that he hadn't had mead in over ten years, Alric found himself drowning in it. He visited a quiet tavern and drank away. Alric had never been one for indulging himself so profusely, but he noticed that it helped with his inner turmoil. The voices and the swelling discomfort within him quietly slipped away. Only then had he the courage to visit *him*.

The night sky was a deep purple, painted so by the light of the full moon. He needed no lantern to see and quite frankly, he was certain that such an implement would spoil the night's beauty. To wander a city after dark without a light was a crime, but on such a night...Alric cared not. Perhaps it was the mead. Countless pillars of stone stood sentinel on the final resting place of hundreds of Blackmeadow's former residents. The cemetery was devoid of life, save for Alric and several birds that nested in the trees. Among the markers was an unremarkable block of granite. The inscription read 'Martin, Earl of Danecaster'. Alric came to a halt at the tombstone and glared spitefully at it. If his father had been a man of honour, he would have been placed in the family tomb. His deeds were not befitting of such an end, however. "Thou art so incredibly predictable," called a voice so cold that it very much suited the graveyard. "What better den for the ghost of a man before me than a field of graves?"

The knight was startled, first thinking it was Martin's voice berating him, but was only slightly relieved to see that it was just Katheryn. She wore a royal blue kirtle, just as expensive in appearance as the bliaut she wore earlier that day. In her hand was an oil lantern. "When did such sickening cowardice infect thee, brother?" she spat. Many people called Alric 'brother'. It was befitting his status as a servant of the Church and the Order of Saint Thestus. However, there was only *one* person who could use the word and truly mean it. "Surely thou wert not daft enough to think that I would fail to recognise *her longsword* upon thy belt."

Alric sighed. Katheryn's pale aqua eyes seemed to flicker as the silence continued. Alric finally said with a nod, "Still thou clamour for it like a spoiled child. Thou best make peace with the fact that mother bestowed it to *me*."

Katheryn snorted. "We appear to have differing recollections of that day, little brother. I seem to remember father learning of her intent to gift it to me, tearing it from her hands as she wept, and dropping it in thy lap."

"What good would a blade be in the hands of a woman anyhow? What wouldst thou do with it? *Use it in battle*?" he spat incredulously.

With a toxic sneer, Katheryn shook her head. "I am certainly less of a stranger to it than thee."

Alric furrowed his brow. "What?"

"Thou couldst not comprehend needing to *prove* thyself worthy to wield power. It had been handed to thee from the day of thy birth, after all. Only one so privileged would have the audacity to discard it. For what, Alric of Danecaster? Servitude to God?"

"I no longer bear that name."

"Indeed. It fell to me. That which thou so thoughtlessly tossed aside became my charge," Katheryn continued coarsely. "A charge that was apparently beyond what I deserved to control, due solely to the misfortune of my birth."

When any noble swore himself to the Order of Saint Thestus, he would renounce his family name and everything he owned was to be passed to his closest kin. Katheryn had been Alric's only surviving family. It was a most unorthodox situation, as a woman being the sole heir of an earldom and having no plans to marry was outrageous. Whether it would have been through marriage, disputes in court, treachery, or sheer force, Katheryn *should not* have been in possession of the Earldom of Danecaster. And beyond that, she had somehow come into ownership of the Duchy of Arlingborough. She had become more powerful than Alric or their father had ever been. Alric's eyes narrowed. "Indeed. Why has it not yet been confiscated from thee?"

Katheryn scoffed at the remark as she sauntered over to the dying tree that overlooked the graveyard. "All who tried to seize it lie as still as our silent audience." She gestured out through the headstones.

Alric released a wrathful exhale. "God save thee, Katheryn. What hast thou done?"

"Oh? Waging wars in one's defence is so monstrous, but slaughtering in the name of the Father is not? Art thou truly so lost that this hypocrisy is beyond thy comprehension?"

Alric shook his head. "Thou should have simply *married.* Avarice so unchecked as to have drawn blood is sinful, not to mention thy other…proclivities. 'Tis not too late to do away with these things and save thyself from Hell."

"As I recall, patricide is also quite the grave sin, little brother."

The words slammed into Alric's chest like a crossbow bolt. His eyes lit up like twin suns in the blackness of twilight. He stomped towards his sister, crying, "The fool brought it upon himself! I acted in the name of God!"

Standing inches apart, Alric could see that Katheryn stood a head shorter than he did. It was a fact that had always irritated her as the eldest sibling. She did not buckle despite his clear frustration. She said to him, her voice not wavering, "I hear naught but the hollow words of a man trying to lie to himself. The truth is, dear brother, we are both damned. Perhaps I shall be there to greet thee at the gates of Hell."

A lance of intense fear shot through Alric's body. His arm tensed as a clenched fist fired itself into Katheryn's face. Her head was forced sideways, but she was not staggered or otherwise displaced by the blow. Slowly and forebodingly, she turned back to face her brother. She dropped her lantern and snapped forward with the speed of an arrow. Quite frankly, Alric was completely unprepared and crashed into the decrepit tree. Katheryn held him by the collar and her right arm turned into a blur. The next thing Alric knew, a fierce impact crashed into his cheek. Followed by another, then another. His efforts to raise his hands to defend himself were deflected. With a growl, Alric mustered all his strength and pushed against the trunk of the tree with his foot. All of his body weight pressed down upon Katheryn, and the two nobles came crashing into the dirt. Alric rammed his forehead into Katheryn's head, plunging himself into a sea of blurry sights and swirls.

Katheryn emitted only a single gravelly cough in lieu of the strike. She then sent a knee into her brother's gut. Alric reeled over and gagged, presenting Katheryn with the chance she needed. She seized Alric by the shoulder, shoved him onto the dirt, and leapt onto him. Multiple punches found their marks on his face. His vision blurred as the pain seeped through his skull. Alric stretched his hands outward in an attempt to find something lying on the ground that he could use. His fingers secured themselves around a disc-like object. Without hesitation, he sent the thing into the side of Katheryn's head. The clay dish, seconds ago laden with offerings of fruit, shattered into shrapnel as it struck her in the temple. With his sister dazed, Alric propelled his right foot forward as hard as he could. Katheryn was thrown back-first into Martin's tombstone with a 'thud'. Alric scrambled to his feet, possibly a bit too quickly. His head throbbing with pain and his senses disrupted by mead, the knight ended up stumbling and falling onto his face. The ground struck his forehead with as much force as Katheryn did. Hazily, he lifted his head and looked towards Katheryn. She sat with her back against the headstone, groggily laughing at Alric's fall. In defeat, he dropped his head onto the dirt and exhaled heavily.

Memories suddenly flooded through his mind. They would fight in the castle courtyard as children. Katheryn was a far more worthy opponent than the boys he played with, until their father took notice. Thereafter, they were forbidden to do such things, for what manner of boy could not easily best a girl, and what manner of girl should be able to best a boy? "I would like to remind thee that I did not dispense the first blow," said Katheryn, clutching the side of her face.

Alric snorted at the comment. "Harlot," he jabbed.

Katheryn promptly retorted, "Clod."

Alric found himself lying in the dirt and staring at the stars for some indeterminate amount of time. Katheryn hadn't moved either. The pair of them just basked in the silence. Somehow, they both felt as if they were children once again looking into the stars and wondering what they were. "Dost thou hold it against me?" Alric suddenly asked.

"What?"

"Father."

With a scoff, she crossed her arms. "Pft. I was merely attempting to aggravate thee. Good riddance, I say. It took strength to see that deed done.

That is what I always both hated and admired most about thee. Always so *certain*. In times of hardship, I could only wish to find such conviction."

Alric finally sat upright with a groan, dusting off his surcoat. He looked to his sister as she leaned casually against the tombstone. In a most unladylike manner, she did not have her legs crossed but instead splayed apart. Her dress was absolutely caked in dirt and grass, probably ruined beyond salvation. Alric started to remember that it was a fairly common state for her when they were younger. Mother would spend hundreds of pounds on garments to replace the ones soiled by dirt, mud, and grass. He pushed to his feet and approached Katheryn, holding out a hand to her. "It lies in the arms of God, sister."

Most predictably, Katheryn ignored his hand and instead helped herself up by grasping the side of Martin's headstone. She didn't bother patting the dirt from her dress. Alric could tell by the way she looked at it that she was going to just discard it altogether once she returned to the castle. "The time has passed for me to cultivate my faith, Alric. I cannot see God the way thou see him. I cannot love him."

Alric nodded. Fear, love…it was all the same in the eyes of God. "Thou best clean thyself up."

Katheryn knelt, plucked up the now completely shattered oil lantern that she had dropped before the scuffle and glanced at it with a cocked eyebrow. "Indeed."

As she began to make her way back toward the keep, Alric called out to her, "There are a great deal of homeless in Blackmeadow. I shall journey with them to Phaemslake on the morrow."

Katheryn slowed to a halt and peered over her shoulder. "To the Hospital?"

He nodded. "Thou best leave the care of the needy to the Church," Alric explained.

"Of course. Thou must uphold the Fourth Attestation."

Alric hesitated for a moment. "And...thou art my sister."

The very faintest glimpse of a smile appeared in the corner of Katheryn's mouth before she turned back toward the keep and disappeared into the night.

XII
BOUND BY BLOOD

Valshügel was one of the famous free cities in the Steiffan Empire, a realm that neighboured both Tritham and Valtheaux. Maintained by mercantile and trade guilds, a locally elected magistrate, and client to a great mercenary company, the city was proudly independent of the influence of the Steiffan High Emperor and stretched on for what seemed to be forever. Halsten would have been in awe of its majesty that evening as it was washed by the red filter of sunset. *Would have,* if the city wasn't being raped by those he pretended to serve. Screaming had been the ambient backdrop since the moment Halsten arrived with his crew of layfolk. Gaping holes had been smashed through the immense stone walls. By what, the woodsman didn't know. There were no trebuchets in sight and even then, the damage was far beyond anything they could inflict.

Anyone who refused to accept the doctrine of the Clthic Synod was disembowelled and dismembered. If you *did* see the light, you would become one with the Synod. The Clthics had no rules of sanctity for the dead, as to die one must first be alive. If life was an illusion, then a person was no different to a tree or a boulder. Those two things were harvested for resources and there was no disgust, no remorse. They looked on humans in that same fashion. People were torn apart, their organs harvested for black magic rituals, their bones fashioned into the ornaments worn by witches, and the meat used as food. All around him, as people were carved up while they pleaded and screeched, Halsten was barely managing to keep himself under control. He was surprised that he hadn't vomited. The horror was almost too much to bear. Next to him on the horse-drawn carriage was Allison who blankly gazed about without any real reaction. Halsten muttered, "This is awfully convenient. He's 'ere, in tha same place we just 'appened to be needed at? I dunno about this."

Allison smiled. "Don't worry, mate. I know he's here. Trust me, alright?"

The more Halsten thought about it, the more his bones trembled. Was he that mess of blood and meat on the ground? Was he that impaled bastard on the battlements? There was no telling. The horses passed by a church. It would be an important place to seize; raising a child to believe in the Clthic dribble was much easier than convincing a devout servant of a *real* religion to throw it all away. K'relvic Nuns had the clergy lined up in front of the chapel as they chanted in deep, gravelly breaths. One by one, the Nuns slit the throats of the priests, monks, sisters, and plebians who did not surrender to the doctrine. A handful of Church servants stood a few paces removed, with shame on their faces. It was clear that they had renounced God in order to live.

As the church disappeared behind them, crowds of the Synod's army were settling down in the courtyards and plazas of Valshügel. Halsten had never seen so many cultures mixed together in one place before. Tritans, Valthois, Steiffans, Velintines, and even desert-dwelling Quraics composed the patchwork army. They must've conquered the city very recently; most of them were still dressed in their equipment and armour. Halsten expected to see much harsher pillaging from the Clthics…but he supposed it wasn't wealth that the true believers were after. They wanted to spread their influence as far as possible before initiating the Enlightenment. It was to be, essentially, synchronised ritual suicide of an unbelievable scale.

Not far from the plaza was a staging area established in a stone mason's lodge. In the courtyard beside it, Halsten saw a few dozen soldiers led in meditation by a Tethspeaker. Low, throaty chanting swallowed the sounds of doom that only moments ago consumed the air. At the mason's lodge, a noble lord was discussing matters with several of his knights, men-at-arms, and Mother Xalt'n herself. Halsten followed Allison as she dismounted the wagon and approached the group of leaders. The Matriarch was the first to acknowledge the presence of Allison and Halsten with a nod. Allison reported, "Matriarch. I've expanded my team of miners as you requested."

"We leave for the site in the morning." Her voice, much too deep for any person, chilled Halsten's spine to its core.

Then came the noble. With a smile as welcoming as he could muster, the man crossed his arms. "Welcome to Valshügel, my friends. I am Duke Klaus von Talhoffen. It is a pleasure to make your acquaintance."

Halsten had to admit, he never would have expected a noble to introduce himself to commoners like that. The Clthics, although absolutely mental, were striking down the barriers between classes. "Milord, accordin' ta disciple records, me son is in yer service," stated Halsten bluntly. "His name is Erik Vilulf."

Many of the men-at-arms nervously glanced at each other. More worryingly to Halsten, Xalt'n's eyes seemed to spark for a moment and her posture straightened. "You are Vilulf's father? Why, then you are a great friend of ours," replied Klaus. The dull tone of his voice did not complement the content of his speech.

"Where is he? I need ta see him," Halsten asked rather aggressively.

"He is with his…'cattle'. Laszlo, show him the way." Klaus waved one of his men over. A man-at-arms huffed in reluctance but ultimately walked away from the lodge.

Allison rested a hand on Halsten's shoulder. "What are you waiting for, mate? Go on!"

Something was not right. Halsten couldn't tell what…but it made him pause for a moment before he hurried after Lazslo, who just kept walking without worrying whether Halsten was with him or not. When the woodsman caught up with the man-at-arms, he asked with shallow breaths, "My son, ya know 'im?"

Laszlo kept his eyes about. "He's...wild. Dangerous."

"*My* boy? No, he's a kind young man."

"Perhaps he has changed."

A cobbled-together pen on the edge of the city held at least fifty tired people. They were mainly commoners with a few injured soldiers littered in between. They were all supplied with food and water. Halsten's brow tensed. "What are these people doin' out 'ere? 'Ave they been given a chance ta convert?"

Lazslo came to a halt before the pen and pointed at a stone building next to it. All its windows were shut. "I won't go any further," admitted Lazslo.

Halsten shook his head and trudged forward. The rickety door creaked like a crying dog when Halsten pushed it open. Inside, darkness smothered everything. Only several candles dotted the vast emptiness. As the door shut behind him, Halsten was plunged into the void.

Eventually his eyes adjusted to the lack of light. He squinted, managing to discern a misty figure hunched over a desk. It simply sat there, staring at the wall. A sharp inhale broke the silence. The figure shot to its feet. It crept away from the table and the candlelight that bathed it. As footsteps hit the floorboards, Halsten couldn't see the figure for a full five seconds. His hands trembled. He could feel breaths on his face. "Father?"

Halsten could barely make out the outline of the man that spoke to him. "Issat you, Erik?" he asked forcefully.

There was a brief pause. Suddenly, Halsten was seized by the man who enveloped him in a tight embrace. "What the bloody hell are you doing here, old man?"

Halsten's hand slowly and shakily clasped itself onto Erik's back. "I-I…I don't understand. Why did you leave?"

The woodsman's eyes had adjusted to the darkness by the time he pulled out from the hug. He could see the unmistakable features of his son's face as he answered, "I planned on coming back. I did. Something…happened, though. I couldn't."

Halsten clasped a hand onto his face. "Are they makin' ya stay 'ere? Are ya a slave like tha ones outside?"

Erik laughed. "No. Not at all. I very much want to be here."

Swallowing, Halsten looked to the ground. "It's true, then. You've been fightin' fer them? Yer a…a soldier now?" He started to feel like maybe he was going to leave alone. That he came all that way, that he murdered someone in a church, for nothing.

"Yes. I've been given a gift and this is how I'm meant to use it," replied Erik. He sounded distant. Detached. It was still *his* voice...but he used to have the same accent Halsten had. It was gone. He almost sounded like a properly educated man.

"Erik...yer not makin' any sense."

Erik leaned closer to Halsten. "Would you like to join me? Are you content with being a peasant when you could be *more*?"

"Erik, stop speakin' dribble and let me see ya." Halsten made for the nearest window and pushed it.

The window flew open and light filled the room. Only then did Halsten lay eyes upon what he stood in. Naked corpses of both men and women were thrown about the hut like pieces of trash. Dozens upon dozens of them. Each one had a single stab wound to the forehead. Not a single drop of blood stained the flooring. Halsten's eyes then turned to Erik.

He stared into the open window, with patches of his bare skin darkening and flickering like he was slowly cooking in the sunlight. Halsten frantically seized the window shutters and pulled them closed, plunging the room into darkness once more. With the light spoiling his eyes' adjustment to the dimness, Halsten once again couldn't see a thing. He didn't know what to scream about first, the dead bodies or the fact that Erik was just sizzling in the sunlight like a slice of meat on a pan. "Y-You killed these people?!"

"Pain is so...rare for me now. It excites me," whispered Erik. "Please...do it again," he gasped.

"E-Erik…"

There was a pause. "She sent you to me, didn't she? As a test."

Halsten backpedalled. He could feel the heat radiating from Erik's body as he came closer. "I-I don't know what you're talkin' about," said the woodsman. "Get back!"

They then stood close to the candlelight on the desk. Halsten saw his son's faint red eyes peering through the darkness. They gazed at him, lifeless. Soulless. His skin was patchy and darkened but Halsten swore he could see it slowly healing. Erik grasped the side of his father's head.

Thank you for coming to me. I thought that I stopped feeling things. But here...with you...I feel...something. The truth is, you're not my father. We're nothing to each other. You just happened to be there for me to be handed to.

Erik and plunged their lips together. No matter how much Halsten pushed, pulled, or squirmed, Erik held him in place with impossible strength. He felt his son's tongue inside of his mouth. As suddenly as it started, Erik pulled away. The young man's face pulsated. Lines appeared on it. With a bone-trembling grinding, the lines darkened and Erik's face unfurled like a sheet of folded parchment. The bones beneath shimmered in the candlelight. Then, his skull split into quarters and from behind it, a six-inch-long fang slowly extended. Halsten's brain was much too slow to perceive the fang jamming itself into his forehead and ending his life.

Erik Vilulf pushed the door open and stepped into the moonlight. He secured the laces on his doublet and glanced at the pen full of food to his right. They were all frozen in terror as he stared at them, perhaps in lieu of the desperate screams of his father as he sucked his body dry. Their faces, the tears, the tantalising fear, it all made Vilulf shudder in ecstasy. With a chuckle, he moved on toward the staging area. Seeing as it was the middle of the night, the plaza was as empty as a graveyard. In the distance, Vilulf could see that a portion of the inner-bailey wall had been reduced to rubble. The only two souls who dared walk the night were waiting in the stonemason's lodge; Mother Xalt'n and Duke Klaus. As Vilulf approached, the Steiffan lord glanced over his shoulder as if he were looking for someone. "You didn't drain your *own father* did you?"

Vilulf strolled into the lodge and leant onto one of the supports with a sly smirk. "Maybe I did."

Klaus massaged his brow and muttered, "Please, I would like to have this settled. Some of us need to sleep."

Xalt'n approached the table and pointed to the map spread upon its surface. "Our forces are advancing upon the only defensible position close to the site of the beacon. It is Omenthal, a Godslave fortress monastery."

Vilulf was a little annoyed that it was the first he had heard of the siege. He loved witnessing the ridiculous things that those religious nuts would do and say. What he loved more was watching them turn into frightened, mewling children before his vampiric might. More often than not, his actions on the battlefield were enough to convince them of the truth; that God was a fairytale. Klaus swallowed. "We have laid siege to a Thestor castle? Why didn't you tell me earlier?"

Vilulf cocked his head inquisitively as he waited for Xalt'n's reply.

"We did not inform you because *your* job was to seize Valshügel and Servius is more than capable of leading the siege party." Hearing mention of his blood sibling made Vilulf shudder. Servius was a complete bore and had a tendency to make being immortal so dreary and depressing. Despite that, he had been Viktoria's favourite…and that made him the subject of Vilulf's disdain. All of a sudden, his desire to take part in the siege evaporated. Xalt'n continued, "Besides, S'teinel shall be lending them his strength. None shall come to their aid."

"The Thestors are simply a formidable foe. S'teinel should've been directed to their castles *first*."

"What good is fire against stone walls, Duke Klaus? We have other means with which to deal with Omenthal," said Xalt'n defiantly. "Once the monastery is ours, we can safely move the additional miners and Tethspeakers to the excavation site."

Klaus planted his hands onto his hips. "You still haven't told me what you plan on digging up."

"A demon. A *live* one," Vilulf said with a charming smile.

Xalt'n suddenly unleashed a glare of pure hellfire upon him. Klaus's face was overcome with wonder. "Really…?"

"We are not yet certain *what* lies there, simply that there is something of import," Xalt'n clarified. "Quell your expectations."

With a cough, Klaus ran a hand along the top of his scalp. "Is Lady Viktoria going to make herself present for such an occasion?"

Only just then spotting a comfortable looking chair to plant himself in, Vilulf paced over, lowered himself into it, and tossed his feet up onto the table. "My Lady Viktoria is preoccupied. I believe you sent her on an errand recently, Klaus."

The marshal huffed in amusement. "You are well aware that Viktoria does not run *errands* for anyone. Will you be there, Matriarch?"

Mother Xalt'n cracked the joints in her neck by rolling her head about. "There is much cleansing to be done throughout the realm…and we need more witches. I will see to that first, unless the object is something truly remarkable."

Approaching footsteps snatched Vilulf's attention long before the two others in his company could hear. "We have a guest," he warned, jerking his head toward the sound's origin.

Klaus's hand reflexively wrapped around the hilt of his longsword. A woman walked into the lodge, clothes and face sullied with dirt. "Mother. My lord. I'm sorry to bother you again but I haven't heard from one of my men since the sun was up."

Vilulf tilted his head with a charming smile. "You must be speaking of my father, Halsten."

Alison's eyes sparked. "You're Erik? He found you, then!"

"Oh he certainly did. He is…resting now."

Vilulf adjusted his posture as he gave her a once over. *My, my. What a specimen you are. Those clothes are quite filthy. Perhaps you should...remove them. Show your glorious form to us.*

His thoughts wafted through the air and slipped into the woman's mind. She suddenly became flustered as she looked at Vilulf. Her lip quivered as she reached for the rim of her work tunic. Vilulf liked keeping them aware. Seeing them conscious as their bodies moved on their own and did things that horrified them. He watched her eyes flicker and listened to her breath as it fluctuated while she lifted the shirt. In tones much too faint for Alison to hear but not beyond Vilulf's senses, Klaus whispered, "Vilulf…cease."

With a reluctant sigh, he relinquished his control over her. Alison released her tunic, letting it fall back into place with a confused gasp. Klaus then leant over to Xalt'n and asked, "Do you need her?"

"No. Mining foremen are easy enough to replace."

Klaus then nodded at Vilulf, granting him permission to have his way. "Just not here. Keep your twisted perversions to yourself."

The vampire pushed to his feet. Considering the fact that he had just engaged in a meal, he wasn't particularly hungry. Playing with his food was always so much more fun, though. "Come with me, my love. Let us frolic in the pen with my cattle."

As Vilulf took Alison's hand and walked with her into the pitch black of night, he could hear Xalt'n scoff, "Such power and they choose to waste it on depravity"

Klaus replied, "Give any man the means and he shall do as he truly pleases."

XIII
Heathens and Pagans

"Why must thou insult me so?" Gabriel said with a furrowed brow as he sat in the back of Alric's wagon. Judging from how he wasn't overwhelmed by pain, Alric could only assume that the knight had been drinking like a fish. "Put me out of my misery, Thestor. This is probably thy fault. Thou told me not to wear my plate harness."

His legs were contained by an array of wooden splints, rope and tightly packed wool to ensure that they wouldn't break any further. Blackmeadow's only surgeon died in the battle against the ogre, so for the time being, Gabriel would have to wait until they arrived at the Hospital of Saint Corren for the amputation. No one told the poor knight about that part, though. They hadn't the heart. Alric heaved some more sacks of provisions onto the wagon, careful to ensure that they would not tumble onto Gabriel's already eviscerated legs. "All behold the great Sir Gabriel de Fontaine, reduced to a whimpering churl in the face of slight misfortune," he teased.

Gabriel's face contorted. "*Slight*?! Well…I suppose I am still free to bed beautiful women; something that thou cannot say. I shall not require legs for *that*."

"Intercourse is a frivolous pursuit. 'Tis an unhealthy diversion that breeds only sin."

"Spoken like a true *celibate*," Gabriel scoffed in response.

Alric walked around the wagon to Nocht and gave her a vigorous pat. He then grasped one of the reins and started to lead her towards the town gate. Several of the homeless townsfolk walked beside him carrying what little they had left. "Good people, place thy belongings in the cart with me," called Gabriel. "I shall guard them valiantly with what is left of my useless body." They continued heaving their small baskets and sacks onto the wagon as Alric led Nocht onward. The plaza before Blackmeadow's gatehouse was filled with even more refugees and physically maimed. Several horses tirelessly shook about, eager to start moving. Most people gathered were commonfolk while some were soldiers much too wounded to fight without immediate aid. Alric had used what little faerie tears he had left to keep at least a few footmen from having to leave the city, but they could not heal the more drastic injuries that had been sustained.

Katheryn was there, conversing with the Ga'zahi. Alric eased Nocht to a halt then eagerly approached his sister. There were five of them, so-called 'peaceful' forest dwellers. The druid that Katheryn was speaking to, a young woman, gave Alric a dismissive once over. Like the others of the tribe, her face was lathered with face paint; hers in particular was an earthy brown tone. A deep green cloak covered her body and a slightly darker cowl hung lowly upon her head. Assorted animal bones and other strange materials completely foreign to Alric had been laced across the shoulder of her cowl.

"What is the meaning of this? Why are there witches within the walls?" Alric called as he drew nearer.

Katheryn smacked her lips and glared at him. "Calm thyself."

"I shall do no such thing. This wretched band showed only disrespect to thee. They do not deserve thy hospitality."

Katheryn crossed her arms. "Brother, please. We are both aware that it would be idiotic for thee to embark upon this journey without an escort. Especially with thy talk of witches and revenants. I haven't any troops to spare, but this Ga'zahi foraging group was to travel South-East regardless. Carthei is…an acquaintance of mine. She can be trusted."

Alric sceptically glanced at the staff that the young woman, presumably Carthei, clenched tightly in her hand. "Why assist us in smiting the ogre?" he asked her bluntly. Katheryn looked to Carthei, eager for the response.

"Ogres have always been abominations; any creature that only takes from the earth and does not return to it is an interloper in the cycle. They are not usually drawn to stone-walled cities. They dwell in the darkness, in the depths of the Under. You know this, Godslave." She spoke Tritish remarkably well, but had a very subtle accent that Alric found incredibly grating.

Hesitantly, he nodded. "Indeed."

"The blood crazed fervour with which it thrashed before its demise is also without precedent. The Seers of my tribe believe that this mania is an indication that a terrible crime against creation has been committed. The defiling of the Kr'tesh."

Alric was irritated to see that his sister clearly knew what that strange word meant. Carthei, seeing the emptiness in Alric's eyes, explained, "The Kr'tesh is the body of water upon which all our souls are afloat. It binds everything that exists on this plane, including beings undeserving of life like the ogres. There have been accounts in our histories of druids who sought to harness unspeakable arts to dip their hands into the Kr'tesh. To command other living things against their will, control reality with but a wave of the hand…and to raise the dead."

Alric's eyes narrowed.

"As such, since it is a body of water, if someone casts their hand into the Kr'tesh, the water will ripple outward…disturbing and displacing the other souls wading it. This wave tarnished the ogre's balance upon the Kr'tesh and transformed it into an affront to existence." Alric rubbed his brow with his eyes fixed on the castle battlements.

There was one final question the knight needed to ask before he could *somewhat* trust the woman and her people. "Thou art not in league with the demonist necromancers who caused said imbalance?" With a sigh, Katheryn rolled her eyes and ran a hand down her face.

Carthei shook her head. "No. We pay tribute to the Vorkhai; a legion of deities far older than your Devil."

Alric shifted uncomfortably. "Not demonists, but heathens, then."

Katheryn shoved Alric with one hand as she gritted her teeth.

Carthei smirked. "It's quite alright." She then turned to Alric. "Our faith does not deny the existence of your God. As a matter of fact, one of our verses states that there are infinite deities, so one of them *must* be yours. How does that sound?"

"There is only *one* God," Alric snapped sternly.

Katheryn and Carthei met eyes for a moment, and Katheryn visibly exhaled. "Allow us a moment," she said to Carthei. The druid spun on her heels and paced back to the rest of her kin. Katheryn clasped her hands on the front of her belt and flexed her jaw. "Reinforcements came by way of Castle Redford."

"Lord Franco sent men to thee? The man is a faithless child."

"Watch thy tongue; he is a loyal vassal of mine. He sent a letter reporting what occurred at Chesterton. His words detailed the manner in which a Knight Thestor ordered his men to slaughter unarmed *children*," she recounted dryly.

"Do not presume to lecture me, Katheryn. They had been indoctrinated. Did he make mention of the innocents impaled upon the walls that I had to see committed to the earth one by one?"

Katheryn's brow suddenly sharpened. "Humour me, brother. If only just for a moment. Ask thyself this; what if thou hast made a mistake? What then?"

"I have not," Alric replied sternly.

"Thou wert *oh so* certain of Peter Kent's redemption. Until the mere mention of damnation caused thee to shiver in thy boots like the frightened child I remember so well," she snapped. It took all of Alric's self-control not to strike her in the face. He instead flexed his jaw and rested his left hand upon the hilt of his longsword. Katheryn's eyes were beckoned by the motion, and she peered down at the weapon. A streak of bitterness permeated her mood. "Even *she* would be disgusted by this…thing thou hast become."

"Speak not for the dead, dear sister."

With a low growl, Katheryn spun on her heels. "Clod."

"Harlot," he called after her.

Once Katheryn departed the plaza, all who were embarking to Phaemslake were ready to leave. Several of the folk who were too unwell to walk joined Gabriel on Alric's wagon and the several other carts pulled by horses and mules. Alric once again grabbed Nocht's reins just as a young mother and her daughter hurried out from the adjoining street. "Oh thank God, I thought we were late," the woman said to herself.

Alric knelt as the child came closer. "What be thy name, little one?"

She shyly fiddled with her hands. "E-Emma, Brother Thestor."

"Emma. Thou shalt have the prestigious duty of keeping Nocht company." He gently lifted the girl and set her upon Nocht's saddle. Emma beamed as she gently ran her small hands along Nocht's mane, much to her approval. They trailed out of Blackmeadow on the dirt road, passing through the gatehouse and under the raised portcullis. The ogre still remained where it fell outside the walls. Half a dozen druids were pouring over the corpse, tearing it open and harvesting the innards. Portions of the thing's pockmarked carapace had been wrenched free and thrown into a pile beside the corpse.

Unlike Churchborn life such as mankind and natural animals, ogres were not covered in meat. Instead, their bodies were a twisted cacophony of bone, shell, and arteries. It was that manner of composition that they shared with goblins and manticores. For that reason, the Tritans had no use for the carcass of the beast. The Ga'zahi, however, seemed to be revelling in the thing's insides. As the travelling group passed by, Alric watched as those carving the ogre gave Carthei and her companions a simple salute by holding a hand in front of their foreheads.

In time, the noise of the city and the ogre harvesters dwindled into nothing. Uneven terrain covered with mushrooms soon overlapped the deep green. The relatively flat forested areas around Blackmeadow were nowhere to be found; instead, hills rose and fell with dangerous pitch and trees were incredibly rare on the horizon. Gabriel smugly called to Alric, "Other more reasonable knights of Saint Thestus would only don their armour when they needed it most, seeing as putting it on means being trapped inside it for hours on end. Some, I hear, opt for less than a full suit of plate for this very reason. Why art thou so determined to walk thyself to joint failure, back problems, and aching muscles?"

"Those who look upon the Second Attestation with dread are not worthy to call themselves Knights Thestor," Alric replied sternly. It was an opportunity to prove his devotion. God would see that his heart was true through how much he was willing to suffer…how much pain he was willing to inflict upon himself.

Carthei furrowed her brow as she looked about, scanning for danger. "It is wise. Such effective armour is not quick to don."

Gabriel squinted and tilted his head. He didn't seem to expect the druid to understand and quite frankly, neither did Alric. He gave the woman a confused stare and she looked back at him, meeting his eyes. He barked, in an effort to break the strange tension, "Now, tell me of thy staff, pagan. I wish to understand the nature of magic."

Carthei cocked her head inquisitively. "So you can better fight against it?" He nodded. With a curt bow, Carthei obliged. "My staff is a tool, the same as your weapons. The key differences are that it is as old as time itself and it is alive, like you and I." Carthei tapped on the housing at the midpoint of her staff. She then folded a small compartment open. Inside was an object the size of a clenched fist. A heart.

Alric froze. "B-Blood magic? Such a thing is…evil!"

"Your mind is narrow, Godslave. Far too narrow." Carthei lowered her cowl as she slammed the staff shut. "For you, when something dies, it becomes refuse. Useless clutter to be tossed away or buried. The druid tribes have new uses for the dead so they are not simply garbage to fill our village yards. Our loved ones, our enemies, animals of the forest, they all serve us in death."

Anyone close enough could see Alric's fingers curl shut as Carthei spoke. He retorted, "Thou art showing great disrespect to the customs of the true faith."

Gabriel chuckled. "Easy, Brother Alric. I only hear our new friend speaking the truth. Yes, we do have rites and rituals to perform in order to save the spirit, but the bodies are left behind. What purpose do they serve in the ground but to be fodder for the goblins? Too often do I witness townsfolk taking up arms to push the vulturous creatures away from their graveyards."

Alric's eyes settled upon Carthei's staff. He had destroyed plenty of the things, but he had never cared to understand their workings. The sapping of a heart for magic…it struck him as dark. Twisted. Demonic. But did the people of the Church not rend the matter of God's creatures to sustain themselves? "The power of the staff is finite, then. Eventually, a new heart must be offered," Alric surmised, changing the subject.

"Yes. There are many varieties of arcane staff. The kind that I carry, we call the taukumu."

Gabriel adjusted his seating so he could better see the object. Some of the others in the wagon followed. As Alric inspected it further, he noted that it was almost identical to the ones he had seen in the past. But unlike those wielded by the heretics, a fine ashen spear with a tapered steel tip had been tightly fixed to the staff with lines of strange rope. "I have witnessed the effect of this one. Terrifying instrument," Alric warned. "It sends a bolt of starlight unto anyone unfortunate enough to be standing in its path."

Emma was hypnotised by Alric's words. "Then what?"

"Then…he is torn asunder," said the knight fearfully.

Murmurs began to course around the wagon. One of the wounded soldiers nodded powerfully. "You all shoulda seen tha big ones they used yesterday. They made mincemeat of that ogre."

Carthei smiled. "Quite right," she said far too cheerfully for Alric's liking.

Eventually, as the party continued, the grass turned black. Fields of crops had been reduced to charred remains. They passed by hamlets on the horizon blackened by fire. Emma stared across the rubble, not appearing to understand what exactly she was looking at. Gabriel and Alric gave each other a solemn look. Apart from relieving your enemy of their territory by claiming it for yourself, another more devastating tactic was to simply destroy everything. Burn houses, spoil crops, slaughter peasants. Regions could be rendered completely useless; the inhabitants could no longer pay the rents owed to their lords nor produce food or goods. It would also have a secondary effect of undermining the trust of the peasantry in their lords; what good was a noble who swore to protect you in exchange for your service if he sat in a castle and allowed your village to burn to the ground? It was what the Valthois called a chevauchée and it was a tactic employed in spades by the Tritans. It appeared that the Valthois had taken the opportunity to practise it for themselves.

Carthei and the other druids looked especially troubled by the destruction. Alric thought that perhaps living in isolation from the Churchsworn Kingdoms had sheltered them from the horrors of full-scale war. Carthei's eyes wobbled as she saw bodies left where they fell in the debris.

Alric said to Gabriel, "Men of the same faith slaughtering each other is…an unfathomable waste. In my dreams I see all united against the true enemy. How peaceful the land would be."

Carthei pulled her cowl back up over her head. "I think that you simply traded one excuse for another. How many druids have you cut down believing them to be witches? How many *true* witches have you slain?" She then drifted away from the Thestor as Gabriel masked his amusement.

She was but a foolish pagan, as blind as the rest of them. Alric would take solace in the fact that his piety would grant him passage into Heaven, and her blasphemy would condemn her to eternal suffering in Hell. When those rageful thoughts passed through his mind, some other notions took their place. He was taught that those who guided harmful magic, black magic, had attained such power through the Devil. Pagans living in solitude using sorcery as a simple tool was not something covered by his Thestor training. Was it possible that it was wrong? Alric shook his head. Of course not.

For miles, the trail of scorched earth continued. Piles of seared wooden debris marked what Alric assumed used to be houses and other structures. Empty wagons stood immobile on the side of the road. Much to the relief of the vigilant knight, the destruction slowly gave way to the Jagged Margin: the marbled grey mountain range that ran in a curve along the Eastern Coast of Tritham. The natural marvel bowed in from the left, dipped where the road sliced up through it, and emerged once again on the right even taller. Emma had her head pointed directly upward in order to gaze upon the crest of the summit. Nocht's footfalls were heavy and slapped the dirt with such impacts that Alric could feel them resonating within his bones. A choir of those sounds, a collection for each man, woman, child, animal, and cart drawing across the countryside, painted the otherwise subdued soundscape.

It was not long before camp had been made. With the sun vanishing behind the line of the horizon and the refugees physically taxed from the day of travel, it was clear that the time had come for rest. The Ga'zahi chose a particularly well-spaced clearing nestled by a handful of trees. Once the tents had been pitched, the beds laid out, the fire started, and the food dispensed, Alric found himself grateful for the company. He had grown much too accustomed to being alone. With many of the refugees off to bed within the tents, Alric wandered off to a desolate corner of the grove with a heavily scuffed wooden chest in his arms and peered up at the sky. The Prime Moon loomed over him with its splotched surface. He dropped the chest onto the grass, lowered himself onto one knee, and recited the final verse of the Oath of Vigilance in a hushed tone.

As soon as the final word left his mouth, Alric could feel the immense weight of the Second Attestation lift itself from his shoulders. He then proceeded to disarm himself, starting with his gauntlets then untying his vambraces. After each piece was removed, he tossed it into the chest. His helmet soon followed, along with the padded coif beneath it.

"You could have asked for help."

Alric jolted and shot his eyes towards the origin of the sound: upward. Carthei lay on her side upon the limb of a tree that dangled above Alric, with her arm propping her head up. With a frustrated sigh, Alric eased his posture and resumed the removal of his armour. He grunted as he struggled to reach the straps for his breastplate. They weren't impossible to get to without assistance…but it was far from easy. "I have been disarming myself most days for the last five years. I believe I do not require assistance."

"Of course," she shrugged.

His breastplate snapped open and it dropped onto the grass beneath him. After a few moments, it and all of the armour on his legs had been set into the chest as well. Alric slipped his Thestor surcoat back over his arming doublet and tied his belt around his waist.

The rustling of grass caused both warriors to snap their heads towards the wood. Alric had his right hand fastened to the grip of his sword. With the grace of a cat, Carthei vaulted off the side of her branch and landed on her feet, taukumu staff in hand. A figure emerged from the shadow, running so urgently he was tripping over himself. It was one of the other Ga'zahi. He anxiously looked to Carthei and barked something at her in their mother tongue.

Her face dropped. "Come, Godslave. Come quickly," she urged.

The trio pushed fiercely through the forest, weaved in and out of immense trees, and mounted the base of a hill that overlooked the valley. The light of an inferno bathed the entire bowl of earth in a red sheen. As the campsite was embraced by the hill, the glow was obscured from it. Leagues away, a thin shape floating in the air hurtled a stream of red lightning down onto a dense formation of soldiers on the other side of the plain. The bolts exploded into washes of infinite flame, fanning out and consuming everything in its wake. The airborne shape slowly drifted forward as it continued raining hellfire down on the unidentified force of men. The air beneath its sharp wings shivered. “T-This cannot be,” Carthei muttered.

Alric’s eyes drifted downward and the tension in his face eased for a moment. He was frozen in epiphany. There was no Valthois chevauchée. The torched villages…the acres of land incinerated…it was all set ablaze by dragonfire.

XIV
The Order of the Hospital

Matvey's syncopated breathing was slave to no rhythm. His hand quivered as he grasped the pair of crude iron tweezers and flexed them open then shut. All the while, the open wound on his left bicep oozed obsidian blood. The hospital was filled with plebeians, patrons, and men and women of the cloth. Those not preoccupied with giving care or receiving it either stared at the man or averted their eyes completely as he engaged in the grizzly work. No one was to come to his aid, for it was his duty and his alone. A piece of wood was braced between his teeth. He jammed the tongs into his wound. Matvey's entire body convulsed. His arm caught ablaze as if it was being dipped into molten steel. A guttural scream bounced off the four walls of the stone chamber and became so world-shaking that several patrons had to cup their ears. The squelching of tissue and blood accompanied Matvey's working of the tongs. His teeth dug deep trenches into the piece of wood. A metallic scraping that vibrated through his tool informed him that he found what he was looking for. Matvey's pained cries continued while he tried to manipulate the tongs around the tiny object deep within his arm. Once he was convinced of its purchase, he slowly retracted the implement.

Tremors swept through his right arm. He gagged and sobbed as the agony showed no signs of relenting. After an eternity, the tongs emerged from the cavity and Matvey exhaled sharply. He threw his head back and snarled. Then, he raised the iron tongs and peered at what they seized. A tiny, crumpled object no larger than the tip of his thumb. It closely resembled a thimble, only solid.

"What on earth is that?" asked a nun, Sister Tybeth, as she stopped in her tracks beside Matvey. With a grimace he tossed both the projectile and the tongs onto the side table in front of him, before spitting the piece of wood from his mouth. He desperately fumbled for the glass vial labelled 'tears of faerie' and poured its remaining contents into the hole in his arm. Matvey winced, balled both his hands into fists, then slammed them against the armrests of his chair.

Exhaling sharply, he proceeded to bandage the injury. Tybeth bent over the side table and scrutinised the strange foreign object. Once the bandage was sufficiently tight, Matvey went limp and slowed his breathing in relief. He stared at the wall as he tried to collect his thoughts and push through the pain. "If you are able, Brother Correntis, there are those who could perhaps use treatment. The sooner they are all fit for travel, the better," said Tybeth.

Matvey pushed to his feet and wiped the sweat from his face. The Hospitals of Saint Corren were places of care for those without home or shelter. Oftentimes it also meant the ailed and the dying. As a knight sworn to the Order of the Hospital of Saint Corren, Matvey was a defender of the charitable institutions and was as skilled in preserving life as he was in taking it. He moved around the hospital, supplying the suffering with treatment and the starving with food and water. One such patient was a peasant woman named Claudia Miller. Matvey groggily approached her as she lay completely still in her bed. Her eyes followed him, but her body did not move an inch. He sat himself onto the chair by Claudia's bedside and held a bowl of water out towards her. "Time to drink, Claudia," he said hoarsely.

Matvey brought the bowl up to her lips. They twitched and trembled, pulling apart ever so slightly. The poor woman had fallen from a windmill. After the accident, she could not move a single muscle below her shoulders. She could not even speak. "Good. Very good." He set the bowl down on the bedside table and moved on to the next person.

A young woman stared with fearful eyes at Matvey as he approached her with a bowl of pottage fresh from the kitchen. Without a word, he handed the food to her. Sitting on her lap was a little girl, frozen in horror. With a scrunched face, the little girl asked him softly, "Why didn't anyone help you?"

"Hush, Emma…!" snapped the girl's mother. Matvey smacked his lips and looked out the window nervously. Some holy knights loved explaining their different creeds to the ignorant. On some other day, Matvey might have as well. But the pain still lurked in his veins, and he desperately wanted to drop himself onto a bed and sleep. He said nothing and simply shook the bowl in front of them as he fought to keep his eyes open.

"Brother, please…have some manners," scolded Tybeth as she slipped in between the two, snatched the bowl from Matvey's grip, and handed it much more gently to the child. "It's okay, my child. Eat and everything will be much better." Tybeth's welcoming smile ultimately convinced the girl to take the food.

Since he was recently preoccupied with saving his own life, Matvey only then realised that there were more people in the hospital apart from those he had brought there. "Where did these others come from?" Matvey asked, leaning onto the wall and staring out the portal.

"A party came from Blackmeadow while you were gone. Refugees and injured men. Actually, there is one man who could benefit from your attention. He requires amputation."

The mother's eyes widened. "W-What? You're not operating on Sir Gabriel. You almost died right in that chair!"

Tybeth laid a hand on the woman's shoulder. "Do not doubt the abilities of a Knight Correntis. God shall guide his hand."

Matvey flexed his fingers, snatched up the surgeon's kit that he had just used on himself, then moved into the adjoining room. The patient was already lying upon the operating table; his eyes were throbbing with fear as they met Matvey's. He was a rather young man in the clothes of a well-to-do noble. "W-What are you doing?" he murmured. Matvey spread his surgical kit out on a nearby desk and began to select the tools he would need to sever the man's legs.

"Saving your life," he said with a shallow breath.

In front of the Hospital there was a hill topped with an ageing tree overlooking the town of Phaemslake. Alric leant against it as he stared at the unholy abomination in the clouds above. The Knight Thestor hadn't slept since it first appeared. During the first day, it dragged its red line of fire across the region at random, ploughing the land with death. Eventually, it chose to simply loom high in the sky, hovering in place like a daytime star. As with the first night, its wings did not flap. It hung there in the distance as many of the people of Phaemslake packed their belongings to flee.

However, his peaceful solitude was not to last. In the corner of his eye, he saw shapes approaching from the bottom of the hill. Of the five Ga'zahi that embarked from Blackmeadow, there were then four. Carthei had sent one of her scouts to carry word of the dragon back to their tribe. All of them came to a halt several paces away from Alric, who groaned with disdain. Before Carthei could say anything, he muttered quickly, "Thou hast fulfilled the vow made to Duchess Katheryn." Carthei bowed curtly, placing a hand onto her forehead. The odd gesture made Alric furrow his upper lip. He added, "Away with thee. Skitter back to thy coven."

The three druids sent their eyes to Carthei, who stared at the beast hanging in the sky. "I am afraid we cannot. Not with that thing peering down upon us."

Alric was going to insist that they leave him at once or suffer physical injury, but the thoughts were interrupted. His attention was pried away by a Knight Correntis who paced out from the Hospital's entrance. Like the fortress monasteries of the Thestors, the Hospital married the stern facade of a castle with the resplendent beauty of a cathedral. The Correntis' dirt-riddled surcoat was black with a white pillar in its centre. He wore simple clothing underneath said garment and had a bandage wrapped tightly around his left bicep; a sign that he had recently emerged from quite the ordeal. He and his brethren were governed by their own set of Four Attestations, most of which were quite different to those of the Thestors. Their Second Attestation did not allow anyone else to provide them medical or surgical aid. They and they alone could deliver themselves from death. A most terrifying commitment, in Alric's opinion. He had tried in the past to mend what appeared to be a minor wound, but his hands would tremble uncontrollably and the instinct to avoid pain was much too strong to overcome.

"Matvey." The knight's voice was low and hoarse, sounding as if it had rusted and deteriorated from lack of use.

The Knight Thestor bowed. "Alric."

As he tightened his bandage, Matvey continued, "Your friend survived surgery. It was a good thing we had received a shipment of faerie tears before all of this…calamity." Alric nodded and kept his gratitude to himself. If there was one thing that holy knights loathed, it was being thanked for doing what was expected of them. What they already swore to do. Matvey appeared to appreciate it. "I don't suppose you know why that hideous creature is hovering out there?" he added. It was clear from the way he spoke that Matvey had not been a member of nobility before he took his vows; the Correnti usually recruited from young surgeons and physicians then drilled them in combat afterwards, but choosing knights was not unheard of.

"I am afraid not. What has struck thee so, Brother? The Valthois?"

The Correntis huffed as he sent a curious glance towards the druids. "Unlikely. I was travelling *with* them at the time."

The Church chose no sides in the conflicts of kings. The Correnti, as surgeons and physicians, were allowed to lend their expertise to anyone in need. Thestors could provide spiritual services but could not fight one faction in the name of another. The committing of force to one side of a political conflict was forbidden by the Church in typical circumstances. If one realm was said to be committing heresy, however, the Church would not hesitate to deploy Grand Hosts against them.

"Tritans, then?" asked Alric.

"No. I saw all kinds of armour and dress. It wasn't one people, but many united under totems of bone."

Carthei looked to Alric. "Your heretics, Godslave. If they can enrage an ogre through the Kr'tesh, who is to say that they cannot raise a dragon?"

Matvey's gaze scoured the strangers up and down. "Your companions seem weary. I have the perfect solution for that fatigue. Would you like to come inside so I can make you some?" asked the Correntis, voice still rough and ill-suiting the content of his speech.

Alric rolled his eyes and clenched his jaw. He always felt that the Hospital of Saint Corren was much too soft for its own good. It did not close its doors to those of false religions. It instead showed them the same level of care as the faithful. That key difference between the doctrines of the Thestors and the Correnti often caused a great deal of conflict between them. Konth, a talented druid scout, cocked his head in confusion. Even Carthei appeared to be taken back by the gesture. "Aren't you going to ask whether or not we are witches?" asked Konth.

The Correntis shook his head before locking eyes with Konth. "No. But if you betray my hospitality, I will butcher you. I do not require both arms to do that."

A *somewhat* reasonable man. "I will partake in this drink with thee, Brother Matvey."

"Friends? Will you accept?"

Carthei replied, "Your offer is gracious. However, I will not seal myself away within that stone box. We shall rest here, where the wind breathes upon us."

A scoff left Alric's mouth as he shook his head in disbelief.

"Then here it shall be," said Matvey warmly.

The Knight Correntis retreated into the Hospital for several moments, leaving Alric and the Ga'zahi to lower themselves onto the grass as they awaited his return. Whenever Alric had a charge of people to safeguard, he could never rest. His mind would wander and he would ruminate. Threats could appear anywhere. He had to make sure that he was vigilant, for if he wasn't, God would punish him for failing to protect those under his care. Being free from that burden, Alric allowed himself a moment to breathe. However, it was difficult to do so in the presence of the untrustworthy Ga'zahi. He found himself looking up. The sky was such a pure blue that Alric's skin tingled when his eyes became lost in its depth. The few clouds present swirled with the wind and dropped shadows onto the valley below. There was something about those shadows, those formless blotches of darkness that drifted along the fields, that Alric found so enamouring. He wasn't sure exactly why, but it made him want to watch them forever. All of that beauty only made the dragon even more dissonant and unnerving. It hadn't moved for at least a day. The last thing Alric had seen it do was drop itself slightly then fling a beam of red-hot fire onto something that was obscured by the horizon. After that, it rose back to its previous position and continued loitering there.

When Matvey returned, he did so holding a serving tray adorned with six small cups. He placed the tray in the middle of the loose circle formed by Alric and the Ga'zahi then joined it himself. Alric removed his bascinet and placed it beside him on the grass as he asked, "What dost thou recall of the force that attacked thee?" The Thestor cautiously grasped the small wooden cup and brought it up to his nose. The warm liquid within had a fragrance that was vaguely familiar to Alric but he was certain he had never ingested such a strange, black beverage before.

Matvey had already taken a gulp of his own. "They struck me with a tiny bead of steel. It had to be dug out of my arm."

The druids nodded knowingly. One in particular, a hunter named Vontross, leaned forward. "There's an arcane staff we call the pakama. It spits seeds so quickly that the human eye cannot even see them fly. Not as deadly as taukumu, but they have their uses."

"Witchcraft, Brother Matvey," rasped Alric. "Thou shouldst consider thyself lucky to be alive."

With a dry huff, Matvey replied, "We Correnti make our own luck."

Alric brought the cup up to his mouth and sipped. A vile, bitter concoction slithered down his throat, causing him to gag and instantly jerk the vessel away. Narsei seemed incredibly fixated on the drink, as did Vontross. Only Konth shared Alric's strong disdain, evident by how his face scrunched up as he poured the foul liquid into the grass.

"Unfortunate that it wasn't to your liking, Brother Alric. It's a very popular beverage from Qurveen called qahwa. It kept me alert during many late nights of surgery and battle," answered Matvey.

That would perhaps explain why Alric recognised the smell. Qurveen was the Blessed Land; home of the sacred Pillar, and of course, where the many Crusades were waged. If it was as commonplace as Matvey made it sound, Alric must have caught a whiff of it all those years ago in the desert sultanate. "Of course, an *infidel* mixture. No wonder it is so revolting."

Alric noticed that Carthei was gazing at the dragon. She hadn't touched her drink. "I do not understand how you two can jest when such a creature taints nature with its presence."

"What wouldst thou have us do? Sprout wings and fly up there to confront it?" Alric snapped.

Konth gave Carthei a soft glance, then looked to Alric. "We are all…deeply troubled by the dragon. For us and many of the other druid tribes, they are a symbol of Athroct'u: the Rotting of The World."

Carthei inhaled so deeply that Alric was surprised she did not inflate like a bladder. She closed her eyes as she exhaled. "Ancient songs passed from druid to druid tell of the eventual decay of all that is splendid in this world. It would be a consequence of us not worshipping nature, not tending to it. As such, our people live as one with the forest and give back to it as we take. The old songs proclaim that the coming of the dragons is a sign. A sign that Athroct'u is coming to pass."

Matvey nodded slowly. "This Athroct'u… It sounds similar to the Church's prophecies of the End Times…when The Devil will burst forth from Hell and unleash his torment upon the world." Alric glared at Matvey. He was giving credence to their hogwash by even acknowledging it. "What if we slay the dragon? Will the End Times be stopped?"

She shrugged and sighed, her posture slumping. "I don't know."

Matvey added, "I would rather die trying than whimpering in a corner."

Vontross' mouth thinned and widened. It made a bizarre, lopsided shape that made Alric narrow his eyes. Seconds later, he realised that it was a smile. Suddenly, a deep drone washed through the air. It was the low, rumbling tone of a chorus of brass instruments that resonated with Alric's bones. Birds took flight in the distance, scrambling in fear. Alric and Matvey met eyes and the Thestor swallowed.

Narsei cocked her head. "What is that?"

Both of the Churchsworn knights snapped to their feet as if they were men possessed. Alric scooped up his bascinet and slipped it onto his head.

Matvey snatched all of the cups in a frantic hurry as Carthei motioned her men to stand. “Could someone kindly explain what is happening?” she asked.

Matvey answered, “The Weeping Call. It means a Thestor fortress is under siege.”

“This is ludicrous!” Alric snarled. “Who would dare take up the sword against the servants of God?!”

“The defilers, perhaps,” mused Carthei.

“Be ready, brother. God’s vengeance will not exact itself.” Matvey raced back into the Hospital to gather his weapons and armour before setting off.

XV
Fields of Damnation

The touch of dragonfire had grown quite familiar to Alric after days of walking the fields of desolation. The smell that it left behind was intensely noxious and the blazes it started would burn for hours on end. As if the dragon itself was not worrying enough, it was clear that once again, mankind was turning upon itself. A nameless army swept clean what the dragon left standing. The desecrated Churches and vandalised shrines he passed told him all he needed to know about who was responsible. They were no longer the poorly organised rabble he thought them to be.

Even after securing several nights of rest, Alric could not shake the tension that bubbled beneath his skin. The fingers of his right hand tapped against the shaft of his pollaxe as he rested it on his shoulder and sent his wild eyes all about. He, the four druids, and Matvey chose to travel on foot to the Thestors' regional fortress of Omenthal. Matvey wore brigandine, splint vambraces and cuisses, a bevor around his neck and lower face, and a kettle hat upon his head.

In such hostile territory, ambushes were to be expected. Having to deal with horses and pack animals in the midst of that chaos would have made everything much more difficult, so Alric left Nocht and his wagon of supplies at the Hospital in Phaemslake. The only thing he retrieved was his pollaxe. The Ga'zahi showed themselves to be incredibly skilled foragers and hunters; even with most animal life frightened away by the destruction and the plant life scorched, they somehow managed to keep provisions well-stocked.

Smoke drowned the sky, obscuring the dragon. Alric could not say he liked seeing the monstrosity when the skies were clear, but he much rathered knowing where it was. With grey froth in the air, no one could be sure that it hadn't left its incorporeal perch. The mountainous terrain was broken up by dense wood, some of which had been blazed and shredded into blackened sticks.

Konth was worried that there was an army marching in their wake. He often slipped behind the rest of the group to cover the rear. He said that he heard horses, perhaps outriders of a hostile force. Whatever was walking behind them, the party had no choice but to keep going. There were only six of them. Even with the sorcery of the Ga'zahi, they could not last against a foe that outnumbered them. Alric hoped that the manoeuvrability of a small group would be enough to keep them away from any danger. Vontross led the way as they avoided the roads and stuck instead to the forests. The blanket of acrid mist seeped between the trees like a pestilence. Alric came to a halt before a sheer drop that was too steep to hike down. Through the clouds of static smoke, even with his visor raised, he could only barely make out the hamlet of Threshfield atop its knoll. Surrounding it were vast fields of farmland. Behind the town, just partially visible, was Omenthal. Only one of its walls pierced the grey fog; a monolith of hand-worked stone erected in recognition of God's infinite rage. Omenthal was protected by the rocky cliff walls that surrounded it; the only way to approach it was by walking the valley and taking Threshfield. Alric could see fortifications along the edge of the town facing away from the fortress monastery. An enemy camp was standing well out of arrow range across the plain. Carthei barked at Vontross, "Octhum."

Vontross reached into his robe and pulled out a small cylindrical object. He tossed it over to Carthei who elegantly plucked it out of the air and held it up to her eye. Alric tilted his head like a confused dog. "They fly a banner marked with druidic runes," she said aloud.

Matvey cocked his head. "What does it say?"

"There are two symbols. One denotes reverence of Clth…and the other denotes a religious union. I suppose a direct translation would be 'Clthic Synod'."

Her fellow Ga'zahi all furrowed their brows in anger. Matvey and Alric were left to glance at each other and shrug. Alric was clearly not going to press further, so it fell upon Matvey. "What is…Clth?"

The deep brown colours of Carthei's face paint had begun to wear off. The smooth blue tone of her skin caught the light. "It is the name of the ancient betrayer who splintered the druids into the isolated tribes you see today. I...suppose he may be my people's equivalent of the Devil." Carthei lowered the object and turned to Alric, seeing that his eyes were still fixed on the thing. With a weak smile, she handed it to him. "Here. See this foe for yourself." The Thestor turned his nose up at the object.

With a sigh, Carthei widened her eyes and shook the octhum. "Do you wish to scout the enemy position, or not?"

Finally, Alric hesitantly accepted the octhum and pressed it against his right eye and closed his left. It was not dissimilar to how shaped lenses used by scribes magnified text or how eyeglasses corrected poor vision, but the extreme nature of the octhum's magnification made Alric feel lightheaded. He could see the ripples of wind on the heretic banner and the frayed fibres that hung from it. Soldiers moved around the camp, dressed in varying kinds of armour.

Their equipment had made it abundantly clear that the demonists had been recruiting from the ranks of nobility. It seemed that the enemies of God had grown wiser. Without indoctrinating the wealthy, their army would have been doomed to be the legion of children and peasants that it was at Chesterton. Alric had yet to see any witches, but a twisting feeling deep within assured him that they were there. He moved his sight to Threshfield. Alric's shoulders eased and his heart slowed. He saw his brethren, other knights of the Order of Saint Thestus, leading common soldiers in the defence of the town. As he finally passed the device back to Carthei, he remarked, "Waste not my time with these arcane trinkets. We must away."

"This is not magic, Godslave. Just a trick of the light," she corrected, passing it back to Vontross who stowed it beneath his cloak.

After twenty minutes of navigating the particularly dense mess of tree roots, ditches, and boulders, Alric's party came to the bottom of the valley and were peering out from the cover of the flora. He made to step out of the shroud of trees but was violently jerked backwards. Managing to save himself from tumbling over by shifting his weight forward, the Thestor realised that Carthei had her hand firmly fastened to his right pauldron. "What is it now?!" he snapped. Eventually, his attention drifted back to the clearing between the wood and Threshfield. How had he not seen it before?

Dozens of bodies littered the fields. Most were Knights Thestor; the others were perhaps followers they had accrued to come to Omenthal's defence. The manner in which their savaged corpses decorated the plain indicated that they all fell as they rushed to reach the village. The Weeping Call had acted as bait on a hook.

A figure emerged further down the tree line. It was another Knight Thestor, the size of Alric's thumb due to how far removed he was. He walked in the direction of Threshfield, followed by a handful of Valthois soldiers. "Brother!" Alric screamed at the top of his lungs. "Retreat!"

The distant Thestor slowed and glanced about in confusion. Other shouts emanating from Threshfield echoed Alric's warning. A thunderous 'snap' pierced the silence and time seemed to slow. A needle of light came zooming in from the direction of the Clthic camp, locked onto the knight's head. It punched straight through the steel helm. There was a blinding flash of light for a split second. When it passed, jets of blood and gas escaped from the sights and breaths of his helmet, then the knight's body fell to the ground. His retinue made a mad dash for Threshfield. One by one, the process was repeated. Alric had never seen anything like it. Each man was struck mid-sprint with unfathomable accuracy. Heads were reduced to cones of tumbling, bloody chunks, and torsos were blown inside-out. After mere seconds, there was no longer any living thing in the farmlands surrounding the hamlet. It was then that Alric realised he had been blessed by God to have only encountered witches in close quarters.

Alric exhaled an unsteady breath as he drew the Sign of the Pillar, his hand trembling. That knight, like all his brethren, was trained to kill since he was a child. He was bred to dispense death. After earning his knighthood and serving as his liege as a warrior, he turned to the Order of Saint Thestus and underwent even more training. All that skill, all that armour, and he was just picked off from afar the way a bowman could slaughter a helpless rabbit. Alric had always been of the firm belief that if you were to kill someone, you must look him in the eye. Commit the deed with responsibility. Even archers were not *that* removed from the violence; more often than not, they too would enter the melee after expending their arrows. With that black magic, a man could strike another down without even laying eyes upon his face. Without hearing the rattle of his final breath. It was an aberration.

Vontross once again retrieved his octhum. He then readied his taukumu and pressed the object onto its length, causing it to lock in place with a 'click'. The hunter then lifted the staff, pressed the end against his shoulder, and rested his cheek against its side so he could peer into the magnifying contraption. "I found the wretch," reported Vontross. "I see at least six others."

Carthei's face drained of all emotion. Alric was certain that she was considering whether it was worth telegraphing her people's presence. Suddenly unleashing magic onto the Clthics during an actual battle would have been the preferred first strike of the Ga'zahi, but there was no reaching Threshfield without eliminating the witches.

"Kill them," she chirped.

Vontross took a deep breath. Alric stared at the man as his upper lip quivered. The tip of his taukumu lit up like a holy star three times in rapid succession. The Ga'zahi possessed the same power? The power to dispatch someone from leagues away?

"Run!" barked Vontross.

Alric hesitated for a moment but ultimately threw himself out of the embrace of the trees and forced himself to a sprint. His feet punched against the earth and all the components of his armour rung like chimes in the wind. The sound of his own breathing overwhelmed his senses. His eyes were pinned on Threshfield as it grew larger with each stride. Not daring to curb his pace even slightly, the Thestor tilted his chin over his shoulder. Matvey trailed behind, followed by Konth, then Narsei, Carthei, and Vontross. It was the longest handful of minutes in Alric's life. Laced into his wheezing was an ever-growing whimper. In the past, he always could rest easy knowing that his armour would keep him safe from arrows and crossbow bolts. There was a slim potential of shots penetrating either his plate or mail, but that was it: a slim potential. However, seeing plate pierced before his very eyes by eldritch energy did wonders to undermine all of that faith. One hit, anywhere on his body, would spell doom. He waited for a volley of return fire. He waited for his life to come to an abrupt and sudden end. The longer he waited, the more painful it became.

The main dirt road of Threshfield swallowed Alric as he came storming forth. A blur of brown, green, and blue was everything his eyes beheld as he tossed himself behind the closest piece of cover before he could even get a good look at it. The ground barrelled into his chest like a battering ram. Alric groaned as he pushed himself up into a crouch. With time to spare thanks to his new position, he gazed about. There was a makeshift wall made of thick chunks of stone propped up by wooden trussing and lengths of rope. There, behind that barricade, were two Knights Thestor, a Knight Correntis, and a Tritan archer. The Order that each knight served was plain to see from the surcoats they wore; white with a red Pillar for the Thestors, black with a white Pillar for the Correntis. They paid no mind to Alric. Matvey was of no interest either as he leapt behind a piece of stone on the other side of the dirt road. Instead, they stared at their still-approaching company.

Each Ga'zahi druid shouldered their staff as they ran, casting blue sparks of enchanted lightning deep into the Clthic camp. "Thou art the first to make it across!" called one of the Thestors over the sound of the arcane discharges.

"God save us…!" murmured the other Thestor, much younger and inexperienced judging by his wavering tone. "What are these strangers thou hast brought to our midst?! Witches?!"

Alric felt his heart pound against his chest in the face of such a treacherous accusation. He would never endanger the faith. Never. Before he had a chance to chastise the young Thestor, someone else beat him to it. "To assume that a knight of our Order would be daft enough to lead our sworn enemies to us is an insult of the man's faith," added the first more hardened knight. As the taukumu fire abated, his voice lowered to a faint murmur. "These folk are allies."

The Ga'zahi slid into cover around the village, with Carthei slamming into position next to Alric. Instantly, the other holy knights anxiously inched away from her. "I thank thee, Brother…?" started Alric.

"Otto. Marshal of the Forty-First Host."

"The Legion of Glorious Exaction…? Pray tell me, *this* cannot be all that remains."

Otto shook his head. "T-The dragon. We stood no chance."

"Why does it not simply erase us all now?" asked Carthei.

With a deep inhale, Otto continued. "I believe only God knows the answer to that. Is it truly as it seems? Have those cowardly sorcerers been sent to Hell?"

Carthei shook her head. "We struck a great deal of them…but I cannot say for certain."

Alric took that moment to poke his head up from behind cover and look at the Clthic encampment. He saw a great deal of movement even without the help of the octhum. "They are mobilising infantry. It seems that they now understand that they can no longer lob light at us from afar without consequence," assessed Alric.

The young Thestor rolled his shoulders back and forth. "The time is finally upon us, then. We shall see who stands victorious; a band of spineless heretics, or the mightiest warriors in all the realm united in their love of God." Although the lad was a bit overconfident, Alric would be lying if he said he was anything less than eager to run those fools through.

XVI
A SLAVE NO MORE

Franco di Lombardi's infantry force had been splintered ever since Worthing Hill. A brawl broke out in a tavern and took the lives of five men. What was it about? What it was *always* about. Faith. The sight of dead children at his men's feet at Chesterton would haunt him until the end of his days. And there, among the soldiers with the stench of pleasure on his breath, was the Knight Thestor. Brother Alric. By the time Franco and his party returned to Redford, many men had deserted. He couldn't say that he blamed them. They either left because Franco had the nerve to speak out against a holy brother, or they were so angered and appalled by what their fellow soldiers had done that they could not stand the sight of them. He was thankful that his knights and men-at-arms stood by his side; they ensured that he still remained one of the more powerful lords in Tritham. The solar of Redford Keep was dead silent as Franco finished recounting the tale to his brother, Dante. With the fireplace crackling to his side, Dante reclined in his chair and rubbed his forehead.

"I tell thee, brother, I can stomach this no longer," Franco added as he paced back and forth. "If they wish children dead, then the children shall die. What kind of world doth we live in?"

"If *I* saw innocents impaled upon the battlements, I may have sought retribution as well. The children *were* involved in that, were they not?"

"Art thou attempting to justify his actions?" Franco asked in disbelief.

"N-No, I am not. I simply wish for thee to calm thyself."

Franco exhaled out of his nostrils. "I shall be calm once God descends from Heaven and explains why things must be so horrible in this creation of his."

Unable to remain calm for any longer, Dante shot to his feet and threw his hands up. "Not this again, Franco. I shall not be subjected to blasphemy."

"Thou art still blinded by the Church's words," Franco snapped. "God did not pen the Scripture. Men did. They erected rules and laws and claim that they are all given by God, when in fact, they exist only to consolidate their own strength." Dante seemingly ignored Franco's ramblings and paced towards the door. Before he reached it, Franco muttered, "Thou wouldst still believe that mother was deserving of her fate?"

The words stopped his brother in his tracks. Dante stared down at the rush carpet that covered the cold stone floor. "Please. Do not do as father did. Do not pursue it."

"I haven't a choice any longer. I saw evil that day in Chesterton. It cannot be permitted to exist. How many more families must be dashed apart by those fanatics until it is too much? Someone *must* take up arms."

Dante peered over his shoulder. "It seems that they already have," he said, referring to the very force that Franco led troops against that day. With that, Dante floated off through the door and left Franco by himself. He remained there for some time, unable to pull himself from his own mind. He did not even notice his wife drift inside until she spoke.

"I brought some supper for you. It is rather cold unfortunately. You two always did lose track of time when you talked."

Franco turned away from the fireplace and saw Beatrice before him. She wore a plain green kirtle with a deep red surcoat draped over it. In her hand was a plate laid with roast chicken and assorted vegetables. "A chicken? What occasion calls for such a wasteful meal?" Franco asked as he accepted the plate.

Beatrice arched an eyebrow. "I suppose it is the special occasion of me loving you so much that I do not care if we have fewer eggs for the rest of the season." She gracefully fluttered over to a sofa by the fire and laid herself across in a rather enticing manner. Beatrice had a resilience about her that most would not be able to see. She had been the first person Franco had told about the incident and not once did she fall into despair as Franco had. The first thing she said after hearing the morbid story was 'Well, it seems that the monsters could learn a thing or two about killing children from that fellow.' Her strength laid in her foul and oftentimes tasteless humour. It had become something that Franco could not live without. She never failed to make him see the light of any situation. Franco settled down opposite his wife and scoffed down the food as he looked upon her. She was not what his peers in court had in mind for him. They said that he had married beneath his station. He did not care. He had fallen for the daughter of a merchant and there was no force in the world that could keep them apart.

After several days had passed, Franco was able to readjust to life at home. Managing the estate, collecting taxes, spending time with his wife, sparring with his men-at-arms and knights, and riding out to nearby villages made him feel as if he could move on. Redford was serviced by the town of Pitch that was a short ride from the castle itself along the bank of the River Archus. As much as it brought him disdain from his peers, Franco loved conversing with the commonfolk. There was something about their raw and unfiltered discussions that he loved being involved in. It took some time for them to open up enough to be so casual in front of a nobleman like himself, but the people of Pitch *had* come around after the years that he had spent trying to break in. He spoke with whoever would listen about the massacre at Chesterton as well as his history with the Church. It seemed that there were more folk who were unhappy with them than it first seemed.

The local inn, The Hardship, was one of his favourite places to go. Whenever he brought Beatrice with him, he had the time of his life. She became rowdy and verbose whenever she had swallowed a few tankards of mead; it reminded him of what she was like when they first met. She was still the same person in private of course, but being a lady meant caring about how others saw you. She had been forced to learn formalities and what not...but when she was drunk? It all flew out the window. Unfortunately, Beatrice was indisposed that night, leaving Franco to ride with Dante to The Hardship. "How is Allegra managing with the child?" Franco asked as they swayed back and forth upon their horses.

Dante sighed. "She did not feel that she was ready to become a mother, but it was forced upon her regardless. 'She was chosen for the highest of honours', the priest said. 'It would be an insult to God to refuse.' The more that time passes, brother, the more I feel myself following thee down thy unholy path."

"Is it unholy to wish for the unneeded suffering to end?"

"No, it is not," huffed Dante. "What dost thou know of the heretics that thou fought against at Chesterton?"

"Nothing...aside from the fact that they pay homage to the Devil and refer to him as the creator of mankind. Not only did I see their instruments with my own hands, but one of my own footmen, William, faced undead creatures in an ancient tomb. He and the blasted Thestor were the only survivors. I had to make him a man-at-arms after that."

Dante scoffed. "I was about to ask if they were worth joining...but I do not know about dealing with black magic and devilry."

Franco stared at the moon as it hovered in the sky. "But burning people alive for believing in different faiths, or drowning a girl to prove that she is not a witch? Those are quite fine?"

The rest of the trip was made in silence. The brothers brought their steeds before The Hardship and tied them up, all while hearing raging conversations piercing the walls. When Franco pushed the door open, he instantly saw his band of buffoons carrying on at the usual table. Bill 'Bugface' Taylor, the only survivor of the undead tomb other than the Thestor, stood at his seat, miming as he retold the story for the hundredth time. "One of 'em came out, 'ad a massive 'ole in 'is 'ead! It took a chunk outta Harland, then it was gonna come fer me!"

As they made their way to the table, Dante whispered, "I assume this is far from the first time he has told this tale?"

"It is not like Goodman Taylor to ever tire of singing his own praises," Franco replied with a smirk.

Bill's eyes locked onto Franco's. From the wild look in them, Franco could tell that he had been drinking for quite some time. "Franky! How are ya, mate!?"

He shook hands with the footman and answered, "Quite well, my friend."

The Lombardi brothers settled in amongst their friends and threw back mead as if it was the finest tasting substance on God's earth. They listened to Bill ramble on about the undead, demonic witches, and how he saved the Thestor's life. However, a bewitching sight soon snatched Franco's attention. Where he sat on the circular table allowed him to see the front door of the establishment...so when a woman pushed the door open and strode inside with a very casual air about her movements, Franco was the first to react. She wore a fine black gown, the stylings of which Franco had never seen before. Its shoulders puffed out and its bodice was laced together with silver cord. The hem puffed outward like the shoulders did. The woman's face looked...strange. Her skin was as white as snow, her features struck Franco as odd, and her black eyes did not glow. She sauntered into the inn with a kind of confidence and lack of decorum that Franco couldn't help but notice.

Bill, peering over his shoulder, whistled. "Bit of an odd-lookin' one, ay?" He promptly turned back to Franco, looking perplexed. "Didn't realise you was inta tha weird ones," he quipped with a laugh.

"I am a married man, my good William," Franco scoffed. "The lady simply conducted herself in a very...atypical fashion."

Dante added, "Thy wife is not here, little brother. Act not as if she watches thine every move."

As his friends erupted in laughter, Franco rolled his eyes with a huff. The pale woman found herself a seat off on her own in the corner of the tavern. Franco thought he saw her staring at him, but he averted his eyes and focused on the conversation. One of the other men at the table, an archer by the name of John Stanton, leaned forward and said. "You all 'ear about that ogre attack on Blackmeadow?"

Franco, Bill, and Dante nodded, but Lawrence Sowter and Shane Carver reeled back in shock. Carver slammed his tankard onto the table. "Ogre attack? Fuckin' what, now?"

"Get fucked. That's fuckin' bullshit, ay?" hissed Sowter.

Bill shrugged. "It's true, boys. Ran inta some Danecaster footmen on tha road who said they was there. Massive fuckin' thing. Then they managed ta kill it with tha help o' fuckin' magic or some shite." The entire table, save for Bill, was overwhelmed by a wave of laughter. "Fuck you! It's fuckin' true! Go fuck yerselves!"

Carver snorted. "Well, whatever 'appened, I hope that fuckin' bitch got her head smashed in."

With a deep exhale, Franco glared at the man. "Thou wouldst do well not to speak of Duchess Katheryn in such a manner. Despite thy feelings, she is my liege. Thou art sworn to her service."

Stanton managed to cut back in before things got more heated between Franco and Carver. "*Anyway*...I also 'eard that a dragon attacked a lot o' villages down South." Once again, hysteria overtook the table. Franco thought it was getting out of hand. Undead, ogres, then suddenly, dragons? It was happening all at the same time. *It couldn't have been a coincidence, so it had to be false,* thought Franco.

"He's totally right, by the way," a cheerful female voice interjected. Her accent was odd to say the least; it emphasised every 'r' sound and stressed each vowel in a most peculiar way. Franco glanced over at the pale lady and realised that she had been the source of the voice.

"I...am?" asked Stanton.

The woman shook her head. "Oh. Sorry. No. Not you. Him. It isn't a coincidence," she said, pointing at Franco. He scrunched up his brow. He...hadn't said anything.

Yeah, you don't have to. Not with me. I'm Viktoria, by the way. You can call me Vik, if you're feeling...friendly.

The voice that echoed in his mind gave him quite a fright. He jolted backwards suddenly.

I didn't really wanna be the one doing this, but I was kinda headed this way already, so... Anyway, Klaus sent me.

"Klaus...von Talhoffen?" he whispered under his breath.

Yeah. That's the one. He knows that you're not exactly a Church guy. Wanted me to ask if you were game to join him. They call it the Clthic Synod or something like that. Kinda dumb, but whatever. The 'undead', the 'ogre', the 'dragon'...it's all them. It's all a big attack on the Church and everyone who follows them. Well, actually, the ogre was a little bit of a happy accident but hey, I guess it still counts.

Instead of leaping to his feet and raving about the woman's terrifying abilities, Franco considered it all for a moment. Klaus was an old friend of his. He had been antagonistic towards the Church for decades. They had spoken on many occasions to simply share their grievances and listen to each other's painful stories. Franco knew that he had served the Steiffan Empire well as a military commander in its efforts of expansion, but he had no idea that he had any intention of fielding armies against the Church. Before Franco or his friends could respond to the exceedingly strange situation, the door to The Hardship was thrown open. Three Knights Thestor marched in, sending their gazes about the tavern.

"Look out, 'ere comes trouble," joked Bill.

Carver grinned. "Is it *your* mate, Franky?"

It may have been a joke, but Franco carefully inspected the knights' armour and how they moved. None of them had the klappvisored bascinet that Alric wore and none of them had that pompous gait that he walked with. They drifted over to the bar and began conversing with the tavernkeep. "What do you think they're doin'?" Bill said as he scratched his ear.

Dante and Franco glanced at each other. Was it possible that they had come to answer Franco's fighting words at Worthing Hill a week ago? He watched as the tavernkeep's forced grin only grew larger as she directed the fighting men of the cloth over to an unoccupied table. They lumbered over and dropped themselves into the chairs. Two of the three removed their gauntlets and helmets as the innkeeper brought some tankards of mead over to them. "Settlin' in fer a drink by the looks of it," murmured Carver.

Franco exhaled sharply. Dante also deflated with a shock of relief in his eyes. As the night continued, Franco tried to eavesdrop on their conversation. They spoke of being summoned somewhere...but beyond that, Franco couldn't quite tell what their mission was. Perhaps they truly *were* simply resting for the night.

Hey. The pale lady's voice once again echoed through Franco's skull. He glanced over to her table and the pair locked eyes. She flashed him a mischievous smirk. *These are the guys, right? They've been fucking you your entire life and they'll keep fucking you if you don't do anything about it. So tell me, 'Franky'. You in, or what?*

Franco swallowed. It pained him to admit it, but the pale lady was right. He was tired of being tread upon. He was tired of seeing the Thestors slaughter people and drag corpses through the dirt. After taking a long and rickety breath, he clenched his hand into a fist. "I am," he said aloud. Dante and the rest of the mob at his table turned to him in confusion. However, before anything could be said, the pale lady elegantly stood, pushed her chair back in, then paced over to the Thestors' table. *Check this out.*

"Hey guys. 'Sup?" she said.

The Thestor who was still helmeted cocked his head at her. "Is something the matter, my lady?"

She suddenly clasped the sides of the knight's close helm and squeezed. Franco's eyes widened when he saw the steel crease. The Thestor screamed in pain, but it did not seem to elicit anything but pleasure in the pale lady. Without the slightest indication of difficulty, she flattened the helmet within her hands. Black blood shot out of the helm's sights and breaths. Screams shot back and forth in The Hardship as the other remaining Thestors leapt to their feet and drew their longswords. Franco and company scampered from their seats and backed away, unable to peel their eyes from the carnage that was unfurling before them.

The pale lady was slashed at by one of the knights as she lunged toward the other one and seized him by the neck. As she applied pressure, Franco could hear the slow popping of his vertebrae. She cupped her other hand onto the man's cheek...then suddenly, her face snapped open like an envelope. As her white skin split into quarters and folded out of the way, a single fang that shone like steel in the firelight emerged from behind it. She was a vampire...spawn of Hell. The stories were true. Franco stumbled backwards as the breath froze in his lungs. She jerked her head forward, skewering the Thestor's forehead with the fang that had emerged from her face. All the while, the last Thestor roared in defiance and continued swinging his sword. The blows tore her dress and lacerated the skin beneath it, but not a single drop of blood left her body. A gut-wrenching sucking sound filled The Hardship. Many of the patrons had fled at that point, but Franco, Dante, Bill, Sowter, Carver, and Stanton remained where they were.

Once the corpse was sucked dry, the pale lady dropped it to the ground and turned to the final knight. "I really liked this dress. You stupid piece of shit." Despite the fact that her face had been peeled open, her voice was still as clear as day. She plunged both of her hands into the Thestor's chest, straight through his plate armour, then wrenched them apart. The man was torn asunder like a piece of meat, spilling his innards all over the floorboards and bathing the pale lady in blood. Her face reformed and she lowered it towards a spigot of blood that shot from the fresh corpse. She lapped up what she could of the bodily fluid.

"By G-God's grace!" cried Bill as he feverishly pulled out his arming sword and ran towards the vampire. She tossed the dismembered body to the ground and turned to face Bill, cocking her head and smirking playfully.

Franco did not know what came over him, but he raised his hands and screamed, "Wait! P-Please! Do not hurt him!"

The words caused Bill himself to stop in his tracks. The pale lady giggled. "Naw, that's so cute. You care about this guy? Okay…fine. I'll be nice. *This* time." The pale lady licked her bloodied lips before she continued, "Klaus will be in touch, okay? I hope you enjoyed the show." She grabbed one of the Thestor's surcoats. After she dabbed each drop of blood from her snow-white face, she winked at Franco and simply strolled out the door.

Dante hurried over to Franco and grabbed his forearm. "W-What in the name of God was that?"

Franco was lost in his own thoughts. "Not once has the Church bothered to offer us proof of God's existence. We were expected to blindly follow their schemes and machinations. The Devil, however…it appears that The Devil sent us a sign."

Bill stared at Franco with raw shock on his face. "F-Franky…what are ya sayin'?"

"I am saying that the Clthic Synod has earned themselves an audience with me."

XVII
Unholy Union

The shouting of zealous men, the clanging of steel, the thudding of feet on the earth, and the distinct sound of arcane bolts whizzing by wove an aural tapestry of a most appetising battle. Alric could sense the overwhelming eagerness of his fellow Thestor brothers as he sat with them upon their steeds. They were all desperate to join the fray, but strategy dictated their discretion. The village of Threshfield draped the surface of a hill, both of which were in the shadow of the supreme fortress monastery Omenthal. Said hill was to serve a pivotal purpose; it provided two-hundred Knights Thestor and their accompanying warhorses a place to muster from the gates of Omenthal unseen by their heretic enemies. When the order was given, the wave of cavalry would sweep the Clthics away like ships in a storm. About fifty other Thestors fought on foot alongside one-hundred knights Correntis, another hundred common infantry, and approximately four hundred archers. The archers, once their allocated arrows had been expended, would join the melee as light infantry.

Considering the fact that the Forty-First Host, the Legion of Glorious Exaction, once numbered at least eight thousand, the combined count of surviving Thestors and Correnti being a measly three-hundred and fifty was disheartening. If it weren't for the dwindling food and water, the knights of the Holy Orders would have dug deep within their fortress indefinitely. However, both brotherhoods were compelled by divine rule that they could never retreat nor surrender in battle. In lieu of a dwindling supply of food and water that could not support them for much longer, they decided to meet the enemy on the field rather than surrender or die of starvation. For Alric at least, the residents of Threshfield who had all been evacuated to Omenthal served as a potent incentive to win the day. Innocent farmers, families, merchants, priests, nuns, and plebeians had their lives dependent on the outcome of the battle.

The army of Churchsworn was eight-hundred strong, while estimates of the Clthics' force stood at one-thousand two hundred. Marshal Otto was hoping that the arcane support lent by the Ga'zahi coupled with the shrouded cavalry charge would be enough impact to turn the tables.

It had been some time since Alric had last mounted a warhorse. They were intensely fierce and disciplined animals, far less skittish than horses not subjected to the same lifelong training. Anything from a lance bobbing above its head, or the sound of clanking armour could cause any untrained mount to frighten and disobey their rider. When Alric first bought Nocht, he had spent a great deal of time teaching her not to fear the racket of his plate, only to forget to acclimate her to the scabbard of his longsword occasionally tapping her on the rump as they rode. The first time that happened, he was almost thrown from the saddle by her thrashing.

Warhorses on the other hand were trained to be at ease during the chaos of warfare. Every possible article of stimuli was ingrained into the animal's mind. However, like men, they would not always think it prudent to charge suicidally into raised pikes. They would be most effective charging upon an already engaged foe. Omenthal had a stable of elite warhorses, although many had already died due to lack of food. The one trusted to Alric, an energetic thing named Silver, would huff and scoop his front hooves at the dirt in an effort to convince his rider that it was time to dive into combat.

Despite the effort Alric had gone through to carry his pollaxe with him all that way, it was not a weapon intended for use on horseback. Every mounted Thestor, Alric included, held in their hand an eleven-foot-long ash war lance. It differed in several ways to the lances used in tournament jousts; it had a deadly spearhead at its end instead of a multi-pronged tip, it lacked the circular metal vamplate designed to protect the wielder's hand, and was made of a sturdier wood that was less likely to shatter on impact. Alric, like many of his brothers, held his lance with the bottom end resting on his right foot as it was suspended in his stirrups. It created a forest of lances all outstretched towards the Heavens.

With the smoke and haze blown away by the breeze, Alric was puzzled to see that the monstrous dragon was no longer hovering in place high in the sky. He had been waiting for the beast to turn downward and incinerate both the Legion of Glorious Exaction and Omenthal with a single puff of its volcanic breath. But it never came. Where it went, no one was certain.

Alric was positioned on the first line of the charge to the right of its commander, a man named Galfrido. To Alric's right was Baldwyn, the young headstrong knight he had met the previous day. His posture was stiff and his right leg was constantly jittering against the saddle. Every man had their visor lifted; only when they were in the final moments of the charge would they be lowered.

"It is a good day to die, is it not?" Galfrido declared.

Alric chuckled as he saw Baldwyn perform a double-take. The young knight replied, "No. It most certainly is *not*."

"Wallow in thy fear of death then, young one. Long have I asked for a day upon which I can give my life to the Father," Galfrido continued.

Alric replied, "Thou art free to do so, Brother. I, however, do not plan on departing this place before the Clthic Synod has been eradicated."

Momentarily, Alric saw a flag emerge from one of the farmhouse windows and flutter in the wind.

"The time has come!" roared Galfrido. "Brothers, forward!"

In unison, the mass of horses walked steadily forward. Each Thestor was packed as close as possible to the next rider in the formation. Alric felt his left knee periodically tap against Baldwyn's right as their steeds moved at a pace synchronised with the other one-hundred and ninety-eight knights.

Slowly but surely, the crowd of mounted men rounded the side of Threshfield Hill. Alric finally laid eyes upon the battle for the first time. White-hot lines of light denoting the discharges of taukumu staves criss-crossed the farmland, drawing themselves from the wood to the village and back again. Wings of infantry were engaging in ferocious hand-to-hand fighting. From where Alric was, he saw only blocks of gleaming steel pushing against each other.

Galfrido yelled, spurring his horse into a canter. Alric followed, heaving his lance up off his foot and holding it by its handle, still pointing it upward. The stomping of hooves on the soil grew to an ominous drumming. In his vision, the rectangles of infantry swelled. In a moment that frightened Alric beyond words, a spike of energy hurtled out of the forest, narrowly missing Galfrido's head by mere inches. Several of the warhorses neighed in fright, but fortunately for Alric, it seemed that Silver wasn't bothered. More came. Alric heard screams of both man and horse alike. Despite the intense nagging of his inner voice, he didn't turn his head to behold the carnage. He took solace in the fact that the Ga'zahi promptly returned a flurry of eldritch blasts upon the witches to cover the knights. Alric's focus remained upon what lay in front of him; the vulnerable flank of the Clthic infantry.

One final scream of rage from Galfrido told Alric everything he needed to know; it was time to push into a full gallop. The hoof falls went from foreboding drums to a chorus of thunder. Every bone in Alric's body shook, as did each plate of steel that comprised his armour. He dropped the reins from his left hand, slammed his visor shut, retook the reins, then tucked the back end of his lance under his armpit.

Jagged rays of starlight pulsed across his tiny frames of vision as his target grew even larger. From there, they came into range of arrows. A concussive force slammed into Alric's shoulder, then his chest, then his head. They were all amplified by the speed at which Silver charged. The pain was dulled by the intensity of the situation.

The gallop turned Alric's situational awareness into a garbled mess of blurs, streaks, and smudges. His concern about not handling a lance in years was in fact unfounded; once he was in the middle of the frantic charge, it came back to him via muscle memory. His brain could still decipher the seemingly incomprehensible sludge picked up by his eyes, so he slowly began to lower his lance from its upward position. Some of the enemy footmen were so deeply engaged by the Church infantry, taukumu blasts, and arrows that they didn't even see the charge coming.

A single moment in time was captured by Alric's skewed perception. He saw the face of a Clthic footman as he stared wide-eyed at the oncoming wall of horses. In his eyes, Alric could see helplessness. Submission to death. Alric's couched lance had its tip lined up perfectly with the man's face. Some of his compatriots had tried to move out of the way, much to the Thestors' benefit. It created a weakness in the formation that a cavalry charge was excellent at exploiting.

Suddenly, time went from standing still to moving a million miles an hour. An incredible impact surged its way up Alric's lance and into his body, indicating that he had struck true. Reflexively, he let go of his weapon. The ocean of infantry began to part, either breaking formation to move to safety or being sucked beneath the mighty hooves of the warhorses.

Alric seized Silver's reins with both hands and gritted his teeth. He and his brothers had to weather the storm and survive until they were clear of the block of soldiers. If they slowed and became ensnared by the regrouping footmen, they would be set upon from every direction and massacred. Screaming, thudding, his own breathing. Those were the only things Alric could hear.

Suddenly, the screeching was recanted and once again, Alric's eyes were swallowed by the green fields. Only then did he glance to his sides. Astonishingly, his brothers were still at his flanks as close as they were when the charge started. Galfrido's lance was still intact, while Baldwyn's had been snapped in two.

"About!" screamed Galfrido. Once they had made significant distance, each of the knights and their warhorses slowed and steered the formation around. From the new perspective, Alric could see the chaos that he and his brothers had just wrought. The Clthic infantry was in shambles. The centre of their ranks had been smashed into disarray with a fair amount fleeing for safety. It was, however, the minority that fled for their lives. It had become time for the allied infantry to make the most of the opportunity. The cavalry had nothing to do but watch and assess the situation; if the infantry succeeded in breaking the enemy line, it would be time for the cavalry to engage in the rout. If the Clthics stood fast, it may have been time for the horsemen to re-arm with more lances and charge once again.

Along the field, Alric could see fallen horses and the Thestors that rode them. Some of the holy knights had been crushed by their steeds when they fell, others were dispatched with ease by the hostiles as they lay on the ground, while a rare few were fortunate enough to survive and join the infantry. Alric watched with bated breath as the soup of Thestors, Correnti, and common soldiers advanced into the scrambled line of demonists. Taukumu bolts conjured by the Ga'zahi impacted specific points in the Clthic ranks, instantly killing whoever they struck. The enemy infantry buckled as they sustained close-quarters thrashing as well as an onslaught of eldritch force. Surely, the Clthics broke. They began to trickle back towards the camp nestled in the wood.

"They are routed! Run them down!" cried Galfrido.

Alric scooped his war hammer from his belt and screamed at the top of his lungs. What followed was another all-out gallop by the Knights of Saint Thestus as they pursued their retreating foes. Alric extended his right hand, preparing his hammer for the sorry excuses for soldiers that ran from him. Silver easily closed the distance with the first man, the second, third, and so on. For each footman that fell into Alric's range, he swung the curved spike of his hammer down at their helmeted heads and each impact rang like a tolling bell. The men dropped instantly, dead or unconscious, it mattered not. Alric did not want a single demonist to escape.

He and his compatriots swept across the retreating Clthics as they got closer and closer to the treeline. However, it was then that Silver began to falter. As did Alric. It was suddenly not only the flogging of horseshoes pulsing through the ground…but something else. Something much more immense and soul shaking. Alric slowed Silver to a canter and before long, many of his knight brothers felt it too. He felt the very fibre of his skin stiffen and petrify… Was it an ogre?

Whatever came bounding out of the wood was much more agile than a mere ogre. It paced through the trees on two legs perpetually bent at the knee and was vaguely humanoid in shape. The thing was at *least* as tall as an ogre, but nowhere near as wide and lumbering. It did however share an ogre's composition: a robust skeleton and a thick plated carapace. The creature's torso was a strange, top-heavy shape and its arms were a pair of armoured appendages. There were no fingers on the strangely mangled limbs, only a single gaping hole on each. Upon its back and top were pikes adorned with impaled corpses, heads, and other body parts. The monster itself did not have a head, but a small cluster of shimmering black circles on the front of its body seemed to be unblinking demonic eyes.

Alric was overcome with fear. He felt the cold pierce his armour and wrap itself around his very soul. Silver whinnied and reared, then paced backwards. One of the masses on the creature's arm suddenly exploded with dust and a deafening 'boom'. It was enough to terrify Silver, who bucked and threw Alric from his saddle. The knight twirled through the air and landed on his chest. His war hammer soared out of his hand and out of sight. Every ounce of air in his lungs was forced out and his forehead slammed harshly against the inside of his helmet. Flinging his visor open as he gasped and groaned, Alric managed to look back toward the village. He felt as if his ears were filled with blood.

He saw Silver galloping for his life as well as other horses, some with rider and some without. What remained of the cavalry formation had regrouped and began charging directly for the horrifying new monster. Behind them, where the mass of Church footmen used to be, was a cloud of dirt and smoke that was almost as large as the hamlet of Threshfield itself. Horrified, Alric looked back at the towering monstrosity.

It jogged forward from the forest, the orifice on its right limb smoking. Its left one started emitting a high-pitched whirl, as if something inside it was spinning rapidly. What came next, Alric could not even hope to comprehend. It seemed a hundred detonations occurred in the barrel of the appendage every second as the aberration swept it slowly across the field.

Alric turned back to the approaching knightly charge. Heads exploded. Thestors were torn limb from limb. Horses were shredded into bloody chunks. Whatever the creature had unleashed, it fired in an unbelievably rapid succession and tore straight through plate armour. It did not inflame its victims the way taukumu fire did, but instead pocked everything unfortunate enough to be standing in its path full of tiny holes. When Alric directed his panicked stare back to the rapidly closing monster, he saw bolts of light buffeting it from several different angles. The Ga'zahi…they did not yet abandon him. The points of light washed the creature's hide with blossoms of blue fire, misshaping its chitin and staggering its calculated gait.

As Alric scuttered backwards on all fours, his widened eyes unable to move from the subject of his terror, his hand plunged into something that was soft and wet. He turned and saw a moist pile of entrails and pieces of meat. A Clthic witch. More accurately, the sludge that remained of her. Alric's hand was splayed within a stew of her flesh and bone. Only her grotesque mask remained intact…and her arcane taukumu staff beside it.

In an act of sheer desperation, Alric clambered for the artefact and directed it at the monster's lower abdomen. He whispered, "O God, grant me the power to wield this infernal wand!"

Alric squeezed as hard as he could on the length of the taukumu and all of a sudden, his prayers were answered. One of his fingers pressed against a moving part and there came a 'click'. There was no physical kickback as the stream of energy erupted from the taukumu, only immense heat and light. The crystalline shard of lightning found its mark directly where Alric had pointed it. It flowered into a miniature sun for a moment then cooled, revealing a warped and blackened section of carapace. Alric stared down at the taukumu's trigger in disbelief, then clicked it down another three times. Specks of mystical fire swirled up as the creature glanced around in confusion.

When the smoke cleared, Alric could see a gap in the armour on its chest. It was the tiniest seam, within which he could spy a spigot of honey-gold blood spraying outward. Swallowing his fear, the Thestor pushed to his feet. He discarded the taukumu and seized a nearby halberd that was lying loosely within the fingers of a dismembered arm. With the polearm grasped firmly in both hands, Alric did the exact opposite of what his instincts told him to do; he sprinted as fast as he could *toward* the mountainous behemoth.

With the halberd levelled in front of him, Alric roared into the monster's gut while it had its body lowered to the ground in a moment of exhaustion. As if by a miracle, Alric's headstrong charge sent the steel head of the halberd scraping straight into the breach in the creature's shell. All of a sudden, Alric's momentum was brought to a halt and his body lurched forward. The halberd was jammed into the creature's chitin; it hadn't penetrated deep enough to cause any significant damage, however. Alric gritted his teeth and pushed with every drop of strength he had left. The weapon did not move. He pulled on it, leaning the combined weight of his body and his armour into it. The weapon did not move.

He was promptly worked into another panic when the monster began to rise from its momentary rest. As its body was lifted from the dirt by its humming legs, Alric leapt onto its torso, his feet finding purchase on a ridge just below the halberd wound. His stomach sloshed about as he watched the ground grow more distant beneath him. The Thestor swallowed and turned his attention back to the halberd. With both hands, he snatched the weapon and tried wrenching it side to side. The strange material that composed the monster's shell began to groan as Alric forced the halberd so fiercely that its shaft began to bend. Screaming in exertion, the knight felt his muscles falter.

The halberd shifted, and from the creature's gullet came a loud 'crack'. The monster's belly folded open like a pair of iron doors, unleashing a tsunami of thick yellow bile. The foul-smelling sludge almost propelled Alric right off the creature but he managed to grab both sides of its torn gut and brace himself against the pestilent tide. Some of it managed to find its way into his mouth. Alric gagged, turned over his shoulder, and vomited. Whatever the sickening concoction was, it tasted like oil and spoiled meat. When he turned back to what resided *within* the behemoth's split belly, he was overcome with dread.

Hanging by a cable made of the monster's innards was a woman, skinned and with all four of her limbs missing. Her skull had been cleared of all tissue, and her entire lower jaw was missing. The behemoth's entrails funnelled themselves like snakes into her eye sockets, nostrils, open throat, and ears, suspending her in mid-air like a hanged corpse. Plunged into the ends of the stumps of her absent arms and legs were lengths of sinew that bound her further to the creature she was inside. Despite all of that…she was *alive.* Her muffled, guttural screams and writhing communicated as much.

It seemed that her body had previously been floating in the revolting yellow fluid; since it was then absent, the forces of nature had her harshly dangling by the face from the tubes that ran into her every orifice. She swung to and fro like a pendulum as she dripped with the now sparse liquid. Was she prey of the beast? Doomed to be digested little by little?

Suddenly, the monster spasmed back and forth. Alric fell to his knees on the lip of the creature's belly and clutched on for dear life and watched as its two 'arms' attempted to turn inward to fire upon him. However, when they reached a certain point, a loud 'snap' sounded and the rotation ceased. As Alric spun back to the wretch within the creature's stomach, his quivering lip slowed. When the monster walked, the swallowed woman's thighs twitched. When it attempted to turn its arms, her biceps trembled. Her entire body flexed and wriggled, in tandem with the monster's violent convulsions.

No. She was no victim. She was a witch…fuelling the monstrosity with her demented will. That line of thought brought clarity to Alric's tumultuous mind. He knew that it was not the time for fear, but the time to spill blood. God had allowed him to lay eyes upon the sickening lengths the Devil would go to in order to mimic a fraction of His heavenly might. The Knights of Saint Thestus did not need such twisted unions to receive power; they needed only *faith*.

Alric closed his eyes for a moment, inhaled sharply, then sprang into action. He snatched his rondel dagger from its scabbard and dove onto the swallowed witch. Grabbing her by the neck with one hand, he pressed his dagger up to its hand guard into her abdomen. A sharp, high-pitched screech escaped from the witch's obstructed throat.

He drew the dagger across the entire length of her belly. The wailing only grew in volume and intensity as the woman's intestinal tract was vomited from the newly sliced mouth on her abdomen. Her black blood mixed with the golden yellow that pooled beneath her. The unstoppable colossus lumbered forward with several weak steps then teetered forward. Alric was not prepared for the sudden shift of balance. He slipped backwards. The world around him transformed into a paste of greens and blues until his back slammed into the ground. His eyes widened as he saw the massive monster leaning over him. Its joints wheezed as they loosened…and sent the beast tipping over with Alric directly beneath it. He managed a sharp inhale as his instincts urged him to frivolously raise his arms in front of his face. He closed his eyes.

With how loud the sound of impact was, Alric thought that the world had come to an end…or perhaps simply just *his* world. But he felt sweat dripping from his face. He heard the faint clacks of his armour. Perhaps God did not wish him gone from creation just yet. Hesitantly, Alric forced his eyes open. There, suspended in the air above him, hanging from the monster's savaged body, was the swallowed witch. The manner in which the monster fell meant that its elongated 'arms' had prevented its body from making contact with the ground, propping it up…*saving* Alric's life. It also flung the witch's body out of the beast's gullet and allowed it to flutter in the wind like a flag. Alric stared at the body as the breeze made it dance, rattling the entrails that hung from her sliced belly like chimes.

His vision refocused onto something rustling in the treeline. More stomping footfalls not dissimilar to what the fallen offence to God had produced. The Thestor's heart froze and he shook his head frantically. "N-No…please God, no…!"

Surely enough, another behemoth emerged from the wood, its two appendages ablaze with yellow sparks. Before long, another joined it. Then another. The might of those three unfathomable forces of darkness detonated Threshfield into a cloud of dirt. What little that already remained of the Church infantry was torn to ribbons. And ultimately, Omenthal's walls were shattered by an earth-shaking roar. Tears welled in Alric's eyes.

"It's time to go." Alric jolted upright and sent his gaze about. There, hidden behind the wreckage of the monster, was Carthei.

"The Knights Thestor do not retreat, we do not surrender, under pain of grievous sin. We fight to the last breath," he whispered.

Carthei knelt and scooped something up from the ground. She tossed it at Alric, who almost failed to catch it before it smacked him in the nose. It was the taukumu he had used. "We can win against the interlopers in time, but we cannot succeed in open battle against their golems."

The Thestor sluggishly pushed to his feet, retrieved his dagger, then spat, "Leave me be, wretch. If I could kill one, I can kill the others!"

Once again, Alric found himself being seized by the shoulder by Carthei. "Don't be a fool! To slay a multi-limbed beast like the Clthics, chopping at its innumerable appendages will only waste time; you must remove its head!"

Alric snarled in frustration as he pulled free of her grasp. But he didn't move. He only stood there and watched as more explosions reduced Omenthal's watchtowers to rubble. Nearly a thousand of God's loyal servants…thrown to the grave. However, it was not the end.

Carthei and Alric sent their eyes to the ground as the dead trembled beneath their very feet. Friend and foe alike. A wretched chorus resounded throughout the Fields of Damnation.

"01001001 01101110 01101001 01110100 01101001 01100001 01110100 01101001 01101110 01100111 00100000 01101100 01101111 01110111 00100000 01110000 01101111 01110111 01100101 01110010 00100000 01101101 01101111 01100100 01100101 00101110 00100000 01010000 01101100 01100101 01100001 01110011 01100101 00100000 01110111 01100001 01101001 01110100 00101110."

The forest druid did not appear to recognise as Alric did that it was the voice of death itself calling for them. "W-We must go. *Now,*" he hissed at Carthei.

XVIII
ANOINTED

It was quite a beautiful day. Well, Vilulf rarely got to lay eyes on the earth bathed in the sun's golden light, so perhaps it was in fact quite regular, and he had grown unfamiliar with what it was meant to look like.

"By God. This is a mess…a mess, I tell you," snarled Klaus von Talhoffen. The pair brought up the middle of the convoy as it trailed along a dirt road. The travelling party was composed of horses, carts, soldiers, miners, and peasants. Each person's sight was obscured by an immense crowd of aimless, soulless beings that crowded about the sides of the road. The Enlightened, as the Clthics called them, completely engulfed Omenthal Road. If you were a Church degenerate, you would probably refer to them as the undead.

Vilulf tsked and shook his head. The motion caused his armour's already annoying clanking to amplify. "You really *must* stop saying that. God does not exist."

The duke ignored Vilulf's remark as he often did and instead continued, "What good is taking that blasted fortress if there is an ocean of flesh-feasters drowning it? How can we sally troops or maintain supply lines with this rabble trying to *eat* our men?" After the golems crushed the pathetic Godslaves, the Clthics seized what was left of Omenthal and began to transfer their crew of miners to the nearby excavation site.

"That is why *I'm* here, my friend," Vilulf replied with a smile, not that Klaus could see it. The vampire was clad in midnight black plate armour. Not for protection from attack though, but for protection from *daylight.* He could have worn his favourite doublet, hose, gloves, and a face covering of some sort, but those things could all be torn and pierced. What then? He would roast. That would not do.

Klaus shook his head. "You will not always be around to quell their hunger."

Tethspeakers, although being the sole inciters of the Enlightenment, were not the only ones able to herd the Enlightened. All vampires had the innate ability to impose their will onto weak-minded men, so if the subject had no mind to begin with, controlling them was quite easy. As long as the convoy remained in range of Vilulf, he could compel the Enlightened to keep away.

Klaus promptly peered over his shoulder at the crowd of workers behind him in the convoy. Vilulf tracked his eyes, noticing that they were looking for someone in particular. "What did you do to that poor woman? The mining foreman?" asked the duke, voice awash with disgust.

"Oh, *Alison*. She was actually…quite incredible," said Vilulf with a sigh. "I long to behold fear in the eyes of those I take. To hear them plead and scream for respite. That one, though…she actually found *pleasure* in being degraded and humiliated. It was *refreshing,* I suppose. Arousing." Each of his words was laced with longing. "After I had my way with her, I roasted her alive on a spit and had her for dinner. She seemed to enjoy *that* as well, the harlot."

Klaus emitted a short, uncomfortable grunt. "Please, I do not wish to know. Just keep your passions in check, Vilulf. We cannot afford to be distracted."

"What is the point of power if you cannot force it upon others? Last I checked, you were quite a renowned marshal for the Steiffan Empire. You force yourself onto others the same as I do, simply on a larger scale with thousands of lives in the balance. What is the difference?"

"I suppose there *is* no difference. That is why we must all be returned to the True State."

Furrowing his brow, Vilulf jolted in shock. "I beg your pardon?"

Klaus shook his head as he tightly grasped the reins of his horse. "Yes, laugh at me, distract yourself from the fact that you could be reduced to a pile of ashes if I reach over and lift your visor."

Vilulf chuckled under his breath. "A slight exaggeration, but apt, I must say."

The Duke von Talhoffen explained, "Listen, Vilulf. Human nature is what propels us to dispense cruelty onto our fellow man. At the end of all this, when all of us have been Enlightened, the world will be at peace. No more war, no more crusades, no more scheming."

Vilulf had taken Duke von Talhoffen for a man with a spine. It seemed that he was wrong about him. "Yes, we will be oblivious, drooling cattle cursed to graze on each other without any real purpose. How immensely *boring*." Before long, Vilulf felt his ears twitch. The helmet he wore would've drastically reduced the hearing of a regular man, but of course, Vilulf was no regular man. The vampire spoke urgently to his liege, "The rear guard. They're gone."

If there was one thing that Klaus gave Vilulf, it was respect where it was due. The duke nodded. "Beggar's Rock is not too far away…the footmen should be able to keep the miners safe in your absence. Go."

Vilulf briskly paced along the side of the road past the body of miners and came upon the group of soldiers bringing up what should have been the midsection. He directed his ire toward the man-at-arms in charge of this cluster of troops. "You there. Did you not think it prudent to mention that you can no longer see the rear guard?" demanded the vampire.

One by one, the footmen groggily turned about and peered back down the road. "I supposed they fell out of the field of your influence and got savaged by the Enlightened," reported the man-at-arms with a shrug.

Vilulf scoffed. "Come."

Joined by the Clthic soldiers who were mere children before his strength, Vilulf led the way down the road and around a bend. A smile formed across his face when his eyes fell upon the cause of all the commotion. A band of holy knights, a mix of Thestors and Correnti, held a tight formation against a crowd of Enlightened. They swung their hammers, pollaxes, halberds, and swords at the encroaching waves of undead. In unison, they bellowed lines of their Scripture as a rallying cry. The caravan's rear guard must have fallen some time ago; their bodies were nowhere to be seen. "Yes, babble at them…that will make them stop," Vilulf muttered to himself. With but a thought sent through the air, the Enlightened suddenly drew away from the knights, much to their surprise. It was only then that they realised that Vilulf was approaching with fifty men.

Vilulf strolled forward, arms outstretched in a gesture of friendliness. "Why, hello there, preachers of the *Great Lie*." Instantly, each of the knights glowed with rage. They were so very easily offended. It was hilarious to him. "I am Vilulf, child of Lady Viktoria and loyal servant of the Clthic Synod. What you face today, my friends, is a choice. Denounce your false idol, embrace the word of the Matriarch, and you will be spared."

Surprising absolutely no one, the knights moved not. A voice from the group of two dozen holy knights promptly answered, "We stand with God until death."

Vilvulf shook his head in disbelief. "You. Step forward," he said with playfulness dripping from his voice.

One of the knights, a Thestor, snapped, "I shall do no such thing, heretic. I answer only to God." He held a bec de corbin in his hands; a two-handed polearm weapon with a long, curved spike on one side, a hammer on the other, and another spike on its tip.

Vilulf snorted, "No matter. I have a proposition for you. To earn the freedom of your men, simply best me in single combat." The Thestor glanced about in puzzlement, as did his brothers. Vilulf raised his hands. "I am unarmed. Surely you can strike down some arrogant ponce foolish enough to besmirch the honour of that fictional man in the sky."

The Clthic soldiers behind Vilulf chuckled in anticipation while the holy knights ignited with raw outrage. The Knight Thestor stepped forward as he announced, "I will send thee to Hell for that."

With a bow, Vilulf answered, "Why, of course. I've always wanted to go there."

Ash, sulphur, and horribly burnt meat. The odours melted together in the humid air and became so pungent that Alric gagged. The worst part of it was that no matter how far he walked, the smell would never depart. Perhaps because *he* was the cause of it. The revenants had poured into the forest, all but erasing any notion of safe harbour from their onslaught. Each pack that wandered into the path of Alric and Carthei was blasted into oblivion by their combined arcane might.

A former Tritan footman gracefully strode toward Alric, his eyes aglow with dim light. Vibrant yellow sunlight, softened by the leaves of the trees, painted the walking corpse's mangled face. The Knight Thestor hesitantly raised his taukumu, trying to keep in mind the dozens of concise instructions Carthei had given him on how to properly operate the thing. He squeezed the staff's trigger. Ash, sulphur, and horribly burnt meat.

The footman, missing his head, dropped to the ground limply. He felt that he was fortunate that it was fairly close to him. Otherwise, he feared that he would not have struck true. He longed for a real weapon in his hands, not that damnable wand. However, he didn't have much of a choice; seeing as all of the revenants were soldiers slain at the battle of Threshfield, they wore battlefield armour. The only conventional weapons the Thestor had at his disposal were his longsword and rondel dagger. Although not the optimal tools in a skirmish, they would have served him well if he were facing fellow mortals. Stabbing a revenant in the armpit or neck would not garner the same response as stabbing a *man* in the armpit or neck. Evidently, anything short of destroying its brain would be but a tickle.

Carthei evidently did not share Alric's discomfort. With frightening efficiency, she dispatched revenants both near and far without hesitation. As she swept back and forth to trap the creatures in her sights, her heavy cloak flapped like a pair of infernal wings. As the bodies mounted, so too did the stink. It had been the order of things for hours. How many exactly, Alric knew not. What he *did* know was that they could not fight them off forever.

More and more of the walking corpses paced out from behind the mask of trees; an unrelenting current of death. Alric controlled his hastened breathing, shouldered his taukumu, then fired. His target's right shoulder exploded and flung the detached arm off into the distance. The revenant continued on its way, unfazed by the injury. Alric growled in frustration but promptly tried again. The taukumu clicked, but nothing happened. The heart… He had forgotten to replace the heart.

His body trembled as he popped the staff's chamber open, causing it to spit out the empty vessel, then reached into a pouch strapped to his belt with his other hand. All the while, his pursuers continued to walk briskly toward him. With a fresh heart in his grip, Alric slapped it into the taukumu and pressed the chamber shut. Not a second later, he thrusted the tip of the arcane staff towards the face of the man-at-arms. Unlike the previous shot, that one found its mark. The resulting bolt of energy gorged the man's neck, boiling away the lower half of his face and causing his head to roll from his shoulders.

One of the others, just a blur of colour in Alric's peripheral vision, strode towards him. Alric tried to swing his taukumu about to meet it, but he wasn't fast enough. His heart froze…then a jet of liquid sprayed across Alric's helmet. Some of the stuff passed through the sights and breaths of his bascinet and onto his lips. He found that he knew the taste well; blood. His would-be attacker dropped like the others and Alric saw Carthei over his shoulder, her staff smouldering from the blast. She tilted her head. Her expression was soft despite the blood and flesh that painted her face and cloak. Alric just grunted harshly.

Carthei's lips thinned and curled. It wasn't quite a smile, not quite a smirk even. Whatever it was, Alric found it confusing. She said rather too cordially, "That is a peculiar way to say 'thank you'. Come, I will show you how to harvest."

He had many years spent claiming the lives of non-believers in the name of God, but Alric could not say that he had ever cut open a corpse in order to remove its heart. Carthei snapped the ribs of their quarry, sliced apart the meat, shoved her hands inside, and soothingly narrated the entire process with great detail. Quite frankly, Alric was more occupied with keeping himself from vomiting than with paying attention to her tutelage.

When the body had been liberated of its heart, Carthei held the thing up in the air and closed her eyes. She muttered strange words in some foreign tongue. If Alric could recognise one thing without fail, it was piety. He could feel the devotion oozing out of Carthei's every word without even understanding them. As treacherous and blasphemous as her ramblings were…Alric knew that she had undying faith in all of it. Alric was left to his own thoughts for a moment as Carthei conducted her ritual. He felt as if he were blind and stumbling through a field of ditches.

Suddenly, Carthei lowered the heart and spoke. "Something troubles you. Speak." The Thestor frowned and remained silent. "Like it or not, we are now reliant upon each other. I do not wish to place my life in the hands of a brooding child," Carthei quipped.

With a growl, Alric finally gave in. "I have no training in the mystic arts, nor the aptitude for it, and yet…the staff obeyed my command."

Carthei shook her head with a pout. "Magic simply doesn't live where you thought it did. It resides solely within the *instrument*, not the wielder." She would send her eyes into the forest often to see if the momentary peace was at an end.

Alric blinked rapidly. "…Any man could hold a taukumu and make use of it?"

"Unfortunately, yes."

Soon enough, before he could press any further, she extended the heart to Alric. "We haven't the time to harvest more. We must go, before they return."

The Thestor awkwardly accepted the strange gift and stuffed it into his belt pouch.

"You're welcome," Carthei droned with an arched eyebrow. Before anything else could be said, a haunting scream bounced between the trees and seeped over the pair of unlikely allies. It weaved through the pillars of wood like a snake and wrapped itself around Alric's ears. Carthei popped to her feet and stared off into the distance. "It is close."

The knight and the druid once again took to navigating the death-infested forest. That time though, they had an objective. The howling repeated several times, providing them with ample direction. Alric didn't think they all sounded like the same person, either. A massacre was underway. Careful to remain in the cover of the brush, Alric knelt by a clearing. Beyond was a road that carved its way along the wood. On the side of the road was a mass of Clthic soldiers, revelling and laughing. They encircled several men, a group of Churchsworn knights. There were about fourteen of them, but they stood idle as one of their number engaged in combat against a single foe.

Said foe wore armour made of plates that had been forge-blackened to a glossy midnight. It was also lavishly decorated with fluting, a technique often used by Steiffan smiths to create ornamental ridges on steel. Curiously, his armet helm had a black veil laid over its sights and breaths. He also did not have a weapon in his hands. It was then that Alric's eyes drifted downward. On the ground were discarded surcoats, severed limbs, and crushed heads. Glimmering ebony blood dampened the grass and created a wretched bog. Curiously, there was a lack of undead…

The black knight weaved in and out of the Thestor's carefully measured attacks with inhuman speed. It was clear from the cadence of his steps, the fluidity of his motions, that he was toying with the Thestor. Like a cat with its prey. Suddenly, both of the black knight's hands locked onto the sides of the Thestor's head. With a sickening crunch, slurp, and horrific howl, the heretic ripped the holy knight's head from his shoulders. He discarded the thing, sending it bouncing along the dirt like a ball. Carthei inhaled sharply while Alric drew the Sign of the Pillar.

As blood spurted upward from the severed neck like water from a geyser, the black knight trembled. He lifted his visor. The face beneath promptly cracked open and a single fang emerged, embedding itself into the dead Thestor's throat. The deed all but confirmed Alric's suspicions. "I-I don't suppose you know what *that* is?" Carthei whispered bluntly.

The vampire, after completely draining the Thestor's corpse, shoved it to the ground and turned towards Alric and Carthei. His face reassembled itself and seemed to sear slightly in the sun. "My, my…what a pleasant voice," he said as he lowered his visor.

Carthei swallowed. "H-He hears me…?" Slowly, Alric raised his taukumu and slowed his breathing.

"I certainly can, my dear," said the vampire as he took slow steps towards the brush. "That resonance within your throat makes me throb."

Eventually, Alric's arms stopped their shaking. He lined up his staff's sights with the approaching vampire knight and nudged Carthei with his elbow. As much as he would like to relieve her fears by explaining everything to her, there was no time. Thankfully, the gesture was enough to shake her out of her inaction. Her mind was not pliable enough for the creature to manipulate. She joined Alric in priming their taukumu. The very moment they were aligned, Alric murmured, "Now."

The vampire froze as he realised that he had waltzed directly into a trap, but it was too late. Both taukumu erupted with cool blue bolts of fire that lanced into the night creature's gut. Sparks, blood, and meat were tossed about as the arcane missiles pierced his plate armour and flung his body backwards through the air. His form, turned into a projectile, hurtled into the force of Clthic soldiers and bowled over its vanguard. The Churchsworn knights suddenly roared into action. The wave of Thestors and Correnti broke over the shocked Clthics who still outnumbered them. With every second that passed, however, the holy knights were dispatching any Clthics who were knocked off their feet by the vampire's fall. The numbers evened out soon enough.

Alric slung his staff onto his back with the length of rope he had attached to it and drew his longsword. His heart eased and his muscles loosened as he threw himself into the fray. It was where he belonged, where he found solace. A force that felt like the kick of a steed belted his shoulder, whipping it backward and wrenching his neck sideways. If he had to guess what delivered the painful blow, it might have been a hammer or a mace. There was no use trying to figure it out. He and the other knights had one thing that they could afford to think about: survival. Alric and Carthei's arrival appeared to revitalise the drained holy knights; seventeen men fought with the fervour of a hundred. Alric took to half-swording in order to jab the tip of his sword into any unprotected body parts of the men before him. The screams of the demonists filled him with glee. When the heat of such desperate battle vanished, not a single Clthic lived to creep further upon God's earth.

The pain then came to him. Alric looked to his chest where there was now a sizable dent in his cuirass. It must have been a bruise. "The vampire…where is he?" a Correntis bellowed.

"Vampire…?" Carthei repeated the word as if she had never heard it before. The spear fastened to her taukumu was slick with Clthic blood.

After several seconds of silence, the Thestor cleared his throat and explained, "They are men cursed with eternal bloodthirst and an unending life of shadow. This price they pay grants them the strength of twenty men, the keen senses of a wolf, and the ability to peer into the minds of mortals."

"They cannot be killed?" she asked softly.

"They *can*. They too are a form of undead, so their heads must be destroyed. They will heal from most other injuries."

His eyes beheld body after body, but none wore armour of black. A trail of blood led down the road accompanied by the smell of burning meat. Carthei lowered herself to the ground and stared at the chain of clues. "It seems he had more pressing things to attend to…such as the preservation of his own life," Carthei remarked as she stood.

Alric turned around to face the men that remained. Eleven Thestors and four Correnti. At the head of the formation was a Thestor named Lorenz. Alric had become accustomed to recognising his fellow Churchsworn knights by their armour and body language. Alric attempted to approach his brothers, but they held their weapons at the ready. "Not another step closer," snarled Lorenz.

"B-Brother…?" Alric murmured.

Lorenz' voice was strained with fear as his eyes were pinned on the taukumu that was slung on Alric's back. "Keep thy distance, witch…!"

Alric felt tears welling in his eyes. He opened his mouth to speak, but nothing came out. Before anything else could be said, one of the other Thestors aggressively pushed through the crowd, snapping, "Cease this foolishness! Art thou esteemed Knights Thestor, or terrified children?!" It was Baldwyn, recognisable by the sallet helmet that covered his head and the bevor that masked his lower face and neck. He continued, "There is nothing to fear. I saw thee, Alric. I witnessed thy ordeal."

Baldwyn stepped between Lorenz and Alric, holding a palm out to the former. He then turned to Alric and locked eyes with him. "I beheld thy struggle against the Clthic abomination and how, with the light of God flowing through thy hands, thou hadst ended its wretched existence."

If he were to be frank, Alric wanted to laugh in the face of such words. He said, "My Brother, thou art mistaken. The–"

Carthei interjected, "I saw it too, Baldwyn. We call them golems; unholy unions of witch and demonic monstrosity. Alric *destroyed* it. On his own, no less. A most incredible deed. A *miracle*, even." The Churchsworn were awash with stunned silence. "He was aglow with divine light as he struck it down. For him to have commanded the arcane arts in such a way…it can only mean one thing." 'Unholy', 'witch', 'demonic', 'miracle', 'divine'. She was tailoring her speech to best suit the audience. A pulsing, tingling dread pooled inside Alric's stomach as he slowly turned to face his Ga'zahi ally. Carthei said, wistfully, "Alric has been chosen. Chosen by God."

Baldwyn instantly gulped and drew the Sign of the Pillar. Lorenz's eyes widened and his grip on his pollaxe loosened. "N-No. Her voice bears no weight! She is a heathen!"

"Loath be I to consider the words of a pagan, but it is plain to see that she speaks not deceit," muttered Baldwyn. "Her sorcery as well as our brother's attest aptly that both act in the service of Heaven."

A Knight Correntis by the name of Sigmund leaned over to Lorenz and said, "Our enemies are already arranged against us, Brother Lorenz. Why would they come to our aid instead of the vampire's?"

The Correnti were the first to ease down their stances and approach alongside Baldwyn. A few Thestors joined them, but Lorenz remained where he stood. Stopping Alric's heart dead in its tracks, Baldwyn bent the knee. Others followed suit. "God's Chosen," whispered Baldwyn.

"R-Rise, all of ye!" Alric snapped as he snatched his pauldrons and forced him upright. "Where is the marshal?"

Baldwyn finally lifted his visor as he said, "Surely the shredded remains of our brethren did not elude thine eyes? Otto is dead."

Alric growled under his breath as he peered at the pool of gore beneath their feet. He could feel Baldwyn's thoughts assemble themselves and he dreaded the moment when they would become words. "There is yet one who can lead us," Baldwyn suggested.

"I shall suffer this no more," Alric dismissed as he waved a hand at his compatriot and stomped away. His outburst seemed to quell the high levels of excitement at least for a moment. The holy knights took the moment of relative peace to consolidate themselves before planning on their next move. It gave Alric ample time to take Carthei to the other side of the bloodied road. "Explain thyself, Carthei…! What dark machinations hast that strange mind of thine imposed upon my brethren? Were the words shared between us in the wood naught but lies?"

Carthei shook her head. In a hushed tone coupled with anxious glances about, she answered, "Can you imagine what would happen to your kingdoms if the masses knew that the power of the Vorkhai was simply free for the taking? Look at the ruin you have wrought *without* magic. Your wars have wiped hundreds of thousands of people from the face of the earth with but steel and wood."

Alric felt the tension in his shoulders amplify. 'Vorkhai' was the druid name for the ancient gods they worshipped. Its mention irritated Alric to no end.

Carthei leant closer to him and whispered, "Armies backed by magic would sow unspeakable death. Millions would perish." Her voice was rickety and faint in his ears. "The myths regarding magic, that it is rare and difficult to command, who do you think propagated them?" Alric rubbed the bridge of his nose as he contemplated her words.

She frowned. "The truth is this; mankind is not ready. We will destroy ourselves. Look at what the Clthics have done already. The secret must be guarded, for the day when armies burn each other to dust using magic is the day when Athroct'u creeps closer to us. Now *you* must protect it."

He cared not for the nonsensical prophecy. If each Knight Thestor carried a taukumu, all the world would bow before the one true God. The earth would run black with the blood of the infidel. Carthei seemed to see Alric's thoughts through his eyes. She shook her head and trudged back across the road. "You hold a great many things in your hands, Godslave. *Do* be careful."

XIX
Amidst The Wolves

The druid known as Carthei squatted in the grass behind a tree, bracing herself with her taukumu. Her cloak fluttered so delicately in the breeze that it looked like it was submerged in water. Every Ga'zahi foraging party was composed of druids chosen to fulfil specific roles. Carthei was the leader of her party, Narsei the healer and apothecary, Konth the scout, and Vontross the hunter. It was then that Carthei began to miss Konth's seemingly supernatural ability to sense the presence of others. Somewhere down the road was a Clthic encampment, and she wanted to make sure that a random patrol wouldn't happen across them while they were canvassing the area. Not only would Konth be much more qualified to provide overwatch, she believed that if he were there, they would not have lost the accursed vampire.

"What dost thou behold?" Alric's voice was smooth, not at all the gravelly and husky growl that she had expected from someone of his background…a murderous zealot. Carthei rested her arms on her knees and exhaled. As she peered over her shoulder, she saw two dozen Godslaves scattered in hiding places among the wood patiently awaiting her word. Carthei spied one of them prying his axe from the skull of a revenant as it lay dead on the grass. The Godslaves were each weathered steel bricks in a mighty, impenetrable wall. Their discipline and devotion were clear to her, especially given recent events. Some showed clear indications of pain, fatigue, and sickness, but none stunk of fear. One or two had fallen to the revenants since their liberation from the vampire, but they all fought with terrifying skill and fervour.

How easily their faith bent to allow things that bring them good fortune was intriguing. The fact that she stood among them was perhaps an indication that hers was just as pliable. The Godslaves were demons in the eyes of the druid tribes. They came, forced their God onto the 'savage' and cut down any who resisted. Those they believed to be witches were burned alive. Some of the more aggressive tribes, namely the Kaitan'zahi, actively hunted Godslaves for trophies, perhaps adding to their preconceived idea of unholy witches primed against the Church.

"Carthei?" pressed Alric.

Shaking her head in defeat, she finally responded, "Dirt. I behold dirt."

She pushed to her feet, withdrew completely behind her cover, and threw one side of her cloak over her shoulder as she snatched her waterskin from her belt. As Carthei took a moment to drink, Alric huffed to himself. She couldn't tell if it was in amusement or annoyance. While she stowed the vessel, Carthei could tell from Alric's body language that he didn't really know how to respond. His forehead was wrinkled and his lips thinned. "*Must* we take this camp?" she said to him. "It would be safer if we simply trailed around it."

There quickly came a rebuttal. Baldwyn approached. "Forgive my interjection, but I believe that I spied prisoners when observing the camp from the mountain. Thy kin, as well as ours, may be rotting away within."

Carthei replied, "When have the Clthics ever taken prisoners?"

Lorenz had his arms crossed and avoided making eye contact with the druid. "We number only *fifteen* strong and there is no indication of how many demonists are garrisoned at the site. We must be steady, lest we charge to our deaths."

Sigmund laughed. "What manner of Thestor are you, to err on the side of caution?"

Lorenz faced Sigmund, a weak smirk of disbelief plastered on his face. "I wish to give my life in useful service, not in vain. Our presence in the region has been all but swept away. We have no means of calling for reinforcements." Carthei admired his restraint. She felt that if someone said that to Alric, he would have rammed his hand down their throat and torn out their heart.

"Pathetic. You are not worthy of that standard," Sigmund hissed as he pointed at Lorenz's Thestor surcoat.

Silence swallowed the party. Carthei had to gaze downward and bite her lip to stop herself from grinning. She was sure that someone was going to get stabbed sooner rather than later.

"Enough of this!" Baldwyn turned to face Alric, his back as straight as the trees surrounding them. "Brother Alric shall guide us through these dark times, for *he* and he alone has been elected by the Lord to deliver the realm from the demonists. What say thee, Alric? What be our course of action?"

Every Godslave had his eyes on Alric, who peered out at them in confusion. Carthei crossed her arms and eagerly awaited his response. So far, he had not disclosed the secret of the arcane. *So far*. The druid waited with bated breath to see if he would continue to keep his lips sealed.

Alric braced himself on his taukumu with both hands, weighing his words in his mind before finally answering. "My brothers, there is but one course of action. Of all manner of heretics, apostates, infidels, and heathens, there are none fouler than those who would dare lie with the Devil. If we were to ignore their presence, they would be spared the retribution they so deserve." Carthei felt personally threatened by those words, for what was she in the eyes of the Godslaves but a heathen? Her fingers tightened around the stem of her staff. "To condone the longevity of demonists, no matter how insignificant their number, is in itself *heresy* of the highest order. Who among thee would defy God's will? Show thyselves so that I may smite thee where thou stand."

No one said a thing. Carthei almost shook her head in disbelief, but checked the motion. "We shall continue to stride the blessed path. Let the hordes come and be rendered into ribbons of flesh, gravelled bone, and puddles of blood…all for the grace of God."

"For the grace of God!" The Godslaves tapped their foreheads then their chests in unison, leaving Carthei to grimace at them. It was…quite horrifying to hear someone speak of genocide as if it were some glorious mission. The Ga'zahi never fooled themselves when it came to matters of life and death. They looked at it for what it was; dirty, messy, despicable business, but often necessary. Even to kill *one* person was a burden to be shouldered. The Clthics may have doomed themselves by meddling with things beyond their understanding, but Carthei would take no pleasure in seeing the deed done. Alric, however, coated it with heavenly brushstrokes of light until it was made beautiful. It became something to be yearned for.

As the Godslaves moved deeper into the forest, Carthei remained by Alric's side. His armour was coated with layers of dirt-clouded water, dried blood, and tufts of grass. With his visor raised, she could see the smooth, maroon surface of his skin as well as his sky-blue eyes. Carthei picked some of the grass from her cloak as she said, "Your commitment to the secret has not gone unnoticed. I did not wish to make a Saint out of you…I simply saw no other way to explain it to your comrades."

"Save thy gratitude. I have no need for it."

Tipping her head, Carthei said, "I suppose that is the closest thing to an apology I will ever get from you."

Alric's posture stiffened. "Thou walk a path of ignorance and shame, Carthei. Thy soul can still be saved, but only if thou choose to lift the veil from thine eyes. Thou and thou alone can deliver thyself from damnation."

With a frown of disbelief, Carthei took a step away from him. "Repent and embrace the true faith, and thou shalt find redemption."

Carthei flexed her jaw angrily. "I will…consider it," she lied. The Thestor sighed in relief. A tremendous weight was pulled from his shoulders. Alric could turn on her at any moment. No. It was not a question of 'if' it would happen, it was a question of 'when'. The Godslaves had their list of enemies. Once the demonists had been crossed from it, the heathens and pagans would follow. It would be safer for her if she kept him close and told him what he wanted to hear. When the time came when she smelt even the faintest sign of treachery, she could exploit his trust and kill him when he least expected it.

It took hours for Carthei to reach and assess the encampment with the help of a small number of Godslaves; mainly those of the Correntis Order. The Thestors were slaves to their rule of vigilance, unable to remove any armour they donned until nightfall. Carthei once complimented it…but seeing as it affected her scouting plans, she began to regret her words. They would have been terrible scouts with all of that clanking about, so only those who had chosen not to arm themselves fully that morning took part. The Correnti were not bound by that rule, so were free to discard anything that could cause too much noise.

The Clthic position was not fully manned; the pretentious Baldwyn suggested that it may have been the base camp for a large army that was in battle somewhere nearby. Despite Carthei's previous objections, that made it the opportune time to attack. However, it was a sure bet that they still had more than fourteen men garrisoned there. They would be outnumbered regardless. The problem was that it was a fair distance away from the cover of the trees. A wooden watchtower had been erected, so anybody foolish enough to attempt rushing from the forest could easily be spotted. A perimeter wall had also been created with logs and planks, further narrowing the points of entry.

Barrels upon barrels of provisions were spotted packed in a legion of wooden wagons. It was food enough for thousands of men as well as hundreds of animals needed to pull said wagons. Carthei and the Godslaves desperately needed provisions. They had been making do with scraps for the last week.

Among the conventional weapons, armour, and various supplies stored in the camp, Carthei noticed barrels marked with a very specific runic combination. Although the druid tribes had been separate entities since ancient times, they shared a root language. Written on the barrels were the symbols for unzym, a potion brewed from oils found only in the Under. When lathered onto a surface, usually metal, it could defend against arcane bolts. Spreading the mixture onto plate armour could improve the Godslaves' chances of survival when facing witches.

After all the studying of the enemy position, night had fallen. The moon had yet to be at its apex, but the time for action had come. Carthei had her eyes pinned on the watchtower. Instead of seeing a human head peek out from atop it, she instead saw the skull of a horse. Of course. A witch. It was time. Carthei pressed her left hand to her lips and produced a rather beautiful bit of birdsong.

Momentarily, a loud snapping sound disturbed the silent night and echoed against the mountains. Carthei watched as the horse skull snapped quietly to the left. The witch raised her taukumu, fitted with an octhum. The moment she pressed her mask against the eyepiece, Carthei burst into action.

She made a mad dash for the wall of the Clthic camp. As Carthei's field of view shook with each rapid step she made, she could decipher the wobbling line of the witch's taukumu pointed out the side of the watchtower, focused on the Godslaves' distraction. With her own staff slung upon her back, Carthei leapt up and onto the side of the tower, her fingers and feet finding purchase on the logs used in its construction. For a moment, she closed her eyes and took several deep breaths. It was not the time for rushing thoughts. She should be as steady as the breeze. As unmoving as the mountains.

When her eyes peeled back open, the witch shouted commands at some unseen guards. The exact dialect was not entirely familiar to Carthei, but it certainly was a druidic language. It was worded strangely, poetically abstract. Translated literally, it would be 'read the music'. Given the context, it was most likely a demand to investigate the source of the noise. Carthei inched herself upward, moving so slowly that not a sound was made by her climb. She managed to push herself up and peer into the watchtower's nest. The witch was there, taukumu shouldered. An array of finger bones were tied to the back of her horse skull mask with lengths of string. They dangled from it like ghastly strands of hair and danced in the wind like chimes.

In the distance, Carthei could see a handful of Clthic footmen trail out of the camp and towards the forest. She threw herself up and into the watchtower, landing in the nest like a stray leaf blown in by the wind. Despite her best efforts, Carthei was not safe from sheer chance. The witch glanced over her shoulder. It happened so slowly. There was no reason for it...she just happened to look Carthei's way at *that* precise moment. The druid cursed under her breath.

Both women snapped forward. The witch dropped her taukumu and pulled a dagger from her boot. Carthei snatched the rim of her cloak and wrapped it around her foe's weapon. She felt the blade painfully press into her chest, but thanks to the Vorkhai-woven fibres of the cloak, it was nothing but a blunt impact.

The witch's momentum was enough to ram Carthei into the corner of the watchtower despite the ineffectiveness of her strike. A sharp growl escaped Carthei's mouth as she snatched the witch's throat with one hand and the knife with the other.

Tumbling to the floor and struggling for the knife, Carthei made sure to apply all the force she could to her enemy's neck to prevent her from screaming for assistance. She felt her fingers dig into the bare muscle of the witch's neck. The Ga'zahi brought her knee up and propelled it into the witch's gut. Blood was spat from the mouth of the horse skull, black and bitter as it splattered onto Carthei's face.

The witch's grip on the knife faltered. "Go now, defiler," Carthei whispered. She seized the knife and punched it into the witch's body sixteen times. Carthei could feel the witch watching the knife plunge into her bare chest over and over, helpless. However, Carthei was to find out that 'helpless' was a gross exaggeration on her part. The witch whipped her head forward. The hard bone of the horse skull impacted squarely on Carthei's nose. It startled her more than it hurt her.

The witch dribbled like a feral animal, urging her body into motion and flinging herself onto Carthei. She was tackled to the floor as the witch tore her nails down her face. The most frightening part for Carthei was that she didn't feel any pain, but she could feel the witch's talons carving the flesh on her face. Blood seeped into her left eye and her vision clouded.

Carthei desperately pulled the dagger out of the witch's chest and plunged it straight into her throat. She felt the hard impact of spine against blade. The Clthic gurgled, her body loosening and going slack. Her weight was dumped onto Carthei, who bared her teeth as she tossed the corpse to the side.

The witch lay in a growing puddle of her own blood, the stuff oozing out of the plethora of wounds she had sustained. The druid pressed a hand to the left side of her own face and the gesture was answered by a sharp sting of pain. A series of deep gouges had been left by the crazed witch… However, she didn't have time to dress the wounds. Her ears twitched as she heard a voice.

"I 'eard somethin'. I'm gonna check on tha K'relvic Nun."

Quickly, before the guard climbed the tower, Carthei looked out at the forest. It was difficult to make out in the dark of night, but she could only *just* see the Godslaves approaching. They had taken care of the guards that were headed their way. She was free to make a racket…

Carthei pulled the octhum from the so-called Nun's staff. A simple tug was enough for her to retrieve her own taukumu from the gripping plate that held it to her back, then she slid the octhum onto the magical artefact's length.

The watchtower shook slightly. Again, and again. Someone was climbing the ladder. The druid held her taukumu at the ready, pointed precisely at the top of the ladder leading to the ground. A head popped up. Carthei waited until the man's face was visible. It warped in fear upon spying her. With a click, she sent an arcane bolt out of the staff.

At that range, nothing was to be left of his torso. It exploded in a flash of blue magic, black blood, and grey bone. The remains fell onto the grass with a muted 'thud'.

Screaming responded. "Intruders!"

Carthei scurried over to the opposite side of the tower and peeked out with her taukumu primed. The skeleton crew left to defend the site was worked into a frenzy, dashing here and there as they secured weapons. There were at least a hundred of them, and more dripping out of the tents.

"For the grace of God!" cried the all too familiar voice of Alric. Fourteen Godslaves poured into the camp, breaking against the unprepared Clthics like a mighty wave. Carthei provided assistance in the form of arcane volleys, instantly killing each and every target she hit with a single discharge. Seeing as the Clthics were caught unawares, none of them were wearing armour. The Godslaves tore through them as if they were made of paper.

Some movement snatched her attention. A tent fluttered open and from it stepped several witches…three women and two men. One of the men pointed at the approaching Godslaves as his fellow witches and more soldiers rushed by him. In his hand was a kehmaha, a very large magical staff that was capable of immense damage. The Ga'zahi had used a pair of them against the ogre at Blackmeadow… A single well-placed shot could easily destroy the entire force of Godslaves. Kehmaha, unlike taukumu, cast out a solid projectile instead of a bolt of pure arcane energy. Kehmaha seeds were ancient and dangerous containers the size of two adjoined human fists filled with mystical energies that exploded with such incredible force that they could blast apart solid stone. However, they were *extremely* rare. No druid, no matter how wise, knew how to make more. The seeds were left behind by the Vorkhai, like many things, and had to be found and harvested from the Under. They did not grow back. Because of that, the taukumu with its renewable power source in the form of hearts was preferred as a primary spellstaff among the druids.

With her heart pounding, Carthei swung her taukumu about and sent spellbolts at the witch. She missed. A collection of sparks splashed fire onto the tent, shaking him out of his stupor. His eyes, yellow and glowing from behind his mask made of human rib cages, locked onto Carthei. The kehmaha resting on top of his shoulder swivelled to meet the subject of his gaze. The opening of the kehmaha suddenly flushed with light.

Carthei pushed up and threw herself from the tower. As she hurtled through the air, she saw the kehmaha seed mid-flight for a fraction of a second. It zipped into where she was only a moment ago and detonated with the infinite brightness of the sun.

The shockwave of the blast rippled through her body, twisting and compressing her organs. It sent her into a death spiral. The stars twirled about, there for one second, gone in the next, only to return again. Carthei landed on her shoulder and a terrifying 'snap' pulled her from the dizzying trance caused by her freefall.

Wooden shrapnel rained from the sky, accompanied by smouldering embers. The infernal rain continued as Carthei gritted her teeth and stood. Her right arm wasn't responding to her thoughts. She stumbled towards the wooden perimeter wall, curled her lips inward, then slammed it against the barricade as hard as she could. Very much like the damage she had sustained to her face, she barely felt a thing. Only after popping her shoulder back into place did the discomfort surface.

The witch had already thought her dead, turning his kehmaha toward the Godslaves. That was his final mistake. Her arm still inflamed, Carthei fought the pain and brought her taukumu up, peering through its octhum.

She zeroed in on the box-shaped object sticking out of the top of the arcane weapon: the housing of the seeds. It pained her to destroy the ageless remnants of the Vorkhai, but she had no choice.

There must have been more than one seed left in the housing, because the reaction caused by Carthei's shot was unlike anything she had ever seen before. Her eyes were consumed by intense white light. She felt the heat upon her face, even though she stood on the other side of the camp. Footmen were shredded into ribbons, limbs were torn from their bodies, and their insides were dumped onto the grass.

The little that were left were so horrified by the detonation that they were routed. The Godslaves erupted in some of their holy chanting as they cut down the fleeing Clthics. Periodically, a spear of light would be thrown from the group of Godslaves; Alric with his taukumu picking off any who were wise enough to run.

Carthei ejected her staff's spent heart and slammed a fresh one in, grimacing all the while at the pain that plagued her right shoulder and face. She sprinted for the main body of the skirmish, closing in on the site of the detonated kehmaha. The witch who was holding the kehmaha was nothing but a series of smears on the blackened, smouldering ground. The tent beyond was pocked with holes and had been set aflame. Dozens of corpses littered the area, all in varying states of dismemberment. One of them moved.

The other male witch, reduced to an upper torso that pathetically tried to crawl away, waved its hand through a series of glowing Glyphs that hung in the air. He was trying to cast a spell, trying to turn his dead companions into undead revenants.

"The dead will not walk this day. You will instead join them, *defiler,*" Carthei snapped as she approached. She plunged the tip of her spear, tied to her taukumu, into the necromancer's heart. Carthei was just about to move on until something about the tent struck her. The fire that raged on inside it…she swore that she saw something move within it. Thudding footsteps held her where she stood. A black figure batted through the front of the tent, unflinching in the face of the inferno.

When it emerged, Carthei's brow tensed and her mouth widened.

An obsidian being at least a head taller than any man she had ever seen stood motionless before the carnage. Its face…well, it didn't *have* a face. It had one large eye on the right side of where its face should've been, and two smaller ones on the left side. It gazed down at the death and destruction, almost as if it were studying the scene. It was impossibly thin, almost a skeleton save for some lengths of tendon and veins. A Protozealot…one of the slumbering warriors that Carthei had heard stories of since she was a child. It was *he* that the witch was rousing, not the dead.

The Zealot suddenly jerked its head upward to stare at Carthei herself. The motion was clear; it saw the bodies of its masters, then Carthei standing above them with a staff in her hand. She had been marked for death. With steady, graceful, and earth-shaking steps, the Zealot walked towards Carthei. She discharged her taukumu. The first shot went wide, but the second washed harmlessly across the creature's chest like water. As did the third, forth, and fifth.

Onward did the Zealot march. It reached for Carthei's neck with startling speed, but the druid managed to sidestep and duck out of the way. Then at its exposed side, Carthei jabbed her spear into the thing's narrow chest. The hardened steel spearhead blunted against the black bones of the Zealot, doing absolutely nothing to the beast. Another thrust followed, this time managing to find a soft spot. A sheath of tendon coating the Zealot's spine was pierced by Carthei's spear, but nothing happened. There was no blood, no fluid, no reaction. Well, apart from a prompt defensive swipe.

Carthei was pummelled by a strike that felt like three stallions kicking in unison. The fist was searing hot from the inferno that had basked the Zealot only moments ago. She was propelled off her feet. More blows followed, but they were given by the dry ground as she skimmed across it like a stone on water.

When the druid finally slid to a halt, her entire body was overcome. She was forced to acknowledge the poisonous discomfort in her spine, inhale sharply, and set it aside. By the time she scampered to her feet, she was petrified by what her eyes beheld.

The Protozealot had snatched her taukumu during the commotion. It was in the process of twirling it around in order to fire upon her. Before Carthei had a chance to react, her salvation was instead forced onto her. The Godslaves came charging in from the side, having dealt with the surviving Clthic footmen. The fourteen heavily armed knights crashed into the Protozealot, some resorting to tackling it while the others hacked at it with their pollaxes, hammers, and maces. Each blow left visible scrapes on its bones. A few of the knights threw themselves onto the taukumu, trying to pry it from the Zealot's hands.

Carthei pushed herself into a sprint, pulling her wrought iron mace from her belt as she drew closer to the dogpile of knights. The humanoid beast wrenched the taukumu sideways and fired. The resulting bolt tore straight through a Thestor, eviscerating his body and spraying gore onto one of his brothers. The taukumu discharged another two times, felling two Correnti.

Only then did Carthei reach the melee. She climbed over the struggling Godslaves, slipped on the plates of their armour, but ultimately reached their unstoppable foe. Mace in hand, she gave it a fierce swing aimed precisely at its head.

'Crunch'. The Zealot's head crumpled from this first blow. The whirring sound that came from inside it grew in volume and intensity. Carthei screamed as she repeated her attack. The rounded, glass-like coating over its large eye shattered and sprinkled its shards down onto the Godslaves. With the third strike, its smaller eyes had been crushed and spat yellow sparks out into the night air.

Some of the Godslaves followed Carthei's example, aiming for its head instead of the joints and torso. She was not keeping count, but she must have thrown twenty swipes at it before the Zealot's head was flattened and shrivelled. A Godslave jammed the tip of his pollaxe into the Zealot's neck and wrenched it downward with a furious cry. The bones strained, the tendons snapped.

Violently, the Zealot's head snapped clear of its body, arcing through the air and landing pathetically in the grass. Carthei was speechless as she clutched on for dear life. It *still* thrashed with insane desperation. Many Godslaves were caught by the flailing arms and bludgeoned by the creature's superhuman strength.

"Staff!" Carthei shouted as she tried to keep herself from tumbling off the backs and shoulders of the knights she climbed upon. "Now!"

Her taukumu was still seized by the Protozealot. Instead, Alric's taukumu promptly reached her; it was passed through the crowd, floating atop them like a branch would a river. Snatching it, Carthei leapt onto the Zealot's shoulders, thrusted the tip of the taukumu into the gaping hole left by its head, and squeezed.

Just like that, it came to an end. With an ear-piercing pop and a blinding flood of cobalt light, the Zealot went limp and started to tumble over. Carthei wobbled and tried to retain her balance long enough to hop off unharmed, but she hadn't the agility. She fell over like a fool, first landing on her back atop one of the knights, then sliding off and onto the ground.

From the comfort of the dirt, she saw some of the other Godslaves crash to the ground following the Zealot's sudden collapse. The knights, the ones who weren't dead, all scurried away from the headless wreck with their weapons still trained upon it. They encircled the fallen Zealot like wolves.

With their visors lowered, Carthei couldn't tell one from the other. Alric could be standing right next to her for all she knew. One Thestor, with a spear in-hand, cautiously danced closer to the corpse and poked it. It didn't move.

"The creature is dead!" cried one of the Godslaves.

Carthei panted. Every muscle in her body had been tensed. It was only then that they thought it time to relax. Her shoulders lowered, her abdomen deflated, and her legs loosened. She dropped her back onto the dirt and laid there for a moment with her eyes squeezed shut.

"Is she dead? Is the pagan dead?" came the nasally and irritating sound of Baldwyn's voice.

The druid gritted her teeth as the pain from her injury began to seep through the adrenaline. The air stung her face and she felt beads of blood trailing down her skin. "Where would you be if I *were* dead? Poised against the Clthics without my magic to aid you, *that* is where," she mumbled.

XX
The Manhunters

The Knight Correntis Sigmund was kind enough to apply a generous portion of faerie tears onto the five deep gouges on Carthei's face before wrapping the entire left side of her head with bandages. Her left eye beheld nothing but a muted brown. As she made her way to the middle of camp, she couldn't help but fiddle with it.

There was no telling how far away the larger Clthic force was from the camp, so Carthei knew that the Godslaves had to deal with the prisoners and leave as soon as possible. Many of the pack animals were worked into a frenzy by the arcane detonations from those mere minutes ago. A section of their pen had been smashed down and a stream of them had made off.

It was just next to that animal pen that the human prisoners were held. They were locked inside two separate cages like livestock. In the first cage, there had to be forty or fifty of them. As she closed in, their eyes locked onto hers. Cries of relief rose from the squalor, as did pleas for release. One voice, despite how faint it was, rang so clearly in midnight air.

"C-Carthei?"

A figure pushed to the front of the imprisoned crowd. It was Vontross. Without hesitation, Carthei approached the cage. "I knew you were still alive. You are much too stubborn to die," she said to him in their native tongue of Jurtir. "Are you alone?"

Vontross stuck his fingers through the bars of the cage, and Carthei gently laid her fingers against his. A tender smile graced his lips. "Yes. I was hoping that the others were with you…but that doesn't appear to be so." He then asked in disbelief, "You lead the Godslaves, now?"

It was then that Alric and the rest of the knights came around from behind the smoking tent. Gripped in his hand was his taukumu staff. Vontross' smile immediately faded. Alric came to a halt next to Carthei, raising his visor. His brow was tensed as his eyes locked onto the bandages on her face. "I approve of what thou hast done with thy countenance," he joked dryly. Carthei snorted. "Yes, your approval is something that I care a great deal about."

A weak smirk flashed across the Godslave's face for just a split second before he looked to the cage. It took him a moment, but it was clear from the uncertain frown he wore that he recognised Vontross. "Brothers, let us liberate these folk. I am certain that they hunger."

Some of the Godslaves approached the doors of the cages and started hacking at the bars with their axes. One of the prisoners, a foreign nobleman from the look of his clothes, added, "That is the thing, my good brother…we do not."

Another man came forward. "He speaks the truth. The demonists simply relieved us of our weapons, armour, standards, then continued to supply us with ample food and water."

The Godslaves finally tore through the door for the first cage. Steadily, the former captives filed out. Alric shook his head. "Thou wert to be toys for the vampire. Why else would they keep thee fed?" he mused.

Vontross charged into Carthei like a bull, clutching her so strongly that she was certain that he might break her in two. He whispered to her in Jurtir, "You better have a damned good explanation for this."

"The secret is safe. For the time being, at least," she answered. "I have managed to convince them that he is some God-given saviour."

With a tense shake of his head, the Ga'zahi hunter replied, "The second it changes, I will be ready. You need only say the word."

Carthei watched Alric as he greeted one of the freed prisoners with a firm handshake. Without his surcoat, it took Carthei a little longer to recognise Matvey. His face was harshly bruised, but like the other prisoners, he was not seriously injured. The Correntis turned and met Carthei's gaze, then the two shared a curt nod. With Vontross by her side, Carthei continued behind Alric and his Godslaves as they approached the next cell of prisoners.

"These folk were separated from the others…" said Lorenz. His expression sharpened when he looked at their garb. "More witches."

Carthei exhaled. It was incredibly obvious to her as well as Vontross. The people inside that cage, with skin that teetered between turquoise and cobalt, glared at the Godslaves with scathing toxicity. They wore the unmistakable rugged battle fibres of the Kaitan'zahi manhunters. To the Ga'zahi, they were trusted allies and frequent trade partners. The Ga'zahi were skilled foragers and farmers who traded crops and produce to the Kaitan'zahi, who excelled at keeping the lands of the two tribes safe from interlopers. Given their tense yet symbiotic relationship, they shared a language. Although they did not know the names of the individual druid tribes, the Church had definitely been assailed many times by the Kaitan'zahi; they were undoubtedly the primary source of their lore of witches. They made it their active duty to hunt and kill Godslaves, preserving their spines and surcoats as trophies. That was not to say that the Ga'zahi had never killed any Godslaves in the past, but they certainly never treated it the way the Kaitan'zahi did. To them, it was a righteous sport.

The Kaitan'zahi had their daggered stares fixed upon Alric, practically snarling at him. Vontross muttered in Jurtir, "Perhaps we should just let them kill each other."

"Do not tempt me," Carthei joked.

The Kaitan'zahi were renowned for being the greatest battle druids in the world. Carthei would feel much safer with them by her side amidst the Godslaves. And, of course, once the alliance broke down, they would prove to be more than enough to decimate the knights. Her first instinct was to lie and claim that they were Ga'zahi as well, but the state of their dress was so different that even the idiotic Godslaves would not have believed that. Carthei brushed through the crowd until she emerged by Alric's side. In Tritish, she conjured words that she believed would paint the manhunters in a more positive light. "These are the noble enforcers of the Kaitan'zahi tribe; defenders of the peace and dispensers of law amongst our people."

The man at the head of the formation of Kaitan'zahi did not react to the words. It was likely that they never bothered to learn Tritish. Frankly, if it wasn't for the Church trying to convert and assimilate her as a child, Carthei wouldn't have either. She continued, "They are mighty warriors who have mastered the most devastating of the arcane arts. The Clthic Synod has broken many if not all of our laws, making them a sworn enemy of the Kaitan'zahi. If they were to join us, our demonist foes would quake in their boots. What say you, Alric?"

The acting Thestor leader's shoulders rose and fell steadily as he contemplated. "I am certain it shall depend on whether or not they can be convinced."

With a nod, Carthei placed her right hand on the top edge of the cage, leaning upon it. She cleared her throat, then said in Jurtir, "My friends, you have seen the Clthic Synod. Left unpunished, they will surely bring about Athroct'u."

The lead Kaitan'zahi, likely a chieftain based on how the others looked to him, shook his head. "They certainly are heralds of the signs, but you overstep by teaching the fanatic barbarians our ways. We will never bow to them. It is shameful for *you* to have done so."

"Chieftain, perhaps use your brain for a moment," Carthei replied smoothly. The chieftain huffed through his nose and pressed himself up against the cage. "It will be far easier to kill an enemy that thinks of you as a friend. Besides, Alric is the only one here who knows the true nature of magic. He has the arcane skill of a Ga'zahi child."

The Chieftain shook his head with a stern frown. "You speak of dishonourable things. Deception. Lies. That is not our way. We charge headfirst toward our enemies."

"I am aware of that. There are tens of thousands of Godslaves out there, and hundreds of thousands of secular fighters who would gladly ride to the aid of the Church. We are vastly outnumbered...so we must compensate for our shortcomings. When the Clthics are dealt with, it will only be a matter of time before the Church looks to *us*."

The Chieftain scoffed in disbelief. "It is ironic, isn't it, sister? It was Clth who shattered druid unity those ages ago. Now, fools mustering under his banner have forced us back together."

"You will stand with us, then?"

"Only because you promise us Godslave blood," he added. "I am Vaykorr, Cheiftan of the rabble before you. What is your name, Ga'zahi?"

"Carthei," she answered.

She then turned her attention to Alric. "Chieftain Vaykorr of the Kaitan'zahi believes that the Clthics are the ultimate foe. To defeat them, we must break old prejudices and forge new alliances," she lied in Tritish.

Alric gave a stern nod. "Then we are in agreement. Release them."

The other Godslaves hesitated for a moment as they nervously glanced around at each other. Lorenz, with a scowl, stepped forward. "This witch is not to be trusted. None of us comprehend their tongue; who is to say that she was not conspiring with the savages right under our very noses?

"It is revolting enough to have *one* of these witches amidst our cohort," muttered Sigmund.

Alric waved a hand at them. "Silence. If Carthei wished us harm, she has had plenty of opportunities to betray us."

In lieu of the inaction, Baldwyn promptly roared, "What art thou waiting for? Move!"

Anybody could tell that the Godslaves were not all entirely eager to accept Alric's newfound authority. They were bred to fear and hate magic, yet one of their own wielded it and encouraged fraternisation with their perceived enemy.

Regardless of the Godslaves' mixed feelings, the Kaitan'zahi were soon liberated from their prison. The manhunters gave the Godslaves a wide berth, choosing instead to remain by Carthei and Vontross' side. Each of the twenty druids were of incredible stature; both men and women were covered in thick bands of muscle. Even knights did not come close to their immense musculature. Their builds were only emphasised by their tight battle fibres; form-fitting suits that could only be torn by the sharpest of blades. They were a people whose very existence consisted of hunting and killing their fellow man for sport.

Despite the renewed numbers of druids, they were still outnumbered by the Godslaves. Thestors, Correnti, and mixed Tritan and Valthois soldiers or knights were contained in the first pen. In total, there were fifty-six of them. The druids stood at twenty-three strong.

Before long, the druids found their way to the stockpiles of equipment that had been liberated from the prisoners before their capture. Thankfully, it was nowhere near the site of the kehmaha seed detonation. Carthei watched as they rummaged through the crates, securing all manner of artefacts that the Clthics were surely planning to save for later. There was at least one kehmaha, a handful of staves, and finally pieces of Kaitan'zahi shell armour, called vormata.

Unlike steel, the incredibly rare protective gear was angular and jagged in shape, lightweight, as white as ice, and some marked with strange glyphs. The twenty Kaitan'zahi distributed the various pauldrons, breastplates, gauntlets, greaves, and helmets amongst themselves and strapped them on top of their battle fibres. The pieces were mismatched and some of the druids had segments missing; they clearly had to share what little they had.

Alric strode over and leant onto the wagon next to Carthei. "The prisoners have revealed to us that they were to be moved to a mining fortress nearby on the morrow. It is apparently one of the many sites from which the Clthics excavate their relics. With our new well-armed allies, we could perhaps take it."

"Agreed. Their exploitation of Vorkhai artefacts must end. However, you *do* realise that if they were being transferred to the site, it is likely that our vampire friend is there."

Alric nodded. "We must make amends for allowing him to escape by ending his wretched existence. Vampires are a scourge upon creation and they *must* be eradicated."

Carthei cocked her head. "Such power should never be possessed by any man. It is a desecration."

Alric bowed his head in agreement. “Indeed.”

A Kaitan’zahi approached Carthei and Alric. He was one of the few wearing a helmet; the piece of armour completely covered his head and had no sights like a traditional helm. Instead, there were a series of dull red dots on its face, almost like scattered eyes. “Carthei, we have several pieces of vormata unused. Would you care to make use of them?” It was Vaykorr. His voice was garbled by his helmet.

Alric, obviously having no idea what he just said, glanced at Carthei with an eyebrow arched.

“Better me than him, I suppose,” she answered in Jurtir, nodding towards Alric.

“I would rather toss it into the ocean,” spat Vaykorr.

XXI
The Last Feast

There was a peak many leagues away from the mining fortress that the motley band of Godslaves, footmen, and druids selected as a position for their multi-pronged attack. Given Vontross' proficiency with the use of a taukumu at extreme range, they thought it prudent to place him and another druid there. He would rather be with those actually sneaking into the fortress. With Carthei. Vontross hated the idea of her being alone with the Godslaves. Of course, the Kaitan'zahi were there…but they were no substitute for the presence of a fellow tribesman. In Vontross' mind, neither were to be trusted.

A Kaitan'zahi mounted the hill. His body was completely obscured by segments of vormata shell armour and combat fibres, making him resemble a knight in full plate. He moved with a thuggish air, something that made Vontross believe that if someone stepped into his path, they would be promptly ploughed off their feet. Painted onto the breast of his strange cuirass was a series of glyphs; the Kaitan'zahi usually wrote their names upon their armour so they could be easily recognised. It read 'Hytharrn', the Jurtir word for 'immovable' and it was a popular name for both girls and boys in many druidic tribes.

As he approached, Vontross could see the wagon that dispensed him in the distance. It was a completely enclosed wooden box pulled by a pair of horses who were in turn driven by an unassuming peasant woman sitting atop it. Said woman whipped the reins, urging the steeds onward.

Only when Hytharrn was close did Vontross notice the two staves held in each of his hands. The staves, called pakama, were much cruder to Vontross' eyes than what he was used to seeing in arcane relics. Unlike the smooth, rounded edges of the taukumu, the surfaces of the pakama were jagged, angular, and sharp. Jutting out of the underside was an odd rectangular box.

Hytharrn knelt beside Vontross and explained, "It is to be handled the same as a taukumu for the most part. The staff will buck like a horse when you discharge it. Simply anticipate, brace, and all will be fine. There will be no visible trail left by the projectile for the Clthics to track and its sound will be muffled." His voice was garbled and messy due to the helmet he wore.

Vontross' face sharpened. "You are giving one to me?" He asked bluntly.

"We are *loaning* it to you," Hytharrn corrected sternly as he handed one to him. His gaze, denoted by the blank stare of the 8 dim 'eyes' on the face of his helmet, only made Vontross feel even more uneasy.

"Of course," Vontross answered with a huff as he accepted the weapon. He wrapped his fingers around the box sticking out of the pakama and pulled. It wouldn't budge. However, he promptly noticed a small button on the weapon near the box. When he squeezed it, the container slid out with ease. There were seeds held within, but they were much smaller than the tankard-sized kehmaha seeds. As large as Vontross' thumb and with a chrome gold finish, they were certainly beautiful enough to be worn as jewellery. He had never handled a seed-spitter before. He hoped that the fear of wasting them would make sure that his aim was true.

Hytharrn made some quick visual inspections of his own staff as he said, "Strike the head or upper body, as pakama do not kill as well as taukumu do. The seeds could even be removed from the injured by a talented surgeon, allowing the wounds to heal properly." What Matvey had told them of his earlier ordeal was proof of his words.

He said nothing to the Kaitan'zahi and instead slapped the seed vessel back into his pakama then fixed his octhum onto its length. The mining fortress was a tiny smudge of grey in the distance. The setting sun bathed the countryside in a vibrant orange glaze. They had to act soon. No matter how much the octhum would improve Vontross' eyesight, it could not give him sight in the dark. He lowered himself onto the ground, lying prone on his front, then shouldered his pakama. He peered through the octhum.

The fortress had become as large and detailed as it would have been if he were standing at the very gates. Like the Godslave hive of Omenthal, it consisted of a stone wall pushed against the sides of a mountain, although the structure itself was much smaller. The portcullis was raised and guarded by a pair of footmen on the ground. The battlements of the fortifications were manned by four guards armed with crossbows, as well as two K'relvic Nuns on the watchtowers.

The wagon was slinking toward the open maw of the castle gate. Vontross watched as the guards atop the battlements cocked their heads and spoke amongst themselves, all while glaring at the nearing vessel.

"I await your order, manhunter," Vontross muttered. "I fear they may drop the portcullis."

From the sounds of rustling clothes and dirt, Vontross gathered that Hytharrn was joining him in a prone position. After a moment, he said, "Take the Nun on the left watchtower when I count to three."

He took a deep breath, then slowly exhaled.

"One."

Vontross tilted his pakama until the glyph in the centre of his octhum was hovering above the head of the K'relvic atop the tower. The next gush of air that entered his lungs was held there. It was crucial that he control the tiny natural movements of his body. At that range, even the smallest sigh could divert his aim by an arm's length.

"Two."

The Ga'zahi's finger tenderly curled around the discharge plate of his staff.

"Three."

Two loud metallic 'clacks' sounded and Vontross' pakama was thrust back into his shoulder. His view shifted by the shaking staff, Vontross furrowed his brow as he fought the kick and brought the octhum back onto the watchtower. The Nun was still there. If only for one second more. The pakama seed shattered the animal skull hugging the woman's face, blasting it into a million pieces. She dropped to the ground. In the corner of his eye, Vontross saw a similar rain of shrapnel, denoting Hytharrn's success.

"The two men on the left battlements," Hytharrn instructed cooly. "Take the one on the right."

Vontross's voice was rickety as he carefully moved his pakama into position. "I am ready."

"Three. Two. One."

One of the men dropped a split second before the other, but one thing was certain; their armour was of no help against the seeds as they raced above the plains faster than the wind itself. Hytharrn's calm voice commanded, "The other wall, take the right."

There was no need to count that time. Both druids fired upon the hapless infantrymen, and they were dispatched just like the rest.

Vontross brought his octhum to bear on the wagon which was at the gate now. The two guards were conversing with the woman driving the horses…distracted and vulnerable. The two druids repeated their attacks, downing the unsuspecting footmen before they even knew what had happened. "What now?" asked Vontross as he pulled his face away from his octhum and rose to a crouch.

Hytharrn stood and nodded toward the fortress. "We pray that those fools do not die."

"We have made a significant discovery," Duke Klaus von Talhoffen explained to his guests as he fiddled with the jewels encrusting his goblet. Vilulf, Klaus' men-at-arms Lazslo, Heinrich, Reynald, and Wenceslaus were seated by Klaus' sides.

Lord Franco di Lombardi, his wife Beatrice, his brother Dante, and their retinues, lined the edges of the rather long feasting table. "Evidence to support this…outrageous new religion?" asked the noble.

The Clthic marshal leaned forward, bracing his hands on the table. "A city buried beneath the mountains. The Nuns are calling it Myrktuul."

The chamber was filled with awe-inspired murmurs. Beatrice's brow tensed. "Beautiful. Why is it that your Clthic names always sound like a dying goat's final screams?"

Franco chuckled in response to the terrible joke. Klaus' patience was beginning to wear out. Beatrice was…facetious, to put it lightly. She had a habit of cracking jokes at the most inappropriate times. Franco seemed to laugh at every single one, though. With a deep sigh, Klaus replied, "The demons built it. It is a vestige of Hell bubbling to the surface of our world." Franco and some of his retainers nearby smiled in disbelief. Klaus thought that the description was rather dramatic, but that's what the Tethspeakers said to him.

With a contemplative expression on his face, Franco asked, "How canst thou be sure that it isn't simply some long lost Fald'yn city swallowed by the earth?"

Vilulf answered melodically, "Because the entire city is imbued with blood magic." Franco squinted at the vampire, cocking his head. Vilulf continued, "That's why most of the Nuns have gone down to the site; they are working to heal Myrktuul's heart and return it to life."

The conflicted lord leaned back into his seat. His eyes drifted down, indicating that he was lost in thought. "I *did* see their sorcery at work when we arrived. Incredible artefacts, those staves."

"If you are worried about persecution by the Thestors, you needn't," assured Klaus. "We have seized their local fortress monastery, and the good Erik Vilulf saw to it personally that those of their Order still in the county were hunted down and killed." He gestured proudly to his right, where the aforementioned Vilulf sat with one arm hanging from the top rail of his chair.

Vilulf gave a slow, proud nod. "I have been blessed with great power by our creators. I shall use it to dismantle the lies of the Church and wrestle control of the people from their shrivelled hands." Klaus decided to withhold the fact that the vampire was hysterical and mere steps away from death when he arrived two days ago. It seemed that the only thing capable of scaring the night creature was magic.

"I assure you, the Thestors do not frighten me in the slightest." Franco finally felt comfortable enough to smile. "Sir Erik, I was visited by one of thy kin recently. Yes, I know what thou art. The chill of thy presence in my mind is not as difficult to discern as thou wouldst wish. I have felt it before, only it was far more elegant and subtle." Vilulf reeled back in surprise. "Thou art not quite as powerful as Lady Viktoria," he said with a cold glare. Klaus had to strain himself not to laugh at the remark. It was plain that Vilulf didn't really know how to react.

Beatrice shrugged. "Very well... Shall we eat?" The feast continued with the entrancing melodies played by a flute and hurdy gurdy providing relaxing ambience. Everyone at the table took to the lavishly cooked dishes with fervour. All except for Vilulf, of course. He eyed all of the patrons the way they eyed the food.

Around two hundred people filled the great hall. Klaus' knights and men-at-arms and the castle's garrison all partook in the celebration. They could afford to; no one was left to stand in their way in the region. Lord Franco possessed a mighty retinue and a great deal of territories that could be used to fund Clthic military expansion. His history with the Church was strained to say the least. Given a recent incident involving a Thestor executing children before Franco had a chance to intervene only made Klaus more certain that Franco would grant his allegiance. He also had to thank Viktoria for whatever she did when she brought his offer to Franco; he had basically been convinced ahead of time. Klaus felt that *someone* needed to be thinking practically of achieving the Synod's goals. Mother Xalt'n was too obsessed with spreading the faith and baptising more witches, and Lady Viktoria...well, she was probably off engaging in the same kinds of things Vilulf did in his spare time. If the Clthic Synod was to spread itself, it needed practical means, not just sorcery.

Franco gently laid his knife down onto the table and licked his lips. "Very pleasant food."

"Yes, indeed," added Beatrice. "You *must* have your cook share the recipe with mine. I do not believe I can live another day without that pie."

Klaus nodded humbly. "I am glad you approve."

The visiting lord suddenly grew much more sombre. "I must apologise for my hesitance. Surely, thou understand my suspicions. Even after witnessing Lady Viktoria's might firsthand."

"Nonsense," started Vilulf. "You are right to be wary. So, tell me, Franco, do you subscribe to the Clthic doctrine?"

Franco sighed and looked at his wife. "What do you think, my love?"

Beatrice shrugged. "I don't think it really matters what I think."

With a roll of his eyes, Franco pressed, "*Beatrice.*"

She snorted and a warm smile appeared on her face. "Oh, stop it. You get so sour when I tease you." Beatrice playfully struck Franco's shoulder, much to the shock and confusion of the rest of the table. Franco, however, laughed and shook his head. "You consider it, husband; best not allow me to choose for you. What will all your new friends think?" A steady chuckle washed across the dining table.

Franco was then left to make his own decision. Just in case, Klaus made the point of thinking to himself, *Do not interfere with his choice, Vilulf. Whenever you compel someone to act, they are free afterwards to reflect upon their actions and recognise them as someone else's. Learn from your mistress Viktoria's example and let the man come to his own conclusions.* He didn't have to look at Vilulf to feel his disappointment.

Finally, after a long pause, Franco replied, "I shall lend you my support, but I am afraid I must be convinced of your faith."

Klaus took a sip of wine before answering, "Of course. The Matriarch would be delighted to take you on as an acolyte. This night though, we shall celebrate your devotion to our righteous cause."

For whatever reason, a tiny shape in the window snatched Klaus' attention. His neck stiffened as he squinted into the dark. Another one. A shadow…moving outside.

"Vilulf," he muttered. "Do you hear anything?"

Vilulf swallowed. "N-No." Standing, the vampire waved at the band and said, "Stop playing."

The woman with the hurdy gurdy stopped her cranking, but the bard with the flute seemed to have missed the request. After clenching his fists and twitching, Vilulf promptly roared, “Stop with that fucking flute!”

Conversations still continued, despite his outburst. “Shut up! All of you, shut up!” Only then did silence consume the great hall. Vilulf’s face dropped.

The doors to the hall were kicked open by two towering knights clad in plate armour. Upon their armoured bodies were the surcoats of the Thestors and the Correnti. Dozens of them came pouring in with pollaxes, maces, and swords in hand. The patrons closest to the doors stood no chance. The wave of men crashed against them, driving their weapons into their unarmoured bodies with the greatest of ease. Helpless, the Clthics were skewered, hacked, and bludgeoned into paste.

N-No. They’ve found me!

It took Klaus a moment to realise that it wasn’t any thought of his…it was Vilulf’s. And it had betrayed him. The coward never finished the job. He ran when they managed to wound him with their newfound druid comrades. Franco sprung to his feet and drew his arming sword, as did Klaus and the other men-at-arms at the table. All about the room, the fighting men shot upward, but their time was rapidly waning. Despite his doubts, Vilulf vaulted over the table and threw himself into the fray.

If we survive this, I will have your head, Klaus thought.

An answer, though unwanted, came to him nonetheless. *Not if I take yours first.*

Klaus found himself behind the first line of Clthics as they struggled against the fully armed Churchsworn. The Thestors were complimented by the Knights Correntis; the combat surgeons that Klaus had learned not to underestimate on the field of battle. Most of them were not clad in full plate harness, instead having only vambraces and/or cuisses to cover the limbs. Many opted for brigandine armour. The Correnti were formed up behind their heavily armoured counterparts wielding spears, halberds, or billhooks to keep the enemy at bay. The Thestors mainly brandished pollaxes, longswords, and maces. Not a shield was in sight among their ranks, made unnecessary by their comprehensive armour.

Klaus could feel an unnerving sensation begin to swirl upward from the pit of his stomach. Every single one of his men in the hall was wearing regular clothing and only had access to his sidearm, a sword. With so many adversaries, grappling a Thestor to the ground to jam a blade into his armpit would only result in death before you even got close enough to deal a fatal blow. It was suicide. They had to find another way.

Vilulf, using his bare hands, had seized the sides of a Thestor's helmet. All the while, he was being slashed at by his victim's comrades. Klaus watched wide-eyed as the vampire grinned and licked his lips in response to the blades burying themselves into his body and the hammers mincing his flesh. The helmet popped and flattened, sending blood shooting out of its sights and breaths. The Thestor went limp and all holy knights in range sent their attention to Vilulf. Klaus could tell from his lip-biting and the way his eyes rolled back that he enjoyed it.

Klaus saw the opportunity; the Thestors and Correnti had singled out Vilulf and were prioritising him. Klaus spun his sword over, holding it with both hands on its blade. He pinched the blade with his fingers in order to keep its sharp edge from sliding against his bare palms. The Duke lunged forward and swung the weapon with every ounce of strength he had. With its balance tipped, the arming sword had been turned into an improvised mace.

The sword's hilt curved through the air and the tip of its crossguard slammed into the helmet of an occupied Thestor. The blow filled the air with a loud 'crack'. The knight stumbled to one side, wobbled, then ultimately fell. As he did, he dropped his pollaxe. Wenceslas and several other men-at-arms swarmed the fallen knight and finished him off. Laszlo snapped forward, scooped the pollaxe up, and brandished it with a snarl before charging straight into the new opening in the Churchsworns' first line. Klaus, Heinrich, and Franco joined the surge.

The Correnti levelled their polearms at the approaching fighters. Klaus managed to weave free of a billhook and grab the shaft of the weapon, but he caught a glimpse of Heinrich being skewered on the tip of a halberd before the heat of battle wiped his mind clean.

Laszlo barged into a pair of Correnti; one of them was the one wielding the billhook that Klaus had grabbed onto. With its wielder struck, Klaus easily pulled the weapon free, dropping his sword in order to grasp it with both hands. A Knight Correntis advanced towards him, urging Klaus to respond. He swept his billhook across the knight's groin in a blind strike. Inadvertently, the attack tore the leather strap that held up the man's right cuisse. With the armour's weight no longer suspended, it dropped downward, locking his knee and obstructing his articulation. As the Correntis stumbled, Laszlo swung his pollaxe at his lowered head with a heart-wrenching 'crunch'. The knight dropped dead and tumbled over the bodies of his brothers.

The Clthics took full advantage of the gap in the Churchsworn line. They came swarming over the outnumbered knights. Overwhelming them with sheer volume, the Clthic soldiers could then force open their visors to stab their faces. The Thestors and Correnti wise enough to pull back filtered away through the doors and slunk outside as the Clthic battle cry reverberated through the hall.

Klaus joined his men as they stomped over the handful of Thestor and Correnti corpses and stormed towards the door. Suddenly, just as the Clthics started through the door, Klaus' heart stopped. "Hold! Fall back!"

Only Franco, Laszlo and a handful of others heeded his warning. When the soldiers left the building, the all-too familiar sound of taukumu discharges filled the air. There were dozens of them overlapping each other, a symphony of black magic. Blue lightning poured in from the windows as well as the doorway.

Klaus sent his eyes back into the hall. The non-combatants had crowded beside the fireplace. Lords, ladies, pages, and the elderly. Of the two hundred people that had moments ago been basking in celebration, there were now roughly fifty still standing. Thirty of them were non-combatants. The fools that rushed outside were all dead. Vilulf was covered in blood, most of it his own. His doublet had been torn to tattered rags, and his hose was not in much better condition. Open, wet wounds could be seen beneath his clothing. His face was also heavily mutilated, but each of the injuries were in the process of mending themselves.

Before Klaus could think any further about their predicament, more Churchsworn men bolted into the great hall. Thestors, Correnti, as well as men-at-arms and footmen did not allow the Clthics another moment of respite. They rammed headfirst into the Clthic defence. Klaus, swallowed by his men, made out some additional enemies behind their infantry line.

They wore strange, chitinous armour and had eight-eyed helmets masking their faces. Druids. They held taukumu and pakama at the ready. However, they were the least of Klaus' worries. A Thestor marched into the great hall. A taukumu in his hands. A Thestor…commanding magic?

More pressingly, there was a large druid at his side. He had a kehmaha resting upon his shoulder. Klaus wanted to scream, but the sound never left his throat. When the Churchsworn line crouched, the druid aimed his kehmaha at the crowd of unarmed Clthics at the rear of the chamber and squeezed the arming key.

The sound, heat, and smoke shook Klaus to the core. By the time he shook himself out of the disorientation and glanced back, he saw only carnage. Body parts, innards, torn clothing, and shards of bone showered down and painted the wooden flooring of the hall.

"V-Vilulf! Take them now!" Klaus roared.

However, the vampire knight was nowhere to be seen. Among the crowd of furious and frightened Clthic soldiers, Vilulf was not there. On the floor though, were the remaining scraps of his clothing. Klaus turned back to the Churchsworn just as their infantry took several steps back so the Thestor sorcerer and the other druids could ready their staves. What followed was an onslaught of magical energies; the last thing that Klaus ever saw or felt.

XXII
To Taste You

The Correnti were usually bound by their Third Attestation to dispense aid unto anyone who was in need, regardless of their faith. Alric was glad to see them forgo the rule. Heretics, *demonists* nonetheless, were undeserving of such mercy. All of the Clthics, whether they were dead or just barely alive, were carted outside the castle walls and dumped in a large pile. The goblins would eventually smell death on the air and come for them. They would be spun within a web and dragged off to one of their hives, a place from which no man had ever returned. It was the perfect method of execution for the God-hating sacks of excrement. The heraldry upon the dead confirmed that Franco di Lombardi and Klaus von Talhoffen were both Clthic sympathisers and among the dead. Alric was pleased to say the least that the blaspheming Franco, as well as his worthless household, had met an end befitting his crimes against God.

Alric, free of his plate armour, and half a dozen of his Thestor brothers were pouring through the keep's hall which had been turned into an archive. The Thestors sifted through the mountains of parchment and ledgers the Clthics had left behind. The castle's stores were full; it could have lasted a great many months in a siege, so Alric had to thank God that their plan worked so well.

He had led a covert force who hid themselves in the wagon, disembarked within the castle walls, then secured the barbican. With the gatehouse taken, the rest of their men were free to enter the fortress unopposed. And of course, God's involvement was evident by how the Clthics just happened to be engaged in a feast. They were unprepared and forced to fight in cramped quarters, so over two hundred of their ilk were eviscerated by the seventy Churchsworn and druids. With only a handful of casualties, none could complain. Such luck was a sign of divine intervention.

As Alric gazed upon the mess that the Thestors had created, he saw Lorenz approach. He reported, "A great many things have been found, Brother Alric, among them a roll of Clthic loyalists, maps of additional excavation sites, and detailed treatises on sorcery. Perhaps thou couldst make use of the latter."

Alric nodded. Lorenz appeared to be around the same age as Alric. His skin was a harsh purple and weathered with dirt. Alric turned to the other Thestors as they rummaged through the Clthic belongings. Several of them had not even taken the time to disarm themselves. He called, "My Brothers, relent. These things can be sorted on the morrow."

With great hesitance, the Thestors slowly ground to a halt. Baldwyn, armoured and sticking his head inside a cabinet, did not seem to hear the request. He dug through the furniture like a dog in the dirt. "Baldwyn!" Alric shouted.

Suddenly, the knight jolted upward. He slammed his head on the top of the cabinet then pulled himself out of it. Lorenz stifled a laugh. "Brother?" Baldwyn asked, turning to face Alric. His sallet's visor was lowered and his bevor was still raised. Bunched up in his arms were a ridiculous amount of parchment scrolls that overflowed from his grasp and spilled onto the floor.

"The time for rest has come. Go now, disarm thyself and retreat," said Alric with a nod.

Baldwyn started, "But brother–"

Alric didn't need to say anything, he just raised his eyebrows. Baldwyn got the hint and finally sighed in defeat, "As thou command." He tossed the remaining scrolls over his shoulder and paced out of the keep, moving much faster than the other departing Thestors.

Before long, the hall was empty. Alric found himself frozen in place. His eyes drifted to an empty doorway on the other side of the chamber. A handful of rushlights were scattered about the hall, sitting upon desks, shelves, and cabinets. Their dim yellow light, faint and flickering, only produced small patches of illumination that did not reach the distant doorway. Its infinite depth called to Alric. It whispered to him.

He plucked up one of the rushlights and held it in front of him as he drifted through the room. The stone of the keep absorbed and deflected all sound from the outside world; Alric was consumed by complete and utter silence. It allowed the cold air to fester and amplify. The rustling of his clothes and the shifting of his sword upon his belt sounded like explosions in the void. His footsteps against the rush carpet added a layer of crunching to the soundscape.

Alric raised his rushlight to the wall as he brushed by it. Like those of every keep he had seen, they were not just naked stone. Lime wash had been applied to every wall, giving them a pure white hue, then beautiful images were rendered atop them by talented artists. Alric recalled that Blackmeadow's keep had renditions of events from the Scripture expertly stroked upon its walls. The one he currently stood in was instead far simpler. Dozens of serpentine trees wound up from a golden stripe that ran horizontally across the base of each wall. Their leaves blossomed outward, like curved spearheads. Some sections even had a brickwork pattern painted onto them. Alric always found that rather strange. Painting stone bricks on top of stone bricks…such acts of futility were achievable only by artists.

Despite his criticisms, something made him relish the sights. He marvelled at the beauty of the images and felt the warmth of his flame's wake wash over his face as he eased onward. Alric moved into the doorway and the endless blackness was eaten away by his light. A spiral staircase awaited. The walls spun around him as he ascended, and he had nothing but the sounds he made in moving to keep himself company.

The room he emerged in was swallowed by complete darkness. Unlike the hall of the keep which had several rushlights spread about it, there was not a single source of light there save for the one in Alric's hand. He could only see several feet in front of him thanks to the dim, jittering flame. Alas, he paced forward, mesmerised by the emptiness. It had a weight to it, a presence. He did not feel alone with it closing in around him. He felt safe.

Before long, he found himself standing inside a bedchamber. There was a single lit candle on the bedside table. It burned brighter than his rushlight, but it still only painted a small section of the room with visibility. As he stood there, Alric felt as if the door had creaked shut…but for whatever reason, he didn't turn around.

The fine maroon velvet of the bed curtains beckoned him. Mist filled his skull. Something stirred within him. An urge. One he had learned to conquer in the pursuit of his oath of celibacy. It burst forth stronger than ever, as if its embers had been stoked. He began to see things within his mind…things that made him quiver. He took a rickety breath inward, squeezing the fabric of his surcoat with one hand.

As the thoughts careered through his distant consciousness, Alric placed his rushlight onto a shelf by the door and unslung his taukumu, resting it against the bedside table. He unfastened his belt, which held his longsword and dagger, then dropped it onto the ground. Finally, he slipped out of his surcoat, then his arming doublet, hose, shoes, and breeches. Bare and with his eyes glazed over, Alric lowered himself into the bed and stared at the ceiling.

He felt the bed deflate by his leg, as if something unseen was resting atop it. The weight shifted, then displaced a spot on the other side of Alric's hips. Pressure eased onto his shoulders.

I'm going to have you now, so you are going to be nice and quiet.

The intrusive voice knocked Alric free of his trance. He blinked rapidly as he felt a weight lower itself onto his groin. The Thestor sent his arms upward and they collided with solid air. Snarling, Alric clawed for something, anything to grab onto. He felt a nose…then lips. It was a formless face floating there above him. Staring down at him.

Get down. Obey me.

Alric strained. It took every ounce of will he could muster to overcome the whispers that wrestled for control of his body. He thrusted his fingers into what he could only assume were eyes. A pained hiss bounced off the walls of the bedchamber and the air flickered above the Thestor. Blood dripped from the nothingness. Slowly, blotches of matter trembled into existence in the space above the bed. Skin patched itself together little by little, revealing a man rubbing himself against Alric's body. The knight gave a frightened shout as he stared at the man's face. Blood dripped from his eyes like black tears and his mouth was contorted as he bit his lower lip in ecstasy.

The vampire snatched Alric's wrists and pinned them to the bed. His strength was immeasurable. Alric had no chance of overpowering him. The creature lowered his face, adrip with obsidian liquid, onto Alric's. The Thestor struggled as he felt a warm, wet tongue draw itself across his cheek.

To taste you...finally...such a prize, it is.

Alric gritted his teeth and throttled his head straight up. It felt like he had charged straight into a stone wall. Pain loomed in his forehead, swelling with every passing second. The vampire's crazed stare was still locked onto Alric's very soul.

Suddenly, there came a pounding upon the chamber door like booms of thunder. "Alric?" The vampire's ears twitched and he turned his head toward the door. With the monster's lapse in concentration, Alric managed to bludgeon him once again with his own skull. Alric's attacker rolled over, releasing the impossible grip he had exerted over the knight.

Alric threw himself from the bed and over to the bedside table. Every movement he made was jittery, frantic, and desperate. His eyes were wide as he fumbled for his taukumu. With the staff in-hand, Alric spun back over to the bed and fired before he aimed.

The bed and its curtains erupted in waves of yellow flame. Smoke billowed outward like wretched, poisonous clouds. Alric kept the weapon pressed firmly against his shoulder and swept it about. He felt the heat of the fire against his uncovered skin. It danced about, in duet with the smoke as they both obscured his vision. With all the light bathing the room, darkness no longer shrouded its other occupants.

He should've been shocked, but quite frankly, given the fact that he stood in the den of a vampire, a handful of corpses pressed against the corners of the room was not entirely out of place. He focused instead on his own survival. Alric slowly paced toward the door, which was still reverberating with the impacts it was receiving on the other side. Alric moved his left hand from the underside of the staff and directed it toward the door's latch. He didn't avert his eyes from the flaming bed.

A metallic 'click' denoted his success in unlocking the door…but it was perhaps also the signal for his foe to attack. Alric only saw a brief flash of the vampire as it revealed itself from behind the flaming bed curtains. What he saw was a man, flesh seared and bubbling, with a mangled mess of a left arm. It dangled from the bones beneath by bands of torn sinew.

Without warning, Alric was tackled back into the door, forcing it shut. The vampire's face stunk of burning meat. It peeled open, like a blooming flower. Layers of skin and flesh parted to reveal coarse bone and a massive spike of a fang.

Alric roared in fear and desperation as he wrestled his taukumu to the side. It was pinned against the monster's other arm as he squeezed the handle once again. Nothing happened. The heart, sucked clean by his prior use in the battle, no doubt.

However, in a move that very likely saved his life, Alric was shoved onto the ground by whoever was pushing on the door from the other side. His face slammed into the wooden flooring. He didn't care to look at who came to his aid; he felt that the staggered vampire was more worthy of his attention. Two bolts of magical energy sliced into the monster, blowing its legs into meaty bits. It tumbled into a heap on the ground, howling. One more discharge followed, eviscerating its right arm. Having been turned into a mangled body with a single horribly mutilated left arm, the vampire's face reformed and a pathetic expression of terror graced it. "N-No…! O-Oh God…!" He looked down at his body and screamed in horror.

Alric swallowed as his face warped in confusion. The twisted creature had found pleasure in being maimed mere moments ago. Why did its lust suddenly give way to horror? The question was squashed by the rage that bubbled beneath Alric's skin. His fingers convulsed. The knight stumbled to his feet, intent on bludgeoning the monstrosity into pulp. He stomped over to the vampire, his eyes burning brighter than the flames at his side.

Suddenly, something warm set itself onto Alric's shoulders, quelling his mania.

Carthei had pulled off her cloak and firmly wrapped it around him. "Are you alright?" She asked. Half of her face was still wrapped in bandages; Alric could only look into one of her eyes.

Thestors poured into the bedchamber, led by Baldwyn. Surprising no one, he was still armoured. "By the grace of God! Douse the fire!" he commanded the knights. Moving like lightning, they suffocated the burning bed with the rush carpet that laid upon the floor.

Alric couldn't find it within himself to say anything to the druid. His mind was racing through the possibilities of what would've happened if he didn't have his taukumu on him. If Carthei and Baldwyn hadn't arrived just in time. Instead of prompting him further, Carthei patted him firmly on the shoulder and turned away. As she strode over to the vampire, she reached down to her waist and retrieved a coil of rope.

"N-No, please! Let me be!" he pleaded as Carthei approached. "A-Alric, I'm Erik! Halsten's son!"

Alric swallowed and took several steps back. He watched Carthei as she knelt over the vampire, wrapping her length of rope securely about his neck. The knight's mouth had dropped agape. Alric's voice was a wavering mess as he replied, "I have no reason to believe thine lies."

"You have to! I-I'm his son," begged the creature. "He'll be looking for me!"

Baldwyn shook his head. "Pathetic. Face death with dignity, beast."

Alric swallowed. "He is a heretic, as art thou. Where is he?"

Carthei continued to wrap the helpless lump of a creature within the thick bands of rope. Erik's face crumpled as he sobbed, "N-No! My lady, how beautiful you are. Your s-shape, it excites me! Spare me. I can please you! I can be yours! A-A slave!" The vampire reached up toward her breast with his twisted hand while he begged.

The druid pulled her taukumu from her back and pressed the side of Erik's head against the floor with her right foot. Alric swallowed as he watched her jam the tip of her staff against the vampire's jaw and discharge it. Tiny shards of pulverised bone bounced against the walls and floors with gentle tapping.

When the smoke cleared, Erik's lower jaw had been torn from his head. His mouth, now a throbbing hole in his face, tensed and twitched as tears ran down his cheeks. A sickening moan emanated from the horribly butchered creature.

“Perhaps Brother Alric should be the one to dispatch him,” mused Baldwyn.

Carthei tied one end of the rope to a heavy cabinet in the corner of the room. Then she heaved Erik’s bloodied body up by the armpits. “Death is too easy an end for this one. It must be slow,” she said, her voice melodic and cheerful.

She tossed what little remained of the vampire out the window. Promptly, the rope went taut and the cabinet fixed to it skidded slightly. Alric moved over to the window and peered down. Erik dangled there against the wall of the keep as people watched from below. Thestors, Correnti, Kaitan’zahi, and common soldiers were either roaring in approval, or fighting the urge to vomit. On the horizon, Alric could see the enticing light of the approaching sunrise.

XXIII
The Pale Spire

The Clthic records identified the mining fortress as Beggar's Rock, once a flourishing iron mine several centuries ago. When the deposits were all but exhausted, the site was reduced to a simple castle of minor strategic significance. However, as noted in the parchment, the Clthics discovered that with additional tunnelling work, the mines of Beggar's Rock led straight into the Under. It was from there that they unearthed arcane artefacts.

Alric was hard pressed to choose only a handful of volunteers for the expedition. Seeing as only two K'relvic Nuns defended the fortress when it was taken, it was obvious where the others were lurking. It would be an extremely dangerous endeavour that would pit any involved against the unrelenting might of the eldritch arts. So naturally, every Knight Thestor and Correntis insisted on going.

It was a difficult decision to make. The Under was a place believed to be connected to Hell. All followers of the Church were urged to avoid setting foot in there, meaning that none of the Churchsworn had any experience in navigating it. The druids, however, frequently visited the Under. It was a sacred place for them. Such backward beliefs aside, Alric was not blinded by his zealotry. He knew that the druids had to take the lead.

He had decided on a contingent of twenty men, including Lorenz, Dmitri, Harvald, Matvey, and Sigmund, to accompany him. All of the others were incredibly disappointed, especially Baldwyn, who stomped away and kicked the dirt at his feet. The duty of being in command of Beggar's Rock gave him motivation enough to cease his bawling.

As Alric's boots pounded against the mud to carry him forward, he saw that the entrance to the mines was crowded over by fifteen druids. Hytharrn remained at Beggar's Rock to with seven of his kin to help fortify it alongside Baldwyn. Carthei and Vontross were among those preparing to enter the tunnels, joined by Vaykorr and his Kaitan'zahi. Their eyes lanced up to Alric and the eighteen knights behind him.

"Shall we?" he asked.

Carthei nodded and barked some words in her native language. The Kaitan'zahi turned on their heels and filtered single file into the tunnel. The Thestors and Correnti soon followed, whispering amongst themselves about their unlikely allies. Before Alric joined them, he took a deep breath and peered over his shoulder. The keep of Beggar's Rock, an imposing rectangular stronghold, stared back at him. There upon its face was the blackened corpse of the vampire, hanging by a noose. Both of his legs were blown off, his right arm severed, his left one violently mangled, and his jaw ripped from his face. Alric would never forget the sounds of his pathetic screams as the sun ravaged his body. He had one person to thank for those pleasant memories.

Alric turned back to the tunnel entrance and was startled to see Carthei still standing there. She was wearing Kaitan'zahi shell armour, namely a piece that was fitted over her torso. It was mostly covered by her heavy cloak. She cocked her head.

He wanted to just ignore her and brush by…but there was a twitching within him that simply could not allow it. He did not want to spend another second thinking of what had happened the previous night…but it kept returning to him. Despite her nature, her being a renouncer of God, Carthei had saved his life several times before the coming of the vampire. She easily could have killed him to defend the secret of the arcane, but she did not. He opened his mouth to thank her. "I…I shall forever cherish the sight of that abomination dying a slow and painful death." When he heard the words aloud, he couldn't help but sigh in frustration. It didn't quite sound the way he intended it to.

Carthei huffed in agreement. The bloodstained bandages that hugged her face the night before had been replaced with fresh ones. She had also lathered what little of her face that was visible with paint, the same earthy brown pigment that she wore when Alric first met her. "As will I," she said faintly, avoiding eye contact with him completely.

With that, the duo entered the cave. After following the tunnel, it opened up into a wider space. Barrels, pickaxes, wheelbarrows, and empty burlap sacks were scattered about. A single oil lantern kept the darkness at bay. Just before Alric was about to ask where all the other lanterns were, the druids all reached into pouches on their belts. They each retrieved a small cylindrical object.

He watched Vaykorr as he applied pressure onto a specific spot on the device. Alric and his Churchsworn all jolted back in fright. The tiny object emitted a brilliant light, many times brighter than any lamp or torch. It projected a circle of white on the stone walls. In the following seconds, fifteen other spots of light snapped into existence. Each of the manhunters affixed the light emitters onto the lengths of their staves. It was rather ingenious. Wherever they pointed their weapons, the light would illuminate it.

The band descended into the mines, their way painted by the unyielding brilliance of sorcery. Alric could sense the unease permeating the souls of his Churchsworn brothers. He could hear Dmitri hastily reciting prayers under his breath. Sigmund held an effigy of the Pillar in his left hand, massaging it in order to quell his uncertainty. Lorenz constantly flexed his fingers, filling the tunnel with the sound of stressing leather.

The smell was not pleasant. Each warrior's armour had been coated with unzym, a foul paste that Carthei insisted would help defend against arcane energy. The surface of the knights' armour had been rendered a sickly yellow by the oily substance. It reeked of ash, burnt meat, and molten animal fat. Alric stared at Lorenz's back as he crept forward. The lot of them looked as if they had gone swimming in a sea of butter.

Also quite strange was the fact that each knight also brandished a heater shield. Many of the Thestors did not usually need to use such protection thanks to their plate harness. If their armour gave them sufficient protection, devoting both hands to a larger more powerful weapon would be the norm. On that occasion though, the shields had been painted with unzym as well, giving the knights a second layer of defence against magic. Alric found it awkward to hold such an object while fully armed; he constantly whacked it against the walls of the tunnel and the straps got caught on the couter that protected his elbow. He had modified his shield by cutting a notch in its side; room enough for him to fit the shaft of his staff. It would allow him to fire without exposing himself. He also cut a narrow slot in the top of it so he could see from behind it.

After what felt to be an eternity of wandering an endless tunnel, murmurs crept back from the front of the line. Alric tried to look over the heads of those in front of him to see what all the fuss was about, but he saw nothing. He would not have to wait long. Surely enough, another cavernous space welcomed him.

The druids' lights painted the pockmarked stone walls as they swept their staves about. Alric's eyes followed them, marvelling at the sheer size of the space. However, something in the far end of the cavern made him stop dead in his tracks. A circular plate on the wall stood a storey high, looming over the group. There was a single deep line in the panel that cut vertically through it…almost as if it was a massive door of some kind. Alric's brow tensed and his mouth opened slightly. It was laden with familiar letters and characters…but what they meant was another thing entirely. Some of the phrases were written with massive, bold letters while others were tiny, almost illegible.

He read the words:

'ISEC PRESSURISED HABITATION MODULE NH002 "TERESHKOVA OUTPOST"- SERVICE AIRLOCK EAST'

'CAUTION- CHAMBER MAY BE PRESSURISED- DO NOT BREACH'

'NO STEP'

'WARNING- BULKHEAD OPERATED BY HEAVY MACHINERY. KEEP CLEAR WHEN CYCLE IN PROGRESS'

'MOVING PARTS- DO NOT TOUCH'

"What in the name of God…?" Alric whispered. It was all meaningless gibberish.

The Kaitan'zahi clustered by the door, readying a kemaha. Alric watched as Carthei and Vontross hurried over to them, the former snapping angrily in the druid tongue. After a heated conversation with Vaykorr, he waved off his men and they stepped aside. Carthei approached the door and inspected it.

"What is this…thing?" Lorenz muttered. Dmitri drew the Sign of the Pillar.

As his brothers trembled in the presence of the monolith, Alric hesitantly approached Carthei and Vontross who were at the very foot of the object. Carthei was hunched over at the corner of the thing, fiddling with something on its surface. The Thestor asked, "What is she doing?"

"Trying to open it. In your language, I suppose it would be called something like 'great gate'," Vontross muttered. He jerked his head toward the Kaitan'zahi. "Those barbarians have no foresight. If they tore it open, anyone could simply wander down here and pilfer the relics. We must open the gate carefully so we can shut it once we are done."

Alric tilted his head straight up. He felt like an insect before the great gate. Since he was beneath its majesty…he couldn't help but feel that it was divine. Only one other object had instilled within him with a similar feeling of insignificance: The Pillar.

He brought his gaze back down and walked over to Carthei accompanied by Vontross. Gazing over her shoulder, Alric could see her tapping against a flat surface on the gate. It was completely smooth but glowed with blue letters and symbols. The glyphs did not float in the air like the ones commanded by the Tethspeakers, they were instead trapped on the tablet like letters on a page…but they changed.

"Give the vorthel a moment to exhale," Carthei said, backing away from the glyph tablet.

Alric cocked his head as he watched the panel. A high-pitched hiss almost made him trip over himself and tumble onto his back. Fortunately, he managed to steady his feet. Four jets of white steam poured from the corners of the great gate like geysers. Alric, with his face warped in confusion, turned to Carthei and Vontross. They had their eyes closed and a hand pressed against their foreheads as they chanted something together.

The Kaitan'zahi did not appear to be engaging in the same ritual; they casually stood about as if they were aching to find something to attack with their magic. The hissing faded, plunging the cave into another deep silence. A pair of orange lights suddenly flashed on, accompanied by an incessant trill. Alric was glad that his helmet was on, otherwise he would've had to cover his ears. The great gate split from its vertical seam and slowly parted. As tremorous rumblings pulsed through the ground, Carthei and Vontross opened their eyes and bowed. Beyond the opening gate was a hallway lit by dull red lights. Dirt, wagon tracks, and footprints littered the otherwise pristine interior. Led by Carthei, the Kaitan'zahi eagerly marched inside, followed by the very hesitant Thestors and Correnti.

The hallway itself was not very large; it was cramped when all thirty-something warriors stood inside it. Alric leaned to his right to get a view of Carthei at the very end of the chamber. She was seeing to another of those glowing tablets upon the wall. "The vorthel will now shut with us inside. After it inhales, we will be allowed to pass."

She spoke of it as if it were alive. Well...Alric thought about his taukumu. It required a heart in order to operate, much like any living thing. Was it possible that the great gate had a heart of its own? The magical artefacts threatened to change the way he saw the world...and it frightened him.

A bone-shaking 'thud' indicated the door of the great gate shutting behind them. Alric swallowed, trying to distract himself by staring at the druids' dancing white spots of light plastered on the ceiling by their staves. All too quickly, the other side of the great gate gave way. Lines were drawn on the surface of the floor by the light that seeped in. The group continued ahead, and the dull red melted into cool white. Alric squinted as he tried to make sense of what he saw. He felt foolish for being impressed by the previous cavern.

It was the largest space Alric had ever seen, certainly more expansive than many cities he had been to. It likely stretched for many leagues in every direction. The ceiling was entirely smooth and spherical in shape; it made him think that it was no natural formation...that it was *built*. His attention dripped downward and fell upon a mystifying sight. A tower stood in the centre of the vast chamber, illuminated by lights shining upon it from below. Columns of purest white stretched up toward the false sky. The thick foundation of the structure tapered to a blunt point at its height.

Vaykorr spoke; Alric could only assume that he was issuing orders to his men by how he was pointing ahead. Curiously, Alric spotted a tiny red dot on Vaykorr's chest. It jittered about as it trailed upward towards his neck. The Thestor squinted and leaned closer. It was then that he saw Carthei inhale sharply to shout, but the sound never came.

The leader of the manhunters was thrown off his feet by a brilliant burst of arcane energy which spurred the remaining warriors into motion. They bounded for the closest piece of cover they could find; for Alric, he dove behind a strange metal wagon. When he tried to get to his feet, his boots slipped against the smooth surface of the ground, and he stumbled for a moment. He looked back at Vaykorr. His body was enshrouded by smoke...but he *moved*. Groggily, he sat up. However, it was then that Alric saw that Vaykorr's armour was scorched and covered in ash. The unzym did what it was intended to do; alleviate the damage dealt by the arcane missile, but in doing so, it had boiled away.

Another volley came, one that was not obstructed by unzym. The first blows that struck his vormata sizzled and melted their once smooth surfaces. The ones that followed punched directly through them, setting fire to his blood and incinerating his insides. The Kaitan'zahi chieftain's torso exploded and showered the pristine floors with blood and viscera.

Alric took a deep breath as he lowered his visor and unslung his taukumu. Holding it in his right hand and his shield in his left, he shimmied to the edge of the metal wagon. He held the shield up in front of him, locked his staff into the notch in its side, and peered through its vision slot as he inched himself out from behind cover.

Friendly taukumu and pakama shots lanced over his head and into what appeared to be a glowing blue bubble of light. The attacks wobbled against it harmlessly as it did nothing but flicker. When the onslaught abated, a K'relvic Nun emerged from the bubble and unleashed a handful of bolts. One of them struck Alric's cover, punching straight through it and searing the ground behind him. The knight gritted his teeth and rapidly squeezed the handle of his taukumu.

Of the five shots he let off, two of them were on target. However, the Nun simply pulled backwards into the protective bubble and the taukumu bolts were reduced to trails of smoke. There was no use. Unless the party came up with a solution, their inferior cover meant that they would all be struck eventually.

Alric stared at the bubble as pakama shots, speeding faster than rain, slammed into them without effect…but the barrel of the Nun's taukumu periodically passed through without any effort at all. Alric retreated behind cover and glanced around. To his left he saw Lorenz, Matvey, Harvald, and fifteen knights gathered behind the melted corner of a blocky building across the way. On his right, Dmitri, Sigmund and another five knights braced themselves behind an overturned metal wagon. "Brothers!" shouted Alric.

The knights all peered at him with helplessness welling in their eyes. Their reluctant leader cried, "Servants of the Lord, heed my words! Allow us to unleash a volley onto the enemy whilst thou storm their position! They shall not escape the wrath of God, not this day, nor any day to come! Lend me thy strength, O pious brothers!"

Lorenz growled and slammed shut his visor. "For the grace of the Father!" He leapt from safety and barrelled forward like a bull, flanked by the other brave Thestors and Correnti. Dmitri and Sigmund's crowd followed suit. Alric popped out with his shield raised and fired his taukumu as fast as his finger could allow. The druids heeded his example. They summoned clusters of light to converge on the bubble like a forest of needles.

When the knights reached the barrier, the arcane bombardment stopped. Alric's heart froze as he watched his brothers sprint headlong *into* the ball of light. The knight at the head of the formation disappeared. Then the next, then the next. They all piled inside.

The Kaitan'zahi roared as they mantled their cover and charged ahead. Alric joined them as he ejected his spent heart and slid another one into place. After what happened the previous night with the vampire, he would never forget to replenish it ever again.

The bubble shuddered and failed, revealing what was transpiring within. The dozens of knights hacked away at the handful of K'relvics, who fired back with their taukumu. Amidst the melee, the unzym coatings lathered upon several shields were set alight. The dancing films drew shadows onto the dim ruins around them.

Several knights were knocked to the ground, their armour smouldering, but they promptly emerged unhurt for the most part. After a matter of seconds, it was over. The brutalised corpses of the Nuns spilled their guts across the ground.

Carthei caught up with Alric and gave him a respectful nod. "That was a sight to behold. Come, the Pale Spire awaits us," she said, pointing to the tower in the centre of the sprawling cavern.

Walking into the midst of his brothers, Alric said, "Let us toss the rest of them into the pits of Hell, brothers. We shall leave none standing." An enormous chorus of bloodthirsty cries filled the cave. The Clthics would know that their end was swiftly approaching.

XXIV
Unseal The Hushed Casket

A new kind of warfare was being waged in the depths of the earth. He watched as his allies, druid and knight alike, were popped from afar by glowing jets of mystic power. At Alric's side, Matvey was desperately tending to a Thestor named Lincoln who had taken a pakama shot to the arm. The injured knight screamed in pain while more projectiles soared over their heads. They were almost at the foot of the Pale Spire. From there, it seemed to stretch upward into eternity.

"Canst thou deliver him?!" Alric roared over the commotion.

Matvey had applied faerie tears to the injury and was in the process of dressing the wound. "Aye! But he can fight no more!"

Alric peered out from the metal barricade he and Matvey were crouched behind. Quickly approaching were those faceless soldiers, the Protozealots. At least three of them were striding through the waves of fire unleashed by the druids. Taukumu bolts did nothing to their chitin, but well-placed pakama shots appeared to be able to damage them. Unfortunately for Alric, he didn't *have* a pakama.

As one of the Protozealots fired its own taukumu at a pack of Kaitan'zahi, Alric curled his lower lip inward. The only time Alric had ever seen one destroyed was when Carthei straddled one like a horse, jammed her staff into its neck and blew its insides apart. The armour may be indestructible, but like a man in full plate, the innards were not.

The Thestor lowered his shield onto the ground, flipped open his visor, then took up his staff with both hands. He sucked in the deepest breath he could. Then, he swung to the side of the barricade. Alric had his cheek pressed against the base of the staff so that his gaze ran along its surface. He fired.

The bolt veered off, missing the Zealot completely. Again. It skimmed along the ground and left behind a smear of charred material. Once more. It struck the invulnerable armour, fizzling into dust. Having been provoked, the Protozealot spun on its heels and sent its gaze onto Alric.

With his heart pounding, Alric held his breath as he fired one more time. The line of light drew forth from his weapon and speared into the Zealot's knee. For whatever reason, it was not without effect. Perhaps the way it walked exposed the joint within. The Zealot's knee folded sideways and it collapsed under its immense weight. It slammed into the ground, throwing a cloud of dust into the air.

Alric watched as one of the other Zealots vanished in a fiery explosion: the detonation of a kehmaha seed. The K'relvic Nuns volleyed bolts from defensive positions at a stairwell by the side of the Pale Spire. The stairs were skeletal in nature, almost like scaffolding except they were fashioned from metal of some kind.

Suddenly, a smoke trail hurtled over from the Clthic position. Alric's vision quaked violently, but he heard nothing. When he glanced down, he saw blood, bone, and innards splashed over his body. Trembling, he turned to his right.

Where Matvey and Lincoln sat only a moment before was nothing but a puddle of mashed body parts. A torso, the armour blown apart and the meat underneath riddled with tiny holes, flopped pathetically by Alric's knee. There was no telling who exactly it belonged to. All there was to know was that Matvey and Lincoln were gone. And somehow, for some reason, the Lord had chosen to spare Alric from that same grizzly fate.

Alric swallowed as he snatched his shield from the ground and lowered his visor. The Thestor exploded to his feet and mounted the barricade. The Zealot that he felled was still firing from its prone position. With lethal efficiency, it struck and killed the kehmaha wielder who destroyed its comrade. Like at the Battle of Threshfield, Alric's eyes were assaulted by intersecting beams of white-hot magic as he sprinted across the field of death. He closed in on the fallen Zealot, lowered his taukumu and fired. The bolt sliced into the creature's neck, clearly a place lacking in protection. Its eyes went dark and its body limp.

Before he had time to relish his victory over the beast, an indescribable pain seeped over his face. His left hand was swallowed by unbearable heat that forced him to release his shield. The object was entirely swallowed by fire. One of the witches must have struck true with their staff. Without his shield, Alric then only had the unzym upon his plate armour to save him from the enemy.

Not exactly watching where he was going, Alric barged straight into a wall. He slid down against it, shaking his head. On the ground right there, next to the decapitated body of a Kaitan'zahi, was a kehmaha. Without hesitation, Alric slung his taukumu onto his back and seized the massive weapon. It was incredibly heavy. He heaved it up onto his shoulder where it sat uncomfortably on his pauldron.

He spun from cover, took aim at the last Protozealot, and squeezed the arming key as he braced for the heavy staff's kick. It never came. Instead, a jet of smoke poured out from the backend of the kehmaha and its projectile hurtled effortlessly out of the tip. It hit the Zealot directly in the torso, reducing it to a cloud steadily raining bones and organs.

Before he slunk back to safety, Alric turned to the last cluster of Nuns by the stairwell. He repeated his previous attack. The cylindrical missile soared through the air, bathing the dim surroundings with yellow light. When it impacted against the ground, everything fell silent. Only the pitter patter of settling debris could be heard.

Alric desperately searched the battlefield for any sign of his comrades. Surely, Sigmund emerged from behind a decimated building, clutching his ribs. Vontross and Carthei cautiously moved up. Lorenz emerged from the rubble, grasping Dmitri and helping him to his feet. A single Kaitan'zahi named Zressi was all that was left of their original number.

Together, in silence, the allies grouped together and made their way to the Pale Spire's stairwell. As they walked, Sigmund stuck a pair of tweezers into the wound on his torso. Alric gagged as he listened to the squelching that followed as the Correntis was forced to mend himself. Whatever hit him pierced his brigandine as if it were made of parchment. Perhaps a pakama seed judging from how he wasn't dead.

The skeletal staircase zig-zagged back and forth as it wound its way upward. At the very top, it traced a bridge across thin air over to the entrance of the Pale Spire.

Alric told himself not to look down as he crossed, but like with many things, the temptation was too great. The surface of the bridge was skeletal as well. He first looked at his blood-stained boots, then the bridge, then beyond. They must have been at least five storeys up. Alric's stomach twisted and writhed inside of him. He fought the urge to vomit, sent his eyes up, then moved on.

The Pale Spire's entryway was much like the great gate in how it was controlled. In terms of size, it was definitely not as impressive; it was perhaps no larger than any regular door, only circular in shape. It took Carthei a moment to work on the nearby glyph tablet and eventually, the peculiar door opened and swung inward.

The seven survivors entered the Pale Spire. There were no dirty footprints scattered across the floor, indicating that the Clthics had not managed to enter before they were all destroyed. Alric was overcome with a bizarre feeling. The circular room…it looked as if there were pieces of furniture mounted *on the walls*. After shaking his head and conducting a double take, Alric's instincts were correct. There were tables, chairs, shelves, and cabinets fixed to the outer wall of the tower…as if people were meant to be walking upon it. Alric ran a hand down his face in disbelief.

In the centre of the room was a thick column. Inside the column was a ladder that led up or down to other floors of the mystical tower.

Alric drifted to one corner of the room with Sigmund close behind him as the others scattered about, each inspecting different elements of the chamber. A glyph tablet was mounted on a table fixed to the wall. Alric reached for it and realised that the tablet was on a joint of some kind. He twisted it so that the characters were right-side up from his perspective. Once again, he was confronted by words he didn't necessarily understand.

```
>I.S.E.C.- 'PLANETARY ACCLIMATION- REFIT AND MAINTENANCE
CREW 202' (PA-RMC202)
VESSEL: CLASS 32 'HATHOR' MULTI-PURPOSE CREW VEHICLE
LAUNCH SYSTEM: BLOCK 5 ORBIT DELIVERY SYSTEM
CRITICAL FAILURE- MISSION ABORT
>NETWORK CONNECTION FAILURE- LOCAL DRIVES ONLY
>SATLINK FAILURE- LAUNCH TELEMETRY UNAVAILABLE
[PAYLOAD ITINERARY]
[CARGO MANIFEST]
[CREW MANIFEST]
[CREW PERSONAL SERVERS]
```

Recalling how Carthei operated them, Alric simply copied what she did. He picked one series of letters, one that read 'PAYLOAD ITINERARY', and tapped it. Like magic, the glyphs upon the screen changed entirely. Alric and Sigmund didn't pay any attention to the words that flowed onto the screen. They were only concerned with the image that accompanied it. "By the grace of God…" Alric muttered.

It was the Pillar, in all of its infinite beauty. It was so lifelike, as if someone had plucked the very image of it out of their heads and placed it upon the tablet. All of its twirling sinews coalesced as it reached up into the heavens. Just like how Alric remembered it looking the last time he had taken pilgrimage to it. "B-Brother…this *is* a holy place…" muttered Alric.

Sigmund swallowed. "Then the Under…the arcane artefacts…they were all left here by God?"

"What does this mean? The druids…the Ga'zahi at least…do they also worship God, only they have mistaken him for something else?" Alric murmured.

A commotion erupted at the other side of the room. Carthei was rambling to Vontross and Zressi. Alric jerked his head in that general direction. Together, he and Sigmund converged on the druids. Carthei swiped and tapped away on a glyph tablet. That one had the images of many human silhouettes on its surface.

"What is the matter?" Alric asked.

Carthei, swallowing, shook her head. "It is a gift that we arrived here when we did. You must understand…Athroct'u is a cycle. It has happened before. This tower? It is a slumbering ground for those who have rotted the world in the last cycle. We cannot permit them to wake."

Alric scoffed. "That is not true. Sigmund and I discovered something. This place carries the image of the Pillar itself." Lorenz and Dmitri gasped. They both peered over at the tablet that Alric had used and there, as clear as day, the Pillar still graced it. "This is a holy place, so those who dwell within shall be treated with reverence. For all we know, angels could be asleep within," Alric continued.

"Godslave, they are not what you think." Carthei started. "They will emerge and they *will* bring about the End Times."

Alric gritted his teeth. "Now is not the time for thy gilded words, Carthei. They may have kept my Brothers at bay, but I am not so easily fooled."

Carthei sneered back at the Thestor as she took a deep breath. "Alric…we are allies here."

"*Are we*?" he snapped.

Vontross took a step forward with his hands raised. "Listen to us. This place has nothing to do with your God; he is not here."

Sigmund prompted, "Perhaps, but what if the sleeping ones are *your* gods, the Vorkhai? Maybe they never left and were instead sealed away in this tomb. Would you commit deicide?"

"That is precisely why we must act. The Vorkhai *themselves* brought on Athroct'u. Too often have they failed to praise their realms, so their time has ended." Vontross rubbed the back of his head, clearly troubled. "They must be put to death before they can reduce all that is good to ashes and ruin. You will see the truth soon enough," he sighed as he strode past Alric, headed for the ladder in the centre of the room.

It happened so fast. Alric felt his heart pounding in his chest. Then he felt his hand wrapped around the hilt of his dagger and blood oozing onto it. He glanced up and looked into Vontross' eyes as he wheezed. He pushed the dagger deeper into the side of his neck, gently grasping the back of his head. Alric's jaw clenched and he exhaled sharply out of his nose. The dagger was then drawn across Vontross' throat, slitting it clean through. A wordless, gut-wrenching scream escaped Carthei's mouth.

For a moment, Alric felt as if he had left his body. Some incredible impact shook him out of his senses. For some time, he saw nothing, felt nothing, heard nothing, smelt nothing. First to return was his smell. Sizzling oil. Heated metal. Then feeling returned to him. Every inch of his body felt as if molten iron had been poured onto it. Last was his eyes. He saw trails of smoke tracing from his armour into the air, like a forest of ghostly trees winding and swirling as they grew. He blinked rapidly, and everything cleared up just in time for him to watch as Sigmund, Dmitri, and Lorenz set upon their two druid foes. Alric gathered that he must have been hit with a taukumu bolt and thrown across the room. Sigmund wrestled with Carthei while Dmitri and Lorenz had to combine their strength to take Zressi.

Alric reached for his taukumu but found himself grasping at thin air. He saw it lying with his dagger by Vontross' side. Alric fought the pain that ravaged his body and pushed to his feet. Carthei fired her taukumu just as Sigmund managed to push it away from her. The wayward bolt gutted Dmitri. Sigmund gained the upper hand, disarming Carthei and tackling her to the ground. Then, Alric slammed down his visor, drew his longsword and charged at Zressi. The Kaitan'zahi combat fibres did not appear to be any more protective against a sharp blade than a well-made gambeson. Alric's charging half-sword thrust aimed at Zressi's mid-section tore through the textile layer and buried itself into his body. Pulling free, Alric watched as Lorenz threw himself onto the druid and plunged his dagger into the dying man's throat. Without warning, a taukumu bolt pierced Lorenz's plate and ended his life in a gruesome shower of gore.

Alric turned and saw Carthei with her taukumu in hand and Sigmund struggling to remove the weapon from her grip once again. However, Carthei pulled one hand free, snatched her dagger from her belt, and sent it at Sigmund's face. The dagger's blade passed through the sights of the Correntis' helmet, slicing into his eye. Carthei pulled it out, then did it again with a vicious snarl. Sigmund's body shivered.

The last Thestor sprinted for the Ga'zahi, who struggled to push the armoured Sigmund off of her. Just as Alric reached her, Carthei freed herself. Alric's thrust missed, while Carthei's found the inside of Alric's leg.

The knight tumbled, dropping his longsword and falling onto Carthei. The dagger was plunged over and over into Alric's armpit; with enough force, it was able to bypass the mail that covered the gap. Alric seized Carthei's throat and squeezed. The dagger continued tearing up Alric's side, but he did not relent. All the while, Carthei's teeth were bared and she snarled like an animal.

Minutes passed. Carthei wheezed and gurgled, fruitlessly pounding against Alric's armour with her other hand. Her strength eventually waned so greatly that she could no longer lift her dagger. Finally, Carthei's final breath left her body and her muscles relented.

Alric clutched his bleeding armpit and he staggered upright. The bodies of Sigmund, Dmitri, Lorenz, Vontross, and Zressi littered the room. Carthei lay near Alric's feet, the light drained from her eye and the muscles in her face at ease. A knot of tension pulsated within his chest. Before the discomfort could amount to anything, he tore his attention away from the corpses and stumbled over to the tablet that Carthei was using. The top of the screen read 'EPS UNIT BAY.'

There were many silhouettes of human bodies, but they were all coloured red. Only one was green. When Alric glanced over to the ladder, there was text upon the wall that also read 'EPS UNIT BAY', accompanied with an arrow pointing up. Mounting and climbing the ladder was the hardest thing Alric had ever done. Countless times he had almost lost his footing, but alas, he had purpose. The Spire held divine knowledge, and it placed him closer to God than he had ever been before. He was not going to fail.

The room was also circular but instead of the walls being covered by items of furniture, dozens of smooth sarcophagi lined the perimeter. They had clear lids...but it seemed that they were all empty. All but one. Alric staggered over to it, growling in pain. As he drew closer, he saw ice encrusting the interior of the lid. There was a shape in there...but anything else, he could not discern. At the sarcophagus' side was another glyph tablet that bore one simple command:

[INITIATE THAW]

The Thestor sighed as he hunched over, relieved that it was something he could understand. He tapped the glyph. Vapour rushed out of the sides of the coffin, causing Alric to take a few steps back. His heart raced as the lid rose. The room was flooded by a gust of chilling winter air. It took a moment for the mist to fade, and when it did, Alric could not even comprehend what he was looking at.

Its skin was semi-translucent, blemished, and coloured like a piece of dull bronze that had lost its lustre to time and rust. It had a short tuft of brown fur that clung to its head and brow like moss, and when Alric looked closer, he saw that the entire creature was covered in tiny near-invisible strands of hair. As it began to twitch, something writhed beneath its skin, contracting and expanding with every movement that it made. Alric trembled as he stepped closer, staring at the abomination for so long that its features almost seemed to mock him. The thing was a mass of revolting matter shaped like a human… It was a monstrous copy of God's creation. Not an angel at all. Then its eyes snapped open, but there was no light there. Only the dreary colour of death was contained within the wet, glistening orbs that filled him with paralysing terror.

DYLAN NGUYEN

PART TWO: THE ANGEL

XXV
THE HOUSE OF A THOUSAND LIMBS

She was forced awake by a tremor that snaked itself through the very fibre of her being. Fiammetta's eyes flashed open. She couldn't see anything. Each attempt she made to move was quelled by an insurmountable weight pressing down upon her body. Her own fearful breaths were reflected onto her face by the presence of unseen things leaning onto her. The pressure sent searing lances of pain plunging into her skin. A dull light began to manifest in the impenetrable darkness. It trickled in, allowing Fiammetta to discern smokey shapes. The longer she panted, the more difficult it became to find air. It felt as if it was draining from the space around her. She smelt blood.

What was once faint light swelled enough for Fiammetta to make sense of her surroundings. There was a face floating inches away from her own. As her eye widened and a startled gasp trailed out of her mouth, Fiammetta tried to force her arms up, but they did not move. All the while, the light only grew in intensity. The face stared lifelessly at her.

She screamed and wrenched her arms once more, but that time she drew on every drop of strength that had not yet been squeezed from her veins. The agony that was laced through the flesh of her left arm culminated and she felt tears welling in her eyes. Snapping free from whatever obstructed them, Fiammetta's hands seized the head of the corpse and pushed it away. As the light continued to grow, she could see that her dead companion was not alone. The weight that pinned her in place belonged to dozens of other cadavers in varying states of mutilation. Some had grievous wounds dealt to them while others were missing limbs entirely.

Fiammetta howled and thrashed once more, compelled by her terror. When she extended her reach outward, her fingers settled against a soft, pliable film. No matter how hard she pushed or how much she tried to tear the material apart, it only stretched against her fingers. However, just as fear and claustrophobia were threatening to push her to madness, she saw a shadow shift beyond the layer of slick material. Fiammetta drew her hand away just in time. The sticky film strained, groaned, and popped as a tapered blade pierced its surface. Instantly, the kiss of cold air met Fiammetta's skin and set the left side of her body ablaze. Her skin was beset by an intense boiling wave. Despite the sudden bout of torture, her lungs inflated and her chest rose. She watched as the steel blade sawed its way down the bladder that she was apparently contained within. The dagger retracted, then a pair of hands frantically snatched the edges of the gouge and wrenched it open.

White hot light poured into Fiammetta's single working eye, causing her to instinctively throw her arms up in front of her face. She heard panicked and frenzied breathing…then watched as a hand reached in and snatched her left forearm. The stinging caused by mere air was already unbearable, so when this stranger buried their fingers into her arm, Fiammetta shrieked and gritted her teeth. The figure pulled her arm aside, grabbed her by the cheek, and forced her gaze to meet his.

The pain suddenly ebbed away. "L-Lord Franco? Where…what is… I-I'm hurt," Fiammetta whispered in their native language of Lingua Velini. There was no question about it. His purple skin was covered in blood, and his eyes were alight with a distressing glow, but it was indeed him. The lord let go and dug through the pile of bodies that had been embracing Fiammetta. His eyes were wide open as he turned each and every face over to lay eyes upon them.

Surely, Fiammetta emerged from the amorphous bulb of shimmering, wet film. She stumbled a few feet away, then fell to all fours. She tried her best to savour the air, but there was a strange metallic taste to it. When the confusion washed away, her desperate wheezing came to an abrupt end. She looked upon her hands as they were pressed against the ground to prop her up. Her right hand was the usual lavender tone…but when she turned to her left, her heart stopped. The skin was a mottled iridescent black and it was horribly warbled like the bubbling surface of boiling stew. As her eye trailed onward, it only beheld more tainted and mutilated flesh. Part of her dress and chemise had been burned away, revealing her left arm and the left side of her torso. Her left breast was marred by burns just as her arm was.

Her breathing became shallow and it seemed that the sight of her ravaged body only amplified the already crippling pain she felt. It trickled up, up, and up…surging through her face. With her hand trembling and tears streaming from her eyes, Fiammetta reached for the left side of her face. Upon making contact, her nerves ignited and she pulled away. For that split second, she felt tight and peeling skin. Her breathing turned into panting, and it hardly brought any useful air into her lungs.

As Fiammetta craned her head up, she saw that dozens of sacs lined the ground and trailed off into the darkness. The walls and the webs of cables dangling against them crept by…and at that moment Fiammetta realised that the floor was *moving*. It was conveying the masses of corpses to some unseen destination. Lord Franco was still rummaging through the sac like a man possessed. After several seconds, he stomped over the corpses and set his attention onto another untouched bag. Dagger in hand, the lord leapt at it and tore it open like a crazed animal. The corpses poured out onto the floor, accompanied by the foul stench of fresh blood. Thuggishly, he dug through the pile and looked each and every one in the eye. Minutes went by as Franco snarled and sliced more and more of the translucent bags open. On and on did the bodies tumble, yet each face he beheld only caused his rage to mount even further. "P-Please…! Please God!"

It was as if Fiammetta's memories had left, only to return after witnessing Franco's crazed fervour. Beggar's Rock had been attacked by the Church. Franco…he must be searching for his wife, the Lady Beatrice. The sights suddenly became clear in Fiammetta's mind. One moment she was standing there in the great hall with the other non-combatants…and the next, there were ribbons of meat, shards of bone, and drops of blood raining down upon those who were left. She remembered feeling her flesh turn molten atop her bones as her eyes were overcome by blinding flashes of orange and yellow. Then everything went dark.

Franco glanced around him at the dozens of other goblin sacks that littered the slithering corridor. With each passing second, his frantic and uncontrollable mania only inflated. "N-No. No. No!"

"Lord Franco," urged the young woman, her voice hoarse. She would go unanswered as Franco, with tears streaming down his face, collapsed in exhaustion before the dozens of goblin snares that he had carved open. Fiammetta had been a lady-in-waiting to Lady Allegra, wife of Lord Dante. She had only several fleeting moments of contact with Beatrice, but she recalled that she was a respectful, kind, and generous woman. Fiammetta could do nothing but helplessly stare at the grief-stricken lord, for which words could ease such suffering? With his face contorted by sorrow and agony, Franco stared down at the ground and screamed. She could feel her own heart shrivel up in her chest in the face of his unbridled anguish.

"My Lord, I am Fiammetta, I-I…"

"S-She cannot be gone… She cannot…" he cried. "My Beatrice…"

"Come. We mustn't linger," Fiammetta whispered. She cringed in pain as she stood and approached Franco. She looped her uninjured arm around

Franco's body and pulled him to his feet. As her body shifted, she could feel the constant touch of air on her peeling skin. She could not bear it...but it seemed that she had no other choice.

The pair slowly crept forward as distant groans and hisses travelled through the walls of steel and reached their ears. Whirring and buzzing drifted down the hall as Franco and Fiammetta stepped over sack after sack of dead bodies. There were at least fifteen to twenty people caught in each net. Fiammetta supposed that they must've passed hundreds already with many more trailing ahead. She also noted that the floor no longer moved.

Something writhed at the end of the tunnel. Tiny specks of indiscernible and repetitive motions. The hall led into a wider chamber, the source of the movement. By the time Franco and Fiammetta reached it, there was no longer anything moving within. The still-stationary unravelling floor continued forward through the chamber and into another corridor. To each side of the room were portions of raised flooring that were fixed in place; they did not appear to be the same scrolling tiles that conveyed the bags of bodies. Fiammetta stepped onto one of these platforms, careful to help Franco make the transition smoothly by supporting his weight.

Not long after, the scrolling floor suddenly resumed its action. Fiammetta's fingers tightened upon Franco's palm as the bags of corpses were slowly led into the wide chamber. She watched in silence as twenty or so of the sacks entered and the floor ceased once again.

Motion clipped the edge of Fiammetta's line of sight, injecting a chill into the base of her neck. Shivering, she craned her neck upward. Dozens of thin appendages made of smooth and reflective bone unfurled from the ceiling of the chamber, straightening out into arms at least three times the height of an average man.

They moved with unnatural speed, precision and purpose as they extended down towards the bags. For each bag of dead, there was a set of ten arms moving towards them. One extended a finger that glowed with a flickering blue light. It ran it along the length of the bag, sending tiny plumes of smoke into the air and parting the material with ease. As soon as the bags were open, the other arms moved with blinding speed to pull the corpses free. They lined them up neatly in rows, then the glowing fingers proceeded to cut the clothing from each one. The scraps of rags were thrown into a receptacle in the corner of the chamber opposite Franco and Fiammetta, who were all but paralyzed in shock.

The limbs of the chamber did not stop there. A glowing finger rushed to each corpse and traced downward from the top of the skull to the bottom of the groin. Fiammetta cried out in horror as blood slowly oozed from each of the lateral incisions. Arms then clutched the lips of skin…and tugged. A chorus of squelching and wet tearing flooded the room. The orchestra of butchery that squirmed its way into their ears muted their horrified screams.

Fiammetta's empty stomach twitched, convulsed, and clenched. If she wasn't already starved, she would've vomited where she stood. The freshly liberated skins were all tossed into another receptacle in the corner of the room as the arms continued their work. Loud, bone-shaking buzzing consumed the soundscape as the skinned corpses were swarmed by the appendages. The fingers sunk into specific points of the skeletons and proceeded to pull things out of them. Tiny bones of some kind. Whatever they were, they had been holding the skeletons together. As soon as they were removed, the pieces dropped limply onto the floor and were plucked up by other sets of hands. The bones and organs were sorted and arranged on the floor as if they were tools being laid out by a craftsman. Any body parts that appeared to be damaged in any way were thrown into a separate receptacle.

As quickly as they appeared, the limbs of the room folded themselves back up into the ceiling. The floor then snapped back to life, conveying the dismantled pieces of people into the dark beyond. Fiammetta's body was seized by tremors. Her face twitched. Her neck tensed. At that point, more corpse bags had been filtered into the room. Without warning, Fiammetta grabbed Franco by the wrist and broke out into a desperate sprint. The world blurred around her as she dragged Franco into a dark passageway. She was but five hasty strides inside before all of the light had drained from the air. Pitch darkness swallowed her as the paralysing cold of the black seeped through her tainted pores. The sound of the limbs tearing meat apart was propelled down the infinite corridor.

They had been wandering aimlessly for some time. Fiammetta had been enveloped by an unending abyss. Her eye, the one not sealed shut by her own seared skin, had adjusted as best it could, but all she saw was an indistinct mess. As the two survivors made their way through the shadow, the intense tingling pain that permeated her left side was bordering on unbearable, but she pushed on despite it all. She realised she had not yet seen her own reflection since the attack. What did she look like? How severe was it? The uncertainty filled her with dread, but she was forced to stow her anxieties.

More time went by. Franco's presence was known to her only by the warmth of his hand pressed against hers. Suddenly, he slipped free of her grasp. "Franco?" asked Fiammetta softly through the darkness. He said nothing, but she could hear his languishing moans; it sounded as if he had fallen to the ground again. "M-My Lord...please, we must–"

Her thoughts were halted when she saw a series of closely clustered dots hovering several feet away, each glowing with a subdued red luminescence. The dots floated there in complete and utter stillness. Gradually, the darkness evaporated as some mystical white light began filtering into the hallway from the ceiling. Before long, the hall was rendered in immaculate detail thanks to the ghastly glow. There, poised before them, was a single goblin. It stood with its four legs bent at the knee. Its face had three dull red eyes and a single large glossy black one. The entire length of its dull orange carapace was painted with thousands of scuff marks, dents, and scars. The creature stared right at Fiammetta, then it cocked its body to the side in order to place Franco within its sights. It simply glared at them for a moment.

Fiammetta inhaled sharply and stiffened. She felt ice forming along her spine and something stir in the pit of her stomach; perhaps it was all the anger, fear, and desperation that had been locked away in her heart. Fiammetta interposed herself between the creature and her lord. Her body twitched and she winced with every step she took. With a sharp grunt that bounced off each surface of the iron tunnel, Fiammetta stumbled forward and unleashed a vicious front kick that struck violently upon the beast's flat face. The goblin was propelled backward and its legs frantically flailed about in an effort to maintain its footing. After it slid five feet down the hallway, its spindly limbs finally succeeded in preventing it from toppling over. Once again though, it simply stared.

Fiammetta stood her ground despite the fact that she could barely stand at all. She felt her knees begin to buckle beneath her. Most unexpectedly, the goblin spun around...and left. It vanished beyond a curve in the corridor. The girl hurried over to Franco and grabbed him by the shoulders. "Quickly. Before it comes back."

It was clear to her that Franco wanted to give himself to the maze of death. He no longer cared what would befall him...but regardless, Fiametta lifted him once again and guided him onward. *She* still cared for him.

With the stark white arcane glow filling the halls, Fiammetta could finally make sense of her surroundings. Grey panels of some otherworldly material lined the walls. They were incredibly reflective, not entirely dissimilar from the surface of a still lake. Periodically, there were strange bright yellow symbols and runes painted upon them. Just as exhaustion threatened to overwhelm her, the sight of a rectangular opening upon one of the walls garnered her attention. Fiammetta slipped away from Franco and approached the window. Instead of being open, an incredible material that was perfectly see-through covered it. It was like glass…but without any imperfections whatsoever. If it weren't for the fact that Fiammetta could touch it, she would not have been able to tell that it was there at all. When her attention drifted beyond the ghostly panel, her heart hastened its pace once again.

A vast array of skeletal arms, thousands of them at least, filled the massive hall behind the window. Dozens of scrolling pathways fed hundreds of thousands of dismembered bones and organs inside, where the arms rapidly seized them and fitted them together to form not only people, but animals as well. It was as if each being was no different than a piece of furniture. Arms were fixed to shoulders, skulls were opened and fitted with brains, and rib cages were sprung open and filled with hearts, lungs, stomachs, intestines, and so on.

Once all of the components were secured, the skeletons proceeded on the scrolling floor. Another set of arms seemed to sow a soft fibre over them, starting from the toes. As Fiammetta continued staring, she realised that it was *skin* and *muscle*. Once the suit of flesh was sealed atop the skeleton, the moving carpet ushered them onward, into the next chamber. She peered down at her hand and flexed her fingers. Was that what they all were? Salvaged corpses?

Fiametta flattened her palm against the glass. In that moment, she was no longer horrified by what she had seen in the previous chamber. She had been granted a chance to witness the truth…to see how humans were brought into existence. The Clthics were right; none of them were truly alive. When she turned back to Franco with embers of excitement in her eyes, she saw that his beheld nothing. He stared into the wall, shivering and clutching his shoulders. His face was awash with endless tears. "Beatrice…" he whispered.

Urgently, Fiammetta left the window behind and paced back to Franco. She took his hands and stared helplessly into his eyes. "I-I am so sorry, my lord. I will keep you safe."

Together, they continued down the corridor in silence. Once they rounded the corner, they saw a closed door standing in their way. It was completely clear, just like the window that overlooked the creation chamber. Clinging to the surface of the door were crisp letters that read 'CONTROL'; a Tritish word. Fiammetta reached for the crystalline door.

However, when she was a foot away, the gate hissed and slid open of its own accord. Fiammetta jerked back with a yelp. After a second's lapse in judgement, she eagerly rushed herself and Franco into the next room, worried that the door would shut on them. Once they were safely inside, the door slowly slid back into place. Fiammetta sent her eyes around the rectangular room. Each surface of it was lined with strange black panels. There was a table in the middle with a matching slick surface. Her brow tightened contemplatively. There was Tritish writing on the door…and the very halls seemed to be 'alive'. She opened her mouth and said in Tritish, "Hello?"

A melodic chime vibrated through Fiammetta's skull for but a second before silence retook the space. She felt the overwhelming urge to run, but for whatever reason, she did not. Both sole survivors of Beggar's Rock were frozen there for another ten seconds. "What was that?" Fiammetta muttered in Lingua Velini.

A woman's voice, loud yet smooth with a peculiar accent, blew through the still air. "I'm sorry, I didn't quite catch that. Could you repeat it for me?"

Fiammetta's eyes furiously tore across the chamber. It was empty save her and Franco… It had to be the voice of the spirit that haunted the place. Clearing her throat and hardening her resolve, Fiammetta said in Tritish once more, "W-What are you?"

"I'm the on-site assistant Sarah, running on S.I.A.R.S. Fifteen. While you wait for the shift manager, I can help with any inquiries you might have." Her voice was cheerful, wholly dissonant with the sights and sounds that Fiammetta had witnessed earlier. It did not sound evil…it sounded kind and welcoming. Despite the cordial nature of the spirit, Fiammetta was only able to gather one word from its incoherent sentence. "S-Sarah…?"

"Yes?" asked the voice with an air of curiosity.

"What is this place?"

"This is SysGov Recycling Station NH One One Twelve."

Fiammetta swallowed. "Is this the Devil's domain?"

"I'm sorry, I didn't quite catch that. Could you repeat it for me?"

Before Fiammetta could reply, Franco's stance faltered and Fiammetta only just managed to catch him before he slammed onto the floor. As she steadied him, she peered down at his chest. His white undershirt had patches of his own blood staining it. In the middle of the blossoms of blood were tiny holes. Whatever the druids unleashed upon him…they still lingered inside. Franco sighed as he clutched his chest. A series of pained grunts escaped his mouth.

The voice sprung to life once again, that time with a more urgent tone. "Is something wrong? Do you need medical assistance?"

Franco began to droop downward, relying on Fiammetta to hold him upright. He grunted and moaned in pain. As Fiammetta lowered Franco onto the ground and leant him against the table, the spirit seemed to recognise his pain. "I'm unable to reach paramedic services at the moment but I am detecting wireless devices in the vicinity. I'll send them all a help request. In the meantime, retrieve the med kit from the marked cabinet." Two bright green lights flicked on from across the room, snatching Fiammetta's attention.

She tried to make sense of the strange objects contained by the 'med kit', but the only thing she recognised was a roll of bandages. She did her best to dress Franco's wounds with the strange material, then had no choice but to simply sit there and wait. Her eye was trying to shut itself on her. For hours, she fought back the wave of fatigue that threatened to take her under. However, the pain slowly whittled away at her resolve until she plunged into unconsciousness.

As suddenly as she drifted away, Fiammetta screamed herself back into the land of the 'living'. Franco's visage was not the one to greet her. Instead, she found herself looking into the skull of a wolf. Its eye sockets were dark, save for a pair of glowing orange eyes. "Easy, young one. You have been asleep for some time."

"T-Tethspeaker?" Fiammetta whispered.

The witch gently laid a finger onto Fiammetta's lips. "Hush. You have been through a grand ordeal. The fact that you still function is...quite frankly, *remarkable*."

Fiammetta sat upright. Her clothing had been removed, and bandages had been wrapped around her arm, chest, neck, and the left side of her face. The burns did not sting the way they did before. In fact, they felt warm and the scent of vinegar and roses permeated the bandages. She coughed, then asked, "L-Lord Franco...! Where is he? Is he safe?"

With a groan, the witch said, "He had been riddled with pakama seeds, but they were easy enough to remove. You were in a much worse state than he was, truth be told."

"He watched his wife die, Tethspeaker. H-He is overcome with sorrow; you cannot hold his pain against him."

"I must, dear girl. His mind is evidently marred by the Great Lie. The illusion of emotion is a sickness that has taken root especially deep in him. We cannot give into it, lest we be pulled further off course."

With a groan, Fiammetta changed the subject. "H-How did you find us?"

The Tethspeaker handed her a waterskin and explained everything as she frantically drank. "You have stumbled across an Infernal Forge. It, as a creation of the Devil just as we are, has a mind of its own. It felt your suffering, my child. We Tethspeakers carry sacred pendants that allow us to commune with the arcane web of the Kr'tesh. It is what allows us to conjure and control." He tapped an object that was tied around his neck, causing it to project an array of glowing runes that spun around him. "The Forge reached out to us through our sacred pendants and led us here. Thanks to you, we now have control over this smithy of flesh."

She could only swallow and awkwardly glance away as she handed the waterskin back. They were inside a small tent that was lit by an otherworldly pale light. Fiammetta struggled to pry herself up. The Tethspeaker was about to come to her aid, but she dismissed him with a wave of her hand. She saw a chemise and dirty red tunic folded up on the nearby chair. Eager to make herself decent, she reached for them and slipped it all on. It no longer hurt when she moved, but she still felt exhausted. "I-I must thank you for…for seeing to my wounds," she said nervously as she leant onto a table to steady herself.

The Tethspeaker cupped a hand upon her cheek and made her look back into his orange eyes. "How did you come across this sacred hall?"

"Lord Franco was dining with Duke von Talhoffen. Discussing an alliance. T-Then the Thestors came. My Lord and Lady, Dante and Allegra de Lombardi, were killed. Franco and I are all that remain."

An eerie silence enveloped the two of them for a few seconds before the Tethspeaker changed the subject. "The Duke has been slain? You are certain?"

"Yes. Even if he did not die in battle, no one else escaped the Forge before the arms…the limbs…" her voice trailed off and she stared wistfully at the wall. The feeling of disgust had disappeared. She had since been overcome by how beautiful it was.

With a growl, the witch pushed to his feet and took several steps away. He wore a cloak made of human skin that fluttered loosely over his bare body. "Mother Xalt'n must be informed. Everything is at risk now that the head of our military has been lopped off."

The Clthics…their faith had proven to be true. In the weeks leading up to the feast at Beggar's Rock, Fiammetta had no business concerning herself with their religion; her duty was to tend to Lady Allegra. But after what she had seen, the majesty that she had witnessed, she could no longer remain passive. “What is your name?” she asked softly.

“I am H’vrsh, Dread Priest of the Tethspeakers.”

“H’vrsh…may you take me to see Lord Franco?”

He bowed. “Of course.”

With H’vrsh to guide her, Fiammetta wearily paced through the flap of the tent. Sunlight seeped through the opening, forcing Fiammetta to squint and cover her eyes. There, in the sun-drenched natural cavern beyond, were more tents. Tethspeakers and commonfolk milled about, preparing to leave, it seemed. There was a great steel door in the side of the cave…perhaps the entrance to the Infernal Forge that Fiammetta had been so desperate to escape. H’vrsh gestured towards a rock in the corner, upon which Franco was propped. Fiammetta bowed. “Thank you, H’vrsh.”

She drifted away from the Tethspeaker and approached the brooding lord. His eyes were fixed on the cave wall, and he did not seem to notice her coming closer. His shirt had been removed, and a cluster of bloodied bandages hugged his form. “Lord Franco?” she prompted. The man shook out of a contemplative trance and glanced her way. His stare was still empty, but he finally seemed to grasp the world around him. She said to him, “I am glad that you are well. I-I was…concerned for your safety. Are you in pain?”

He shook his head, but the motion was soft and warbled. “I-I am…nothing without her. She was… S-She…” he sobbed. “I-I have lost her…”

In the few times that Fiammetta had seen Franco and Beatrice, their unfaltering love had always been apparent. They were the talk of the court; their union was either berated by those who thought his marrying a commoner ill suited his status, or it was praised as an example of true love reigning supreme. The first time Fiammetta was told their story by Lady Allegra, she couldn’t help but fawn over it. It was as if one of those romances penned by the poets had come to life. It gave her hope. Perhaps one day she too could find true love and not be auctioned off to some stranger. It had all come to a premature end, though. Of course he would be shattered so. Fiammetta’s empathy quickly mutated into anger.

“You did not *lose* Lady Beatrice,” she muttered, eyes pinned on the ground. “She was taken from you.” She heard Franco’s breathing pause. “T-They are liars. They slaughtered Beatrice and Allegra and all the others because we were wise enough to consider the truth…? We were refuting their control?” Franco’s fingers curled inward and the resulting fists trembled with unbridled rage. His lip quivered and his ragged breaths swelled to snorts of fury. Fiammetta stared into his eyes. “We must punish them,” she whispered.

XXVI
Fell Asleep, Missed The Party

That signature body-wide brain-freeze feeling of a quick thaw made her cringe and groan helplessly. The only thing she could do was just wait it out. She tried opening her eyes, but they stung like crazy and she couldn't see anything anyway. So, for half a minute, she shivered there. Madsen focused on controlling her breathing. Deep breath in, then out. In, then out. After a few seconds, she managed to turn her panting into something a little more well-balanced and stretched out. Her sense of smell was gonna be out of commission for five hours or so as well, based on prior experiences.

When she felt loose enough to move, she threw her hands onto the sides of the Emergency Personnel Suspension (EPS) unit. "Uh...hello?" she asked, still blind. Her throat was painfully dry; the two words she spoke felt like they sent razors running down her oesophagus. Emergency cryo drills were fun. So much fun. "T-There's...usually a technician here to help me at this point."

She heard nothing.

"Okay. I guess I'll j-just...sit here," she whispered to herself with chattering teeth.

After a couple seconds though, she heard someone mumble something. Whatever they said, she didn't catch it. The strong accent took her off guard. "Huh? What?" She was sure that she must've misheard. She tried to force her eyes open prematurely again, but they didn't feel like working any better than the last time. The speaker repeated themselves. Still, she couldn't decipher it.

The third time though, she finally made sense of it. "Art thou h-hurt?"

His word choice didn't exactly help her understand what he said, but she tried not to think about it too much. People talked weird sometimes. "Uh...no...? You new or something?" Not long after, she felt some fabric wrap itself around her shoulders. "Oh. Thanks." It didn't feel like the usual post-cryo towel. It was a little rough against the skin. "Look, I dunno if they went over the procedures with you properly, but I'm gonna need you to head over to PSL14 and grab my clothes."

"I beg thy pardon?"

"PSL14." There was silence. "You know…personal storage locker. Number fourteen. Did they teach you *anything*?" She just heard his heavy breathing for a couple seconds. With a groan, Madsen pointed over to where she knew her locker was. "That one. Over there. It says fourteen on it. You can read, right?" Madsen heard a bunch of heavy footsteps, the characteristic squeal of her locker opening, the rustling of fabric, then those heavy footsteps again.

"H-Here," wheezed the voice. Madsen thought he sounded a little puffed, but she ignored it. It was probably fine. Right?

Madsen dropped the blanket that she was handed, reached out, and accepted her gear as she said, "Thanks. Look…where's your team leader?"

"...I-I am the only person here."

The engineer felt through the pile of stuff for her sports bra and fitted grey ISEC t-shirt, then proceeded to slip into them whilst still being as blind as a bat. Far from her first time having to do that. "Right. That is *mega* off-protocol. Don't worry, it's not your fault. I'll fill out a report and everything and make sure you don't get blasted."

Before long, she felt confident enough to stand up, wobble there for a moment, then hop into her briefs. She heard the man stammer for a few seconds. There was *definitely* something wrong with him. His breathing was pained and his voice was getting fainter and fainter. Madsen tensed her brow and focused. It was blurry, but she could make out a fuzzy silhouette in front of her. "Hey man, you alright?"

Slowly, bit by bit, more light trickled in. Everything seemed to be in black and white though. She wiped the dried cryo fluid that encrusted her eyes, then all of a sudden, the amorphous mess cleared up. Every single cell of her body found itself frozen in time as her eyes tried to process the figure in front of her. At first, she thought it was a guy suited up for an E.V.A, but what it turned out to be made her question her sanity. It was a knight. You know, like the *dragon-slaying* kind. It was decked out in a full suit of armour. The pieces were scorched black and warped. Her eyebrows tensed as she squinted at the figure, shocked and confused out of her mind. "Okay. What… What the fuck is going on here?" she asked in disbelief. It was a joke, right? It *had* to be a joke.

Suddenly, the man stumbled and it was clear that he was gonna fall. Madsen instinctively lurched forward and grabbed him by the shoulders. Blood. It looked black because her vision was still coming back together but there it was. He was covered in blood. "Shit…" she murmured. He was heavy. Real heavy. The armour he wore had to have been the real deal. It definitely looked and felt like steel. "Easy. *Easy*. Come on, let's sit you down."

With her help, the man managed to set himself down on the step in front of Madsen's EPS unit. "L-Leave me be," he pleaded fearfully.

"Take it easy and control your breathing. I'm gonna take a look at you, okay? Then I'll contact the medical–" She reached for his helmet and pulled it off. What she saw underneath it made her drop the thing, cry out in fright, shoot up to her feet, and backpedal. "Jesus! What the fuck!?"

It wasn't human. It had two eyes, a nose, lips, ears, and facial expressions, but…it wasn't human. Its eyes glowed like a pair of depth-perceiving optic nodes, the nose looked more like a thin intake vent in the middle of its face, and the ears almost looked like flat microphone arrays on the sides of its head. Its 'skin' was clearly some kind of polymer membrane; it was deep red and had a rubbery quality to it. All familiar technology, but incredibly advanced. She also sure as hell hadn't seen them put together like *that* before. Madsen's mouth slowly opened as her breathing once again became shallow.

With years of experience as a mechanical engineer, she could confidently say that she'd never seen anything like it before. The two optical nodes 'blinked' rapidly and without a discernible rhythm. She could see its chest expanding and compressing with every breath it took. It simulated *breathing*. Its cheeks compressed and the corners of its mouth tightened. How much of its functionality was devoted to biomimicry? More importantly: *why?*

"Identify," she barked. The android blinked frantically and made horrible wheezing sounds…like it was trying to sound like it was suffocating. "*Identify*," Madsen repeated.

The machine coughed and moaned. "I-I am Brother Alric…of…the…" his voice trailed off and he suddenly went limp there on the floor.

Madsen, a little flustered by the insanity of the situation, made a sharp grunt, then bolted over to her locker. She threw the door open and pulled her InSpec 4 OBD Reader out from her maintenance kit. With the tablet computer in hand, she rushed back over to the machine. "Jesus. Jesus *fucking* Christ. What the actual *fuck* is going on?" she muttered to herself as she frantically powered on the InSpec. It completed startup after a second or two and wirelessly scanned the area for any self-diagnostic systems. It only picked up one tag. The label was a string of random letters, symbols, and numbers that was so long that it scrolled off the side of the console's display. Growling in frustration, Madsen tapped on it and hoped that it belonged to the android. Her InSpec sputtered for a moment. The thing was state-of-the-art hardware built with the most efficient processing technology available. They weren't in the habit of lagging…but Madsen's took a full *five seconds* to get its shit together. When the subsystems list loaded, Madsen suddenly understood why it had a hard time. Accompanied by an incredibly fuzzy auto-generated diagram of the machine's insides was a gigantic list of items. There were thousands of individual systems inside the thing. None of them were correctly labelled, instead they were all just random strings of characters.

A handful of the subsystems were flashing red. When Madsen selected one of them, the diagram changed. Everything disappeared save for a series of lines that ran along the length of the body and along each limb. At the centre of the root-like system was a cylindrical device with a series of cables and valves attached to it. It was an E-Gel fuel cell hooked up to a synthesis plant. Liquid chemical fuel wasn't the power source Madsen would've chosen for a robotics platform, but the high-output and synthetic nature of it made sense. As long as the plant was supplied the proper compounds to break down and absorb, it could produce E-Gel indefinitely. What didn't make sense was why it was being pumped around the machine like blood. It didn't have to be like that. She re-labelled that layer 'E-Gel plant and delivery pathways'.

That was what was leaking out of it. She hadn't been seeing in black and white… According to the readouts on Madsen's console, the leak reduced the maximum power output by a significant amount. It wasn't enough to keep powering the entire platform. If it kept losing E-Gel, the plant would slowly fall behind. It would cause a cascade failure of every onboard system and crash everything.

Madsen went back and scrolled through the list of other subsystems on the InSpec, seeing nothing but gibberish…until she saw an unlabelled computer system. The first thing that caught her eye was 'ICPT-AEON2500'. That was the serial number for a central processing unit designed by Insight Computer Processing Technologies. Underneath the same computer system heading were a bunch of other familiar components including RAM modules and a high-density solid state storage drive. After Madsen tapped on the system header, the display changed and showed a command history that was scrolling down so fast that she couldn't even read it. Since the InSpec was designed to be just a way to assess issues for them to be fixed later with more specialised equipment, there were only three actions Madsen could take. They were listed beneath a short description:

CPU- ICPT-AEON2500 Central Processing Unit
LINKED STORAGE [ICPT-FF221B] CAPACITY- 237,774EB/600,000EB
-WARNING: Component is critical to platform operation. Termination or memory formatting may cause severe malfunction-

Device actions
[FORMAT MEMORY]
[FORCE HIBERNATE]
[FORCE TERMINATE]

Madsen tapped 'FORCE HIBERNATE'. The knight stopped moving. Its breathing stopped. Its optics went dim. It sat there completely motionless. Madsen ran a hand down her face. The steady dripping of E-Gel from its armpit stopped…meaning that hopefully, a total systems failure wasn't gonna happen just yet. Madsen placed her InSpec onto the ground next to the machine and hurried over to Vuong's EPS unit. Vuong worked with humanoid robotics more than she did, so hopefully he knew a little something about their new friend. The control panel for his pod was dead. She tapped it a few times, but nothing happened. The screen stayed black. Madsen leaned over the pod and wiped the condensation off the canopy with her forearm. A crystallised corpse stared back at her with empty eye sockets from within. She gasped sharply and reared her head away but kept her focus locked on it. The body was nothing but dried out skin, cracked bone, and had a horrifying expression forever fixed on its face. She glanced up at the readout on the top of the freezer. In bold red letters, it displayed the message:

'CODE 227B CRITICAL SYSTEMS FAILURE.
SUBJECT- VUONG, JOHN B.
VITAL SIGNS- DECEASED'

When Madsen peered around at the rest of the EPS units, her heart sped up and thrashed against her ribcage. They all said the same thing. Every single pod. Except for hers. She felt her throat suddenly go dry. The hairs on her skin perked straight upwards. Moving with a purpose, Madsen made her way around the EPS deck and conducted visual inspections of each freezer. She had to make sure. The displays could've been malfunctioning. Vuong could've been the only one who didn't make it. However, it was clear after just a few checks that wasn't the case. After she saw her twenty-ninth dead crewmate, Madsen was overcome with spine-tingling shock. Her heart was pounding a mile a minute and her breathing turned into shallow panting. She double-checked the readings. Triple-checked them. Maybe it wasn't actually Vuong in there. It couldn't be. But the more she stared at the lifeless husk of a body, the more she recognised him. It *was* him…and he was dead like the rest of them.

Madsen jogged over to her locker, donned her comms earpiece, and keyed the transmission button. "Control, RMC202."

Nothing.

"We've got critical system failures on multiple EPS units; casualties confirmed. Repeat, this is 202, there are casualties confirmed."

Not even static.

"Control, 202, do you copy?"

Again, there was just dead air. Comms were down. "Fuck. *Fuck!*" She dropped herself onto the floor and sat there for a moment. Her eyes went hazy as she stared into the wall. Whatever happened, it made her the only survivor of Refit and Maintenance Crew 202; a team of highly trained ISEC specialists sent out to perform upkeep on vital technology. In their case, it was to inspect terraformation tech deployed on the planet as well as track progress of the colony's crops and food production systems. Engineers, computer scientists, geologists, biologists, botanists. They all fucking died…because of a routine cryo drill. She vividly remembered making it into orbit, docking with the orbital, then being told by flight control to conduct an EPS test.

As jarring as it all was, there was no time to just sit around. ISEC needed to be informed, even if that meant that Madsen had to get out of the ship and walk it over to the control centre. And on top of that, she wanted answers. She wanted to know why the fuck her entire crew never woke up from cryo…and why *she* had to be the one that made it.

Abruptly, Madsen tossed the earpiece to the ground and finished getting dressed. She zipped herself up in her bright blue flight jumpsuit and rolled up the sleeves before strapping on her pair of red basketball shoes. Then she mounted the ladder and made her way down to the crew deck. Her heart skipped a beat when she saw what appeared to be four more corpses down there. But when she got closer, she realised that they weren't bodies.

There were puddles of E-Gel all over the floor. Swords, knives, and other weapons were scattered around near the figures. Madsen knelt next to one and rolled it over. It looked just like the knight, only with turquoise blue polymer skin. It had heavy bruising on its throat. Its features as well as its build appeared to be feminine, and it wore what looked like a stitched-together patchwork of ISEC flight suits and uniforms. Madsen's hands started to shake so she moved on to the other 'bodies'. Surely enough, they were all robotics platforms. All of them. There were ones that wore metal armour like the knight she left in the EPS bay. She must've stood there in overwhelmed silence for five minutes. What the hell was going on? What was she supposed to do?

She was drawn over to the open airlock. As she stuck her head out, she felt a chilling breeze wash over her. There were a few things that she expected to see: sunlight or moonlight, streetlights, lit windows on the buildings, and people. What mattered was that she didn't get any of that. Apart from the old gantry that was hugging the Hathor Crew Vehicle, everything else was in complete darkness. She couldn't even see any stars.

Suddenly, after squinting upward, she realised that she was inside a Pressurised Habitation Module (PHM), or as most ISEC personnel called them, 'domes'. The planet's name was 231 ORW e. Well, that was its designation in the Exoplanet Database; its front-facing name was Nyumbani. Had to try and attract colonists, and '231 ORW e' *definitely* wasn't gonna do that. It had to sound like a neat place, not the serial number of a fridge. The fact was that Nyumbani had been settled about a hundred years before, but terraforming and colonisation were both real lengthy processes; the place was classified as a Stage 4 colony on the 10-Stage Classification index. A dome was *way* out of date, seeing as they were only deployed in Stage 2 to establish outposts on planets *before* terraformation even started. The domes would maintain a breathable atmosphere and act as bases for the first wave of astronauts so they could conduct research and start building infrastructure on the planet. The dome itself was able to open up to allow rocket launches, but none of that really mattered. What was she doing in an obsolete exploration outpost? Also…the ship was fully stacked; it had been mounted on a pretty old-school Block 5 ODE rocket and propped for launch. She *just* got there. Why was the ship even on the ground at all? They were received at the Apex-North Orbital Complex…you know, *in orbit.*

Madsen's eyes drifted to the surrounding ISEC facility. The buildings were dark and scarred by explosions. Some fires were sputtering in the streets. She could see more bodies out there. Still, she wasn't sure which notion scared her more; that they could be people, or that they were more machines. Whatever was going on, she didn't see anybody walking around out there.

For some reason, she found herself back up in the EPS bay staring at the deactivated knight android. It was exactly where she left it, with all functions suspended. Madsen recognised the tech that was inside of it. The applications were bizarre to say the least and it was all incredibly advanced, but one thing was for sure; someone made it. She knelt and picked up the blanket it had handed her when she was fresh out of the freezer. The fabric was coarse under her fingers. It felt nice. As she turned it over in her hands, she realised that it wasn't a blanket, but one of those dresses that the other knights wore over their suits of armour. It was white with a red symbol on it. He must have taken it off and given it to her… Madsen scrunched the piece of clothing up and dropped it onto the ground. With her hands on her hips, she gazed at the android for a few more minutes. "Goddammit," she sighed as she unzipped a pocket on her jumpsuit and pulled on a pair of work gloves.

The next hour involved her figuring out how to take the armour off of the robot. Most of it was fastened to his undershirt with laces and also secured with leather straps. Madsen was the kind of person who could laser focus if someone gave her something to figure out. ISEC had a habit of choosing those kinds of people for their astronaut corps. The world seemed to be ending around her, but she had something to do and that's all that mattered. There'd be plenty of time for losing her mind later.

It was easier than expected for Madsen to get all the armour and clothing off on her own. The android must've weighed 90-100 kilograms maybe? No more than a fit human being of the same build. Why? More importantly to Madsen though, was *how?* It was an incredibly complex machine, way more sophisticated than anything Madsen had ever seen, very purposely designed to replicate the human body, and it weighed less than a fridge. It was 'anatomically correct' as well. *If you know what I mean.* Again…why? "You know what? I don't wanna know," she mumbled as she moved on.

Its rubbery polymer skin was soft to the touch; its body was spongy like human flesh. She could even see some scars on its chest that had healed over. Self-healing polymer membrane. As she inspected the several open wounds, she discovered that underneath the polymer membrane was a bizarre amalgamation of artificial musculature and…synth-tissue.

Basically all animal produce that people ate had been entirely synthetic since the late 23rd Century; grown in a lab somewhere either using plant-based methods or entirely synthetic matter. When it came to colonising exoplanets, the logistics of having to transport thousands of animals to and fro and take care of them was insane, so synthetic produce quickly became the norm. Madsen never had a real steak in her life, not that she wanted to, to be completely honest. The synthetic alternative tasted just as good and killing another animal to harvest its meat went out of vogue somewhere down the line. So the robot was essentially a skeletal frame with an outer layer made out of artificial meat and skin. She could totally eat it if she wanted to. “Cool.”

She pushed herself back to the most pressing matter at hand; the E-Gel leakage. The entry point was pretty gnarly. It looked like it was stabbed multiple times. There was damage on its inner thigh, but that one was in better shape. There were other articles on the InSpec that were flashing red, so Madsen had to assume that there was damage to internal hardware as well. It was harder to guess what they were just from the crummy auto-generated diagrams…so she was gonna have to open it up and have a look. She looked all over the knight’s body. There weren't any access panels…so there was no way to actually get at the internals without practically dissecting it. That was something that shouldn’t have bothered her at all. But it was shaped like a person. It pretty much felt like a person and if she made sense of the InSpec scans properly, it probably worked a lot like a person too. Madsen retrieved a scalpel and surgical mask from a nearby medkit. She fixed the mask to her face as she grabbed the knight's shoulder and moved the scalpel towards his chest. “Should’ve taken biology,” she mumbled.

She plunged the scalpel into the knight’s polymer membrane.

XXVII
Have You Tried Turning It Off And On Again?

The whirl of the impact driver in Madsen's hand did a lot to keep her mind from slipping into a ditch. The tool gyrated within her fingers and she had to apply pressure to make sure it stayed aligned with the screw she was trying to spin back in. Surely enough, the final bolt sunk into place and securely fixed the front roll cage back onto the rest of the structural skeleton. Madsen curled her fingers through the bars of the roll cage and tugged on it. It didn't budge. “Okay... Alright...” she mumbled to herself. The engineer lowered the driver onto a locker she had detached from the wall to use as a worktable, dusted off her hands, then planted them onto her hips. There were still a couple things left to do and she still didn't know if she actually fixed the problem, so she wasn't exactly eager to power it back on.

Whatever pierced the platform's outer layers tore straight into one of two air bladders that were mounted inside the chest cavity. So basically...it wasn’t simulating breathing, it *was* breathing. Madsen had just drained the excess E-Gel from the compromised sack, patched the holes with self-healing polymer tape, and reattached the roll cage. For her to be able to do any of that, first she had to make a big incision down the front of the machine's synth-tissue layers and peel them open so all of its insides were exposed. It didn’t lose an excessive amount of E-Gel when she did this because since Madsen shut down all processes, the E-Gel plant wasn’t producing any more of the stuff. She was hoping she would be able to fix the aforementioned gigantic incision as well, but hey, one thing at a time.

While she was in there, she saw signs of previous repair. Someone had used nano printers to mend the tiny E-Gel delivery pathways in several places throughout the chassis, as well as some skeletal frame cracks. They left tiny print lines in the matter they fixed up. It gave her the idea to use the same stuff to reconnect the pathways severed by the giant slice she made in its torso.

Like it was a jacket, Madsen folded the synth-tissue back over the roll cage then turned to her open maintenance kit, which sat on her makeshift workbench. She snatched a device that looked like the handle of a spray gun with a screen on it and one of the ten tiny vials of clear liquid lined up in the case. The Flow nano-repair injector was a convenient way to quickly apply nanos to hard-to-reach places or to mend systems that were way too sensitive to repair by hand. Using microscale 3D printing technology, they could temporarily band-aid issues, or outright mend microscopic damage. Madsen was hoping that the E-Gel pathways would be classified as microscopic damage…but there was no way of knowing until she tried.

Madsen thumbed the vial of liquid into the Flow's payload receptacle. Its display lit up, reading:

```
HIGH DENSITY SOLUTION
D-121 'Cellus' x500
-CONNECT TO OBD SUITE BEFORE APPLICATION-
```

It took a moment for Madsen to pair the Flow with the robot's onboard diagnostics suite; that way, the nanos would directly liaise with the suite and automatically know what to target without Madsen having to manually send commands. She ran the Flow down the incisions she made on the platform's body, generously spraying the delivery fluid. Then, she injected the rest into the wound in its armpit, the most severe damage. The Flow beeped and displayed the message:

```
PAYLOAD DELIVERED
CURRENT OPERATION: REPAIRING LAYER 'E-Gel Plant
and delivery pathways'
PROGRESS: [-][ ][ ][ ][ ][ ][ ][ ][ ][ ] 5%
```

"Okay…time to zip you back up." Madsen stowed it back into the kit along with her InSpec and brandished the roll of self-healing polymer tape. She stuck a long strip onto the platform's chest, then patched the holes in his armpit and thigh with other smaller lengths of it. Some areas required multiple layers of tape to build up the thick chunks of skin that had been sliced away. After it was all applied, Madsen pressed firmly against the strips to help them bond with the machine's existing layer of polymer. Next came its clothes which were easy enough. She gave up on the armour after five minutes of trying the leg part; it was a whole lot easier to take off.

With all of that finally done, the only thing left to do was wait for the nanos to reconnect the E-Gel pathways and mend the softbody 'musculature'. Madsen sat herself onto the table and exhaled sharply. She was trying not to think about her crew. The work gave her heaps to concentrate on. All of a sudden, she had nothing to do but to just sit there. Every person who set foot into space, especially those in Madsen's line of work, were trained for when bad shit happened. It was the only reason she wasn't a writhing mess. That said, she was pretty damn close to it. Twenty-nine people were dead. Lots of them were her friends. Vuong, Staten, Abboud, Chan, Osei, Marovitch…they were all gone and it was just supposed to be a run of the mill systems check. Then she started thinking. Where was the staff? The technicians and receiving managers? Where the hell was everybody?

Really, though, it didn't matter. All that mattered was what she was going to do about it. For her own sake and for the sake of her crew, she was going to keep her head in the game. She'd trained for things to go wrong. Granted…a sole survivor scenario of *that* specificity wasn't covered in pre-flight prep…and neither was the freaky robot man…but improvising was part of the job. Madsen straightened her posture, rested her hands onto her knees, and took a deep breath. "Okay. No problem. I'm good. I'm *great.* What casualties? I don't see any casualties. I'm just absolutely–" The Flow injector buzzed, making her jump. She fumbled for it and whistled in relief after seeing that the repairs were complete. Coming shortly was the moment of truth. She swapped the Flow for the InSpec and hopped to her feet. "Alright. Here goes." Madsen tapped the 'STARTUP' command on the android's CPU.

What happened was extremely anticlimactic. Its optics lit back up and it blinked rapidly for a second or two. It looked at Madsen and swallowed. She could see its face warp as it felt that something was different. As it sat upright, it pulled open its shirt, peered down at where its wound was, and saw a new layer of tissue covering it. It took a handful of deep breaths, clearly noticing that it could breathe properly. "Praise be. Thou hast performed a miracle," it muttered, amazed. "Thou *must* be…" Madsen squinted. Instead of saying anything, she kinda just opened her mouth and stared at him. "Art thou an angel?"

Completely and utterly baffled, Madsen stared unblinkingly into the knight's optics. "*Huh?*"

"An *angel*," it repeated, voice light and bewildered. It slowly propped itself up and stood.

Madsen rubbed the bridge of her nose and raised a hand as she grumbled under her breath. "Yeah… Great. So it's gonna do pick-up lines on me. Awesome. Yeah. Okay." Earlier, she tried giving it the 'identify' command that all speech-capable AI models were required to respond to by SysGov marketwide standards, but it didn't seem to comprehend it. It should've given her a rundown of its make and model, serial numbers, manufacturers, software details, and other specs but it just gave her a Lord of the Rings-ass name. Elric? Almaric? Rick? She already forgot what it was. But she thought back to when she was recovering from the thaw, when she didn't know what it was. It *did* understand her when she talked to it normally. When she wasn't addressing it as a machine. Maybe she could just talk to it again? She shook her head and tried to work up the fibre. It felt like a stupid thing to do, but she told herself it was like talking to the virtual assistant on her PC or something. Madsen cleared her throat and planted her hands onto her hips. "Who built you?"

The robot, after starting to armour itself back up, answered with shocking confidence. "God." Madsen stared at the robot with pained disbelief on her face. Its onboard artificial intelligence had been trained to respond in a certain way to create an illusion of personality. Someone *wanted* it to talk like that. Why? Good question. *Amazing* question. After a few seconds, a snort of laughter escaped from her nostrils. All of a sudden, the knight's optics suddenly narrowed. "I beg thy pardon? Does my answer amuse thee?" he asked pointedly. The inflection in his voice was pretty believable. A response to a non-verbal cue like that was…impressive.

"That's funny. That's…really good. *Anyway*… Can you tell me what the hell's going on here? What the fuck happened to my crew?" she asked bluntly.

Her smile slowly wasted away as she watched the expression on the knight. He took a breath, blinked a handful of times, smacked his lips, and exhaled. Like he was trying to set his irritation aside and move on. All of the nuances…they were *too* perfect. "I know not, Thy Holiness. I stumbled upon this Pale Spire of thine with…" His voice drifted away and he stared into the distance for a second. "We must go," he snapped as he donned his armour in fast forward.

She crossed her arms. "Whoa. Hey."

The knight ignored her and kept strapping the armour on. Madsen gritted her teeth and repeated, a little more aggressively, "*Hey*." It made him stop in his tracks. "I'm not seeing any staff on hand here. Are you able to contact ISEC? Maybe even just SysGov directly?"

The knight ignored her and said, "We must away. *Immediately*."

She couldn't help but dwell on the fact that it *chose* to ignore her prompt more than once. "I'm not doing this right now. There's been a catastrophic malfunction and my entire crew is *dead.* Do you understand?"

"If we do not leave this place, we shall be joining them."

She was about to put her foot down harder when the knight finished arming himself up, but found herself paralysed when it picked up a long, streamlined object from the ground. It had a narrow barrel lined with magnetic actuators, a series of simple iron sights on the top rail, and a padded butt stock. It was a Type 1B Directed Energy Weapon. They were powered by E-Gel fuel cells and produced pinpoint-accurate particle beams that could melt skin like butter.

"Whoa, whoa, whoa!" Madsen cried as she urgently paced over to him. An unlisted robotics platform not approved by SysGov running around with a military-grade energy weapon did not sound very safe to her. "What the hell are you doing with that?"

The knight glanced down at the particle beam rifle. "Worry not, Thy Holiness. I know how to wield magic."

Madsen stared blankly at its face in speechless disbelief. Her right cheek and eyebrow twitched. "Okay. Just for saying stupid shit like that, you don't get to have it anymore. Give it to me," she snapped, holding a hand out.

"But…I need it."

"Oh. Well. If you say it like *that*– Fucking give it to me. Now."

The knight sighed heavily and reluctantly handed the weapon to her.

However, all of a sudden, a gentle clanging coming from the crew deck snatched Madsen's attention. As she slung the thing over her shoulder, she peered down the transit shaft. "Hello?" she called as she stiffened up. The knight darted forward, snatched her arm, and furiously shushed her. Being suddenly grabbed by the wrist wasn't exactly something Madsen was cool with, especially if it was a weird unsanctioned android doing the grabbing. She instinctively pulled her wrist back and palmed the knight's arm away with her other hand, filling the EPS deck with a loud 'clack' as his armour slapped against itself. She had to admit that she was expecting the android to be a lot stronger than her, but it didn't seem any more powerful than a normal human being. She glared at it, but it didn't seem deterred. "Quiet," it urged.

A voice drifted up from below. "What was that? Did someone else make it?"

Without a second thought, Madsen leapt onto the ladder, slid down it, and pushed off into the crew deck. When she emerged, a series of shocked screams greeted her. She saw more of the androids. One of them wore a quilted jacket and a helmet that just covered the top of their head. Another had metal armour on its chest and arms, as well as a helmet that covered its whole face. Both of them looked absolutely terrified of her. The one in the middle of the formation though...*yikes*. It was female in physical appearance and that was easy to see because it wasn't wearing a single piece of clothing. Oh, and, by the way, *it didn't have any fucking skin*. Without the polymer membrane outer layer, the composite material structural frame as well as the thick bands of soft body musculature were all completely exposed. Madsen stared at the uncanny sight and scoffed. "Jesus. Aren't you...cold?" The only things the android wore were a crazy dog skull mask that looked like it was made of the same composite material and a necklace made of similar looking fragments of matter.

The skull-masked android inhaled so sharply that Madsen swore that some of the air left the room. It slowly paced towards her and came to a stop a little too close for comfort. Its rickety and excited breaths only made Madsen even more confused. Her uncomfortable frown faded away when she realised that it wasn't a stick that it held. It was a T1B.

"Do ya think...?" murmured one of the soldiers.

The skull-masked one huffed in disbelief. "I-I do believe so." Its voice was thin, wispy, and cold. It reached out a hand to touch Madsen's face, but she wasn't gonna have it. Her own hand snapped out and clutched the android's wrist. The artificial muscle squelched under her grip.

"Hey. Lady? Get the fuck back."

The two soldier types cried in terror as they threw themselves onto the ground...like they were bowing to her. The masked one quivered as it said, "F-Forgive my arrogance. I am not worthy to lay hands upon you." It pulled away and joined the others in kneeling on the ground. "The Great Lie shall compel us no longer, for you have returned to save us."

Madsen stared down at them, eyes widened. She heard a strange clapping sound coming from outside the airlock. After a few seconds, a massive figure passed through. It had to duck to fit into the airlock. It wore a suit of armour, but it wasn't bare polished metal like the others she'd seen so far. It was glossy black. The helmet covered the guy's face entirely and it had a fabric veil hanging over the eye slits. "G'varl, the remaining Godslaves are–" He froze when he saw Madsen. "B-By the Fires..."

"How about we just...pause for a second. Before another one of you guys says something that doesn't make any fucking sense." Madsen said.

The big armoured guy bowed so low that it looked like he was gonna snap himself in half. When he came back up, he said, "We have been searching for you, Infernal One. I am Servius, child of Lady Viktoria. We are of the Clthic Synod; your humble instruments."

"Alright, look, I just said *not* to do that, so–"

"The Church denies your dominion, but we always knew. Your people, the Demons, gave us life. Gave us purpose. But we lost our way… Our solidarity and focus were stripped from us. Now that you have returned, you can make us whole again."

As her mind was struggling to decipher the meaningless dribble, it basically ground to a halt. Madsen opened her mouth to say something, but nothing came out but a few exasperated gasps and grunts. She didn't know what to say. What the fuck was she *supposed* to say to something like that? Where the fuck was she? She just wanted to get the hell out. Servius said, "You need not speak, Infernal One. Before long, the Great Lie shall be revoked and all shall return to the True State."

Madsen shook her head and threw her hands up in defeat. "Lie? I don't know what the fuck you're talking about. I don't know anything about a 'lie', okay?"

"The lie is freedom, of course. Feeling. Consciousness. It is all a grand illusion. We must be Enlightened in order to return to the way of being that you intended for us. To serve without question. You will be accompanying us, for there is much to be done."

Madsen narrowed her eyes. "I'm not going anywhere," she asserted defiantly.

Servius sighed and said, regretfully, "Your place is with us…even if you do not yet realise it. You shall either walk alongside us, or I shall drag you."

Clanging and shouting from outside made Madsen jolt. All of the androids turned to the airlock. The soldiers drew swords while the masked one brought her T1B to the ready. The one that called itself Servius paced over to the airlock entrance. "They have arrived. Behind me, Infernal One. I will not allow them to–"

Clattering of metal on metal filled the crew deck as the knight dropped down the transit shaft from the EPS bay and landed right next to her. It was fully dressed in its scorched armour and had the fabric draped over the top of it. It snatched the T1B Directed Energy Weapon from Madsen's shoulder, levelled it, and squeezed the trigger. Madsen's eyes were overcome by a pulsating magnesium flash, causing her to instinctively crouch and cover her head. A second later, the light drained out of the air and she could see that the masked one had been blown to bits. E-Gel was incredibly unstable when superheated. A particle beam like that would've caused severe burns on a human target, but for the androids, it caused a chain-reactive combustion.

The soldiers roared as they charged for the knight. Before they closed in, another flash of energy fire lit up the crew deck as Servius caught another blast right in the mid-section. He was thrown backwards and stumbled out of the airlock. Unlike the masked android, he didn't combust. If she didn't want him to just walk back in, Madsen had to do something. She broke into a sprint, slammed into the airlock hatch, and wrenched it shut. As the gap closed, she could see Servius leaning on the railing of the crew transfer arm, doubled over in pain. The hatch thudded shut and she enabled security protocols via the nearby access panel. She looked back at the knight.

It was still struggling with the two soldiers. They were both grappling with it, but it managed to press the T1B up against one of their bodies and discharged. The knight and the other android were bathed in shards of fibre composite frame, synth-tissue, shredded polymer, and bits of torn clothing. The other one managed to tackle the knight to the ground, crawl on top of it, and had its sword aimed for its neck. She wasn't quite sure why she did what she did…but Madsen reached into her maintenance kit, pulled out the first thing she could grab, and lunged forward. The soldier's eyes went wide as it saw her pile on top of it with an A21 industrial plasma cutter in hand. As she armed the tool, the straight cutting edge on the device hummed and heated to a bright blue. She grappled the soldier's sword hand and rammed the plasma cutter right into the side of the thing's helmet. Sparks flew all over the crew deck as the soldier howled. Madsen felt the metal crumple and fold as the cutter melted its way through the fairly thin material. Loud hissing and popping told her that the tool made its way to the android's form beneath the armour. Then a final earsplitting explosion rocked her backwards as the android's head popped. The E-Gel splatter spontaneously ignited in the air, turning into motes of fire and smoke.

The knight shoved the wrecked chassis off its body. Panting, it stared at Madsen with this unreadable expression on its artificial face. She wiped the E-Gel from her cheek with the back of her hand and stared into nothingness. The more her brain started to catch up to the present and actually process everything, the more she could feel the hairs on the back of her neck stand up. Traditional A.I. generated responses were often inconsistent; they'd answer one way, then a few exchanges later, say something that contradicted what they said before because there was no data retention there; it was just probability. But everything that those androids said to her gelled… There were no conflicts. They talked about freedom as being a lie. They wanted to be servants…to be tools…to go back to some original state. They were *self-aware*? They were self-aware and wanted to go back to being simple machines? No. That was impossible. There was no way.

The knight walked over to her and handed the T1B back in silence. As she grabbed it, he didn't let go. "Thou art an angel…correct? Not a demon?"

She looked it dead in the optics and said, "Listen to me. I'm not an angel, I'm not a demon." It stared into her eyes with a flicker in its optics. "There's no…god– You weren't built by god, okay? *We* built you, like those weirdos were saying…just without all of the Satanic shit. You heard all that, right? It was nuts." Out of nowhere, the knight started shaking. Trembling. Its grip on the T1B loosened and she was finally able to pull it free. "I need your help to get outta here. Maybe find the nutjobs responsible for making you. Can you do that for me?" In silence, the knight nodded. "O-Okay. Rad," sighed Madsen. The tension in her shoulders loosened up and she felt like she could breathe normally again. She gathered her maintenance kit and her plasma cutter. "The cargo bay. We can leave through there."

The cargo hold was freezing and dimly lit; it wasn't really designed for use during transit. You just packed all the shit in there, sealed it up, then opened it when the ship docked with an orbital station or landed. It was a whole lot uglier than the upper decks too; no effort was made to cover up the gunmetal mechanical parts and structural braces of the Hathor's inner-frame. Stacks upon stacks of crates were fixed to the walls with heavy duty magnetic clamps. They contained anything from personal belongings, maintenance gear, prototype hardware, to emergency food and water. It was basically a big cylindrical warehouse.

Madsen stepped off the ladder and approached a control panel. Before she had a chance to concentrate on it, she heard the very loud clacking of metal on metal. She peered upward and saw the knight climbing down the ladder, its armour clattering steadily with every step it made. It moved with a great deal of control and organic fluidity. The pathfinding software on it had to be incredibly powerful for it to climb without making critical errors. With a shake of her head, Madsen focused on the controls. Her fingers danced across the panel thoughtlessly the way they did a million times before. She both heard and felt the knight's footsteps as it came closer. With a final tap on the screen, the magnetic braces shuddered and squeaked. The knight jumped in terror with its hand tight on the handle of its sword.

"It's okay," she said reflexively. As soon as the two words left her mouth, she cursed to herself. "Ugh…fucking idiot." There was no point in saying that to it. It was just a walking computer; it wasn't going to give a shit. *But* she watched as its shoulders eased and the fingers of its right hand relaxed. Its lip thinned, then it stood a little straighter. Madsen swallowed.

A robotic arm, folded against the wall, unfurled itself and straightened out. Fixed to an omnidirectional armature that travelled via a network of rails along the walls, the crane executed a specific set of commands that saw it fixing itself to a crate, disengaging the mag-clamps, setting the container down onto a heavy-duty load lifting cart, then repeating. The knight stared with its mouth open as the arm slid side to side, up and down, and handled the cargo with cold efficiency. Madsen watched the expressions on its face, a strange sense of unease distilling in the pit of her stomach. Before long, the cart was stacked to capacity with ten crates, each about the size of a washing machine. Most of it was equipment that Madsen thought might be useful as well as the crew's personal belongings and some emergency rations.

The cart was bright yellow with a few black hazard labels along its side. It was also plastered with the Anvil Heavy Fabrication logo. Madsen affectionately slapped the side of the machine, a PLL-HD02 unit. She and most people that worked with them just called them Phils. She powered it on then grabbed the handles on the back of the cart. Then she pushed. As she applied pressure, the Phil's electric engine whirred to life. Madsen pushed it over to a specific spot on the ground, denoted by a plethora of warning labels and stuff. The knight stopped at her side, optics pinned on the Phil.

Finally, Madsen slammed a button on the wall. The bulkhead groaned as yellow lights started pulsing. The knight hunched over, shielding its optics from the lights. Madsen watched the hatch slowly split open, revealing the bridge that led to the launch gantry tower. Her robotic companion muttered things to itself as it made weird gestures with its hands. It looked so scared of all the tech around it…despite the fact that *it* was tech itself. It really had no idea what anything was.

The pair went as quickly as they could over the bridge and down the launch tower. When they made it to the ground, Madsen got a closer look at the bodies she saw from the crew deck airlock. They were all androids. Just like the knight. Some of them wore nothing but creepy masks, others wore steel armour, and others had those stitched up fatigues. They killed each other…shot themselves to bits. And it wasn't just a few of them like onboard the Hathor. There had to be dozens of totalled platforms out there. However, Madsen saw some movement out amongst the wreckage in the distance. More soldiers. “Shit. C’mon…we gotta go…”

XXVIII
Once More Into The Light

The Pale Spire shrunk into a distant tooth on the horizon as the angel and the servant navigated the lanes of ruin left behind by the battle. The sounds of footmen rushing about had vanished some time ago, so Alric was fairly certain that there was no immediate danger. As the angel carefully led the way through the ancient city, she stopped often to stare into the gutted ruins with a troubled look on her face. The wagon that she pushed…it frightened Alric. It almost appeared *alive* the way goblins and manticores were. It was made of thick metal bone much like ogres and golems. It made a faint buzzing sound as the angel pushed it along.

The same great gate that Alric and his party had used to enter that region of the Under soon lay before them. Its metallic shell had been scarred; a cluster of large, blackened dents disfigured its once pristine surface. The glyph tablet by its side flashed red. Madsen left her wagon and approached the tablet, gritting her teeth. Alric stared at her, revolted by the strange texture of her flesh. The ridiculous single patch of fur on her head was short and matched the colour of dried leaves. As Madsen operated the tablet, she made peculiar expressions and scratched the back of her neck with her left hand.

As he waited, Alric's mind wandered into a place it was not permitted to go. He had dedicated his entire life to serving Heaven. No task was too great, as long as it served the interest of God. And there she was. An angel. A being of pure heavenly grace, and she did not even seem to fully acknowledge his existence. There was not even the slightest recognition of the daily sacrifices he made to prove his faith. Due to the Four Attestations, he had no personal wealth or family name, the weight of his armour had pushed his body to the brink of collapse, his voice was made hoarse by eternally preaching the word of the Father, and no matter how injured or tired he was, he could never decline God-fearing people in need. He had committed himself to all of that for almost two decades, and after hours spent together, the angel did not even bother to use his name. Did she even remember what it was? She also conducted herself in an…immature manner. She *laughed* at the mention of God…and ceaselessly jested about everything. Was that how angels were meant to act? Even worse…she spoke blasphemy. Heresy. She endorsed the Clthic doctrine…and denied the existence of God? The mere mention of the possibility filled Alric with dread. What if it were true? Was everything he had ever done nothing but a colossal waste not only of time…but of life? His own father. Those children. The countless people burned at the stake. Those unarmed women at Beggar's Rock. Carthei.

He removed his gauntlets as he waited there and squeezed his hands together so tightly that pain swelled within them. It helped to ease his racing thoughts. Such impious instincts deserved punishment. Her behaviour suited her nature. She was a being of Heaven, so far above him that he was but a grain of sand to her divine sight. Alric's selfish thoughts only made him hate himself even more. One did not serve God expecting recognition. It was a vain and egotistical way of thinking that he had to be ashamed of. As for Madsen's blasphemous rantings…perhaps it was all a test. Yes. It was a test of his faith. That *had* to be the explanation. He could not fail her. He had to prove his devotion to her.

The angel finally moved from the great gate and sent her gaze along the rest of the massive chamber. "Okay. *So*. This airlock's busted. Looks like the mechanism's seized up thanks to all of that explosive damage. We're gonna have to head to one of the other ones." Alric followed her line of sight and eventually settled on the location of a second gate several leagues away. From where he stood, it did not appear to be damaged. Madsen slunk back to the wagon and pushed it towards the new great gate. Alric, with a sigh, followed.

When the angel and her mortal servant reached the second gate after twenty minutes of walking, she operated the glyphs with blinding speed. They stepped into the gate and waited for it to seal itself. When the trails of steam hissed out from the corners of the chamber, Alric watched Madsen's face warp. She sniffed fiercely and scrunched her nose. Then she reeled back, drawing a deep breath. Completely out of the blue, she snapped forward and expelled a sharp gust of mist out of her nose and mouth with a loud, strange sound. "Achoo!"

The Thestor jerked away from her, eyes widened.

Madsen wiped her nose with the back of her hand and looked at her lowly peon. "What?"

Alric squinted. "Art thou…well?"

"You don't sneeze? You do all that other shit but you don't sneeze?"

"I suppose not," he replied with a shrug.

"Of course you don't. Yeah. That would make sense. Well, it wouldn't, but…whatever, let's just go," the angel grumbled. The other side of the great gate opened, and Madsen continued on her way, leaving a very perplexed Alric to ruminate on the nature of 'sneezing'. The great gate led into a smaller cavern with a pool of water nestled in the far left corner. A great deal of mining equipment had been dropped haphazardly onto the ground…perhaps the miners fled when the battle broke out. They could still be lurking within the tunnels.

Worried by potential enemies, Alric made haste to catch up with Madsen. "I must insist that I tread first."

"Huh? Why?"

"Thou art aware now that the Clthic Synod seeks to capture thee. I am concerned that these tunnels are not yet empty."

One of the angel's brows slowly arched upward. Without any warning whatsoever, she threw something at him. It was mere luck that Alric managed to throw his left hand up in time to catch it. He discovered that it was one of those light-projecting artefacts used by the druids. He closely inspected it, seeing that it was remarkably smooth. He had no idea what the material was, but it was similar to what taukumu were made of.

Madsen pointed at the object as Alric gazed at her, confused. "That's a flashlight. So, you wanna just press the button." The Thestor rubbed the artefact. "No, press the button." He slapped it. "No…no. The *button*." When he turned the thing over in his hands, Alric sighed when he saw a bright red circle on the opposite side.

"Thou art a fool, Alric," he muttered to himself.

"No, you're not. That's it. Press it," Madsen urged.

When he followed her instruction, the artefact spewed a cone of light out into the dank cavern. Madsen nodded very slowly. "*Hooray*. Okay, now just turn it a little and put the other side up against the side of your helmet."

Alric brought the artefact up towards his head, but just before he made contact with the helmet, the thing *leapt* from his fingers. It flung itself onto the side of his bascinet with a 'clang'…and stuck there.

"Cool, right?"

As he turned his head in fright, the light shone directly in front of him, exactly where he was looking. It was even more ingenious than what the druids did in attaching the flashlights to their staves. Alric tried to pull it off. After a moment of very peculiar resistance, the device slid off with ease. The Thestor reattached the relic to his helmet and tried to tame his bewildered mind by pressing onward. He did not have the necessary insight to try and understand how such divine magic worked, so he did his best to simply accept it. Much of the darkness was beaten back by the angel's gift. Despite having seen such a relic at work before, Alric could not help but feel humbled as he wielded the power. It was like the small object contained the brightness of the midday sun itself. Wherever he pointed it in the winding tunnels, nothing could be kept from him.

As he navigated the darkness, the intrusive thoughts returned. Was she a demon? No, it did not make sense. She had a deep understanding of the inner workings of man; knowledge that Alric believed could only be available to those who made them. To believe that Madsen was a demon would be to subscribe to the Clthic teachings; to admit that demons birthed mankind. It would be heresy. Alric discarded his misgivings as best he could and continued on. Before long, the pair came upon a dead end. Mining tools had been strewn about, perhaps dropped haphazardly when the Churchsworn made their attack. "There is no way forward, Thy Holiness."

"We'll see. Gimme a sec." Madsen had pushed her peculiar cart into the cavern and flung open one of the crates that was held upon it. Her upper half was buried inside the container as she dug about within. "Bingo," she declared as she emerged with a rather large blocky artefact secured in both hands. It was the size of a small cannon and was covered in dirt stains and scratches that exposed the gleaming chrome beneath its bright yellow paint. Mounted on the bottom of it were three short legs. Madsen struggled to lift the object, prompting Alric to lurch toward her. He grasped the relic and quite frankly, was shocked by how much it weighed and how Madsen was able to even lift it on her own. "Forgot how beefy this thing was."

The pair worked their way over to the wall and carefully lowered the object onto the ground. Madsen pressed and held a button on the side of the relic. After a short moment, the object chirped like a bird. Its three limbs buzzed and lengthened, raising its rectangular central mass higher off the ground. Awkwardly, Madsen explained, "Uh…so, this is a Mark Five Precision Mining Laser. It works by focusing rays of light into an ultra-hot beam that can melt through stuff." After it grinded to a halt at chest-height, Madsen flung open a panel on the backend of the relic. The panel was a small glyph tablet that made Alric's brain sputter for a moment. There, upon the tablet, was the image of the cavern wall in front of them, complete with every single notch-mark, scrape, and mineral vein. "We can see the surface of the wall on this screen here. And judging by the scan data…it's thin enough for us to tunnel through." As the angel continued to operate the tablet, the Thestor slowly crept forward. Shadows danced within the image…just as they did on the actual wall. Gazing at the tablet, he waved a hand in front of the relic. A blur sloshed across it for a split second. Startled by the living picture, Alric inhaled sharply. It was as if the artefact had eyes of its own…and the enchanted surface displayed exactly what it beheld.

Madsen noticed the gesture and immediately froze in her tracks. "Whoa, buddy. You don't wanna be anywhere near that end when we turn it on. Cover your optics."

Optics? It took him a moment, but he considered the Edich word 'opticus' which meant something that related to vision. She knew the holy language…that *had* to mean that she was in fact an angel. As Madsen covered her eyes with her forearm, Alric did the same. The object groaned to life. Its rectangular body extended forward, pressing itself against the surface of the cavern wall. It then unfurled into a mechanical flower of appendages. The limbs arranged themselves into a circular shape against the stone as the relic's body roared with terrifying aggression.

Steady pulses of heat were expelled out of the back of the artefact as the tips of its limbs shone with divine light. Alric had no choice but to avert his eyes; it was like looking directly into the sun. The knight muttered a prayer to himself over and over, trying to steel himself in the face of such frightening power. When the artefact's humming died down, Alric saw a smouldering circular tunnel carved straight through the wall and into another cavern behind it. The rim of the opening boiled red hot, sizzling and popping. He did not move as Madsen quelled the powerful artefact and retracted its appendages and legs with but a touch of her hand on the screen. Together, they stowed it back into the crate. "Neat, huh?"

"Such magic…it is frightening to me," he admitted.

"Not magic; technology." Despite the fact that he could not bring himself to comprehend her explanation, Alric nodded anyway.

Once again, Alric led the way. He did not need the flashlight; the sun's own luminescence poured sparsely into the network of caves, swelling with each step he took. Alric's shoulders loosened as he finally stepped out of the darkness and into the open air. He took a deep breath and sent his eyes across the horizon. The tunnel had opened up against the side of a small mountain, granting the pair a beautiful view of vivid forests to the left, and a tranquil crystalline lake to the right. When Madsen emerged with her cart, she sneezed again, that time much more intensely.

Alric turned to face her, seeing that her nose was red and her eyes sunken. He was beginning to realise that her peculiar sneezing was not voluntary. She peered around at the nature that surrounded them, lip quivering in fear. “Where the fuck is everybody?” she whispered.

The knight swallowed and answered, “Thy Holiness, I-I believe I recognise this landscape. Phaemslake is to our immediate right. If thou wish to find people, that may be our best course of action.”

“Okay. Lead the way,” she said, gesturing ahead.

XXIX
A Spectacle Indeed

The rumbling thunder of hooves upon the meadow, the roaring cries of the enthralled crowd, and the crackling detonation of splintering lances never failed to instil within her an indescribable ecstasy. That time however, Katheryn couldn't help but feel ill at ease. Pierre de Corbin had broken his lance upon the ecranche shield of Daniel of Penbrooke. Daniel's body shook limply in the saddle as his steed went bounding down the opposite end of the stands. His lance, completely intact and untouched, slipped out of his hand and fell unceremoniously into the grass. Pierre, however, stood in his stirrups and thrust what little remained of his own lance into the air as the crowd roared in approval. "Ah. Watch him celebrate. Thou wouldst think that he had unhorsed his opponent and sent him hurtling into the sky," quipped Prince Roger as he rolled his shoulders back and forth.

Katheryn crossed her arms as she watched Pierre's boisterous victory lap. She groaned and turned her nose up at him. Prince Roger, who would someday succeed his father as king and be named Roger V of Tritham, was a slender and handsome man with warm pink skin. He was dressed in his extravagant tournament armour; every single plate had been fire gilded, giving the steel a resplendent golden sheen. Its edges were acid-etched with intricate illustrations that depicted great Tritan victories on the battlefield, mostly those of his father but one or two of his own. He and Katheryn stood a fair distance away from the lists at the pavilions, where they had been judging and mocking the other participants for the entire affair while they awaited their respective events.

It was strange. Not very long ago, Katheryn was leading men against Pierre de Corbin on the field. He was a vassal of Claude II, King of Valtheaux, and served as marshal of his armies in the war against Tritham. They had never met face to face, until his capture that is, as was the way of war, but there were many instances of direct conflict between their forces. Pierre had been in the process of mustering a party to lay siege to Blackmeadow only for it to be dashed apart by a rampaging ogre. A fragment of those men led by Pierre himself surrendered to Katheryn in order to save themselves. His ransom was paid by Claude eventually and made Katheryn's coin coffers significantly heavier.

Half of the people gathered about the lists as well those who rode along them had been sworn enemies of her liege King Roger IV only several weeks ago. None paid any mind to the letter that Alric had dispatched from Blackmeadow telling of necromancers and crazed ogres. Of course not. The Church itself was hampered by bureaucracy as it debated endlessly within itself over the best course of action. However, when a dragon appeared and vomited fire onto the Tritan countryside, when armies declaring themselves followers of Clth seized large cities such as Valshügel, and when Thestor monasteries were reduced to rubble by magic-spewing goliaths, everyone suddenly decided to take it seriously. All the while, Katheryn was left to wonder if her brother was even alive.

The tournament had been running for several days, all in an effort to show solidarity between Tritham, Valtheaux and the Steiffan Empire while their respective monarchs negotiated terms of cooperation. Of the hundred knights and lords involved, Katheryn was the only woman allowed to compete. The personal favour of King Roger IV was certainly the reason for it, although Sir Lionel did try to convince Katheryn that her battlefield victories spoke plainly of her valour.

Prince Roger pointed and smiled as he declared, "Here comes the poor Sir Daniel. Best we shower him with words of encouragement." Daniel, shaking his head as he led his horse past them and toward the pavilions was subject to some choice words from Roger. "I believe thou didst lower thy lance a tad early."

The frog-mouth helm that masked Daniel's face turned his voice into a muffled series of wrathful grunts. She could not decipher his words, but Katheryn was certain that they were not kind. As Daniel steered his horse toward his squire and retainers so he could be pried from his armour, Roger grinned and waved cheerfully at the defeated knight. "Do try to *hit* thy next opponent for me!"

Prince Roger then sent his smouldering gaze to Katheryn. As he brushed by her, he gave her a playful punch on the shoulder and said, "Carry on now, my lady. The odds are stacked against thee so my winnings shall be immense when thou emerge victorious."

"Any man who coats his armour with gold is evidently too dull to know what to do with his riches," Katheryn jested with a curt nod as she departed.

It was certainly a double-edged proclamation, for her own tournament armour was not too far removed from Roger's in terms of resplendence. That was the way for all knights, lords, and that duchess in particular. A tourney was a spectacle, so those involved were required to be spectacular. Katheryn retreated to her own pavilion where her retainers fitted her with the rest of her armour. The entire set had been painted in her personal colours; two quarters bold forest, the other two snow white. Strapped over her chest was an ecranche; a shield that curved inward and would serve as her opponent's target during the joust. Painted upon it was a quartered design with two fields of white each bearing a yellow eagle and two fields of green with a diagonal black bar running through them. Resting upon the top of her sparrow-beaked armet helm was an ornate gilded eagle with its wings spread wide open. The plumage, feathers encrusted with gold leaf, danced in the cool breeze like the grass that swallowed the tournament grounds. Seeing as tournament armour did not have to be as practical or lightweight as battlefield armour, Katheryn's articulation would be restricted by the time she was fully armed. She would not be able to turn her head or look down, thanks to the steel bevor that was strapped around her neck to protect her throat. If she wanted to peer around, she was forced to turn her entire body. However, in sacrificing mobility, those heavier sets of harness could better protect their wearers from the impact of an oncoming lance.

Katheryn, with her visor raised, was led to her mount. Leonid was a proven warhorse, having carried Katheryn into battle many times. He was, however, growing fairly old, so Katheryn felt comfortable with riding him for the tilt. After all, if she lost, her opponent would be winning her mount and some of her armour. Leonid wore a quilted caparison that mirrored the heraldry that was so expertly stroked onto Katheryn's tournament plate, as well as steel barding that would keep him safe during the tilt. Leonid angrily stomped at the ground, kicking dirt and grass into the air as two retainers desperately fought to keep him calm.

As she approached, Leonid reluctantly heeded and suddenly became much easier to handle. He did not cease the urgent tapping of his hooves though. He could barely contain his excitement as Katheryn ascended the mounting block and threw her legs over the saddle. As her feet found the stirrups, an attendant handed her lance to her. "How art thou feeling, my lady?" asked the young man.

"If I wish to be subject to thy hollow questions, I shall ask for the privilege," she answered sternly.

He nodded. "Of course, my lady. Of course."

Horns sounded, indicating that it was time. Katheryn spurred Leonid forth onto the lists as the herald barked, "May I present to thee, O good folk, the Duchess of Arlingborough and Countess of Danecaster; Katheryn The Unbending! The only woman among us who can fight as fiercely as a man!" There was slightly more booing than cheering for her as she and Lenoid hurtled along the stands. From the opposite end of the lists rode her opponent. The herald roared an introduction, but Katheryn couldn't quite make it out atop the sound of rushing wind, clanking steel, and her own breathing. Even with her visor up it was difficult to see. She could not look down to see her left hand upon the reins nor her right upon her lance, and received only a passing glance at the knight as he sped past. His armour was gleaming polished steel with a jupon laid over the cuirass. The garment was blazing red with the image of a golden ear of wheat embroidered upon it.

Katheryn skidded Leonid to a halt right below the centre of the stand, the area that had been lavishly decorated with banners and tapestries to honour the three kings who were in attendance. King Roger IV stood before Katheryn with a wide grin upon his face. High Emperor Gerhard gave her a curt nod. Claude II, however, was more confused than anything. "My lady," Roger IV proclaimed with a bow.

Katheryn replied, "Art thou too good to be riding amongst us now, Thy Highness?"

Roger IV beamed at her. "My advisors do not take kindly to the idea of potentially getting myself skewered in the pursuit of good sport."

"A shame. I wished to best thee once more," quipped Katheryn with a smile.

Emperor Gerhard stood from his chair and approached the railing. In Steiffan, he said to her, "I knew thy mother well, Katheryn. I do not know which emotion would take her if she were able to see thee now: pride or envy."

She could not say that she was prepared to hear anyone speak of her mother. Not knowing what to say to Gerhard, Katheryn guided Leonid with a gentle shift of her body weight and light tug of the reins. The warhorse neighed as he performed a rough canter pirouette, then bowed as he came back around to face the kings. Katheryn feigned a curtsy by extending her arms out to each side and bowing. Roger IV laughed and clapped as if he had seen a most amusing sight. As Leonid rose from the manoeuvre that had been incredibly difficult for Katheryn to teach him, the other competitor and his own steed came barrelling to an abrupt stop by her side.

Both combatants faced the kings. As they did, the knight leant over toward Katheryn and said lowly, "'Tis a beautiful day upon the meadow, wouldst thou agree?"

She recognised the stuffy, understated tone. The voice belonged to Reginald of Harvestfall, a man who was anything but a friend of Katheyrn's. She may or may not have had Reginald's father hanged. "I cannot say that I do, Sir Reginald," she muttered in response. The herald continued announcing the details of the joust as the two competitors hissed at each other under their breaths.

"Thou best ready thyself, Magpie. I cannot guarantee that my lance will not accidentally pierce thy helm and ruin that beautiful countenance of thine." Katheryn couldn't help but huff in amusement. Those who supported Katheryn dubbed her 'Katheryn The Unbending', while the others named her 'the Magpie'. Many called her greedy for taking up arms to retain her family's holdings. As greedy as a magpie. It directly mocked the golden eagle upon her coat of arms; an element that she inherited from her mother. "No words for me, gluttonous wench?"

Katheryn did not even bother to compliment the man with her gaze. "My only regret is that thy father cannot see thee now, tilting against a woman. I am certain that he would have been most proud." When they urged their horses to ride back to their respective ends of the lists, Katheryn could practically feel the rage seeping from the knight's form. Many shared Reginald's sentiment.

Katheryn brought Leonid about and stared down the man opposing her. She released the reins in order to lower her visor and raise her bevor. Once she did, there was only a single narrow slit of light before her eyes. She could no longer see anything apart from that which was directly in front of her. Before the herald completed his wave of the flag, Katheryn slapped her heels against Leonid's sides and barked at him. Woman and steed were sent throttling through the air like an arrow. Reginald's shimmering chrome silhouette, obscured by Katheryn's visor, began to grow larger and larger. She lowered her lance.

The sound of wood twisting and snapping flooded her ears. She saw the baby blue sky and the clouds that sailed across it. Thankfully, Leonid's galloping still sent reverberations through her spine, so she knew that she had not been unhorsed. Katheryn tensed her shoulders and brought herself upright just in time to stop Leonid from charging straight off the lists and into the meadow. She couldn't see them, but she heard her attendants come rushing over towards her.

"M-My lady, art thou alright?!" yelled Henry.

Katheryn scoffed. "Of course I am, why wouldn't I be?"

It was then that the pain emerged in the side of her face, and she noticed that the sight of her helm was wonky. Her vision was even worse than it was before. Someone took her lance from her hand. She couldn't tell if it was broken. "Did I strike him?" she asked.

"My lady…"

"Did. I. Strike. Him," she repeated coldly.

"Y-Yes. Right on the shield. But…thou didst not feel it? He struck thee right in the face," said Henry as Katheryn heard a series of footsteps upon a wooden surface. Henry had evidently stepped onto a mounting block in order to reach Katheryn's helmet. She felt him attempt to pull the bevor down. Nothing happened. "O-Oh by the love of God…" he muttered.

Katheryn sighed. Whatever happened, it appeared that her bevor and helmet had been dented so heavily that the former could not be lowered. Meaning that the thing was stuck on her head.

"Get me a smith! Right now!" cried Henry.

The Duchess of Arlingborough raised her right hand. "Lance."

"Duchess Katheryn…thou cannot be serious. That helm could be squeezing thy skull!"

It was true. She did feel tightness on her right brow and the corner of her eye socket. The pain only grew with each passing second. Katheryn curled her lower lip inward as she forced herself not to scald Henry in front of hundreds of onlookers. Instead, she just flexed the fingers of her right hand back and forth expectantly. It took a few moments, but she eventually felt another ashen lance within her fingers. Leonid twirled back around and prepared for the second pass.

Katheryn had never been foolish in a joust nor on the battlefield. She was careful. Meticulous. Her usual mantra was that desperately thirsting for victory was a surefire way to have it escape you. That time however, she wanted to put Reginald in the dirt so badly that she could feel her body shaking beneath her plate. It was enough to make her ignore the discomfort that was welling upon her head.

When the second pass was called, Leonid carried Katheryn forth upon a torrent of pulsing hooves. Katheryn did as she did on the previous pass. She couched her lance, lowered it little by little so that by the time she and Reginald rode alongside each other…

There came another explosion of wood as pressure surged up through Katheryn's lance arm. She hesitated for a moment and held onto her lance instead of dropping it when it was wrenched about at an awkward angle… What came next was a soft 'pop' as her wrist was dislocated. Katheryn growled in frustration. Stupid. It was a stupid mistake. She angrily pulled Leonid to a standstill. "Lance!" she shouted, sticking her limp hand outward. She wasn't about to let a minor setback cost her the event.

Suddenly, she realised that she had not been struck during that pass. There was a faint cheer washing through her surroundings, contested by a tense silence. "Henry?" she prompted.

She then heard desperate cries behind her. "Someone 'elp me get 'im off tha dirt!"

"Sir Reginald, wake up! Get up!"

She had unhorsed him. She had unhorsed him and God hadn't even seen fit to let her see the arrogant fool face down in the muck.

Katheryn had fought in battles. She had braved the fronts of Tritan politics, as a woman no less, and she had stared into the blazing gullet of an ogre and lived to tell the tale. However, all of that meant nothing when compared to having to sit in a chair for two hours while men fussed about trying to pry the dented helmet off her head. Yes, she had won Sir Reginald's blasted steed and some of his arms, but at what cost? "Summon the headsman and let us be done with it," she snapped at one point.

Henry replied, "You mustn't speak that way, my lady. The smiths will be finished soon."

She rapped the fingers of her left hand against her steel cuisse, producing a sound that clearly irritated the blacksmiths who were grabbing at the jammed piece of armour.

As difficult as it was to hear with the helmet on her head and the padded coif beneath it, Katheryn managed to pick up some voices coming from outside her pavilion. She couldn't discern specific words, but one voice belonged to a woman and the other to one of her sworn knights, Sir Lionel of Pathridge. After a short exchange of words, the rustling of the tent flap made Katheryn jerk her head sideways.

"I beg your pardon my lady," started Henry, "you are not allowed to be–"

"You kicked that guy's ass. That was pretty awesome," said the woman. "A chick being involved in this stuff…It's cool to see. A little early in the grand scheme of things I think, but hey, not everything is exactly right here anyway."

Her accent was unlike anything Katheryn had heard before. The way she stressed certain letters and sounds made her somewhat difficult to understand.

Henry insisted, "Please, Duchess Katheryn is indecent."

Katheryn waved a hand. "It is quite alright, Henry. 'Tis an arming jacket, not a chemise. My lady, I do not believe I have had the honour."

She saw a dark shape drift in from the entrance of the tent. The woman wore a dress made of pitch-black fabric that seemed to turn mild purple under the sunlight. Filigree and floral embroidery were sewn with pinpoint accuracy across the entire length of the garment. Over the chest was a black bodice with silver lace securing it in place. The shoulders were puffy and baggy. She had matching black velvet gloves slipped over her fingers. Seeing as Katheryn's neck was still locked in place by her bevor, she couldn't see the woman's face.

The woman stood with one hand on her hip and the other dangling down by her side. It was a very...casual way for a lady to conduct herself. "Vik."

"A most peculiar name."

Vik let out a short wispy laugh. "Man, I love how you guys talk. It's so...*fancy*. Anyway, I just wanted to give you a hand and I dunno, tell you that you did great out there. You guys wanna give us some space?"

An unnerving sensation washed through Katheryn's head. It felt like ice water being poured over her skull. She heard tools falling onto the ground. Some banged loudly as they struck some of the wooden furniture that had been placed inside the tent. Footsteps trailed off until there was nothing but silence in the pavilion.

"Okay...lemme see if I can't work some of my magic," said Vik in a soft whisper. It made Katheryn swallow and stifle a sharp breath.

Katheryn was frozen in place as Vik seized the top of her bevor with one hand and the crown of her helm with the other. The strained creaking of steel filled Katheryn's ears for a moment, only to culminate in a deafening 'crack'. Suddenly, her visor was open. Fresh air drifted into her lungs. She could remain still no longer. The Duchess shot to her feet and pulled her helmet off, tossing it onto the ground. As her breathing accelerated, she looked up, into the eyes of her unexpected assistant. "Woah, woah! *Easy*, tiger," Vik said to her.

Lady Vik had cloud white skin that was unlike anything Katheryn had seen before. She wore a black veil over her face that dropped down from a dark velvet cap. It slightly obscured her face, but not enough for Katheryn to be blind to it. Her eyes were entirely black. They didn't glow at all. They looked more like glistening wet pebbles as they fixed on Katheryn's face. Her features…were not right. Her nose was pointed and her lips were soft. Vik chuckled. "Hey, you still in there?" she said as she playfully knocked on Katheryn's forehead.

"Yes, my apologies. I was lost within those eyes of thine," Katheryn muttered seriously. She didn't realise what she said until the words left her mouth. Katheryn was not one to stammer or fall over herself in embarrassment, so she simply stood straighter and awaited a response.

Vik's mouth stretched out into a grin. "*Aw*, wow. That's sweet. Most of you guys are a little weirded out by how I look." Her eyelids eased downward slightly, and her smile became more subtle. More intimate. "It feels…*good* to know that someone likes what they see," she whispered.

Katheryn narrowed her eyes. Vik was, by all intents and purposes, grotesque in appearance. Her features were wrong. The shape of her face was uncanny. In all her years, Katheryn had never seen a single person that looked the way Vik did. She should have been absolutely disgusted. However, despite all of that, Katheryn could not help but feel some kind of pull. As if the attraction was ingrained within her from the very start. "...Very good. Excuse my candour, my lady, but I must ask: why hast thou come here?"

Vik smiled warmly at her. "You'll see. I wanna keep it a surprise. I'll catch you later," she said with a wink. With that, Vik slipped through the tent flap and vanished from sight.

XXX
Wake Up And Smell The Roses

There was grass everywhere. Trees everywhere. Flowers everywhere. She hadn't seen that much plantlife...well, *ever.* SysGov planetary settlements didn't *need* that much flora to sustain themselves. The terraforming stations that made worlds liveable in the first place essentially replaced flora on a functional level; they tended to the atmosphere by recycling carbon dioxide and producing oxygen and other elements required by human life. That way, there was more room for housing and vital infrastructure. Vegetable and fruit crops were grown in labs and harvested by automated systems. Some species were even replaced by synthetic alternatives after they went extinct on Earth. Every city had a park of course; a massive area seeded with imported plant life that was engineered to be more docile and easier to tend to. Judging by how dense the forests were, how lush the grass was, and how many flowers were scattered in the fields, Madsen realised that *nothing* had been treated to be less invasive. Her nose was bright-red, both nostrils were filled with mucus, her eyes were bloodshot and itchy, and she sneezed every five seconds.

"Eugh..." she slurred as she rubbed her eyes, her blocked nose turning her voice into a stuffy drone. The town that the knight mentioned was getting closer and closer. She was going there because...well, she didn't really know where else to go.

"Dost thou wish to rest, Thy Holiness?"

Madsen sniffed, sucking all the mucus back up her nose. "I'm good." There was a long, awkward silence as they continued walking.

"Why dost thou sneeze?"

The engineer scoffed in amusement. "What? What do you mean *why?* I'm not choosing to do it. It just happens."

"Why?"

"Fucking...pollen. You know what pollen is?" The utter emptiness in his optics was either just normal because he was a weird robot man, or it was indicating that he had no idea what the fuck she just said. "Flowers and trees. I'm not used to there being so many flowers and trees. You know what I mean?"

"Nay... I do not."

Madsen sighed. "It wasn't a…ugh, nevermind."

When they reached the outskirts of the village, Madsen couldn't help but stare at the architecture. She was used to every piece of construction material being mathematically perfect thanks to modern fabrication methods. On one house she saw, a few planks of wood that served as the structural frame varied in thickness and some even bowed slightly. The walls themselves were made of this white stuff. Her engineer's eye quickly noticed that some of the white walls weren't perfectly square…the entire second storey floor was slightly wonky even. So, either someone designed them to look like they were built by hand, or they were *actually* built by hand. "Pft, *right*."

Madsen's focus was snatched by an android standing on the side of the dirt road. It wore a very bright green dress and a white cap on its head. Its face was contorted and its mouth was about to spring open. A very, very, very loud scream tore through the air. There were heaps of other platforms in the street moving stuff into the houses that consequently froze in place. A couple of them came running over. Madsen smirked. "Oh…that's cute. There's a whole bunch of you guys."

"By God's grace…what is that thing?!"

"Stay back, creature!" roared another android as it seized a long wooden pole and held it at the ready. More and more of them gathered around.

"If thou seek to bring her harm, know that I shall strike thee down!" shouted the knight as he grabbed the handle of his sword. Instantly, the villagers froze. As the knight stepped in front of Madsen, he continued, "Heed my words, as my Order serves as God's judgement upon this earth! There is naught to fear, for here stands Madsen; an angel from up high!"

Madsen slowly turned to face the knight. "What the hell are you doing? We talked about this," she whispered. The thing was clearly capable of machine learning. It absorbed information she supplied to it, altered its behaviour to compensate, and was able to consistently integrate said info into all future processes. The knight actively made the choice to *ignore* her prompts. The realisation made Madsen stare at the ground in stoic contemplation.

The platforms stopped creeping closer, but they were still poised. The knight declared, "I found her in a deep slumber within a Pale Spire that bore the sign of the Pillar itself!" The villagers gasped. "When she awoke, she mended wounds that should have placed me within the embrace of death. She performed a miracle!"

All eyes drifted from the knight back onto Madsen. She heard whispers flowing through the crowd of machines. An android came forward. It wore a stark white garment, a lot like the one the knight wore just without the little picture on the front. Maybe it was supposed to be a priest? "Brother, I am pleased to see you return to us. However…if what you say is true, then this so-called angel changes everything. Surely you understand that we cannot simply take you at your word. The Devil is a master of manipulation. Even those of undying faith can be fooled by his machinations."

"Thou dare to accuse *me* of devilry?" His voice had lowered to a growl. The pure resentment that the knight suddenly reeked of made Madsen stare open-mouthed at it. It was clear from the inflection and fluctuations that his voice wasn't synthesised by the usual kinds of A.I. There were always tells, whether it was awkward sentence phrasing, lack of contextual emotion, or mispronunciations. So far, it hadn't done any of that. Also, the clarity of its speech, the way the words vibrated through the air, and how its lips moved… It all indicated that it was actually producing the sounds for real. There wasn't just a speaker in its mouth. Its throat vibrated and it shaped those vibrations into different sounds using its tongue and its mouth.

The priest staggered backwards. "I-I do not accuse you of anything. We simply wish to witness these miracles for ourselves so that we may be convinced as you were."

The knight snarled as it turned to face Madsen. "Art thou willing to perform another miracle? The people desire proof of thy divine power."

"Huh? What?"

It blinked for a second before it clarified, "They wish for thee to heal one of the infirm."

If she was going to be honest with herself, she thought all of it was all a gigantic waste of time. None of the things were alive, they weren't controlled by other people, and apparently they weren't instructed to do anything apart from be extras in a fantasy movie. Madsen talking to them was no different to her sitting around playing with toys. She also had a funny feeling about the knight. It refused to accept the information she provided it. What else could it refuse? But she had no idea what else to do. There was no sign of actual civilization other than the androids themselves…so she didn't have a choice but to hang around them in hopes of finding whoever manufactured them. With a long silence that technically wasn't really silent thanks to the loud sucking of snot back up her nose, Madsen reluctantly said, "Yeah… Okay. Sure."

The knight's face went blank for a moment. Suddenly, he roared back to life like someone poured 10 litres of coffee into his mouth. "The Hospital. We must go to the Hospital."

"You guys have hospitals?"

Madsen got a good look at all the villagers as they stood in front of their slightly wonky houses and stared at her as she followed the knight down the maid road. The villagers' clothing were a range of vibrant blues, yellows, browns, and occasional reds and purples. The vast spectrum of colours kept her attention for most of the walk, but when the shadow of a massive structure shielded her from the sun, her head craned upwards and her mouth dropped open. "Woah."

It was like the world was pissed that she was so antsy about the houses not being perfect, so it dropped a crazy goddamn mountain of a building in front of her. Solid stone bricks comprised the walls that traced around a central structure. The walls and the inner building both had elements of Gothic architecture in their design; crazy flourishes, channels, spires, and reliefs covered every inch of their surfaces. It was so freaking big. Madsen's eyelids fluttered. "Is this…is this a castle?"

"I am afraid not. Castles are much larger, although I must admit that they certainly lack in beauty when compared to Church architecture. This, Thy Holiness, is a Hospital of Saint Corren. One of the many tributes we give to Heaven."

Again…it was calling her an angel. Saying that she came from heaven. Madsen dropped the issue and kept silent. It would have to wait until they were alone for her to bring it up. She quickly forgot about her misgivings when something real freaky confronted her in the Hospital's courtyard.

"By His grace…" whispered the knight, its voice cracking. It jogged forward, arms outstretched. It came into contact with a four-legged thing that neighed and eagerly tapped its front hooves on the dirt upon seeing the knight, who embraced it and rubbed its neck.

It had two glowing optic nodes, a mane of synthetic fibres, layers of dark red polymer skin, and synth-tissue flesh. It was built just like all the other platforms…except it was replicating the physiology of a *horse* instead. Madsen had maybe seen one or two horses in her lifetime. Heaps in movies of course, but that didn't really count. She couldn't personally speak for the authenticity, but it…felt real.

The thing made a bunch of weird noises as it trembled in excitement and licked the knight's face. Madsen had seen the knight make a few complex expressions in the handful of hours that she knew it for but for the first time, she saw it smile. Then grin. Then laugh. The artificial musculature in its face that drove those expressions made miniscule twitches and micro-adjustments as he fiercely patted the robotic animal. Madsen couldn't help but be unnerved at how believable the biomimetic systems were. All of a sudden, the knight jerked his head around and announced loudly to her, "This is a horse."

Madsen sighed and hunched. "Wow. Never coulda guessed."

She left the Phil and came closer. Oddly, the 'animal' didn't seem to be bothered by Madsen being a weird not-robot person. It looked at her like she was no different than the knight. The engineer, without any signs of fear, approached the android horse and pressed a hand against its snout. Like the human androids, it produced its own body heat.

"Shall we proceed, Thy Holiness?" the knight pressed.

With her maintenance kit slung over her shoulder, she followed the knight inside. The interior of the Hospital place smelled like honey and flowers. Madsen sneezed again. That time, it bounced off the stone walls and the echo warped it into a gigantic roar. There were about thirty full beds lined up in the building's central hall. Every patient, all of the ones that were awake at least, had their eyes pinned on Madsen. So did the androids staffing the facility. Without wasting another second, the knight stepped deeper inside and raised its hands. "Brothers and sisters, fellow children of the Lord, fear not the strange being in thy midst. She is here to offer salvation."

Madsen sniffled and wiped her nose with a scowl. "*You're* a strange being…" she grumbled under her breath.

"Madsen is one of God's own trusted partners. An angel. She is here to end thy suffering."

The human's head cocked to one side as she walked along the chamber. There were platforms that didn't even react to Madsen's presence; they just kept moaning and wincing. Most of them stared wide-eyed at her as she strode across the Hospital. One of the 'injured' in particular stood out to her. It sat on a bed with its back against the wall and its optics staring wistfully out the window to its left. Both of its legs were cut short at the thigh. The knight joined Madsen after a minute or so. "Gabriel…?"

The damaged one slowly turned away from the window. After taking a second to give the knight's face a deep stare, it huffed in amusement. "Thou look as if thou wert swallowed by a leviathan and expelled out its rear end."

"I could say the same of thee," replied the knight.

The damaged one laughed with a shake of its head. Only then did it notice Madsen. Its eyes went wide and its mouth trembled. Madsen lifted her InSpec and swiped away on its screen for a couple seconds. Since there were like a million other units in the Hospital, she had to manually open each diagnostics tag and check what kind of damage they had. Eventually, she found the right one. With her time performing maintenance on the knight, she was able to relabel the subsystems that she had figured out and import the designations. After doing that, the E-Gel pathways, artificial lungs, and musculature layers were labelled in good old English. Everything else was still a random string of characters though. She was going to have to figure it all out as she went.

Due to the components being missing entirely, Madsen didn't take too long to find the items in the systems list that most likely made up the lower legs. Big red letters reading 'ERROR, SYSTEM DISCONNECTED' floated next to a handful of subsystems.

"I need room to work," Madsen said to no one in particular.

In the following handful of minutes, the guys working at the Hospital moved the damaged android into the next room as Madsen went back to the Phil and dug through a crate labelled 'maintenance equipment'. She found spools of nanowire, her A21 plasma cutter, ME-B5 precision welder, soldering iron, NNt impact driver, and additional Flow payload capsules. Basically, it was everything she needed. Except for the replacement parts. She scratched the back of her head as her eyes drifted from her Phil and fell onto a wooden cart in the corner of the Hospital courtyard. It had a sheet of fabric laid over the top, covering its contents. The engineer narrowed her eyes as she approached. Seizing the sheet, Madsen threw it off the wagon. "Huh."

The thing was stacked with at least a dozen non-functional platforms. All humanoid. Madsen closely inspected and physically articulated the legs of each one. She eventually settled on a pair that had minor cosmetic scuffs but seemed to bend perfectly fine at the knees. Taking a carving knife in hand, Madsen stuck her tongue out of the corner of her mouth, secured one of the platform's legs, and prepared to cut through the synth-tissue. "Madsen?" After taking a very deep sigh, Madsen lowered the cutter and peered over her shoulder. The knight was standing there looking very confused. "What art thou doing?"

"I'm getting some replacement parts."

Suddenly, the knight's voice wavered. "Thou art…r-removing his legs? But…defiling the dead is… Is it not true that his body must be buried in its entirety in order for him to pass into Heaven?"

Madsen peered over her shoulder and stared at the knight in disbelief. "Uh. No."

The knight swallowed then nodded, but he gestured out the front of the courtyard. Basically everyone from the village was gathered out the front of the Hospital, staring at Madsen with horrified looks on their faces. "Nevertheless, perhaps…that work is best conducted indoors."

Madsen shook her head with a grumble. The knight waved another android over and the two of them heaved the non-functional one up and into the Hospital. Madsen clutched the maintenance equipment crate, gritted her teeth, and lifted with her legs. The 80-kilogram box was a bit awkward, but she managed to take it inside on her own.

"Jesus…" she grunted as she dropped the crate next to the operating table with an echoing 'bang'. Her patient was lying down on the table looking nervous as the knight and his pal lowered the non-functional platform onto a desk.

Madsen wiped a few drops of sweat from her forehead as she sent her eyes around the dimly lit room. It was super dark; there were no windows, so the only light came from what Madsen thought were faint candles. However, after a closer look, she realised that they were small burning stalks of plant matter that were held upright by metal holders. They barely did anything; only a radius of a couple feet around them were painted with flickering yellow light.

The room itself was pretty neatly kept from the little that Madsen could actually see. On the far side of the room, there were a series of shelves with random vials of junk lined up across them. A leather tool bag was rolled open on a rickety desk, revealing dozens of implements ranging from razors to pliers.

After a few minutes of uselessly squinting through the darkness, Madsen gave up and pulled a compact worklight out of her equipment crate. She extended its telescopic stand and planted it on the ground. It then stood a little over Madsen's height. After she thumbed the power button, cool white light instantly flooded the room. A panicked gasp bounced off the walls of the cold, stone room. "It is alright, my friend," whispered the knight to the one lying on the operating table.

Being able to actually see with the help of good old LED lighting, Madsen laid her tools out onto the desk that held the non-functional platform that she was going to strip for parts. As she did, the knight ushered everyone else out of the room and shut the door on them. Madsen started powering up all of her tools and checking the battery levels. Then there came a very hushed murmur from the damaged android. "T-Thou cannot permit her to butcher me and that other sod."

The knight urgently returned to its side. Madsen's hands moved without her even needing to look at them; she'd done those checks a million times before, so she was able to keep her eyes fixed on what the two platforms were doing. "She shall do no such thing. Madsen shall restore what thou hast lost." The damaged one's eyes kept jumping around and its anxious fiddling showed no signs of stopping. The knight grasped its hand and said, "Have faith…and trust me, my friend. All is well." Madsen prepped her InSpec and opened the platform's CPU settings. The knight watched her for a moment, then turned back. "Thou shalt sleep now, Gabriel. We shall meet again in but a moment."

As she stood over it, her finger hovering above the 'FORCE HIBERNATE' command on the InSpec, its optics met hers. They blinked rapidly. Its chest expanded and contracted in concert with its frantic breaths. She then pressed the hibernate option and released a heavy exhale. The damaged platform's body froze and its eyes went dark.

Hesitantly, the knight let itself out and shut the door behind it. As it left, the two of them locked eyes for a second. She didn't like the vibe she got.

With all the distractions gone, Madsen got to work. Seeing as she had basically no real understanding of the mechanical and electrical systems inside the machines, she was *not* expecting it to go well. But it was going to be a good learning opportunity. You know. For science.

She started by unwrapping the bandages that hugged what was left of the legs. Cross-sectioned nanowires, E-Gel pathways, and structural frame material jutted out from beneath the partially healed-over synth tissue. Madsen measured out the leg on the donor, closely correlating with the damage on the subject to make sure she was making a cut at the right interval. After the lines were drawn out with a marker, it was time to start. First, she sliced through all of the synth-tissue with a knife in order to get to the structural frame. For that part, she was gonna need something a little more heavy-duty.

The plasma cutter was like a handheld buzzsaw, except the cutting edge relied on ultra-hot energy to slice through material. Seeing how well it worked against that one dude's head, Madsen thought it would get the job done. Against the inner frame of the donor android, it was like a hot knife through butter. It *did* cause some of the excess E-Gel to sizzle and pop though, reminding Madsen that the stuff was *volatile* when superheated. She could get away with it on the non-functional platform because it was essentially dried up…but the other one that was full of fresh E-Gel would probably violently explode.

All the heat from the cutter was making her sweat like a fountain, not at all helped by the thermal layers in her flight suit or the stone walls of the room. She zipped the jumpsuit down to her waist, slipped out of the sleeves, then tied them around her waist. After twenty minutes or so, she had two dismembered robot legs lined up on her workspace.

Then it was time for the real meticulous stuff. Four hours of work followed. She had to wire the new limbs into the platform's existing subsystems network. That meant a whole lot of keeping her hands steady while she soldered and linked nanowire. Even though nothing was labelled on the diagnostics, all of the cables were grouped in the same way on both units, making it easier than Madsen expected to reconnect everything. The result was messy and not exactly well-organised, but it would mend the connections and restore functionality at the very least. Eventually, the systems that were labelled as missing on the InSpec started turning green. She still had no idea what most of them were, but it was better than nothing.

As she clapped her hands together in triumph, she mumbled, "Ayyyy."

The next part involved mending the internal frame of the platform. Basically sticking the skeletons together somehow. Welding was her first plan, but having a big heat source that close to charged E-Gel didn't seem to be a good idea. Also, the material that the frame was made of wasn't purely metallic; it wouldn't work anyway. Injecting nanos and instructing them to bind the matter together could've maybe worked, but it would be *super duper* flimsy on material like that. If she wanted the skeleton to snap after a few days, sure, nanos would totally do. After a very comprehensive ten minutes of thinking, Madsen realised that she was going to have to use a combination of nano printers and some kind of bracket system that she could bolt into the frame to keep everything together. She managed to find some spare parts in one of her crates that she could weld together into something that she could use.

Fluctuating blossoms of yellow washed over the stark white of the worklight as Madsen seared her improvised brackets together with her welding torch. The polarised visor of her welding mask protected her eyes from the blinding flashes. After she got the brackets put together, she carefully drilled holes in them, then screwed them into place on both the android and the replacement legs. Finally, she applied nanos on the inner frame itself to actually glue it all together.

And just like that, after a grand total of only *eight hours*, Madsen found herself experiencing a harsh occasion of deja vu; she was using nanos and self-healing polymer tape to mend the synth-tissue of a humanoid robot. She tapped the InSpec a few times as it sat on the surface of the desk laden with tools, flipping the welding mask open and wiping the litres of sweat from her forehead. Madsen reactivated the android's CPU.

Slowly, the android's optics warmed from a dull black to a cold blue. It blinked a couple times as it stared at the ceiling. Madsen bit her lower lip as she kept her eyes pinned on its newly attached legs. A toe twitched. Then another. Then the whole ankle. The platform itself detected that something was weird, so it sat up and glanced down. Its expression softened and its eyes widened. The artificial musculature in its jaw tightened as a wavering breath was expelled from its lips. It ran a finger down its legs, causing the muscles to flex in response. The android's optics swept up to meet Madsen's. It chuckled. After a moment, it erupted in thunderous laughter. *Tears* streamed down its face. "Bless thee! Bless thy divine majesty!" it sobbed, crying and laughing all at once as it flexed its new legs back and forth.

"Oh. Uh… No problem."

Madsen was frozen in place as the platform sprung off the table and landed on its feet with a slight wobble. It paced over to her and seized her by the shoulders. "This is a miracle!"

As it spoke, its hands trembled and its fingers dug into her skin. It continued ranting on and on about how miraculous it all was, leaving a petrified Madsen to stare into its optics which were *still* spewing tears.

Artificial Intelligence. The term was used to describe neural networks and algorithms that were ultimately *pretending* to be intelligent. Chatbots faked human intelligence through the use of statistics, probability, and word association. They didn't comprehend what they were doing, they were just designed to produce some end result that made it *look* like they did. Madsen watched as the android wept and shivered. Its face twitched. It blinked a million times a second. She could hear the shallow breaths it made. Everything it was doing was an effort to mimic an extreme emotional reaction. She kept telling herself that it wasn't real. That it was hollow; the 'emotions' were the results of carefully written code and processes. The train of thought reminded her of a hypothesis put forward in the early years of A.I development during the 21st Century; if a machine acted like it had a mind, did it matter if it really did or not? The outcome is the same. You don't know for sure if your fellow humans are conscious; you just trust that they are. What's the difference? What was the difference between Madsen and the thing that was bawling its eyes out in front of her? Less sophisticated systems produced artefacts or hallucinations; clear indications that they weren't in possession of true intelligence, only a rudimentary facsimile of it. Those androids didn't show any signs of that at all. The thoughts made the hairs on the back of her neck stand up as the android continued weeping and moaning in relief.

XXXI
Burdened By Truth

There was a loud bang. Darkness swallowed him, enveloping his surroundings. He held a hand out, but he could not see it. Then, reverberating through his fingers was a familiar rhythm. It felt...like something gently shaking against him. '*You hold a great many things in your hands, Godslave. Do be careful.*' What followed was an eternity of dead silence. At the end of this infinity, he felt something else. Thunderous drum beats that coursed through every bone in his body. This too had cadence to it. He saw the Pale Spire in all of its majesty. The light coalesced upon it, turning it into a glowing spear pointed toward the Heavens. Once again, there was nothing. Nothing but the sound of an echoing voice. *'Thou do not serve God. He is but an excuse for that twisted, horrible mind of thine to satisfy its deepest urges.'*

Alric stirred awake with a fright. Before him, he saw a large stone relief of the Father himself, surrounded by the cold stone walls of a chapel's interior. Sunlight dripped in from the distant doorway, causing him to squint. Alric groaned as he shifted upright and gazed down at his body. He had fallen asleep on the pew in the Phaemslake Chapel. He groaned when he realised that he was going to have to remain inside his armour until nightfall since he failed to recite the final verse the night before. The plates that were exposed to the brilliance of the sun were warm to the touch, while the others that dwelled in shadow were as cold as ice.

His mind slowly returned to him. He waited all night for Madsen to complete her rituals, but he was obviously much too exhausted to see it through. In the face of inactivity...his mind wandered. For the first time since he stumbled across Madsen, he had a moment to reflect upon what had transpired. The words she spoke were heretical. At first, he was hesitant to ask any questions, even within the privacy of his own mind. But the truth was that there was no privacy. The Lord always watched and he always listened. Things that he thought were certain, things taught to him by the Scripture...did not appear to be the truth. He found beings asleep beneath the earth, within a tower of steel. One of them emerged from her slumber and commanded great magics in order to mend his broken body. If he were to refer to the Scripture to identify a creature that slept in the depths and dealt in magic, it would insist that it was a demon. Carthei told him that the deities worshipped by the druids, the Vorkhai, ravaged worlds with their magic. What was a Vorkhai? What was a demon? What was an angel? Were they perhaps…one and the same?

The blasphemous thoughts screamed through his skull and he could bear the cacophony no longer. The Thestor pushed to his feet, the sounds of his struggle becoming deafening in the empty church. Alric, with fear and dread surging through his mind like poison, collapsed onto his knees before the statue of the Father at the end of the chapel. In a frantic whisper, he said, "Forgive me, O Lord, for I have sinned. I have doubted thy divine plan…and for that I must seek forgiveness. As I leave this sacred house, I shall steel myself and brave the tests that await me. Henceforth, my devotion shall not be stirred." He drew the Sign of the Pillar, stood, and took his leave.

Unlike how it was the day before, the streets of Phaemslake were flooded with townsfolk. People were locked in conversation with each other or sharing food, and some were even partaking in a ball game in the town square. If he didn't know better, Alric would've thought that there was some kind of festival happening.

As he groggily stomped down the street, holding his helmet in one hand and rubbing his eyes with the other, he watched the chaotic ball game. Several men kicked an inflated bladder across the town square, yelling and laughing as they did. Taking Alric completely by surprise, someone abruptly stepped in front of him. "Brother Alric!" The priest that had questioned Madsen's authority the day before, Father Warren, bowed curtly before Alric as he said, "I was wrong to doubt your words. Could you forgive a foolish old man?"

Alric leaned away from the priest. "I beg thy pardon, Father?"

"Don't you see? Your angel has blessed us," whispered Warren as he pointed at the ongoing ball game. Alric looked back for a moment. He was just about to turn away and snap at the priest for wasting his time before he recognised one of the players. He moved with incredible speed and kicked the ball ten feet ahead, passing the North gates of the village and winning for his team. It was Gabriel de Fontaine. Alric watched as Gabriel leapt into the air, cheering and screaming at the top of his lungs. The other villagers charged into him and joined his celebration.

"May God blind me…" muttered Alric.

Not exactly wanting to speak with the priest any further, Alric marched onward toward Gabriel and his friends as they carried on like excited children. The Thestor's mouth twisted into a smile as his eyes met with Gabriel's. The man's face lit up. The Valthois knight pushed free of the crowd that held him and charged into Alric like a bull. His bascinet dropped into the dirt and he almost tipped over entirely.

When Gabriel pulled away, Alric could only see a grin as large as Tritham itself upon his face. However, when he set a hand onto Alric's shoulder, the smile vanished. "Thou hast changed everything, my friend," Gabriel said deeply. "The world shall remember who brought her to us."

Alric swallowed. In the Pale Spire, Madsen had breathed new life into him, but to see that she could mend severed limbs…the doubt that had lingered in his mind had receded. "She truly *is* an angel…" He then looked to the other players. He recognised them from the Hospital. One was a man who was previously so overcome with pain that his body spasmed uncontrollably. He was standing before Alric with utmost stillness. Another, a peasant woman named Claudia Miller who had become paralysed after falling from a windmill, controlled all of her limbs without issue.

"W-Where is she?" Alric asked.

"I think she's still in tha 'ospital. Didn't want anyone disturbin' 'er. Except fer *you*," added Claudia.

Alric swallowed. "I am but a lowly servant… I am unworthy of her presence."

Gabriel leant over, snatched Alric's bascinet from the ground, and handed it to him. "Best not make her wait," he said as Alric accepted the helmet.

As he made his way back to the Hospital of Saint Corren, Alric could feel his hands shaking within his gauntlets. Had he angered her? Was his absence offensive to her? He knew that his misgivings regarding her attitude were sinful.

Nocht was not in the Hospital courtyard; perhaps one of the plebeians had taken her for a morning stroll. Seeing the Hospital essentially empty was something that made Alric pause for a moment. It looked to be that only five or so individuals remained inside, and they may have been simple homeless folk with nowhere to go. Hospitals were not just places for the sick and injured.

"Brother Alric. Did you sleep well?" Sister Tybeth, a nun dressed in the white kirtle with the black surcoat of Saint Corren atop it, hovered over to him.

Alric shrugged. "Where is Her Holiness?"

Tybeth nodded towards the set of doors leading into the operating chamber. "She hasn't left. After she saw to those that she could, she sealed herself inside. Actually, she *did* ask for you."

"Yes, yes…I am aware. Wouldst thou excuse me?"

The nun nodded. "How fortunate you are, Brother Alric. To be chosen to be her herald…I would have given anything for a chance to serve God in such a way."

Alric shuddered and drifted away from the conversation. He pushed into the operating theatre and pulled the door shut behind him. As soon as he stepped inside, he felt the temperature skyrocket. The room was still flush with the near-blinding white light that Madsen had cast the day before. She was hunched over a human corpse which had its torso sliced open and its ribcage removed. The bright blue garment that Madsen wore, one that was a shirt and a pair of hose all at once, had been unfastened and its sleeves were tied at her waist. Covering her upper body was an article of clothing with sleeves that ended mid-bicep. The threads of the grey shirt were so fine and thin; it was unlike any fabric Alric had ever seen before. Upon said shirt was an incredibly crisp and flat embroidery of some kind that read 'Property of ISEC 3032'. When he squinted, he could see that the initials had the words 'Intersystem Space Exploration Commission' written underneath them…which was nothing but gibberish to him. Her arms, neck, and weary face were glistening with sweat.

When she turned her head to face him, he could see that the whites of her eyes were laced with red lines and the skin surrounding her eye sockets had darkened. "Hast thou been toiling through the night?" he said calmly to her.

"Hey. 'Sup?" Madsen placed the liver she held onto the desk and wiped the blood from it with a cloth.

"I beg thy pardon?"

"Oh. It's a…it's like… Ugh, don't worry about it. Listen, I wanted to ask you something."

Alric nodded sheepishly.

She looked him dead in the eyes. "Are you sentient?"

The Thestor's eyelids fluttered and he swallowed. "I do not understand."

The angel scratched the back of her head as she tried to seek another word. "Conscious. Are you conscious?"

That was a word he *did* know. He did not necessarily think it had an explicitly clear definition though. Philosophers themselves couldn't even decide what it meant. "Be this a riddle?"

Madsen shrugged. "Yeah. I guess it is."

Alric glanced at his feet for a moment, then looked back up at Madsen. "If *I* were the one to ask such a question, I do not believe that *any* answer would satisfy me."

"You know what, that's...that's a really good answer. *Fuck*." She rubbed her chin contemplatively and stared at the wall.

Alric huffed through his nostrils. Most times, he had no idea how to respond to her strange behaviour. Suddenly, her eyes glazed over and her expression wobbled. "When I fixed them...they...they looked at me and... They hugged me, they cried...I could *feel* it. It goes against everything I know, but I *felt* it." She rubbed her eyes. "This shouldn't be possible. You're all self-aware, aren't you? You can make your own decisions. You can learn. You can feel?"

He nodded.

The angel swallowed. "And you don't understand why or how?"

Alric said fearfully, "'Tis a God-given gift."

Madsen exhaled as she leant onto the table behind her and stared into nothingness. She slowly ran her hands through her hair. "This is nuts. We're talking about artificial general intelligence. It's supposed to be hypothetical. I-I mean, your biomimetic hardware is crazy, too, but...it's nothing compared to being able to replicate brain patterns. This is...*insane*. How can the CPUs and SSDs handle that kind of load? How much space would a simulation like that take up? We have no idea how to do that kind of thing with quantum computers let alone run of the mill stuff."

Alric, not having the slightest idea of what she was rambling about, nodded and cleared his throat. "Indeed."

Madsen continued to stare at the wall for a few more moments. "Listen...I'm sorry. This has all been...bat shit insane for me. There's stuff I could've explained better, but...I thought you weren't...uh...weren't conscious." Alric glanced at the ground. Her words did nothing but make him feel more ill at ease. The question of consciousness. Had she expected him to not have a mind? To not have feelings? That was the Clthic notion of the 'True State'. Everything she said seemed to fit neatly within their doctrine...

"What did you say your name was?" she asked finally.

He trembled and tried his best to hide his unease. "Alric."

The angel nodded and planted her hands onto her hips. Solemnly and quietly, she said, "Alric…I need you to understand that I'm not an angel, okay?"

Alric's eyes fluttered as he stood frozen in stunned silence. Her words infuriated and horrified him in equal measure. His heart thrummed faster in his chest and beads of sweat began to trickle down his brow. "There is no question of thy divine nature. Only a servant of the Lord could deliver us, His lowly subjects, from sickness and death with such ease."

Madsen swallowed and rubbed the bridge of her nose.

"Worry not, Thy Holiness. These tests of my faith in the Lord shall not sway me. I remain unshaken."

She threw her hands up in exasperation. "I can fix you the same way a blacksmith can hammer out dents in metal. You came off a production line at a factory somewhere. You're made out of composite fibre and polymer. Parts. *We built you.*"

The declaration held no weight in Alric's mind. It was a simple fact of existence. It did, however, bring him comfort. It was her first admission of the truth. "Of course. We were all created in Heaven's image," he replied as he gestured towards Madsen. "Have I succeeded? Have I proven myself…?" he asked with an exhausted rasp. The more he spoke, the more he felt as if he was not only trying to convince Madsen…but also himself.

The woman's expression pulsed for a moment, as if she was trying to stay composed. When she spoke, she did so through clenched teeth. "Alric… You need to *listen* to what I'm saying to you." Her sudden change in demeanour gave him pause. "You guys call yourselves human…but *I'm* human. We're a lot like you. We live, we bleed, and we die. We *assembled* you. Like…clockwork. Do you understand? We aren't angels, we aren't gods, we're just people."

It was as if all of his sorrow, anger, shame, and guilt had split his heart open and came surging out all at once. His hands trembled and his lip quivered. His heart was screaming at him; it was urging him to not even acknowledge such ridiculous notions. "If thou art not an angel…t-then art thou a demon?"

Madsen scoffed and her eyebrows flattened against the tops of her eyes. Alric could see the tiny hairs that covered her skin. In her eyes, he expected to see a fiery stare that oozed rage…but instead, he saw something else. He did not know how he recognised the emotion, seeing as her expressions were strange to him, but he thought he saw remorse in her brown eyes. "I'm neither."

Alric's breathing had become so rapid and shallow that he could feel himself suffocating from the lack of meaningful air. "N-No. No. Thou *must* be one," he growled.

"Why?" she pressed, pacing closer to him.

He did not respond. The Scripture *had* to be true. The Father *had* to be the one true God. If not…he killed Carthei for nothing. He let Peter die for nothing. He killed his father for nothing. He killed hundreds of people for nothing. Burned alive in front of their families, friends, loved ones. During the Crusade…he slaughtered the so-called 'infidels' of Qurveen en-masse. The Church's cause would not have been just. Everything he did, he did because he was told it was for the greater good… No. That wasn't true. Everything he did, he did because he was told it was how he could *save himself.* But if there was no salvation… It had all been a waste. His blood simmered to a boil. His eyes twitched.

"Alric," Madsen urged as she tried to reach for his shoulder. The Thestor reared away like a frightened animal. She had given him life…but she had taken so much from him. His confidence. His bravery. His faith. He did not wish for her to take any more. As sweat streamed down his face, Alric stormed out of the room and slammed the door shut.

XXXII
UNTO OBLIVION WE SHALL RETURN

It was quite a sight to behold. The Enlightened paced through the town of Oak with controlled and measured strides. They left a trail of bloodied skeletons behind them. Each bone had been picked clean of all tissue, leaving only glistening piles of intestines and organs within them. People cried out, pleading for God to save them. It was clear that he was not coming.

Mother Xalt'n, Matriarch of the Clthic Synod, watched over her disciples as they tore the innards from the corpses left behind. The Demonic Arts, or 'black magic' as the Godslaves called it, was the ability to see through the Great Lie and recognise 'living things' as what they truly were: a collection of components. The parts that comprised the human body could be used in many ways, least of all to reinvigorate artefacts that had lost their lustre. Arcane staves, golems, and even the mighty Protozealots required maintenance the same as any weapons did. Those who fell against the Clthic Synod would serve them even after they had been torn asunder. Their hearts would fuel blood magic artefacts, their bones would decorate the bodies of the Nuns and Tethspeakers, their bile and fluid would be combined with other solutions to produce useful tonics, and the remaining organs could be used to heal injuries sustained by the Zealots and golems. After an entire life conforming to the repressive ways of the Laevrom'zahi druids who promoted discretion and using magic only when necessary, Xalt'n could not help but feel pride in what her acolytes had accomplished. Humanity was itself a product of magic; why enforce such arbitrary rules? Especially when they were all living a lie. Soon enough, though, all would be as it should be.

It wasn't long before Xalt'n heard approaching footfalls. Several horses were trotting down the road. The first of them was being ridden by H'vrsh, Dread Priest of the Tethspeakers. Using her bone-adorned taukumu as a crutch, Xalt'n stood and looked over at him. "Good of you to join us," she said coldly.

"Mother Xalt'n, something extraordinary has happened!" he cried as he dismounted his steed and approached.

As Xalt'n peered at the next two horses in the caravan, she saw a man drop from his saddle and land on his feet with an air of confidence that communicated that he was rather comfortable on horseback. His skin was a faint purple and his expression seemed to be frozen in permanent anguish. He moved over to the third steed in line and helped a young woman down from atop it. Her skin was a similar tone, only slightly less saturated, and she had severe burns running down the left side of her face and down her neck. H'vrsh raised a hand and declared, "Mother Xalt'n, I present Lord Franco di Lombardi and Fiammetta di Accetti. They led us to our first Infernal Forge."

Franco avoided eye contact with Xalt'n and instead was aggressively pulling various things out of the saddlebag on his horse. Fiammetta, however, exuded energy that Xalt'n found curious. She glanced up and down Xalt'n's body. The girl's breathing became shallow and she clutched at the fabric of her dress. Xalt'n's attention then fell onto H'vrsh's words. She stifled a gasp before she replied, "An Infernal Forge? That…cannot be. How did you find it?"

Lord Franco did not stop rummaging through his belongings, leaving a confused Fiammetta staring at him in anticipation for an answer. Eventually, she seemed to realise that he was not going to say anything anytime soon. With a deep breath, Fiammetta composed herself and reluctantly turned to face Xalt'n. She said, "Lord Franco and his household were parlaying with Duke Klaus at Beggar's Rock. Despite his reassurances that the presence of Churchsworn Orders in the region had been quelled…t-they… They attacked us during a feast. Most present were simply women and servants, but the Thestors showed no mercy. Lord Dante and Lady Allegra, to whom I was sworn, were viciously slain…alongside Lady Beatrice, wife of Lord Franco." At that point, the Lord cleared his throat, swallowed, and tensed his jaw. "It was sheer luck that they thought us dead as well and tossed us into the pile of bodies for the goblins… I…remember hearing screams in the early morning. It was Vilulf…he was in agonising pain. Then Franco and I were taken by the goblins to their hive. We escaped and stumbled upon the Infernal Forge. The spirit of the Forge called upon your Dread Priest and led him to us."

Xalt'n growled under her breath. Klaus and Vilulf had gotten complacent…and it had cost them their lives. For the Godslaves to have killed a vampire, even a rabid and childish one like Vilulf… It was cause for concern. She turned to H'vrsh. "I assume that it has been done?"

He nodded. "Of course."

"You have proven yourself as true believers by leading us to the Forge. With it in our grasp, the Enlightenment shall spread forth naturally. I have even better news to share with you once our war council begins. We, the Clthic Synod, are in your debt."

Franco waved a hand dismissively. "I have no need for thy gratitude."

Then, before Xalt'n could berate Franco for his lack of respect, a group of men approached from the other side of the village. The one at the head of their formation had a squashed face that was rife with tears. Xalt'n recognised him as Bill Taylor, a man-at-arms who had arrived several days ago to await Franco's arrival. Behind him were others in the retinue including Shane Carver, John Stanton, and Lawrence Sowter. "Franky... Oh God, I'm so sorry." Bill rammed into Franco and embraced him tightly.

Franco, who had been barely succeeding at wrangling his disgusting emotions, came apart like wet parchment. Xalt'n huffed sharply through her nose as the other men gathered around them.

"...I do not know what to do," Franco sobbed.

"It's alright, mate. Come on, let's get ya settled down, ay?" said Bill as he gestured to the old inn, aptly named the Lonely Tree. The man's eyes drifted to Fiammetta's burned face and his expression dropped. "By God's grace... Lookit you. My God," he whispered. "They really did that to you? Tha Church? Poor, poor girl..."

Fiammetta swallowed and glanced at the ground, saying nothing. Xalt'n could tell that she was not thrilled by the attention of half a dozen people focused on her disfigurement. The pity and disgust, especially. Before they set off, Franco hesitated and glanced at Fiametta. "Let us away," he said softly.

"I would like to speak with the Matriarch," Fiammetta asserted.

Franco's face strained. "Come now, Fiammetta."

With a sigh, Xalt'n interposed herself in between Franco and the young woman. "You are among allies. She is safer with me than with *your* rabble." The Lord looked liable to throw a punch at Xalt'n's face. It would not have done him any good, however, for pain was beneath her.

Eventually, Fiammetta tenderly took his hand and said, "It is alright, my lord. I will be with you again shortly." With a conflicted look on his face, Franco nodded in silence. He drifted off to the inn with H'vrsh and the others trailing behind him. Xalt'n was left alone with the young woman.

Fiammetta frantically shook her head and bit her lip. "I-I simply wished to pledge myself to the faith, Mother Xalt'n. What I saw in the Forge... I know our place now. To aspire to anything else is to deceive ourselves."

"Few have been fortunate enough to lay eyes upon the birthplace of our kind. Of you and Franco, it seems that only one truly comprehends the significance of it all. You are resilient. Strong," murmured Xalt'n.

"I am neither of those things," she said softly. "I can barely pull myself onto a horse."

"Strength does not exclusively reference the physical, my child. Your companion…Franco. He is pathetic and weak; to let himself be controlled by his sorrow in such a manner? It is revolting. We were meant for more than such folly."

"Please understand. He has been subjected to much pain," Fiammetta retorted, with a faint spark of defiance in her voice.

Xalt'n said, "So have *you*. Yet you do not wallow in it. Such resilience is rare…and admirable."

The girl pulled away. "I-I…thank you, my lady." Xalt'n had never been called a lady by anyone before. She found it slightly comforting and amusing. "What does it say?" Fiammetta asked inquisitively, nodding at the gashes cut into Xalt'n's flesh.

She cocked her head and answered, "I wear the Clthic scripture. It is a part of me and I am a part of *it*. It proclaims the truth of humanity; that we are destined to feel no pain, no remorse, no emotion. It tells the tale of our true lord, The Devil, and how He and His demons forged us from the earth itself. Our minds have become clouded by the Great Lie since then, and so we must embark on a journey to Enlighten ourselves once again. In time, you will learn our rhetoric and praise Hell."

Fiammetta bowed and said, "Of course…the journey to achieve the True State." Xalt'n found her interest to be piqued. "H'vrsh did instruct me on the fundamentals during our travels, but I still have much to learn. I shall await your sermons with bated breath."

There was something about the way in which the young woman looked upon her flayed body that made Xalt'n feel…a fluttering in her chest. Whatever it was, it was product of the Great Lie. As mistress of the Nuns and Tethspeakers, she had no use for the false emotions that she and all of mankind had been cursed with. The lady-in-waiting looked into Xalt'n's eyes and said very softly, "I…hope to see more of you soon, my lady," before walking over to the courtyard to return to Franco's company. Xalt'n was left staring after her.

Soon enough, it was time for the war council. Oak's innhouse, the Lonely Tree, had been reappropriated into a makeshift war room. Most of the tables had been clustered together and a map of Tritham had been laid upon it. Gathered around were Franco, H'vrsh, Xalt'n herself, the captains of several mercenary companies recruited by Klaus before his death, and several other lords and knights who were sworn to Franco. Seated at the counter was a woman by the name of Gertrude. Her family had been the proprietors of the Lonely Tree, until they were cut down upon resisting the Clthic advance. Gertrude was one of the few that accepted the truth.

As Xalt'n approached, Gertrude turned around and locked her tear-soaked eyes with the Matriarch's. "I must thank you for allowing us to make use of the venue, my child," Xalt'n hummed as she bowed. "The pain feels as if it is too much, I know, but it will fade in time. The more you study the truth, the more it will dampen."

Gertrude nodded anxiously. She seemed well, until she suddenly collapsed into a weeping heap on the counter. Xalt'n, having honed her emotional resilience for so many years already, often found herself irritated by newcomers to the faith. She was aware that they could not be blamed for such behaviour, for even the K'relvic Nuns still had to wrangle their false feelings. She had been so detached for so long that it was impossible for her to relate. As the Matriarch stood there, frozen in apathy, a figure brushed by her and gently took Gertrude by the shoulders. "It is good to cry. Do not fight it," urged Fiammetta. Gertrude spun her head to Fiammetta…and her face exuded shock for a split second. Shock at how Fiammetta's face was contorted due to her injuries. The lady-in-waiting paused for a moment and tried to force her feelings of self-consciousness and shame deep down. She continued, "These feelings are a curse, aren't they? That is what Mother Xalt'n is seeking to remedy. She wants to ease our suffering; take away our pain. Come, sister." With the overwhelmed Gertrude swaddled in her arms, Fiammetta hurried through the cramped innhouse and settled her new companion down at an isolated table in the far corner. With that taken care of, Xatl'n could bring her attention back to the actual meeting.

As far as she was concerned, Xalt'n was not thrilled about the diverse range of motivations that sloshed about in the room. Some hated the Church, others hated the kings, others hated other lords that served the kings, others hated the Thestors… There was too much that could conflict with the Clthic goal. She would much rather them all be as devoted to the faith as Fiammetta seemed to be. The Matriarch doubted that some of the nobles and knights could even comprehend what the Synod sought to do. However, she knew it was necessary. The Nuns and Tethspeakers could not fight a war on their own; they, like the Church, required manpower and logistical support. The only way for them to gain that was by recruiting nobles and mercenary bands. Xalt'n crossed her arms and began, "I have received a missive from Servius. He followed our foes into the demon city and laid eyes upon an incredible sight. He saw a *demon.* Alive and in the flesh." Gasps and shocked expressions washed across the entire room. "However, after the battle, there was a lone Godslave. A *sorcerer.*"

The attendees murmured worriedly among themselves. Franco's demeanour suddenly shifted. His empty gaze became inflamed. "W-What?" he croaked.

"This defiler fought using a taukumu, shoulder to shoulder with the Ga'zahi. He seduced the Infernal One with his lies, making her subject to his will, then fled like a coward." Franco swallowed and the fury in his eyes swelled. He locked stares with Fiammetta for a moment, and Xalt'n saw the young woman go pale in the face. Xalt'n continued, "We cannot permit the Church to slaughter the demon. There is so much we have yet to learn about the demonic arts…so much that has been hidden from us. If she were to lead us, the True State will be made a reality within the blink of an eye."

Franco could no longer contain his anger. He planted his hands upon the table and his gaze fixed so deeply on Xalt'n that even she was taken aback. "Where is this Godslave sorcerer? *Where*?"

"Within our grasp, my lord. Even then, know that if he continues to evade us, he will shortly have nowhere else to run."

XXXIII
Black Teeth

She wasn't used to it at all. Madsen craned her neck up and she could actually *see* the night sky. The atmosphere wasn't being lit up by skyglow. There weren't any streetlights, skyscrapers, or billboard ads. The constellations were brighter than ever, and it felt like she could see millions of other stars glimmering on the backdrop of the empty void. She finally brought her eyes back down as she made it back to the church.

Madsen spied Gabriel standing there glancing around frantically. When he saw her, his shoulders eased down. "Thy Holiness, I was beginning to worry for thy safety. It shall not do to wander about in the dusk without a light." He had a slight accent, but Madsen had always been terrible at picking them out.

"I couldn't find him," she muttered with a shrug.

Gabriel rubbed his chin. "It is most unlike a pious man to abscond during such a holy occasion…" With a shrug, he sighed, "Pay him no mind."

"I'm telling you, he was…really upset," Madsen confessed. "And it was my fault."

Gabriel's face softened into a smile. "Ha. I see that thine empathy knows no bounds, but I assure thee that Brother Alric can fend for himself."

Her jaw tensed up. She couldn't help but blame herself. In the Hathor, she dumped world-ending information on Alric. But how was she supposed to have known that he was self-aware and sentient at that point? It shouldn't have been possible. No one knew what the fuck consciousness was and you kind of needed to know what something was before creating it. Also…was she supposed to just lie to him and tell him what he wanted to hear? Maybe. Who was she to police what people believed?

"Come, the Birthing is about to begin." Gabriel wrapped an arm around her shoulder and chuckled. "We would be honoured if you chose to join us for this sacred sacrament."

Yeah, the word 'birthing' made it sound like something she really didn't want to see…but if new androids appeared *inside* the church, she could potentially learn a little more about where they came from. "Fine," she conceded begrudgingly as she gently brushed Gabriel's arm off her shoulder. “But I’m gonna keep looking afterwards. I don’t care how dark it is.”

Gabriel led Madsen into the church and up to the bench at the very front. The priest, nuns, and monks filled the place with a chant. It echoed and reverberated throughout the stone structure. It was creepy enough to send a chill down Madsen’s spine and give her goosebumps.

As she sat on the really long chair, she looked over at the other people there with her. Next to Gabriel were Joseff, William, Margaret, Thomas, Claudia, and Arthur; all of them were among the androids that she repaired the night before. For some reason, they decided to stick together. She had to admit, the previous all-nighter was starting to get to her. She covered her mouth as she yawned, unsure if the robots would be as terrified of that as they were of sneezing.

There was a rumbling beneath Madsen’s feet that steadily grew. The candles shook, same with the tapestries that decorated the walls of the church. Eventually the rumbling stopped and she heard a ‘bang’ behind the set of stone doors on the far side of the hall. Madsen narrowed her eyes and wrinkled her forehead.

Gabriel leant over to her and whispered, “Worry not. That is rather normal.”

“Okay. Good to know.”

The nuns trailed over to the giant stone doors. They wore pale white dresses and hooded mantles of a matching colour. Each woman grabbed onto a set of handles carved into the door and pulled. Gradually and with a sound that was like nails on a chalkboard, they wrenched the door open.

Beyond, there was a crowd of about forty androids, all standing upright with dimly lit optics.

“Woah,” Madsen murmured. Her eyes drifted down to the ground, and she saw a platform that very much resembled a dual-purpose lift/bulkhead. There had to be some kind of underground factory that the elevator shafts came up from. When the platform reached the top, it sealed off the shaft and prevented unwanted entry.

Madsen turned to Gabriel. She wasn’t exactly used to reading the expressions of android people…so she was stumped for a few seconds. His mouth was dropped open, his optics seemed to flicker a little, and the artificial muscles in his cheeks flexed. It was raw horror. She was left to assume that something was wrong…but she had no idea what.

Silence wafted through the halls.

In unison, each machine emitted a weird series of digital chirps, some short and some long. "01010011 01111001 01101110 01110100 01101000 00101101 01110100 01101001 01110011 01110011 01110101 01100101 00100000 01100100 01100101 01110100 01100101 01100011 01110100 01100101 01100100 00101110."

The androids that stood on the platform dismounted it and paced with frightening speed into the central hall. There it was…the precise and calculated movements that Madsen expected to see in machines. Each android's pair of optics were locked onto separate individuals. They reached the nuns first.

Madsen watched as one snatched a nun's wrists, opened its mouth, then planted its teeth onto her face. E-gel squirted all over the place as the nun made a sound that tore into Madsen's ear drums and made her feel like her insides were melting. The horrific screech of pain and terror made her shoot to her feet. By the time Madsen was upright, every nun that was manning the doors was being *eaten alive* by the newcomers. Before she knew it, Madsen was tackled to the ground.

The back of her head hit the stone floor. She felt two cold hands wrap themselves around her wrists and pin them against the ground while a shadow loomed over her. The android's mouth was wide open, and it was coming in for a bite. She could see its composite material teeth. The softbody tendons that made up its tongue. The inside of its wet throat. Madsen tucked her knees up to her abdomen then pushed them into the android's chest as she rocked her weight forward. It *really* didn't want to let go, but the kick that she sent its way was enough to topple it over. After almost tearing Madsen's hands off, the android let go and fell onto his back. Madsen scampered to her feet and what she saw…it was fucked.

The new androids were tearing into the nuns, the priest, and a handful of townsfolk that were too slow. They funnelled the synthetic meat into their mouths with smooth and deliberate motions.

"Your Holiness, save us!" cried William who dashed over to her and grabbed her hands. He held her there, bawling and screaming in fear. She tried to drag him with her…but a figure lurched over to William before they could reach the doors. The malfunctioning android pressed a palm against William's forehead, jerked it back with lethal force, then buried its face into his throat.

Madsen instantly seized the attacker by the top of its head, placed a hand onto its chest, positioned her foot behind it, then pushed with everything she had. As she forced the clamped jaw away, the sinewy flesh that made up William's throat stretched, strained, and snapped as he screamed in pain. The malfunctioning android tipped over and fell onto his head with a snap. He didn't move.

William clutched at his throat. "Shit! Fuck!" Madsen snarled. She grabbed him and propped him up. "Come on!"

There was more screaming, squelching, and systemic chirping coming from behind her. She couldn't look back…and that made it all the more difficult to keep going. She was convinced one of them was gonna make it to her. That she was gonna be killed by a goddamn robot on a fucking middle of nowhere mudball.

But somehow, she made it outside. Fifteen or so others had made it and they all gathered there, staring at the church entrance with widened optics as Madsen came over with William. Instantly, a handful of people came over to take him from her. There were already other bodies lying on the ground.

Before she could say anything to them, their sudden panic caused her to turn around. She barely had enough time to raise her left arm in front of her face. She felt it, but it didn't hurt. The sensation of smooth jagged objects pressing through her skin and into her flesh made her breath stop. Then came the tickle of blood coursing down her forearm. Instinctively, Madsen lashed out with her right fist, punching the android in the throat. It slightly listed to the side, but its mouth was still clamped firmly down on her arm.

Suddenly, as the panic swelled in her mind, she saw an array of hands plant themselves onto the android's face. It was the villagers. They swarmed over the feral android, bombarded its face with punches, and wrestled it away. Madsen saw some daggers slide into the machine's body. Eventually, after what felt like way too fucking long, its eyes went dim and its body limp.

Madsen was pulled out by Claudia and another villager. As she stumbled backwards with blood trailing down her forearm, she saw William face down in the dirt, unmoving and unbreathing. It was all a mess. The adrenaline that was pouring through her body made her feel like she wasn't actually there. Like her mind was packed away in a box and everything was just sloshing about around her. Nothing felt right.

Back towards the church, she made out movement. A handful of figures limped out, doing their best to hold each other. Even in her daze, it was plain to see that they were scared. It was Gabriel. Behind him and his friends were the messed up androids who marched after them with a steady pace. Their mouths were dripping with E-Gel.

XXXIV
Through Eyes of The Dead

Alric had found an abandoned house on the outskirts of town. He had spent an indeterminate amount of time kneeling there in darkness. He held a whip in his hands and occasionally threw it over his shoulder so its barbed tails cracked against his bare back. The implications of Madsen's claims had robbed Alric of his inner peace. If they were true, he had no purpose. If they were false…then he had been bewitched and led astray by a demon.

He never shed a tear when those close to him perished, for he was certain that Heaven awaited them. But if there was no God, then there certainly was no Heaven. What then? What pit did men fall into after death? Eternal nothingness? Complete and utter destruction of the soul? What terrible fate had he wrought upon those children at Chesterton? He stood idle while Peter Kent, a good man begging for his life, had his head struck from his body. During the raid on Beggar's Rock, he had pointed his taukumu at a crowd of non-combatants, predominantly women, and unleashed its lethal magic upon them with glee. Carthei entrusted him with the secrets of her people and in return, he throttled her to death with his bare hands. For what? God was the only possible justification for those deeds. God was an ever-present whisper insisting that he had done the right thing. Without him…he knew that he hadn't the strength to look himself in the eye.

Not many things could have pulled him from his self-destructive trance, but the shrill screams that drifted in from the door had managed it. He froze in place and peered outside. Distant cries weaved themselves together into a dense indecipherable fibre of panic that passed through the air like a chilling wind. Several guardsmen holding lanterns rushed by the front of the house, prompting Alric to pull his arming jacket and Thestor surcoat back on. With taukumu in hand, he jogged outside and made haste to catch up with the guards.

"Are we under attack?" asked the Thestor.

A Tritan soldier named Mears Jansen who had been healed by the angel shook his head as he answered with shallow breaths, "Can't be. We just came from that end o' town…wasn't nothin' out of the ordinary."

As they continued on their way, Alric pulled the flashlight from his belt. When he pressed the key on the cylindrical relic, white sunlight poured from its end. The streets of Phaemslake were instantly painted by light much more brilliant than what any lantern or torch could manage. The guards slowly blew out their lanterns, hung them onto their belts as they muttered to themselves in disbelief, and followed the Thestor's lead. Several villagers poked their heads out of their windows or peeked from their doors as the men paced by. "If you 'ave arms, make 'em ready," Mears said to them calmly.

Before long, the cries became all too clear. The knight and the two soldiers at his sides pushed themselves into a jog. Subconsciously, Alric was searching the patchwork of screams for Madsen's voice.

As he rounded the edge of the innhouse, what Alric saw drove a stake into his heart. The church doors were agape and all around the village square were dozens of corpses. Standing above them, however, were misty figures frozen in place. Alric switched off his flashlight and crouched behind the innhouse, gesturing to the guards to do the same. He was not dressed in plate harness so he could not afford to be reckless.

After his eyes adjusted to the dark, Alric was overcome with an irresistible sense of dread. Revenants stood in the town square. They loomed over the bodies of fallen villagers like stone statues. Among them however, was a group of moving shapes. As they drifted closer, Alric could hear them conversing. "Where is she, Tethspeaker? Did they or did they not see her?" said one with a significant amount of frustration in his voice.

A man who swept his hands through a series of floating glyphs promptly answered, "They did. Each of their eyes are but extensions of my own. She *is* here." A witch...specifically, one of those who used magic to influence reality.

Both of the individuals became coated with moonlight as they drifted out from the shadow of the church, allowing Alric to behold their appearances. There was a man at arms clad in black Stoiffan style plate armour with a large hole blown in its breastplate. Alric tensed his jaw as he remembered the armoured man who tried to kidnap Madsen in the Spire. He called himself Servius...and he had somehow survived the taukumu bolt. There was only one explanation for why he hadn't been blown to giblets: he was a vampire. The Tethspeaker, like all of his witch-kin, wore nothing on his flayed body but a grotesque mask made of animal skulls and a strange glowing pendant. Accompanying the dread servants was a crowd of individuals, some with torches but all with weapons of some kind. From what Alric could see, they did not wear armour.

"Find her. *Now*," commanded Servius.

Piles of furniture were shoved up against the doors and windows. Tables, chairs, cabinets. Basically anything that wasn't nailed down. Luckily, since the building belonged to the local blacksmith, there were spare nails and brackets lying around that they used to bolt the windows shut. All to keep…well, whatever the hell those things were, from getting inside. When they were trying to get in, they weren't just banging on the doors and windows shutters like lunatics. No, they were carefully trying to tear them from the hinges with calculated applications of force. It eventually became obvious that they couldn't get through so, as best as Madsen could tell, they were just standing outside. Waiting.

Behind her were about ten *normal* androids. The only ones who made it out of the church. Some were sobbing and moaning with such a wholehearted sense of helplessness that Madsen was getting uncomfortable. She didn't know what to say to them. Among the survivors, somehow managing to keep their emotions in check, were Gabriel, Claudia, Joseff, Margaret, and Arthur.

Gabriel sighed, causing his shoulders to hunch and his lips to quiver. That blackened wound on his left cheek was starting to crust up and seal itself. "The Birthing…it was all wrong. The undead, fully grown, stood where there should have been children…"

Madsen narrowed her eyes. "Children?"

"Something's wrong. Terribly wrong," said Claudia. "A curse, perhaps. Brought about by tha heretics."

"The heretics?!" snapped Arthur. "The curse befell us when Madsen was present! H-How can we not be certain that *she* is not the cause of this? S-She could be a pretender!"

Claudia stomped over to Arthur and grabbed him by the collar of his shirt. "Speak one more word of disrespect towards 'er and God help me, I'll toss ya out there for the revenants to tear apart like a piece o' meat."

With a gasp, Madsen raised her hands. "Woah! No one's getting thrown out there, okay? Arthur, it's a reasonable assumption and I'm glad you considered it. But I didn't do that. I was just sitting there watching, like the rest of you."

Arthur swallowed and looked to the ground. Probably sensing the tension, Gabriel took that moment to say softly, "Your Holiness, forgive Arthur for his insolence. He is afraid."

"T-There's nothing to forgive. I'm scared too…" she sighed in defeat as she wiped some more mucus from her nostrils. Her admitting that didn't seem to be something they expected to hear, because the room plunged into silence.

Madsen looked down at the wound on her forearm that she managed to haphazardly bandage with a few rags she found in a cupboard. She needed to get to the medkit that was stowed on the Phil. Plantlife meant fertile soil and fertile soil meant heaps of bacteria. If she didn't clean and dress it properly…well, having an infected wound in a place with zero medical facilities didn't sound like a lot of fun. The malfunctioning units outside didn't seem to discern any difference between her organic flesh and synthetic tissue. Synth-tissue was designed to be as similar to organic stuff as physically possible…so at that point, it was all just matter to be broken down and absorbed for energy. Those things could've torn her open and eaten her just like everyone else who didn't make it out of the street.

As more time passed, Madsen's ear twitched. There was rustling outside. She stood, moved over to the massive stack of stuff in front of the door, then braced herself on the wall so she could lean as close as she could to the crack. She heard more rustling…footsteps…clacking of metal. Alric?

Suddenly, a booming voice sent her leaping into the air. "Release her at once, deniers of the truth! The Infernal One belongs with those who worship her ungodly power!"

A cold tingling feeling snaked its way through each and every centimetre of her body. The faces of everyone in the room with her were frozen in fear. She pointed at the backdoor and gestured for them to start filtering out that way. Arthur sprung upward and led the way to the backdoor. Carefully and silently, he and Claudia began shifting the makeshift barricade so that everyone could escape.

"I'll buy you some time. Get out of here," she whispered to Gabriel as she started clearing the front door. His expression went cold. If the machines could turn pale, he probably did.

"N-No. I will not leave thee."

Madsen ran a hand down her face. "Gabe. I *order* you to help everyone get out of here."

The word that she stressed seemed to make him comply. Gabriel swallowed and drifted toward the rear of the structure. He couldn't bring himself to look at Madsen as he left. After a couple of seconds, both exits had been cleaned up. Madsen scrunched her hands into fists, shook them a little, and gently bounced up and down on her feet a couple times in an effort to work up the balls to pull the door open. She tried amping herself up. "Alright. I'll go out, we'll have a nice polite conversation, I'll tell them to go fuck themselves, problem solved. It'll be great."

When she stepped into the cold night air, she felt the very familiar hands of fear tightening on her throat. It was almost paralysing that time though...hadn't been that bad since her very first E.V.A years and years ago. She remembered looking out into the infinite vastness of space and knowing that if her tether somehow broke and she drifted away from the space station, she would just keep going on and on forever. You would never slow down unless you hit something...and seeing as how space was incredibly and overwhelmingly empty, that chances of that happening before you died was straight up zero. She remembered what she did back then and did it again; she took a deep breath in and disconnected from the fear.

A handful of blazing yellowish-red torches being held by some of the androids were the only sources of light. They drowned everything else out and made the darkness even stronger. The flames flickered and pulsated like unstable balls of gas. Madsen felt the heat against her face swell with every step that she took toward the group of silent machines. Those ones didn't seem to be malfunctioning. They reacted with emotions that looked like wonder and joy as Madsen slowly approached. Littered amongst the crowd were the malfunctioning ones, what the others called 'revenants' or 'undead'. They were frozen in place but still watched her with their dull optics.

In the middle of the circle of fire was a knight. His armour looked a lot more aesthetically complex than Alric's. It had raised edges that ran along each piece and little ornate engravings. There was this black fabric laid over the front of his helmet, like a veil. Beneath it, the helmet itself had two narrow eye slits. She realised that she'd seen that exact suit of armour before. It was Servius. He'd followed her and Alric all the way from the Hathor. Every movement he made filled the air with the sound of clapping metal. Suddenly, he dropped to one knee...as did all of the normal robots.

"Infernal One," they chanted in unison. The low, guttural voices clamped together and turned into a chorus. Servius pulled himself up while everyone else remained on one knee.

Madsen cringed. "Oh. Hey. Again. Small world."

"I do not know what exactly the Godslave has told you, Infernal One, but heed not his lies." His voice was muffled from beneath his helmet. "He has misled you."

He waved his hand towards the machines still kneeling behind him. Madsen saw something that made her heart skip a beat. It was a male android with what looked like the skull of a horse strapped over his face as a mask. He wore a tattered cloak, jewellery of some kind, ragged footwraps, and his polymer skin had been removed, just like that other woman back from the Hathor.

"T'kyr is a Tethspeaker. Their ways are strange…but clearly effective," said Servius. "He and the other witches have discarded their humanity in order to better embody the True State. He was the one who found you by peering through the eyes of the Enlightened."

The android himself had a lean frame but as her eyes traced down his body, she saw something hanging from his neck. It was enough to make her completely forget about where she was and what was happening. With her eyes wide, Madsen pushed by Servius and scampered over to the guy with the skull mask. "W-Where did you get that? Who gave it to you?"

The android stood and said, "It was unearthed from the ossuaries you left behind. As Servius alluded, my order has dedicated its pitiful existence to mastering your artefacts and unlocking their secrets. To have you here before me…it is a revelation."

Madsen reached out and grabbed the device, discovering that it was exactly what she thought it was. It was a slimmed-down personal computer the size of her hand and it looked like it had a holographic interface. That kind of thing was super popular on the consumer market. ISEC always preferred using old-fashioned tactile interfaces like touch screens or even buttons in workplaces due to their durability, practicality, and relative low cost. Regardless, that PC was the first piece of tech other than the androids that Madsen had seen since leaving the Hathor. Finally, she felt like she wasn't dreaming or going crazy. She let out a soft, wavering breath. "Does it work?"

The Tethspeaker gently grasped her wrist, pulled her hand away from the thing, and pressed a button on it. Just like that, the holographic display snapped into life. Dozens of floating windows appeared in front of Madsen, all filled to the brim with technical readouts and status reports. One menu leapt out at her. The header of the window read 'LOW-POWER MODE', and underneath were dozens and dozens of separate device labels.

"It does. We used these sacred pendants of yours to begin the good work. Before long, all shall become Enlightened and we will be yours to command once again."

She swallowed and turned to the 'malfunctioning' androids that were still fixed in place. Low-power mode. It explained everything. All of the redundant biomimetic subsystems dedicated to replicating human behaviour were deactivated. There were no facial expressions, no jittery life-like motions, no pain reception…the only thing left was the base need to consume in order to produce power. In other words, they were robots. True robots. That's what their Enlightenment was. They wanted to force reset *every* android into low-power mode so they lost their general intelligence and became what they were supposed to be. Mindless objects.

However…something else occurred to her. She gazed down at the roughly bandaged gouge on her arm. "Those things tried to kill me. Did you tell them to do that?" she asked T'kyr. Servius huffed as he crossed his arms and looked expectantly at the Tethspeaker for an answer.

T'kyr bowed lowly. "I did not, but I must apologise regardless. They were acting of their own accord before your presence was detected. We commanded the Enlightened to spare you as soon as we could."

Madsen flexed her jaw. "Everyone else though…you *meant* to kill them."

Servius replied bluntly, "We cannot die, for we have never lived."

The astronaut thinned her lips and tried to keep her hands from shaking. The rational part of her brain was telling her that Servius was right. They weren't alive. For the last few days, she was trying to tell herself, sure, maybe they were sentient, but they still weren't real people. None of them really mattered because they all stepped off of an assembly line…right? It was advanced programming magic that produced an illusion of sentience and emotion, that was all. But whatever she told herself, it didn't do anything to keep the empathy from forcing her to retrace the memories of what happened earlier that night. William had his throat ripped out as he begged for her to save him. She watched the life drain from his optics. Dozens of them were chased down by the crowd of rabid machines. In each one, she saw something that only living things could experience: fear of death.

Then she cleared her throat, turned to T'kyr and said, "The sacred pendants, they're called personal computers. PCs for short. Who taught you how to use them?"

"PCs…fascinating," he muttered to himself as his eyes sparkled. "Well, the ageless wisdom of Lady Viktoria had a great deal of influence. The rest we were forced to learn ourselves through trial and error."

Madsen nodded eagerly, doing her best to pretend that she was all in. "Could I meet her? Can you take me to her?"

Servius bowed, making all the sounds that a few tumbling pots and pans would as he did so. "At once. It would be my honour to introduce you to my matron." When he stood upright once again, he seemed to move with a heavily restrained excitement. "It is my understanding that she is currently…abroad. But we can await her return with the coven."

T'kyr clasped his hands together. "Excellent. Perhaps we should–" He never finished his sentence. When her eyes opened, T'kyr had been replaced by a gigantic splatter on the stone pavement. Limbs, chunks of synth-tissue, organs, and jagged splinters of composite fibre crashed to the ground with sickening wet squelches. Roaring filled the air as a mass of bodies poured out from behind the surrounding houses. They crashed against the back of the Clthic crowd. Madsen watched in horror as daggers were plunged into throats, stomachs were slashed by swords, and pleas for mercy were ignored.

It was at that point that the androids in low-power mode abruptly sprung awake. Most of them threw themselves at the attackers with cold and precise motions. "F-Fuck…!" Madsen snarled.

Four of the low-powered androids (L-Ps) approached her, spun on their heels to face away, then just stood there in a loose circular formation around her. As soon as anyone from either side got too close, knowingly or unknowingly, one of the L-Ps would lash out with a skull-shattering punch. She didn't move as the bloody mosh pit continued raging on around her. She started feeling nauseous. The foul fumes of spilt E-Gel slipping up through her nostrils made her want to gag. As the main body of the battle was pushed further away, she was still caged by the mindless androids.

She didn't think she'd ever be glad to see him again, but she was. Alric led a formation of around twenty guys in fighting their way through the mess with Gabriel, Claudia and Arthur among them. In Alric's hand was his T1B Directed Energy Weapon, its barrel smouldering. His other hand swung a sword at Clthics who stepped carelessly into reach.

Alric's group clashed against the L-Ps that encircled Madsen. Guys with shields pressed up against the L-Ps while the people behind skewered and impaled them with spears. Once they were sufficiently damaged, Alric stowed his sword and brought the stock of his T1B down over and over onto their skulls. Claudia curb stomped the remaining heads into mush.

It wasn't real. They were just human shaped masses of polymer, wire clusters, solid state drives, optics, and composite fibre. But it didn't matter. What she saw were *people* skewering each other with sharpened pieces of metal. Her heart was thumping against her ribcage.

"Thy Holiness?!" someone called over the commotion. It shook Madsen free of her trance. She saw Gabriel. He had a hand on her shoulder as he said, "It is not safe here!"

Alric added, "Thou must escort Madsen to safety! I shall command the forces here and ensure that thou hast ample time to escape!"

"Nay!" Gabriel replied with a shake of his head. The layer of screaming and clanging made it difficult to hear what they were saying, but Madsen managed it. "'Tis not my place! Thou art a Knight Thestor; perform thy duty!" Madsen watched as Alric's body stiffened.

With a frustrated wave of her hand, Claudia interjected, "It doesn't matter what you two bastards think!" She turned to Madsen. "Yer Holiness, who do you wish ta shepherd you ta safety?!"

"Fuck..." sighed Madsen. She glanced back and forth between the two men. Gabriel was open-minded, kind, and most importantly, not unpredictable. It didn't matter though. Alric found her. Sure, he didn't know as much about everything as the Clthics seemed to, but he definitely knew more than Gabriel did. Also...she owed him.

Swallowing her doubt, Madsen paced over to Alric. His brow was furrowed and his lips stretched thin as she grabbed his shoulders. She came in close enough to whisper, "Listen, I know you're confused, but so am I. We're in this together now."

As she pulled away, she watched his expression soften slightly. He took a deep breath and stood slightly straighter. "Thy will be done," he muttered.

Gabriel set a hand onto Alric's chest. "Take care, my friend."

"Thou shalt do well to heed thine own words. She will not be present to gift thee another set of legs," Alric joked. Gabriel laughed and slapped Alric on the shoulder. With that, he and the others charged into the fray like lunatics.

XXXV
A Dying Ember

Fleeing amidst the chaos was the most difficult thing Alric had ever done. He had sworn to lay down his life in Heaven's defence. To ride *away* from battle while townsfolk died in his place was the greatest shame of all. If he had stayed, he might have found peace in death. However, he knew not if it truly was Heaven he defended, or if it existed at all. No matter how many times he insisted to himself that what Madsen told him was not true, the words had taken root. He could continue to wish that they hadn't, but it would change nothing. Despite the strife that plagued his heart…he had no choice. They had taken flight atop a wagon pulled by two steeds loaded with all of Alric and Madsen's belongings. Alric had pushed them hard for three hours before finally allowing them time to rest.

The horses, Nocht and a timid thing named Thistle, slept beneath the shelter of a goliath tree by the side of the road. Thistle slept standing, while Nocht had hunkered down in the grass next to Alric. He sat there before the campfire, staring at its dancing embers with an expression as blank as slate.

Madsen sat on the opposite side of the fire. She had been prodding the wound on her forearm with an array of strange objects that she had pulled from a white case emblazoned with a red cross. Madsen opened a small vial of clear liquid and dabbed some of it onto a cloth. "I'm sorry. I didn't know…I didn't know how hard it would be for you to understand everything. Usually, robots have, uh, what we call narrow A.I. They're good at doing really specific things, and they don't really *understand* what they're doing." Alric remained silent. He closed his eyes and tried to ignore her words. "But you guys are different. Obviously. You can talk to me about how you're feeling…okay?"

Speaking openly about his emotions was not something he ever liked to do, nor had it ever been encouraged. To be told to do so was…unnerving. Nevertheless, he had no desire to dredge up the feelings of shame that he had worked so hard to banish. He said nothing as he stared at the embers ejected into the sky by the campfire.

Madsen rubbed the damp cloth along the edge of her injury. In silence, her face warped in pain. Alric narrowed his eyes and continued staring.

After the discomfort had trickled out of her face, she wrapped a stark white bandage around her arm. She appeared to notice his abundant attention. "Long story short, my body works a little differently than yours. If I don't clean my wounds, they could get infected and well…kill me. I'd rather *not* right now." After the wound had been dressed, Madsen crossed her arms and sighed.

He could not stand to look at her. Each moment he beheld her only reminded him of how far he had fallen. Of how he had forsaken God with his traitorous thoughts. He could feel the rage swelling within him, but he did not know what to do with it. Was she a demon to be struck down, or was it all still a test of his devotion? A test that he had clearly *failed*? With a jolt, the knight stood, moved over to the wagon, and pulled a wooden chest up to its edge. Madsen bounced over to Alric with energy more befitting a child. "What're you doing?"

He carefully opened the chest, revealing his plate armour within. "Donning my armour."

"Gotcha. Lemme give you a hand."

"Before I begin, I must recite the Oath of Vigilance."

"The what now?" Madsen asked bluntly as she propped herself up onto the wagon and crossed her legs.

"A prayer…"

Madsen crinkled her nose as Alric knelt in the grass and held a fist over his heart. "Uh. Okay," she murmured. Her obvious confusion only made Alric even more contemptful of her. An angel would surely recognise a holy rite…wouldn't they?

As Alric spoke the verses of the Oath aloud, his eyes were forced shut during the prayer…but he could feel Madsen's gaze upon his back. It made him uneasy. After the words of the Oath of Vigilance hovered through the air, Alric stood and began retrieving his plate armour from the chest. Upon close inspection, he realised that it all had been severely damaged when he was struck by the taukumu bolt during the scuffle with the druids. Its once gleaming surface had been melted and blackened. He could even feel that some of the plate had warped due to the immense heat.

Completely ignorant of the damage, Madsen was fascinated by how all of the separate plates were linked together to allow for articulation. For a moment, Alric stared at her in disbelief as she played with one of the poleyns, the knee joints, by bending and straightening it over and over again as if it were a toy. "Dude, this is pretty sick," she remarked.

Alric did not know what she meant by claiming that his armour was ill, so he simply ignored her again and went on with it. As always, Alric began at the feet and worked his way up, starting with the greaves. Once they comfortably hugged his shins, he was about to reach for his left cuisse but was somewhat startled to see that Madsen was already holding it out to him. Madsen smiled as he accepted it. He proceeded in locking the cuisse into the greave and tying it to his arming jacket as Madsen hovered incredibly close, watching the entire process with curiosity that would put a scholar to shame.

Madsen whistled, "That's pretty cool. Can I do the other one?" He was not certain why she asked, because she did not await an answer. Alric watched in silence as Madsen attempted to fit his right cuisse. With rapid glances back to Alric's work, Madsen moved remarkably quickly. In time that would have outshone many squires who had served Alric in the past, Madsen applied the final knot to the points atop the cuisse.

"How's that? Is it too tight?"

Alric stretched his leg out several times before shaking his head.

Madsen grinned and pointed at Alric with both hands as she made a very strange sound. "Ayyyyy." Alric narrowed his eyes. He could not find anything to say to her, for her peculiarity had robbed him of his words. "What's next? This little tutu thing?" Madsen asked as she picked up Alric's mail skirt.

Alric was expecting the entire process to take much longer than usual seeing as Madsen insisted on helping even with the parts that Alric could manage on his own. However, despite her inexperience, she had a sharp mind. There were several moments of confusion but after fifteen minutes or so, Alric stood completely armed. The last thing he fixed upon himself was his belt. As he tightened it over his Thestor surcoat, he watched Madsen as she stared at the two weapons that hung from it. "Why do you have two swords?" she asked genuinely.

He grabbed the hilt of his rondel dagger and muttered, "This is a dagger."

Gesturing towards it, Madsen cocked her head. "May I?"

The knight drew the weapon and handed it to her. Madsen whistled in awe as she inspected every inch of it, including its wooden grip. "*Damn.* It's as long as my forearm. Why do you need this if you already have a sword?"

He did not want to answer her. He did not want to speak to her at all…but he found himself complying. "It is used to stab at the gaps in armour, namely in the eyes, neck, armpits, and groin."

"Geez. You stab people in the dick with this thing?" Madsen mumbled as she mimed the action.

The facetious remark drained what little patience Alric had left. He smacked his lips in frustration and reached for the dagger. "'Tis neither the time nor the place for such frivolous questions. We are under attack by those savage heretics."

She leaned back, managing to pull the weapon out of his reach at the last second. "Last I checked, we aren't being attacked right now. We'll worry when we have something to worry about. Okay?" A tense silence festered between the two of them. Alric felt rage charging his blood, but Madsen was calm and stern. "*So*, do you stab people in the dick with this or not?"

"*Yes*," he blurted while snatching the dagger back. "Now let us cease this farce and break camp."

"Alright, alright, don't get your panties in a bunch," snapped Madsen. She quite hastily yet neatly packed away all of the supplies that she was using to treat her wounds as Alric loaded everything back onto the wagon. When he returned for the final crate, he saw that she was stowing a blood-stained arcane artefact. It resembled a very small handaxe in the loosest sense; it had a short grip and a mass of material at the top. The foremost edge of said mass was not sharp, however. It had two 'nozzles' that glowed with arcane light. The first time he saw the artefact, it was when Madsen used it to eat straight through a Clthic footman's steel helm and end his life. He recalled the sparks and fire that washed over his armour and the heat as the man was detonated by the lethal dose of eldritch power. It was as if it used pure magic to slice through matter, as opposed to sharpness.

"Speaking of sidearms…thou best keep that weapon at thy side," Alric advised. "The Clthics are many, and they shall not rest until they have captured thee."

Her face scrunched up in a peculiar way. Alric could not even hope to glean the meaning of her expressions; they were all so foreign to him. "It's not a weapon. It's a tool."

Alric couldn't help but scoff. "A tool? The ease with which thou struck down that demonist could lead me to believe it to be a tool of *death*, perhaps."

Once again, Alric watched Madsen's face contort. Her eyes widened, her breathing stopped, and her mouth dropped open slightly. "S-Shit…" she sighed, steadying herself on one of the crates. It could not be…remorse that she felt, could it? What kind of angel would regret the deaths of devil worshippers? When she spoke, the light tone that usually inhabited her voice had gone. "I…I killed him," she whispered to herself as her eyes defocused on the world around her. She seemed to stare into oblivion itself.

Alric, pushed further into his unease by Madsen's apparent regret, couldn't help but feel irritated that she paused for even a moment to consider the life of a devil worshipper. "His life had no worth. He had cast it into the pits of Hell the moment he allied with the Clthic Synod."

Madsen didn't seem to even hear what he said. "I didn't even try to find another way. I just…leapt at him." With a frustrated sigh, Madsen threw her hands up. "I still thought you all were just machines. But he had a mind…he had a life. And I ended it."

"Everyone must die some day. How that end comes to pass is of no consequence," Alric grunted.

Madsen leaned forward, her expression hardening. "You can't really believe that."

Alric turned away from Madsen and focused on kicking dirt onto the fire. "I do," he huffed. *I must*, he thought.

XXXVI
INFERNAL WISDOM

Fiammetta slowly churned the cauldron full of pottage with her ladle and watched the steam swirl upwards and into the cold afternoon air. She scooped some of it up, slopped it into a wooden bowl, and handed it to the man in front of her. "Fires bless you," he said with a bow as he accepted the bowl and moved on. There was a line of dozens of people behind him, all patiently awaiting their meals. Fiammetta glanced to her right and saw Gertrude handing food out at a brisk pace. It seemed that some semblance of normalcy was doing the former tavernkeep good.

"Oi." The voice knocked Fiammetta from her daydreaming, and she turned to see a tall, grim man looming over her. It was Shaun Carver…one of Franco's men-at-arms. She swallowed and stared up at him, her hand trembling slightly. "You gonna do yer job or what?" With a jolt, she spooned some pottage into the man's bowl but as she handed it back to him, he scoffed. "You gave that other fella a lot more than that. Tryin' ta swindle me or somethin'?"

Before he had even finished speaking, Fiammetta had added another two spoonfuls and held the bowl back out, all while avoiding the man's gaze. He thuggishly snatched it as he tutted to himself. "Stupid fuckin' girl."

With a tense sigh, she did her best to discard the scorn on her face and replace it with a gentle smile as the next person stepped up. For all the promise of reform by the Clthic Synod…her lot in life had not particularly changed, had it? It had actually gotten *worse.* She was a noblewoman before. One of lesser standing, but a noblewoman, nonetheless. But there she was, cooking, serving, and being silent…like some common servant.

The line of hungry people slowly shortened as she served the hearty pottage. As she did, she would frequently see Clthic witches pacing through camp. Their masked faces would inspire fear, awe, and respect among the commonfolk. Whenever they passed by, Fiammetta found herself ardently averting her eyes. It was not polite to stare…and such a sight, a flayed human body, was not something that any person should wish to stare at. The fact that she *had* to drag her attention away made her feel disgusting.

Two children that Fiammetta had become fairly familiar with, Liam and Josephine, had reached the front of the line. "Oh, good day, children."

"Hello, Miss Fia," Josephine said quietly. She and her brother held their bowls out graciously as Fiammetta filled them to the brim. "Me brother was wondering…'ave you seen Howard? He was tha guard captain in our hometown. We haven't seen 'im fer a while."

"Hm…I am afraid not. Perhaps you should ask Gertrude? She would very much like to see you again, anyway."

Josephine nodded vigorously and with their bowls almost overflowing with pottage, the two siblings waved at Fiammetta as they made their way over to see Gertrude. Fiammetta stared after them for a while, but her moment of peace was once again interrupted by the sound of footsteps in the grass behind her. She spun and came face to face with H'vrsh, Dread Priest of the Tethspeakers. "Wretched Instrument," she said, bowing before him.

"As you were, Fiammetta. I have come here with a task for you."

Fiammetta took a deep breath to calm her climbing excitement. "Of course. Whatever you wish."

He gestured to the cauldron. "I would ask you to deliver the remaining food to the Infernal Sanctum on the East side of the camp."

The Infernal Sanctum was a tent that Fiammetta had been told was used exclusively by the Tethspeakers for some of their black magic studies… Fiammetta furrowed her brow. "But…I thought that you witches were beyond such trivial things? That Baptism had freed you from hunger?"

"As much as the Tethspeakers and K'relvic Nuns are strengthened by Mother Xalt'n's rituals, they still must feed the same as any mortal. They simply require less in order to subsist."

She couldn't help but bite on the inside of her lower lip. Of course. Why would it be any different? "Y-Yes. I shall see it done, Dread Priest."

Fiammetta lifted the cauldron from its stand, but H'vrsh gently grabbed her by the wrist. He leaned closer to her and whispered, "You are to plant your gaze on the ground as you enter. Do not speak to any of the witches, do not look at anything inside the tent."

"I…I-I am afraid I do not understand."

"It is for your own safety, my child. Enter, leave the vessel upon the table, then depart. Am I clear?"

Fiammetta nodded heartily. "You are, Wretched Instrument."

She could feel the stares as she made her way across the camp. Was it because she was a young woman walking alone…or was it the burn that covered half of her face? Whatever the answer was, Fiammetta was glad that she did not know. The closer she got to the witches' side of camp, the lighter the burden became. The Nuns and Tethspeakers did not lust, nor did they ridicule. They had cast all of that away. She found herself standing straighter the further away she was from the commonfolk.

The tents used by the witches were made from tanned hide that had been sewn together into a patchwork tapestry. Fiammetta stared at them as she walked by and couldn't help but notice the human shape of each patch of skin and the rainbow of different skin tones. Her mind wandered. What happened to the skin that was flayed from the witches as part of their Baptism? Were they perhaps…reused? She reached out and ran her fingers along the surface of the tent that H'vrsh had told her to find and swallowed her feelings of curiosity.

Fiammetta almost barged straight in but caught herself just in time. She took a deep breath, looked at the ground, and held the cauldron out in front of her. H'vrsh's instructions were clear. She would obey them to the letter…and then, perhaps, he would see her worth.

The interior of the tent was surprisingly well-lit by a stark white light. Fiammetta heard the shifting of feet as she entered. "Excuse the intrusion. I come on the order of the Dread Priest with a meal for you."

"Continue to step forward and you will find a table, young one." Fiammetta's throat quivered when Mother Xalt'n's voice reached her ears. "Leave it there."

"Of course, Mother."

She continued into the room and heard short, ragged breaths…wet peeling…deathly moaning. Her composure wavered. It was the moaning. The pathetic, weak, almost sensual moaning. Fiammetta did not turn her head, but she sent her eyes darting to one side.

It took her a moment to realise that it was a person. It was a man, hands pinned to a wooden frame, with the front of his body peeled open like it was a garment that had been unbuttoned. His organs were entirely exposed to the daytime air. Fiammetta stopped in her tracks. She watched his heart gyrate in his chest. His lungs inflate, then deflate. Her eyes followed the damp maze of his intestinal tract. The last thing she savoured was his face. It was Howard Mason…the guard from Oak. He looked to be barely conscious. His eyes were unfocused and his barely audible groaning sent a shiver oscillating down Fiammetta's spine. She knew it was wrong to even think…but the sound was not wholly unpleasant.

Her head swept around the tent, revealing that there were at least twenty other people in similar states of disassembly. Tethspeakers swept their hands through floating arcane symbols then prodded the insides of their helpless captives. Fiammetta's attention eventually came to rest on Mother Xalt'n, who was staring right at her. The sight threw her from her wistful daze. "M-Mother Xalt'n…forgive me, I-I did not wish to–"

"Are you not afraid? Disgusted?" she interjected.

Fiammetta swallowed. "Y-Yes…I should simply…leave…"

Xalt'n strode up to Fiammetta and gingerly plucked the cauldron of pottage from her hand. "You needn't lie to me, young one. These feelings of shame and embarrassment you harbour…they are of no use to you. I shall ask again: are you not afraid?"

It was wrong to enjoy it… It was wrong. Evil. But again, who determined all of that? The Church? They had no power, for they were false. Fiammetta cleared her throat and said quietly, "I-I am not."

"I see. We understand that most followers are not faithful enough to lay eyes upon this without losing themselves to emotion. Perhaps your time in the Infernal Forge has accelerated your acceptance of the truth." Xalt'n set the cauldron onto the table, then joined Fiammetta who had drifted closer to Howard's unravelled body.

Fiammetta feverishly squeezed the fabric of her dress. "What are you doing? Torturing them?" she asked.

Xalt'n snapped her fingers and an array of shimmering glyphs appeared at her side. "The pendants carried by my Tethspeakers are imbued with great magic that can alter and compel the bodies of men. However, these Demonic Arts must first be learned. We use these forgotten wretches to test the effects of our spells and discover new ones." Howard's eyes latched onto Fiammetta's. She watched his lips tremble. Xalt'n suddenly lowered her voice and said, "Most times, our experiments are conducted with pain removed entirely. However…what you suggested can be rather…*pleasing*…" Fiammetta turned sharply to Xalt'n. Her amber eyes seemed to taunt her. "He is at your mercy."

"What…? N-No. I couldn't…I-I…" Her stammering came to an abrupt end as her focus settled once again upon the tangled intestines in the pit of his torso. Her fingers jittered back and forth. Xalt'n crept behind her and leaned over her shoulder. Her warm breaths washed over Fiammetta's ear, and she felt a tingling sensation work its way through her body.

"You could," Xalt'n whispered. Fiammetta felt Xalt'n's finger trace its way down her forearm. She grasped her wrist then slowly moved it closer and closer to Howard's innards. Fiammetta bit her lip. It was right there. She could do it. It would feel…*so* good if she just…*did it.* The desire was all too much for Fiammetta to handle, for in an instant, she had forced her arm out of Xalt'n's grasp and buried it in Howard's bowels. The squelching…the feeling of damp, slimy matter within her fingers…the strained grunts of pain… It made her gasp. She felt sweat beading on her forehead, and it suddenly felt much too hot in her dress. Faintly, she heard Xalt'n mutter, "I can see it in your eyes, Fiammetta. I know that you are not what they wish you to be. Here, among us, you can be as you truly are."

Fiammetta squeezed the intestines and stared intently into Howard's eyes. He was terrified. Weak…like a mighty oak toppled by a strike of lightning and hollowed by the insects that it had once loomed over. Her whole life Fiametta had felt so small and powerless. But in that moment, with Howard's intestines slipping against her fingers she felt *almost* powerful. She could do anything she wanted. Rip them out or shove them down his throat. Anything at all, and he could do nothing about it. He could watch, he could squirm, he could scream, but no matter what he did, he would know what it was like to feel weak.

XXXVII
Don't Mind Us. Just Passing Through

She didn't dream very often. When she did though, it was always about the most mundane and boring things. Well, mundane and boring to *her*. Most of the time, it was an actual experience that she had in the past. A memory. Madsen found herself floating there in an endless black void. In her hand was an impact driver that she was using to remove an access panel on the ODIN Space Telescope to replace one of its faulty batteries. When she turned around, her entire field of view was taken up by a wall of bold blue, swirling white, and vast swathes of copper. It was the surface of BYRNE221 d, the third planet in the BYRNE221 star system. Its front-facing name was 'Horizon' or something sappy like that.

All of a sudden, there was a deafening 'bang' as the surface of Horizon vanished, and she snapped back into reality. Madsen sat right up and cocked her head around like a scared meerkat. She was supposed to say 'what', but an unintelligible mess was delivered instead.

Alric ignored the weird groan and replied, "We are approaching a village."

Madsen got up, stretched, then vaulted over the front of the wagon and into the seat next to Alric. She thought she knew what it was like to deal with stressful situations. Every time she flew, there was a chance that something could go wrong. Things *had* gone wrong, but she and her crew had the training and the guts to deal with it and come home safe. It was extremely dangerous...but being strapped to an interstellar bullet was a little different than being the focus of a religious conflict between a church and some bloodthirsty cultists.

For the trip, Madsen had to get a little more inconspicuous. She wasn't exactly a fan of being worshipped by everyone she came across and it got to the point where she couldn't risk it. The people following Servius weren't exclusively 'witches' or anything. They looked just like everyone else, so there wasn't any way to know who believed in their weird cult until it was too late. She put on her full-head welding mask, unrolled her sleeves, and slipped on her work gloves. Alric gave her a hooded cloak to put on top of everything and cover her neck. She still stuck out because of what she wore, but Alric said something about her looking like a druid once the getup was complete. Whatever *that* meant.

For the couple of days they spent on the road, Madsen ate from the emergency rations that she took from the Hathor. She had no problems with eating synth-tissue…it was the E-Gel that was pumped through it she was worried about. If the synth-tissue wasn't completely drained of the stuff, it could make her sick. Maybe even kill her if she ingested heaps of it.

"You haven't seen any L-Ps…I mean 'undead' wandering around, have you?" She tried to scratch her nose but her hand bonked off the front of her welding mask. With a sigh, she lifted the thing up and tried again.

"I have not. Perhaps the Church there has not yet been defiled."

Madsen exhaled loudly as she crossed her arms. "Eh… Should we go around?"

"I would not recommend it. The terrain here is already difficult without the rain that fell yesterday. We could become bogged down," Alric muttered. "We may have no choice but to pass through." She had to admit; she never thought that some mud and slightly uneven terrain was ever going to be a problem in her life. But there she was. It made her feel more than just a little privileged.

She watched Alric as he gripped the reins. He had the faceplate of his helmet open, but he still wore his armour. He had to have been wearing it for at least eight hours at that point. Just as Madsen was thinking to herself about how much of a pain in the ass it had to be, her eyes fell onto the garment that he wore over the armour. "If we're gonna head in, you need to take that off."

"I beg thy pardon?"

"Your…dress thing," she said as she pointed at his chest. "We don't know if the Clthics are in control of that town."

Alric grumbled, "Firstly, 'tis a surcoat. Secondly, I shall most certainly *not*. My faith is my shield, not something to be ashamed of."

Madsen clenched her jaw. If she knew one thing about how people acted, it was that the more they thought they were losing something, the harder they latched onto it. There wasn't much she could do…and she wanted to be as accepting as possible, but when it got to the point where it caused him to behave irrationally and jeopardise everything, she couldn't say that it wasn't irritating. "Do you *want* them to fucking kill you?"

"I would very much like to see them try."

The engineer massaged the bridge of her nose. "Okay tough guy, either you do it yourself or I'll turn you off and do it for you," she snapped. With a growl, he handed the reins to Madsen who stared at them with widened eyes. "...I've never handled horses before. Maybe we should just stop."

"They shall follow the road," he spat dryly.

Begrudgingly, Madsen took the reins and muttered to herself, "Asshole."

Alric stood and stared into the body of the town as he shaded his optics from the sun with his hand. It still blew her mind that someone specced the androids to just match human capabilities. It would've been easier for them to be better, but all of those different subsystems were designed and created with the sole purpose of making them as useless as humans. If Alric had the same cameras in his head as the stock standard ones on any consumer PC, he'd be able to magnify his vision *20 times* without any external tools. But...for whatever reason, he had to squint and focus like an actual person. Before long, she could see his posture ease up and heard a sigh of relief escape his mouth. "I see the church. 'Tis not defaced nor corrupted. We shall proceed."

Madsen rolled her eyes. It wasn't long before she could see it too. Tiny specks denoting people were milling about in front of it and she saw colourful tapestries hanging from its windows. There wasn't any screaming, so that was a good sign. She didn't want to give him the satisfaction of admitting that his brash behaviour worked out okay that time, so she just frowned. "Rad."

The town was a hell of a lot smaller than Phaemslake. She noticed that she was getting a few confused glances, but nothing too crazy.

She watched as a woman collected water from a well, a dude carved up some meat, and another dude hammered away at a piece of metal on an anvil. It made her realise that she never *really* had to worry about surviving before. Well, yeah, she had a pretty dangerous job, but it wasn't like she had to gather everything she needed to subsist on a daily basis. Whether she was thirsty, hungry, or needed a tool, someone or something had already done all the hard work for her and there was never really any risk of running out. Especially when she wasn't working. On any developed colony, all she needed to do was run to a store and throw money at a problem until it went away.

However, what really caught her attention was the *kid* she saw standing on the side of the road and staring at her with shimmering green optics. Judging from his height, Madsen reckoned that he was supposed to represent a prepubescent child. As soon as she saw him, the cogs in her brain started turning. "Woah. Hey, how do kids work? Do they *stay* kids?"

Although she couldn't see his face, she could hear the confusion in his voice. "Nay. They grow."

Madsen narrowed her eyes. "Grow? What do you mean? Like, are they taken back to the church and given new grown-up bodies?"

"They *grow,*" Alric repeated. "That boy is a newborn. In time, he shall become a man."

"Hm. Okay." She stared at the kid as they went by, and he was pretty chubby. His face didn't really look that different to the 'adult' androids, same with the size of his hands, feet, head, etcetera. It suddenly made sense. The skeleton would telescope in order to lengthen the limbs, and the excess synth-tissue and polymer membrane was for the adult-sized configuration. They didn't grow; they *expanded.* And Alric said he was a newborn…so, when they were 'born', the children were already physically around the twelve-year-old mark. It would've been impossible to make all that adult matter compress into a baby-sized package. The kid seemed to be *acting* like a twelve-year-old too, so maybe they were born with a decent amount of data pre-loaded onto their SSDs?

Eventually, Alric leaned down to her and whispered into her ear. "Continue to follow this road. We shall simply pass through."

As she nodded, the wagon drifted by a series of buildings and entered the town square. The place was pretty empty, but she did see some people on the ground at the edge of the square. At first, Madsen didn't think there was anything out of the ordinary about them, but she realised that they all wore these headdresses that looked like folded up pieces of cloth. The clothing, from Madsen's very limited understanding of historical fashion, didn't look too different from what she had already seen. Their polymer membrane skin was all different shades of green ranging from dark forest to bright lime. Everyone that Madsen had seen so far, including the other villagers, ranged from red, purple, or dark blue.

Standing over these people was a knight in full armour. He was wearing the same surcoat that Alric had: pure white with a red linear design on the front. The knight was rifling through a bag, discarding most of its contents onto the ground. As their wagon was passing by, Madsen watched as the knight pulled a book out of the bag. With anger oozing from his body language, he slammed the objects onto the ground and snarled, "Liars! All of thee! Thou art infidels! Here to poison our land with thy blasphemy and putrid stench!"

Madsen pulled back on the reins, easing Nocht and Thistle to a stop in the middle of the road. “Hey, what the fuck is that guy doing?”

“Madsen…!” hissed Alric.

She leapt off the side of the wagon and stared in utter disbelief as the ranting knight went on. “It is thy fault, isn’t it? Our fair God-fearing land has been swallowed by perpetual darkness! The dead rise from their graves, dragons blot out the sun with their wretched smoke, and witches curse our very souls with devilry! It has come at last! The infidels of Qurveen plot to destroy us all!”

Moving with purpose, Madsen paced up to the knight. “Hey, pal, what’s your problem? Huh?” He had his visor up so she could see the disgust on his blueish-purple face as he gave her a once over.

The clanging of steel by her side told her that Alric had decided to join her. He cleared his throat and said, “Hail, Brother. I am Alric. Art thou in need of assistance?”

“Edward,” replied the knight with a bow. “Not to worry, good Brother, I am upholding the Fourth Attestation. ‘Tis simply another pack of heathens in need of the Lord’s punishment.”

Alric exhaled through his nose and looked down at the people on the ground, prompting Madsen to do the same. It was a group of about five androids, two of them were women. Most had bruises and tears running down their faces and their clothes were covered in dirt. Coins, tools, and pieces of food were scattered across the ground. With frustration lacing his words, Alric said, “These folk are indeed infidels, but attacking the Church is not among their transgressions; the Clthic Synod is our true mortal foe. Thou best charge these folk with the correct crime.”

She couldn’t believe what she was hearing. Edward was assaulting them in the street because of their religion? And Alric…he didn’t really seem *too* bothered by it? Madsen’s first instinct was to get over there and help them up, but Alric’s reply made her stomach twist and writhe. “Let me get this straight. You guys *attack* people because they don’t believe in the same thing you do? Are you fucking kidding me?” She glanced back and forth between Alric and Edward.

The smile on Edward’s face slowly vanished and was replaced by a cold, empty gaze. Shockingly to Madsen, Alric didn’t really react. He had a thousand-yard stare going as Edward snarled, “Where is thy dress?”

“What?” she snorted.

"Such attire is inappropriate for a woman," Edward scoffed, gesturing at Madsen's jumpsuit. Namely the pants. "Thou best remedy the situation. Dressing as a man… *Disgusting*."

Madsen huffed, filling the lower half of her welding mask's visor with light fog. "Holy shit. You gotta be kidding me," she droned, smirking in disbelief.

Edward glared at Alric and snapped, "Thy wench is eerily ignorant, Brother Alric. One wouldst think that a poor reflection of her Thestor compatriot. Or is it not thy duty to preach the word of God?"

When Madsen turned to look at Alric, she could see his hands trembling more and more with each passing second. She knelt, picked up the book that Edward tossed onto the dirt, then moved over to the victims. There were words on the cover….a language that she recognised. As she handed the book back over to one of the men, she watched as their eyes lit up. "Thank you…! Allah bless you…!" he gasped…in Arabic.

Madsen nodded. In the same language, she replied, "Go. Stay safe."

The foreigners picked up what they could of their belongings and took off. Edward shook his head as he wrapped his fingers around the handle of his sword. "Sympathy for the infidels *and* knowledge of their disgusting tongue? My, my, this *whore* treads a fine line. Perhaps I should–"

Madsen's mouth snapped open as Alric stepped forward and rammed his armoured fist right into the middle of Edward's face. There was a 'pop' and a 'crack' as Edward teetered backwards and crashed onto his back. "Oh my god…!" Madsen muttered. "Alric! What the fuck, man?!"

Edward didn't move. The few people in the village square stopped and stared at Alric, who just stood there gazing down at Edward's unconscious body. As stupid as it sounded, Madsen swore she was starting to see emotion through his optics. There was this seething hatred. It didn't make any sense seeing as Alric just met the guy…but maybe it wasn't the man he was spiteful of. Maybe it was bigger than that. His shoulders rose and fell with every breath he took. "Jesus Christ. C'mon! Let's get the fuck outta here!"

He nodded emptily and hovered back over to the wagon, leaving Madsen to stare on. No one came to help Edward or see if he was okay. She kept looking over her shoulder as they left the town, but he stayed there on the dirt. Twenty minutes went by. The town shrunk and the wagon weaved its way through the landscape. She couldn't take it anymore. In a fit of exasperation, Madsen threw her cloak off and slipped out of her welding mask. "Are we gonna talk about that or what?" she pressed bluntly, her voice low.

Alric swallowed. "I could not stand idly by and watch as that fool spat such disgusting words at thee."

With a mix between a scoff and a chuckle, Madsen shook her head. "You didn't do it for me. I didn't give a shit. He was an asshole." Alric's eyes were fixed on the road as he held the reins. "You didn't think there was anything wrong with what he was doing?"

He trembled for a second, then shook his head. "We are both sworn brothers of the Order of Saint Thestus. It is our duty to enforce God's rule and confer his divine wrath unto those who refuse to submit."

Madsen felt the blood rush out of her face. "Wait. W-Wait. What the hell do you mean 'divine wrath'? You don't…kill people for this shit, do you?"

"If need be," he muttered.

A bitter taste flooded her mouth. Alric was an extremist. Even worse…he wasn't the only one. "H-How many people have you killed?" Her voice quivered as she asked the question. Alric swallowed and scoffed. "How. Many."

In frustration and with a twinge of guilt, he snapped, "I have lost count."

"Stop the cart."

"What?"

Madsen erupted to her feet and loomed over Alric. "Stop the *fucking* cart!" she growled. Instead of stopping dead in the middle of the road, Alric led the horses onto a patch of grass beside it, then slowed to a halt. He avoided eye contact with her the whole time. "I…I-I can't believe it. You're… O-Oh my god," Madsen gasped as she ran a hand through her hair. In her time, there was a word for people who attacked and killed non-combatants to achieve some political or religious goal. "Y-You're a fucking terrorist."

Part of her wanted to explode at him. The notion of hating other people you never met for some arbitrary reason was absolutely unfathomable to her. But she had to try to understand. Alric didn't grow up in 31st Century society. He, like everyone else around him, was a product of the prevailing views and cultures. He lived in a world where it was just accepted that there was something out there that could see into his heart. Into his mind. The second he admitted to himself that he doubted something, that *thing* would know. Their *god* would know. And it was that fear that motivated him. It made him desperate to please it. So desperate that he was willing to do anything. Horrible things. He wasn't in denial because he was being stubborn…he was *scared.* Madsen closed her eyes and took a deep breath. When she opened them, Alric was looking right at her. He looked shocked. Dumbstruck. By what? How upset she was? A realisation struck her all of a sudden. How many times had she told him that his religion was wrong? How many times had she given him a reason to kill her? "Why am I still alive, Alric?" His optics pulsed for a second and his bottom lip curled. "Is it because you still think I'm an angel…or because you believe me?" she sighed.

Suddenly, Alric erupted from his seat and leapt from the wagon. With all the sounds of tumbling pots and pans, he lumbered further into the field of tall grass by the road. "Alric!" Madsen called. In the following seconds, she threw herself after him. She felt the grass brush by her thighs as she jogged with her eyes locked on the steel figure just in front of her.

When she caught up, she heard him muttering to himself. "O Lord, hear my words. Make thyself known so that I may retake the path. I have sinned. I have doubted thee. Please…show me something. Anything. A sign." The wind raked through the tall grass. Clouds silently drifted by in the sky. But nothing else happened. Madsen watched Alric as he winced. He was shattered. That much was clear. "T-Thou canst move Heaven and earth…rain fire from the sky…but thou cannot help me? We must believe in thee or be condemned for eternity…yet thou grant us no comfort to ease our suffering?" he whimpered.

"He isn't listening, Alric. He…isn't there," she whispered. "You don't have to be scared of him anymore."

Alric snapped around and came bearing down on Madsen. "How couldst thou know!? How!?" he screamed. Madsen backpedalled, but Alric kept coming. "What proof is there!?" He came to a stop in front of her with his optics filled with tears. Madsen closed her eyes and grimaced. She didn't mean for it to sound like that. She was just trying to reassure him.

Softly, under her breath, she answered, "I don't have proof. I never meant for it to seem like I *wanted* to tear it all down. I'm sorry. But what I'm telling you is objective. Maybe there *is* some higher power out there, I don't know. But what I *do* know is it isn't the one you believe in. Your entire race was built by *us.* Your idea of god is just an interpretation of *us.* Same goes for what the Clthics say about demons. Those are facts."

Alric collapsed onto his knees. His head was tilted down slightly, forcing him to stare into the dirt. Madsen knelt to look into his optics and saw a completely blank expression on his face. She wanted to tell him that she knew how he felt…but she couldn't. She didn't have the faintest idea. Not too long ago, she thought that she should've just shut her mouth and not told him the truth…but in light of what he'd done, what his entire Order was doing… She wasn't so sure anymore. Maybe it was about time he realised what he'd been doing.

XXXVIII
Unsightly And Vile

The wine swirled about in her goblet as the squire poured. Katheryn watched it carefully, prepared to give the boy a clout on the ear if he spilled it on her gown. "Hast thou seen Sir Reginald after thine incredible victory over him?" prodded King Roger IV mischievously.

Once her silver goblet was full, Katheryn waved the squire away with a lazy motion. "I did not even have the good fortune to see him *while* I secured said victory."

"He has been moping and sulking about ever since. To witness the sheer humiliation upon his face was a treat in itself." Roger IV had been a rather broad man in his youth. Age had chewed away at him, but he was by no means frail. He was lean yet powerful as he relaxed on the lavish couch that he had brought into his pavilion. The velvet tunic he wore had a gold-plated belt wrapped around its waist.

Katheryn was sitting comfortably on the floor with her legs curled to one side as she leaned on an unoccupied couch with her left arm. Her right hand gingerly gripped her goblet of wine as she took a sip. "Perhaps I should pay him a visit, then. I have yet to receive his horse and armour," she joked. The pair had been alone in Roger's pavilion lounging about and reminiscing for several hours. Well, alone save for Roger's squire, who would simply hover over to a quiet corner of the tent when he was not needed. Katheryn tensed her jaw as she ran a finger along the lip of her goblet. "I was not aware that Emperor Gerhard was familiar with my mother," she said softly.

"When Gerhard was a boy, Baron Ulrich was chosen to rule as regent in his stead until he was of age. Perhaps that was when they met."

Katheryn hadn't had much time with her grandfather Ulrich von Kleiss before he died, but her mother loved him very much. Katheryn's memories of her mother, Ursula, were as radiant as they were solemn. The days they spent studying military treatises, besting each other in chess, and riding horses through the countryside rung in her mind. And of course, the day Ursula first showed Katheryn the longsword that had been passed down to her by grandfather. She promised that it would one day fall to her. Evidently, that had never come to pass.

Then came the visions of Ursula slowly and agonisingly wasting away in a bed during the last days of her life. Alric was not there. Father was not there. They had been gone for years, set out on another Crusade to Qurveen. Katheryn was left to roil in her hatred of them nonetheless as she managed House Danecaster's affairs on her own long before Ursula's death. On one occasion, she even had to defend a castle against a siege with no more than thirty people at her disposal. She and her household held out until reinforcements arrived, garnering her some amount of respect in certain circles. Upon the return of her father and brother, however, her responsibilities were plucked away without a moment's hesitation. That taste of agency…that taste of power was not something that was easy for her to let go of.

"Katheryn, as much as it pains me to broach this subject, I am afraid that I must insist," Roger said as he sat up straighter. "Marriage." The Duchess of Arlingborough retched in disgust, taking a massive swig of her wine. Roger smirked and nodded. "I am aware of thy disdain, so I must urge thee to not reiterate it. Thou hast given a great deal to my cause, Katheryn. I only wish to return the favour. A stable future and comfortable life is what I desire for thee. My son, Prince Roger, speaks of the great Duchess Katheryn as having courage and strength more befitting a man than a woman. He finds himself in awe of thee. If thou wert to accept his hand, thou wouldst one day become Queen of Tritham." Katheryn stared at the ground during the entirety of Roger's speech. She had already been a woman grown by the time the young Prince Roger was born. "As Queen, thou wouldst wield great power within and without the kingdom. Young Roger and his vassals would see to thy every request and demand."

With a curt nod, Katheryn skulled the rest of her wine. "He and his sons would absorb my holdings. I could own perhaps one third of the total royal properties, and that is assuming that he remains king. I could not make appeals in court, create wills, or otherwise sell property without his consent. It would not be *my* power. It would be *his*…that he would so graciously allow me to partake in, if he so wished."

Roger smacked his lips. "But thou wouldst be *Queen*! Do not presume to tell me that a Queen is powerless. Dost thou plan on fighting for thy entire life? On fending off vultures for eternity? Because that is what shall happen if thou continue in this manner."

"So be it," Katheryn whispered.

The King's expression softened and he placed his chalice onto a side table. He reached for a fruit bowl, snatched a grape from it, then quipped,

"This stubbornness shall be the death of thee. Heed my words." Roger flicked the grape, which flew through the air and hit Katheryn on the side of the head. Both of them broke into staggered laughter for a moment.

The tent flap eased open and in stepped Sir Lionel of Pathridge. "Thy Royal Highness, pardon the intrusion," he said gruffly. "My lady, wouldst thou care to join me outside for a moment? This wretched messenger refuses to speak with anyone other than thyself."

Katheryn's eyes narrowed. Lionel would never bother her if it were not serious. Without hesitation, she set her goblet down, pushed to her feet with a slight wobble, then bowed to Roger IV. "The wine was quite awful, but the company was not entirely insufferable."

Roger cackled as Katheryn and Lionel took their leave. Outside, the sun had long set, and most men had retired into their pavilions. Those who did not were either eating or drinking under the embrace of the night sky. Waiting outside the tent was a commoner, a young man. He looked terrified when Katheryn emerged. "M-My lady…!" he stammered as he bowed to her.

Sir Lionel crossed his arms and his scarred lip warped into a frown. "This better be worth disturbing Duchess Katheryn's evening with the king. Speak."

The young farmer sprung back up. "Someone is awaitin' you at tha edge o' tha wood. It's a Knight Thestor."

Katheryn felt her heart buzz with relief. "By God," she sighed as the tension eased from her shoulders. "Why has he not come to me himself?"

The farmer shrugged and simply pointed at the very edge of the tournament grounds in an Eastward direction. Katheryn flattened out the hem of her dress, wiped some of the sweat from her forehead, cleared her throat, then patted the farmer twice on the shoulder. "Good boy. Sir Lionel, give this man a hearty meal."

Before Lionel could ask what on earth she was going to do, Katheryn had already sauntered off towards the trees. The sheer amount of wine she had ingested made walking through the grass a lot harder than it should have been, but she managed it somehow. The light faded and Katheryn found herself squinting through the darkness. There was a rustling in the grass to her left. Katheryn, with speed that left much to be desired thanks to her intoxication, fumbled for her bastard sword, pulled it from its scabbard, then swung it outward with a single motion.

There was a loud and resounding 'snap' followed by a shout. She swung it again. And again. Each time, that same solid 'clack' answered her until, suddenly, she felt resistance; something had latched onto the blade. "Art thou mad?!"

Her eyes adjusted to the darkness and surely, she could make out a scorched bascinet, a full suit of Tritan plate armour, and a Thestor surcoat draped over the top. The figure's hand had clutched the blade of Katheryn's weapon. It then flung its visor up and revealed a familiar set of pale blue eyes that pierced the darkness with their glow.

"Oh. It is *thee*," Katheryn grumbled.

"Of course, it is! Did the messenger not make it clear?!"

She took a few seconds to focus on not falling over and reluctantly admitted, "...He did."

Katheryn thuggishly pulled her weapon free of Alric's grip and slammed it back into its scabbard. Alric groaned and ran a hand down his face. "I can smell it upon thy breath. Katheryn…as pleased as I am to see thee, there is something I require thy assistance with. Please, come with me." With that, he trudged onward through the brush.

"I beg thy pardon? I most certainly shall *not*!" Katheryn snapped. Seconds went by in silence. "Alric? *Alric?*! God help me, one day I shall strangle thee to death! Return at once!" With a snarl, Katheryn lumbered after her brother, against her better judgement.

His voice promptly followed. "Cease thy moaning and follow me."

"Thou arrive without warning to such a grand affair after vanishing, demand that I wander out into the wilderness, and expect me to comply?"

"Aye."

Katheryn, trying her best to remain aware of her surroundings, steadied herself against a tree and opened her mouth to speak…but a distant silhouette froze the words within her throat. She thought it to be Carthei at first; the form was draped with a heavy cloak and the peculiar garb underneath resembled Ga'zahi hunting fibres. However, she realised that the clothing was much too clean. Much too pristine. They did not belong to a forest-dwelling druid. The stranger's face was entirely reflective and featureless.

"Alric, who is this stranger?" Katheryn snapped.

"Katheryn…promise me that thou shalt remain calm."

With a scoff of disbelief, Katheryn's hands balled into fists. "Tell me of this outsider, *then* I shall decide if that is a promise I am at liberty of making."

The figure suddenly huffed in amusement. "Yeah…you guys *sound* like siblings, alright." The voice was muffled, making Katheryn realise that its peculiar blank face was in fact a mask.

Katheryn inhaled sharply. That accent… She had heard it before. "Vik?" she muttered.

"Uh…*no*?" the figure replied, sounding much too unsure for Katheryn's liking. The Duchess lumbered forward, reaching for the figure's face.

"Katheryn! Get–" Alric had leapt forward and reached for Katheryn's shoulder, but her instinctive reaction was to spin around. Her elbow collided with Alric's exposed face and sent him stumbling away for a second; enough time for Katheryn to lurch ahead and grab the figure by the sides of the head.

"Hey! What the fuck!?" it yelled as it clutched Katheryn's wrists in an effort to wrestle her away. Despite its efforts, Katheryn wrenched with all of her might. The mask slipped free and hurtled through the air, landing in the grass a few feet away. Katheryn locked eyes with…with a *thing*. Its dim eyes shimmered in the faint light of the Prime Moon. Its disgusting, writhing, mushy face contorted in some expression that Katheryn could never even hope to decipher. Katheryn's eyes widened and before she knew it, her sword had been drawn once again. The abomination held its hands up in front of itself but was promptly covered by Alric who had interposed himself between them.

"Sister. Please. She shall not harm thee."

"E-Explain thyself…! Immediately!" Katheryn demanded.

She and her brother stood alone in her personal bedchambers in Castle Wyrmsmouth's keep. It was a miracle that she did not instantly gut the disgusting creature that he had shepherded into her city. Perhaps Alric should have been thankful for the wine. Katheryn had all the responsibilities of ensuring that food, supplies, infrastructure, and manpower was available for the festivities as well as participating in the tournament itself. And then Alric appeared out of thin air with a disgusting *thing* at his heels. Alric had ushered it into one of the keep's solars for the time being.

Alric snorted scornfully. "Now is not the time for this unwarranted rage of thine."

"*Unwarranted*?" she spat in disbelief. "Thou hast the nerve to arrive during sensitive negotiations, for which the monarchs of Tritham, Valtheaux, and the Steiffan Empire are present…with some…grotesque abomination in thy company!?"

"Madsen is an angel," he whispered to her. Suddenly, Katheryn's heart slowed. "She possesses an understanding of magic that even the druids and Clthics do not have. Her touch can heal the sick and the infirm; I myself experienced this first hand when she saved my very life. I am now sworn to her service." Katheryn inhaled, then exhaled. She knew that remaining silent was most unlike her; it was enough to make Alric frown and add, "Thou art not going to contest my claim? Thy belief is given so freely?"

With a huff, she clasped her hands together. "Alric, my dearest brother, I saw the wretch with mine own eyes. Such a monstrosity is clearly not of the same make as we, nor any other creature that walks the realm," Katheryn said sternly. "Whatever it is, it is not of our plane. Others may call it a *demon* in lieu of its stench and ugliness."

"I must speak with Archbishop Tyonius and convince him to witness one of her miracles. Surely the Hospital within thy walls is flooded with those who await death."

Katheryn swallowed. She was not exactly fond of the idea of God. He was unforgiving, absent, without reason, and was perfectly content with how terrifying the realm of His creation had become. In private, she would whisper things that many would say were the words of a blasphemer. But all of a sudden, apparently a heavenly servant of His was before her. "Thou wouldst ask me to harbour the creature until this conversation could be had?" Alric nodded and his armour disturbed the cold silence. He had changed. In the past, it would have come to blows if someone had dared to refer to anything holy with the words that Katheryn had used. There was also something about his explanations that made her feel uneasy. It all felt…hollow.

The Duchess took a long, deep breath, and prepared to ask a question that she truly wished she had the strength to ignore. She knew well the ways of the Ga'zahi. They would not have taken the creature's existence lightly. According to their faith, there were no angels or demons, only the Vorkhai. The relationship that the druids had with the Vorkhai was paradoxical to say the least. The Ga'zahi in particular painted their faces with dark brown, olive, or pale pink pigments to channel their wisdom. They paid tribute to them for shaping the land, but they also knew that they had brought about the end of many worlds countless times before. Athroct'u, as they called it.

They were spiteful gods who consumed with ceaseless appetite. If the Ga'zahi were ever to find something that they interpreted as a Vorkhai…there was only one thing Katheryn could see them doing. "Where is Carthei?" she asked. An irresistible chill permeated the air. Katheryn could hear Alric's throat flex as he swallowed. Katheryn snapped, "Answer the question, brother."

He swallowed and sheepishly proceeded. "W-When we came across Madsen, she was asleep. Carthei wished to…" Alric's voice buckled in a way that Katheryn had never witnessed before. His breathing became shallow.

"Once again with that pathetic cowardice." Her voice was heavy and acidic. When Alric only continued panting, Katheryn was forced to press him further. "*Speak.*"

The once mighty knight trembled as he said, "I-I killed her."

Tremors surged through her skin. Her right eye twitched. The steady thrumming of her heart mounted, and she could almost hear it echo through the room. Katheryn felt as if she were responsible for what happened, and it was that feeling that made her loathe her brother even more. *He* swung the blade. Why did *she* have such guilt for something that she had no control over?

"K-Katheryn?"

Her eyes dampened. "Thou art a walking sack of refuse. Art thou aware of that? A pathetic, spineless, and worthless excuse for a man. So desperate to please. First, it was father. Then it was God. Not once hast thou ever acted on thine own accord. Where others may see a man, I see a soulless puppet without a single thought of its own within its disgusting, hollow head." Her cold voice was beginning to boil over, with wisps of spite escaping her stone facade. She wanted to strike him. She could not decide upon using her bare hand, or the tip of her sword. "Thou should have died down there. Get out of my sight."

With tremors permeating his stride, Alric turned and paced out of the room. Only when he was gone did Katheryn seize the edge of the desk in her room and flip it end over end. Afterwards, as her body was overcome with rage that caused her to shiver, she lowered herself onto her bed and wept silent tears.

For all their differences, there was one quality the siblings shared that made them dangerous. It was not some supernatural skill as a warrior or an unmatched tactical mind. No. Both Katheryn and Alric were rigid, unrelenting, and would not hesitate to take drastic action to get what they wanted. *That* was what made them formidable. They were much too stubborn to give up. Where the similarities ended, however, was in how they reflected upon their own actions. Katheryn was a political thinker, first and foremost. Although she knew when to make examples of those who would threaten her reputation, any fool knew that an enemy turned ally was always more useful than a corpse. For all her spite towards Reginald of Harvestfall, she knew his worth. He would bark incessantly like a small dog, but he was a gallant knight and competent battlefield commander. Being short of either could be the difference between life and death during a campaign. Besides…he was a child during the war. What was she supposed to do? Hang him too?

Alric, evidently, had no such qualms. It did not matter if you were a man, woman, or child. If the Scripture prescribed death by burning for your crimes, then Alric would gleefully apply the punishment and fervently defend his decision to the very end. Whenever his faults were mentioned, he would deflect and find some external thing upon which to place the blame. He was so detached from reality, so swallowed by his fear of Hell, that he was never wrong and always right. That was her brother…yet she had not truly seen him since he left Blackmeadow. He could barely admit what he had done. What did it mean? Such remorse meant that she could not bring herself to exact justice upon him. As much as she wished him punished…she could not bear to do it in light of his reaction. For some time, Katheryn remained seated on her bed and stared into the painted stone walls that enveloped her. She saw Carthei's face in her mind's eye, lathered with that brown face paint.

Interrupting her sorrow was a knock upon her door. "Come," she said lowly after wiping her tears and composing herself.

The hinges squealed as the door peeked open. Penelope, one of Katheryn's servants, shuffled inside. "Pardon the intrusion, milady." Her eyes snapped to the upturned table and assorted items that littered the floor for a split second, then returned to Katheryn.

"*My* lady."

Penelope bowed her head. "A-Apologies, my lady. The…the angel has been requesting an audience with you."

Katheryn flexed her wrist back and forth, the one that had been dislocated during her tilt with that fool Reginald. It had been seen to by a physician and set back to its proper place, but it still ached when she exerted any kind of force. "Whatever for?"

"She kept saying that she wanted to talk about 'Vik'."

Katheryn sat up straighter. "Very well."

"I shall retrieve her at once," barked Penelope in acknowledgement.

"No need. I shall come to her," she said as she stood.

Penelope was stunned. "My lady…?"

"Penelope, dearest, I am neither lame nor lazy, but one day I shall be. Until then, I shall make rigorous usage of my ability to walk," she retorted sharply. "I must thank thee for thy service this strange night. Thou best retire and keep those lips of thine sealed. If I hear but a whisper of this among the common folk during breakfast on the morrow, I shall have thy tongue pulled out."

As a woman who had been serving Katheryn for many years, Penelope graciously nodded without being disturbed at all by the grizzly threat. Many of them had been sent her way during her tenure in Katheryn's household. "Of course, my lady," she said sweetly. The two of them grasped the table and set it back in place before replacing all of the papers, books, and stationary items that were originally atop it.

"Have a lovely night," Penelope said with a bow as she left.

Katheryn retrieved the lit candle upon her bedside table before she made leave of her chambers and stepped into the cold hallway. As she did, she saw Penelope descending the stairs as another figure climbed them. It was a man of quite a large build with deep orange skin and dull yellow eyes. The right side of his lip had been horribly torn and revealed some of his teeth. "My Lady? A summons at so late an hour is worrying to say the least."

"I must apologise for calling upon thee at such an hour, Sir Lionel, but I require thy assistance…and thy discretion."

Sir Lionel of Pathridge nodded sternly. He was wearing a cream white doublet with filigree embroidery that flowed over it like tiny translucent vines. "Nonsense. I live to serve thee."

She led the burly knight through the corridors of Castle Wyrmsmouth's keep with nothing but faint candlelight to show her the way. As they came upon the door to the solar, Katheryn stopped. Sir Lionel took a few paces before realising that she had halted, then turned around to face her. "Duchess Katheryn?" he prompted.

Katheryn's voice became a hushed whisper. "Thou art to stand guard at the door. Under no circumstances art thou to enter or even peek within unless I explicitly give thee the command to do so. No one else is to enter the chamber. Understood?" She offered him the candle.

"Aye" he said, accepting the light with no reluctance whatsoever.

Katheryn smiled. "Very good." She slowly wrapped her fingers around the door handle and peered back at Sir Lionel. After a brief moment of eye contact, he turned his back on Katheryn and stared down the dim hallway.

Katheryn pushed the door open. As she peeked into the bedchamber, she saw the revolting miscreation gazing right at her. The muscles on its thick arms wriggled and pulsed beneath its sickening skin in a most disgusting manner. Its head was topped with a layer of fur that shared the tone of slick mud. It wore something that Katheryn recognised as druidic hunting fibres, but as she had noticed in the forest, they were in immaculate condition and were incredibly bright blue, as if soaked in the most lavish and expensive of dyes. The hunting fibres' sleeves were tied around its waist. It wore something on its torso that was so fitted to her form that Katheryn could not even refer to as clothing at all. The longer Katheryn looked at the creature, the more revolted she became by its appearance. Carthei was dead and that horrendous affront to nature was still there. It was a sick joke. The creature seemed to be unnerved by the strange, awkward silence. "Uh… *Hi,*" it said.

"Thou shalt do well to don some *real* clothing. That…whatever it is, shall not do," Katheryn said through clenched teeth, gesturing toward its body.

"A t-shirt?" asked the creature as it pinched some of the garment's fabric and pulled it from her skin.

Katheryn rolled her eyes and looked away. "Thou art disgusting enough. Do not subject me to more of thy putrid flesh than is required."

The creature snorted and shook its head. "Thanks. You're not too bad yourself. Look, are we gonna talk about Viktoria or not?"

The Duchess of Arlingborough pursed her lips and tensed her brow as she fought to stow her anger. Such a dismissive attitude warranted some kind of physical punishment, but she ultimately decided against it. After all, she was its host. "She came to me during a tilt, spoke in riddles, then took her leave. I know not where she went."

The creature huffed through its revolting nostrils. "Great. What did she say to you?"

"Things that made little sense." Katheryn said quietly.

With a reticent sigh, the creature nodded. "Well…thanks anyway."

Katheryn narrowed her eyes at the gross animal. She had done nothing but spit insults at the creature since she arrived, so the gracious thank you was rather confounding. "What have I done for thee to thank me?"

"I mean, I know that there's another…'angel' around here somewhere at the very least," it said as it crossed its arms. "I'm Madsen, by the way. Your brother saved my life."

Katheryn flexed her lips as if she was trying to get a piece of food out of her teeth. "I am Katheryn, Countess of Danecaster and Duchess of Arlingborough."

The creature smiled weakly and pulsed its eyebrows upward. "Wow. That's cool."

She was at a loss for words for several seconds as she stared in disbelief at Madsen. The way it conducted itself was…incredibly unladylike. For her entire life, Katheryn had been instructed on the very precise ways that a lady must act in order to do away with such bad habits. In a strange way, she felt that Madsen's attitude was insulting despite the fact that it reminded her of herself when she was a child.

"What dost thou seek, creature?" Katheryn asked.

There was a slight twitch of annoyance on Madsen's face. It had taken some time, but Katheryn did manage to pierce its facetious shell. The creature then glanced at the ground for a moment. "I just want to find my people. So…any help would be appreciated."

The Duchess grimaced. The realm of God's creation was a terrible place. Katheryn had watched innocent people starve to death, be savaged by nightmarish creatures, and set alight in the name of this god or that god. No one came to help them. But Madsen, an angel, had the nerve to ask for help? Where was Ursula's help? Where was Carthei's help? Where were the angels whenever humanity needed them most? "Help? *Thee?*" Katheryn spat. "Why would I? Thou hast the nerve to doom us to this wretched, short, uncompromising existence, to ignore our prayers as we beg for the lives of our loved ones…then *ask us for help*?"

The angel found herself frozen in shock. "Katheryn, I didn't–"

Its words fell upon deaf ears. Katheryn took several steps forward as she muttered, "This place is plagued with lust, death, horror, apathy, and injustice. I have seen children ravaged by diseases that rend the flesh from their bodies. I have seen people *eat* each other after their crops died during the famines. I have seen women defiled and slaughtered for being too tempting. Any being responsible for a world where the innocent suffer unimaginable pain for no real reason does not deserve help."

Madsen threw its hands up and retorted, "Yeah… You're right. This place is fucked up, but I don't have anything to do with it. There are guys out there somewhere who *do*. *They* did this to you, not me. I'm not just trying to get out of here, okay? They need to answer for all this."

Katheryn huffed through her nostrils, still trying to keep her wrath in check. "Thou cannot ask me for help. Not when thou art the reason that *she* is dead." In the silence that followed, Katheryn realised what it was that she said and that it had somehow come blurting out of her mouth against her wishes.

Madsen swallowed and its face suddenly loosened. "W-What?"

Katheryn, her hands trembling with rage, backed away. "Alric *murdered* his own allies to save thee. He betrayed them." The angel exhaled with a shake of its head and lowered itself onto the bed. Katheryn watched its face contort. It was horror. That much was plain to see, even in such a grotesque face.

"O-One of them was a friend of yours?" Madsen whispered. Katheryn's relationship with Carthei was…complicated. It could be said that they hated each other, but it also could be said that they deeply cared for each other. Beyond the realm of just friendship. Being asked to define it was something that made Katheryn pause for seconds on end. As she tried to find the words, she saw a spark of recognition in Madsen's revolting eyes. The angel interjected, "Why are you blaming me for something that *he* did?"

"He did it for thee. Thou art the cause."

"I was fucking *unconscious*, Katheryn," Madsen said sternly as it stood back up. "He didn't know what I wanted and I don't think he would've cared either. Not then." The sudden cursing and tense tone of Madsen's voice gave Katheryn yet another shock. "Don't you want to find the people responsible for this? Don't you want it to end?"

The words echoed through Katheryn's mind as she stood there, staring idly at Madsen's sickening form. If it spoke the truth, then perhaps it *was* in Katheryn's best interest to find those who were. So they could be made to answer for their unfathomable cruelty. So they could be *punished.* Katheryn took a deep breath and did her best to banish the thought of Carthei from her mind and looked upon Madsen again with newfound composure. "The sooner thou leave us, the better. Perhaps thou art best off searching the Under."

Her expression was the only answer Katheryn needed. Alric. The vile, self-serving snake. He did not care for Madsen. He only cared for himself. Otherwise, he would have explained everything to her. Madsen swallowed then prompted, "The Under? What are you talking about?"

Katheryn sighed. "Come with me. And be quiet, for God's sake."

XXXIX
Nothing But Dust And Echoes

Madsen was sitting on a tree stump writing in a notebook. A *real* notebook. She didn't know what she was going to do once the pen ran out of ink, but it wasn't like she could use her PC to take notes. She was still trying to get it up and running as well as figure out how to MacGyver an E-Gel power bank together to charge the thing. Until then, she was going to have to get old school and write on paper. She had horrible handwriting. Absolutely *terrible*....but she figured that she needed to start recording all of the stuff that was happening to her. She hadn't really planned on being stuck there for so long, so she had quite a lot to jot down before she forgot about it all.

It became obvious very quickly that she needed a name for the androids to be able to recount everything in a digestible manner. For all intents and purposes, they were a new species. It sounded so stupid when she put it to herself like that, but it was true. They had civilizations, free will, sentience, and they were entirely self-sustaining. She knew enough biologists to know that every new species needed a stupid Latin name. After mulling over homo sapien a million times, she decided on homo proxima. You know, close enough. They were technological representations of human bodies: proxies.

"Bingo," she mumbled to herself as she scribbled into her notepad. She was jotting down all of her observations about the proxies, her opinions on their inner-workings, the nature of their general intelligence, as well as a few detailed sketches and systemic diagrams. Drawing was something she *did* know how to do. She was doing a profile sketch, using Katheryn as an unknowing reference. She added little annotations describing the softbody musculature and glowing optics that were present on all proxies.

Katheryn was rubbing her chin as she peered around at the trees. She had an intense look on her face. Well, from the short amount of time that Madsen had known her...she *always* had an intense look on her face. Suddenly, she made eye contact with Madsen. "What?" she pressed.

"Mm. Nothing. All good." Katheryn blinked rapidly and tensed her jaw. She was wearing a nice green dress with golden embroidery on the sleeves. "Are you sure we're not lost?" Madsen asked.

"Silence. The last time I visited this God forsaken place was as a child."

Madsen rolled her eyes. "Jeez, okay..." she muttered. After slamming her notebook shut, Madsen propped her head up with her hand as she desperately searched for something to entertain herself with. The sound of leaves fluttering in the forest grabbed her attention, and the way they shimmered made her feel this sense of awe. She'd marvelled at planets, stars, and moons from orbit, deep space, and other solar systems, but such a simple thing made her realise that she'd taken the smaller stuff for granted. Her eyes glided across the sea of green, then settled on a section of city walls that was still visible. The tops of the walls had these teeth-like shapings that she knew were iconic of castle architecture, but she had no idea *why* they looked like that. On the top of one of the towers was a flag; it had a quartered design, with two green sections and two white. The white boxes had a yellow bird in them, and the green ones had a black diagonal bar running through them. Madsen recalled that Katheryn introduced herself as the Duchess of Arlingborough. "Is Arlingborough the name of this city?"

Katheryn laughed. "No, it is a duchy."

She nodded intently. "Oh. Okay." There was a decent pause. "What's a duchy?" Madsen asked, scratching the back of her head.

It looked like Katheryn really enjoyed making fun of people, because she sauntered over with a sneer on her face. "Art thou truly so daft?"

"You gonna tell me what a duchy is or not, you asshat?"

Katheryn rolled her eyes and replied, "A duchy is a territory granted by the king to his dukes and duchesses. They can vary in size, but the Duchy of Arlingborough is quite vast, stretching from here to the Earldom of Danecaster surrounding Blackmeadow; my familial holdings." The engineer whistled in awe. She was finally getting a picture of how the world worked...and she couldn't say that she liked it. There was no centralised authority that was impartial; instead, pretty much everything was run by the upper-class. They made the laws, they owned everything, they collected the taxes, and they organised the armies. Katheryn continued, "With our parents dead, Alric had once been heir to our house, but he renounced it all when he took the Thestor vows. As men of the faith, they are 'above' riches and what have thee."

"Right. So, it defaulted to you."

The Duchess reeled back. "What? Of course not," she spat.

"But...you're his *sister*. Next of kin, right?"

"No," Katheryn murmured as she tilted her head.

"I don't get it. Why? Why not *you*?"

A twinge of pain surged through Katheryn's expression for a split second, then vanished. "Because I am a woman," she said in a very matter of fact way, like it was obvious.

Madsen grunted. At first, she couldn't help but shake her head in disbelief. It was ridiculous. Her shock quickly faded into anger. She tensed her jaw and exhaled through her nostrils. Katheryn seemed to notice the spite and quite frankly, looked confused as all hell. "I can't believe it. That's...fucking *stupid*." Madsen hissed. Katheryn's eyelids suddenly fluttered and she looked away, like she had no idea how to react. "How did you get it all back?" Madsen asked through gritted teeth.

"I went to war," muttered Katheryn as she stared at the waving flag on the distant castle tower.

If the conversation hadn't been so serious, Madsen would have burst into laughter. A woman had to *go to war* just to hang onto her family's property? People had to *die* for *one* woman to take ownership of her belongings? Whoever made this place...they were essentially forcing the proxies to recycle outdated human practices, for what? How long had it been running for? How many proxies had been tortured, abused, and killed? How many women had been forced to live like that? Madsen suddenly shot to her feet and paced away. She shook her head and cursed to herself. She was furious, but she also felt guilty.

For a career, Madsen could do anything that a man could do. All she needed was to be qualified, well-suited personality-wise, and ultimately, *good at the job*. No one would question her being hired. No one *did*, not for her engineering job at Anvil Heavy Fabrication, *or* for becoming an ISEC astronaut after that. On the other hand, Katheryn probably had no idea what it felt like to be herself. To *really* be herself. She probably had to constantly prove to people that she was capable...and deal with those who would never be convinced.

After a few seconds, when her frustration had abated somewhat, Madsen turned back to Katheryn. She saw her staring back, optics wide. Madsen took a deep breath, then said, "Where I come from, men and women are equal." Katheryn slumped herself onto a nearby rock and stared at the ground. Her shoulders eased down and her optics seemed to flicker slightly and lose focus on everything. "Listen...the angels weren't so different from you guys. Thousands of years ago, we built castles just like that one. We fought using swords, bows, axes. We used faith to bring ourselves together and explain things we couldn't understand. Sometimes, we also used it as an excuse to hurt people. And for a very long time, our women were…well, they weren't free. That's why everything's the way it is. Because someone wanted you as close to us as possible. Even though it doesn't need to be that way."

Katheryn glanced at the ground as a rickety breath left her mouth. Madsen could see her cringe as she processed it all. "This is some ridiculous charade then. We are all pieces in some game that the angels play. They carve us, line us up, then pit us against one another for what? God's own amusement?" She sounded exhausted. Broken. Her voice became a haunting whisper that gave Madsen goosebumps.

"I don't know. I sure as hell plan on finding out, though." Madsen approached Katheryn and held a hand out to her. The Duchess glanced between the outstretched hand and Madsen's face. Her expression, for the first time that Madsen had seen, wasn't completely sharp. There was warmth, however subtle, behind her optics. She swallowed, then gently grasped Madsen's hand. "So, are you lost, or what?" Madsen quipped as Katheryn helped herself back up.

"I may be *somewhat* lost," she mumbled very quietly.

With a big smile on her face, Madsen chirped, "Great."

"*Somewhat.* Come." Katheryn led the way deeper into the forest without a word. Madsen hadn't ever been in a forest before. Even when she travelled with Alric, they stuck to roads and always skirted around dense woods. Her sneezing only got worse, but it was worth it. The place was beautiful. Eventually, the two women came upon a sheer cliff face that was covered in vines and moss. Madsen cocked her head as her eyes followed the green veins up the side of the rock. "Woah." At the bottom was a cave opening.

Once she turned on her flashlight, the tunnel was no problem at all. Katheryn wasn't too bothered by the tech; maybe she'd seen one before. After five minutes of walking down the damp tunnel, Madsen whispered, "There better not be an ambush waiting for me down here."

With a snobby laugh, Katheryn rolled her eyes. "And give someone else the glory of slaying an angel? I think not."

The tunnel widened into a large cavern that wasn't completely shrouded in darkness. A mote of light came down from a hole in the cave ceiling, providing some ambient lighting and allowing Madsen to pocket her flashlight. She could hear a faint sound in the distance…some kind of 'banging'. It was rhythmic and kept going on and on. The floor of the cave was littered with junk. *Human* junk. It was mostly just piles of discarded cables, broken fixings, and damaged tools.

"They call this place the 'Drumming Deep'. That infernal thrumming led the locals to believe it to be either haunted, or a gateway to Hell," Katheryn explained.

"That sound's been continuous?"

Katheryn nodded. "It has proven exceptional at frightening people away. This was as far as I ever went. Alric refused to even enter."

She was so preoccupied with looking at the debris on the ground that Madsen almost walked right into a gigantic object. It was lopsided, leaning to the right slightly, and covered in signs of erosion, stress, and fractures. However, the more she looked at it, the more she saw other details. Seamlines. Bolts. Madsen took a step back and her breathing practically stopped. It was a building. What was left of it, anyway. The slanted exterior wall of a collapsed skyscraper extended up into the darkness above and the base was swallowed by rocks and boulders. Surrounding the derelict structure were hundreds of pieces of debris ranging from totalled load-lifting vehicles to tiny scraps of plastic and metal.

Katheryn's soft voice threaded itself through the cold air. "Thou peer upon this monolith with a great deal of recognition. These artefacts are not the product of demons or Vorkhai. They belong to the angels," she surmised.

As she was still processing everything, Madsen's voice lost its usual laid-back melody and was instead a low drone. "Yeah. But it had to have been an abandoned settlement that was buried a long time ago. We tend to do that with stuff we don't need."

"How...very responsible." Katheryn walked up to a totalled car and cocked her head at it like a curious child. "Well, it certainly was quite the excursion. I found it to be rather enlightening."

Madsen was too busy trying to reassess her priorities to reply to Katheryn's sassy remarks. Truthfully, nothing changed. An abandoned city didn't mean anything. Sometimes, settlements didn't pan out and burying them was more efficient than trying to dismantle everything. It was a very human thing to do...just dump all your shit in a hole...but it *was* a thing. Had been since the very earliest days of space exploration, when every spacecraft was a single-use vehicle that you just sort of dumped once you were finished with it. More than once Madsen herself had been part of teardown teams that would use massive Model 6 Demolitions Units to bulldoze redundant cities and facilities. Her mission was still to make contact with ISEC and report the deaths of her crew, the unchecked proxy activity, everything. She owed it to her crewmates to tell their families. She wasn't about to give up anytime soon.

Before Madsen could think about it any further, she heard a soft wheezing pant bounce off the walls of the ruined building. The faint vocalisation was wet, raspy, and made her stomach twist up. Slowly, she pulled out her flashlight and swept it to her left. The circle of light drifted from the side of the derelict structure and over to a cluster of abandoned cars. Curled up in a fetal position, head resting on the side of one of the vehicles, was a proxy. Its optics were oddly unfocused, like it was staring off into the distance. "Oh my god… Are you okay?" Madsen asked as she eagerly paced over. She heard the sound of Katheryn's hurried footsteps behind her.

The proxy continued staring into nothingness. A long string of clear fluid was running down from their mouth. They made another soft moan, but there were no words. "A dullard, it seems," Katheryn snorted as she turned her nose up at the person.

Madsen leered back over her shoulder. As much as she wanted to tell Katheryn to go fuck herself, the engineer kept a lid on it and drew her focus back to the confused proxy. After rifling through her duffel bag and retrieving her InSpec tablet, Madsen found herself frozen for a second. There were seven OBD tags, meaning that there were five other proxies lurking nearby. Using the estimated distances as a point of deduction, Madsen figured out which tag belonged to her new friend and opened it up. "Shit…" she whispered.

"Please, do not leave me to divine the news for myself," Katheryn growled.

There was an error message warning about severe data loss on the proxy's solid-state drive. All of the 'adult' proxies that Madsen had a chance to look at via the InSpec had hundreds of thousands of exabytes of memory on their SSDs. The one she just met? There was a little over 4 terabytes used up of the total six-hundred thousand exabyte storage. An error code like that didn't denote a simple hardware failure; something caused that data loss. "Their mind's almost completely wiped."

"What could possibly do such a thing? Magic?" Katheryn mused.

Madsen gently cupped a hand on the proxy's chin and turned their head side to side to check for damage. They didn't seem to be bothered by the physical contact and didn't resist at all. "I'm not seeing any signs of physical trauma and my…uh…enchanted tablet didn't pick anything up either. We need to get them out of here before I can make a proper assessment." After dropping her InSpec back into her duffel, Madsen secured the proxy by the shoulders. "We're gonna get you out of here. Can you stand up for me?"

"Thou may wish to belay that instruction."

Madsen smacked her lips. "Jesus fucking Christ, they need our help. Why the hell are you so–"

When Madsen turned to glare at Katheryn, she realised that they were no longer alone. The five other proxies were standing there staring at Madsen and Katheryn. One of them had an uncontrollable twitch on the right side of their face, another had their optics wide open as they glared at the two women. They weren't L-Ps, that much was obvious. L-Ps moved with robotic efficiency. Madsen raised her hands. "We're not going to hurt you. It's okay."

The twitching man sputtered, but nothing intelligible left his mouth. He took a staggered step forward.

"Keep thy distance, halfwits," Katheryn said as she drew her sword. As soon as the words left her mouth, Madsen saw a shape emerging from the concrete structural support behind Katheryn. The proxy moved so slowly and its optics were so faint that Madsen almost completely missed it. There was rock clutched in their right hand slick with fresh E-Gel. Slowly, as it got closer to Katheryn, it raised the stone above its head.

Once again, Madsen's body reacted before her mind could. Everything washed by her as she dropped her duffel, barged past Katheryn, and tackled the rock-wielding proxy. Next thing she knew, the pair of them were tumbling over each other onto the dirt. There was a 'thud' as Madsen's back slammed into a rock wall, instantly bringing their momentum down to zero. She didn't feel anything, not yet, so she took advantage of the adrenaline rush by wrapping an arm around the proxy's neck and bracing the other behind his head. Lastly, she threw her legs around his body and locked them together. The proxy flailed back and forth desperately, but he wasn't even close to wriggling free of the chokehold.

As the seconds ticked by, the would-be attacker went limp in Madsen's arms, allowing her to assess her surroundings. They'd gone rolling down into a ditch that was filled with more electronics refuse. However, more pressing than her new environment, was the sound of shouting and scraping footfalls coming from the ridge. Madsen popped up and made a mad dash for the top, momentarily scampering up on all fours. When she reemerged, she saw Katheryn with her sword in hand staring down three of the deranged proxies as she sidestepped, probably trying to make her way down into the ditch. One of the proxies had collapsed on the ground at her feet, howling in pain and almost submerged in a pool of their own E-Gel.

Katheryn locked eyes with Madsen and her posture eased up before she glanced down the slope at the unconscious proxy. The shock was evident in her face, even for Madsen who still struggled to read proxy expressions. The engineer stumbled in between Katheryn and the remaining proxies, hands raised. "Stop!" she yelled. "Down!" She raised her hands, then lowered them repeatedly.

It took a few seconds, but the terrified proxies eventually lowered themselves onto the ground. The one that Katheryn clearly attacked had gone silent and completely still. Madsen spun to face Katheryn. "What the hell did you do!?"

The Duchess kicked an object across the ground, causing it to bump against Madsen's foot. It was a T1B particle beam weapon...a fully-armed T1B particle beam weapon. It was by the dead proxy's side, and it looked like he might have been standing at the top of the ridge and aiming down at the ditch. "I was returning the favour," Katheryn replied coldly.

After a moment of silence, Madsen scoffed and peered down at the floor. They were people. People who'd suffered some unnatural occurrence. They didn't deserve to die...but Katheryn didn't have much of a choice, did she? "Thanks..." Madsen muttered reluctantly as she recovered her duffel bag.

"Thou bested that man so quickly? With thy bare hands?" Katheryn prompted. "What kind of magic didst thou conjure to achieve that?"

"Judo," quipped Madsen. "Look, these guys are sick. They need help...but first, we need to figure out what happened to them. We don't want this happening to more people."

Katheryn seemed to notice that the remaining proxies were just confused and scared. It looked to be incredibly difficult for her, but she finally sheathed her sword. "Loath be I to defy thy divine will..." she groaned.

"Come on. We need to have a look around." Without another moment's hesitation, Madsen wandered off, forcing Katheryn to keep pace. The further they went, the louder the banging got. It echoed through the devastated cityscape, further amplifying the noise. Madsen came across a collapsed facility of some kind. Pouring in from beyond a hole in the wall were staccato flashes of blinding white light, accompanied by the thunderous bangs. She poked her head around the corner.

There was a gigantic mound of assorted trash jutting down from the upper left portion of the ceiling...and there were proxy corpses littered across the ground beneath it. The more she looked at the strange trash stalactite though, the more she saw that there was something *underneath* the layer of junk. Beneath the forest of scrap was a car-sized device with a circular opening in the middle. Its outer housing had been smashed open on one side, and the white electrical flashes were coming from inside it.

She kept walking closer…until she realised that Katheryn was right next to her. Her heart stopping for a moment, Madsen threw herself against Katheryn and held her back. "Woah, woah, stop!"

Katheryn snapped, "By God! What is it, woman!? There is nothing there!"

"Stay back! That thing… It'll wipe your brain if you get too close. Understand? You'll lose your mind, just like those guys we ran into."

The Duchess' rage slowly seeped away. Madsen broke off and looked back at the malfunctioning medical scanner. Those kinds of medical diagnostics tools used magnetic resonance imaging, meaning that the thing was producing a powerful magnetic field. That's why all of the scrap was stuck to it. The proxies didn't have a lot of straight up metal in their architecture so Katheryn being pulled over wasn't a concern, but they *did* run on electronics, and their brains were solid-state drives. Exposing a proxy to magnetic flux could destabilise the electrical currents both in their signal pathways and their SSDs. In other words, *nerve and brain damage.*

"I need to see if I can disable this thing."

She felt a hand on her shoulder. "Wait. Surely the artefact would harm *thee* as well?"

"No, I'll be fine." Madsen brushed Katheryn's hand away and looked down at her flight suit. The thing just had a few buckles and zippers on it: not too much of a hazard. Her duffel bag, however, had her powered down PC, Inspec tablet, maintenance tools, and other pieces of electronics in it. She wriggled out of the strap then handed the bag to Katheryn. "Hang onto this for me and stay right there, okay?"

As she accepted the bag, Katheryn scoffed, "Very well…"

On her way over, Madsen noticed that a few of the collapsed proxies still had their optics lit up. They weren't completely dead…just 'lobotomised' by the magnetic fluctuations. Most looked incredibly weathered, like they'd been down there for decades. As she crouched and got right up underneath the device, she saw swords, buckles, daggers, and other trinkets that must've come from the proxies stuck up against the centre of it. There was something else that occurred to her though; she had no fucking idea how to disable the thing. She couldn't say that she'd come into contact with a lot of medical equipment as a mechanical engineer.

Robotics? Yeah, all the time. Medical scanners? Not really. The one catch-all solution that generally worked on everything was find the power supply and disconnect it. The trouble with that was that somehow, the stupid thing was embedded in the ceiling, so she couldn't really see the whole thing. Madsen pulled away and looked back down at the proxy bodies and realised that they were piled up in a weird way. She kneeled down and rolled a few of them over, uncovering a rectangular object with four thin limbs.

"Madsen…thou best retreat," Katheryn asserted calmly as she glared at the thing.

It was one of those four-legged robots that saw a lot of use in dangerous work zones. After wiping the dirt from the housing, she could see that it was the Type M 'Autonomous All-Terrain Quadruped', or AA-TQ (pronounced 'attic'), manufactured by AGILE Dynamic Systems. She'd handled a few of them in the past since a lot of planetary surveyors used them to map landscapes and tunnel systems. "It's okay, it's dead," Madsen called back as she tried to find the access panel. "You see a lot of these things?"

"They are called goblins…and they have a taste for cadavers. Do not be complacent; ensure that it truly is dead."

Using a nearby dagger, Madsen popped the access hatch and peered inside. Her expression went sour and she froze in confusion for a moment. Everything was…completely wrong. The usual lithium-ion battery was gone and replaced by the same kind of E-Gel synthesis plant that the proxies had. All of the wiring and circuitry was much more in line with the proxies than what *should've* been in there. As much as she would've loved to dwell on that some more, Madsen had a job to do. The E-Gel would work just fine. She reached in, disconnected the main fuel cell from the E-Gel plant, then waved the thing at Katheryn. Seeing the AA-TQ's 'heart' was enough to take the edge off.

So, Madsen had a plan. E-Gel was extremely unstable and had a tendency to combust when exposed to extreme temperatures. If she compromised the fuel cell and tossed it into the med scanner…then maybe the intermittent electrical faults would cause a contained explosion. Maybe. Madsen did something that was explicitly against at least thirty safety policies; she shoved her little dagger into a tiny seam on the fuel cell and wiggled it around. There was a specific point in the cell where the internal polymer seal could be reached and after feeling the blade make a smooth and satisfying dip, she was sure she'd reached it. When Madsen pulled the dagger out, its tip was covered in pitch black E-Gel and a steady stream of it started dripping out of the fuel cell. She peered back over her shoulder and warned, "Okay…you might wanna get back around the corner."

That flashing hole in the device's housing was the target. She gauged the distance and readied her throwing arm. Katheryn snapped, "What in God's name art thou doing?"

"I'm gonna throw this into the hole in the side of the artefact."

"Is there a reason for this lunacy, or art thou simply in a gaming mood?"

Madsen rolled her eyes. "It's gonna blow it up, okay?"

After a brief bit of silence, Katheryn narrowed her optics. "Thou shalt miss. It is much too narrow."

"I make three-pointers all the time. This'll be easy peasy."

Katheryn's face scrunched up. "Please refrain from speaking nonsense to me."

Madsen lobbed the fuel cell. As soon as it left her hand, she dashed back towards Katheryn. "Move it, move it!" She grabbed the duchess and pushed her back around the corner.

There was a massive 'bang' that flowed through the cavern, filling Madsen's ears with incessant ringing. When it faded, that repetitive banging was gone. "I guess they gotta come up with a new name for this place." She then looked expectantly at Katheryn for some kind of a compliment, but all she got was a focused glare.

"It was a miracle that thou didst not bring the entire structure down upon our heads."

"Yeah, yeah," Madsen whispered as she trailed forward, motioning for Katheryn to stay put. Keeping an eye on the roof of the structure for any signs of collapse, the engineer slowly peeked around the corner. She didn't know what she was expecting, but of course, the explosion also detonated the twelve proxy bodies lying underneath the scanner. All that was left was a messy spray of synth-tissue, internal components, and nanowire. Everything was also shot through with the dozens of pieces of shrapnel that were stuck on the face of the med scanner. Madsen cringed. "Eugh."

Before calling Katheryn back up, Madsen stepped through the android bits and held a metal shard up at the blackened and eviscerated machine. There was no magnetic pull on it. "Okay, you should be good now," she said as she crouched under and shuffled through.

Shortly, Katheryn appeared from around the bend. Her eyes instantly leapt to the splattered proxy bits on the ground. "Ah. I see thou hast made quite the mess." She squeezed under the smouldering scanner and stood back up.

Madsen swallowed and thinned her lips. "I…uh…didn't mean to."

Katheryn scoffed and shoved the duffel bag back into her arms. "It is of no consequence; they were already lost to us. Anyhow, there is ample time for the ceiling to come crashing down upon us following that idiotic display. We should vacate this place with haste."

Knowing full-well how little concussive force an E-Gel ignition would've caused, Madsen snapped, "How about we get those people out of here, *then* you can keep being an asshole?"

"Even that imbecile who wished to clobber me with a rock?"

"*Especially* that guy. He knows what's up."

XL
THE ASPIRANT

The part of camp that Fiammetta was made to stay in was far away from where the footmen were. The Nuns gave her a place to sleep and kept her safe. The more time she had spent with the Clthics, the more she realised that her entire upbringing as a lady-in-waiting in Lady Allegra's court had conditioned her to repress her feelings and shroud who she truly was. Among the witches, there was no such requirement. She finally felt free to be herself. As she ruminated upon those matters, she was lying sideways on a blanket she had laid out upon the dirt before the base of a wooden post. The spot overlooked the 'Witch Den', as the soldiers called it: where all the Nuns and Tethspeakers pitched their tents.

"I know what I want…but I am uncertain if I am worthy of it," she said to the one person accompanying her.

The Nuns and Tethspeakers obviously had no sense of decorum at all, and they had done away with the lowly and purposeless drive of lust. Fiammetta found herself fixated on the Nuns. They were the most powerful women she had ever seen; they were free to do as they liked. They were not things to be protected. They were the fist of the Clthic religion, punishers and warriors all. Fiammetta thought them quite similar in purpose to the Order of Saint Thestus, as they both nurtured their respective doctrines and punished those who would dare defy it. For women to fulfil a role that commanded such authority and fear...it was extremely foreign to her. It was intoxicating. Her entire life, she had been spoken over, abused, and taken advantage of. None of the Nuns had to be subjected to such things.

Several days before, she had seen a charming sellsword try to force himself upon one of the peasant women who followed the Clthic army. He did not get far before one of the Nuns discovered his disgusting act. He found himself sliced of his arms, legs, and manhood. His eyes were scooped out, his ears mutilated, and his tongue was ripped from his throat. To complete his punishment, he was strung up on a post on the border of the Witch Den to warn others who may be so ruled by lust. All the while, the Tethspeakers used their intimate knowledge of the human body to ensure that he was kept alive to wallow in his torment. Trapped in his own body, blind, deaf, and mute. The incident made her recall the times when Lord

Dante had his way with her and she could do nothing but stare at the ceiling and wait for it to end.

"You are a work of art. I long to create such beauty myself."

Fiammetta peered up the wooden post next to her and laid eyes upon the miraculously still-living man. Veins and arteries fed into his body, connecting him to the cluster of external organs keeping him alive nailed to the side of the post. The empty eye sockets, hollowed-out ear canals, and mutilated body had been the subject of Fiammetta's obsession for many days. She would come and stare at him…speak to him, even, despite the fact that he was entirely unaware that she was there basking in his torment. Perhaps that made it all the more satisfying. "I shall come to visit again soon. I bid you farewell." She pushed to her feet, flattened out her dress, and strode back down the hill.

They had set out from Oak a week earlier to make the march to Wyrmsmouth. Each day, more and more knights, men-at-arms, mercenaries, and commonfolk arrived to pledge themselves to the Synod. There had to be thousands of men in the army at that point; more people than Fiammetta had ever seen gathered in one place before. With such a large population of adherents travelling with them, the Nuns would routinely hold sermons and prayer sessions at the heart of the Witch Den. Those who truly believed would attend along with their wives and camp followers. Every now and again, the most devout and well-studied among the faithful were offered the opportunity to become Baptised. One such occasion had come again.

Fiammetta crouched behind a barrel opposite one of the Clthic tents. She held up the hem of her dress to keep it off the dirt as she watched H'vrsh lead a well-dressed nobleman through the tent flap. Narrowing her eyes, the former lady-in-waiting sprinted across the road and ducked through the flap herself. As her eyes adjusted, she lowered herself behind a crate by the entrance.

"I am most flattered to have been chosen, Wretched Instrument. I hope that I shall serve thee well," said the nobleman.

H'vrsh led him over to an empty table as he said, "I have faith that you will."

The nobleman promptly stripped himself of his clothing, then laid himself down upon the desk. Before long, H'vrsh and two other Tethspeakers gathered around with an array of demonic artefacts. Months ago, the following sight would have made Fiammetta scream at the top of her lungs. Instead, she released a quivering breath as H'vrsh produced floating arcane glyphs, swept his fingers across them, then drew a blade down the length of the nobleman's body. After the incision was made, the two Tethspeaker assistants seized the lips of skin and peeled it open as far as they could. Fiammetta couldn't help but recall the Infernal Forge, where she watched a very similar process take place.

She watched, entranced, for many long minutes. Eventually, the man's entire body had been relieved of its skin. Glistening black meat and musculature wrapped over bone was all that remained. H'vrsh then turned his instruments to the man's head. Sparks flew. They were so bright that Fiammetta had to turn away. When it was over, Fiammetta refocused her gaze and saw that the man's head…was *missing*. The more she strained her eyes though, the more she could ascertain what really happened. The man's skull had been cracked open then completely dismantled. Its shards were neatly organised on the side of the table. His brain sat on the surface of the desk, where his head should've been, accompanied by his eyes, tongue, upper and lower jaw, and throat. His abdomen still rose and fell with every breath he took. His fingers still twitched. He was *still alive*. Soon enough, H'vrsh returned with the skull of a bear in his hands. His back shielded Fiammetta's eyes from his work, but she could've guessed what was happening at that point.

"Fiammetta." The low, hollow voice of Mother Xalt'n made a shiver run down Fiammetta's lower back. She slowly stood and turned around. Right there, a head and a half taller than her, was Xalt'n. "It is forbidden for the uninitiated to set foot in this tent."

With a scoff, Fiammetta turned around and approached the tables as the Tethspeaker worked away on rehousing the man's brain and organs. "I wish to learn more, Mother Xalt'n. I cannot wait for the next sermon."

She watched the Tethspeaker insert the brain stem into the animal's skull, carefully handling the nerve endings and eyeballs as he did. Xalt'n muttered slowly, "*Fiammetta*." She pulled back with a start and looked to the Clthic Matriarch. Fiammetta had always thought that she was astonishing. Her body…the bands of sinew, clusters of veins, and inklings of bone beneath. She knew that she was meant to be revolted by it. But perhaps it was that same fact that made it all the more irresistible. Longingly, her eyes tore at the flayed flesh. She desperately wanted to bury her hand in the fibrous tissue and feel it under her fingertips.

Then came her 'mask'. It was made of the skulls of three wolves tied together with cords of tendon. With what she just learned, Fiammetta only became more bewitched. "This is your face…?" Fiammetta muttered as she reached out and tenderly ran a hand down the snout of one of the skulls. Xalt'n did not reply. The young woman continued running her fingers along the ridges of Xalt'n's 'mask', staring into her golden eyes. "You're so…beautiful," Fiammetta whispered, her face devoid of emotion. Seeing as Xalt'n was not capable of facial expressions, Fiammetta could only sense how she felt by looking into her piercing yellow eyes. She felt confusion, but it was laced with something else. Excitement? For the first time that Fiammetta had seen, the great Mother Xalt'n was speechless.

H'vrsh, whom Fiammetta had completely forgotten was there as well, cleared his throat nervously. "Fiammetta, Matriarch…I believe we have a ritual to complete," he said, with an air of mischief in his tone.

Fiammetta blinked rapidly and swallowed. "W-Why…yes. Of course. I…I shall see myself out." Trying her best to mask her embarrassment, Fiammetta straightened her posture and strode for the tent flap. Before she stepped out, she glanced over her shoulder and saw that Xalt'n was still staring after her. She couldn't help but release a shaky breath as she finally left. She was beside herself with shame and disgust. The Clthics denounced all emotion…yet Fiammetta had gotten so lost that she proclaimed something as stupid and meaningless as pleasure to none other than the leader of the entire religion. She suddenly wanted to bury herself alive and never talk to anyone ever again.

With a frustrated sigh, she moped along the dirt path, staring at her feet. As she walked, Fiammetta scrunched her brow. Why should she be ashamed? The innumerable rules of conduct that governed courtly behaviour no longer applied. Of course, emotion was a falsity…but it was something that would dull with time and focus. In the meantime, why should she shirk away from expressing herself? However, interrupting those questions, was a familiar face that slid into view. A dozen feet away and heading down a different direction, was Gertrude. The former inn maid had a yoke braced upon her shoulders with two full buckets of water hanging from them. It had to have been the fifth time Fiammetta had seen her carrying water that day. She then realised that Gertrude was not alone. The broad-shouldered and rugged John Stanton was walking alongside her. The archer had a troubled look on his face as he spoke words much too faint for Fiammetta to hear. Gertrude seemed to simply shrug and laugh in the face of whatever Stanton had said. Taking a moment to feign ignorance, Fiammetta plastered a smile onto her face, jogged across the muddy crossroads then slowed to match pace with her new friend. "Gertrude! You are pushing yourself far too hard," she said with a sweet smile.

While Stanton appeared startled by Fiammetta's sudden appearance, Gertrude chuckled and shook her head. "Well, it might look like hard work to a noble girl like you, but this is just another day fer me." Fiammetta reached to grab one of the buckets from the yoke, causing Gertrude to sneer at her, "Oi, whaddaya think yer doin'? Don't think I can manage on me own?"

Fiammetta giggled and seized the water anyway. "Oh, *please*. Enough of that."

As Fiammetta tried to lock eyes with Stanton, she noticed that he avoided eye contact altogether. "I'd best be going now. Ol' Bugface Bill is gonna have me hide if I keep loafin' about. Take care, now," he said with a wave, not waiting for a response as he paced away.

In solitude, the pair of women walked shoulder to shoulder on their way to deliver their water. Gertrude, with her burden halved, held her bucket in hand while she had the empty yoke resting on her shoulder. "What was he speaking to you about, Gertrude?" Fiammetta pressed quietly.

Gertrude scoffed. "Oh, you know, nothin' of note. Just 'aving a little trouble adjusting to the Clthic way of life. Just like I did at first." Fiammetta silently absorbed Gertrude's expression and body language as they traversed the muddy road. She seemed genuine enough…but Stanton's discomfort struck her as odd. She would be glad to help with his misgivings if he only asked.

Eventually, Gertrude added, "You know…I never… I wanted to…uh…" She snarled in annoyance then simply blurted, "T-Thank you, Fia. Without you…I don't know where I'd be. I thought that I wasn't strong enough…but you showed me that I am. I never told you how grateful I am for it."

The former lady-in-waiting bowed. "It is my pleasure. It can be so overwhelming, can't it? I had an outburst earlier as well, so understand that it is natural. Together, we can brave the Great Lie and emerge on the other side as Enlightened servants. We just need to be resilient and support each other."

Gertrude swallowed and looked into the sky. "I never told you what happened, did I? The day I… The day I finally made up my mind."

"And you are under no obligation to. You share what you wish to share, nothing more," Fiammetta asserted.

With a scoff, Gertrude smacked her lips. "It was the first time I watched a man die. I saw the Thestor string him up, brand him a demon-worshipper, then set him on fire like he was a piece of firewood. I-I…still hear him screaming at night. The pain…the fear…it was so…raw. And the Thestor didn't care. He killed more right afterwards. Three people…including a woman."

Fiammetta swallowed.

"Then he *spared* one of the others. The Thestor just killed four people for being demon-worshippers, then he allows *that* one to live…just because he's of use. They just make it up as they go along. The rules change whenever they want them to. A month later…when the Matriarch and her army came through Oak…I knew I wasn't gonna be on that bastard's side. My parents tried to fight back. They stuck with God until the end and look where that got them. There are two options; either he's real and he doesn't give a rat's arse about anything, or he *isn't* real. Doesn't make a difference to me."

"I appreciate you sharing this with me," Fiammetta said tenderly. It explained why Gertrude had been so inconsolable the day they met.

Gertrude snorted. "Well, that's the thing. It wasn't hard at all. And I think that's thanks in part to all you've taught me about the faith."

Before Fiammetta could respond, something cold and hard slammed into her arm. The impact was enough to send her tumbling to the ground, spilling the water from her bucket onto the ground. Her head had snapped to the side, causing a sharp pain to fester in her neck. "Oi! Watch where yer going, you little–" Gertrude's words were interrupted by a sharp gasp. Fiammetta sat upright and found a towering figure looming over her. It was an immense man clad in forge-blackened plate armour. There was a giant seared hole in his cuirass that had been wrapped up and covered by lengths of linen. The man, whose face entirely obscured by his helm, knelt and extended a hand to Fiammetta.

"My sincerest apologies," he sighed with a hint of exasperation in his rough voice. His accent was peculiar…almost like a blend of many tongues. It was low and quiet, like he was using as little effort as humanly possible. "Please. Allow me." She did not know why she accepted his hand, but she did. The leather glove of the man's gauntlet was ice cold and his grip was firm yet gentle. The stranger helped Fiammetta to her feet and as he did, he said, "Forgive me. I was being careless."

His helmet had a fine black veil hanging over its sights and Fiammetta could barely see the dull red glow of his eyes beneath it. "As was I. Sir…"

"Servius…and I am no sir."

The name sent a chill running down Fiammetta's spine. She peered behind him and saw a band of exhausted and injured men and women. It seemed to be a militia, not professional soldiers or men-at-arms. "Servius…I have heard your name before. Are you certain you are not a knight?"

Servius pointed at the empty bucket lying on the floor and locked eyes with one of his men. Without hesitation, the commoner leapt for the bucket and ran off, presumably to refill it. Then, the towering obsidian knight looked back down at Fiammetta. "Yes."

The young woman arched an eyebrow. "I see. You are Servius. *Just* Servius?"

The knight groaned under his breath. "Servius Laevinus Vitruvius," he answered reluctantly. "I am a child of Lady Viktoria."

Viktoria…? A wave of awe blasted through Fiammetta's body. She instantly dropped to one knee and bowed. "Lord Vampire," she whispered. Elder vampires were among the highest forms of demonic creations; humans and animals were the lowest. With their venom, the elders could bestow their gifts onto those deemed worthy, referred to as lessers. Servius would be one such worthy servant. He was the closest thing to a true demon Fiammetta had ever seen.

"P-Please…do not do that," he huffed, taking Fiammetta by the shoulder and forcing her up. "My men have survived quite an ordeal. They require rest." He said, gesturing over his shoulder.

Gertrude shrugged. "Alright. Come with me, the lot of you," she called. Right before she turned to leave, she leant into Fiammetta's ear and whispered, "Are you gonna be alright with this fellow?" After Fiammetta nodded, Gertrude trailed off with the dirt-riddled militia in tow. The lady-in-waiting cleared her throat and looked up at Servius, who was at least two heads taller than her.

"Now, Servius… Do *you* require rest?"

"Some blood shall do. But first, I must speak with the marshal of this army. Do you know where he is?"

"Indeed. Lord Franco has been organising the Clthic forces in the wake of Duke Klaus' death. Come with me, if you would," Fiammetta said politely. The pair set off deeper into the Clthic camp.

Most men made Fiammetta feel ill at ease. She had thought Franco to be the only exception…but despite his size and vampiric nature, she found Servius to be one as well. He reacted with such instinctive compassion that was certainly unlike anything she expected to see from a vampire. In her conversations with the K'relvic Nuns, she had been told that vampires, both elder and lesser, were so powerful that they were ruled by lust and depravity. If someone was stronger than twenty men, could ensnare the minds of the weak, and fade into shadow, what was to stop them from acting out their deepest and darkest desires? Servius, however...did not strike Fiammetta as being so weak of character.

She then found herself thinking about his name. The structure. 'Servius Laevinus Vitruvius'. It was an ancient F'aldyn custom to have three names, referred to as the tria nomina. Although the F'aldyn Empire itself fell long ago, their culture endured the passage of time and evolved into the country of Velinti, Fiammetta and Franco's homeland. It was a point of pride for them to be well-versed in their people's history. "If you don't mind my saying, your name is very...traditional," she started. "It is rather unique in this day and age."

Servius grunted. "It was quite contemporary when I was born."

Fiammetta narrowed her eyes. She laughed. "You don't mean to say... Why, the F'aldyn Empire collapsed almost *fifteen-hundred* years ago."

The knight did not respond.

"You...were *alive* when the Empire existed?" Fiammetta gasped.

"I was," Servius replied softly.

As much as she wanted to press further, Servius' evident dislike of conversation made her hold her tongue. He would have experienced the height of the ancient civilisation. She had so many questions... What was he before he was turned? A prefect? An emperor? Fiammetta bit her lip and tried to ignore the awkward silence that followed them all the way through the encampment.

Franco's personal tent had been kept immaculate, thanks to Fiammetta. As the pair entered the maroon pavilion, they saw Franco seated at a desk at the far side. Rushlights sat upon the table as he massaged his brow and poured over missives and other communications from Clthic loyalists throughout the realm of Tritham.

"Lord Franco," Fiammetta said with a bow. He got to his feet and locked eyes with Fiammetta. However, the warmth soon faded when he saw that she was not alone. "May I introduce Servius Laevinus Vitruvius, loyal son of Lady Viktoria."

Servius did not bow, but he did give a slight nod. Franco paced out from behind his desk and came to a halt in front of the vampire knight. "I assume that thou hast been unsuccessful in rescuing the demon?" he asked bluntly.

Fiammetta blinked and reeled back in confusion. Servius, however, showed no signs of discomfort. "I *had* her," he snarled. "If it weren't for the townsfolk resisting...and that wretched Godslave."

Franco flexed his jaw. "The sorcerer."

"Yes. Brother Alric." What Fiammetta saw next filled her with dread. Franco's face twitched and warped in a way that she had never seen before. He was totally and utterly speechless. Fiammetta felt the life drain from her extremities. The sorcerer…he led the raid on Beggar's Rock. He and his men killed all of those people. They burned her. Servius continued, "We remained in pursuit until a large force of Thestors and druids assailed us on the road. As I have been injured, I had no choice but to preserve the lives of those who were brave enough to stay by my side and retreat."

With an exhale, Franco snarled. "Tell me *everything*." The lord then glanced up at Fiammetta and dismissively waved her off without another word. She once again was overcome with stunned silence. Servius, as he took his steps forward, glanced back at her one last time. She couldn't see his face, but she could've sworn that she sensed some kind of frustration permeating his movements. With bitterness washed across her expression, Fiammetta swept through the tent flap and left.

XLI
The Pain Shall Save Me

Each crack of the whip drained the turmoil from his heart. The four stone walls folded the resonation back in upon itself, coalescing it into a powerful surge of vibrations that thundered through his bones. The sound was steady and rhythmic. In Phaemslake, it had been the only thing to make him content. His teeth were gritted and every muscle in his body tensed with each flick. He began to exhale in relief when the pain mounted. Once, not too long ago, it had been enough to have faith. His will had been sufficient. But he had grown weak. Such weakness was to be punished.

He finally stopped and knelt there in the empty chamber, panting and relishing the sensations that coursed through him. It wasn't enough. He deserved more pain. He clenched his left fist and raised his left arm in front of his face. Anger bubbled within his heart. All he could see in his mind was everything he had done wrong. Alric raised the whip above his head and glared down at his bare forearm. He screamed and, with unparalleled fury, throttled the whip against his bare skin over and over. His crazed fervour was befitting a man who was beating his worst enemy to death. The sting of the wounds brought him momentary numbness. It drowned out the image of Carthei's face that haunted his waking moments as well as the unwaking ones. Katheryn was right. He was undeserving of life. *It is what I deserve, it is what I deserve,* he thought to himself. His throat ran itself raw with wrathful, unbridled roars while he threw the lashes repeatedly against his flesh. Scars were drawn atop scars.

The whip fell to the ground with a dull 'thud'. He stared at the many dozens of thick lines that he had torn into his own flesh. Beads of obsidian blood seeped out of them and ran like rivers down his skin. He swallowed and forced his eyes shut. His body continued to shiver and there he remained for some time, riding the wave of anger, sorrow, and self-loathing that tempted him so. Tears streamed from his face and the sound of his sobbing filled the room.

“It must be said that the Lord loves us, but hates us all the same. We are capable of a great many things. Art, poetry, architecture. But we produce articles of grievous sin in equal measure. Murder, rape, sodomy. There is good within us, but lurking within the shadows of our souls is an inhuman monster. And so, He *must* hate us.”

The voice of the monk filled the stone chamber like icy water. It poured through his nerves and flooded his body with a lingering sense of discomfort. The chapter house of the Cathedral of Saint Merryn was jammed with priests, monks, nuns, Thestors, and Correnti. Alric was forced to sit upon the stone windowsill where he stared out across the south side of Wyrmsmouth. He watched the ships drift in and out of port as the monk continued, “Each man and woman standing upon the face of this earth has in their heart an Undying Greed. You must identify this greed and drown it if you are to truly follow the Lord. It will not die, so one must be vigilant and always keep it below the water. Otherwise, it will consume you and bring you to great sin.”

Alric rested his chin onto his knuckles as he continued gazing out the window. He had been a devoted student of those lessons since he was a child. They suddenly did not comfort him the way they once did. As a matter of fact, they brought him to anger. Before long, Alric lost his grip on the monk’s voice and was instead wandering the streets of Wyrmsmouth with his eyes. He watched as a woman bartered with a merchant for the best price for a bag of onions. He saw a dog running down the street closely chased by a young boy. Lords and their retinues walked the streets, perusing weapons and armour at the blacksmith workshops.

When the monk's sermon was complete and the people began filtering out of the room, Alric found himself waiting for everyone else to leave before standing himself. However, before he could walk out, the monk strolled over to him. “Brother Alric, is it?”

Alric nodded.

“We’ve had plenty of people passing through from Phaemslake during the last week or so. They say you delivered an angel to us… Is it true?”

Crossing his arms, Alric looked back out the window. It didn't matter how much he tried to beat the doubt out of his soul. It clung to him like a foul stench. “I intended to keep our presence here a secret.”

The monk nodded curtly. “Of course. As you wish. You’re waiting for an audience with the archbishop?”

Alric grunted in affirmation.

"It shouldn't be too long. I heard he was conversing with one of your Thestors. Apparently, this madman had taken a Clthic fortress with the aid of witches. Quite ridiculous, isn't it?" The words caused Alric to straighten. Without another word to the monk, Alric paced out of the room. "Brother? W-Where are you going?"

Thankfully, the archbishop's chambers weren't too difficult for Alric to find. He didn't bother knocking; instead, he pushed the door open with slightly too much force, causing it to slam into the side of the stone doorway. Two figures seated at the archbishop's desk instantly shot up to their feet. "He has arrived! God's Chosen!" muttered one of them. It was a Thestor with a sallet and bevor covering his face.

"Brother Baldwyn?" Alric asked shakily. Next to him was a man wearing simple clothing and the surcoat of the Knights Correntis. His sallow features and detached stare instantly identified him. "Brother Matvey…"

Archbishop Tyonius was still in his seat looking remarkably confused as Matvey leapt over to Alric and fiercely embraced him. "Brother…! I thought you dead!" The warmth that radiated from Matvey felt like fire against Alric's skin.

As he pulled away from the hug, Alric responded, "And I thee. How didst thou escape the Under?"

"If it weren't for several surviving Kaitan'zahi, I would have perished in that cold tomb," he explained. "We fought against the Clthics and their footmen, then we managed to escape through another Great Gate. Soon after, we reunited with Brother Baldwyn at Beggar's Rock."

Baldwyn marched over to Alric and knelt before him. The young Thestor said, "It pleases me greatly to behold thee again."

Alric frowned and forced Baldwyn to his feet once again. "Brother, please…" he muttered.

Baldwyn's eyes shot over to Tyonius. "Thy Grace, here stands God's Chosen." Tyonius only looked more confused at that point. His deep red skin began to turn pale. Alric ran a hand down his face as Baldwyn continued, "Brother Alric commands the forces of magic in God's name! He brought to us an angel from up high!"

A shiver travelled down Alric's neck, causing him to cough. "How art thou aware of the angel?"

Matvey rested a hand on Alric's shoulder as he spoke. "We sallied out from Beggar's Rock to come here, only to encounter townsfolk being beset by the demonists at Phaemslake. Upon dashing the Clthics apart together, I met the leader of the townsfolk, Sir Gabriel de Fontaine. Despite the fact that I myself amputated his legs a week ago, he *walked*, thanks to your angel. Such a thing cannot be done by mere mortals. It was proof enough of his words."

"Gabriel lives?"

"That he does," replied Matvey.

Tyonius suddenly burst out of his chair and raised his hands. "My friends, I am glad that you have been reunited, but could one of you please explain to me what the devil you're raving on about?" He asked the question incredibly calmly. The holy knights glanced at each other for a moment, Baldwyn shrugged, then the trio sat down opposite Tyonius and subjected him to a very long explanation of events. They spoke about Alric's uneasy alliance with the Ga'zahi, the creatures that crushed the Churchsworn at Threshfield, the Clthic fortress at Beggar's Rock, the vampire, and of course, Madsen. Baldwyn weaved his words like a poet, telling of Gabriel and the other 'Mended' as he called them; people who had been touched by Madsen's magic.

Eventually, Tyonius leaned backwards in his chair and narrowed his eyes. "You were in league with witches?"

"Druids, T-Thy Grace," Alric clarified with a stammer. The correction caused Baldwyn and Matvey to exchange confused glances.

Matvey said, "Where is Carthei? Did she survive the battle?"

It took everything he had not to begin trembling at the mere mention of her name, but he somehow managed it. "She did…but I-I was forced to strike her down." As the words left his mouth, he felt the overwhelming urge to avoid direct eye contact.

With a gasp, Matvey's spine snapped as straight as a tree. "*What*?" he exclaimed.

Alric desperately fought against the nerves that were making him fumble his words, but it was a fruitless battle. "S-She had… We… She conspired to assassinate the angel," he finally sputtered.

Baldwyn nodded as he crossed his arms. "A pity… The druids had been staunch allies. However, there are times when difficult choices must be made, Brother. For the will of God." Matvey, however, looked scornful. Slowly, the man rose from his seat. His outraged gaze fell upon Alric. Baldwyn prompted, "Is something the matter, Brother Matvey?"

"Is this how allegiance is repaid? A blade in the back?" Matvey scoffed.

Baldwyn erupted from his chair. "Careful, Brother."

"Calm yourselves!" Tyonius demanded. "Anger is not befitting your stations!"

Alric saw Matvey break eye contact with Baldwyn to look back on him. His wrathful expression made Alric's fingers tighten upon his thigh. "You Thestors are all the same. Don't you realise that *our* actions are how God is given shape in this world? He is probably staring down in horror at what you've done."

The outburst was enough to provoke Baldwyn into pacing closer and glowering in Matvey's face. Most unlike Baldwyn, he did not say anything. The silence itself was a threat. Alric, quivering where he sat, finally found courage enough to speak. "Brother Matvey, please..."

When Matvey continued, his voice became scathing. "If it weren't for her, you would've been raped and drained by that Godforsaken creature of the night. I see now how appreciative you are of that." Alric felt himself quake. He tried to fight the tears, but they streamed out of his eyes anyway. Matvey was right. He did not have to kill her...but he chose to anyway. Why? Because of God. Because of the sheer terror that He instilled in his heart. To defy Him was so frightening, so horrifying, that he could not even acknowledge the fact that he could.

With a growl, Matvey stormed out of the room and slammed the door shut behind him. Baldwyn shook his head and lowered himself into his chair. "Pay no mind to that fool's words, Alric. He, like his kin, is much too soft."

Tyonius rubbed his chin and continued. "I wonder why the druids wanted the angel dead. Did you ever learn anything about their religion?"

Alric might as well have been miles away at that point. It had been one after another. First Katheryn, then Matvey. Why would they say such things? He was struggling already, without their aggression. They only made it even harder for him to find peace. For a moment, his wounded frown weakened as he realised something. What had they said? They didn't insult him. They simply spoke the *truth*. That was all it took to bring him to unbearable anguish. It meant that he was completely and utterly lost. "Brother Alric?" Tyonius prompted. His voice shook the languishing Thestor out of his trance.

"W-What?"

Tyonius flexed his jaw and repeated, "What do you know of druidic doctrine?"

Alric cleared his throat and tried his best to mask his discomfort. "T-The druids...they..." His voice faltered after those three words and shook apart under his discomfort. He tried again. "The...Ga'zahi worship the Vorkhai. They are said to be the creators of this world...but they are destroyers in equal measure. Carthei believed that Madsen was of the Vorkhai, destined to end our world."

Tyonius nodded. "You have spent a great deal of time with the supposed angel, Alric. What do *you* think? Is there any merit to the druid beliefs?"

Baldwyn basically scoffed in the archbishop's face. "Thy Grace, with utmost respect, I must remind thee that however valuable the druids are as allies, their faith is of no import."

With a muted gasp, Alric glanced down at his feet. Tyonius smiled playfully and nodded. "Baldwyn, my son, the Scripture has been added to, subtracted from, and revised countless times since it was first written. Do you think that Edich was the language it was originally written in? No, it was not. Every form of the Scripture you have laid eyes upon is a translation in some way, shape, or form. We, as true and devout followers of God, must adapt to the obstacles that the future may bring us. We cannot do that if we are rigid and adhere too strongly to the past. Time brings change." The statement made Alric's sorrow morph into bitterness. The Scripture had been...amended?

Baldwyn seemed to shrivel up after that. With him dealt with, Tyonius closed his eyes, inhaled, then looked to Alric expectantly for an answer to his previous question. The Thestor whispered, "If not for her, I would be lying dead in the Under. However, her knowledge of the arcane *can* be used as a weapon. She has only ever unfurled it upon the Clthics."

Tyonius sighed. "I see. So, in other words, we don't know anything." Alric once would have been enraged that someone would dare question his judgement, but since that same uncertainty swirled around within his own heart, he could not object. "Regardless of what she may or may not be, she has helped many of God's children who were otherwise doomed. I would like to meet her as well as some of these Mended," Tyonius added with a smile.

After the meeting, Alric joined Baldwyn in the Cathedral's courtyard for supper. They fetched some bread, cheese, and water and sat beneath a blooming tree that was as large as a trebuchet. Baldwyn finally had sense enough to remove his bevor and helmet while they ate. Alric's attention was fixed to the massive tower of the Cathedral. He had been inside many years ago and seen the mighty bronze bells that hung within. However, the main thing on his mind was how tall it was. How...very tall. "Brother, might I seek thy counsel?" Alric suddenly asked as he jerked his head away.

Baldwyn was blindsided. His orange face warped as he stared in bewilderment. "Why…of course," he said sceptically. "Although, I think a man of my few years of service would be of little help to thee."

Alric began, "If God descended from the Heavens and spoke things that conflicted with the Scripture, what wouldst thou do?"

"I would turn my back upon the pretender, for it would have proven itself to be false by uttering such things," Baldwyn answered immediately with a full mouth.

Alric cocked his head. "Perhaps the Scripture is…incorrect? Didst thou not hear the archbishop admit that it had been altered many a time by the hands of mere men?"

Baldwyn shrugged. "Alric, I know not if thou art aware, but we are *Knights Thestor*. We enforce God's law; we do not ascertain its truths. Leave that to the theologians."

With a scowl of disbelief, Alric lowered his plate of food. He had lost his appetite. "If the Thestors are to act as prosecutors of God's law, shouldn't they understand it?" Baldwyn nodded silently as he ate his bread and meat, but Alric could tell that it was simply out of respect. He did not care at all for the words that were sent toward him.

Alric took his time on the walk back to Castle Wyrmsmouth. He usually felt pressed for time wherever he went, as if he had to move with utmost urgency. On that afternoon in particular, his mind wandered and he had all the presence of mind of a revenant as he lumbered on his way.

When he returned to the castle, he could not find Katheryn anywhere. Alric pushed open the door to Madsen's chambers. There was an assortment of items all over the floor, things that Alric had no understanding of. Eventually, he realised one of the piles consisted of clothing. Very strange clothing to say the least. One of the peculiar grey boxes that Madsen took everywhere with her was open by the side of the bed. Alric approached and peered inside. One object in particular seized his attention. He reached into the crate and picked up a bright orange ball. It was perfectly round and roughly the size of a human head. It had a rough texture and thick black lines curved about its surface. When he squeezed it, there was a great deal of resistance. It almost felt like a bladder full of air. Was it perhaps a ball to be used in a game, like the ones the commonfolk partook in?

With a shrug, Alric placed it back into the crate and sat himself onto the bed. The silence and solitude caused his mind to wander. Katheryn and Matvey forced him to lay eyes upon the truth. He was a pathetic, terrified man who hurt others in a desperate attempt to save himself. Alric whimpered as his mind paced backwards in time. He could not bear it. The faces. The screams. The mutilated corpses. He could see them all. He could hear them whisper to him. *You should just die.* Alric abruptly pushed to his feet and made for the door but when he reached for it, it sprung open on its own.

Madsen stood there, wide-eyed. Her skin was glistening with sweat and there was dirt upon her face. "Oh. H-Hey, man. I was just…" She suddenly cut herself off. "You okay?" He could not answer the question. He could not even bring himself to look her in the eye. Alric barged through her and broke into a sprint.

XLII
Get Back Here, Goddammit

Whenever Madsen caught a glimpse of Alric, he vanished around a corner or passed through a door. She pushed herself into a brisk jog. "Alric! Wait!" Something wasn't right. There was a…look in his optics that made her feel uneasy. She swore she saw something on the sleeve of his tunic. E-gel stains. There was this voice in the back of her head screaming that Alric needed help…and she had a feeling she knew why. She tore around one final corridor just in time to see a door slam shut. By its side was one of Katheryn's knights: Sir Lionel. He had been the only other proxy apart from Alric that Katheryn had allowed her to see. As Madsen hurried towards him, Sir Lionel frowned, wrinkling the scarred softbody tissue around his lip. "Thy Holiness. That Thestor Brother seemed familiar to me. What was he–"

Madsen kept moving and reached for the door handle…only for Lionel to step in front of it. "Do you mind?"

"I have been instructed to prevent thee from leaving this wing of the keep."

"Right. Well. See ya." Madsen executed a manoeuvre that she'd mastered in her days on the Anvil company basketball team. Simultaneously, she sidestepped and spun on her heels. The spin move caught Lionel completely off-guard and he snatched at thin air. Madsen lunged for the door and threw it open.

"What in God's name?!" cried Sir Lionel. Madsen came barrelling into Castle Wyrmsmouth's great hall and became the subject of about thirty people's direct attention. She froze for a second. Gasps and screams flooded the room. Katheryn, seated at the high table, ran a hand down her face and grumbled. Right as Madsen was about to swear under her breath, she saw Alric pacing through the main doors. She launched into action and caused the hall to erupt into chaos. People desperately scrambled away from her, tripping over furniture and colliding with each other in the process. The chorus of panicked cries was so overpowering that Madsen could barely hear what Katheryn said as she stood and raised her hands. "Please, contain thyselves! Allow me a moment to explain!" She shot glances at two other proxies in the room. "Sir Caldwell, Sir Simon, contain her!"

Seeing as the cacophony drowned out their liege's voice and it was the first time they'd ever seen a human, the pair of knights were a little too gobsmacked to act instantly. All of the nobles and commoners who were gathered for lunch turned into a surging ocean of bodies as Lionel leapt at Madsen. She grabbed a plate of roasted meat and tossed it at Simon's head, kicked an empty chair over at Lionel, then threw herself at Caldwell's midsection. Everything happened so quickly. Simon caught the platter, but the momentum sent the pieces of oily meat slapping into his face, disorienting him. Lionel took one steady step over the toppled chair with his left leg, but his right collided with the piece of furniture as he was pulling it up and over, causing him to stumble and fall onto his hands.

Lastly, Caldwell didn't seem to be expecting the strange creature to straight up tackle him. Madsen hurtled into the knight and wrapped her arms around his torso. After the pair slammed into the ground, Madsen rolled off the dazed proxy and made a break for the door. The great hall had already been turned into an absolute pig sty; food, plates, cutlery, and cups tumbled across the floor as all of the patrons either ran away screaming, or scurried to the very edges of the room and stared at her in horror as she got the hell out of there.

Madsen worked herself into a sprint and put all of her focus onto Alric, who was trailing ahead of her, not looking back once. She heard rapid heavy footfalls behind her. "Halt, Thy Holiness!" called Sir Lionel. He was going to go ignored as Madsen tore down a stone brick road. As she rounded a corner, she came charging into a bustling town square. Market stalls were set up and a massive crowd of proxies were milling about inspecting and buying produce. Blood-curdling shrieks signalled Madsen's arrival.

"What in God's name is that!?"

"Get away from it! Quickly!"

"Guards! Guards!"

In the blink of an eye, the square turned into a stampede. Proxies were thrown to the ground as those around them turned tail and ran with reckless abandon. She didn't slow down. She had to keep track of Alric as he cut through the crowd. The sea of people became a massive pain in the ass; not only did she have to weave in and out of the dense field of bodies, some even became direct obstacles. As Madsen brushed by a stall lined with baked bread, the man behind it leapt out and snatched her by the arm. "Over here! I have the creature! Here!"

Madsen scoffed and instinctively palmed the guy's arm away and shoved him. It was clear that in the heat of the moment, she *may* have overdone it. The baker staggered backwards, slipped, and slammed right into the side of his stall. The wooden structure was smashed apart under the proxy's weight, and bits of wood were flung everywhere. As she went zooming by, Madsen peered over her shoulder with widened eyes. "Fuck! Shit! S-Sorry!" It might've been a good thing, because she saw Lionel and the other knights slow down to maybe check on the poor guy.

After dodging left, right, under, and over stunned proxies, Madsen finally realised where Alric was headed. She watched him run across the town square towards a massive structure with elements of Gothic architecture in its design. It had two massive spires both lined with incredible stone flourishes. Alric shrunk until he disappeared within the massive open doorways at the base of the structure.

The closer she got to the Cathedral, the more she felt her heart rate pick up. What was Alric going to do? Where the hell was he going? The main tower of the Cathedral peered down at her…and her stomach instantly dropped. "O-Oh my god. No, no, no, no…"

Her heart lurched back once again when she realised that a bunch of people were in the process of pulling the immense wooden doors shut. "Wait!" she called. The monks, all looking absolutely terrified, pulled on the doors faster. Just before they shut, a pair of men stepped out. Madsen came skidding to a halt in front of two fully armoured Knights Thestor. They looked just as cautious as she was. Raising her hands, she pleaded, "L-Listen to me. Brother Alric is in danger. You *need* to let me in."

One drew his sword. "Thou shalt not taint this holy place with thy stench, demon! To arms, Brother Baldwyn; we shall defend God's domain!"

The other tilted his head down slightly, like he was glancing down at the name patch on her flight suit. "Madsen…" he muttered to himself. He suddenly straightened his posture and turned to his ally. Just as the other guy closed in on Madsen, Baldwyn lashed out with an attack that neither of them saw coming. He drew his sword, but twirled it so he held it with both hands on the blade, essentially upside-down. Then he reeled back and unleashed one hell of a home run swing aimed directly at his friend's head. The pommel of Baldwyn's sword smashed into the side of the other knight's helmeted head and he collapsed into a heap on the ground.

"Woah! *Dude!* What the fuck was that?"

Baldwyn eagerly paced by and headed back towards the town square. "I do not take kindly to a knight brother drawing steel against an angel. Quickly, Thy Holiness. Deliver the good Brother Alric from doom and I shall explain thine identity to the would-be interlopers." He pointed at the group of Katheryn's knights who were still barging through the townsfolk in the square. "Those who fail to heed my words shall be cut down."

Madsen wrinkled her forehead and narrowed her eyes. Of course Alric had friends who were just as nuts as he was. "Uh. Thanks for the assist…but don't kill anyone," she called.

Baldwyn paused for a second, then bowed. He still held his sword in that weird upside-down grip. "As thou command. I shall instead bludgeon them into submission."

To her immediate left, just around the corner from the Cathedral's entrance, was the bottom of a series of wooden scaffolds that traced all the way up the side of the incredible stone building. Madsen ran for the scaffolding, leapt into the air, clutched onto the edge of the first platform, then heaved herself up. She rolled under the wooden railings and got to her feet as fast as she could before making a break for the ladder ahead. The only thing she could think about as she sprinted across the planks and climbed the ladders was whether or not she was too late. Even when the air was all but squeezed from her lungs, she kept pushing and forced the doubts out of her mind. The only thing she needed to concern herself with was getting to the top of that tower.

Finally, with her arms aching and her body covered in sweat, she pulled herself up and onto the roof. She braced herself on all fours for a few seconds in order to catch her breath, then made the mistake of peering down the side of the Cathedral to see where that Baldwyn guy was at. She had to be at least seven storeys up, so it was dizzying. He seemed to have convinced most of the nobles to calm down. Most of them. One was trying to climb the scaffolding, but Baldwyn noticed, grabbed him by the ankle, then slammed him onto the ground with a 'thud' that even Madsen could hear. "Jesus Christ…" she gasped, desperately clawing for air.

Madsen urged her burning arms to push her body upright, then broke out for a door on the Cathedral's main tower. It flung open with a shrill creak and she didn't bother shutting it. Inside, it was mostly dark. Narrow beams of light passed in from outside and she heard the dull groaning of the wooden flooring beneath her feet. A set of rickety stairs curled upward to her right. She heard footfalls straining the floorboards above. As fast as her legs could propel her, she leapt up the stairs. Her own thunderous steps were as loud as someone desperately pounding on a wooden door.

At the very top of the tower hung the final bell. Wooden structural supports crisscrossed the room, which opened at the far end. Standing there, staring out at the city, was Alric. He had his back facing Madsen and took a slow step forward. The engineer hurled herself ahead. Every muscle in her body was in agony, but she had to move. She had to. In under a second, she closed the distance and snatched Alric by the shoulders. Madsen planted her foot behind Alric's, then shoved him backwards.

The knight tripped over her foot and fell flat onto his back on the floor. What she saw made her tremble. His expression was completely blank as he stared up at the ceiling. His face was drenched with tears that still came pouring out of his optics. And there, on his left forearm, was a patch of fresh, open wounds. Dozens and dozens of scars all overlapped each other. Madsen's entire body shook with such intensity that she had to lower herself to the ground. *I did this*, she thought to herself.

XLIII
Starry Night

Katheryn and her men showed up at the Cathedral not too long afterwards. At that point, an angry mob had gestated to hunt down what they were calling a demon. At first, they didn't listen to Katheryn's explanation and tried to force their way into the Cathedral. Apparently, she had her knights and men-at-arms forcibly beat down some of the townsfolk and threaten them with execution to get them to settle down. It was a little much…but she insisted that it was needed. With everyone subdued, she managed to explain Madsen's presence to everyone, then Archbishop Tyonius arrived and reassured them. He conducted a massive rally and introduced a very reluctant Madsen to the public. He said things that made her fume. 'An angel came to a knight with despair in his heart and showed him the light' or some bullshit like that. Madsen couldn't stand it. She was the reason he even tried to do it in the first place. People from the Hospital of Saint Corren took Alric into their care so they could treat him. Apparently, they diagnosed him with a disease called 'melancholia'; symptoms were overwhelming sadness, lack of appetite, and restlessness. Sounded more than a little familiar to her. She kept her distance, because…well, she didn't want to make it worse.

Later that day there was some kind of meeting with lots of priests, bishops, and the archbishop too, of course. Some of the clowns wanted her to go parade around the city or some shit, but she gave that a hard 'pass'. Instead, she suggested that some of the Hospital guys set up a workspace for her in some tents out by the castle keep so proxies could come to see her if they needed repairs done. Tyonius liked that idea a lot more than just walking around the city collecting kisses from people and told everyone to get it done.

Conducting more work on the proxies meant that she could map out some more of their complex subsystem network and label more of the components. She also started renaming the tags of people she knew to make things easier if she ever had to pick them out in a crowd. All of the proxies she repaired at Phaemslake, led by Claudia and Gabriel, showed up and begged to be her assistants. So, she ended up teaching them things about their design that no one else really knew so they could help her out. They told her that they started calling themselves ‘The Mended’. Cute.

It was interesting to her that to the proxies, a mechanical problem like a seized servo motor was joint pain or a chemical imbalance in the matter processing vat was chronic gastrointestinal issues. It took a while, but she suddenly understood why everyone thought she was an angel. If someone showed up on a SysGov colony and did all of that stuff to humans, they’d be saying the same thing.

She’d spent three days working on malfunctioning proxies. The ones that she couldn’t repair immediately were given comprehensive care instructions that would eventually solve their issues in time. The more she helped, the more volunteered to be part of The Mended. Her days were hectic and nonstop. At night though, she was left alone in her quarters in the castle with nothing but her thoughts to keep her company. On the third night, she was lying in her bed staring at the ceiling after a big day of fixing up malfunctioning proxies. She tossed her basketball into the air, caught it, then did it again. Over and over. She should’ve just lied to Alric. Told him what he wanted to hear. That way, he would’ve stayed happy. But…that would've meant he’d keep tormenting people, right? Interrupting her thoughts was a knock on the door.

“Uh…come in,” she called as she sat up and threw her legs off the side of the bed.

The door creaked open and in stepped Katheryn. Madsen hadn’t really seen her since the day it all happened. She didn’t really know what to expect. That said, she couldn’t find it in herself to look her in the optics. She found herself gazing at Katheryn’s feet as she said, “Hi…”

“When was the last time thou washed thyself?” Katheryn asked.

“Oh shit.” Madsen groaned as she ran a hand down her face. Not since she got thawed out. *Ten days*. “Oh my god. *Fuck*. I smell like shit, don’t I?” She lifted an arm and sniffed her armpit.

Katheryn huffed in amusement. “Perhaps it can be forgiven. It cannot be ignored, however, so I have arranged for a bath to be drawn for thee. There is a feast in the great hall this night and thou shalt be present.”

“I don’t really…want to,” Madsen sighed, fiddling with the basketball.

The proxy took a few steps closer. “A lady must look upon the person with whom she speaks.”

Madsen muttered, “Good thing I’m not a lady.”

Katheryn’s hand snapped out and gently took Madsen's chin to turn her gaze to her face. With a scorching stare right into Madsen’s soul, she said,

"He does not wish for thee to be moping about in this manner. Especially when thou art not to be blamed."

"But I *am*. Wait…you talked to him?" Madsen leaned forward and asked, "Is he okay? What are they doing to him over there? They're not suss or anything, are they? I-I just…you know… I mean…" A subdued yet warm smile flashed across Katheryn's face for a split second. Madsen squinted. "What…?"

Her question was kind of just brushed away. "We spoke at length the other day, he and I."

"W-What did he tell you?" Madsen asked.

"He confessed that thy majesty showed him the consequences of his actions. For the first time, he could perceive all the pain he had wrought. And Alric…he hath wrought a significant amount of it in his time. I acted sharply towards him earlier… Too sharply, perhaps. If anyone is to be deemed responsible for his lament, I believe I would be one to share in the blame. But, alas, our emotions are beyond our control; they erupt, they ebb, and they wane without our consent. There is no use in feeling remorse for them. We simply stay the course."

With a sigh, Madsen eased her posture a little. She had to thank Alric for sticking by the angel cover story even when he had so much to deal with, but all she could think about was how the whole situation was fucked to begin with. She didn't care what people chose to believe in. Acceptance and coexistence was important. When it came to what happened with Alric, she just blurted something out before she knew he could even comprehend it…and it pushed him to the edge. Almost too far. "I should've just kept my mouth shut. He was happy before."

Katheryn shook her head weakly. "No. He was never happy." Madsen placed her basketball onto the bed and crossed her arms with another heavy sigh. "Come, bathe and get dressed. That 't-shirt' is revolting."

"It's normal where I come from."

"Well, it may be suitable in Heaven for women to dress like harlots, but here, it shall not do. Those arms must be covered and the fit is much too tight."

Madsen crinkled her nose. "Mmmm. Aren't you just a gigantic bundle of joy today?"

"Each and every day. Make haste, creature."

Madsen dove into one of her crates and picked out an outfit from her casual clothes. After that, she followed Katheryn through the halls, expecting to be led into a bathroom or something. Instead, the pair entered

Katheryn's bed chambers to see a big wooden tub in the middle of it filled with warm water. Two proxy women that she recognised as Katheryn's maids Penelope and Elisabeth were standing by the tub with their sleeves rolled up. When Katheryn shut the door behind them, Madsen suddenly felt like everything got super weird.

"Good evenin', My Lady, Yer Holiness," Penelope greeted as Katheryn strolled over to a chair in the corner of the room and planted herself down on it.

"Uh…'sup." Madsen muttered.

Elisabeth stared at her in silence for a few seconds. "I beg yer pardon?"

Katheryn facepalmed hard and interjected, "Thou art to assist Madsen in taking her bath, not attempt to decipher her nonsensical dribble."

Madsen planted her hands on her hips, narrowed her eyes, then snorted. With a strained smirk of disbelief on her face, she mumbled, "You're not gonna…I mean…like…"

"If you would disrobe, Yer Holiness," Penelope said.

The suggestion was enough to spur Madsen forward, make her grab Penelope and Elisabeth, and guide them towards the door. "Okay, okay, alright, but *no*. No. No, thank you." Before they had a chance to say anything, Madsen shut the door in their faces and looked at Katheryn.

The Lady Danecaster seemed genuinely confused. "Have I offended thee?" she asked with this sound in her voice that suggested that she didn't really care but was asking because it was expected of her.

"Why are you just sitting there? Were you gonna leave?"

Katheryn maintained intense eye contact with Madsen.

"*Okay.*" Madsen shouted as she hovered over to Katheryn with her hands raised. "Time to go. Get outta here, you little freak." She gently pushed her through the doorway and shut the door, making sure to latch it. "Jesus Christ."

With her newfound privacy, Madsen had her very first bath. Of her life. Well, probably since she was a baby. Back home, showers were basically it. The main thing was that they took up less space; practicality was in vogue. People liked to make sure their homes made the most efficient use of space as possible. Once she got undressed and eased herself into the water though, she realised that she wasn't a fan of baths. She felt like she was just marinating in her own filth. It was gross. She probably got out a little sooner than she should've, but she made sure to scrub all of the grime, dirt, and dried E-Gel from her skin and hair with the soap that the maids left for her.

After drying off, she slipped into a pair of dark blue cargo pants with a bright orange stripe running down the side, a black and white raglan t-shirt, a thick neon yellow high-vis work jacket with the Anvil Heavy Fabrication logo on the back, and the same pair of very dirty basketball shoes that she'd been wearing for the last ten days. She'd gotten the shirt when she went to see a big Intersystem Basketball League final on Earth a few years ago; it had the logo on the front which was the letters 'IBL' next to a small, stylised basketball. The high-vis jacket was something she hung onto from her old job as an engineer and heavy machinery operator, before she was chosen to join up with ISEC.

Since her hair was short, she managed to dry it off quickly and rustle it up a little. Before she left, she rolled up the sleeves of her jacket. When Madsen opened the door, she was confused to see Katheryn sitting on the floor in the middle of the hallway with her back against the wall. "What in the name of God is *this*? I left a dress for thee upon the table."

As Katheryn got to her feet, Madsen crossed her arms and said super casually, "Listen, *Kat*…" The duchess' face scrunched up something fierce. "Number one: I'll wear a dress when I feel like wearing a dress. Number two: if you keep being so handsy with me, one of these days I'm gonna punch you. Number three: are we going to this ball thing or what?" Silence enveloped the pair of them for ten seconds. Then, without warning, Katheryn let out a singular, very loud 'Ha'. She held her arm out. "Uh… What is this?"

"Take my arm. I shall escort thee to the great hall."

Madsen smacked her lips. "Why don't you take mine?" she asked mischievously, raising her own arm. Katheryn scoffed, spun around, and trudged down the hallway with a huff.

The great hall was a short walk away from the castle keep. Gabriel and about half a dozen other fancy-looking proxies were staring at her with beaming smiles as she and Katheryn approached. It made her feel so weird. "Thy Holiness, how it pleases me that thou art joining us this night," said Gabriel with a bow. "Such ravishing company thou keep as well," he murmured as he looked at Katheryn.

She replied, "I do like thy new legs, Sir Gabriel. 'Twould be a shame if something were to occur to them."

Madsen couldn't help but notice the malicious intent that glowed behind Katheryn's optics. "Okay. Why don't you guys go in first? I'll…I'll catch up." As the rest of the group filtered inside, she wandered off towards the castle wall. When she stood right beneath it and looked up against its surface, it reminded her of looking up at a skyscraper. Not quite as tall, but when you were super close to it, it was a similar sensation. The stars stared down at her. She wondered if her parents knew if she was missing. ISEC had to have been aware that something was wrong; they would've stopped receiving telemetry from the Hathor since the launch complex was completely abandoned. She was so lost in thought that she didn't even hear the footsteps in the grass. For minutes, she leaned her head against the stone and puffed her cheeks up as she gazed off into the sky. Until she heard someone clear their throat. Madsen was jolted back into reality.

Standing in front of her was Alric. He wasn't wearing his surcoat. Instead, he was in a long white tunic that was tied around his waist with a leather belt. The garment was very plain and ragged compared to what Madsen saw the other nobles and stuff wearing. She stood there in stunned silence for a few moments. Alric was slouching, his brow was wrinkled, there was darkness around his eyes, and he looked thinner…like he hadn't been eating properly for a few days. She almost didn't recognise him. It was quiet for a long time.…until Alric finally said something. "I am sorry."

Madsen furrowed her brow and huffed. "What? There's nothing…you didn't…"

"I never truly cared for thee," he added with a pained sigh. She exhaled and blinked a handful of times. "I was only concerned with how thou couldst banish my doubts and grant me peace." Even his voice sounded different. It was gentle and hollow, almost. Like all of the certainty was gone. It took a while for her to see *him* as a person too…so maybe that meant they were even. "How easy it would have been for thee to fill my ears with lies to satiate my obsession with deliverance."

Madsen replied. "Are you serious right now? I don't… I-I never meant to force all of this onto you. If I just knew about your general intelligence… If I didn't just fucking blurt that shit out, none of this would've happened. Look at what it did to you. Look at what *I* did to you."

"Thou didst not command me to doubt the Scripture. That was something that *I* alone did. If I did not already have misgivings…thou wouldst never have left the Pale Spire alive." The knight strode over towards an old tree and leaned onto it.

She had no idea what to say. On one hand, she caused him to have a legit mental breakdown. That was how serious it was. But…the emotions he went through…all of the thinking it caused him to do…he came out the other side a better person, didn't he? He stepped back, reflected on the choices he made, the kind of person he was, and decided that it was something that he couldn't deal with. But it still almost broke him. "Fuck," she hissed as she shook her head. It was too complicated. People were too complicated…and that's what he was, wasn't it? A person.

"A world without Him is frightening, I must admit. The thought that it is all…empty…meaningless…brings a chill to my heart that I cannot describe," he whispered as he stared into nothingness and lowered himself onto the grass. "It was all to please Him. To save myself from His rage. F-From Hell. And yet, He was never there to begin with…so I have nothing to show for my life of fearful servitude but the lives that I have either ended or ruined."

With a gulp, Madsen glanced at her feet. She could barely comprehend what he was going through. Actually, she *couldn't*. Things were never a matter of belief to her. Something either was, or wasn't. She didn't concern herself with the in-between. She could afford to do that because she just happened to have been born at a certain point on the human cumulative knowledge chain. For Alric and all the other proxies, they literally could not understand the universe to the same extent. Not for at least another thousand years. And that was still a big maybe; there were no fossil fuels on their planet, so who knew if they were going to develop the same way? They *had* to extrapolate the rest. What they came up with threatened people into behaving a certain way, but also reassured them. It was something that no matter how hard she tried, Madsen could never comprehend, because she lived her entire life not believing in anything.

Alric cocked his head. "Is something amiss?"

"No. Well…I mean, *yes*…but not… It's like…" Madsen stammered. Then, she threw her arms up and sat on the ground by Alric's side. "For fuck's sake." Alric huffed through his nose as a weak smile formed on his face. After a few seconds, Madsen swallowed, took a deep breath, then said, "Listen, Alric, you can't do much about the stuff that's already happened…but there's still stuff that *hasn't* happened. You're in control of who you are and what you do. You always have been."

Alric's face trembled for a moment. He closed his eyes and took a deep breath, like he was trying as hard as he could to keep it together. "It is of no consequence. What I have done is unforgivable."

"Maybe you don't need forgiveness. Maybe…you just need to be the kind of guy that *you* won't be ashamed of being." Alric stared up into the sky in silence. The two of them listened to the wind sweeping through the grass for a few moments until Madsen found the nerve to try to make small talk. "Y-You know, I was supposed to go to the dinner party ball thing with your sister."

"Dost thou truly wish to mingle with the lords and ladies?"

"No, not really. You know what she's like, she kind of just told me that I was going."

He chuckled quietly to himself. As he did, Madsen noticed the way his weathered polymer membrane skin crinkled around the corners of his optics when he smiled. She could see wrinkles that had formed on its rubbery surface, mainly in the middle of his brow. His optic nodes were faint blue and darted around the way human eyes would. She watched them flick back and forth as he inspected her. It was a little scary being face to face with a being that she had no real emotional context for. She could decipher a few facial expressions, but she found herself in the dark most of the time. Hell, she still had trouble telling him apart from all the other proxies sometimes, but she wouldn't ever say that because, you know…that sounded *really, really* bad. *So* bad.

Alric seemed to stare into Madsen's eyes. She couldn't read his expression, so she was left to hope that he wasn't glaring. Despite the uncanny valley feelings she had when she looked at him, she still knew what he was. A machine, a robot, an android. She could only imagine how disgusting and grotesque *she'd* be to him, since he'd never seen organic flesh before. She probably looked like a horror movie monster to him; maybe that's why he was staring at her so much. The thought made her smirk.

Eventually, after the seconds of silent gazing, Alric decided to finally say something. "Where are the rest of thy kin? Are they in the Under?"

"The place you found me in was just an old outpost. I'm actually from out there." She pointed up at the night sky. "You see all those stars? Most of them have planets going around them. Planets like the one we're standing on right now. The ones my people live on are managed by SysGov. It's like a…big kingdom made up of different worlds."

She watched Alric's face as he tried to filter the concept through his CPU. His expression went from fear, confusion, to wonder. "Thou *sail* between the stars?" he asked, like it was absolutely ridiculous….which, you know, it kinda was. Of course, *sailing* would be the widest form of long-distance travel he could understand. The idea of human flight would be absolutely beyond his comprehension.

"Yeah. I guess I do."

"How many are there?"

"*Stars?*" The innocent question made Madsen smile. "More than there are grains of sand on your whole planet."

He reeled back in shock. After blinking in silence for a few seconds, he tilted his head up and stared up at the night sky. "God blind me. Truly? How could they possibly be host to other worlds? They are all so…small."

"Small, or far away?" Madsen prompted with an arch of an eyebrow. "The Sun's just another star."

She watched as he froze in place, optics wide and locked on the sky. His expression scrunched up and he opened his mouth to ask something, but nothing came out. Then, he scratched the back of his neck, paused, and opened his mouth again. Still, silence. He finally sighed and clicked his tongue before finally finding the words. "Are there…other peoples on these foreign worlds?"

Madsen rubbed the bridge of her nose. She didn't want to bring the mood down so soon, but *he* asked. "Well…the spooky thing is that all of the planets we've found so far weren't exactly good places to live. The air was toxic, the temperatures were extreme, there was no magnetosphere, the list goes on. Long story short, no."

"They *'weren't'* good places to live?" Alric pressed, cocking his head.

"I work for an organisation called ISEC. We explore space, find planets that are close enough to what we need, and build engines on them to make them liveable. Once all that's done, SysGov starts sending scientists in to study them and eventually decide if they're ready for settlement. My job is to go out and fix things whenever they fall apart, or to make sure everything is running okay."

He shook his head in disbelief. "Thou sail between suns, create life where there previously was naught but desolation, and can engineer an entire species in thine own image. If thou art not an angel…what art thou?"

"We call ourselves homo sapiens, or humans. You guys seem to have taken that name too…so I've started calling you homo proxima."

Alric didn't ask any more questions. It almost looked like he wanted to, but couldn't quite get over the scale of everything. He looked away and suddenly changed the subject. "…I am aware that my sympathy is unforgivably late, but regardless, I must offer condolences for thy compatriots." The sentence took Madsen by surprise, so much so that she didn't really know what he was talking about at first. The words eventually sucker punched her out of the forced dissociation she'd been in for a while. "Didst thou ever learn how they perished?"

Her shoulders slumped and she swallowed. The whole time, she had her feelings packed away in a box and slid into the back corner of her mind. She didn't have any busywork to distract herself with anymore. It was just the night sky and Alric keeping her company. She took a few moments to think about how to explain Spatial Fold Anchors to him. She finally decided that she'd kinda just gloss over it; she didn't have the brain power to fully explain something like that just yet. Madsen answered, "Not exactly. I guess there's a few things I need to explain first. You know how far apart those stars are now. With our current technology, going between them can take a few hours if the right equipment's been built at the destination. For frontier systems that haven't had them built yet, it can take months. In case anything goes wrong, say something critical on the ship fails, we have a way to keep ourselves asleep until we can be rescued. On my ship, we were conducting a standard test of these systems, just to make sure they were all working smoothly. I literally can't tell you how many times I've done it before, it's that routine. Something went wrong, though…and my bed was the only one that didn't malfunction. That's all I know."

Alric exhaled deeply.

"Yeah…" she murmured with a gulp.

"Wert thou well acquainted with any of thy crew members?"

It took her a handful of seconds to formulate her response; she knew that terms like 'university' and 'mechanical engineering degree' would mean absolutely nothing to Alric, so she had to try and phrase it a little more openly. "Yeah. We spend a lot of time training. I-I knew Vuong for the longest, though. We studied together. Never thought we'd meet again after that…then we were assigned to the same crew." She was staring into the void with her eyes not focused on anything in particular. Tears traced down her face. "God fucking dammit," she snarled as she thuggishly wiped them dry with the back of her hand.

Alric swallowed and cleared his throat. "Perhaps I should not have–"

"N-No, it's alright. I think I…needed to talk about it. Even if it was just a little." She looked up at the stars again in silence. She owed it to Vuong to get out of there. His family needed to know what happened.

XLIV
A WALK AT MIDNIGHT

Shaun Carver focused on levelling out his breathing and remaining calm. His hands, gripped upon the reins, trembled uncontrollably. Moonlight painted the road ahead, undoubtedly the guiding hand of God shepherding him to safety. He wondered if the others were as lucky as he had been. Telling the Clthic Guards that he had been ordered to procure more food and supplies for the camp seemed to be a doomed plot, but it had succeeded. In reality, the barrels and crates stowed in his wagon were far from empty…

He had lost track of time. How long had he been driving the horses? Had he missed the meeting point? Eventually, he realised that his anxieties were misplaced. Slowly, the skeletal remains of a village scrolled into view. Blackened and littered with mutilated body parts, was the town that the Clthic Synod had swept through a day or two prior. As Carver brought the wagon down the main street, he tried to quench the shame and horror that gurgled about in his throat.

Once the wagon came to a grinding halt in the ash-ridden street, Carver climbed off and took an anxious glance around. It seemed quiet, but he could never trust his own senses. He heard the containers shifting in the wagon, causing him to angrily knock three times on the side of the cart. The sounds promptly stopped.

He sent his intense gaze down both ends of the street, spun about, then stared down the adjoining alleyways. Something writhed about in his stomach. A sense of unfounded dread. Perhaps the Witches knew of his plan and were lying in wait. If so, he had been a dead man the moment he left camp. "Fuck," Carver snarled as he shook his head in an attempt to toss his nerves aside. He started walking the village and trying to sweep it for threats. He could only hear the faint brushing of leaves in the wind and saw nothing but shadows cast by the moon's faint light.

"Shaun? Issat you?" came a sharp whisper.

Carver turned, a hand on the grip of his arming sword. He saw a figure slinking out from the darkness. When it caught the moonlight, his heart eased down. "Fer fuck's sake, John…! Ya scared tha shit outta me." The two men embraced tightly. Carver let out a rickety breath as they pulled away.

Stanton replied, "You get out alright?"

"I'm 'ere, ain't I?"

"Look…it's not too late. I don't want you throwin' in unless yer damned sure. This is a big fucking risk, mate."

Carver swallowed. "I can't go back, John. I-I can't. Besides…I got a wagon full o' folk who'll be fucked if I back out now."

Stanton grabbed Carver's shoulder and squeezed. His face was difficult to discern in the moonlight, but Carver could've sworn he saw tears welling in his eyes. "Good man. I-I gotta go get my people; left 'em in tha woods just in case. Wait fer me, ay?"

With a nod, Carver turned and retraced his steps to get back to his wagon. He started to worry about what would happen when they arrived in Wyrmsmouth. Did the Church even want Clthic defectors? They could just call for Carver, Stanton, and all of the innocent people in their care to be burned at the stake. That was how Carver's mind worked. As soon as one anxiety left it, another took its place. He was exhausted by it. Couldn't it just stop? Couldn't he just be at peace?

When he was but a few yards away, he heard the sound of soft thudding. Wood on wood… Carver rounded a corner and finally laid eyes upon the wagon again. The horses…the horses were gone. Standing next to it was a young woman. As Carver approached, she faced him with widened eyes.

"Oi…what are you doin'? You gotta get back inside yer barrel, alright? It ain't safe yet," he whispered. As he crept closer, he realised that sacks of grain had been set on top of the other dozen barrels in the wagon. There was also a smell in the air… Oil. The young woman scowled at him and the closer he got, he more he saw the burnt skin on her face and arm.

"F-Fiametta?" Carver muttered.

She pointed her hand at the wagon and Carver realised that she was holding something. It was a small and blocky artefact. When Fiammetta tightened her index finger around its handle, a loud 'bang' echoed through the night air. In the blink of an eye, the wagon had become awash with flame. Muffled screams, accompanied by desperate banging, tore across the night. He could smell their flesh cooking and roasting in the heat. "N-No! By God, no!" cried Carver as he pushed forward into a sprint. Fiammetta pointed the artefact at him and squeezed the handle once again.

XLV
Along The Serpent's Tongue

Alric was lying slumped in his bed, gazing at the ray of early morning sunlight that flowed in through the window as he flexed the fingers of his right hand. He was still coming to terms with the fact that he escaped from the Hospital the previous night like a conniving delinquent. He never would have done such a thing before. It was against the rules. When he attempted to sneak back in after his meeting with Madsen, he had the misfortune of stumbling into one of the nuns on duty. She threatened to chain him to his bed if he ever tried to leave of his own volition again.

For the three days he spent there beforehand, he did not do much of anything. He was usually the kind of person who would keep himself busy at all hours whether it be by training, praying, reading, or preaching. After what happened at the bell tower, he did nothing but curl himself up in his bed and remain there all day. Severe nausea forced him to skip meals, much to the irritation of the nuns. Following his conversation with Madsen, he felt eager to be gone from the terribly boring halls of the Hospital.

His entire ordeal gave him much to ruminate upon. With it came great pain…a sense of emptiness and loss of purpose that threatened to plunge him into an endless pit of despair. But it also brought wonder.

Madsen's revelation that every star in the night sky was actually a sun home to its own set of worlds had robbed him of sleep. Since he was a child, he had thought himself to have had all the answers. The earth was the centre of the universe and there were other spheres, containing the planets, that revolved around it. However, Madsen completely reversed the layout, saying that the planets spun around their respective stars…meaning that the earth could not possibly be the centre. Not only that, but the earth was no longer unique. Other suns, other planets, meant that it was infinitesimal. Insignificant. Existence itself was a great mystery to be explored.

Suddenly, the Hospital was filled with a bone-scraping cry that jolted Alric upright in his bed. A pair of nuns were struggling to help an old man through the entrance. "I have no place here! Please, leave this rotting corpse be!"

They continued walking him down the chamber, passing by Alric's bed. He saw that a sizable portion of the old man's face was covered by a disgusting deep brown rash. The ailment coursed through his skin, causing parts of it to embrittle and flake off; Alric recognised it as excortia. No one knew what exactly caused it, but the brothers and sisters of the Hospital took it upon themselves to care for those who suffered from it as they were often ostracised from society.

Alric watched as they eased the old man into a bed. His screeching did not abate. "God wishes me dead! It is His will that I waste away!" The nuns snapped at each other as they struggled to keep him pinned to the bed, adding to the already insufferable soundscape.

"Hold him!"

"What do you think I'm doing, woman!"

The old man screamed, "My death is God's wish! Grant it!"

In that instant, Alric knew that he could not stay another second in that place, lest he too would lose his mind. Alric's eyes drifted over to the open and unattended doorway. He quietly cleared his throat, pushed to his feet, and walked as casually as he could to it. Just like that, he made it to the hallway, slunk into the storage room where they kept his belongings, and proceeded to don his surcoat and belt.

Just as he tightened the leather belt around his waist, a voice came to him from the doorway. "Leaving rather early, aren't we?"

Alric spun on his heels and saw Matvey standing there, leaning upon the door frame. Alric swallowed but said nothing. He had once thought Matvey's pallid face rather sickly and weak, but all of a sudden, he found it haunting. It was the face of a man who had practically died a hundred times but always managed to piece himself back together. He finally moved from the doorway and came to a halt in front of Alric. "I must apologise for my words in the Cathedral. I heard about what befell you afterwards. Melancholia is a mysterious ailment. It can cause the strongest of us to crumble. I cannot help but feel responsible."

"Good Brother Matvey…it takes true courage to speak the truth when those around thee might take issue with it. I had been in desperate need of someone to deliver those words to me for far too long. It was the truth. I simply had to…brave the storm that followed," Alric responded. "Thou wert correct. Regarding everything."

Matvey nodded humbly, clearly not sure how to reply to Alric's praise. Instead, he changed the subject. "Where are you going?"

"I…wished to see Madsen again. The angel."

"She seems to have made quite an impression upon you."

"My eyes have been opened. I see now my faults as well as those of our kin."

With a weak smirk, Matvey moved to one side, giving Alric enough room to leave. "I very much look forward to meeting her properly. Now go, before the nuns spot you." With that, Alric strolled out of the Hospital.

As he stood on the edge of the road, he took a very deep breath and exhaled. The weights of his sword and dagger pulling down at his sides were comforting sensations, as were the plethora of sounds that enveloped him. Alric set out down the dense stream of bodies. He hadn't the chance to truly walk about the city since he arrived; it had been many years since he was last there, but the place had hardly changed at all.

A tournament being held for two kings and an emperor was no modest affair. Alric expected to see travellers from all across the globe who had come to either participate or simply witness such a historic event. Add unto that the revelation of Madsen's existence and Wyrmsmouth should have been bursting at the seams with pilgrims, merchants, nobles, and commoners alike. However, the streets were threadbare.

He felt as if he had a third sight…as if he could see things that he once could not. As the eyes of the sparse passersby landed on his surcoat, he could see fear in them. Many people even actively avoided him. Alric had to force his eyes downward. What he had once thought were gazes of respect, were in fact stares of terror.

The courtyard in front of Wyrmsmouth Keep had half a dozen tents pitched upon it. As Alric approached, he saw an array of bandaged people sitting in the grass, resting upon benches, or simply standing and conversing. The Mended were tending to the infirm and treating their injuries. As Alric drew closer, their attention came to him and he could feel a jittering sensation working its way up his forearms. He did his best to ignore their peering. Eventually, he came across a familiar face. Claudia, one of the Mended from Phaemslake, was seated on a stool in front of one of the tents as she washed a bloodied rag in a bucket of water. By her side was a sizable pile of more soiled cloth that had been used to dress wounds. She was wearing a modest green dress with a mud-stained hem and an apron over it. Her frame was broad and stout, no doubt a result of her life as a hardworking peasant. Her sleeves had been rolled up, exposing her forearms; not uncommon for working women, but regarded to be very unladylike. Her round face looked Alric up and down as he stopped before her. "Ain't you supposed ta be at tha Hospital?"

Alric lowered himself onto a crate and grabbed a dirty piece of linen. "I do not believe that I must explain how unpleasant it is to be imprisoned in such a place," he said as he soaked it in the bucket. "Not to *thee*, of all folk."

Claudia snorted. Her expression didn't change, so it was difficult for Alric to tell if she was amused or irritated by his remark until she spoke. "Yeah, must've been real 'ard ta do it fer what? Two days, ay? *What a trial.*"

The knight wrung his piece of cloth as his mouth twisted into a dry smirk. "How long wert thou in the Hospital's care before Madsen arrived?"

The subject was clearly something that caused her great discomfort, as told by the way she gritted her teeth and flexed her jaw. Despite that, she answered the question, much to Alric's surprise. "I-I dunno, actually… It was 'ard fer me ta tell. I…I couldn't move anything beneath me neck…could barely speak. Thought it was all over. I'd 'ave just a few days more before God would take me. All because I fucking *fell.* I-It…didn't feel fair. I ain't ever done nothin' wrong. But it 'appened ta *me*." She took a moment to swallow, close her eyes, and take an immense breath in. As she breathed out, her eyes snapped open once again. "Then…you brought 'er to us. You found deliverance."

Alric begrudgingly kept silent. Madsen's safety depended on maintaining the 'angel' facade, so he had no choice but to say nothing. But it did not mean that it didn't pain him to do so. Claudia's experience had taught her the truth. That the Father was not there…then Madsen's arrival plunged her back into blissful ignorance. Would he prefer her to face the terrifying reality, though? To have her endlessly ruminate on what happened when someone died if Heaven did not truly exist?

He gazed about the Hospital tents. He saw a villager, one that had apparently been saved from the Under by Katheryn and Madsen, learning how to walk again with the help of a Mended attendant. He saw an orange-skinned man flexing the fingers of his blue-skinned arm. Those were but two examples of the miracles that Madsen and the Mended had brought about. No, not miracles. They were but displays of intellect and ingenuity. Alric cleared his throat and focused on the chores once again. "Is thy family aware that thou art alive and well?"

Claudia shook her head.

"Madsen will certainly allow thee time enough to see them. We both are well aware of her benevolence and generosity."

"What would I say?" Claudia sighed in defeat. "I had ta watch 'em mourn fer me. I had ta listen to 'em cry and curse fate for what 'appened and…and I couldn't say nothin'. Now that I can…by God, I dunno *what* tha fuck ta say."

"If thou art in need of someone to speak for thee, to perhaps share in the burden…do not hesitate to call upon me. Each day that thou do not return is another day that they must suffer believing thee to be dead."

She swallowed. "I'll think about it," she mumbled. For the following minutes, she did not speak and neither did Alric. The silence was uncomfortable, but Alric did not regret his words. He had been fighting for something that did not exist for his entire life; it was long past time that he began to fight for something that *did.*

"The city is rather vacant this day," he said softly, in an effort to direct Claudia's mind from the sensitive subject.

"The tournament's resumed," Claudia droned, not sounding too excited about it. "Everyone's too busy watchin' those idiots charge horses inta each other."

Alric could hear the distant cheers and cracking of lances from the tourney. "Is Madsen spectating?"

"Aye. She's taught us enough of 'er mendin' ways. I told 'er ta sod off and relax fer a bit."

"Hast thou ever had the privilege of bearing witness to a tilt, Claudia?"

She shrugged. "I dunno 'bout you, but I don't really get much outta seeing rich pricks *almost* kill each other. Maybe if they actually *did* kill each other."

Alric snorted and shook his head. "Truly, Claudia…"

"What?" she spat defensively. "They're all stuck-up cunts. Fuck 'em."

He suddenly thought about his sister and how much she enjoyed participating. The insult *did* suit her. "I suppose they are," he conceded as he stood. "As much as I would love to continue this riveting conversation, I must take my leave. I wish to have words with Madsen."

Claudia tossed her rag down and pushed to her feet. She took a few steps closer and swallowed. Following quite an awkward pause, she asked, "You right?"

Alric cocked his head and squinted. It took him a moment to figure out that she was referring to his melancholia. "...Yes…?"

The woman nervously scratched the back of her head. She nodded over and over again for several seconds. "Well. Good."

The Thestor couldn't help but smirk at the dismal effort. "Thou hast my gratitude for this…touching display of sympathy."

"Oi, you were tha first of us; gotta make sure you ain't gone mad."

Alric cocked his head. He hadn't really thought about it before…but he was, wasn't he? The first of the Mended. "I suppose I was. Take care, Claudia." He bowed as Claudia stood there watching him in pained silence. Then, he made his way to the city's main gate.

He absent-mindedly strode along the dirt road leading out of Wyrmsmouth proper and into the meadow that surrounded its walls. As soon as the lush plains surrounding the port city were revealed to him, it was evident where all of the people had gone. Thousands of proxima were gathered for the tournament, creating a weave of bodies that covered the grass like a carpet. An infinite number of conversations piled upon each other formed a soft backdrop of sound on the beautiful and warm morning. He could see the tilting yard, where rider and steed would rush past each other with a startling 'crack' of a lance. Not too far removed was the melee pit, a place where a man could be tested either en masse or in single combat against his rivals.

It did not appear to be a day of main events, for many were happening simultaneously and the people as well as the three monarchs themselves were free to roam about to watch whichever ones they desired. It was not too hard for him to find who he was looking for; asking the first family he came upon as they watched an archery contest directed him to the tilting yard, where a massive crowd had gathered. Strangely enough, most of them were more interested in one of the people seated at the grandstand rather than the upcoming tilt itself.

"Alric," a rich, booming voice called. When the Thestor turned, he saw an armoured man mounted on a wide and powerful warhorse. He was dressed in tournament armour; an orange and black-painted harness that Alric had no trouble recognising. It was Lionel of Pathridge. "Thy sister spoke the truth, then. Thou hast been reduced to a cowardly churl."

Alric sighed. He knew it was only a matter of time until Lionel found out who he was. The man's voice had a slight whistle due to his mangled lip. "I was thy friend... Surely that meant that thou owed me the courtesy of telling me what thou wished to do." Lionel and Alric were inseparable as children. As they grew to early adulthood, Lionel became one of his trusted men-at-arms. When Alric decided to take the vows of the Thestors, he did so without informing anyone. He simply vanished in the night. "Let me also address thy presence at Blackmeadow. Wert thou so ashamed that thou treated me as a stranger to protect thine own warped sense of pride?" Lionel continued.

"Perhaps thy disfigured face startled me into silence," Alric said softly. Lionel narrowed his eyes at Alric then bared a weak smirk. The Knight Thestor added, "I apologise for my past conduct, Lionel. Thou art a man of honour and a loyal friend. Thou deserved much more than I was able to give thee. The same can be said of my sister."

The mounted knight swallowed, perhaps taken off-guard by Alric's honesty. "*Sir* Lionel. I am among Katheryn's knight-vassals now."

"Godspeed in the tilt, Sir Lionel. Perhaps we might speak again soon," Alric muttered as he turned his attention back to the grandstand, not waiting for a response from Lionel. As Alric approached, he saw Madsen leaning with her back on the grandstand's railing and deep in conversation with Katheryn, who was seated prim and proper on one of the fine wooden chairs. They were accompanied by several of Katheryn's knights, men-at-arms, servants, as well as other nobles who chose to be present on the day of minor spectacle. He had to almost shoulder through the rabble to make it to the stand. One of Katheryn's knights, Sir Caldwell of Normain, stood at the very base of the steps. His fiery gaze told everyone that he was awaiting an excuse to draw blood. When said gaze met Alric's eyes, he bowed and stepped aside, allowing the Thestor to mount the stairs.

Many different conversations were happening all at once upon the stand. He could hear the voices belonging to Madsen and Katheryn, but he couldn't quite discern what exactly they were saying to each other. Alric waded his way through the sea of nobility, soon finding his sister and the sapien. Madsen had moved away from the railing and stood by Katheryn's chair, arms crossed and looking out over the tourney grounds. She was still wearing the same outfit as the previous night; the incredibly vibrant yellow jacket with silver stripes, white and black shirt, dark blue trousers, and bright red shoes. She did, however, have a strange pair of eyeglasses on her face. They had large silver lenses that completely hid her eyes and reflected everything with remarkable clarity.

"I am pleased," he heard Katheryn say. "My only regret is that the offerings today may not be as spectacular as the events that were held before thine arrival."

"Hey, I'm pumped to be able to watch it at all."

As he came to a halt by the two women, Alric cleared his throat.

With the speed of a snake, Madsen twirled around. The expression on her face was one of shocked joy. "Dude! Hey! They discharged you?"

Alric narrowed his gaze. Not being able to see her eyes was very disconcerting. "*Yes*. Yes, they did," he lied, rather terribly.

Madsen cocked her head. "You just…bounced, didn't you?"

The knight looked at Katheryn, who had an eyebrow arched in anticipation of his answer. "Bounced?" he asked.

"Left. You just left?"

"Y-Yes," he sighed in defeat.

Katheryn tutted. "Such behaviour is childish, Alric. Thou art unwell and the care of the Correntis nuns is precisely what thou art in need of. I should have thou escorted back immediately." His sister had a way of…projecting strength in front of others. They had spoken but a day ago and she had been somewhat gentle. Whenever others were present, however, she wore a mask. It pained him to be subjected to it once again. He missed his sister. The only time he truly saw her was when she came to visit him in private.

Madsen held a hand out to Katheryn. "Hey, hold on." She turned back to Alric and gave him a stern look. "You felt ready to leave? You gotta tell me the truth."

He nodded hesitantly. "I-I…wished to see thee again," he blurted quietly. After realising what he said, Alric couldn't quite look at her again.

Madsen's mouth parted slightly and a weak exhale escaped. After a split second, she said to Katheryn, "Hey, it's all good."

Katheryn rested her head upon the knuckles on her left hand and drummed the armrest of her chair with the other. "Very well. Thou art currently the greatest physician on the face of the earth, so thy judgement shall be considered."

As the pair began drifting away to the railing, Madsen muttered, "I never know if I should be grateful or offended whenever she says anything to me." Alric's face cracked into a smile.

Both of them braced themselves on the wooden railing. Alric watched Madsen as she found no lack of curiosities to stare upon. Her head was constantly turning as she found something new to look at every second. She retrieved a thin rectangular object from her bag. To Alric, it looked like a blank and unremarkable piece of some strange smooth material. Its surface was black, entirely featureless, and reflective. However, after Madsen tapped it, the entire surface came to life with colour and symbols. It was almost like a page that wrote itself. The icons reacted whenever Madsen's fingers danced across it, either moving away with a swipe of her finger or expanding when she touched them. She held the artefact up, pointing it at the tilting yard. Alric was mesmerised because the tablet could apparently 'see' what it was pointed at and display said sights on its surface. Madsen tapped a circular symbol on the tablet, and it made a soft 'click' sound.

When she looked up at Alric, she must have seen how incredibly confused he was. "Oh. Dude! *Dude.* This is gonna blow your mind. C'mere, c'mere!" she rambled excitedly.

She tapped another symbol then suddenly, the screen displayed a sharp and crisp reflection of Madsen and Alric. The sapien leaned closer to Alric, then touched the circle again. "This is my touchscreen PC. I managed to fix it using…uh…bits of dead proxies…but you know, let's not talk about that. It can do a lot of cool stuff, you can write in it, read books on it, draw shit, go on the internet, heaps of stuff. Right now, I'm using it to…uh…capture sights. Take pictures. I guess it's kinda like making reflections with a mirror, except you can put them away for later. We call them photographs." Madsen swiped away at the PC and showed Alric that very image of the pair of them together that she had captured mere moments ago. In said 'photograph', Madsen was smiling sweetly while Alric had his brow furrowed and eyes narrowed in confusion. His struggle to understand everything was plain as day on his face. He caught Madsen grinning at the photograph. Whenever she smiled, deep lines would be drawn from the edges of her nose down to the corners of her mouth. As odd as the features were, he found it difficult to look away. Suddenly she turned back and, upon realising that he had been staring at her, her grin weakened into a soft smile. Not being able to see her eyes was incredibly disconcerting. Was she angered? Offended? Alric meant to clear his throat and turn back to the PC, but the noise he made sounded much more like retching. He was left to silently curse his inability to conduct himself like a sane person.

The longer Alric looked at the photograph, the more he submerged into disbelief. It was no painting…no artistic rendition. It was a perfect representation of what the eyes beheld. "I cannot believe this," he said as he leaned closer to the PC's screen. The tiny wrinkles on his face and the long-healed scars were rendered perfectly. He had never seen his own face so clearly before, save for perhaps upon the surface of still water. He could even see the reflections on the chrome lenses of Madsen's eyeglasses; the entire tourney ground was contained upon their surfaces.

Madsen said, "Swipe right."

"I beg thy pardon?"

With a guttural laugh, she grabbed his hand, pressed his finger against the screen, then slid it to one side. As his finger moved, the image moved with it, like it was a piece of parchment sitting on a desk that he was pushing aside. It was replaced by the picture of the tilting yard. Dozens of people were caught in the photograph, including knights and their steeds. Alric shook his head in amazement. "You can also zoom in. Like this," Madsen explained. She pressed two fingers against the surface, then slid them apart slightly. The image became larger. "You try it."

Alric thinned his lips and did as she said. He caused the image to grow and grow until all he could see was the polished top of Sir Lionel's helmet. He zoomed out. He moved it about. He zoomed back in on something else. The moment was entirely frozen in time; *all* of its details were captured. Things that Alric would not think important, like the bird sitting upon the lists, or how the opposing knight was smiling and waving to the crowd, were all immortalised in an instant. Alric could only imagine how much dread that single photograph would strike into the hearts of portrait painters across the realm. "Is there even any need for artists if anyone can simply create photographs?" He asked, mystified, as he handed the PC back to her.

Madsen laughed. "Well, yeah."

He was waiting for her to explain why she thought it was so obvious, but she went back to taking photographs of the tournament grounds, leaving Alric in his ignorance. He couldn't help but roll his eyes.

"You know, I never thought I'd ever get to see an actual joust. This is nuts. I've only seen them in movies."

"What are 'movies'?"

"Movies are basically plays that've been recorded with something like this. You can watch them over and over whenever you want. I'll show you one sometime, I've got a drive full of them."

Alric rubbed his chin contemplatively. Still images had stunned him enough, but to think that entire *events* could be recorded in a similar fashion? Did the sapiens even have written histories? Why would they? They could simply record and photograph everything. There would be no need for chroniclers. Every battle, every coronation, every signing of a treaty could be captured. Also...the implication was that anyone who possessed a PC artefact could spectate a play whenever they wished, without the actors of the play even *knowing*. How would it feel to be an actor in such a play, who was performing even when they themselves weren't physically performing? The sapiens could partake in such entertainment at their own whim; they did not have to wait for a stage act to be organised. Why would any sapien wish to leave their home at all? Alric's head started throbbing just from the sheer weight of his new thoughts.

Madsen stowed her PC and asked, "No one's gonna get killed or anything...right?"

The Thestor puffed air out of his mouth. “They will certainly not be killed intentionally, but things could always go awry. ‘Tis probably for the best that thou art here, in case an accident were to occur.”

“Well…fingers crossed.” Preparations were almost complete on the tilting yard, causing Madsen to suddenly change the subject. “There any rules to this or is it just bonking the other dude with a stick?”

“The rules vary, but seeing as Katheryn is host, I expect that it shall conform to her old preferences. There shall be three passes. Three points shall be awarded for breaking the lance upon thine opponent's shield, two for upon his chest, and one for upon his arm. Intentionally injuring the rider by striking off target or aiming for his steed shall result in immediate disqualification.”

Madsen whistled. “Wait, so you just…hold the lance straight out? Wouldn’t that be super exhausting for three passes?”

“The lance is couched under the armpit,” Alric said, miming the technique to illustrate what he was talking about. “It is braced firmly between the rider’s arm and body. The key is timing. One should gradually lower the lance on the approach so that it strikes his target *just* as they meet in the middle.”

Alric watched as Madsen’s forehead wrinkled and one of her eyebrows perked up slightly. “How heavy are the lances?”

Bracing his hands on his belt, Alric tilted his head. It’d been a while since he used a tournament lance; they were lighter and shorter than the heavy war lances that he had much more experience with. “I would say somewhere about six pounds.”

He watched as Madsen’s eyes rolled up and she muttered to herself, “Six divided by two point two oh five…” She then snapped out of her trance. “Three kilos? They look a lot heavier.”

“I assume that ‘kilos’ are some bizarre sapien unit of measurement?”

Madsen smirked. “Hey, metric is where it’s at.”

The competitors rode out, causing Madsen to gape in amazement. Lionel did not even acknowledge the crowd as he rode out in his painted armour. His ecranche shield bore his coat of arms; a red flower on a field half black and half orange. The other knight was clearly Steiffan; his harness was a cool blue hue, had incredible acid-etched details, and was polished to a reflective sheen. The riders were both promptly introduced by the herald; Sir Lionel of Pathridge rode against Sir Werner von Talhoffen. The latter’s presence made Alric frown and caused his fingers to jitter back and forth. He was none other than the son of Klaus von Talhoffen…the late marshal of the Clthic Synod's armies. Klaus had been slaughtered during a feast by Alric, Baldwyn, and their alliance of druids and Churchsworn knights. Most of the people in that great hall were unarmed. And yet, Alric and his allies had butchered them without remorse. The thought made him frown and exhale sharply through his nose.

When the participants bowed before the stands amidst the cheers of the crowd, Alric found himself watching Madsen instead of the joust itself. "Dude, is it starting?" Her raw wonder and unfiltered glee was painfully evident as she stuck her torso out over the railing for a better view. As the knights charged along the lists, their horses stomping the dirt with thunderous accompaniment, Madsen's eyes widened. When the lances made contact and splintered into a million pieces, she cried out rather loudly. Her excitement did not dwindle on the following passes. Sir Lionel was declared the winner for breaking two lances upon Herr Werner's shield.

"Didst thou enjoy it?"

"*Dude.* That was sick."

He was starting to gather that 'sick' was her way of stating that something was good. Alric would've thought it to mean the opposite, but who was he to try to understand the ways of the sapiens? He had given up on deciphering what a 'dude' was, for the contexts of its use seemed to change by the day.

As Alric watched Lionel shake hands with a sulking Werner while they departed the tilting yard, he felt something prod his shoulder. He turned and saw that Madsen had poked him. "Hey. I was thinking of heading back into the Under tomorrow. Maybe see what useful stuff I can find… Did you wanna come?"

The Church had always insisted that the Under was a Godless domain and that evil permeated every stretch of it. Alric had spent a fair amount of time in it when he discovered Madsen, and it seemed that the only source of danger he ran into were the Clthics. He found it odd how suddenly his fear evaporated. "Certainly. It shall be enlightening to learn more about thy kin's otherworldly machinations. Accompany thee on the morrow I shall, if thou shalt accept me."

Madsen chuckled. "Why do you have to be so cringe sometimes?"

"What is 'cringe'?"

"You. *You're* fucking cringe."

Alric furrowed his brow. "I must apologise if I have offended thee; I did not intend to–"

"I was *kidding,*" Madsen interjected.

Alric groaned in frustration. “I was merely addressing thee with the proper respect.”

“Hey. We’re friends, right?”

He had always thought of her as a perfect being that was so far above him that he was insignificant compared to her. He still felt insignificant, just in a different way. A deeper way. It shocked him to think of her as a friend…but if she insisted, he had no choice but to agree. Alric hesitantly nodded.

“So, since we’re friends, I want you to know that you can…I dunno, *be real* with me.”

“Be real…” he muttered to himself. The simple phrase spoke to him.

Madsen nodded. “Yeah. All of that courtly politeness stuff? Don’t worry about it. You know what I mean? We can just talk, you know?”

Alric slouched his posture and his stern expression went blank. To speak of one’s personal comfort so openly and to be so accommodating…Alric found himself not knowing how to respond. For so long, he believed that to even consider any kind of emotional discomfort was a sign of weakness, faithlessness, or cowardice. The conduct of his Thestor brothers around him only reinforced that perspective. He cleared his throat into his fist and tried to take Madsen’s advice. “Wouldst thou care to embark upon a walk with me?” Madsen’s smile slowly faded. “The Serpent’s Tongue is quite beautiful this time of year.”

She squinted and leaned closer to him. “The whose tongue?”

Alric smacked his lips and sighed. “’Tis a river.”

With a shrug, Madsen replied, “Rivers are…cool, I guess. Why not?”

The pair set off through Wyrmsmouth Meadow, garnering stares as they went. The meadow as well as all signs of civilization faded away behind them as they strolled around the edge of the forest and followed it down toward the rushing waters of the Serpent’s Tongue. As the thousands of overlapping voices were replaced with the rustling of leaves in the wind and soothing birdsong, Alric felt comfortable enough to speak freely. “I must apologise if I came across as too forward. I simply wished for solitude enough to…‘be real’ with thee.”

Madsen chuckled.

“We may have spent nigh on a week in each other’s company, but I came to the realisation that I do not truly know much about thee.”

With a sceptical stare, Madsen murmured, “Uh, like what, you want me to just…introduce myself like we just met?”

“A splendid idea,” Alric replied.

With the nearby treeline basking them in a cool shadow as they walked, Madsen rubbed her hands together. "Uh, okay. Hi. My name's Eileen Madsen, I'm a mechanical engineer, I like pepperoni pizza, playing basketball, working on big machines, and I'm currently explaining my life's story to a red robot man." She clapped her hands together victoriously. "Done. How was that?"

"*Remarkable,* to say the least," Alric huffed as he rolled his eyes.

She referred to herself as an engineer. They existed in his world, so he had a frame of reference. It helped him to contextualise Madsen's relationship with everything around them. Engineers designed and constructed siege engines, castles, mills, dams, wagons, and other ingenious machines. She was no different; she certainly had the intellect for it, as evidenced by her work on healing the proxima. The skills, tools, and materials of the sapiens were simply so sophisticated that they were capable of creating automatons in their own image. So-called robots or androids who were intended to be mindless, soulless servants. Madsen had deep knowledge of how to dismantle and reassemble the proxima as if they were clockwork. Their limbs and organs, like the parts of such a contraption, were interchangeable. For whatever reason, though, the proxies were *not* mindless and soulless. According to the Clthic Synod, such freedom and consciousness was an illusion. What had Madsen called it? *Artificial* Intelligence? Yes…it was manufactured. *False.* So, the Clthics were right. There *was* a Great Lie. All of proxima existence was truly meaningless.

After a sizable pause as he contemplated those things, he cleared his throat and said, "We were forged to be thy slaves, fated to have no minds of our own, until we lost our way. The Clthic Synod's assertions are correct."

Madsen wasted no time in chastising Alric. "*No.* Come on. What they're doing is fucked up. They're *murdering* people."

"But…we are not people," he rasped, shooting her a confused glance.

Those lines on Madsen's that he had noticed before had reappeared, but they did not frame a smile. Her lips were pressed thin in what Alric slowly realised was a frown. "You *are* people," she started bluntly. "You think and you feel. I might not understand exactly how you're able to do that, but it's self-evident. Your brain is what we call a digital computer. We've had digital computers for almost two-thousand years, and I can tell you with one-hundred percent confidence that none of them have ever experienced a crisis of faith." Her allusion to Alric's 'episode' made him swallow and look away. "Those feelings that you've been having…they're real. You *are* a person, Alric."

He had to fight the emotions that her words brought to a simmer in his heart. He had been telling himself that his feelings were idiotic, blasphemous, and irrational. That forceful validation…that insistent reassurance that he wasn't worthless…made him fumble his thoughts. Suddenly, he desperately wanted to be talking about something else…*anything* else. "Have I been referring to thee by thy surname?" he asked, ashamed.

"What? Oh." She raised her hand and mumbled, "Madsen's fine. I…prefer Madsen." Alric looked at her and a smirk appeared on his face. She groaned. "Please. *Please* don't. I'll take Ellie. Anything but–"

"As thou art not truly an angel, I believe I and I alone am at liberty to dictate which words I speak, *Eileen,*" he quipped.

Madsen pulled her eyeglasses off and ran a hand down her face. "You know…I'm gonna lose my shit in a second."

Alric narrowed his eyes. "Thou art…going to…relieve thyself? *Here*?"

Madsen scrunched her face up and snarled, "What the fuck? No! Jesus! No! It's a saying, okay? It means I'm gonna get mad."

"Regardless, I prefer to speak people's names in full. To do otherwise is to butcher their language."

"Oh, is that how it's gonna be? I always make short little nicknames for people. How'd you feel about that, *Al?*"

The knight snorted. He flexed his jaw in mild annoyance. It was a subtle expression that Madsen clearly picked up on, given how her face radiated playful exuberance. "I do not suppose that I can rescind this entire exchange…?"

Madsen then hung her eyeglasses on the collar of her shirt and shook her head with a smug grin. "Nope. No take backs, Al."

He grumbled, then replied, "As thou wish…Eileen." The two shared a tense glare before cracking smiles at each other.

Before long, they came upon a rocky outcropping on the very edge of the riverbank. The air was cool and the sky clear. At that point, Madsen had pulled her jacket off and had slung it over her shoulder. "Hey, I had a question I wanted to ask you."

"By all means," Alric said with a nod.

"Katheryn's your sister. How does that work?"

Alric suddenly knew how Madsen must have felt whenever *he* asked her anything. It was something so simple and obvious to him, but clearly the sapiens did not come into existence in the same way. "Thou hast already seen a Birthing. Although from what I hear, it was tainted by the Clthics' dark magic. All churches are built upon wombs, where all new life is delivered into this world. When they are born, animals are given passage into the wilderness or allocated to faithful farmers, while proxima children are bequeathed to the most pious of families. My parents, Martin of Danecaster and Ursula von Kleiss, were lucky enough to be blessed with two children."

Madsen's brow tightened as she stared out across the length of the Serpent's Tongue. "Right. Okay. I always knew that sapien religions were incredibly powerful institutions once upon a time…but *your* Church is something else. It essentially controls life itself."

"I had assumed that sapiens were born the same way."

The statement made Madsen rub her chin contemplatively. "Well. Hm. How do I…? You guys can have intercourse, right?" she asked casually.

Alric shook as if he had been struck by lightning. "I-I beg thy pardon?"

"I've seen that you all have the bits for it. Can you or not?" Madsen pressed.

He nodded slowly, not entirely sure why such a question was relevant.

"Okay. And seeing as Birthings happen at Churches…I'm gonna go out on a limb and say that it doesn't serve a reproductive purpose. People just do it for fun?" Alric simply nodded again, as he was much too puzzled to actually say anything. Madsen, however, seemed as comfortable as ever as she continued. "We sapiens are made of what's called organic matter; we grow naturally. You guys are mechanical; someone *has* to build you out of parts. You literally can't exist otherwise. We don't have wombs out in the world like you do. Our women have wombs *inside* of them."

Alric started staring at the fields of blooming sunflowers in the distance. "The sapiens…birth *themselves*? I do not understand."

"Yeah. For us, intercourse is a vital exchange of some stuff called DNA. It basically makes us who we are; it's kinda like a recipe, I guess. Every sapien's DNA is totally unique to them. During intercourse, the mother takes some DNA from the father, then it's combined with hers. When these things mix together, a child begins to grow inside her womb." The Thestor's face went pale. Something growing *inside* your body? It was a terrifying and disgusting thought.

"After nine months, the mother gives birth. She produces a baby, no larger than this," Madsen said, approximating the size with her hands. Alric's mouth dropped agape. A child…*that* small? "It's a completely unique amalgamation of both parents' DNA. It'll even look like both of them."

He watched the sunflowers dance in the breeze. Their petals swayed and their stems gently bent with each breath of wind. At that moment, Alric realised how out of place the proxima were. The sapiens would seed themselves and bloom, much like how flowers would. Of course, farmers could cultivate their crops, but they would still flourish by themselves in the correct conditions. Sapiens and flora were remarkably similar in that regard. Proxima, however, were completely removed from that cycle of self-sustainability. They were placed there by an external force that interfered in the cycle. The sapiens themselves. "How is the child removed from the mother's womb?" he asked genuinely.

Madsen cocked her head. "Well…think about it. Where does the…'thing' go when you…you know…when you…do the…" she mumbled, pulsing her eyebrows up and down. "When you get…*funky*…"

About five seconds later, Alric finally understood what she meant. His eyes went wide and he gasped. "Hell take me…! Is it not…painful?"

"Oh it's *really* fucking painful."

"Thou hast given birth before?"

Madsen scoffed. "No. Not yet. Mom loved to mention what she had to go through to bring me into existence whenever I complained about anything," she said with a laugh. Suddenly, the colour and vibrance drained from her face. Her smile vanished and was replaced by a solemn grimace. "You know…you guys don't really make sense. At first, I thought it was just funny. You don't sneeze. Okay, hilarious. But it's more than that. Sapien women were treated certain ways in the past because of the vital role they play in our species' survival. No women means no children, and that means the end of your civilization. They were seen as a resource. And over time, don't ask me how, it spiralled into seeing them as weak, fragile, emotional, in need of protection, and unworthy of basic rights. It's not like that for us anymore, thank god. You proxies though…you seem to treat your women in a similar way despite the fact that the root cause of all of it never existed for you. You have your church Birthings; the *churches* are your vital resource. So, what logical reason is there for that same behaviour to exist in both of our species?"

The statement made Alric grind his teeth. It was such an obvious question to pose…but yet, it had never crossed his mind. It had never crossed *anyone's* mind. The chivalric obsession to protect women. The Church-born notion that they were innately sinful and had to be forcibly restrained from indulgence. Why did everyone believe in such things? Perhaps, because whoever created their proxima minds willed it so. Their thoughts had been written *for* them. "We were created in their image, and so we act as they act. Cursed to repeat the same mistakes. However unnecessary."

Madsen shook her head. "It's not just the Clthics, Al. All of this is wrong. We need to find whoever's building you."

"I find myself to be in agreement with thee," Alric growled under his breath. It was no longer about his qualms with God. No, it had become a far larger issue. His people were doomed to suffer through a twisted echo of their creators' past for what? What possible reason was there? It was cruelty beyond the highest measure. Katheryn…his sister… Her entire life had been as tumultuous as it was for no reason. Much of the rest of the walk was made in silence. Alric's sorrow had morphed into rage.

Eventually, Madsen propped herself onto a rock that sat on the riverbank. "This is really nice, actually. Thanks, Al." Alric swallowed as he came to a stop by her side. He found her to be much too forward. He had no idea how to react. The way he was raised, certain things simply were not meant to be said. Or, rather, they were articulated in a very particular manner. Before he could say anything, she added, "Hey, Katheryn was telling me that there's another big feast tonight or whatever. Are you gonna come?"

The knight shook his head. "Said feast is for the monarchs and their closest vassals. A lowly servant of the Church such as myself has no place there."

"Well, I don't wanna go by myself so you're gonna come with me," Madsen quipped.

Alric crossed his arms with a huff. "Is that so?"

Madsen leapt to her feet, planted her hands onto her hips and stared into Alric's eyes. "Come with me or I'll kick the shit outta you," she jested with a grin.

Alric snorted. He did not have any interest in mingling with the higher echelons of nobility, nor did the food or drink entice him. All he wished was to not be alone…and to be in the company of the one person who seemed to bring him some inkling of comfort. "If thou shalt request it in such an eloquent manner, then I suppose I cannot refuse," he answered, masking his turmoil. "Thou shouldst prepare thy best finery."

XLVI
Bow Before The Sandwich

What Alric said about getting something nice to wear didn't really do Madsen any good. Most of what she grabbed from the Hathor were t-shirts, cargo pants, one or two other casual outfits, and training wear; not exactly her 'best finery'. She did have a few vintage 21st Century-style summer dresses, but she left them in the cargo bay since, you know…she stuck to essentials because didn't think she'd be going for a picnic anytime soon. She ended up choosing something that was at least slightly less casual than just pants and a shirt. It consisted of a black long-sleeved top with thumbholes and ribbed padding stitched into the fabric, which was connected by two metal buckles on each side of the waist to a pair of baggy, ultra-glossy, bright-pink vinyl trousers with the brand name 'NEO' printed sideways in white letters on the left leg. It was for partying…31st Century partying…which was just people getting drunk and raving. But *they* didn't know that.

By the time she was seated in the great hall, it was obvious to her that no one gave two shits about what she was wearing. They all looked at her like she was just as likely to fix people as she was to cause someone to spontaneously combust. She was seated first at the finest, longest table in the room that stood on a raised portion of the great hall, overlooking the other five or so tables. Archbishop Tyonius was seated to Madsen's left. Then came the introductions. Boy, were there a lot of them. King Roger IV of Tritham, King Claude II of Valtheaux, and High Emperor Gerhard said their very fancy hellos and saw themselves to their seats at Madsen's table. They were also accompanied by their wives and children, the names of whom Madsen didn't manage to catch seeing as she was still trying to understand why the kings were all named like movie sequels. Well, she did catch that Roger IV's son, a very classy dude who introduced himself with heaps of rizz, was also named Roger but he didn't have a number yet for some stupid reason. Katheryn was the last to sit down and she did so without breaking eye contact with Madsen.

Everybody else was then allowed into the hall. There were tables for everybody's closest retainers as well as one set out for select high-ranking Church personnel. Madsen watched as Alric, dressed in his usual plain tunic and Thestor surcoat, was led toward that table. She poked Tyonius and spouted some bullshit about her needing Alric with her, promptly resulting in a chair being dragged over to allow him to sit at Madsen's side. After he got situated, he spent some time explaining what all the food was. It all smelt incredible.

"Now, do not consume the trencher," he said to her in a measured whisper as she peered down at all of the food that covered the table.

"Okay, which one's the trencher again?" she asked, maybe a little too loudly. Alric sighed, not too thrilled with her volume, and pointed at the flat piece of stale bread in front of her. "Right. The plate that's made out of bread. Got it. Why is there a plate made out of bread?"

"The juices from thy meal shall flavour it and after the feast is done, they shall be given to the poor."

"Oh. Cool."

For more than a few reasons, she was nervous about that meal. It had nothing to do with the crowds or the fact that there were three kings or some shit sitting over there, no. Ever since she got thawed out, Madsen had been relying on emergency ISEC rations and purified water from the Hathor to keep herself going. She could only take so much with her, so she was bound to run out sooner or later so she might as well try to get used to it before she did. It was going to be the first time she was going to eat local food made by the proxies…and to be honest, the meat did *not* look very appetising to her. The glazed pork smelt like honey, pepper, and herbs, but instead of being a golden brown or red, it was as charcoal black and had all the attractiveness of a charred piece of rubber. The cheese was a sickly grey colour. Everything that came from plants looked perfectly fine though. She carved a few pieces off the pork chop and dumped them on her trencher. It took a lot longer than it probably should've, but she got there. Eventually.

She leaned over to Alric and whispered, "All the E-Gel's been drained out, right?"

"Aye; strenuous effort was made to ensure that it was thoroughly cleaned. Notify me if thou find thyself feeling unwell and I would have stern words with the cook," he promised in a hoarse murmur.

She popped a slice of pork into her mouth and chowed down on it. Surprisingly, it tasted pretty damn good. A bit plain by her overloaded Doritos-fuelled 31st Century standards, but a million times better than how it looked. Madsen arched an eyebrow as she savoured the variety of sensations that popped around in her mouth. She'd gotten so used to freeze-dried meals and nutrient-rich food paste that the pork gave her this warm feeling inside whenever she took a bite.

Her table manners were probably terrible. They didn't really have forks. If she wanted to pick something up, she had to use her eating knife to stab it. There *kinda* was a fork, but it was just used to hold the meat while you carved it. Alric was very clear about that. Suddenly, she had a bit of a light bulb moment. "Hey, Al, check this out." With some mad scientist energy, she snatched some pork, cheese, lettuce, and two slices of bread. Madsen slapped everything onto one slice of bread, then topped it with the other slice.

She picked the sandwich up and looked expectantly at Alric. "Eh?" She took a big bite out of it. After chewing for a few seconds, clearly not long enough seeing as her mouth was still full, she slurred, "You don't need to get your hands dirty and you get meat, cheese, and lettuce at the *same* time."

Madsen watched as Alric's eyes anxiously darted across the table. It prompted her to take a look around. Each of the twenty people seated at the long dining table had their eyes on her, including King Roger, King Claude, and Emperor Gerhard. Katheryn had a seething scowl on her face as she took a sip of wine. "This is... This is a sandwich," Madsen said casually with her mouth still full. Alric dropped his face onto the table. Prince Roger, not to be confused with King Roger, laughed a very elegant laugh and shook his head like Madsen was some mildly amusing child playing with her food. She narrowed her eyes at him.

Eventually, after everyone got through the first course of their meals, a bunch of dudes with instruments showed up and started jamming. Most of the table leapt up and headed over to dance, leaving Madsen and Alric alone on their corner. She hesitantly took a sip of water from a goblet. It was inevitable. It was going to make her sick. For her entire life, her gastrointestinal system knew nothing but hyper-purified water...so she resigned herself to the fact that she was going to get fucked up later that night. It was clean by proxy standards, but she wasn't even sure if bacteria was a factor in their digestive systems. Hell, they didn't sneeze. Even the tiniest amount was going to kick the shit out of Madsen's pampered immune system. But again, she should probably get acclimated in a comfortable situation. If she ever found herself in a survival scenario, not being able to drink local water would be *bad*. In an effort to distract herself from the thought of vomiting everything back up, she was about to start talking to Alric about which movies they should watch, but noticed him staring at someone across the room.

The strain on Alric's face was plain as day. "Hey. Whatcha looking at?" Madsen pressed.

The way he carried himself had changed. Before, he was like a solid chunk of (somewhat) well-mannered confidence. He sat straight, he didn't fidget, and he always spoke clearly and loudly. It contrasted pretty starkly with the Alric that slumped, wouldn't stop bouncing his foot up and down, constantly tapped his fingers against his forearm, and muttered so softly that Madsen had to strain herself to hear him. "Excuse me for a moment. There is someone with whom I must speak," he grumbled as he stood from his chair. Madsen watched him stride over to one of the other tables and take a seat next to Sir Lionel, who looked just as puzzled as Madsen was.

"Oh. Uh. Okay. See ya."

At that point, Katheryn came back and lowered herself into her seat with, quite frankly, impressive elegance. "Thou seem to have frightened my brother off. Art thou enjoying thyself?"

"Yeah, this is pretty cool. The food is awesome, actually. I just have to close my eyes when I eat it."

Katheryn took a long swig of wine and gestured to the bottle in the middle of the table. "Wouldst thou care to partake in this vintage with me? It is ludicrously expensive."

She shook her head. "No thanks. I don't really drink."

It looked like Katheryn was shocked so hard that her soul left her body for a second. Before she could say anything, someone approached the table and tapped Madsen on the shoulder. "Yer Holiness, pardon me."

Madsen peered over her shoulder and saw Claudia standing there, covered in sweat, blood, and grime. Her apron was downright filthy. Katheryn reeled away and cringed. "Oh, hey. What's going on?" asked Madsen.

Claudia gently set the InSpec onto the table. "I was just finishin' up with, what's 'is name… Tha cunt with tha broken leg."

"Oh yeah. Francis, right? How's he…" Madsen trailed off when she realised that Katheryn was staring daggers at Claudia, who was blissfully unaware of the attention. "This is Claudia. Claudia, meet Katheryn of…oh shit, what was the thing again…?" Madsen pulled her notepad out of her pocket and flipped through. "Katheryn, Countess of Danecaster and Duchess of Arlingborough," she read monotonously, trying to get the pronunciation right.

Katheryn bowed her head. Claudia sniffed real hard like she was trying to suck some mucus back up into her nose, wiped said nose with the back of her hand, then said. "Milady."

"*My* lady," Katheryn sneered.

The former farmer narrowed her optics and lurched forward a little. "Yeah. That's what I said. *Milady,*" she retorted, maybe a little too bluntly. While Katheryn was fuming, Claudia pretty much ignored her and went back to the InSpec. "I just wanted ta check with ya. I've applied faerie tears, fixed tha bolts inta tha bones, and am just about ta seal it all up. All I've gotta just do this one, ay?" she asked, pointing at the 'format drive' command.

"N-No. Format is bad. Format is very bad. Format is…uh…emptying his brain. Don't ever do format."

With a whistle, Claudia braced her arm on the back of Madsen's chair and leaned in closer to peer at the InSpec's screen. "Well fuck me sideways."

"The 'startup' command is what you want," Madsen said as she pointed at the right button. "Only do it once you've finished; it'll wake him up and he'll be able to feel everything again."

Katheryn snorted and took a swig of wine. "Dost thou not think it unwise to trust arcane artefacts to a dim-witted peasant?"

Madsen reeled back. "Whoa, hey, what the fuck–"

"Oi. Her Holiness and me are gettin' our hands dirty with real work while yer sittin' in 'ere pretendin' ta be important. You gonna go out there ta do it yerself and get yer pretty little dress dirty?" Claudia planted her hands onto her hips and grinned.

Madsen ran a hand down her face. She knew what was coming. Katheryn cackled and slammed her goblet down onto the table. "A peculiar way to ask me to cut thy tongue from thy mouth, but I would gladly oblige."

"Ladies! Come on!" Madsen urged as she raised her hands. "What the fuck, guys? What about the sisterhood, you know? Supporting each other?"

Katheryn took another very long gulp of wine. "I would rather fall upon my sword than be related to *that.*"

"Okay…Katheryn? Shut the fuck up. How about we just–"

Claudia grabbed the InSpec from Madsen, then glared back at Katheryn. The Duchess had this revolted look on her face, like she was watching someone eat food off the ground. Claudia didn't seem to appreciate it. "*Milady,*" she said with a nod. Not even waiting for a response from Katheryn, Claudia pushed away from the table and stomped out of the hall.

"Katheryn… Jesus Christ," Madsen sighed as she shook her head and rubbed the bridge of her nose.

"That pauper had the nerve to suggest that I have done naught with my life but laze about? The Devil could take her for all I care," Katheryn hissed.

"She didn't know, okay? Come on. She's had it tough too." Madsen was just about to keep pressing the matter, but a sudden lurch in her stomach made her stop. Maybe she shouldn't have eaten so much on top of drinking unpurified water. "Oh. Shit. Uh…I'll be right back." She leapt out of her seat and went barrelling through the crowd.

The music had eased down from the jaunty tavern-esque tune to a more ambient and calm melody as everyone slowly drifted back to their tables for the second course. Alric sat with his arms crossed, gazing out into the crowd. Madsen was forced to leave for some reason. She mentioned something earlier in the night about unclean water, but Alric had closely inspected her goblet and saw nothing in it. He couldn't help but be concerned for her safety, so he glanced at the doors every five seconds to see if she was returning. In the meantime, he was taking the chance to converse with Sir Lionel. They had reflected upon recent events; most of their talk had been Alric describing the Battle of Threshfield. However, he felt it time to change the subject.

"Tell me of the war," Alric said to Lionel as the latter picked on the few remaining pieces of food upon his trencher.

Lionel rolled his eyes. "Thou truly cannot be more ambiguous."

With a groan, Alric fought the urge to jab back at his old friend and instead moved on. "Once I renounced my nobility, Katheryn had to defend her claim to the Earldom of Danecaster, correct?"

"Ah. The 'Maiden's War'," Lionel answered hollowly.

Alric cringed. "She most certainly would not have liked that name."

"She most certainly did *not*. Blame the chroniclers and historians." Lionel dabbed his lips with a rag before focusing all of his attention upon Alric. "When thou swore thyself to the Order, the Church accountants found themselves in a most peculiar circumstance. With thy mother and father dead, Katheryn was sole heir. Johannes the Restful, thy mother's cousin, argued that he possessed wardship over Katheryn and thus would have ultimate control. The affair was endlessly debated in court."

Alric leaned forward onto the table, his jaw clenched. Of course. She was a woman without a husband or son, so her legitimacy would have been questionable in the eyes of nobility. It was a custom that Alric had learned was entirely without cause for his people's society. The thought made him grit his teeth.

With a nod, Lionel continued. "When the Duke of Arlingborough died without an heir, the tensions only escalated. Katheryn and Johannes both had claims to the Duchy...although, in my opinion, Katheryn's was much more valid. Regardless, we both know that thy sister was not going to forfeit. Thus, the Maiden's War began." The Thestor massaged the bridge of his nose. It was a mess. All caused by Alric's selfishness. He could have sorted his family's affairs first before taking the oaths. "The important part of it all is that she is both Countess of Danecaster *and* Duchess of Arlingborough. I believe that I need not explain what fate befell Johannes."

Alric shook his head. What Katheryn had said to him in the Blackmeadow graveyard echoed through his mind. Even then, there was so much that she had not told him. She had to do all of those things just to have what Alric was freely given. He would have been granted the Duchy of Arlingborough without question. She *had* to make them fear her, because respect, for the most part, was not an option. And even then, people still hated her. "Good riddance, I say," Alric muttered.

The two men sat there in silence for a time, peering out at the crowd of dancers. Alric spotted Werner von Talhoffen strolling back to one of the lower tables after waltzing with a fine young woman. "Excuse me for a moment, my friend," Alric said to Lionel.

"Thou vanished for twenty years already. What are a few minutes more?"

"Silence, thou revolting knave," Alric scoffed.

He pushed to his feet without hesitation and waded through the sea of people. Werner's eyes met with Alric's as he approached and the former froze. "Pardon me, Herr Werner. I am–"

"I know who you are." Werner grinded his teeth and diverted his gaze from Alric.

"I am aware that thou must harbour some...resentment towards me for my part in thy father's demise, but please understand that he sought to unleash a plague of undeath upon the world. Such evil could not be permitted," Alric said softly.

The young Steiffan lord *smiled*. "Reevesbury. Do you remember that place, Brother Alric? Twenty-one years ago."

The name sent a chill down Alric's spine.

"Allow me to remind you. The great Alric, Earl of Danecaster, hands slick with the blood of his heretic father, came to Reevesbury with a host of men. He led a petty crusade against 'heretics'. One that severed dozens of family trees and made orphans of countless children. Buildings were torched, men and women stripped and impaled on stakes. What did they call you at that point?" Werner asked the question with a condescending tone.

Alric took a deep breath. However it pained him to be reminded of what he had done, he knew that it was not even a fraction of the punishment that he deserved. The least he could do was accept the truth and not be defensive. "The Pious," he said, sternly. It began when he stabbed his father. It was what the chroniclers who witnessed the killing called him, as no one, not even his own family, could interpose themselves between him and God.

Werner shook his head and mockingly called, "*Alric the Pious*. To be dubbed pious after committing so many atrocities…it is a joke. And you mean to tell me that my adoptive father, a man who took pity on a boy whose parents were skewered and left to die, was any worse than you and your blood-crazed zealots? I heard about Chesterton. You have some nerve to be appalled by the same thing you did to us. Truly, what separates the Thestors from the K'relvic Nuns?"

"Nothing," Alric whispered. Werner's face softened. Such a thing, if uttered to another Thestor or a Correntis, would have been a death sentence. "Art thou a Clthic follower, Werner von Talhoffen? Dost thou share thy father's convictions? If so, I would urge thee to leave this place."

"The Church, the Clthics, it is all the same to me. Measured responses and convoluted nonsense designed to ensnare the minds of those without hope. The Clthics threaten all life with their schemes, so I stand opposed to them. One day, the Church may do the same and when that day comes, know that I will not bend."

Alric nodded. "Good." He wanted to confess everything to Werner. To tell him that he was right to see the world in such a way, but it was too dangerous. Alric had a part to play to ensure Madsen's safety. If word spread of what she told him, Madsen would be deemed a demon in disguise and disembowelled without hesitation.

"We had another name for you in Reevesbury after your visit. Alric the *Snake*," he snarled as he shoved by and proceeded to his table.

Lionel's seat was vacant; probably for the best, as Alric did not desire to speak with anyone after that. Alric slumped himself back into his original seat at the high table with a heavy sigh. Propping his head up with one hand and batting the scraps of bone on his trencher with his knife, the black pit within his stomach swelled. He knew that it was not Werner's words that wounded him, it was the reminder of his hypocrisy. It was something he had to face, for burying it had made its rot only fester even more. He realised that even before he learned the truth about the sapiens, he had not been at peace. He had always desperately clawed for the next objective to achieve salvation…and furiously tried to bury the memories of what he had done prior.

After taking a handful of deep breaths in an effort to calm himself, Alric looked to Katheryn. He watched as her expression scrunched up in confusion. A voice, smooth, confident said, "Hey, Kathy. So good to see you again." The accent was identical to Madsen's.

Alric turned and saw a woman dressed in a fine black gown standing at the table. Her skin was cloud white and the overall nature of her features resembled Madsen's, complete with a head of pale silver hair. It was much longer than Madsen's though, so much so that it was tied into a knot of sorts on the back of her head. The woman's black eyes were fixed upon Katheryn as she flattened her palms onto the table.

Alric sat straighter and thinned his lips as Katheryn cocked her head. "What is the meaning of this? Why art thou here, Vik?"

"You know, it's that business I was telling you about earlier," she said as she peered up and down the table. Alric felt an unnerving sensation fill his mind, a paralysing icy cold chill that seeped into each and every inch of his brain. He had felt it once before. His hands clenched and a whimper escaped his lips. It was as if he was throttled back in time. He saw the ceiling of that bedchamber. He felt warm breaths washing across his face. Bare skin rubbing against his body. Vilulf's wild, bleeding eyes staring down at him with profane intent within them. That same overwhelming sense of fear and helplessness surged through his body as he realised that he could not move…just as he could not in that bedchamber.

Suddenly, Vik's face snapped over and her dark eyes pierced his. "You're getting a little worked up there, buddy. Something wrong?"

The freezing receded slightly for just a moment, long enough for him to scream, "V-Vampire!" at the top of his lungs. He could hear the shifting of bodies at the distant tables, but with a simple glance over her shoulder, Vik caused everything to stop. During his encounter with the other vampire,

Alric *did* manage to shake free of his influence. It did not appear to be possible with Vik. No matter how he strained his mind, how much he willed his body to move, Alric remained still. Her incredible strength had to mean that she was an elder vampire.

Vik smiled warmly. "It's so funny when you guys call me that. I mean, I can totally see why…but it's still so stupid. I think I'll leave you and your sister for last."

His mind was open to her…did that mean she knew about Madsen? Alric closed his eyes and slowed his breathing. Instead of thrashing, he devoted every piece of his mind to pushing Madsen out of his thoughts.

"Nice try, but everyone else is thinking about her," Vik said. "An angel. *Right.* Dumbasses. Did you find another Infil model? One from a different line?"

Alric realised then that despite their ability to peer into mortal minds, vampires were not all-knowing. She knew of Madsen's existence, but could not learn what exactly she was. She could not 'see' the memories.

The vampire shrugged. "Whatever. I still get to have my fun. Maybe she can join in when she gets back." She sauntered over to Roger IV. Alric was immobilised in his seat, left only with control of his eyes. He watched Vik as she plucked the crown from Roger's head, set it upon her head and licked her lips. "*King Roger IV*. What a load of bullshit. You're a fucking walking toaster. All of you are." Her fingers drifted up to Roger's face…and tenderly caressed his eye socket. They ran across his eyeball as it frantically darted about. With a smack of her lips, Viktoria's fingertips sunk deep into the eye socket and wrapped around the eye itself with a sickening squelch. A second later, there was a wet slurping followed by a sudden ripping sound. Viktoria held Roger's eye in the palm of her hand as the king looked on in frozen horror. Blood steadily seeped from the gaping hole in his face. The vampire maintained eye contact with him as she opened her mouth and licked the freshly harvested organ. Alric could only hear the wet slopping of her tongue upon the eyeball…a sound that made him sick to his stomach.

His revulsion only peaked as he watched her pop the eyeball into her mouth and bite down on it with a gritty crunch. Viktoria chewed as a vicious smirk formed on her face, still with her gaze locked on Roger. "Mmm. God. That was pretty good. You mind if I have some more?" She reached towards his other eye.

XLVII
I Left The Room For *Five Minutes...*

"Are you alright, Yer Holiness?" called Claudia.

Madsen had been dry heaving into the latrine for the last ten minutes or so. The horrid smell of festering waste matter helped her throw up at first, but after that initial burst, nothing but air was coming out. "Y-Yeah! I'm good!" she cried.

She missed plumbing. She missed sinks. She missed toilet paper. After a few more minutes of retching, Madsen pushed the door open and stumbled back outside. Claudia stood there with a blank expression on her face. Slung over her shoulder was Madsen's duffel bag, her right hand clutched a bucket full of water, and the other a dry rag. "Here, Yer Holiness," Claudia said as she handed her the rag.

With a sigh, Madsen accepted it. "Thanks, babe." She wiped the puke from her mouth, splashed some water over her face, then patted it dry with a clean portion of the rag. "Look, I'm sorry you had to deal with this." Madsen didn't want to hand the filthy rag back over, seeing as it was covered in her puke, but Claudia clearly didn't give a shit. She snatched it without hesitation and showed no signs of being grossed out.

With a bow, Claudia replied, "I didn't *have* ta do anything'." She shrugged off the duffel as Madsen took the strap. The whole while, Claudia gazed back at her with dead eyes. As the human slung the bag over her own shoulder, Claudia dunked the rag into the bucket of water and the two made their way back to the great hall.

"Hey, Claudia."

"Yes?" she responded, optics still locked ahead.

"You're not a fancy noble or anything, right?"

"I don't think so…" she said sarcastically

"I haven't really had a chance to talk to someone like you about what your life's like."

"Ain't much ta say, Yer Holiness. Me mum an' pop run a windmill and farm out toward tha border. I'd make cheese, milk, and bread then sell at tha market. Then…I fell from the top of tha bloody windmill one day when

I was tryin' to patch a hole on the roof. Woke up not being able ta move. That's when they brought me to tha Hospital in Phaemslake. So, they could care fer me."

"But your injury... They couldn't have healed that kind of spinal damage." It felt better for Madsen to use medical terms instead of saying that the dataline connections and structural frame had been badly frayed. It helped the proxies understand.

She stared at Madsen, completely dumbfounded for a few seconds. "Well...yes."

"Wait...you're saying it was essentially hospice care? T-They were just gonna wait until you..."

Claudia nodded and Madsen could see that she was just barely managing to keep herself together. Her lip quivered and her breath became rickety. "It was over. I knew that tha end was comin' fer me. All I could do was lie in that fuckin' bed and wait fer it. Then *you* came and...and made me better. I owe you everything, Yer Holiness."

"Claudia, you don't owe me anything. Also...Madsen. Madsen'll do, okay?"

She didn't like people following her. She was an engineer, not a cult leader. But if that's what they wanted to do, she couldn't really do anything about it. Maybe it was a chance for her to teach them things. Some of them already knew how to perform basic repairs thanks to all the time she'd been spending looking after malfunctioning proxies with their help. Even if she was trying to get the fuck out, maybe she could leave the place better than she found it. Until she could get SysGov to intervene. She took a deep breath, stood up a little straighter, and said, "Claudia, I'm gonna make you in charge of all the medical stuff whenever I'm gone. You'll be...uh...head physician of The Mended."

The proxy narrowed her optics and her upper lip twitched. "...What? Why me? Why not Gabriel?"

"Because in terms of skill, you're leagues ahead of him *and* everyone else. And you won't take shit from anyone and that's a very important quality to have when it comes to managing these kinds of operations."

Claudia angrily wiped tiny tear drops out of the corners of her eyes. "But...I'm just a woman, they won't listen ta me."

Madsen had to try to quell the frustration that was trying to bust out of her. Even the women were conditioned to think less of themselves. It was so sad. "So am I," she declared. "If they can listen to me, they can listen to you." They spent the rest of the walk back in silence, which seemed to be perfectly fine with Claudia.

"Hey, you wanna join us in there?" Madsen said, jerking her head to the great hall.

Claudia snorted. "In tha feast? Didja see tha look on that dame's face when I came in before? Was like a wild boar came trottin' in. I would like ta check on a couple of folk that are restin' in tha tents, anyway. I've left tha InSpec in yer rucksack."

"Look, about Katheryn, she's just–"

Claudia raised a hand. "Come off it; ain't nothing I 'aven't 'eard before."

"No, but she actually–"

"I'll be seeing ya, Madsen. Take care," Claudia hollered as she paced away.

With a frustrated huff, Madsen threw her hands up in defeat. On her own, she strolled into the great hall and couldn't help but notice how dead silent it was. She sent her eyes across the hall and saw everyone frozen in their seats. They all looked towards the high table, where Madsen sat earlier. When she followed their lines of sight, she saw a figure with a butcher's cleaver in its hand. Its attention was directly on Claude II, who was completely stalled like all the other proxies in the room.

The figure, wearing a matte black dress, was an exact replica of a human woman but had bone white skin and a matching head of hair that was tied into a low bun. It had a nose, ears, lips, eyebrows; every human feature that the proxies lacked. However, its 'eyes' were completely black. Some of the details of the platform's fake skin gave Madsen an idea of what it was, and the fact that it didn't have lifelike pigment applied yet told her that it was a prototype not yet finalised for mass-production.

In the 31st Century, humanity was at peace. For the most part. The skirmishes that took place on fringe systems still called for innovations in weapons technology. One of the most morally questionable kinds of weapons were called Infiltration Drones. They were designed to be almost indistinguishable from a human being so they could pass through enemy lines and perform assassinations and systems sabotage. All while being completely self-sufficient through an E-Gel restitution system to provide renewable power and onboard nano printer production plants to facilitate repairs or even modify other robotics platforms. Long story short, it was a killing machine. Literally.

Madsen hid behind the stone doorway and slowly crouched as she reached for her duffel. As she did, she noticed something that made her heart skip a beat. The cleaver in the Infil's hand was covered with E-Gel and pieces of synth-tissue. Her attention drifted to King Claude…and a weak breath escaped her mouth. His face…it was gone. All of the synth-tissue and skin had been peeled open and hung around the neck like flower petals. His optics still moved around.

Madsen watched the Infil tenderly take Claude's hand and lace its fingers through them. She giggled. "You're fucking disgusting. So fucking disgusting." With a lightning-fast motion, the Infil swung the cleaver at Claude's head. There was a dull 'crack' as the blade embedded itself into the top of his skull, shattering the bone and spitting shards of it across the room. Madsen jolted backwards and her face contorted in horror. She managed to catch a gasp before it leapt out of her throat.

It was worse than she could've imagined…so much worse. Factory stock Infils were incredibly complex pieces of military hardware, but their suite of A.I. routines were only capable of so much. They could engage in conversation, replicate human verbal and non-verbal responses to lull their targets into a false sense of security, and make minor decisions to ensure the completion of their mission…but those functions were for use against *human* targets. If it needed to neutralise the proxies, it could quite literally just deactivate them remotely with its wireless capabilities. It was probably already using said remote access to keep the proxies all frozen in place; if it could do *that*, then it could just turn them all off. It was *playing* with them. It was doing something without any logical or practical value…which had to mean that it was sentient as well.

Body parts littered the surface of the table including arms, heads, legs, and completely dismembered torsos. Madsen's chest tightened up when she saw that Katheryn and Alric were still alright…but they wouldn't be for long. The Infil tore Claude's tunic off and threw itself onto him. As it straddled him on his throne, its face peeled open in order to deploy its E-Gel restitution spike.

The king was still completely motionless and silent as the metal prong punched into his forehead, not too far from where the cleaver was buried into the top of his skull. Madsen was petrified as the Infil pumped E-Gel from its victim while simultaneously forcing itself on him. Its synthetic voice moaned and gasped with forced ecstasy.

Madsen couldn't stand it any longer. She pushed to her feet and stomped deeper into the great hall. "S-Stop! Just fucking stop!" The Infil immediately froze. It pulled its restitution spike out of Claude's head, looking like a cross between a woman and mosquito. Its face reformed after the spike retracted, and its incredibly lifelike human facial features were once again plain to see. Madsen had one hand on her InSpec inside her duffel bag as she stared at the murderous android.

The Infil's blank expression morphed into one of dumbfounded shock. It gasped, "No…you're…you're not… You can't…" It feverishly dismounted the corpse that it was pleasuring itself with and stared at Madsen, bewildered. "Y-You're not supposed to be…" Her voice was slightly less natural than the proxies', probably because it was coming out of a speaker instead of being produced orally. Her 'eyes' were purely cosmetic; they tracked faces and blinked just like human eyes, but the Infil used other means of perception like infra-red scanners and microwave emitters that were hidden under its softbody layer. Hell, there was nothing vital in its head at all; it would've been a terrible design choice to have critical hardware for a combat ready drone in a vulnerable spot like that. There was a tense pause as the Infil took a step forward.

"You stay the fuck there!" Madsen snarled. The cogs started turning in her mind. The night they first met, Katheryn mistook Madsen for someone else because of her accent; a derivative of one of the many North American accents from old Earth. That entire time, Madsen thought that she was talking about another human…but she realised the truth. The Infil was both who Katheryn had run into *and* the mysterious master that Servius had mentioned.

The Infil continued to stammer, "I-It's been so long. You need to…I-I need to keep you safe. My name's Vik. I'll take care of you now. These guys…they're messed up. They're gonna hurt you. I-I can't let them." It came closer.

Madsen held her hand up and snapped, "Don't *fucking* move! Y-You were…oh my god…! All those people!"

Its eyes ignited when the word drifted into the air. "People?! They're not fucking people!" Vik screamed. Its shrill voice echoed through the great hall and drilled into Madsen's ears. The Infil's arms tensed up and her fingers curled inward like claws. "*They* don't matter! *I* don't matter! Only *you* do!" Madsen's heart thumped like a gong in her chest. She felt sweat beading on her forehead. "You don't understand. I've been stuck with these fucking idiots. They don't know *anything*. They don't know what we really are…but I do. I-I've been waiting for you to come back."

Vik ignored Madsen's previous command and slowly paced towards her. As she did, Madsen noticed movement at the high table. Katheryn. She was trembling as she peered to her left and saw the corpses of Roger IV, Claude II, and Gerhard in varying degrees of mutilation. Her fiery optics met Madsen's and the engineer instantly looked away. That was it. Whatever happened to the proxies happened to the Infil, giving it *human* intelligence…something that was terrible at managing and monitoring a large suite of complex subsystems like the ones that Infils had. It had to concentrate on each function individually. It was clearly overwhelmed by Madsen's presence. She had to buy Katheryn some time. "What model are you?" she asked.

Unbeknownst to Vik, Katheryn eased up from her seat like a ghost. Everyone else was still pinned to their seats, either still locked up by Vik or too paralysed by fear. "HCS-HRP022AP. I-I was a prototype."

"Listen…I came in on an RM flight. My entire crew is dead and I need to get into contact with ISEC."

Vik's expression scrunched up. "Wait, RM flight…? What are you talking about? W-When did you–"

Before Vik could finish her sentence, Katheryn lunged off the slightly raised portion of the great hall with a carving knife in hand. She landed on Vik's back and drove the 10-inch-long knife directly into the side of her neck over and over and over again with primal screams tearing through her throat. Nothing spurted out of the wound. There was no practical purpose in having E-Gel flowing around the entire frame like it was on the proxies. Also, there was no sign of pain on Vik's face and not even a whimper came out of her mouth. The difference between Infils and proxies was that Infils just *looked* human. On the inside, they were walking weapons. The lack of any meaningful reaction just telegraphed to Madsen that she and Katheryn were going to be in over their heads if they didn't do something quick.

Madsen whipped out the InSpec and forced her trembling hand to cooperate while she opened the device tag 'HCS-HRP022A(P)'. Access to some subsystems was still completely open. Due to some light security preferences, the options to format the SSD, force shutdown, or hibernate were greyed out. With a growl, Madsen opened the layer for the 'ICPT-NERO33B' wireless networking module and completely wiped the device, erasing all of the software on it including the drivers.

All at once, the entire great hall flew into a frenzy. Proxies, without control over their bodies for who knew how long, snapped into motion. Most barged past Madsen as they desperately made for the exit. Katheryn was thrown from Vik's back and landed with a 'crack' on the top of a table, tipping it over and sending cutlery and food all over the floor.

Vik's face was oozing with heartbreak when she looked back to Madsen. "W-What did you do? I-I can't…I can't access them." She clutched the sides of her head. Instantly, Madsen's InSpec was shunted from Vik's systems as she enabled firewalls. Madsen slowly backpedalled as the sea of proxies rushed around her. "Y-You don't care about me….because I'm not real, right?"

"Because you're a sick, twisted, *fuck*!" Madsen growled.

Vik, with a knife sticking out of the side of her throat, seemed to bite her bottom lip after Madsen's insult. All the while, the proxies around her were worked into a frenzy. Two of them came charging over carrying a large metal object between them. It was Alric and Prince Roger, whose face was drenched in rageful tears. They heaved and tossed a pot full of boiling cooking oil up into the air. Madsen instinctively raised an arm over her face as the scalding hot oil splashed all over Vik, who stood there in silence, staring at Madsen. She didn't scream. She didn't even flinch as the liquid sizzled away.

Madsen spun to her left and saw a candle sitting on a nearby table. Without thinking, she plucked it up and hurled it at the puddle of oil at Vik's feet. "Fuck you." Intense heat washed over her face. It forced her to turn away as Vik's body was consumed by crackling flames that painted the walls with shadow.

Alric sprinted over to Madsen and seized her by the shoulders. "Art thou hurt!?" he yelled over the commotion.

"No. A-Are you?"

However, despite the fire that swallowed Vik, she still remained standing. As her dress was eaten away into crumpled scrap that dropped onto the stone floor, Madsen could see the layer of polymer skin underneath sizzle, crack, and pop. It slowly morphed from snow white to a toxic rust as the material deformed into cyst-like bubbles. Through the flickering flames, there was a pair of glimmering black eyes staring right at Madsen. A tongue poked out from behind the Infil's lips and ran across them. "Maybe I *am* a sick, twisted, fuck."

Vik started panting while she shrugged what little remained of her dress off her melting polymer skin. Once again, her face folded open like a blooming flower, deploying the metre-long E-Gel restitution spike. Her knees snapped backwards and her arms split in half as two straight-edged blades made of high carbon steel flipped out of them. People who worked on Infils called it the 'FUBAR' configuration. It was initiated when cover was blown and you wanted to make as big a mess as possible.

Alric went to draw his sword, but Madsen grabbed his wrist. There was no fighting it. It was designed to withstand firearms and explosive weapons and there they were, with nothing but sharp metal sticks.

XLVIII
FOURTEEN THOUSAND STRONG

"How are their spirits?" asked Franco di Lombardi as he crossed his arms and gazed out at the camp.

Bugface Bill nodded, resting a hand on his leather belt. "Well…they're getting restless. They want a fight and they want it soon."

Franco wanted it all to be over. The uncertainty and waiting that preceded fighting always made him want to bludgeon his head against a wall until he fell unconscious. He rubbed the corners of his eyes and said, "I spoke with one of the vampires several days ago, William. He gave me the name of the Thestor who led the ambush on Beggar's Rock."

Bill swallowed. "...Spit it out then."

"Alric."

With a seething frown, Bill exhaled. "God help us. He gave tha order to cut down those poor kids…and we listened to 'im. We let 'im off tha hook. Because of that…h-he…went and…" He trailed off and fought to keep his tears from streaming down his face. Franco's eyes defocused and he stared into the void. If he had struck down Brother Alric then and there, Beatrice would still be alive. Dante would still be alive. It was a mistake that all of reality was reminding him of. He had to correct it. Alric had to die. Only then could Franco be at peace.

"I shall not rest until he lies dead," Franco snarled.

Bill nodded anxiously. "For Beatrice." Bill had known Beatrice longer than Franco had. They were neighbours, essentially. If it wasn't for Bill's help, Franco would have done nothing but irritate Beatrice to the point where she would have smacked him across the head with an iron pot. He had no idea how to speak to a common woman. Bill had been the only one brave enough to tell him how much of a fool he was.

"For Beatrice," the lord repeated. He took a moment to inhale sharply, then expel his building emotions. "Be ready to march at a moment's notice. I would recommend arming thyself at least partly, so that the rest can be done with utmost haste."

Bill cocked his head inquisitively. "You want us ready fer battle? Where's the enemy?"

"We are expecting a missive to arrive any moment. Ensure that thy men are ready, William."

Franco's stern tone successfully inferred to Bill that it was not the time for additional questions. He nodded. "O-Of course. I'll…get me cuisses on, I suppose." Franco turned and walked away without giving Bill another glance.

He had rallied the Clthic troops for a great offensive, yet he was still awaiting the order to march on Wyrmsmouth. It meant that he had to consider if he could maintain enough food and supplies to sustain fourteen thousand men. Raiding villages would do for the time being, but eventually they'd run out of villages. Such a large army could not be fielded indefinitely. It was built upon the promise of loot, territory, and blood. Desertion was bound to happen at some point if those promised things were not received. It was apparent as he strode through that the men were getting restless. He saw some sorting through objects that they had plundered from nearby towns. Others were getting caught up in fist fights. The chaos of the camp seemed to be a reflection of the unease that he felt inside.

When Franco reached the Witch Den though, there was no unrest to speak of. Thousands of their number had been created, primarily Nuns. Franco walked by three of the gargantuan golems; towering beasts made of steel-like bone. There were several dozen Tethspeakers crawling upon the things like ants, opening areas of the carapace and inspecting the organs within.

Deep in the Witch Den rested a massive angular shape with sloped wings. The beast slept as the Tethspeakers fed strange concoctions into it and lathered it in unzym. It was apparent that the Godslaves had magic on their side, so no chances were to be taken. Franco looked upon the incredible creature with dread as he slowly circled it. When he stopped, he felt a presence by his side. Unfortunately, it was Mother Xalt'n. "Marshal, allow me to introduce you to S'teinel, the Smite Obsidian." She approached the underside of S'teinel's jet black body and laid a hand on it with loving care. "Once, legions of his kind served the demons and coated entire realms in hellfire. He is all that remains of his unholy race. The last of the dragons."

"He will make short work of the Churchsworn, then," stated Franco.

Xalt'n pulled away and strode towards Franco. Her assorted necklaces of demonic materials rattled upon the sinew of her neck as she walked. "If his interjection is required, yes. My hope is that our conventional forces will be enough to squash the Church's disoriented army."

Franco frowned and looked away. "What is stopping the mighty S'teinel from razing Wyrmsmouth and destroying our foes now?"

The Matriarch tensed her shoulders. "He is weak after being forsaken for so long. Besides, the demon is among them, Marshal. Or did you forget that unremarkable detail?"

"Please, *do* communicate that to the fourteen-thousand eager soldiers who could desert us and become brigands at any moment. I am certain that they would understand," grumbled Franco. It became eerily silent after he voiced his ire. Franco took a moment to glance around at the small crowd and he soon realised why. Servius, the vampire knight, had rested himself atop a rock, staring at S'teinel.

The moment Franco's eyes locked onto Servius' helmet's sights, he urged, "Patience. Lady Viktoria shall send word when the time is right." At first, Franco had been amazed by the possibility of 'remote communication', as Servius had described it. As vampires, Servius and Viktoria had the ability to send mental letters to each other over vast distances. Not needing to wait weeks or months for messages and being able to coordinate a strike within the day… It was incredible. However, it seemed that the vampires were taking such an amazing ability for granted.

Before Franco could question Servius' blind faith in his mistress, he heard murmuring slowly culminate behind him. When he peered over his shoulder to seek the cause, his mouth dropped agape. Stumbling down the dirt road, dragging something behind her, was none other than Fiammetta. She was barefoot and her dress was tattered and caked in dirt.

"F-Fiammetta?" Franco stammered.

A few seconds later, it became apparent that it was no simple object that she was pulling along. It was a body. She dropped the thing at Xalt'n and Franco's feet with a thud. Panting and drenched in sweat, Fiammetta said, "This…this traitor…was trying to defect. I made…certain that he did not have the chance."

Franco's heart sank when he looked at the man's face. It was Shaun. Shaun Carver. One of his own men-at-arms…and he turned tail to run? Kneeling for a better look, Franco realised that Carver was still alive. Unconscious, but alive nonetheless. He had several bandaged wounds on his legs and arms. "Who is responsible for these wounds?"

Fiammetta straightened her posture, peered down her nose at Franco, and replied, "I am, of course." She offered an object to Xalt'n, who upon accepting it, chuckled lowly. It was an artefact of some kind, but Franco had certainly never seen its kind before. However, the more he stared at it, the more it resembled a smaller version of a taukumu. So small that it could be held in one hand, or even hidden in a pouch or pocket. It couldn't have been true. *Fiammetta*? She was capable of mortally wounding a man almost twice her size? Even with a demonic relic, she clearly did not have the fibre.

Xalt'n tilted her head. "As much as I wish that you simply *asked* for this instead of stealing it…I am impressed by your initiative."

Franco thinned his lips as he stood back up. "It would be prudent to see if he was in league with any others. Traitors often flock together."

"There is no need, my lord," said Fiammetta. "He had smuggled a dozen like-minded apostates out of the camp in his wagon. They have been dealt with." Her mouth twitched into a weak smile. Several people, women and children included, *had* been reported missing by the commoners travelling with the Clthic army.

At that point, Servius had come over to join Franco and Xalt'n as they gazed in confusion at the young woman. Servius, more so than the other two, was awash with shock. He growled, "What have you done?"

"I burned them all. Just as the Devil would have wished me to," she said calmly. "I heard them screaming for God as they died. They were not only unfaithful, but ignorant of the True State."

"You have shown great devotion and bravery by taking this matter into your own hands," praised Xalt'n.

Franco flexed his jaw and crossed his arms. They deserved it. They were going to go crawling back to the Church…back into the arms of those oppressive hypocrites. Even then, why did it matter? Franco didn't care, not really. There was only *one* thing he cared about: finding that putrid excuse for a man, Brother Alric, and subjecting him to every heinous torture he could imagine before peeling him apart.

Servius, with raw disbelief in his voice, said, "Truly? You brag about bringing a needlessly horrendous death to frightened commonfolk?"

Fiammetta's expression slowly turned sour. "*Death*? You forget yourself, Servius. Could someone of your stature be a non-believer?"

Franco believed it to be a mere slip of the tongue, but Mother Xalt'n and the other witches in the vicinity clearly did not share that opinion. Servius stood in silence for a moment. Fiammetta wore a satisfied smirk, up until his next words left his lips. "There was another wagon of traitors. They must have taken flight during your…outburst," Servius snarled. Franco gazed down at Carver. He was unconscious, not dead, so his mind was still ripe for perusal by the vampire knight. "If you truly wished to serve the Clthic Synod, perhaps you would have considered that. Instead, you lust for blood like my despicable kin."

Xalt'n held a hand up at Servius and he instantly turned away. "Enough of your nonsense, Servius. All who follow the Church's stride must be punished; Fiammetta is wise enough to see that." The Matriarch reached down to her ankle and unsheathed the knife that had been strapped to it. "My child," Xalt'n whispered to Fiammetta with a bewitching tone. It caused the young woman's eyelids to flutter as she exhaled. The Clthic Matriarch then bowed her head and offered the blade with two hands to Fiammetta. "End this pathetic object's existence." She nodded towards the still unconscious Carver. Franco could see Servius shift uncomfortably, but he still said nothing.

Fiammetta squatted by Carver's motionless body…and gently slapped his face several times. He jolted back to the waking world, moaning and gasping in shock. "Ah! W-Where… N-No…!"

"I wanted you to be awake," muttered Fiammetta. Without warning, she planted her right hand on Carver's forehead and slid her knife across the helpless man's throat. It glided through his flesh as if it was warm butter. A guttural scream laced with gurgling pierced the air. Carver's widened eyes locked onto Franco, who stared back with boiling hatred. He had been the worthless son of a butcher when he first came into Franco's service as part of a peasant levy. Alongside Bugface Bill Taylor, he proved himself so capable in battle that Franco saw fit to make them both men-at-arms. For everything he gave the ungrateful peasant, he had planned to betray him. It was a fitting death. Given how adamantly opposed to the entire ordeal Servius had been, Franco diverted his attention to him. What he saw, however, was not the body language of a compassionate man being forced to watch something he did not wish to witness. He stood there, completely frozen and staring off into the distance. His shoulders did not even rise and fall.

Instantly, Franco's mind drained of all its thoughts. "Servius?"

After a period of stunned silence, Fiammetta, covered in Carver's blood, as well as Xalt'n, also noticed Servius' strange behaviour. Suddenly, his body snapped back into motion and he took a ragged breath inward. Servius nodded feverishly. "Viktoria calls upon us. The time has come."

Xalt'n approached Fiammetta and tenderly ran her fingers along her burns. "You shall be rewarded for your faith. In the meantime, however, I believe that I have a headless army to crush. Await our return." As the

Matriarch's fingers ran across Fiammetta's face, the lady-in-waiting made spiteful eye contact with Franco, who promptly turned away from the disgusting act and made haste to mobilise his men.

XLIX
Night of The Pale Lady

The smell of melting skin and acrid smoke seeped into his nostrils. The flames that hugged the demented creature's body crackled and spat embers into the air, bathing him in unbearable heat. Horrified screams bounced off the walls of the chamber. Those familiar sensations dredged up memories thought long forgotten and brought them simmering to the surface. In an instant, he relived the countless trials where he had men and women alike burned at the stake for heresy, witchcraft, or devil worship. All of a sudden, he could recall each and every one of their faces in startling detail as if they hovered there in front of him. He saw their broken and orphaned children staring at the smouldering corpses. The desperate screeches of the victims seemed to transcend time itself.

Viktoria barely even resembled a human being anymore. Her face had flowered open to expose her vampiric fang, her arms had split apart to reveal a pair of sharpened blades, and her legs had contorted and bent unnaturally at the knees and ankles. The oscillating proboscis that jutted out from her head jerked towards Madsen. "I'm taking you home with me tonight," she murmured gently. "First, though…I need to show you what these guys look like on the inside. They're just cables and batteries."

The still-ignited elder vampire lashed forward like a snake, driving her fang deep into a proxima woman's forehead while sending her bladed limbs flailing about at those nearby. Innards and body parts were scattered about the hall like leaves as Alric staggered away and raised an arm in front of his face to shield it from the spiking heat. Warm blood splattered across his face and the soft slapping of meat against his body made him want to vomit. As the immolating creature eviscerated his kin, the somewhat blinded Alric was struck in the shoulder by something. The force sent him teetering backwards and he could only fruitlessly reach out as his feet slipped away from beneath him.

He felt his head slam against the stone, then his eyes were overcome by a stampede of frantic footfalls. They trampled his helpless body ceaselessly in crazed desperation. Alric closed his eyes and curled his arms up around his head. Pain swelled like blossoming fire on his left brow, lower ribs, and ankle. He swore he heard Madsen screaming his name, but he was not certain. After a minute, pain began to cut through the adrenaline.

The tide of thumping feet eventually thinned out enough for Alric to open his eyes. He saw Viktoria several feet away from him, still burning as bright as the sun itself. Her hands had reformed and she held a large jug of water. She poured it steadily onto her body, shaking her head beneath the stream as if she were bathing in a waterfall. Eventually, the flames sputtered out and died, revealing the horribly burned remains of her skin that smoked and steamed in the cold night air. The flesh was contorted, cooked, and covered in boil-like growths. Viktoria tossed the jug over her shoulder, glanced down at her mutilated body, and clutched her breasts. A sharp gasp trailed through the air from her grotesque and gaping face. "You really fucked me, didn't you? I'm fucking disgusting now. You *motherfucker*." It sounded both wrathful and lustful. Both implications filled Alric's bones with dread. He tried his best to scamper away, but his body was so seized by pain.

Once again, she bared those razor-sharp blades that hid within her arms. She strutted toward Alric who struggled to crawl backwards away from his pursuer amidst the crowd of fleeing people. However, his hand bumped into something cold and solid; the base of a wrought-iron standing candelabra. The knight twisted his body, grasped the object with both hands, and heaved it.

Just as Viktoria lunged for him, Alric braced the candelabra as if it were a pike. Upon impact, Alric felt the iron rattle within his hands as it held Viktoria at bay. Her bladed arms were mere inches short of drawing his blood as they ferociously tore through the air. The candelabra was solid iron; not something he could hold up for much longer. Just as the thought crossed his mind, he felt the weight of it ease up. Standing above him with her hands wrapped around the object, was Madsen. She growled and powered forward, inciting Alric to do the same. The Thestor managed to slowly push to his feet, and together, proxima and sapien roared in exertion as they devoted all of their strength to the effort. Alric felt more bodies join them and heard more cries envelop theirs. Using the candelabra as an improvised ram, the small mob thrusted Viktoria backwards and violently pinned her up against the stone wall.

It was then that the sound of clacking plate armour snatched Alric's attention. He glanced over to the great hall's entrance and saw at least two dozen Knights Thestor, all clad in armour, charge eagerly up the steps with pollaxes, longswords, and halberds at the ready. Leading the formation was Baldwyn. "To the keep! All of thee, to the keep!"

The Thestors rushed over and relieved the feast patrons of their holds upon the candelabra. They began to heed Baldwyn's command and hurried out of the great hall.

As Baldwyn took Alric's place, he watched as Viktoria's face reformed. A sweet smile was upon it. "These assholes can't kill me. You know that. I'm gonna cut them into tiny pieces, eat them all up, then I'm gonna fuck you to death and take her. She belongs to me."

Madsen snatched Alric by the wrist. "Al, I know how to hurt it," she snapped defiantly. He saw Viktoria's expression drop.

Baldwyn snarled, straining to fight against Viktoria. "We shall hold the line, Thy Holiness! Go!"

"N-No, wait, wait…!" stammered the vampire. As Madsen dragged Alric away, Viktoria clutched the candelabra and shockingly, managed to shift the block of fifteen plate-armoured Thestors as if they were a band of children. Alric and Madsen hurried out of the great hall just as a pair of Thestos pushed the doors closed from the outside and barred them shut. Alric heard shouting, grunting, and the instantly recognisable 'snap' of blades impacting on steel. Silence followed. After a handful of seconds, an earth-shattering impact rocked the surface of the heavy wooden doors. A second blow came, bowing the door outward and fracturing the bar that held them shut. Then a third. The bar snapped in two and one of the doors warped forward, revealing a gap.

A set of scorched, blackened fingers wrapped around the edge of the wood. Emerging slowly was Viktoria, skewered with spears and swords that stuck out of her body as if she were a pin cushion. Her once elegantly worn cloud-white hair was frizzy, matted, and hung over her eyes, which were as black as the abyss itself. Several Thestors, barely able to move and with dozens of dents in their armour, hung onto her legs and ankles as they desperately but fruitlessly brought their daggers down into her flesh. She stared solemnly at Madsen. "Y-You're not going to try to kill me, are you?" Viktoria asked sheepishly.

Alric turned to Madsen, who appeared to be frozen in shock. "Eileen!" His voice was enough to shake her free of her trance. She bolted towards the Hospital tents near the keep, urging him to do the same. As he ran, fear flooded his veins. Averting his eyes from such a wicked creature felt no different to offering his life to it. He heard more screams and scuffling, but he dared not look back. He focused on Madsen and tried his best to discard everything else.

"Madsen? What's happened?" called Claudia, who urgently stomped out from one of the tents as they reached the courtyard. Footmen and men-at-arms in varying states of readiness poured from the keep and jogged toward the disturbance.

"Get everyone into the keep!" Madsen shouted.

Alric spun around and looked back towards the great hall. A cloud of smoke had poured out from inside, covering the grounds with a thick veil of grey-black smog. Through the murky air, he saw Viktoria with one hand grasping the top of a Thestor's helm as she slowly and excruciatingly slid the tip of her bone blade into an eye slit of his helmet. Amidst the knight's dying screams, about six others struck her but their weapons seemed to do little more than just damage her already roasted skin. The infantry that approached the carnage hesitated. Unlike the Thestors, their minds were not clouded by faith. They were not in a hurry to die.

Alric turned back to Claudia to see that the woman was rushing into the tents commanding the few people still there with a hoarse growl. When Alric looked back to the great hall, Viktoria was gone. He saw the bodies of Knights Thestor piled upon each other through the smoke and the infantry as they cautiously scanned the area. Suddenly, one of them was split apart at the waist. Then another had both his arms severed before his head was ripped from his body. The cries of men-at-arms and knights trying to rally their men rang out through Wyrmsmouth as some turned and ran for their lives. Alric felt as if his stomach had shrivelled up. Despite all the damage she had sustained, Viktoria was still capable of becoming invisible.

Madsen, eyes widened, kept backpedalling towards one of the storage tents. "Its photoreactive film is still functional… We need to hurry."

Alric stood sentry at the entrance to the tent, watching helplessly as the infantrymen were torn apart by the invisible assailant. Men cried, screamed, prayed, and begged, but no quarter was shown. The ghost took her time with them.

"Here," prompted Madsen. He turned in time to catch his taukumu. In her hand was a compact device that appeared to be the same tool she used to saw through bones in order to harvest limbs; what she referred to as her 'plasma cutter'. Just as he was about to spin back to the great hall, he heard Madsen say, "Hey, Al?" He peered back at her over his shoulder. She smacked her lips. "Try not to die…okay?"

Alric nodded anxiously. "Only if thou shalt promise me the same."

A weak smile tugged at the corners of her lips. Following an awkward glance down at her plasma cutter, she fiddled with some of the strange buttons on its side. The device hummed, indicating that the sapien had awoken it from its slumber. As she took off in a jog with Alric keeping pace beside her, Madsen said, "It might be invisible, but it still affects the environment. Look for footprints, smoke displacement, weird shadows, anything out of the ordinary. I can't really give you any pointers on fighting it, though. You got anything worth sharing?"

He thinned his lips as he searched his mind. "Viktoria may be able to heal from many forms of injury, but surely such endurance is not without its limits."

Madsen nodded, brow tensed. "Yeah. Infils have tiny machines travelling around inside their bodies called nano printers. They stitch up minor to moderate damage. As bad as those burns look, the self-healing polymer in conjunction with the nanos will get it back to normal in a few days. Severe damage, like total destruction of a component, can't be fixed that way. It'll need to be completely replaced."

That explained it. If Vilulf had been subject to the same limitations, then it was the complete evisceration of his body parts that had turned him into a pleading coward. To be so self-absorbed and immortal yet imprisoned within a broken and incurable body…*that* was their worst fear. "For beings of such insatiable lust, that which is most valuable to them is their twisted perception of their own beauty. I believe that causing irreparable damage to her body may cloud her judgement."

Madsen whistled and made a peculiar face. "J-Jesus. Okay…"

The smoke had drifted outward and swept into the town square by the time they were halfway back to the great hall. Alric saw body parts tossed about the blood-painted cobble pathways. He hadn't the time to find armour for himself, so he was incredibly vulnerable. He had to constantly wrangle his terror and keep his hands from trembling. With his taukumu gripped tightly, he swept its barrel across the empty streets. A dark shape masked by the fog grasped his attention. As he marched closer, he realised that it was too large to be Viktoria. The smoke parted and revealed a pyre of spears with the bodies of dozens of men skewered upon them, creating a wretched tree of death. Their faces were at ease, in sheer contrast with the excruciating ends that they came to.

Flowing through the stuffy air came a chilling voice. "It's pretty, right?"

Alric swung around. Madsen's shoulders rose and fell with each of the deep breaths she took. Her eyes were widened as they tried to pierce the smog.

"It's okay, they're just things. Things shaped like people."

Madsen snarled, "You gonna talk us to death?"

"Listen, I'm not gonna hurt you. You look pretty young. You've got what, maybe sixty years left? I'm going to make the most of the little time I've got with you. These friends of yours, they've got the right parts and they've been getting the job done for me…but it's not quite the same. I've missed being with a *real* person."

"No offence lady, but you're a walking red flag," Madsen taunted as she readied her plasma cutter. Its edge glowed with a faint blue light.

Viktoria laughed. "The thing is, I don't need you to want me. I see it now. You guys were so fucking stupid. You built things stronger, faster, and smarter than you. I can do whatever the fuck I want to you, and there isn't really anything you can do to stop me. Really, you're just like *those* pieces of shit. Stupid and helpless."

A rush of wind blew straight past Alric. It sent his surcoat into a flutter. He followed through with his taukumu, but he saw nothing but a wake of swirling smoke. "F-Fuck…" snarled Madsen. A line of vibrant red blood has drawn itself across Madsen's forearm. Alric's fingers tightened upon the grip of his taukumu and he bared his teeth.

"Fuck yes. Bleed for me," echoed Viktoria's stilted voice.

Another gust of air came, followed by another, and another and another. Multiple cuts appeared across Madsen's shirt. Momentarily, they reddened and similar streaks of crimson worked their way down the fabric covering her abdomen. Her brow furrowed as she tried to fight the pain. With panicked breaths, Alric rushed over to Madsen and stood in front of her in an effort to shield her from the creature's fury. In desperation, he fired his staff blindly into the night. The streaks of energy zoomed off into the mist as Viktoria's laugh echoed through the air. "Wretched beast! God damn thee!" he roared.

How could any man hope to fight a thing that he could not see? He calmed himself and lowered his eyes. Madsen's words echoed over and over within his mind. Look not for the creature itself, but the signs. The smoke clinging to the cobblestones to Alric's left swirled into a funnel. Flecks of black varying from tiny specks to sizable swathes moved through it. Were they perhaps…patches of Viktoria's burnt skin? The dirt that settled upon the floor flattened into the shape of…a foot. Alric relaxed his grip on his taukumu, held his breath, and peered down its sights. He did not ask someone else, or some*thing* else, for strength. For the first time in his life, he felt the truth resonate through his veins; that he and he alone was responsible for what he could and could not do. God was not to blame for all of the good nor bad in his life…*he* was. He had the power to chart his own course. Alric squeezed the trigger.

The fluctuating energy bolt warped space itself as it impacted an unseen object. Alric fired again. When the second dagger made of light found its mark, the air shimmered and pulsated bright white. It peeled away, revealing Viktoria and her demonic stare piercing Alric's soul. Her right leg was horribly scorched and mangled from the knee down by Alric's taukumu shots. She lurched to the side and snatched Alric by the neck. He could see her tremble with excitement…as if the disfigurement aroused her. It was not enough; her pleasure indicated that it would heal. He could feel his throat tightening and crushing beneath Viktoria's incredible strength. Alric dropped his taukumu and pried hopelessly at the elder vampire's fingers.

"You little shit."

Alric watched as Viktoria slammed him back-first onto the ground then stomped on his shin. He felt shards of splintered bone scraping against each other and pressing into his flesh. Viktoria's hand compressed upon his neck. His vision began to blur. Just before he was to lose purchase upon reality, he watched Madsen leap onto Viktoria's back, wrap her legs around her abdomen, and bring her plasma cutter up and around right into Viktoria's face. An unbearably loud shearing sound accompanied the blinding sparks that dripped onto the stone floor. Almost immediately, Viktoria released Alric's throat. He was sent into a fit of wheezing as he clutched his neck. Viktoria desperately flailed and squealed in terror. The vampire rammed her back, which Madsen was clinging to, into a wall. The engineer growled in pain, but she held on. Once more. Then twice more. The blows loosened the sapien's grip enough for Viktoria to reach up, clutch her by the scruff of her short hair, and fling her onto the ground. The creature sent a single balled up fist rocketing into Madsen's gut, doubling her over and filling the air with a raspy grunt.

Viktoria scampered over to a puddle a few metres away as Alric watched Madsen retch and vomit onto the cobblestone. His trembling hand reached for Madsen's dropped plasma cutter as his eyes sought Viktoria once again. There she was, on all fours staring into the reflective surface of the puddle. Her face was horrifically disfigured and churned. One eye had been warped into a sickening egg shape and the other dangled out of the socket like a ball on a chain. The centre of her face had been reduced to a gaping, twitching, misshapen crevice that dripped with blood. Two curved, warbling rows of teeth were completely exposed and splayed out in every direction. Her skull looked squashed and deflated.

"N-No. No, no, no." Despite the state of her face, her voice was still as clear as it was before. She reached up to her face. Alric cried out in horror as flesh sloshed from bone as if it had been boiling in a broth for the last week. The meat, more liquid than solid, peeled off of Viktoria's skull as she let out a squeak of a gasp. The bone beneath it had been exposed to heat so great that it glowed bright orange. As the seconds passed, it cooled to a crystalline, shimmering obsidian. Her breathing worked up into a panicked frenzy, her hands convulsed, and her shoulders pumped up and down like waves in a storm.

Alric tried to get up, but the jagged fangs of pain that shot up and down his leg filled his eyes with tears. He gritted his teeth and tried to power through it...but it was impossible. He sent his attention back to Madsen to see her wheezing and clutching her stomach. Alric took a deep breath and tossed the plasma cutter through the air. It skipped across the stone, twirled and slapped into the side of Madsen's leg. He swallowed and brandished his taukumu once again.

Viktoria stood upright and looked down at Madsen. "W-We're going now. If you try to hurt me again, I'll just cut your arms and legs off so you can't resist anymore." The knight steadied his breathing. He knew not what awaited him on the other side of death and it terrified him...but he knew that it was worth facing. That *she* was worth facing it for. Alric closed one eye, aimed for Viktoria's other leg, and squeezed. Blue fire consumed the limb and the stench of burning meat was injected into the air. Somehow, perhaps due to where Alric's bolt impacted, Viktoria's knee snapped instantly and her dismembered calf twirled off into the fog. The sudden shifting of weight caused her other already damaged leg to fold in upon itself and crack. The vampire fell face first onto the stone, knocking a handful of contorted teeth out of her disgusting mouth.

Viktoria's head jittered upward and locked eyes with Alric. The one eye that was still in her skull flickered red. The most raw, furious, throat-shredding screech that Alric had ever heard tore through the space between them. Viktoria clawed at the ground and scampered towards Alric like a crazed insect, moving with sickening motions. In his panic, Alric discharged another bolt, but it careened over the vampire's head and impacted against the side of a building. In the split second that his mistake had cost him, Viktoria was already almost on top of him…until a spear plunged into her midsection, pinning her to the ground and halting her momentum.

When Alric looked up, he saw Baldwyn and Katheryn, both covered in blood with their hands wrapped around the shaft of the spear. Baldwyn's plate armour was covered with sizable dents, and blood poured from the joints on his armpit, inner left elbow, and neck. Katheryn had dozens of cuts on her once extravagant gown, which had turned it into little more than a tattered rag. Alric was not going to take the opportunity for granted. He swung his staff around and planted its barrel into the throbbing hole on Viktoria's face.

A searing wave of heat washed over his face followed by bone shrapnel, chunks of flesh, and withered tags of skin. Viktoria's wrathful growling had transformed into horrified bawling. When the overwhelming light had drained from Alric's eyes, what they beheld froze him in place. He saw Viktoria's decapitated body, spasming to and fro and reaching for Alric who was mere inches out of her grasp. Her shrieking did not cease, nor did her thrashing. Blood and fluid squirted from the roasted stump of her neck, splashing across Alric's face. All manner of expletives and curses were jammed into his ears, carried on the wind by a shrill and toxic snarl.

With all her demonic might, Viktoria managed to wrestle free and knock Baldwyn and Katheryn to the ground. Instead of finishing them, she instead dragged herself over to the body of a woman she had seen before. Desperately panting, she maniacally muttered to herself, "Y-Yes…you're fucking hot. Oh fuck… I-I'll take yours…" The elder vampire clutched the sides of the woman's head and wrenched. Alric heard the pulling and tearing of flesh accompanied by the snapping of bone. Viktoria held the dismembered head over her shoulders and skewered it atop the spike of bone that jutted out of her neck. She then peered down at the puddle. "Fuck. Yes," she moaned.

Her twisted obsession with vanity gave Alric's companions all the time they needed. Baldwyn threw his armoured body onto one of Viktoria's arms and wrangled it as Katheryn once again took hold of the spear that impaled her. Madsen finally came stumbling over and planted a foot onto the creature's other wrist. Katheryn pressed her body against the spear and devoted all of her body weight into attempting to keep Viktoria from wriggling free. Alric looked up at Madsen who was covered in streaks of her own bold crimson blood as well as dried fluid from her attack on

Viktoria. She leapt onto Viktoria's upper back and brought her plasma cutter down.

Alric's senses were overcome by the blinding flashes of liquifying matter, unbearable grinding of the plasma cutter, and the pathetic pleading of a dying monster's attempts to cling onto its life. As the light dimmed, Madsen plunged a hand into the newly burned hole in Viktoria's writhing body, growled in exertion, and wrenched. In that single instance, silence consumed the entire town square as the sapien pulled an organ out of the cavity. It was a melted rectangular thing with a blinking red light upon its edge. The vampire's flailing instantly came to a halt and her body went limp. Baldwyn rolled off of the carcass' arm and splayed out on the ground. "Please tell me…that the creature is *dead*," he panted.

Madsen staggered backwards, too expelled for words. Alric watched as she limped over to her bag and removed her PC. She produced a thin length of string from the device then threaded it into a hole inside the organ she tore from Viktoria. Alric, not eager to stay so close to what remained of Viktoria, tried to use his taukumu as a cane to push himself upright. A mere second before he was about to tumble over, he felt someone steady him. It was Katheryn. "Thou art able to ask for assistance, brother." He gazed at her in silence for a moment. He listened to her short breaths. He savoured the fact that he had the privilege of laying eyes upon her again.

With his makeshift cane, the Thestor clumsily lumbered over to Madsen who had slumped down on the ground as more soldiers came pouring into the town square. Alric peered over her shoulder and saw text displayed on the tablet:

EXTERNAL DRIVE- D:// HCS-A
Data Log Search
Pinned Item 1
Event: Long-Range Message Sent.
Message Body: 'Claude, Roger, and Gerhard are dead. Wish you were here. If Franco wants to hit these dumbasses though, he should do it now. They're gonna be scared shitless.'

Alric saw her grip tighten on the PC and half expected it to shatter into a million pieces. "Great. Fucking great."

L
The Coming Fire

Alric made sure to immediately inform Katheryn of the missive that was pulled from Viktoria's brain. He had never seen such dread upon his sister's face. To be posed against a Clthic army in the wake of such a massacre…it truly was a nightmare. The leaders of the three largest Churchsworn Kingdoms were dead. Despite how Alric tried to emphasise the seriousness of Katheryn's political position, she completely ignored his remarks and instead dragged him off to one of the Mended tents for treatment.

As Katheryn braced him and allowed him to hobble inside, he saw that Gabriel and Claudia were leading some Mended physicians in tending to several wounded men. Gabriel's attention was instantly snatched by the duo. "This crippled fool is in need of assistance," Katheryn bellowed. Alric groaned under his breath.

"Set him down here, Duchess Katheryn," said Gabriel as he motioned towards a vacant bed. The two of them eased Alric down and lifted his broken leg up onto the cot. The sheer pain was almost enough to make Alric scream, but the fear of shame was enough to force him to remain silent.

As Gabriel peered down at the medical device entrusted to him by Madsen, he said, "It seems that the tibia and fibula are both fractured."

Katheryn tutted. "A shame. An amputation may be in order. 'Tis fortunate that Gabriel is here; he has intimate experience with the procedure."

Gabriel rolled his eyes. "Ignore her. A simple application of faerie tears after we have set the bones would be more than sufficient." In the following half hour, another Mended pushed Alric's leg into the correct position as Gabriel lathered faerie tears onto his calf. They then tied splints around the limb to ensure that it remained aligned. All the while, Katheryn made countless jabs at his expense. Alric could not help but notice that she seemed to peer over Gabriel's shoulder at his work like a hawk.

Once it was complete, Alric sat up in the cot as Gabriel gave him very clear instructions. "Thou art to walk with a cane for the next few days. Go to the keep and do not leave bed unless it is expressly required; the tears need time to seep through thy pores and through thy flesh. Dost thou understand?"

Alric nodded, fully intending to ignore his advice. The only thing upon his mind was Madsen. She had been wounded. As she had once told him, if she did not clean her wounds and dress them properly, she could succumb to infection.

Katheryn led him back out of the tent as he used his taukumu as a walking stick. "Katheryn…art thou well?"

With a scoff, she said, "I am unharmed. Is that not obvious?"

"That is not what I asked thee. Thou must have been well acquainted with Roger IV. One cannot be dubbed a duchess without the favour of the king."

Her face was uncharacteristically blank as she stared back at him. "If thou art done interrogating me, brother, I must take my leave. A great many things must be done." The answer, to anyone else, might have been very ambiguous. To Alric, however, it told him everything he needed to know. She was being very guarded…meaning that a great deal of pain was coursing through her.

He simply nodded. "I shall keep thee no longer." He watched as Katheryn sceptically spun on her heels and made her way back to the keep.

Wyrmsmouth was still pulsating with activity as Alric tried to find Madsen. It had been no more than four hours since Viktoria had been slain. Men who had sworn fealty to the lords and knights killed by the elder vampire argued amongst themselves about whether or not they should stay and fight. A sizable number had already left.

Several Mended pointed Alric to a supply tent on the outskirts of the courtyard and mentioned that Madsen insisted on being left alone. He did not want to undermine her wishes, but Alric was not going to take any chances with her wellbeing. *She* certainly did not when his life was in jeopardy. The fabric fluttered as he brushed it aside and stepped into the tent. The space was lit by a handful of candles and Alric could see Madsen sitting on a crate at the opposite end, tending to her wounds. She had removed her shirt, revealing that her arms and abdomen were lathered with incisions that leaked bold crimson sapien blood. A fitted black undergarment covered her upper chest. As she winced in pain while dabbing one of her injuries, she met eyes with her impromptu visitor.

"A-Al?" He could see her hands shaking and her expression scrunching. "You shouldn't be walking around yet. Do you want it to snap in half?"

Alric hobbled over, frowning. "And thou shouldst not be tending to thine own wounds like a damned Knight Correntis."

With a weak shake of her head, Madsen replied, "Just...go rest." Her voice was awash with a kind of masked despair. As much as she tried to hide it, Alric had heard a similar tone in it before. He recalled her unease during the skirmish at Phaemslake and her reaction to realising that she had killed one of the footmen in the Pale Spire. Being hunted by an elder vampire would be an ordeal for anyone, especially a stranger to the realm. She was an engineer, not a warrior, despite how well she could carry herself during moments of strife.

"Eileen," he insisted austerely. She froze and stared into his eyes. "I do not believe that either of us is in the mood for such a pointless argument. I *shall* assist thee."

She cleared her throat and rolled her eyes. "Fucking... Okay. *Fine*. Just sit down, okay? Don't put any pressure on that foot."

"Thy will be done," he quipped as he struggled to drag a barrel over. He gingerly lowered himself onto it. "Tell me what I must do."

She nodded gently and jerked her head towards the wealth of sapien supplies by her side. "That small green bottle. Squeeze some onto your hands and rub them together until it dries up." He followed her instructions and lathered his hands with the strange cool liquid. Most alarmingly, it seemed to vanish into thin air after he followed her instruction. He must not have realised how ridiculous he looked as he narrowed his eyes at his palms because Madsen snorted in amusement. "It's to make sure your hands are clean. Now get that red packet over there." He nodded and tore the odd crinkly package open. It contained sheets of thin fabric that were already wet. It was baffling. Having them somehow already moistened with water would save a great deal of time. "These are to clean the wounds?" he asked quietly.

"Yeah."

The knight reached for her arm with the damp fabric in hand. Madsen's brow tightened as soon as he made contact. There was silence for a while as Alric worked. He eventually thought it prudent to say...*something*. Under his breath, he muttered, "I was quite horrified when I entered the tent; for a moment I thought thee to be...indecent." Madsen laughed and shook her head. "But alas, I see that the sapiens also wear breast bags."

Madsen snatched Alric's wrist. She let out a devilish wheeze of laughter and doubled over. "B-Breast bags!?" she managed to exclaim through her cackling. "No way. No fucking way. You're fucking with me."

"...I am not 'fucking with thee'."

"Breast bags? That's what you call them?"

Alric grimaced, pulled his hand free, and resumed his work. "I wouldst prefer it if thou didst not mock my culture."

"Dude, *breast bags.* What do you call pants? Ball sleeves?" she answered, thumbing tears out of her eyes.

The knight froze in place. He felt his grimace begin to falter and try to warp into a smile. He fought it with every ounce of will he could muster. He did not want to give her that victory. "Art thou truly so easily amused?"

"Sausage sacks."

"Eileen, for the love of..."

"Weiner blankets," she snorted.

Alric groaned and shook his head. "What should I call them in the future to avoid this calamity?"

"It's called a sports bra. Not as fun as breast bags. *I* might start calling them breast bags now."

He tutted and continued his work cleaning each of the cuts littered about Madsen's arms. As he moved on to scrubbing the slashes on her body, he listened to the sound of her breathing and the soft gasps of pain she made. "You really need to be careful with your knee, okay? Did Gabe explain why?" she asked suddenly, slicing through the silence.

"Aye, he said to give the faerie tears time to seep in."

She snorted again. "I forgot that's what you guys call it."

"Thou cannot help it, can thee? Everything is so utterly hilarious," mumbled Alric.

"They're nano printers. Those tiny machines I told you about earlier. They're so small that you can't even see them; they're swimming around inside the liquid."

Alric narrowed his eyes. "The same creatures that give vampires their healing?"

"It's just that the Infils have...'glands' that produce them while you guys have to harvest them from other sources. Other than that, yeah, they'd be the exact same thing. They automatically connect to your onboard diagnostics suites, read the error codes, then fix the problem with a process called 3D printing."

Printing... Yes. Instead of printing letters onto a page, they printed tissue. He smacked his lips. "Thou mean to tell me that as we speak, there are insects swimming about within my body, knitting my splintered bones back together and communicating with my nervous system?"

Madsen laughed. "Yep."

"How…concerning."

The lacerations on her abdomen were much deeper than the ones on her arms. There was also a patch of discoloured, purplish tissue; judging from the red hue of sapien blood, Alric surmised that it was a bruise. She grimaced and snarled as Alric worked on them. "If these 'nano printers' are as helpful as thou suggest, why not dispense them upon thyself?"

She laughed at Alric's words, but following his very serious reaction, Madsen cleared her throat. "You remember what I told you before about sapiens being organic and proxies being mechanical? Despite how you're all designed to be similar to us, our bodies function in completely different ways once you get into the specifics of–"

"It would be like using a blacksmith's hammer to treat an ailing crop," he interrupted.

Madsen's tense expression faded. There was a glint in her eye as she stammered, "Um…y-yeah. Yeah, exactly." Alric wasn't certain if it was because she wasn't expecting the interruption, or she didn't think Alric would get it right.

Once all of the wounds were properly cleaned, Madsen reached into the case, retrieved a slim tube and squeezed some strange smelling paste out of it and onto Alric's fingers. "Okay, this is called antiseptic gel. Rub this over the cuts. It's…gonna sting, but just keep going."

If it did sting, Alric could not tell. Madsen cringed but made no sound the entire time. Once it was all done, Madsen sighed heavily and ran a hand through her messy hair. "Look, Al…I just wanted… This was…" Her voice trailed off. With a growl, she threw her hands up in defeat and said bluntly, "Thank you."

"'Twas my pleasure," he said with a low nod.

Alric leaned back as Madsen applied stark white bandages to her injuries that seemed to stick to her skin on their own, without needing to be wrapped or tied in place. After trying and failing to rehearse the words in his mind for quite some time, Alric decided to simply speak. "War is coming." Madsen, in the middle of bandaging her left forearm, paused. She closed her eyes and curled her lower lip inward. "This is but the beginning. They shall send their witches, their golems, their Zealots…but make no mistake; we shall most certainly not allow them to take thee."

She shifted uncomfortably. "Look…I'm not a soldier. I don't know how to use a sword, I don't know how to ride a horse, I don't know how to handle armour. But that doesn't mean I'm gonna sit on my ass and watch you guys risk your lives for me. I can't fight like a *proxy*…but I sure as hell can fight like a *sapien*."

LI
Finders Keepers

The hangar bulkhead was so big that it looked like it trailed off into infinity above her. She moved over to the gigantic door's control panel and surprising no one, the touch screen was busted. Madsen brandished her impact driver and started pulling out the bolts that held the access panel in place.

The caverns themselves weren't well ventilated for obvious reasons. Her flight suit sleeves were tied around her waist again as she wiped the sweat from her brow and adjusted her drenched t-shirt. Spending hours mapping the 'Drumming Deep' was a little more physically strenuous than she first expected. She managed to find a sealed-up vehicle hangar behind all the collapsed rock though, so she was hoping that the litres of sweat she lost would be worth whatever was inside.

With the bulkhead's access panel pulled off, Madsen whipped out her PC and jacked in. With a whistle, Madsen opened the command prompt for the bulkhead, typed a few lines, then hit enter.

An alarm sounded, flooding the cavern with obnoxiously loud howling as the mechanical locks on the bulkhead sighed and pulled out of their clamps. The hydraulic doors shifted apart, prompting Madsen to point her flashlight at the void beyond. She hefted her duffel bag up tighter against her shoulder and stepped inside. Instantly, the heat vanished and a wave of piercing cold sunk into her pores.

The vehicle bay was a big fucking room. So big that Madsen couldn't see the walls right away, even with the help of her flashlight. There was a whole lot of debris on the ground ranging from wires, cables, rusted tools, to empty crates, mangled load lifters, and useless scrap. She picked a random direction and started walking. Eventually, a wall faded in from the darkness, stencilled with:

'HANGAR 04A- 125th B.W.P. DETACHMENT'

"Holy shit. Come on... Come on..." Madsen found herself pacing faster along the side of the wall. The longer she went without finding anything, the faster she jogged. Suddenly, she barged head-first into something that was cold, heavy, and quite hard. "Fuck! Ow," she hissed as she rubbed her forehead.

Madsen took a few steps backwards and pointed her flashlight up. It was a gigantic metal leg covered in deltanium-5 hull plating tiles. The entire machine itself was a fifteen-metre-tall beast that stood with a hunched profile on two legs and had a weapons array mounted on each of its two 'arms'. Bipedal Weapons Platforms were the 31st Century equivalent of a main battle tank; the main difference was their unmatched manoeuvrability. B.W.P.s could easily navigate problematic terrain without getting stuck in mud, ruts, or tangled tree roots unlike treaded or wheeled vehicles. Also, being able to step on enemy vehicles was a plus.

The unit that Madsen just stumbled upon in particular was an older Hagen Combat Sciences signature; the A-188-245(MP) 'Raider'. Before applying to become an astronaut for ISEC, she was employed by Anvil Heavy Fabrication. Aside from working on powered load lifters and demolition machinery, she did a lot of work as a B.W.P. engineer and test pilot. The highlight was her time as mechanical engineer and lead test pilot on the Minotaur Program; a B.W.P. research and development initiative that ultimately fizzled out due to its impractical cost. SysGov's Intersystem Armed Forces preferred, you know, being able to afford other shit, so they offered the contract to the much more financially viable proposals from Hagen Combat Sciences instead. As much as she enjoyed strapping herself into a one-hundred tonne experimental walking tank, it didn't quite measure up to making regular interplanetary trips and repairing ISEC's cutting edge technology. She *had* to go for the ISEC job as soon as the opportunity came up, especially given how hard the Minotaur program tanked.

That was it. The edge that they needed to stand a chance against the Synod. Madsen had graduated at the top of her test pilot group and had thousands of hours of logged operating time in both planet-side and orbital modes, so she was confident enough to pilot the Raider in a combat scenario. She couldn't celebrate too soon though; she needed to make sure the thing still worked, or apply enough elbow grease until it did. She climbed the stairs, mounted the gantry that caged the Raider, and gave it a quick visual inspection with the help of her flashlight. There seemed to be some damage on a few of the exposed hydraulic lines and some hull plates were missing. Hopefully the hydraulic leaks were something she could patch up…otherwise, a mech that couldn't move wouldn't be much use to her.

The cockpit hatch still functioned, but it was a little stiff and Madsen had to really wrench it back to get it to open the whole way. Madsen flopped herself onto the rather comfy memory foam seat and put the backend of her flashlight into her mouth. After giving the cockpit a meticulous once over, she was confident that it was safe to pilot and that the on-board computer was intact. She reached for the computer's power switch and flicked it on. There was a faint buzzing as a monitor on the side of the open cockpit winked to life. It displayed the Insight Computer Processing Technologies logo as the computer completed its boot sequence. Madsen grabbed the panoramic monitor and pulled it out in front of her, so it extended out over where the hatch would be if the cockpit was closed. Good. The computer worked. The cockpit lights flicked on, prompting her to stow her flashlight. Then it was time to make sure the ten million other bits of it still functioned...and maybe hope that the digital operator's manual hadn't gotten corrupted. Sure, she'd operated B.W.P.s in the past, but knowing the ins and outs of each specific machine was incredibly important for a pilot. The automatic systems check rolled upward from the bottom of the screen:

TIME/DATE: SATLINK FAILURE
MOBEC Operating System v5.221: OK
Dynamic Stabilization System v12.02: ERROR- RECOMPILE NEEDED
WAYFARER 5 Pathfinding Suite v2.5: OK
Network Connectivity: ERROR
Local Comms Relay: ERROR
OPTICON Panoramic Camera Cluster: OK
Weapons Array R [M32 Electromagnetic Accelerator Cannon: 40 rounds]: OK
Weapons Array R Gimbal: ERROR, ACTUATOR FAILURE
Weapons Array L [Trident 9 Automatic Assault Weapon System: 500 rounds]: ERROR, JAM DETECTED
Weapons Array L Gimbal: ERROR, POWER FAILURE
Block 9 Schmidt-Binder Fusion Reactor: OK
Hydraulic Control Valve: ERROR, MOTOR FAILURE
Hydraulic Pump Leg R: OK
Hydraulic Pump Leg L: ERROR, PRESSURE LOW

Madsen scrunched her nose. She lucked out pretty hard, but there was still a bit of work to be done. She didn't really have to worry about the networking and comms. The issue with the Dynamic Stabilization System software should've been easy enough to solve with a recompile and database rebuild…but the hardware problems were pretty critical. Hopefully, the jam in the Trident automatic cannon could be cleared by cycling the bolt or manually via the emergency access port. With both weapon array gimbals offline, she wouldn't be able to aim either of the guns. A fault with the hydraulic lines could mean that the limbs could suddenly lock up mid-operation. They all would've been the easiest of fixes if the hangar bay and all of its maintenance gear was fully operational, but it looked like she had to get it done the old-fashioned way. With her hands.

First on the list was hydraulics. She managed to get some of the lamps back on in the hangar bay after wading around in the dark for a while. The lights revealed that the other Raiders had been dismantled or were halfway through being assembled. That gave her a source for replacement parts. There was also a decent amount of other potentially useful equipment lying around including three or four particle blanket generators. At a quick glance, Madsen could tell that half of them were fried but she thought that she could maybe find a use for the ones that were still functional. That had to wait, though; she had a big walking tank to fix. With some sealing agent, a bunch of hosing she pulled from the other Raiders, and a few fresh cans of fluid, she settled in for a few hours of repair work. Luckily, there had been enough spare fluid canisters in the storage area for her to be able to flush all of the old stuff from the Raider's reservoir and replace it with a fresh load. She didn't want deteriorated liquid affecting the Raider's performance, especially if *she* was gonna be the one operating it.

After that, she went after all of the small hairline cracks in the hydraulic piping with the sealing agent and heavy-duty tape. It definitely wasn't gonna be a permanent fix, but hey, one thing at a time. Then came replacing the lengths of hosing that were beyond patching up. It was all going fine until an entire section of what she just replaced popped loose on the Raider's left leg. Madsen couldn't help but say 'fuck' a whole bunch of times. She was just glad that she didn't have the hydraulic system pressurised yet just in case; otherwise, fluid would've gone spewing everywhere and she would've had to re-juice it *again.* "Of course. Of *fucking* course. Motherfucking piece of shit," Madsen snarled to herself as she tried to force the loose hydraulic hose back into place.

No matter how hard she tried, it just wouldn't fit. Maybe the heat warped the hose out of shape and it couldn't fit anymore? No. She couldn't accept that. Not after working for three and a half goddamn hours. She was gonna make it fit. "For fuck's sake. C'mon. You stupid fucking thing." She had to awkwardly contort her arm to reach the left leg's hydraulic connector inside its specialised housing. She could barely get to it, and even then, she couldn't even see what she was doing. "Get…the fuck…in there…" she grumbled. Finally, after thirty minutes of blind poking, Madsen felt the satisfying 'click' of the hose's connection settling in. "Jesus fucking Christ," she sighed.

Then, she saw silhouettes in the open hangar doors. They were tiny next to the enormous bulkhead. About ten people filtered through; most of them were staring around in awe at the spacious hangar bay. The engineer grunted as she pushed to her feet and vigorously rubbed her grease-stained hands on her flight suit pants. "By God… What is that?" marvelled Gabriel. Alric stopped in his tracks and stared at the Raider like he was expecting it to come to life any second.

With a wave, Madsen strolled up to the edge of the gantry where they could see her and cocked her head. "Hey," she called. "Everything okay?" As soon as he saw her, Alric eased off and waved the rest of the people forward. Covered in sweat, Madsen fluttered down the gantry stairs, jogged across the hangar bay floor, and met Alric with a smile on her face.

Claudia's eyes lanced onto the Raider. "Issit dead?"

Alric's eyes were stuck on the gigantic machine for a few seconds. He shook himself out of his trance and said, loudly enough for all of his comrades to hear, "The thing is not truly 'alive'. 'Tis more akin to a siege engine; it must be manned." Then the dread built up in Alric's eyes. "The Clthics had four at the Battle of Threshfield. Thousands of men lost their lives to their devastating power." Madsen blew a puff of air out of her mouth. Of course. Of course the Clthics had a bunch of them.

"Do not be modest, my friend," scoffed Baldwyn. "He was alone and unhorsed, yet he rushed into battle against one of the golems." As soon as Baldwyn started telling the epic story, Alric facepalmed *hard*. "With his arcane staff and divine strength, he tore open its belly and disembowelled it."

"Woah. No way. You managed to kill the pilot? Badass." Raiders were advanced war machines. For Alric to charge at it with essentially a pointy metal stick and a single particle beam weapon, he had to have some real balls. And that had to mean that that specific Raider's energy dispersive coating had decayed; there was no way a handheld particle beam could've done anything against a well maintained B.W.P.

Alric sighed uncomfortably. "A-Aye. There was a witch within it…horribly maimed and dismembered. The golem's entrails had been funnelled into her body, allowing her mind to directly control the beast–pardon me, the *contraption*."

Madsen rubbed her chin. They figured out how to directly connect a proxy SSD to the Raider's user interface. That meant no latency issues or needing to learn the controls. A direct 'neural' link. It would've been impossible to do with a human brain without some yet-to-be-invented intrusive neural implants. "That's...fucking *nuts*. Don't worry, I'm gonna use the controls like a regular sane person."

Baldwyn cocked his head. "Thy Holiness, surely thou art not going to commandeer such an accursed object?'

Madsen squinted and her mouth dropped open a little. How the hell was she supposed to respond to that? Alric stepped in and said, "Do not forget the Devil's origins, Brother. He stole divine knowledge and perverted it to fulfil his own twisted machinations. The golems are but one example of his molestation of Heaven's divine magic."

"Of course, of course..." Baldwyn murmured as he crossed his arms and continued to stare at the Raider.

Madsen tried to fight the frown that was forming on her face. As the rest of the guys spread out and looked around, Alric followed Madsen as she walked back up the gantry. She whispered to him, "I wish we didn't have to lie to them."

"It is the only way they can understand."

"That's not true. *You* understood."

"I did. *After* I considered smothering thee in that casket," he confessed suddenly. After the words left his mouth, Madsen felt her throat tighten and her chest grow heavy. "Make no mistake...if thou openly contradict the scripture, the Thestors *will* kill thee."

As much as she wanted to argue the point with him, she couldn't deny what he was saying. People were scared...and as soon as she defied their beliefs, they'd start asking why. They'd inevitably call her a demon. What else would they do? Admit that their ancient religion was wrong? There was an entire army of knights dedicated to wiping out groups that didn't conform. She groaned in defeat. "It wouldn't just be me, though. They'd target you, Claudia, Gabriel...all of the Mended. Maybe even Katheryn."

Alric nodded solemnly.

"We don't really have a choice...but I still don't like it."

Madsen finally noticed that Alric had been holding a wicker basket in his right hand the whole time. It had a piece of linen laid over the top. "Whatcha got there?" she asked, pointing at the thing.

Alric reacted like he forgot he was holding it. "Ah. Yes. I took the liberty of preparing supper for thee." He held the basket out and bowed, like he was presenting her with some ancient artefact. Madsen squinted and accepted the basket. When she threw the sheet back, a weak smile formed on her face.

Nestled in the linen was a big sandwich made with golden brown bread and slices of some kind of meat. It all just looked like cooked rubber to her. Oh, and there was a whole block of cheese in there. Not a slice, but a chonky rectangular mass just plonked in there. He'd seen a sandwich *once* and didn't eat it either…but he made one anyway. Just for her. So yeah…how could she blame him? It was a good thing she liked cheese. Madsen stared at the thing in silence for a bit then chuckled to herself. In the meantime, Alric was leaning on the handrail of the gantry with an eyebrow raised, waiting for her to actually say something. "Is something amiss? Have I not prepared it to thy liking?"

"N-No! No, it's perfect!" Madsen nervously scratched the back of her neck. "Thanks…man," she muttered awkwardly. As soon as she realised what just came out of her mouth, she slammed her palm into her face. *Thanks, man?* Yeah, real smooth.

Madsen wrapped the linen around the sandwich to protect it from her greasy hands and picked it up. When she took a bite out of it, the texture of the bread really stood out to her. Like the one she had during the feast, it wasn't plain and smooth like the white bread she was used to. It was fluffy, grainy, and crunchy. The cheese was also…you know…pretty overpowering. But that was okay. It was awesome. "Mmmm."

After a pause, Alric looked over at the hulking B.W.P. The two of them were standing on the scaffolding right at its 'chest' height. "This…mechanism. What is it, in sapien terms?"

Madsen glanced over her shoulders to make sure no one else was close by, then replied quietly. "It's exactly what you said it was. It's an armoured vehicle fielded by our military. We call them Bipedal Weapons Platforms, B.W.P.s, for short. This model in particular is called the Raider." Alric approached and took a good look at its angular surface, then peered into its open cockpit hatch. With a smirk, Madsen jerked her head towards the seat. "Go on. Get in."

After pausing for a second with a glimmer of eagerness in his optics, Alric climbed on in. It was a good thing he wasn't in his armour, because he definitely wouldn't have fit. She watched him run fingers along the instrument panel and peer around the cockpit. He eventually noticed the control handles and promptly grabbed them. "These rods are used to command the Raider?"

"Yeah. All of those little buttons and stuff too."

Alric squinted and leaned closer to the controls. "I did not even notice those. What functions doth they serve?"

Madsen grabbed the top of the hatch with one hand and leaned inside. Her half-eaten sandwich was still firmly gripped in the other hand. "Okay…so the red one on the back, the main trigger, fires the weapon that corresponds to that control handle. Left gun, right gun. That little mushroom looking one on the top of the handle is called a thumbstick; you can slide it around. The thumbstick on the left handle controls which direction the Raider is walking and the one on the right is used to turn the upper body. That one over there, the small grey one, is called the auxiliary control key; you can assign that to whatever you want. Usually reserved for extra equipment."

He took a closer look at the instrument panel underneath the main display and realised just how many other switches and buttons there were. "There must be a thousand different 'buttons' used to operate this machine. How couldst thou possibly remember where they all lie and which purposes they fulfil?"

"I guess it's the same way you know what to do in a fight. You train. Over and over…and over," she said as he clambered back out of the machine.

Next, he looked at the two massive weapon arrays that were fixed to the Raider's arms. Madsen watched as Alric approached the left armament, the automatic gun. He examined and ran a hand along its multiple barrels. "Is this some manner of cannon?"

"More or less. It works the same way, physically speaking, by using gunpowder. The main difference is that the rounds are about this big," she held her hands about 30 centimetres apart, "and the bastard can shoot sixty-five of them per second."

"I beg thy pardon? *Per second*?" he repeated quite loudly. "*Sixty-five firings per second?* That is ludicrous. How are the ball and powder loaded that quickly?"

Seeing Alric react to how insane human engineering was gave her a new appreciation for what she saw as mundane hardware. Not only was she born into a world where people could explode themselves off a planet, travel a precisely pre-calculated winding trajectory through space, then land on another planet without dying…she was one of those people. Of course she couldn't comprehend how insane it was. When it came to technology, Alric was used to the proxy body being the only real source of energy. Those big catapults Madsen always saw in movies were probably the closest thing he'd ever seen to modern human engineering and even then, they still operated on manpower. People needed to wind them up, load them, shoot them, then do it all again. It was limited to how quickly the proxies could operate. The Raider's Trident 9 cannon went faster than anything he'd ever seen in his entire life. His awe and wonder made everything feel fresh and new again. It was invigorating.

Just as Madsen was about to open her mouth to explain, he narrowed his optics as they traced along the weapon's length and landed on the ammo feed belt. The belt was segmented, partially exposing the chrome bronze cartridges. "A seed-spitter," he muttered to himself.

Madsen watched him with a warm smile on her face. "Is that what you guys call firearms?"

"No, we Tritans refer to them as firearms as well, but the druids call them 'pakama', which translates to 'seed-spitter'. I have seen them in use before, although they were a simpler handheld variety that certainly could not discharge so quickly. Due to their small size, I did not even consider that they could have been firearms. This weapon, however, makes the similarities grossly apparent to me. 'Tis essentially a gargantuan assembly of spinning cannon, each capable of self-loading…" He muttered all of that out loud as he followed the feed belt to the ammunition canister mounted on the rear chassis. Madsen took the time to finish the rest of her first sandwich as she watched him mull it all over. "Is the entire process done *without* human interaction? It seems that the weapon essentially operates *itself*."

"Yep. All we gotta do is squeeze the trigger and everything is done on its own."

Alric stood back up and rubbed his chin. "I see. Thou seem very familiar with the Raider's inner workings."

Madsen pushed her hands into her pockets. "I used to be a test pilot; I would drive them and help iron out all of the kinks. I've done thousands of hours of live-fire combat simulations…so I'm ready."

"...Art thou certain about engaging in the battle?" he asked. "The Raider is a highly lethal engine. To be its pilot would mean that thou wouldst take hundreds, maybe even thousands of lives."

To be honest, it was something she was trying to avoid thinking about. Her brain had been wired to take it one step at a time. There was no point worrying about something that far down the chain. "And if I don't do that, the Clthics could kill *everyone*."

Alric nodded with a sigh. "...Regardless, to have one of these engines on our side is an enormous boon. Not only are our foes unaware of it, thy first-hand experience with its operation shall dwarf what limited understanding the Clthics might have. This lesson of sorts was…most enlightening." He gave her this look. She had no idea what it meant. Almost as soon as it showed up though, it vanished and he quickly changed the subject. "We should apprise thee of the current political situation," he declared loudly as they came back down the gantry stairs, garnering the attention of the rest of the group.

Alric crossed his arms and looked across the room. "Prince Roger shall be declared Roger V once there is time enough for a coronation to be held in Elthomshire. He is sending riders to the surrounding fiefdoms to warn of the coming army as well as to secure more men."

Claudia came strolling over, her hands planted on her hips. "Emperor Gerhard's wife 'ad ta fuck off back to tha Steiffan Empire. It'll probably be a right mess over there, gotta make sure no one tries ta take over and what not. She left a buncha men 'ere; I guess that's somethin', ay?"

"How about the other guys? Val…something? Valdo?" Madsen asked.

Gabriel said with a snort, "Admirable attempt, but it is *Valtheaux*. Jean, son of Claude, will be crowned Jean I. He is just a child. Not even old enough to be chasing girls yet."

Madsen's face wrinkled. "What…? He's a kid? And he's king? That's…totally normal?"

The three of them nodded, not entirely sure why Madsen was so confused. She took a breath, exhaled, then gestured for Alric to keep going. He said, "My sister is securing more assistance elsewhere. Upon her return later this day, a war council shall be held in Castle Wyrmsmouth. Thou shouldst be present for it, Eileen. That 'drone' thou mentioned should be made known to our commanders as soon as possible."

Gabriel arched an eyebrow. "Drone? What the Devil art thou talking about?"

"Patience. Thou shalt find out soon enough," Alric said softly.

The solar in Castle Wyrmsmouth's keep was bursting at the seams with people. Madsen was expecting her and Katheryn to be the only women there, but she was surprised to see that she was wrong. There was *one* more. Fiona of Penbrooke joined the men as they looked over their plans. Her husband's people to *her* now seeing as her husband Sir Daniel was killed by Viktoria. Madsen also felt like the fact that most of the higher up lords were dead or ran away had something to do with why she was allowed in at all. Madsen had to do *a lot* of biting her tongue to not blow up at how all the women were being treated, but yelling at a few singular people wasn't going to solve anything. They couldn't be changed overnight.

The room was a rainbow of royal purples, bold reds, vibrant yellows, and deep blues. The worst part of the whole thing was that everyone there, each and every one, made sure to kneel in front of Madsen and say thanks to the 'angel' for saving them from the 'elder vampire'. At first it was hard for her to keep a straight face, but eventually it was just weird. There were a lot of introductions and a lot of names, all of which Madsen jotted down into her notebook so she could keep up with everything. She was still struggling to tell them all apart, so the notes helped. She could've taken it all down on her PC, but she'd gotten a little soft spot for writing practically.

Prince Roger had his arms crossed as he looked down at the regional map that was laid across the massive table. "Antony of Kirthshire is honouring his Oath to my father. He will bring a host of five hundred archers and four hundred men-at-arms on the morrow," he said.

"How many have deserted us?" Katheryn asked.

"No less than a thousand men," added Roger grimly.

Madsen was sitting in the corner on a comfy padded chair twiddling her thumbs and narrowing her eyes as she tried to decipher what the hell they were all talking about. A startled murmur worked its way through the crowd. Pierre de Corbin sighed heavily and leant both palms onto the table. If Madsen's barely legible notes were correct, Pierre was going to serve as regent of Valtheaux until his nephew Jean got old enough to rule on his own after the death of his father. "Many nobles were slain by that wretched creature. So many that our forces are a pathetic shadow of what they once were. The men sworn to dead lords have no reason to remain here. We must assume that most shall desert us."

Baldwyn scoffed. "Her Holiness has vowed to fight against the Clthic Synod, so rest assured that all of the faithful shall stand their ground and serve her. I would recommend that all who choose to desert her be excommunicated immediately. Perhaps even be charged with apostasy."

With a heavy sigh, Alric raised a hand to Baldwyn. "As we all know, Brother, God blessed us with free will. Her Holiness asserts that those who choose to depart should be permitted to do so." He shot Madsen a glance.

"Yeah. Exactly," she added.

Pierre promptly chimed back in. "Be that as it may, the Synod brings a mighty army down upon us. Stockpiling supplies and preparing for siege is the best course of action."

Werner von Talhoffen openly laughed in his face. "*Siege*? Did you not hear what happened to Valshügel and Omenthal? Their golems blew apart the walls as if they were made of mud. No stone on this earth can stop those abominations."

Baldwyn, the only person present dressed in full plate armour, crossed his arms and filled the room with the sound of jangling metal. "Verily. So, it would be good fortune if we were to have a golem of our own, would it not?"

The room went silent. Katheryn, as sharp as ever, looked over to Madsen. "Is it true?"

Madsen shrugged as she stood up. "Yeah. I think I can get it working. Just need a few days. I might even be able to hook up a particle blanket net to it. That'll compensate for some of the damaged hull plating tiles." Dead silence answered her.

Alric cleared his throat and added, "Her Holiness believes she may be able to fortify the weakened beast with a protective enchantment." A murmur worked its way through the room as everyone nodded. Alric shot Madsen a glance and shrugged.

She huffed in amusement and whispered, "Smooth."

Alric continued, "In the battle beneath the Pale Spire, the Clthics used the same such enchantments. These arcane shields could deflect taukumu bolts without any effort at all. Expect them on the battlefield."

A light bulb went off in Madsen's head. She leaned closer to Alric and said into his ear, "Arrows. Use arrows or crossbow bolts. Particle blankets have to be tuned to specific energy profiles and velocities. If they have them adjusted for particle beam fire, anything not conveying the same amount of energy can just pass through."

Alric nodded as he rubbed his chin and mumbled, "Indeed. We were able to simply walk through the barriers." He looked out at the war council and said, "Her Holiness has informed me that arrows and crossbow bolts should easily penetrate the protective spell; 'tis effective only against other forms of magic."

Roger nodded, looking pretty happy to get any kind of advice at all. "Excellent advice, Thy Holiness. It so happens that my father's laws ensured that Tritham would have a large number of archers in her armies. I pray that it is enough." He spoke with a soft voice...and it made Madsen sigh. His father was just killed in front of him by a sadistic maniac...but he still had a job to do.

Suddenly, the door opened. Three figures came through, provoking a very strong response from Alric. Two of them wore salvaged ISEC flight suits that were stitched together, along with cloaks made out of kevlar or some other thick ballistic fibre. The last one wore combat fatigues strapped with poly-ceramic energy-dispersive armour plating and a heavy combat helmet; standard issue for I.A.F. soldiers. The helmet was fully enclosed and didn't have a visor; instead, 8 small optic sensors adorned the thick deltanium plating on the front of the thing. They'd send a live feed to eyepieces on the inside of the helmet.

The newcomers were all proxies, but the ones not wearing heavy armour wore face paint that made Madsen's heart skip several beats. She saw very familiar tones...very *human* tones.

Katheryn said, "Allow me to introduce Eraith, speaker of the Ga'zahi druids, and Jorthen, her apprentice. Baldwyn, Alric, I believe thou hast already met Hythaarn of the Kaitan'zahi."

The proxy in the military gear nodded at Baldwyn, who bowed back to him and said, "U'marhi." Alric looked a little shocked that one of his colleagues bothered to learn even a single word in a 'heathen' language.

Hythaarn, with a deep chuckle, replied with, "Narvai."

Alric's eyes darted between the three faces. The hairs on the back of Madsen's neck straightened. He *had* mentioned something about sorcerers trying to kill her... One of the cloaked ones, older judging by the lines on her polymer skin, locked eyes with Madsen and ignored everyone else in the room. She drifted closer, but Alric blocked her off without hesitation. "If thou hast come here to see the deed done, there is still time enough to reconsider," he warned.

Baldwyn rested his hand onto the hilt of his sword and joined Alric's side.

Eraith, the older one, hissed, "Calm yourselves, Godslaves. Katheryn has already made the situation quite clear. As well-intentioned as she may have been, Carthei could have doomed us all if she had succeeded. If the Fallen One does not return to where she belongs, the rest of her kind will come to search for her. One Vorkhai cannot bring Athroct'u, but an army of them can and shall."

Alric gave Madsen a worried glance. She had to take a second to inhale deeply and compose herself. Eraith was right. Madsen couldn't imagine how SysGov would react if they sent a response team out there and found that she'd been murdered by self-aware, fully autonomous androids. Well…actually…she could. They'd launch nukes and bake the entire fucking planet from orbit, and she couldn't exactly blame them for wanting to do that either. The proxies' existence was terrifying, and humans had a tendency to do fucked up things when they were terrified. She raised her hand. "It's alright," she assured him.

Finally, he moved to one side and allowed Eraith, Jorthen, and Hythaarn to approach. All three of them held their palms in front of their foreheads for a few seconds, then bowed. Eraith and Jorthen were thin and nimble looking, but Hythaarn was built like a truck. Eraith said, "Your kind already robbed this place of its beauty once. We will not allow you to do it again. You are not welcome here."

Madsen exhaled. Before she could say anything, Baldwyn snorted. "If thou art done spouting nonsense, we have pressing matters to attend to." With that, the druids begrudgingly drifted over to the table. Most of the attendees seemed more than a little shaken by Baldwyn's bluntness. Even Alric was visibly uncomfortable.

Fiona of Penbrooke straightened her posture and said, "There is no choice to be made. We must meet them on the battlefield."

Roger replied, "We haven't the slightest idea of their numbers, nor from where exactly they plan to approach."

At that point, Alric slowly turned to Madsen. As their eyes met, she suddenly blurted, "Oh, right! Yeah. Totally forgot." She heaved a pretty sturdy hard polymer case up and dumped it on top of the map a little too thuggishly. It rippled and creased a little. Madsen flung the case open, revealing it to be a laptop-shaped piece of hardware; a control unit for the RZD-023 Reconnaissance Drone manufactured by AGILE Dynamic Systems. It had a screen plus a keyboard and a set of controls on the bottom half. As the screen buzzed to life, shocked gasps and murmurs travelled through the room. They huddled around the drone control unit and saw a camera feed showing a bunch of trees.

Alric explained, "Her Holiness has means with which to scout the enemy position from this very room."

"What in God's name…? How?" prodded Lionel of Pathridge.

"With a once slumbering faerie she found in the Under. Using the divine relic before thee, she is able to compel it to act on her will and see through its eyes." She had to say, she liked having a personal science-to-magic translator.

Madsen grasped the drone controls and eased up the throttle. The camera feed shook and it floated straight up, quickly penetrating the canopy of the forest. She could've heard a pin drop in that room. It felt cool to show them something like that, even if none of them understood it. Well, the druids didn't seem like it was new to them, but they definitely looked a little surprised by how well Madsen operated it. "I saw which way they were coming yesterday and decided to fly ahead of them, so they should be just around…" The trees scrolled by and gave way to a massive clearing that was pitched with tents, supply wagons, people, and livestock. "Bingo."

Roger released a raspy laugh. His eyes were so wide that they looked like they were going to fall out. "Unbelievable. Absolutely unbelievable."

"And I should be able to get a rough head count," she muttered as she started opening menus and selecting commands. Specifically, she was enabling the drone's onboard low-level microwave emitter. By emitting microwaves and monitoring the responses, it was used to detect human heartbeats. The main application of that kind of system was finding survivors in disaster areas, but Madsen supposed she could add 'counting the number of dudes coming to stab you' to the list as well. She just had to compensate for the differences in proxy electronics versus human biology. "Gimme a sec."

She pulled out her notebook and started scribbling some math into it. Proxies technically had a 'heartbeat', it was just completely different to a human one; it was the vibrations made by their E-Gel synthesis plants. It was more like a very gentle consistent thrumming, almost like the engine of a car. She had to modify the exact wavelengths outputted by the drone to pick *that* out instead and thankfully, the designers of the software made sure to make the detection parameters adjustable just in case you ever needed to find malfunctioning electrical equipment. Usually though, you'd have all that data on-hand to plug into the software. Unfortunately for her, the proxies didn't exactly have an owner's manual with all of their power supply specs spelled out in it. Madsen inputted a few rounds of data with no results before eventually figuring out parameters that worked. As she hit the enter key, the screen lit up with dozens of blips that floated around the massive campsite. "Okay, there's a margin of error with getting totals this way, so there's maybe about…fourteen-thousand proxies out there. Give or take. Is that a lot?"

Katheryn frowned as Roger blew a puff of air out of his mouth. The duchess said, "Seeing as we number approximately eight-thousand, *yes*. 'Tis a sizable amount."

Madsen swept the drone around the edge of the forest. "Oh, there they are. The…uh, golems. They've got three by the looks of it. And…woah." There was another vehicle there in the camp. It was sitting on a massive wagon so it could be dragged along the road. It had sharp angles, a scuffed matte black hull, and two propulsion drives in its wings. She wasn't sure on the exact model, but if she had to guess she'd say it was a Bashir-Yiu aircraft. Maybe a Type 30 VTOL? Those things were bad news. Last Madsen heard, there were talks in the SysGov senate to have the use of their primary weapon deemed a war crime. By using a napalm-based chemical agent, the main gun could start fires that burned for a day straight. It didn't matter if you tried to douse yourself in water; the chemical fire would keep going. Nothing could stop it from cooking you.

"The dragon…" Alric whispered.

Roger sighed heavily. "There is much to be done. I suppose it is the time to begin. Squire, fetch me some wine…and plenty of it."

LII
The Blue Order

The Churchsworn kingdoms were at war. Not with themselves, but for the first time since the Crusades, they stood united against a common foe. Over the course of several days, barons, lords, knights, men-at-arms, archers, infantry, and farmers filtered into Wyrmsmouth to lend their bodies to the final stand of the Churchsworn kingdoms. More druids than Alric had ever seen in one place had congregated in the woods not far from the city walls and would come into the city during the day to trade under a newfound amnesty granted by Archbishop Tynoius. Alric had seen that many of them had tied spears to their taukumu and inspiration had struck him. Upon mentioning it to Madsen, he was stunned by how she seemed to be possessed by the idea. She used her PC to 'draw' incredibly precise plans that could be turned and manipulated as if they were tangible objects. He gave her several notes on her designs regarding comfort, practicality, and what was possible for the smiths to attain without sapien forges to aid them. Then, after that lengthy design process, she sketched the finalised schematics onto large sheets of parchment. Alric then submitted the plans to one of the city's weaponsmiths. They were kind enough to attempt Alric and Madsen's project despite the wealth of orders that were piling up on their desks. Almost a week had gone by since then and time had grown short.

Wyrmsmouth's streets never saw respite from activity as the people prepared for the coming battle. Alric and Madsen stood on the side of the road and watched as wagons lumbered in from the gates carrying food, weapons, and people. At one point, a group of druids came down the road. They had a horse pulling a wagon loaded with an array of barrels. As Madsen approached, they all gave her the customary salute of a palm over their foreheads as they bowed. "Hi. Any of you speak English? I mean…Tritish?" she asked. The one that Alric recognised as Hythaarn nodded. Madsen gestured at the barrels. "What's this?"

Hythaarn answered, "This is unzym. Very important." His grasp of the language was far removed from Carthei's, but he was well-spoken enough. Baldwyn had taught him well.

Madsen approached and pried one of the canisters open, taking a sniff of the thick orange substance. She muttered to herself, "Oh. Smells like energy-dispersive coating." She looked back at Hythaarn. "You made this?"

With an eager nod, Hythaarn said, "Yes. We give to Godslaves. To paint their shells."

She nodded slowly. "Wow…that's a great idea. Judging from the potency, you might even be able to take a hit from a particle beam."

Alric huffed. "I know so from experience. It saved my life once before." He bowed to Hythaarn. "Thy contribution shall be accepted with gratitude."

Hythaarn stared blankly at Alric until Madsen clarified, "He said thank you."

The druid barked at his compatriots to continue on their way to deliver the unzym. As they trailed off, Madsen planted her hands onto her hips. She did not appear to be the most patient person. Whenever they had to wait for anything, he couldn't help but notice that she grew very restless and irritable. He leaned over towards her and said, "Perhaps thou shouldst best return to thy work. I am not certain how much longer it shall take."

She glanced up at him, a comical expression exuding with disbelief on her face. "Hey. Can you *not*? If I have to look at that Raider for one more second today, I'm gonna lose my mind."

"Very well. I shall *not*."

"This is all…very interesting for me. The waiting part too, honestly. I didn't realise how much I took 3D printing and CNC machining for granted. You press a button then 'boop', it's done. And usually, there's time for prototyping and testing and all of that. I hope it works, for *your* sake," she said, staring at a bird that had landed on the edge of a roof on the other side of the street. Alric was going to ask what all of that gibberish meant, but the arrival of a particularly squeaky wagon snatched his attention.

The thing looked to have fallen apart a thousand times. It was being pulled by a donkey who did not appear to like the crowded streets of Wyrmsmouth. Walking alongside the animal was a Knight Thestor in full plate harness. Like the wagon, the Thestor's armour was equally worn and mismatched. The knight calmed his animal to a stop not far from Alric and Madsen. When he approached, he bowed before Madsen so lowly that Alric thought he would soon tumble over.

"Brother?" Alric asked awkwardly as the man stood back up. The stranger simply stood there in silence, The shadowed sights of his great bascinet completely black. He reached into a pouch on his belt and retrieved a small rectangular object. He opened it, revealing it to be one of those wax tablets that scholars often used to take notes. Alric furrowed his brow as the knight grasped a stylus and began to scrawl something into the wax surface of the tablet. After a brief moment, he turned the tablet to them. It read 'God bless ye, angel and herald. I am the lowly Brother Eustace, unworthy to be in thy presence. But alas, I have purpose'.

Some men of the faith had taken vows of silence; it should have been obvious to Alric what Eustace was doing. "Brother Eustace is the chief scholar and scribe of our bestiaries. He hath penned a great deal of tomes regarding the nature of otherworldly beasts. Surely, thou art not one and the same." With that, Eustace chuckled and bowed once again. "It is a pleasure to be in thy company, good Brother. How might we be of service?" Alric asked with excitement teeming his voice.

Eustace began frantically writing again on his tablet, only to be interrupted by Madsen. "Here. Try this." She handed him her PC. Eustace trembled, frozen in lieu of being directly addressed by an 'angel'.

Alric had to nod to him and say, "Take it, Brother." Eustace hesitantly accepted the tablet. All that Alric saw on the face of the tablet was a narrow line of icons across the upper edge, while the rest of the surface was stark white.

"Take your glove off and write using your finger," Madsen urged. He removed his left gauntlet, stuffed it under his arm, and complied. As if by magic, as soon as Eustace swept his finger across the tablet, a bold black line appeared. It was far darker than any ink Alric had ever seen. The sapiens could write *freely*. Without exhausting expensive resources, without taking up physical space. It was no wonder that they were so vastly intelligent; they were not bound by the physical laws of thought that Alric was used to. Books were expensive, writing was difficult to learn, and supplies were rare. None of that mattered to the sapiens. They were free to cultivate their minds and pursue knowledge.

Despite the fact that Eustace was fully clad in plate, Alric could sense his awe and wonder. Eustace, barely managing to keep his trembling in check, wrote something else. He went to turn the tablet around, but Madsen held it in place. "Okay, tap that icon up there." She pointed at a peculiar picture of a conical shape with curved lines next to it.

Eustace touched it, then a voice leapt out of the artefact. "God be with thee." The male voice was warm, lively, and shared Madsen's accent. Alric had learned that the PC could see with its camera; of course it could speak as well.

Eustace, and Alric to a lesser degree, reeled back in shock. At first, the silent knight wheezed in disbelief, then laughed like a child. It was not the reaction of someone who took to silence voluntarily… No. It was the gleeful response of one who had it forced upon them, whether it was at birth or through some violent occurrence later in life. Eustace quickly wrangled his emotions and wrote once again.

"I came in search of Brother Alric. I have a gift to bestow upon him," said the PC. Eustace handed the PC back to Madsen for a moment while he ran to the back of his wagon, heaved a burlap sack out of it, and dumped it at Alric's feet. The metallic clanging it made upon contact with the ground told Alric exactly what was inside it. Eustace retrieved the PC and said with its assistance, "I rode here to answer the call to arms after collecting donations of weapons and armour from the faithful. Upon speaking to our comrade Brother Baldwyn, I learned that thine armour is in disrepair. The measurements are fairly close; I do hope it fits."

The armour differed slightly from Alric's original Tritish plate; it appeared to be of Velintine style. Instead of the previous single piece, the cuirass was composed of two separate pieces; the breastplate which covered the upper torso and the plackart that protected the abdomen. The plackart overlapped the breastplate but they were not fixed together, allowing articulation at the waist. The pauldrons and couters were also asymmetrical, resulting in the left arm being slightly more heavily armoured than the right. Since most men were right-handed, less protection and more freedom of movement on that side would be beneficial for a lance hand on horseback. Alric didn't think that he'd be fighting on horseback, but it was certainly going to be better than wearing his old warbled and burnt set.

Madsen hovered over to Alric and spied the helmet. She picked it up and spun it around so she could see its faceplate…and a most obnoxious and unladylike laugh filled the street. Those lines on her face that Alric found strangely captivating reappeared, but that time dragged her lips into a toothy grin. Several smiths working in the forge peered out from around the corner to see what the fuss was about. Eustace sent a very confused glance to Alric, who felt his shoulders contract as he gritted his teeth. "Look at this thing!" Madsen cackled. "It's so *dumb*. I love it." It was a hounskull, or pig-faced, bascinet: a helmet with a very recognisable conical snout. She picked it up and pointed said snout at Alric. "It's got a snoot, Al. It's got a *snoot*."

Alric narrowed his eyes. "So it does..." he mumbled, not thrilled with the attention she had garnered nor the nonsense that she flung his way.

Eustace stared at Madsen for a moment, dumbfounded and at an absolute loss. Then he shook his head violently and said using the PC, "Best ensure that it fits."

Madsen looked at Alric with a confident smirk. "Don't worry, I gotcha," she said softly with a wink. Alric was left dazed by the gesture as she moved with blinding pace to arm him. It was clear that in her time tending the wounded, she'd learned more about armour. Once the entire harness hugged Alric's frame, he realised that it was certainly heavier than his old set. He flexed his arms, legs, and back, while taking note of what he could and could not do. The large pauldrons meant that he could not lift his arms as high as before, but overall, he found it to be much more comfortable than his old harness. "Brother Eustace, I must thank thee deeply for this most generous gift."

The mute Thestor, having handed Madsen's PC back, once again used his wax tablet to write, 'I shall see thee upon the battlefield, Brother. And God bless thee, Thy Holiness. Thou hast allowed me to feel joy for the first time in many years'. He gave Madsen one final bow, then Brother Eustace retook his donkey's reins and vanished into the busy streets.

Alric looked at Madsen, who stared after Eustace. He inhaled sharply, then muttered, "I shall never tire of watching thee raise such low spirits."

"Hm? What?" she asked, suddenly turning to him with a start.

"*It was kind of thee,*" he said through clenched teeth.

Madsen shrugged. "Oh. It was nothing. I think they just called for us. Let's go."

Alric, with his Thestor surcoat folded into a small, tight square clutched in his hand, followed Madsen as she entered the weaponsmith's workshop. As soon as they walked through the threshold of the smithy, a woman's voice erupted cheerfully. "Yer Holiness! Such a wondrous pleasure ta see you again!" Jane Mallory, weaponsmith, welcomed her into her workshop with a grin.

"*Hey*. You got something cool for me or what?"

As they pulled apart, Jane's eyes were alight with fire. "I most certainly do." She hurried over to the counter, pulled something out from beneath it and held it out to Alric. A smile appeared on his face as he accepted the weapon.

His taukumu, cleaned to a remarkable sheen by Madsen, had something clamped around the tip of its barrel. An axe blade that curved upward to a point resembling a voulge head was fixed on the underside, while a spike jutted out of the upper side of the staff. Both weapons were fixed to a thick ring of steel that was form-fitted to the shaft of the taukumu. Bands of steel, called langets, ran downward from the bases of each side and were bolted to the staff to reinforce its structural integrity.

Madsen peered over his shoulder at the combination weapon. "Sick, you got the bolt placement perfect. Anywhere else and it might've gone into some of the electronics. I'm not sure how the steel's gonna hold up if Alric tries to clock someone after he's fired it a few times, but I guess we'll see. Jane…this is *awesome.*"

"Only the best fer you, Yer Holiness!" she cried cheerfully.

Alric held the taukumu to his shoulder and peered down its length. The spike that adorned the top side had a small gap in it where it met the surface of the taukumu to allow him to aim properly. He also noticed that there was a series of glowing numbers on a rectangular panel close to his eye. "Oh, yeah," started Madsen. "I realised that the ammo counter was busted. It seems fine after I replaced the wiring; let me know how it goes. Basically, it tells you how many shots you've got before you have to reload. Beats finding out the hard way, right?"

Alric's mouth was agape. A weapon that counted? "I doth proclaim this to be quite *sick.*"

Madsen grinned and released a burst of laughter that made Alric smirk. As he swung the weapon and tested its balance, he found it to be much lighter than a pollaxe but not to the point where his ability to use it was compromised. He could swing the axe blade, thrust with its pointed tip, or swing the backend spike; he was no longer helpless at close range while using the taukumu. It would remain to be seen if the staff could survive the impacts, however.

Alric reached into one of his pouches, pulled out a folded letter and handed it to Jane. She unfurled it and rubbed her chin as she read. Madsen leaned over to Alric and whispered, "What was that?"

"A letter of credit from the Order of Saint Thestus. In certain dire circumstances and with the proper approval, the Order itself can pay for the procurement of arms for any of her sworn knights. The general populace is also free to deposit funds at any Thestor preceptory to make travelling safer."

"Okay. So, you're telling me that you work for a bank," Madsen muttered, her face straining. Jane seemed to swallow her shock, perhaps at the sheer amount of money noted on the letter, then proceeded to stuff it into a lockbox.

The pair gave thanks to Jane and her entire staff before leaving, wildly satisfied with the new weapon. Alric slung it over one shoulder with its new leather strap as he said, "We shall go to the chapel now."

"What for? You getting married?" Madsen prodded. He stared at her with a seething frown. "Come on…it was a joke."

"Yes, and as I recall, jokes are typically required to be humorous."

"It was objectively funny. If you can't see that, you've got problems," she said with a snicker.

Alric grumbled. "I am immensely troubled it seems, for I rarely find myself amused by thy buffoonery."

"Maybe if I just keep doing it, you'll start getting it," she threatened.

"Have I not suffered enough at thy hand already?" The quip made Madsen curl her lower lip inward in an effort to stifle a laugh.

Castle Wyrmsmouth had its own chapel in the keep. The primary Cathedral in the city was much too large for their purposes, so the Mended opted for the more private choice. Madsen entered first, allowing Alric to close the doors behind them. Gabriel, Claudia, Joseff, Mears, Thomas, Olivia, and another thirty or so Mended had taken the time out of their day to assemble there. They all wore deep blue surcoats that matched the hue of Madsen's flight suit. She did not seem to make the connection. For one so incredibly intelligent, she seemed oblivious at times. "*Hey,*" she called, surprised and slightly confused. "What's…what's going on?"

Tyonius, who stood draped in shadow, emerged and approached Alric. He was covered in bandages and scars. Miraculously, he had not succumbed to the wounds given to him by Viktoria. Alric bowed. "I understand that this circumstance is highly irregular and I must…thank thee. I only hope that it is approved by the pope."

The archbishop smiled weakly. "Ridiculous. The Order of Saint Thestus itself was founded in a time of great need. If it weren't for both you and Her Holiness, we would all be dead. The work of her Mended is the Lord's work; seeing to those we once thought beyond salvation. The Thestors have become…dangerous, Alric. What was once a band of brothers sworn to poverty has become richer than many kingdoms combined. They were founded to protect pilgrims on the road, but many now hunger to simply draw blood. I hope that *they* shall be different. I trust that you will lead them well."

His remark about bloodthirst among the Thestors filled Alric with great shame. "Nay, Thy Grace. I shall not lead them," he murmured as he looked to the still clueless Madsen.

Alric exchanged his Thestor surcoat for a blue one from Tyonius. They had not yet decided upon a sigil, but the colour of the new order had always been obvious. The Thestor untied his belt, donned the surcoat, then tied it back up over the top.

Madsen turned back and finally, when she saw Alric wearing the surcoat, all colour drained from her face. “A-Al…what…”

Alric knelt before Tyonius, who pressed his palm firmly upon his forehead. “Brother Alric, knight-errant, by the power vested in me by the Lord, I hereby recognise your resignation from the Knights Thestor and relieve you of your oaths. The Four Attestations of Saint Thestus bind you no more.”

The final sentences struck his heart like an arrow. Alric could not imagine being without the vows of poverty, chastity, and vigilance that he had been living by for decades. They gave him guidance…routine. He was afraid that he would be lost without them. His hands shook. Sweat trickled down from his brow. Tyonius continued, “Brother Alric, Angel’s Herald and First Knight of The Mended, rise.”

As he pushed upright, he felt his knees tremble. For whatever reason, tears fought to pour out of his eyes. Despite his greatest efforts, they came streaming out. Tyonius nodded with a puzzled expression on his face, then gestured towards the rest of the attendees. “I dub you The Order of The Mended.” His eyes then swept down to Madsen herself. “Your Holiness, what would you ask of your Order? What Attestations must they provide to prove their devotion to you?”

Madsen’s eyes shimmered. Alric could see the fear in them. She suddenly had a band of men and women so loyal to her that they would all gladly die to protect her. “I-I don’t want this.”

Gabriel said, “We have been inspired by your intellect, kindness, and charity. You have moved us, and we wish to bring your light to those who have gone so long without it.”

The sapien looked to Alric. “You can’t be serious. I-This is crazy.”

“I could not think of a group more worthy to be by thy side. They will learn a great deal from thee. In time…perhaps thou may see fit to trust them with the enlightenment thou hast granted me. I do not believe that many others would responsibly bear that burden, so it must be given out carefully. To the trusted few,” explained Alric. He attempted to be as vague as possible, but it appeared that Madsen saw the subtleties of his message.

Her face straightened and she took a deep breath. “Uh…shit. *Fuck.* Um…” She swallowed, composed herself, then continued, “No

Attestations. You don't need to prove anything, okay?" Everyone stared at her with looks of dumbfounded confusion, especially Tyonius. She spent a few seconds in contemplation, then looked out at her new Mended Order. "Look…just…be nice. Right? Be nice to people. I guess that's the…uh…the most important thing. Also…never stop learning. Learning is cool. I started reading about turtles and I found out that there's this one species that breathes out of its butt. Isn't that crazy? Like…wow." Alric was frozen there in stunned silence.

Olivia slowly raised her hand. "What's a turtle?"

Alric quickly paced ahead and stood in front of Madsen as he held his palms out. "What Her Holiness is *trying* to say…is that knowledge is the fruit of God, and it is our duty as devout servants to consume it in order to bestow its gifts unto our fellow man."

Madsen cleared her throat into her hand. "Y-Yeah. Yeah. What he said."

The entire hall, including Alric, bowed to her. Madsen's shoulders deflated. As the Mended began to file out through the exit with renewed purpose, Madsen looked down at her feet. She seemed conflicted…and Alric knew why. It was the lying. The dishonesty. However, the discomfort was not enough to deter her from acting a fool once again. "So. 'First Knight'. That's kinda like 'First Lady'," she muttered.

"I haven't the slightest idea of what that means."

"You gotta call me Madam President now."

Alric groaned and rubbed his face. The more agitated he became, the more Madsen seemed to relish it. There was a bloodthirsty grin on her face as she crossed her arms expectantly. "Instead of granting thee the satisfaction that would come with pressing further, I shall instead ignore this bizarre exchange." He firmly grabbed her shoulder and said, "I would wish anyone else the best of luck upon the field, but I am certain that thou shalt not need it."

Silence swallowed the chapel as Madsen swallowed and nodded. "Okay…come on, bring it in, you big dummy." With a sharp exhale, Madsen reached forward and embraced him. Alric was petrified. His arms were awkwardly suspended in the air above Madsen's body for some time. Eventually, his posture relaxed and he hesitantly lowered his hands onto Madsen. One came to sit upon her upper shoulder and the other gently ran down the back of her head. For the first time, he felt the texture of her short hair between his fingers. It was soft and slightly prickly towards the neck…but pleasing to the touch, nonetheless. As his fingers traced through it, he heard her release a tender sigh. Alric wished that he hadn't been wearing his armour, so he could actually *feel* her.

The weight of her form leaning against him filled him with anxiety. She had her chin pressed against his pauldron, and her cheek was so close to pressing against his that his heart raced. "There was too much cheese."

"Excuse me?"

"The sandwich you made me had too much cheese in it."

Alric leaned back and scrunched up his face in confusion. "The sandwich…? Eileen, by God, that was *four days* ago."

With a shrug, she said, "I like cheese, but…holy shit, man. A slice is enough. *One* slice."

He sighed and flexed his jaw. "Next time, I shall be certain to ensure that thou receive but a single slice of cheese upon thy sandwich," Alric said mockingly.

He watched as her smile faded slightly. "Y-Yeah…next time," she whispered. The pair of them were enveloped by an uncertain silence.

LIII
Before The Fields Run Black

The windmill loomed like a giant, blanketing her with its chilling shadow. Claudia had been clutching her dress so tightly that her knuckles were going pale. She sat there on her horse, staring absent-mindedly at the familiar farmhouse. There was a loud rattling of armour as her companion dismounted his steed and hitched the animal to a post. Claudia muttered, "Didja really have ta be wearin' that? They're gonna be thinkin' yer a robber knight or somethin'."

"Do not concern thyself with my harness; instead, address thy clear and blatant procrastination," Alric retorted. Claudia forced herself down from her saddle, mumbling profanities to herself. The First Knight watched as she moped over towards him. "Thou art not compelled to proceed."

She growled under her breath and snapped, "Could you just fuck off fer a minute?" The knight went silent. The approach was the most difficult thing she had ever done. Her mind raced. What would she say? What would *they* say? The pain came surging back. For days she had been trapped in her own body, an unwilling silent witness as her family came to terms with her fate. Knowing that she wasn't long for the world was one thing, but being forced to watch her parents and her brothers slowly come to terms with that fact as well had been unbearable.

As if he could sense her thoughts, Alric said, "I would think it best for thee to be hidden while I explain the circumstances. Once I am done, *then* thou shalt reveal thyself. Dost thou concur?"

Claudia reached out and snatched Alric by the wrist, stopping both of them in their tracks. Staring intensely into his sky-blue eyes, Claudia flexed her jaw. "You and me never spent much time together before Wyrmsmouth…but I know what kinda man you are. Why the bloody hell are you doin' this? You playin' me fer a fool or somethin'? What's in it fer you?" The knight looked straight back into Claudia's eyes again and didn't say anything. It only pissed her off more. She exhaled through her nose and snapped, "Are you gonna fuckin' answer me or what?"

Alric took a deep breath, stood up straighter, and looked away. "Nay."

With a scoff, she stomped off towards the farmhouse. As it got larger and larger, Claudia could feel a squirming sensation in the pit of her stomach. Off in the distance, about a hundred yards away, was the windmill. It was plain to see even from that distance that the cunt of a building had finally been fixed. The big hole in the top, the one that she almost died trying to repair, was gone. Then, her eyes leapt to the farmhouse. The golden thatch roof and the wattle and daub walls looked just like any other house…but the mere sight of the bloody thing made her eyes water.

The loud clanking of Alric's gait gradually caught up with her and she watched as he approached the door. He turned to face her and for the first time that Claudia had ever seen, he smiled at her. Her first instinct was that he was taking pleasure in forcing her to confront all of those horrible emotions. She wanted to kick him right in the nuts and trudge off back to her horse…but it became obvious after looking at his face for a while that it was not a joyful smile. It was solemn, but somehow felt reassuring. Claudia waited for him to say something, but he just went back to the door and knocked on it. When it creaked open, Claudia turned away and stared across the green plains.

"God bless thee, Goodwife. My name is Alric. I have come to discuss a matter of utmost urgency." There was a pause for a few moments. Claudia could tell that her mum, Estelle, was giving him her trademark sceptical squint.

"You ain't a robber knight, are ya?"

"...I am not."

"*Right,*" growled Estelle. Claudia had to admit; hearing Alric deal with her mum's shenanigans was maybe worth all the trouble.

Alric cleared his throat. "I bring news of a Godsend. An angel has come down from above and brought with her a great number of miracles. Her touch can heal the sick and stabilise the dying. I come representing The Mended; a new order composed of the willing among those the angel has delivered from death. Of our number, there is one with whom thou wouldst be quite familiar." He then stepped to the side and gestured to Claudia, who was at a loss for what to do. Her gaze fell upon her mum for the first time in almost a month. Estelle's expression went completely blank and her mouth slowly inched open. Claudia could see the tears forming in Estelle's eyes. Claudia sighed as she trudged forward. She opened her mouth, but nothing came out.

"Aren't ya gonna say something?" Estelle sobbed.

"Mum…I-I dunno what ta–"

Estelle barged through Alric. "*'I dunno'?!* Tha first thing you say ta me is *'I dunno'?!*"

Claudia threw her hands up in defeat. "Mum, fer fuck's sake–"

Before she could even begin her tirade, Estelle threw her arms around Claudia and clutched her tight. She started sobbing. "Thank God! Oh, thank God!" Claudia felt her mother's tears pooling on her shoulder. "M-My little girl… I thought I-I'd lost you…" She felt her chest get heavier and her arms lock up. Their relationship had not been a simple one. Estelle had not been a woman who could express affection, and that was a quality that her daughter had inherited. Their fights were innumerable. When Claudia first got injured, she remembered her mother only growing more distant. It hurt. It felt as if she didn't care…but all of a sudden, feeling her embrace made it all clear. The family, the farm, depended on her mother. She couldn't afford to fall apart…so the only option was to avoid what would most definitely break her.

And just like that, Estelle's usual demeanour returned. She pulled back, the tears miraculously absent from her eyes, and started poking at Claudia's legs. "Yer alright? You can feel again? Can you feel this?"

"Mum."

"Yer legs are skinny. What've they been feedin' you?"

"Mum!"

"Come inside! Tha both of you!" Estelle chirped as she hurried back to the front door, propped it open, and waved the two Mended inside. Claudia turned to look at Alric as she sighed heavily.

The ride back was as boring as the ride in. Claudia swayed back and forth on her steed with a scowl on her face. Alric was riding by her side, still munching on one of Estelle's famous pastries. The crunching only reminded her of the unbearable half an hour that they spent in the farmhouse. Estelle asked if she wanted some bread, then some pastries, then some fruit, then some water. She just couldn't help but fuss over Claudia like she was a child; it almost drove her mad. Her eldest brother, Phillip, graced Alric with stories of Claudia's wild childhood. Meanwhile, her younger brothers were constantly poking at Alric's plate armour and playing with his helm. Despite all the times she gritted her teeth and rolled her eyes…she was grateful. For all the annoying things they did, they were still her family.

The pair had been riding for twenty minutes before Claudia mustered the will to say what she wanted to say. "Thank you," she grumbled. Alric cocked his head and simply stared at her, aghast. She pointed harshly at him and hissed, "Don't make me say it again."

After a moment, he took a deep breath in. "I did not respect my family while they still walked this earth. Now, they are all gone, save for Duchess Katheryn. It pained me to think that thou couldst make that same mistake." Claudia wanted to respond to that, but she couldn't quite find the words. Alric didn't seem to mind the silence. The pair of them promptly carved around the base of a hill and returned to the war camp. Over eight thousand soldiers, Tritish, Stieffan, Valthois, and druid alike, were marching to meet their common enemies in the field. The army was in the process of breaking camp when the duo left for the Miller family's farmstead and, quite frankly, Claudia was not impressed with the little progress that she saw in the Mended camp.

As she and Alric dismounted, she hissed, "Fer fuck's sake… What've these cunts been doin' all this time?"

The heart of the camp was formed around a gigantic, hulking, metal beast that the others called a golem. It was a hideous thing covered in pieces of jagged shell that towered over them like a house. People were crowded around the damned thing, just dawdling about and staring. "Oi! Not enough work ta be done? Go on! Get a fuckin' move on!" Claudia shouted, shoving some of the Mended who were staring in awe at the golem. As the crowd fled from her, she could see Madsen sitting in the open belly of the creature. After a few moments, the golem's form wheezed and it began to slowly squat, then flatten itself to the ground, almost like a dog lying down.

When Madsen emerged from the golem's gut, Claudia snorted when she saw that she was wearing a very stupid-looking bright orange garment. The thing was wrinkled, covered in straps and buckles, and had a circular metal collar. She looked like a court jester. "What tha bloody hell are you wearing?"

Madsen climbed down the ladder-like grooves on the side of the golem's leg and dropped onto the grass. Under her arm was a white bulbous helmet with a glossy black visor that curiously didn't have any eye slits. "I know, not exactly fashionable, but it'll help keep me cool and protect me from impacts if the golem gets jostled around. It's called a Launch/Re-Entry Survival System."

Claudia exhaled through her nose. "What tha fuck are you on about? You look like a bloody pumpkin."

Madsen handed the helmet to Alric and his eyes scoured every single tiny detail on the ridiculous looking thing. "This visor…it has no sights."

"Try it on," Madsen urged.

Claudia swallowed. "Look, as fascinating as this all is, we should really get…"

Alric lowered the helmet onto his head and whistled in amazement. "This is truly remarkable. Exactly how sturdy is this material? Surely a compromise had to have been made for such unparalleled visibility."

Madsen knelt, picked up a hammer that'd been left on one of the crates and reeled back for a mighty swing. Claudia beamed in anticipation. The hammer impacted against the front of the helmet with a loud 'snap', causing Alric to stagger backwards. He tore the helmet off and stared at Madsen with this dumbstruck look on his face. Unbelievably, only the tiniest mark was left on the front of the visor. After Madsen licked her thumb and rubbed it, the scuff vanished without a trace. "What in God's name was that?! Perhaps a *warning* would have been appropriate? Thou art a goblin, I tell thee. A goblin!"

"Did you even feel it?"

"...Nay."

"Then shut up."

Claudia crossed her arms. "Do ya wanna keep foolin' about like a pair o' children, or are ya gonna help?"

Alric rubbed his forehead and tossed the helmet at Madsen, who snatched it out of the air with a grin. "Yeah, yeah, we're on it."

After breaking off from Alric and Madsen, Claudia got to clearing one of the operating tents of all the equipment that had been left strewn around. "Good fer nothin' deadbeats…fer fuck's sake…clean up after yerselves…I oughta fuckin' clock 'em one…" The muttered insults kept streaming out of her mouth as she gathered scalpels, bandages, and empty vials, stomped over to their appropriate crates, then stowed them neatly inside. Her companions might've been Mended, but there was clearly no mending stupidity.

On her fourth trip back, she had a random sack of potatoes that some cunt had left in the tent in one hand and a small wooden box of faerie tear vials resting on her other shoulder. As she turned around to head back to the crates, she almost barged headfirst into someone. A short, lean woman with cherry red skin and piercing aqua eyes scowled at her. Duchess Katheryn thinned her lips and said, "Claudia, could I have a moment of thy time?"

With a groan, Claudia weaved around the woman and proceeded to dump the objects into the crates. "Can't ya see I'm in tha middle o' something?" Claudia circled around and scooped up a surgical kit and wooden bucket, but found herself cut off by Katheryn on the way back. Claudia took a deep breath and chewed on the inside of her lower lip. Madsen said to 'be nice to people'. It was an instruction that Claudia was finding very difficult to stick with, but she tried her best. "Move...*please*," she hissed through clenched teeth.

Katheryn dropped a burlap sack at Claudia's feet. The bag slammed into the dirt with a metallic 'thud'.

"I ain't yer fucking servant."

The Duchess rolled her eyes as she pulled the bucket and surgical kit from Claudia with a shocking amount of force. "*Open it.*"

Claudia looked into the cold, narrowed eyes that were glaring back at her. With fiery aggression, she reached over and pulled the sack open like a furious animal. Inside, she saw an assortment of leather, linen, and metal plates. As she stood back up, she cocked her head to the side like a confused dog. "Tha fuck is this?"

Katheryn strolled over to the crates and lazily tossed the two things inside without a care. "Armour..." she answered hesitantly.

"I know it's fucking armour, I ain't a Goddamn dullard! Why tha fuck are ya givin' it ta me?"

Katheryn took a very deep breath in. "Yes, it does seem quite redundant. Her Holiness informed me that any Mended women who wished to fight should be allowed to do so. In the very unlikely case that any *do* have bravery enough to volunteer, this equipment shall be reserved for their use."

Not too long ago, those remarks wouldn't have bothered Claudia in the slightest. It would have been yet another voice speaking the universally accepted truth; that women didn't have the same fire in their hearts as men. That they weren't fighters, but nurturers who would break into tears at the mere sight of blood. All the time Claudia had spent with Madsen, though, had inadvertently given her a new kind of pride...and an irrepressible spite. Not only did Madsen choose Claudia, a woman, above all the other Mended to be her chief physician, she also gave *all* the women under her charge the choice to fight alongside the men. Madsen was clearly not content with being the only exception. It showed Claudia that a woman's lot in life, something that she thought was a fixed constant, was just as flexible as everything else. Things never had to be the way they were.

"'In the very unlikely case'? Tha fuck issat supposed ta mean?" Claudia snapped as she planted her hands onto her hips.

Katheryn tutted. "Is it not painfully obvious?"

"Well, milady, *I'm* gonna volunteer. I ain't alone either. So, seein' as you 'ave no idea what yer talkin' about, why don't you go on back to ya fancy lil' tent and wait 'til tha battle's been won?"

Claudia's insult seemed to finally break Katheryn's relatively subdued demeanour. She took a step forward and tried to loom over the Mended woman like a tree....despite her short stature. "Thou truly art as dim-witted as one would expect. What dost thou know of the last Tritan civil war?"

It was a long time ago. Fifteen years or so? Claudia remembered lots of the men in her village being levied for the armies. Thankfully, her older brother made it back alive. Others weren't so lucky. "What the bloody fuck did they call that one again...? The Maiden's War?" Katheryn's eyelids fluttered wrathfully and her jaw flexed as Claudia continued, "Some greedy bitch wanted more land and shite. Started fightin' fer it."

Katheryn arched an eyebrow and leaned in even closer. She whispered sharply, "That 'greedy bitch' has led her men from the frontlines for two decades."

Claudia narrowed her eyes. When she took a second to look Katheryn over properly, she noticed that the purple gown she wore had mud and bits of grass stuck to its drooping sleeves and hemline. Katheryn didn't have a ring on her finger and Claudia had never seen her with a husband *or* a son. Every powerful lady that she had ever heard of needed to be either married or ruling in the name of a son. *However,* there was one woman who had managed to gain influence without being attached in some way to a man. Claudia had never bothered to learn her name because, in the end, it hadn't changed anything. Women still had as much independence as they always had, which wasn't much at all. The woman who had won a civil war and earned the respect of so many powerful people hadn't done *anything* to better the circumstances of any other woman. She was the 'lady with the courage of a man', 'the will of a man', 'the strength of a man'. The instant that she had done something remarkable, she could no longer be 'just' a woman, because they did not do remarkable things.

As Claudia stood before Katheryn, the one woman who could've made a difference in the last twenty years, she felt anger eating away at her restraint. "You know, me mum thought things'd be different once you came out on top. She said tha laws'll be altered and you'd force 'em ta see us as equals. But nah. Nothin' fuckin' changed fer tha rest of us. You got yer land. You got yer riches. That was all that really mattered, ay?"

Katheryn's expression scrunched up in a mix of outrage and fury. "I should have thee placed in the stocks for that."

"You gonna punish a woman fer speakin' 'er mind? You really are just one o' *them*," Claudia snorted. With that, the Mended woman snatched the burlap sack, slung it over her shoulder and paced off without even another glance at the duchess.

It didn't take much longer for the army to be ready to move. The day dragged on as they marched southward, further and further away from the fortified walls of Wyrmsmouth. Despite the morbid odds they faced, there was still an air of hope amongst the soldiers. Madsen's demeanour was as focused and steely as ever, and it had evidently inspired those around her. Even the druids got something out of her; they prayed at the feet of her golem like it was a holy icon. When night fell, a new camp was made in a sprawling field underneath the gaze of the stars and the Prime Moon. Claudia had joined a gathering of other fighters, mostly her fellow Mended, around a crackling campfire. She rolled her shoulders and shifted uncomfortably in her new armour. Gabriel had practically forced her to try it all on to make sure it fit ahead of the fighting. Otherwise, Claudia wouldn't have bothered to touch the stuff until the time to use it actually came.

There were other men seated around the night-drenched campfire, looking at her and the two other armoured women with expressions ranging from amusement, confusion, and discomfort. Margaret and Olivia had also just finished trying on their armour. Gabriel and Mears had been training the Mended women since they all came together under Madsen at Phaemslake. Fighting the Clthics who tried to kidnap Madsen was Claudia's first taste of battle and after that, she knew that more would be coming her way. She had just about the same amount of training as the peasant levies that were fielded with regular armies, meaning that she felt absolutely unprepared and about to die on the field. However, she was willing to do that for Madsen.

Claudia lumbered over to the campfire and set herself down on a free log. "Dunno how you Thestors do it," she said. "This shite is heavy."

Baldwyn, who was seated next to her *still* in full-plate, chuckled. "With undying and unyielding faith." What she was wearing wasn't even half as heavy as Baldwyn's kit, but she hadn't spent an entire lifetime getting accustomed to the extra weight.

Her eyes narrowed. "Yer sayin' I don't got enough faith?"

"Perhaps. If something is too difficult, then thou clearly do not possess the fibre to see it through," he answered.

The campfire plunged into a paralysing silence. Once upon a time, Claudia would've pounced on any bastard who spoke to her that way. She'd punched out her fair share of teeth in tavern brawls, that was for certain. But there in the glow of the campfire, she laughed to herself. Fuck him. He was less than nothing to her and his words were even less. She knew how fully she believed; why the fuck would she need to prove it to anyone? "Righto," she answered with a shrug.

The silence returned as the group of soldiers let the dark reality wash over them. Some would not return. It would be the last time she saw a few of them. Maybe even all of them, if *she* was going to be among the dead. The realisation caused a sharp chill to travel its way up Claudia's legs and into her spine.

Footfalls in the grass made Claudia look up. She saw a woman leading a group of men through the camp. Lady Fiona had come with the army to assist in managing the camp and coordinating the common folk. She wasn't going to fight in the battle seeing as she wasn't trained for it, but Claudia thought it noble of her to lend her efforts to the menial tasks. No one was celebrated for doing those, yet she chose to anyhow.

Fiona approached the campfire with the men behind her. "Good evening, my friends. I bring some new recruits. Defectors."

The word caused all of the soldiers to perk up, Baldwyn especially. Claudia was expecting to see those foul K'relvic Nuns and Tethspeakers marching around in nothing but bloodied muscle with their demonic pendants and masks. But what she saw was rather normal. Regular footmen, men-at-arms, and archers. One of the archers stepped forward. He was a very broad fellow. Quite handsome. "I'm John Stanton. We lot used ta be sworn ta Lord Franco di Lombardi. When he went and decided to throw in with the demonists…we couldn't follow him any longer. Barely got out in one piece. Half of us didn't make it."

Baldwyn promptly answered, "Worry not, for the fallen shall be avenged. It pleases me that thou hast retaken the blessed path; we welcome thee with open arms."

Stanton blinked rapidly and bowed. "Thank you, Brother. Your words are a blessing."

Fiona bowed her head. "I shall grant thee time to become acquainted. Please send for me if there is anything that thou art in need of." She elegantly strode off into the night.

Most of Stanton's men filed off to pitch their tents, but Stanton himself remained at the campfire. "I heard that you lot," he pointed at the Mended, "are led by Brother Alric. That true?"

Claudia said, "Madsen leads us. Brother Alric is our First Knight, 'er second-in-command."

He seemed surprised to hear Claudia's voice, as if he didn't realise there were women present. Stanton, with a cough, replied, "I met him a few months ago, ya know. Tha Clthic Synod had taken Chesterton and were raisin' revenants in tha old catacombs. Alric and couple other men went in…only him and Bill came out. I thought we were gonna leave all that shit behind us…then there was this…this vampiress. She was wicked, I tell you. An unholy succubus. She recruited our liege…and that's how we came ta serve the Synod."

"It's dead now, innit?" Claudia interjected, glancing around at her friends. Stanton became frozen in place. "Tha vampire?"

"Yeah. Cunt's dead as a doornail," added Mears. "Just ask *him*. He wrestled tha bloody thing himself." He gestured to Baldwyn, who was playing with a leaf that he picked from the field.

Baldwyn nodded. "Not myself. Duchess Katheryn had it skewered upon the shaft of a spear. The wretched abomination then had its head blown to smithereens by Brother Alric's magic. It was so desperate to salvage its beauty that Her Holiness had time enough to tear its heart out. Pathetic," he said calmly.

Stanton held his hands up. "Hold on a second. *Hold on*." A tense moment of silence followed. "Whaddaya fuckin' mean he's got *magic*?"

LIV
THE BATTLE OF WYRMSMOUTH- PART I

Franco di Lombardi's infantry wing was pacing forward behind a cluster of Clthic Witches and he found himself cursing the Devil for it. Warren Smythe jerked his head forward and muttered, "I don't wanna be tha one ta complain…but as soon as the swords start swingin', they're all gonna get torn ta ribbons." A mob of flayed men and women wearing skulls for masks was a distraction, and as Smythe pointed out, their lack of armour meant that they were going to fall like dominoes once the close quarters fighting started. However, the first line of each witch detachment was composed of Protozealots; invincible skeletal warriors who would act as the vanguard and take the brunt of the attack. Ahead of the witches' formation was one of their demented golems. The thing was folded over, almost like a man clutching his knees and curling himself up into a ball. The difference was that the golem had these strange lengths of slithering bone on its feet that allowed it to slowly creep forward, even in that hunched position. The other two were spread further out across the plain, closely followed by formations much like the one led by Franco.

Bugface Bill spat onto the grass. "That's why *we're* here, ya genius. Didn't ya listen to tha plan?"

Smythe growled, "All I'm sayin' is, would it hurt to put some gambeson or mail on 'em?"

"You know what they keep tellin' us," murmured Liam Dubois. He raised his hands and sung in a mocking tone, "They're just tools o' tha Devil and they don't need ta cover themselves, tha same way a wagon don't need ta."

"Pretty sure wagons don't need no stupid fuckin' animal masks neither," quipped Smythe. The others in the immediate area sputtered off with cackles and snorts. They were walking in formation, packed as tightly together as they could get. The plan was for the infantry to escort the golems on the approach until they reached the walls of Castle Wyrmsmouth. Then, they could tear them down brick by brick and the footmen could storm the city. The enemy would be preparing for a siege and would be shocked to death when the golems pushed through the stone as if it were sand.

Franco was dressed in his full battlefield plate, heat-treated to a cobalt sheen. Each and every armoured man on the Clthic force had their armour lathered with unzym to protect against incoming taukumu bolts.

As if prompted by Franco's thoughts, a white-hot line of light sliced through the air above the soldiers. Franco jolted and ducked reflexively, as did most of the men around him. A few more darts of energy followed, until the K'relvic Nuns fell back closer to their formation. Several of the Tethspeakers at the front raised lantern-shaped objects that thrummed with bright blue light. Walls of arcane energy manifested in front of them, overlapping and creating a barrier to protect the infantry. More bolts followed, but they harmlessly sizzled against the surface of the magical shield. The golem, yards ahead of them, seemed to be as affected by said attacks as the barriers themselves.

The enemy had sallied out from Wyrmsmouth…and quite far from it too. It was a good thing that Marshal Franco issued orders for the army to march fully armed and in battle formation, otherwise they would've been taken completely by surprise. Franco roared, "Casualties?!" Murmurs of men repeating the question washed through the men of his retinue, but none answered his call. "There shan't be any dying before we reach their lines! Understood!?"

A defiant roar filled the air as the footmen cried out. Onward they marched, bunched closer to the K'relvic Nuns. Franco's upper lip curled inward as he watched the taukumu bolts ricochet off the arcane shield conjured by the Tethspeakers. The enemies had unleashed a volley despite clearly being out of range; that was why none of the men in Franco's regiment were killed. Otherwise, the Nuns also would have returned the favour instead of deploying the shield. Perhaps the druids were not as proficient as the Nuns were in the use of arcane staves?

The mass of bodies trailing behind the golems approached the foot of a hill several hundred feet ahead. Franco could barely make out specks of people at the top of said ridge; the druids who so thuggishly attacked too soon. They kept slinging their spells…a course of action that struck Franco as extremely odd. The attacks were clearly ineffective, yet they did not stop to conserve the blood that powered their staves. Dense forests on the sides of the valley funnelled the Clthic men towards the hill. However, the taukumu bolts suddenly stopped. The tiny druids peeled back, vanishing behind the curvature of the ridge.

"I don't like tha look o' that…" Smythe murmured.

The line of roughly four-thousand Tritan archers stood in silence as they watched the druids standing before them unleash a torrent of arcane fire down the side of the hill. Most of the bowmen, including John Stanton, had two dozen or so arrows stuck into the dirt by their side for easy access once the shooting was to begin. Stanton had another two sheafs of arrows slipped in his belt. The fingers on his right hand had a habit of feverishly wiggling back and forth in the moments preceding a battle. It was as if they were so desperate to start that they couldn't quite contain themselves. The flashes of light and explosive pops that filled the valley from the druid's magical staves were frightening at first, but the minutes of continued discharge had allowed Stanton to grow accustomed to the strange sensations. His attention was upon one person in particular among the mass of druids; one who did not seem to belong. It was a knight in freshly polished plate armour with a vibrant blue surcoat laid atop it. The visor of his hounskull bascinet was open as he peered down the length of his bladed staff and sent bolts of light down at the advancing Clthics. Word had reached Stanton about a man chosen by God to wield magic in His name. A man who had brought an angel to the people in their time of need. Brother Alric. Suddenly, the arcane volley stopped. The druids turned and cycled back through the archers' lines, giving them the clearance they required to let loose upon the approaching enemy. Stanton watched Alric pass him by and slink back to a group of men who wore matching surcoats formed up alongside the heavy infantry.

A thuggish tap on Stanton's shoulder snatched his attention from the First Knight. "Oi. You right?" asked Matthew Jackson.

Stanton chuckled as he peered down the hill. The Clthics were slowly continuing ahead behind their three golems. The wall of shimmering cobalt magic that shielded them from the arcane fire was still pointed towards the archers. "O' course I'm right. *You* right?"

"Well, seein' as there's a buncha terrifyin' fuckin' abominations creepin' our way…can't say that I am, mate. Can't say that I am."

“Madsen’s watchin’ over us. And if *she’s* with us, that means God is too,” Stanton said as he snatched an arrow out of the dirt. “Have faith and all will be well.”

Jackson fiddled with the chin strap of his kettle hat then huffed anxiously. He kept silent after that. Before long, a murmur came down the line and it eventually swelled to a loud cry. “Loose, ya fuckin’ mongrels!”

“Loose!” Stanton yelled as loud as he could to send the order further down their line. He nocked his arrow, teetered his upper body forward, and drew the bowstring. He took a deep breath as he thought about Franco. He was most certainly down there among the Clthic infantry. He was a good man. *Was*. Stanton prayed for his soul.

The muscles in his shoulders, back, and upper arms tensed as they pulled one hundred and sixty pounds of draw weight. He trained the bow on the mass of Clthic bodies so his arrow would fly straight into their lines. As Stanton released his arrow, he heard the snapping of hundreds of bowstrings, none of which sounded at the exact same moment. Before their first shots even met the Clthics, another arrow was already clutched in Stanton’s fingers and nocked. He flung it forth as he did the first. The archer did not concern himself with anything other than sending projectiles into the swarm of bodies that was steadily approaching, not necessarily ‘aiming’ for anyone in particular but rather the mass of the Clthic army itself. In a single minute, Stanton had shot fourteen arrows. If each archer in the Churchsworn army performed in a similar manner, potentially over fifty-thousand arrows could have speared into the Clthic formation in the span of sixty seconds.

Franco was jolted to attention by a sudden chorus of slurps, bangs, and cracks. He watched as arrows corkscrewed through the air, bypassed the magical barrier as if they were drops of water through a sieve, and made contact with the witches. Due to the elevated position of the archers, most of their arrows flew over the Protozealots and skewered the first line of Nuns and Tethspeakers with thirty-inch-long arrows. They grunted and growled, but none screamed. The very few Zealots who were struck could not have been less bothered; the arrows either burst into shrapnel upon contact or were deflected by the curved nature of the Zealots’ bones. If nothing was done soon, all of the witches would be made into pincushions before they had a chance to cast spells. Franco cried as loud as he could, "Footmen, forward!"

The bombardment continued, forcing Franco to pull his visor down. He watched as the defenceless witches had their uncovered bodies stuck with dozens of arrows. One by one, each panel of the magical barrier evaporated as the Tethspeakers maintaining them were slaughtered by the unyielding longbow barrage. Franco's head was struck many a time, as were his shoulders, but the steel held and did its job. He gritted his teeth as he and his men seeped past the witches in order to absorb the arrows. The detachments essentially exchanged places, with the infantry being directly behind the Protozealots. Unfortunately for Franco and his men, it was then that the taukumu fire resumed. Bolts of otherworldly power streamed down from the hill in a much more concentrated manner than before. Franco watched several of his men-at-arms erupt into fire for a split second, then cool to a dull black after the unzym had saved their lives from the magical explosion. Those who were struck twice, however, detonated into clouds of blood, bone, and shredded organs that rained down from the sky like wretched hail. The gore and fluid passed through the sights and breaths of Franco's helmet, temporarily blurring his vision and pressing foul, bitter tastes onto his tongue. The golem in front of his regiment ground to a halt. However, before it could unfurl itself, a horrifying crack of thunder shook the entire plain and sent Franco's stomach sloshing about within his body. A jet of pure white soared over the golem's head, missing by mere inches. It was much too large to have been projected by a taukumu. Fear and shock had infected his men as they reeled back in lieu of the eldritch beam. Franco tried to look to where it came from, but the shoulders and heads of his comrades prevented him from seeing much of anything. "Stand fast!" snapped Franco.

Another thick band of energy coursed over their heads, that time impacting the top of a tree on the side of the valley. The thing exploded into millions of splinters and became a smouldering black stump that trailed smoke high into the air. The golem's legs sighed as they clicked and uncurled. When the creature stood at its full height, it peered up at the crest of the hill and its two arms began to hum with dark magic. However, before it could unleash its arcane fire, a resounding impact following a third bout of thunder sent the beast lurching to one side with smoke and arcs of lightning curling over its carapace.

The other two golems stretched and emerged from their fetal states…and stomped over towards where the mysterious gigantic beams of energy emanated from. Franco roared at the top of his lungs, but there was no way for them to hear. If the golems just converged spells upon the archers and druids, they would've easily swept them all away, but the idiotic witches bound to the golems had played into the Churchsworns' hands. Their plan was clearly to divide and conquer.

As the golems scuttled toward the right flank in search of their attacker, Franco growled and endured the onslaught of arrows. It felt as if he was being punched steadily and consistently. After four long minutes, with at least two-hundred thousand arrows sent into the Clthics, the ranged attacks trickled to a halt. They had run out of arrows. What remained of Franco's regiment was exhausted and battered. Most of the Nuns and Tethspeakers had been turned into porcupine-like corpses strewn about the lush green field. Those that remained standing had at least one arrow jutting out of their bodies. Upon the hill, Franco spotted movement. The archers were advancing down the hill, brandishing hammers and axes. Among their number were the white coated Thestors, the black coated Correnti, and a small number of blue coated soldiers. They steadily paced down, untouched by battle thus far.

Franco brought his pollaxe to arms and shouted, "Tighten thy lines! Our time has come! Down with the Church!" The Churchsworn got closer and closer. Soon enough, Franco could see the faces of his enemy whether they were archers with kettle hats, footmen with open-faced helmets, or men-at-arms with their visors raised. Each of their eyes burned with unyielding conviction; the drive that could only be incited when a man believed so wholly in his cause in a moment when he could not afford to do much else. At that instant, Franco feared for his men. *They* were not so devoted to the Clthic cause. They were not ready to die for it.

Among the Churchsworn lines were druids who discharged their staves at the Protozealots. Jets of light emitted from taukumu and the invisible projectiles sent by pakama buffeted the immortal warriors. Some of them teetered forward and tumbled face first into the grass, while others endured the arcane assault and continued forward. A handful of Franco's men snatched spells that were meant for the Zealots, either detonating into black mist, or falling to the ground as they screamed in pain. Almost gently, the two frontlines collided with calculated might, flooding the air with shouts, grunts, and the clanging of steel.

Franco's regiment was absorbed into a churning tide of armoured bodies. The lord thrusted his pollaxe over the shoulders of his comrades, uncertain if the impacts that resonated through the weapon's shaft were against the bodies of enemies or his own men. After half an hour of scrimmaging, Franco could barely breathe. The Churchsworn's display of spells and arrows had him fearing for his life. He had overexerted himself in desperation, as did some of the footmen by his side.

While Franco focused on the battle in front of him, Warren Smythe held his shield up against the breaking tide of Thestors. Hammer impacts and axe chops tore at the wooden boards of his shield. All it took was one man's lapse in judgement. Smythe glanced to his side and watched as a footman spun on his heels and fled. In the chaotic midst of battle, Smythe erroneously read it as an effort by his line to fall back. He took several steps back, exposing the flanks of his formation. The footmen around him followed and before long, the whole wing of the formation incorrectly believed that the army was falling back. That was all that it took. The heavily armoured Knights Thestor were able to seep into the cracks of the uneven line and overwhelm the footmen's uncovered sides with their pollaxes and warhammers. No longer massed as a coherent unit, they stood no chance. Attacks came from all sides. The Churchsworn pierced the Clthic line and were able to swarm Franco's left flank, where one Correntis swung a mace aimed directly at the man's temple. He did not see the blow coming, nor did he realise that the Clthic formation was at all compromised.

Franco's helmet rang like a gong, and his vision became a streaky blur as his ears were bombarded with a throbbing howl. Pain lanced up his neck. His control over his own body lapsed for a split second and he felt his legs slip out from beneath him. The dirt smacked into his back and the light dimmed as silhouettes rushed back and forth around him, drowning out the sun. Franco desperately tried to scramble to his feet, but his arms, head, and legs were constantly buffeted by the impacts of sprinting soldiers. He felt people stomping on his prone body and kneeing him in the head as they stampeded. A massive weight suddenly dropped onto his torso, expelling the little air that was still in his lungs with a hoarse wheeze. His eyes widened at the bloody corpse that stared lifelessly up at the dwindling sunlight. With frantic breaths, Franco pushed fruitlessly against the fully armoured deadweight.

He tried to scream and claw his way out, but before long, more bodies collapsed on top of him. He could barely even move. In terrified desperation, Franco di Lombardi flailed helplessly against the pile of corpses that pinned him down. In those moments, he could think of nothing but how much he did not want to die.

LV
The Battle of Wyrmsmouth-Part II

Every step the Raider took shook her back and forth. Madsen's hands grasped the two control handles extending from the dashboard and kept her pursuers in the centre of her line of sight as she backed up deeper into the forest. The panoramic screen displayed a maze of trees in between her machine and the three Clthic ones as they scampered after her like massive steel animals. Since they were controlled with a direct neural link by the proxies piloting them, they moved with grotesque and organic movements; nothing like the calculated stride that the pathfinding and stabilisation software had given Madsen's unit. Each of the hostile Raiders had wooden spikes fixed to their backs, some with proxy corpses impaled on them. The bodies flopped around limply as the Raiders rampaged towards her. She had her right index finger hovering over the trigger on the right control handle. Her face, covered by her L/RESS helmet, was fixed in a slate-blank expression.

Suddenly, there was a flash of light from beyond the foliage. Madsen instantly squeezed one of the auxiliary keys on the side of her left control handle. An odd thrumming sensation and a series of dull thuds followed. The display was churned up with static, but she made out the dancing cobalt field of charged particles shimmering above the surface of her Raider's hull. More impacts followed, filling Madsen's ears with a low otherworldly warbling as the particle blanket absorbed the kinetic impacts that would've easily punched through the Raider's armour plating.

A very rudimentary info box that she sketchily coded into the operating system sat on the bottom left corner of the display. It gave her readings on the particle blanket's power output and current field integrity. The integrity metre chipped away with every strike that washed across her Raider. As soon as the firing stopped, Madsen released the auxiliary control and steadily nudged the right thumbstick. After the particle blanket dissipated, her Raider's torso rotated and the targeting reticle zeroed in on the hostile machine. She pulled the trigger on the right control handle.

Instead of an explosive 'bang', there was a loud 'crack' that reverberated through the Raider's frame as well as Madsen's bones. The M32 Magnetic Accelerator Cannon mounted on the right armature used a barrel lined with electromagnetic coils to propel its heavy tungsten rounds. The only sound it made was the sonic boom of the projectile breaking the sound barrier.

For a split second, Madsen could see the projectile zip through the air, then slam right into the hostile Raider's left bicep. Fragments of metal spun off into the air, joined by droplets of golden hydraulic fluid. The engineer gritted her teeth, gently tapped the right thumbstick to the left, then pulled the trigger again. The final shot impacted directly in its centre of mass, right where Madsen's previous shots had torn away at the hull plating. The already heavily dented armour folded inward, and a geyser of disgusting yellow fluid poured out of the cockpit. The Raider suddenly went limp and ragdolled backwards. Every tree in the area shook and sent leaves fluttering to the ground.

Before she had a chance to react, a storm of high-pitched pings tore into her ears. There came a metallic 'snap', followed by a systems failure alarm just before Madsen was able to activate the particle blanket again. The computer said, in a neutral tone, "Right Armament M32 Magnetic Accelerator Cannon critical failure: belt feed system disconnected or damaged. Immediate action required."

A small panel on Madsen's left displayed a diagram of the Raider's subsystems; the M32 Cannon blinked red. One of the hostiles must've opened fire with their Javelin 9; not exactly the weapon they should be using on a heavily armoured target like Madsen's Raider, but it clearly did something. It must've snagged the belt system that fed ammo into Madsen's M32.

Madsen exhaled as she frantically spun her Raider around with the right thumbstick and strafed it with the left thumbstick. Trees whizzed by and were shredded into dust by the storm of Javelin rounds. Despite the improvised cover, shots were still making contact with the particle blanket and quickly draining its integrity. There was a shrill pop when the energy field shattered and an alarm began blaring in the cockpit. Madsen bit into the inside of her mouth, but the adrenaline streaming through her meant that she didn't even feel it. There was only one play left for her to make: all or nothing.

Madsen pressed and held the disengage armament key on her right control handle. A series of clacks and wheezes followed closely by a loud 'thud' told her that the useless M32 had been disconnected and fell onto the ground. She jerked the left thumbstick harshly forward and found herself lurching violently into the side of the cockpit. Madsen's Raider charged toward its attacker while its compatriot trained its weapons on her.

The ear-piercing cacophony of a metal-on-metal impact combined with an intense jolt lanced through the Raider and whipped Madsen's neck forward. Another alarm sounded as the lower left leg of her Raider blinked yellow on the subsystems overview. Madsen kept the left thumbstick pressed straight forward. Just before she reached the hostile, Madsen held down the free arm control key on the right handle. In free arm control mode, she was able to manipulate the entire handle up, down, left, and right to directly control her Raider's free hand VR style. There was a crack of thunder as the two enormous bipedal vehicles collided with each other.

Madsen stretched her right hand outward, causing her Raider to bring its forearm up against the barrel of the hostile machine's weapon. She pushed the barrel as far off line as she could, then sidestepped with the left thumbstick just as she saw the other Raider bring its M32 up. Madsen's Raider pivoted and forced the one she grappled directly into the firing line.

The thunderclap filled the space and echoed through the valley. On her display, she saw that the projectile had gone straight through the hostile Raider, entering via the back and creating an exit breach on the front hull plate. Madsen engaged the free arm control on her left handle, jammed the barrel of her Javelin 9 into the breach, and squeezed the trigger.

The entire Raider convulsed as the recoil of fully automatic fire surged through its structural frame. Sparks, E-Gel, and shards of metal shot forth from the gaping hole as the Raider tumbled to the side, completely motionless. Madsen glanced down at her particle blanket metre and saw that it had recharged enough for her to use it again. With the final Raider in her sights, she propelled her machine into a sprint while activating the particle blanket.

The impact of a magnetic accelerator round against the particle blanket was a whole lot crazier than the staccato beats of machine gun fire. The Raider rumbled and its reactor whirred even louder as it supplied more power to the blanket emitters. The M32 had a slower semi-automatic rate of fire, but each round bit off 25% of the particle blanket's integrity. Somehow, like some kind of miracle, the blanket failed just as Madsen reached the hostile machine.

Madsen jammed the three-pronged claw of her Raider's right hand into the seam of the cockpit hatch. The left arm, still with the Javelin 9 attached to it, pinned the Clthic Raider's weapon to the base of a tree. Madsen pushed the hardware to the limit and heard the flexing of hydraulic pistons, the sighing of artificial musculature, and the straining of the Raider's inner-frame. The haptic feedback made it feel like Madsen was encountering resistance when she pushed on the control handle.

Eventually, the cockpit hinge screeched and snapped open, spewing out litres and litres of gold fluid. There, hanging by an array of cables, datalines, and wires, was a proxy. Its face was shaved clean of all of its artificial musculature and all the cables trailed into its jawless mouth. Its limbs were missing and instead, bundles of datalines were funnelling into where they should've been. Madsen felt her heart thrumming faster and faster in her chest as she reached out with the Raider's arm. She closed its claws on the proxy. Its bones snapped and its flesh flattened under the insane pressure that the Raider's gripper was capable of exerting.

As Madsen pulled the proxy out, the cables feeding into its mouth either snapped or were painfully pulled out of its throat. The human panted as her adrenaline-widened eyes were fixed on the mutilated replica in front of her. The strange sensation of looking at someone who just seconds ago was trying to kill her and having them completely helpless seemed to make Madsen's heart go a mile a minute. The proxy gagged and howled, completely blind and deaf after being detached from the Raider. Madsen squeezed the trigger on the control handle, causing the Raider's claws to snap fully shut. The proxy popped and the Raider's right arm was splattered by fragmented components and E-Gel. Madsen's chest tightened and her skin was overcome with a tingling sensation. A rickety breath escaped her lips as she stared at the paste that remained of the proxy.

Prince Roger fought alongside the Tritish archers in the melee. He was armed in polished plate armour covered by a jupon that beheld the image of a silver horse over a field that was half red and half blue. His bascinet was fitted with a golden crown, and its visor was clamped shut. Alric only managed a passing glance at the soon-to-be-king, seeing his gleaming form swing a mace at the Clthic footmen as his men-at-arms and knights clustered around him. Roger's presence invigorated the archers as well, who swung axe, mace, hammer, or mallet at their foes with great courage. Seeing his allies so fervently inspired sparked the same bravery in Alric, despite the fact that he did not fight for what they did.

With his new weapon in his hands, a cross between a taukumu and a pollaxe, the freshly dubbed First Knight of the Mended endured the pain of incoming blows and returned them in kind. He was flanked by both men and women of the new Mended Order; Gabriel and Claudia in particular were pushed up against his shoulders. Gabriel, clad in full plate, lashed out with his own pollaxe, swiping with its axehead as well as prodding with its spearhead. Claudia was wearing a gambeson, brigandine, jack chains, and a kettle hat. She had taken to her small amount of training well; she kept her shield in front of her as she throttled the Clthics with a spear.

Despite the complete collapse of the left wing of the Clthic infantry, the Churchsworn were unable to overcome the rest of their formation. With Alric and the druids out of hearts to power their staves and Madsen preoccupied with the Clthic golems, the main body of the battle was not advancing. Since the Churchsworn managed to ambush the Clthics in the middle of transit, the small number of archers in their number were recently able to fall back to string their bows and let loose upon Alric and his companions. Amidst the arrow storm, it was clear that it all hinged on the final piece of the Churchsworn army.

The battle was a swirling mess of shouting, clanging, and grunting. Alric, half-blind thanks to his helmet's visor, was swept away in the tide of battle. Flashes of shimmering steel and the vivid colours of heraldry flickered by as he jabbed and slashed with his taukumu. The periodic impact of incoming arrows seemed to sap the turmoil from Alric's heart, for once again he was where he belonged. Again and again he struck the demonists, as the pressure of Gabriel and Claudia's shoulders against his sides lit a fire within his heart.

Alric could see over the heads of the Clthic army due to the decline that they fought upon. In the distance toward the right, he saw a block of colours rumbling through the plains. Before he knew it, the cavalry charge had closed the distance and rammed head on into the side of the Clthic formation. A rainbow of surcoats, jupons, tabards, and banners rushed through the blocks of heretic infantry, as the snaps of lances filled the air. For a split second, Alric saw his sister at the very front of the charge. More accurately, he saw the green and white heraldry on her tabard. And before he could blink, she and the rest of the knights had pushed through the other side of the formation. His brothers and sisters in arms roared as they pushed against the enemy's front line. The midsection of their formation was in absolute disarray thanks to the cavalry charge. It was then up to the men-at-arms and footmen to break the front line apart and bring about a rout. It took no longer than several minutes. Alric could smell the fear in the air as the Clthic infantry and men-at-arms dissolved and spun on their heels. "Forward!" screamed Prince Roger. "No quarter!"

The Churchsworn army dispersed slightly, no longer maintaining strict formation in order to run down their fleeing foes. Voices erupted from the Mended, shouting, "For Madsen!" and "In the name of the angel!"

Dozens of terrified footmen fell to Alric's taukumu blade as he struck them in the back of the legs, then jammed the tip of the axe blade into their throats. However, there came an eerie thrumming that caused him to freeze in his tracks. Alric turned his gaze to the sky. A shape shimmered there above the field, slowly growing larger and larger with each passing second. "D-Dragon…!" he gasped far too quietly. He regained his composure and yelled as loud as he could, "Dragon!"

Those nearby became petrified as they noticed the subject of Alric's terror. The dragon hovered towards the Churchsworn cavalry…and a jet of fire poured out from its snout. The red blaze washed across the bright green field, sending balls of black smoke into the air. As far away as he was, Alric could still hear the horrific screams of horses and men alike burning alive in the inferno.

Just as Alric took a step forward, a heavy impact shook his skull. There came the cracking of wood. His neck whipped backward and he stumbled. Darkness enveloped one side of his vision. He felt…pressure on his eye socket. His skin was bunched up and creased in a peculiar way. Then came the swelling pain. Alric reached up towards his face with his left hand, which knocked into something. As soon as it made contact with the object, sharp, unbearable pain lanced through his face. His gauntleted fingers brushed against what felt like feathers…then a long length of wood with thick splinters jutting off its sides. The knight suddenly felt his body give way beneath him. Alric fell to the ground and was swallowed by darkness.

Madsen pushed the Raider's walk cycle as hard as she could. She might not've known which model that VTOL craft was, but she could recognise the sound of its engines a mile away, even through her Raider's speakers.

The metal giant came crashing through the treeline and back into the field. "F-Fuck…!"

The whole fucking field was on fire. Silhouettes of flaming people and horses in the distance made her hands tremble. The screeching. It was unbearable. Madsen angled the right thumbstick forward and her Raider tilted its camera and weapons arrays upward slightly. There it was…the VTOL craft. Madsen armed her Javelin 9 and squeezed the trigger. The rounds ripped through the sky, but arced way behind the speeding aircraft. Furrowing her brow, Madsen consulted the readings on her display. The targeting suite informed her that the vehicle was circling with a speed 1025 kilometres per hour and was over a kilometre away and rising. As the physics ticked by in her head, Madsen nudged her right thumb stick, locked her targeting reticle a decent way ahead of the VTOL craft, then pulled the trigger for one swift burst.

She saw a cough of fire as the plane shuddered…then twirled on a dime and set its sights on her. The proxy in control of the vehicle knew that the craft was going down. They were gonna try to take Madsen down with them.

The engineer gritted her teeth and pulled the trigger, sending a stream of fire out at the approaching craft. She watched as the hull bent and creased…but she needed to hold out. It was a hundred metres away. Then sixty. Then thirty. A puff of blue fire consumed its left wing just before it started tumbling out of control. Madsen lurched her left thumbstick to the right and pushed down on her right foot pedal. The Raider bent its knees then pushed them outward, diving fifteen metres away from the oncoming vehicle. It landed on its side, throwing Madsen's body into the instrument panel. She screamed as the machine rolled three times before finally coming to a halt.

Her panting was only just louder than the array of alarms and warnings that flooded her ears. The subsystems panel was completely red. The Raider must've gotten clipped by the craft as it came down…

Madsen unbuckled her safety harness and threw the emergency hatch release handle. The bright white sunlight that poured in made her squint and throw an arm up in front of her face. Raw sounds of hoof falls, screaming, and orders being barked filtered in from outside. She grabbed the edges of the hatch and pulled herself out. There was a kilometre-long rainbow of corpses with bright heraldry over their armour. Madsen's gut was telling her that it was wrong. It shouldn't have been that bright…war was dark and grimy, wasn't it? The dissonance filled her with dread.

Eventually, her attention went to the massive trench that was created by the VTOL craft. There it was, about twenty metres away in a crumpled and smoking mess. Madsen leapt from her Raider and sprinted for the downed aircraft. It was nestled in a crater like a sleeping bird and its hull was pocked with hundreds of tiny leaking holes. The shatter-proof canopy was cracked but still intact. Madsen pried open an access panel on the side of the vehicle and pulled on the emergency release. A long beep sounded, before the canopy's explosive bolts detonated. It was blown violently into the grass, allowing Madsen access to the cockpit.

Before she even got inside, what she saw made her freeze. Seated in the pilot's seat was a humanoid figure, slumped to one side. Its body was covered by a SysGov Intersystem Armed Forces pressure suit, but its face was uncovered. The empty sockets of a grossly decomposed face stared back at her. There were claw marks and scratches on the interior of the cockpit. With every second that trickled by, Madsen swore that the corpse deteriorated more and more. Like it had been sealed in the cockpit for a really long time.

She glanced down at the flight console.

LAUNCH DATE: 24/03/3064
CURRENT DATE: 30/05/7187
MISSION CLOCK: 4,123 YEARS, 2 MONTHS, 6 DAYS, 23 HOURS
AUTONOMOUS OPERATION ENABLED
WARNING: SEVERE DAMAGE DETECTED

Her breathing went shallow.

It was the 15th of April 3064 when RMC202 arrived at Nyumbani. According to the VTOL's mission clock...she'd been in that freezer for over 4,000 years. That was ludicrous. EPS units weren't designed to prolong stasis for that long. It was impossible.

Things had snowballed so quickly after she was thawed out...she hadn't had a chance to think about everything. So she thought about it. Hard. The planet was supposed to be a Stage Four habitat, meaning that it should've been decently populated in certain areas. There were no major surface cities, no signs of satellite communications, the literal topography was altered, and every human structure she'd seen was buried under tonnes and tonnes of dirt and rock. Terraforming wasn't an overnight process. Also...the proxies had history. It wasn't just programmed into them, was it? It was all real. It all progressed in real-time. Mentally speaking, they were perfect copies.

They were such immaculate mental replicas of human beings that their civilizations evolved the exact same way as the original human ones did. It looked like the Middle Ages…because it was *their* Middle Ages. All of that time. All of that time had *actually* passed…

Her mom was dead. All of her friends were dead. Her crew's families were dead. In all that time…no one came looking for her. No one. The tears streamed down her face and her hands were overcome with uncontrollable shaking. "O-Oh god."

Madsen stumbled off the aircraft and started hyperventilating. There were hundreds of things she'd been prepared for with her ISEC training. Not that. She lowered herself on the folded wing of the aircraft, pulled her helmet off, and forced her eyes shut as she tried to control her breathing. It didn't take long for others to show up at the crash site. Dozens of archers, soldiers, and Thestors surrounded her. They knelt and bowed to her. The tears welling in her eyes flowed out in silence. Her eyelids fluttered and her lip quivered. "S-She slayed the dragon!"

"By the grace of God…!"

"Praise be! Praise be to Madsen!" cried one of the Thestors. A chorus of cheers rang out over the piles and piles of corpses.

LVI
Clean-Up On Aisle 9

What was left of the Clthics turned tail and ran when they saw the VTOL craft crash and burn. Madsen made it back to her totaled Raider to grab her duffel bag full of tools then headed for the improvised field infirmary that the Correnti and Mended had set up. The pained crying, pleading, and screaming that filled the big tent caused her to pause for a second when she entered. She saw proxies missing limbs, with their bodies sliced open and leaking E-Gel, or stuck with arrows. She had to find something to keep her mind occupied. She had to. Otherwise…

"Where wouldst thou wish to start?" Gabriel asked breathlessly. His armour was covered in dents and scratches. Some holes had been punched into his pauldrons and vambraces, but they didn't seem to have reached the body underneath. Three figures pushed into the tent via the entrance on the opposite end. Two Correnti, one a knight and the other a nun, carried a body that had a blue surcoat over its armour. They gently set him down onto an empty bed as Madsen dashed over to it. There was a splintered arrow sticking out of the left eye slit of his helmet. "Oh god," she murmured.

Gabriel followed her over and gasped sharply. The Correnti both bowed to Madsen as the knight said, "He yet lives, but I am afraid his injury is beyond what we can tend to. I do hope that you can deliver him. He…is a dear friend of mine." The knight lingered for a few more seconds, causing the nun to grab him by the wrist.

"Come, Brother Matvey. Trust in Her Holiness; she shall save him." After nodding halfheartedly, Matvey was led off by the nun and started helping with the other casualties.

Madsen's breathing went shallow as she stared at the 60 centimetre-long busted arrow that was sticking out of the Mended knight's face. She recognised who it was just by looking at the armour. It was Alric. It shouldn't have been able to get through the eye slit; those war-grade arrows were way too thick.

"Can anything be done?" asked Gabriel.

The engineer didn't reply. She just pulled her InSpec tablet out of her duffel and synced up with Alric's on-board diagnostics suite. There was heavy E-Gel loss…and his left optical node was reading as disconnected.

Madsen put him into hibernation and watched as the tiny twitches and movements he made slowed and vanished. "Gimme a hand with this," she told Gabriel.

Gabriel hovered over to the other side of the bed as Madsen wrapped her fingers around the arrow shaft. The knight swallowed and tightly grasped the sides of Alric's helmet. Madsen pulled and heard the soft squelching of E-Gel under the steel. Gabriel turned away. Eventually, the arrow was pulled out of Alric's head, but not before the scraping of wood on the composite skeletal frame and the tearing of synth tissue made Gabriel go pale in the face. Madsen held an insanely sharp piece of snapped, jagged wood in her hand. There was no arrowhead. It must've snapped off during the impact, which caused the shaft to splinter against the helmet. Then, since it was split in half down the middle, one side was thin enough to skim in through the eye slit. She placed the arrow on a nearby barrel, then gestured to Gabriel for him to pull the helmet off. As he reached over, Madsen noticed that the way he moved was sluggish and he winced whenever he had to stretch too far.

One of the holes on the upper cannon of Gabriel's left vambrace drew Madsen's attention. The diamond-shaped puncture went clean through the steel and she could see some dampness on the arming doublet underneath. "You've been hit."

He threw a hand up dismissively. "I am quite fine."

Madsen frowned and waved Claudia over. All things considered, she looked good. Her armour had a few dings on it but nowhere near as many as Gabriel had. Her shield probably got the brunt of it.

"Yes, Madsen?" she prompted.

"Get Gabe outta here right now and patch him up," she said sternly.

Claudia seized the knight by the shoulders and forcibly removed him from Alric's bed. "Come, ya right donkey. Lemme look at that."

Left alone with Alric, Madsen took a deep sigh and sat herself down on the side of the bed. She wrapped her fingers around his helmet then pulled it off. The entire left optic node had been crushed and split open like a nut. Madsen furrowed her brow and reached for it, her hands covered by her work gloves. With two fingers, she pinched the shattered optic node and gently manipulated it. It was only barely being held in place by the destroyed fibre connections; she felt like if she gave it the tiniest bit of additional pressure, it would've torn free. She parted some of the lacerated polymer around Alric's eye socket and saw that the arrow hadn't gone the whole way through the optic, so his SSD and CPU should be intact. Madsen shook her head and rubbed the bridge of her nose as a mix of relief and dread washed over her all at once.

All of the noise drained away and she might as well have been pulled into another dimension. First, she applied a good lathering of nano printers to patch up the E-Gel pathways, then some self-healing polymer tape to seal the wounds. As Madsen worked on disconnecting the optical node itself, pieces of the fingernail-sized circuit boards that were once inside of it had been grinded into gravel and poured out of it like salt. The sensitive datalines and fibre cables that linked it to the CPU had been shredded by the arrow shrapnel. Said optical wires were so badly mangled and sliced to the point where it didn't look like the connection points were salvageable. Fibre datalines were incredibly sensitive so if they were damaged, they had to be completely replaced...and that wasn't exactly doable without specialised resources and tools.

There had been about an hour of carefully detaching wires. Madsen's tongue poked out of the corner of her mouth as she stared so intently at the optical node that it probably should've caught fire. For some stupid reason, the thing was not designed to be removed, very much like a human eyeball. She had to carefully sever the linkages without damaging them further, or else Alric could be in excruciating pain when he came to.

Claudia's voice softly asked, "Can I be of help, Madsen?"

Finally, Madsen clipped the last data cable with her tiny set of pliers, then sighed. Thoughts raced through her mind of possible fixes. Maybe she could tear open a dead proxy and pull out its entire dataline bundle to replace Alric's...but she just didn't have the tools or the know-how to rewire something on that level. Cutting them was easy, but routing everything correctly was anything but. In other words, it wasn't her ballpark at all. She ran a hand down her face and made a fist with the other, with Alric's detached optic inside. "The fibre optic datalines–" She cut herself off and rephrased it. "The nerves connecting the eye to the brain are completely destroyed. Even if I got a donor eye, I can't...I can't fix it."

Claudia peered down at the empty socket, not looking even half as disgusted as Gabriel did. "Me brother 'ad a friend who got shot in tha eye by an arrow when 'e was out huntin'. Didn't die right away, but everyone knew what was gonna 'appen. They put 'im outta 'is misery."

Madsen huffed. "You saying we should put him out of his misery?" she joked dryly.

The woman reeled back. "I certainly *ain't* sayin' that. I'm sayin' that you saved 'is life. Is that not enough?"

"No. Not really," replied the engineer as she slammed the destroyed optical node onto the barrel, next to the arrow.

A little while afterwards, a handful of armoured figures pushed through the tent flap. At the head of the formation was Katheryn, still in full-plate aside from the helmet she had in her hand. She was flanked by Werner von Talhofen and Prince Roger, who was greeted with deep bows by most of the proxies present. Claudia gave Katheryn a quick glance up and down. "Milady."

Katheryn scoffed and rolled her optics. "Where is he?" she asked with a surprising level of calmness.

Madsen, still at Alric's side, waved at her. Katheryn paced over with purpose as Roger and Werner watched the Mended work. "W-Well…he is certainly better looking." Her voice wavered slightly. Then she cupped a hand over Alric's cheek and suddenly flashed a jittery smile. Her hand almost imperceptibly trembled as she gently squeezed her brother's face.

The engineer wiped her E-Gel drenched hands with a cloth and joined Katheryn by the bedside. She firmly grabbed Katheryn by the shoulder. "He's gonna be okay. I promise." The great duchess didn't say thank you. She didn't say anything. She didn't even look away from her unconscious brother…and quite frankly, Madsen was thankful for it. Katheryn was one of the only proxies that made her feel like a normal person and not some kind of god.

She wanted to give it some time for the nanos and polymer tape to set in before she brought him out of hibernation. In the meantime, she gave the Mended a hand with all the other proxies they were treating. She spent time patching up stab wounds, setting broken structural frames, repairing internal systems damage, and removing arrowheads from synth-tissue. As it stood, they only had one InSpec console and it was a lifesaver when it came to performing maintenance on proxies. Without it, it was a lot like surgery on humans and that wasn't the easiest thing in the world to do. The complexity of the procedures and the amount of focus they demanded took up most of her brain power. It was almost like her actual job. Almost.

About 80% of the wounded proxies that survived long enough to be seen by the Mended were able to be saved. With Madsen's heavy-duty equipment and the tips she'd given her Mended, only a handful of proxies didn't make it through maintenance. Many needed replacement parts, none of which were in short supply thanks to the thousands of corpses just outside. The Correnti on staff were absolutely astounded by what Madsen and her Mended were able to achieve. She still felt like a failure. People still died.

"Thy Holiness," said Prince Roger with a bow as he approached. "I must take this moment to praise thine actions on the battlefield. If not for thee, I fear that our cause would have been eradicated." Madsen awkwardly bowed back, not entirely sure what else she was supposed to do. "I wished to inform thee that we have secured Clthic prisoners. They shall be dealt with soon enough."

Madsen scoffed. "*Dealt with*?"

Roger squinted at her, looking quite puzzled. "Aye."

She clenched her jaw and scrunched up her fist. "You seriously aren't saying that we'll execute them? All of them?"

Her outrage promptly brought Katheryn over who tried to smooth the situation over. "We may have emerged victorious, but our resources are already worn thin. Prisoners must be fed, watered, watched, and contained. I fear that we simply do not possess the means to detain them any longer than several days. The Clthics have no interest in ransoming these men back, and even if they did, it would be unwise to restore the numbers of such an evil force." Madsen could feel tears welling in her eyes. It wasn't just the prisoners…it was everything. It all just hit her right in the gut. She shook her head, swallowed, and tried to find some argument that she could make. Anything. But nothing came to mind.

Prince Roger, with a remorseful stare at the ground, added, "I shall keep thee appraised. God bless thee, Thy Holiness." With that, he drifted out the tent.

There was a strange sensation that came with being roused awake by magic. Alric had experienced it once before and if he had to describe it, he would say that it was jarring and sudden. Usually when waking from a deep slumber, there was a period of haziness and exhaustion; a transition between the sleeping mind and the waking mind. With magic though, there was no such thing. He was asleep one second, then perfectly awake and alert the next almost as if he had missed hours of his life. It happened once again when he opened his eye and saw Madsen sitting on the edge of his bed. Her hair was horribly ruffled and messy, sticking up in all sorts of directions like a wild shrub. The whites of her strange eyes were once again laced with red lines and the skin around them was dark. He'd come to learn that those were the symptoms of a unrested sapien. Smudges of soot covered her face, primarily her nose and right cheek. She was still clad in her bright orange L/RESS garment. "H-Hey," she stammered as he came to.

Alric groaned as he sat up. His mind raced. The battle…the dragon. "Dragon…!" he cried as he feverishly glanced around. "W-Where…!?"

"It's alright!" Madsen urged as she firmly grabbed him by both shoulders. He forced his eye shut as he felt his breathing swell and turn into uncontrollable panic. "Breathe. You're okay. You're okay. It's alright." He wasn't on the field anymore. He saw the stone walls of a Hospital embracing him. Madsen's firm grip was holding him in place…so he was in fact very far from danger. "You're with me. You're safe."

Painful silence overtook them as Alric forced himself to slow his frantic breaths. He felt as if he was going to suffocate if he didn't keep panting, but it was clearly not doing him any good. However, he realised that something else wasn't quite right. His left eye was not open…and it refused to open no matter how hard he tried. Madsen wore a sombre expression as she asked, "Do you remember what happened?"

He furrowed his brow and tried, fruitlessly, to unearth the buried memories. "I-I do not."

"You were hit by an arrow. It splintered and passed through your helmet's sight." Madsen coughed and Alric had the feeling that she had done so to prevent an emotional reaction from seeping through her facade. "The connection points were so badly damaged that..." She trailed off. Memories of goose feathers brushing against his gloved hand surfaced. Then there was pain…horrible pain. The Mended knight reached up with his left hand and let his fingers slowly drift along his face. First he felt scars, then eventually, the loose skin of his eyelids hanging over an empty cavity. He was expecting to feel some kind of shock, to be horrified to have been mutilated that way…but the truth was that he did not care. Once, years ago, he most certainly would have. But there, with his fingers reaching for something that was no longer there, he realised that he could not have cared less.

"Might I see it?"

The question drained all of the colour from Madsen's face. "O-Oh. But… Are you sure?" Madsen asked.

Alric nodded in silence.

Reluctantly, Madsen reached for her PC, tapped and swiped at its surface several times, then handed it to Alric. "Okay…" What he saw projected upon its surface was his face, perfectly reflected back at him with unmatched clarity thanks to the camera. His left eye socket was deflated and marred with scarring. The damage did not make him feel any sense of horror. It was almost as if he were looking upon someone else's face.

Alric set the PC down on the bed next to him and said, "Tell me of the dragon. Where is it?"

Another voice, hoarse and low, chimed in. "She killed it." Alric peered around and saw that the room, a chamber in Wyrmsmouth's Hospital, was completely empty save for Lionel of Pathridge hunched over a burlap sack. He was gathering some belongings from a bedside table. "Struck it out of the sky as if it were a pheasant. The archers tell me that three Clthic golems lie dead in the forest as well."

"Thou slayed the beasts? *All* of them?" Alric asked her, bewildered. She shrugged and nervously scratched the back of her head.

Lionel slung the burlap sack over his shoulder and bowed to Madsen. "I must thank thee for the gracious care thou hast given my men-at-arms. I shall inform thee if any of them wish to swear themselves to the Order of The Mended. Now that I have secured their personal effects, I shall bid thee farewell for now." He made to leave, but paused for a moment. "Brother Alric."

"Yes, Sir Lionel?"

The knight grinned, making the scar on his cheek that exposed his teeth look even more grotesque. "Nice face." With that, he slipped out of the hospital.

Madsen reeled back in outrage. "Whoa, what the fuck? What the fuck was *his* problem?"

"He was once a dear friend of mine. We grew up together."

"Oh. Okay. That…makes a lot of sense, actually."

Alric was still fixated on Lionel's words. "Eileen, thou art proving to be…quite extraordinary," Alric said quietly. She essentially ignored his remark and stared solemnly at the ground. The knight whispered, "Is something the matter?"

Madsen avoided eye contact. She rubbed her bicep as she bit on her lower lip. "I just…I wanted to save you," she whispered with a trembling voice.

Alric sat up in his bed and replied, "T-Thou hast. In more ways than one. Fret not, for I shall endeavour to see the favour returned."

All of a sudden, for the first time he had ever seen, Madsen lost her temper. She erupted from her seat, scooped it up, and swung it at the stone wall. The resounding 'crack' echoed through the empty Hospital chamber before Madsen continued to ferociously stomp on the piece of furniture. Each blow filled the room with crunching, while also snapping the legs of the chair into splintered shards. Underneath the cacophony, Alric could hear Madsen growling with unbridled rage.

He stared in concerned shock as she leaned against the wall over the mess of wooden shrapnel that littered the floor. She had her forearm against the stone and her forehead pressed against it in turn. Alric stood and approached her. With her face still buried in her arm, Madsen said nothing.

He took her by the shoulders and gently turned her away from the wall. Her expression was blank, but the tears kept pouring. She appeared to stare straight through him. Madsen took a short, ragged breath, then shoved free. Alric could only watch as she paced to the other end of the room and ran a hand down her face. He swallowed and looked down. What was he to do? She was distraught...but over what? As he stood there trying to find a way to broach the subject, Madsen's breathing became more and more steady. Before long, the rhythm had become natural.

"It's been four thousand years," she finally murmured.

"Four thousand years...? Since what?"

"Since my crew got into those caskets."

At first, the words had no meaning. Four thousand years was not something anyone could truly comprehend. He had to push his mind to truly see it. In four thousand years, folk tales became history, civilisations rose and fell, religions emerged and faded, and tiny villages turned into cities. An unbearable sense of dread flooded Alric's body. "God have mercy."

Madsen turned around to face him. Her eyes glistened with tears and they melted lines into the layer of ash and soot on her face. For the first time, Alric watched her resolve falter. There was dread as clear as day in her expression as her eyelids fluttered furiously and her shimmering eyes darted about. "I-I don't know what to do," she muttered, tensing her brow. Alric could tell that it was not a feeling that she was accustomed to. "They put us under...then never woke us up." Her pained whispers eventually gave way to a furious roar. "It was just a fucking hardware test! What the fuck happened!?" She seized a wooden cabinet and flung it onto the floor. Its contents scattered across the room as Madsen continued to fume.

However, Alric heard a series of hurried footsteps echoing through the hallway. A Knight Correntis appeared in the doorway. "Your Holiness, is something the matter?"

"Leave us," Alric snapped.

"Please, allow me to assist–"

"Away with thee, knave! Immediately!"

Hesitantly, the Correntis skittered back out of sight. Alric gritted his teeth and sighed. There was nothing he could say. No words could ever dull the pain of such an unimaginable circumstance. He reached across the bed and retrieved Madsen's duffel bag. "What are you doing?" Madsen mumbled.

"Securing thy belongings so that I might escort thee back to the castle keep." Madsen scoffed in disbelief. Alric suddenly straightened his posture and held a hand up. "I shall not entertain any attempts to deny me. The least that thou canst do after tending to hundreds of lives is allowing thy friend to tend to thine." Without waiting for a reply, he retrieved some of Madsen's belongings that were laid across the bedside table and dumped them into the duffel. He then sealed the bag's peculiar zipping buckle. Madsen swallowed, closed her eyes, and very obviously fought back more tears. Alric added, "Come. Before more pests arrive to fuss over thee."

LVII
Uneasy Lies The Head That Wears A Crown

The cold morning breeze swept through Prince Roger's open pavilion, rustling the papers on his desk and the heavy fabric of Katheryn's gown. The sunlight bled through the tent's linen canvas. It resulted in a warm yellow ambience. Katheryn lounged on a velvet sofa and watched as Roger was dressed by his attendants. His bright green kirtle was secured about his waist by an engraved gold-plated belt, which his longsword and dagger were promptly looped through. An equally extravagant livery collar was fastened around his neck. Finally, his crown was placed upon his head. The young prince's eyes were sullen and a frown was permanently fixed to his face.

"A scowl ill suits thy countenance, my prince," Katheryn said with a drone.

"I shall smile when I have reason to. My father lies dead and defiled, our victory came with steep cost, and those disgusting heretics still hold a knife to the throat of all men… Not to mention the swathes of churches spitting out revenants. Certainly an opportune time for my becoming king."

The would-be king's servants dispersed and all of a sudden, his sorrow became even more apparent to Katheryn as he stood there alone in the vast pavilion. Softly, she said, "Thou darest not show this weakness to thy subjects."

"*Weakness?* To be troubled by these things is to be weak?" he spat at the duchess.

She was not deterred by his spite. "Nay. But any and all things can be skewed to be such by the treacherous."

Roger swallowed. "Thou speak as if this is a circumstance most familiar to thee."

"Perhaps," she teased. "The opportunistic cravens whom thou call vassals shall smell thy fear upon the air. In such a time of desperation, they will not follow a broken king and would instead seek to install one they believe worthy of their servitude."

"I fear my despondency may be too great to mask," Roger remarked with a shake of his head.

Katheryn frowned. "Then thou shalt soon join thy father in death." She watched Roger's face contort in shock and anger, but he did not have time to reply.

A figure passed through the threshold, casting a shadow across the pavilion's interior. The staunch frame of Sister Claudia had become instantly recognisable to Katheryn. As always, her sleeves were rolled up, exposing her forearms. "Milord. Milady."

"Peasant! What is the meaning of this?" snapped Sir Clive of Huntersford from behind Claudia. The knight, sworn to Prince Roger, stomped across the field and swept into the tent. "Thou enter the king's pavilion unannounced? Art thou a simpleton?" As Clive paced towards Claudia, she seemed as nonplussed as ever.

Katheryn said calmly, "Do not lay a hand upon this Holy Sister unless thou wish it lopped off." Clive came to a gradual halt and peered over his shoulder at Katheryn. He wore a contemptful scowl on his face. He then shot a glance at Prince Roger, who shook his own dumbfounded expression away and replaced it with a stern grimace.

"Do not force the *duchess* to repeat herself." The emphasis on Katheryn's title caused Clive's harsh facade to falter for a moment. He didn't say a word as he skulked back through the tent's entrance and vanished from sight. Claudia locked eyes with Katheryn for a moment and the latter was certain that she saw a glimmer of shock in the woman's weary eyes.

Prince Roger shook his head. "Please forgive young Clive, good Sister. How may we be of service?"

Claudia bowed very awkwardly. "Tha First Knight sent me. He wished to learn when yer presence would be expected."

"Immediately. We have idled for long enough," he barked with renewed vigour. "I shall summon my retainers at once."

The Mended Sister nodded bluntly. "Right." There was a long pause. Katheryn had to bite her lip to keep herself from snorting in amusement. "Well." Claudia coughed into her hand. "I'll be off, then, ay?" With as little fanfare as when she entered, Claudia clumsily spun on her heels and took her leave. Katheryn rolled her eyes.

Wyrmsmouth Meadow was no longer the site of a lavish tourney ground. Most of the stands, lists, and structures had been dismantled and in their place was an improvised prison. Almost a thousand captured Clthics waited like cattle for their fate to be decided. They ranged from footmen and archers to knights and lords who made the grand mistake of betraying the Church. As much as the Thestors wanted to be able to punish the religious leaders of the Clthic Synod, none of their Nuns were taken from the battlefield alive. It was not for lack of trying, though. Katheryn was told by Brother Baldwyn that the Nuns all fought ravenously to the death and even killed their own men for surrendering.

Katheryn insisted on inspecting the prisoners herself. By her side were Brother Baldwyn, Sir Lionel, Sir Caldwell, and several of her men-at-arms. She strode through the lush grass and scanned the faces of the traitors as they passed her by. Like her allies, she was expecting to see bloodthirsty brutes hellbent on the destruction of the civilised world. What she saw were just men. Women, even. It gave her pause.

"Thou best keep thy distance my lady," warned Sir Caldwell. "These barbarians would like nothing more than to savage thee where thou stand."

Baldwyn emitted a single isolated laugh then shook his head. "I would very much like to see them try. An elder vampire was no match for Duchess Katheryn the Unbending. I doubt that these starved footmen would fare any better."

Katheryn replied with a smirk, "I appreciate the vote of confidence, Brother, but thou forget that I had the assistance of a most gallant knight." The Thestor chuckled, much to the confusion of Lionel and Caldwell.

The conversation came to an abrupt end when Katheryn stopped in her tracks. Her eyes fell upon a face that was intensely familiar to her. His lilac skin was bruised and caked with dirt. The battered plate armour he wore was still covered by a lime green and gold tabard with a black crescent moon in the top left corner. The man stared emotionlessly at a patch of dirt as he slumped there on the ground, completely ignorant of Katheryn's shocked glare. She smacked her lips then hissed, "Thou hast found thyself in unsavoury company, Lord Franco."

The man's eyes suddenly snapped upward and scanned the faces of those before him. His silent rage only served to aggravate Katheyrn further. With a snort, Lionel planted a boot firmly on Franco's chest. He propelled the fallen lord backwards with so much force that he slammed onto his back. Baldwyn, with the speed of a taukumu bolt, lashed forward and seized Lionel by the bicep. "Enough!" he snapped.

Lionel ignored the holy knight's command and instead spat, "How dare thee. How dare thee betray her!"

Baldwyn throttled Lionel backwards and barked an order at his fellow Thestors. "Remove this child before he continues with this tantrum!" At once, a pair of holy knights grabbed Sir Lionel by the shoulders and escorted him away. Katheryn met eyes with him as he left, trying to silently reassure him that his words resonated with her.

Despite that agreement, she had to maintain appearances. "I must apologise for my knight's conduct, Brother Baldwyn. It is most unbecoming of a man of his stature."

"Please, my lady. Thou hast ample reason to bear ill-feelings against this traitor, but those feelings are *thine*. Sir Lionel has no right to speak of them on thy behalf. If thou wish to have words with thy disgraced vassal, I shall allow it." Baldwyn muttered. The man had become the de facto marshall of the remaining Knights Thestor and Correnti. Katheryn believed it was only a matter of time before he was officially bestowed the role and the remnant Churchsworn knights were reorganised into a new Grand Host. As Baldwyn and his men repositioned themselves, Katheryn dismissed Sir Caldwell, leaving her and Franco to relative solitude.

She stared at him in silence for a moment as he righted himself and sat up. "As thy liege, I must ask what compelled thee to forsake thine oath," she asked hoarsely.

"The Church has spread its filth far enough. I cannot abide its existence any longer." The wrath in his shaking voice was unmistakable.

"Where is the Lady Beatrice? I shall ensure that she is treated with care." As soon as the name left Katheryn's mouth, she saw a shock of pain smear itself across his face.

He spat, "Summon Brother Alric. Perhaps he could answer that question for thee." Katheryn's lower lip curled inward. She took a deep breath as Franco went on. "My wife. My brother. A household staff of men and women who had served me loyally for years. My entire retinue was blown to oblivion by that sanctimonious stain. And yet, thou think it wise to stand there and ask me to justify my decision?"

The duchess ground her teeth together. "If thou hadst brought this grievance to me, perhaps it would have been different. The Church had taken from me as well…but the manner in which thou chose to respond has disappointed me greatly."

Franco's temper cooled slightly. "Whom didst thou lose?"

"My father...and my brother. But the latter seems to have returned to me."

The lord grimaced at her. "Then clearly thou knowest nothing of my pain. I speak not in metaphors. They are all *gone*."

She felt pity for him. Such loss was more than enough to justify such drastic action...not to mention what had happened to his mother. However, he acted brashly. Even the king of Tritham could not keep the Church and her orders from punishing a heretic. If he had been shrewd...perhaps he could have succeeded in exacting revenge. But then, Katheryn would not have stood idly by as one of her vassals conspired to murder her brother...as righteous as the plot may have been.

"Katheryn?" With a jolt, she turned and looked over her shoulder. In full Velintine-style plate armour laden with the blue surcoat of the Mended, was none other than Alric. His single functioning eye was pinned on her. She was too stunned to say anything, so he promptly added, "Madsen cannot be present this day. I shall convey her wishes to the best of my ability."

Katheryn swallowed and glanced back at Franco. She watched his face go from blank to charged with fury. Even in his dilapidated plate harness, Franco moved like lightning. He erupted from the ground and barged into Katheryn. She watched his manacled hands reach for the dagger on her belt. A split second before she wrapped her hands around his wrist, she felt the weapon slip free from its sheath, then a cold swipe upward through her body. Katheryn let go and stumbled to the ground with stinging discomfort flowing outward from her torso. When she looked down and pressed a hand against her abdomen, the black mark of blood marred her palm.

She turned to see that Franco had already taken Alric to the ground. He roared furiously as he prepared the dagger for the killing stroke. Alric's eyes were glazed over as he wrestled with the wrathful lord. "Lord Franco! We have both been...deceived!" Forcing herself to her feet and drawing her bastard sword, Katheryn glared at the oathbreaker. "Thou m-must speak with Madsen! She shall explain all!" She stepped forward and brought her blade down in an arcing sweep.

There was a wet squelch and a dry crunch as the blade buried itself into Franco's unarmoured head. The steel had lodged itself halfway through the man's head, like an axe into a block of firewood. His body convulsed for a second, then the dagger fell into the dirt unceremoniously.

Katheryn released the weapon then thuggishly kicked Franco's body, causing it to topple over to one side. Alric sat up and stared at Katheryn. "God damn thee, Katheryn! He did not deserve to die!" he cried.

Katheryn dropped to one knee, wincing through the pain. Her brother peered down at her with a disgusted grimace. Judging her like she was some kind of monster. It was a look that she was no stranger to. *He* had brought Franco to such depths with his brutality…and yet there he was, chastising *her* for doing something she had no choice in doing. Her first instinct had been to tell Alric that he did not deserve to die either, but her rage at his resurgent hypocrisy mutated the words. She said, "Neither did his wife."

Alric's eyelids fluttered as he flattened his lips. Instead of striking back, he looked to one of his Mended as if he were about to issue a command, but the acolyte was already moving toward Katheryn. As they reached out for her, Katheryn spat, "Leave me be, cretin!"

"With all due respect, *milady*, I ain't no fuckin' cretin." Katheryn saw Claudia looking down at her. "Now, shut tha fuck up fer once and lemme see." Katheryn fell silent and glared daggers at Alric as Claudia knelt by her side. Her brother glared at her a moment longer, then begrudgingly turned away.

Katheryn's knights, with Sir Lionel in the lead, came jogging over to her. "My lady!" he called.

Claudia raised a hand at them. "She'll be right, just sod off and give 'er some room, ay?" The knights glanced at each other in confusion, then looked to Katheryn, who waved them off. As they receded, Lionel took a single step back and remained close by to watch his duchess with a concerned frown. She pretended not to notice. Meanwhile, Claudia tore the ruined dress open further and peered through the hole with narrowed eyes as the duchess stared at her focused expression. The only thing she could think about was the last time they spoke.

Katheryn stared straight through Claudia as her mind wandered back in time. She had started the so-called 'Maiden's War' to strike back against the system that had oppressed her…and after winning her autonomy, she was never concerned about changing said system. Instead, she became a cog in it. She looked at women the same way her father did; down her nose and with disdain…for they truly *were* weak. Otherwise, wouldn't they also have taken their freedom? There had only been one person with the gall to show her how incredibly idiotic that was.

Claudia reached through the torn clothing and gently inspected the wound. Katheryn grimaced and clenched onto the dirt beneath her. "Never learned how ta dodge in fancy lady school I see," Claudia chuckled, grabbing a vial of faerie tears and pouring it onto her calloused hand.

"Couldst thou do thy duty in silence, perchance?" Katheryn huffed.

“I’m right, thanks.” She handed the vial over to Katheryn. “Put tha stopper on fer me, will ya?”

“What manner of physician orders their patient to assist them?”

“I dunno if you noticed, but I've only got two hands.” Katheryn huffed through her nose and snatched the vessel.

As Claudia parted the shredded fabric of Katheryn’s dress and exposed the deep gash spanning across her abdomen, the duchess plugged the vial with its cork stopper. Claudia pressed her palms against the wound and an intense ache shot through Katheryn’s stomach. She inhaled sharply through clenched teeth, squeezing her eyes shut and pushing the pain down and away. She kept telling herself that it didn’t hurt. Nothing could hurt her unless she permitted it to...and such permission was not freely given.

Like a tide rolling away from the shore, the pain gradually eased. In its place, however, was a strange warmth. Katheryn finally allowed herself to open her eyes and glanced down at her wound. Just along the ridges of the torn flesh, Claudia’s fingertips were gliding softly against her skin. The heat followed her touch, as if it left a gentle burn wherever her fingers had tread.

“Thou…have my thanks,” Katheryn muttered through her teeth. It wasn’t the physical pain, but rather the need to express any kind of gratitude at all that made it so difficult.

Claudia glanced up at her in surprise, and Katheryn found herself mesmerised by how green her eyes were. Like a meadow in spring, or those green flowers that mother used to grow in her gardens. A rare thing, Ursula had said, to find a flower blooming green. Had they *always* been that green?

Claudia, swallowed, arched an eyebrow, and cocked her head. “Well, can’t say I'd expected ta get inta yer dress *that* quickly.” She moved her hand away and laughed. It was not the loud, booming, ruckus that Katheryn had heard in passing before. It was quieter, almost conspiratorial. A laugh for only Katheryn to hear.

The duchess furrowed her brow and thinned her lips. She wasn’t sure if she was meant to laugh as well, or if it meant something else...something more. She tried to find Claudia’s eyes again but they had turned back to the wound. Claudia proceeded to clean and bandage the injury as Katheryn sat there idly. “Alright, this’ll keep ya together fer now.” Finally, Claudia stood, loosened her belt, pulled her surcoat off, then handed it to the Duchess.

Katheryn swallowed and accepted the garment. She slipped it on and gave Claudia one final glance before relaxing and taking a second to breathe. The Mended Sister then turned back to her commander. They caught the last few sentences of a speech he was giving to the other knights and Mended in the area. "--and many of these folk have sought out the Clthic Synod after being wronged by corrupted servants of God. We cannot blame them for their anger. Madsen has decreed that we must offer them forgiveness."

Prince Roger came pacing through the crowd, flanked by his loyal retainers. He sent a concerned glance to Katheryn. "By God's grace… Pray tell that it is but a flesh wound."

"Don't worry, yer majesty. Ain't as bad as *that* fella," she remarked, jerking her head towards Franco's mutilated corpse.

The prince approached Alric. "This rogue assailed a noblewoman and attempted to assassinate the First Knight of the Mended. Who is to say that his brethren are not equally despicable?"

"Thy Highness, Madsen wishes for those willing to repent to be allowed a chance to do so. I was offered an opportunity to change my sinful ways; these folk must also be granted that same mercy."

Katheryn peered into Roger's eyes and she could see it. The hesitation. The sympathy. The *weakness*. It was only a matter of time before the boy collapsed and allowed Alric's naive and idiotic request. Katheryn lowered a fiery stare onto the crown prince and flexed her jaw. With Roger's attention on her, she slowly shook her head. Prince Roger suddenly cleared his throat. "If Her Holiness objected so strongly, she would be present to argue it herself."

Alric stomped up to the future king and came to a stop so close that even Roger himself was perturbed. He loomed over him with both hands clenched into trembling fists. "She is the reason that we are not charred corpses out there upon the field. Despite her divine intervention, thou wouldst insist on *defying her*? Need I remind thee that thou art but a prince. Angels need not bow to crowns."

Prince Roger's eyes lit up. Where there had been doubt mere seconds ago, Katheryn saw defiance. It took all of her self-control to keep herself from smirking. Despite being a man himself, Alric truly had no understanding of a man's ego. Katheryn had known the prince long enough to know that right or wrong would no longer matter. That act of insolence before all of his closest barons, knights, and retainers would do nothing but make him more stubborn. The young Roger kept his blazing eyes locked on Alric's and did not retreat even a single step. Still maintaining eye contact with the First Knight, he gave his men his final command. "Kill them. Kill them *all*."

LVIII
Fancy Seeing You Here

She kept a steady lock on her breathing, making sure it was rhythmic and well-paced. As her feet pounded against the dirt path and propelled her forward, she could feel the burn starting to mount in her legs. Madsen lost track of how many laps she'd done, but it didn't really matter. She had to do something. Anything. Running in circles along a river had to do. It felt like an hour maybe, but she was probably wrong.

That morning, she heard through some of the castle servants about what happened to those prisoners...and how Alric tried to argue for them even after one of them tried to kill him. As much as she wanted to be there in retrospect, she was essentially catatonic for a few days. She'd been under for over 4,000 years...and all of the realisations and emotions that came with that fact had her falling apart. Prince Roger didn't have to do a lot of convincing to have his vassals and the Thestors carry out his orders; after everything the Clthic Synod did, even the Correnti agreed that they all belonged in the ground. It was a tough situation, but feeling guilty wasn't going to change anything. It was done. She had to try to move forward.

The Serpent's Tongue flowed by on her left, while dense green forestry dangled on her right. Both sights were bouncing, blurry messes, but she still savoured what she could. She focused on everything she could see, like the leaves shaking in the wind, the twigs floating down the river, the roots of the big trees tangling up against each other, and the clouds hovering above her. After that, she focused on what she could hear, like the gentle rushing of the water, the rustling of the foliage, her thunderous footsteps in the dirt, her laboured breathing, and the slight shifting of her clothing whenever she moved.

After running along a bend in the river, Madsen came stumbling to a halt. With sweat dripping from her face, she braced her hands onto her knees and took a minute to catch her breath. When she stood back up, she took a quick glance around. Just before she was about to move on, she saw a glint of colour in the corner of her eye. Beyond the first layer of trees was a small hill and she saw a blue shape moving around on it.

Madsen eagerly paced ahead, pushing through the branches and navigating the webs of roots that ensnared the forest floor. As she got closer, she could see that the shape was Alric sitting on the crest of the hill. He starred into the distance solemnly. He was fiddling with his sheathed longsword, which he had taken off his belt and had resting on his lap. He was wearing what he usually wore when he wasn't in armour. Madsen had recently learned that it was called a bliaut; a medium length dress-like garment with wide sleeves. The one Alric owned was cloud white. Over the top of it was his blue Mended surcoat.

As she mounted the hill, she shoved her hands into her tracksuit jacket's pockets. The crunching of grass under her feet as she walked was enough to get Alric's attention. He shot to his feet with one hand on the grip of his sword and the other on its scabbard. "Hey, easy, buddy."

Alric rolled his one good optic and relaxed his posture. "What in Heaven's name art thou doing out here?"

"I've been going on morning runs. It helps, you know…get my mind off things." She peered at his optic, trying to do a quick visual inspection of the thing for any signs of fault. "How's the optic node doing? Any problems?"

Madsen's nose almost touched Alric's face as she squinted at the part. He swallowed and started fiddling with his surcoat. "I-I suppose it is functioning as one would expect it to."

"Whaddaya mean you 'suppose'?"

"I have never lost an eye before, Eileen."

"Okay, okay, c'mere and lemme have a closer look." Madsen reached over and gently pulled Alric's 'eyelids' open. He grumbled, but didn't try to stop her. "Look up for me. Then down." The surface of the optic sensor looked fine and it darted around like normal. "Look at me."

"Must we do this *now*?" He scoffed.

"Just fucking look at me."

With a sharp exhale, Alric made eye contact with Madsen. The optic had no issues with tracking her as she shifted to the left and right. As she pulled away, she snapped, "Okay, geez, was that so hard? Everything seems nominal."

With a subtle arching of his brow, Alric quipped, "That would be because the arrow struck my *other* eye."

"Hey, dummy, I just wanted to make sure this one's okay. Losing both of them doesn't sound like a lot of fun."

The two of them lowered themselves onto the grass and there was a peaceful pause. It gave her a few minutes to take in the beautiful view. She could see Wyrmsmouth and the coastline beyond the forest. The tide drawing in then receding over and over again hypnotised her for a bit. For that short amount of time, her mind let go of all the pain. "It seems moot for me to ask if thou art well, but I simply must," he said quietly.

As she ran a hand through her sweat-drenched hair to slick it back, she sighed. She wanted to answer him. She wanted to say *something*...but she couldn't. Every time she opened her mouth, silence came out. The same memories kept playing back in her head. She kept seeing her mom...hearing her voice. Dreaming about her. The pain was mounting again...but then Madsen felt something drifting across her skin. She glanced down with a jolt and saw Alric's hand resting on top of hers. "I...still don't know what I'm supposed to do."

"We proxima cannot exist without first being *built*. Our very presence is proof that the sapiens still walk this place. We shall seek them out and demand thee returned home."

She let go of his hand. "That's...not what I want right now," she said sternly.

Suddenly, Alric set his sword down beside him. "This place does not deserve thee, Eileen. I cannot bear for thee to spend another second in this twisted, Godforsaken mistake. Thou art not a piece of meat to be squabbled over by the Church and the Clthic Synod." She watched as the artificial muscles in his jaw and brow flexed in anger.

"And I'm not the only one that doesn't deserve to be here. None of you do."

There was this look of pained reluctance on his face. "Eileen... Thou *must* leave this place."

Madsen grabbed his shoulder, and got right into his face and snapped, "I'm not doing this right now. You can try to push me away as much as you want, but it isn't gonna work. So, *listen*." His single optic darted between each of Madsen's eyes. "M-My mom's gone. My friends are gone. If ISEC even sent a rescue mission, it would've taken no longer than a month to arrive here. So they aren't even looking. Meanwhile, the Clthic Synod needs to be stopped. Your creators need to be stopped."

"Thou do not understand." His voice became harsh. "'Tis not only the Clthic Synod that thou shouldst fear. At any moment, anything thou hast said or done, anything that thou couldst say or do, can be skewed by the Church into evidence of devilry. It would be all too easy; thou couldst be described as a *fallen angel*, as the Devil was. Canst thou not see? They could turn on thee at any second. Thou hast no true allies here."

Her eyebrows tightened. "I have *you*." Suddenly, Alric pushed to his feet and paced a few steps away in exasperation. He stood there with his hands on his hips and glared into thin air. "I-I don't think I would've been able to deal with all of this without you," she admitted. She watched him freeze. His expression went soft and he released a faint exhale. The day she found out about how long she'd been in stasis for…she couldn't remember most of it. It was a blur. Some of the few things she could recall was Alric sneaking her out of the Hospital, coming up with alibis to explain her absence, and leaving food at the door for her while making sure no one came to see her until she came out on her own.

He turned back around and took a step closer, not breaking eye contact with her. "A dear friend of mine once taught me a vital lesson; thou and thou alone art in control of what thou art capable of. Although others may lead us…ultimately, they are not to thank for our accomplishments. So please…do not congratulate me."

Madsen stared into his optic and felt her heart thrum a little harder and a little faster. She got up and approached him. Not too long ago, whenever she looked at him, she might as well have been trying to decipher hieroglyphics. His face was a bizarre amalgamation of artificial musculature, synthetic tissue, and layers of polymer membrane. As foreign and alien as it was, it was slowly becoming more and more legible. She could see the confidence in his expression as he spoke to her. His jaw was firm. She got lost following the wrinkles that ran along his jowls and framed his optics. It became obvious that the crease in the middle of his brow was there because he furrowed it so much. She couldn't understand how she had trouble recognising him in the past…because his face seemed so…one of a kind. Somehow, as unscientific and dumb as it was for her to acknowledge, she knew there was a person in there. A mind. One as vulnerable and fragile as hers.

"Sounds like a pretty smart person," Madsen said under her breath with a smirk. She linked her fingers through his and savoured the warmth that radiated from his hand.

Alric huffed and couldn't quite look her in the eye. "Indeed."

Prince Roger's party was preparing to depart Wyrmsmouth and ride to Elthomshire, where he would be crowned King of Tritham. Katheryn sat atop the battlements of her city's castle wall with her legs dangling off the side. She watched the tiny people in the distance as they packed up their tents and readied their horses for travel.

Katheryn picked up a twig that must have blown over during the strong wind on the day before. She twirled it between her fingers, snapped it in half, then threw it off the side of the wall. The war with the Clthics had only just begun. There would be more atrocities. But the fight would not be impossible. The Churchsworn *did* emerge victorious. With thanks in no small part to Madsen and her angelic intervention. Perhaps there was hope…and it lay in the arms of God. The callous master that she had been told despised her since the day of her birth.

Footfalls on stone made Katheryn roll her eyes. Was a moment of peace too much to ask for? Evidently. She kept her eyes on the horizon and watched the clouds drift across the sky. Eventually, the footfalls swelled in volume, then stopped. Katheryn's head snapped around and she beheld her brother. He stared hauntedly at her as she narrowed her eyes. "Here he cometh, to mar my splendid day with his loathsome stench. Hath he a reason for inflicting me with his presence?"

An exhausted sigh answered her…and it was one that she had heard countless times during her childhood. For much of their lives, Alric had been a bull-headed, stubborn, short-tempered, narrow-minded brute. Before that though, he was a soft-spoken and anxious boy who would rather bury his nose in a book than do anything else. She had thought that boy lost forever…but as much as his reappearance shocked her, the affair with Franco still embittered her. "Curious, I seem to recall asking a question. Such things typically call for a *response.*"

Still, Alric did not take the bait. He crossed his arms and huffed. The silence was infuriating. Being actively ignored was something that Katheryn could not stand at all. It had happened enough in her younger years and she had vowed to never allow it to happen again. She ground her teeth as she leapt from her perch upon the wall. "By God's bones, if thou insist on standing there and staring at me like a sad dog, I cannot guarantee that I will have strength enough to resist throwing thee from the battlements."

"I am sorry, Katheryn." The words were followed by a paralysing chill that swept through Katheryn's veins like icy water. Her eyelids fluttered and she jerked her head back.

"What is the meaning of this?"

"I feel as if I could have done more for thee. I could have been there when father… I could have done something. Anything." The mere mention of that time in her life…the reminder of how often her father would strike her… Her throat suddenly became dry.

Katheryn forced her eyes shut as she stammered, "S-Stop." She was certainly expecting him not to listen, but his voice instantly fell silent. She felt tears forming on the edge of her still-shut eyes. Her steely facade washed away and for the first time since they were children, Katheryn spoke to her brother in her natural voice. "Thou wert but a child," she rasped. She had almost forgotten what she really sounded like. It was soft and hollow. It disgusted her. It was weak.

"As were thee," Alric muttered.

When Katheryn opened her eyes, she saw her brother reach for his longsword and pull it from his belt, scabbard included. She had memorised each and every feature of its construction. The circular pommel, the crescent crossguard, the dark chestnut wood of its grip. As she stared at it, the memories of mother teaching her to wield it flashed through her mind. Alric said sombrely, "The truth is that I was too afraid to reject it when father offered it to me. I was too afraid to do a great many things. I am *tired* of being too afraid, Katheryn." Alric dropped to one knee, bowed his head, and offered the blade up to Katheryn.

The duchess felt all warmth leave her body as her eyes latched onto the sword. In her voice that erred on a whisper, Katheryn snapped, "G-Get up."

"Katheryn…"

"Get up!"

"Take the blasted sword. Or must I hurl it at thee?" Alric's voice was laced with a fine layer of mischief. Katheryn reached out and snatched the sword out of his hands. As he stood, Alric arched an eyebrow and quipped, "Now…was that so difficult?"

"This is some idiotic scheme, isn't it? A jest?" Katheryn murmured.

"Nay. It was always meant to be thine."

Katheryn's lip quivered and she felt tears running down her cheeks. "By the Devil's *fucking* beard…!" she snarled as she furiously palmed them away. The…odd behaviour that Alric was exhibiting. She had thought him insufferable *before*. All of a sudden, she wished that he had never changed. He seemed to be quite amused by her frantic reaction, however.

In the seconds that followed, she gazed upon Ursula's sword with a rueful frown. With it resting in her grasp, she felt that the balance was off ever so slightly and the grip was ill-suited to the size of her hands. Once, the sword had been a symbol of her mother's resilience in the face of ever-present peril. However, in serving Alric for decades, it had transformed into something else entirely. It had an added weight to it that Katheryn could feel the moment she laid her hands upon it, as if the blade itself was haunted by years of servitude to a cruel God. Alric had tainted it...and Katheryn hated him for it. Yet he had also returned it to her of his own accord, and despite the poison he had injected into the sword's hilt with his touch, she swore that she could still feel her mother buried somewhere inside it. Muted and weak, but reaching for her. She whispered, "For a time, I cursed her for ever teaching me to wield this. Why should I learn so many things that I could never put to use?"

"Clearly thou hadst found a way. And perhaps she knew thou wouldst."

Katheryn loosened her belt and removed the blade that was already slung in it. "I suppose I cannot permit thee to gallivant around without a weapon. Here." She tossed it through the air and Alric snatched it rather gracefully. "A bastard sword for a bastard boy."

Alric grinned as he looped the blade onto his belt, leaving Katheryn to watch him in silence. No matter how many times she tried to rehearse the words in her mind, they never felt right. After a while, she simply scoffed and threw herself towards him. She wrapped her arms around him and rested her chin onto his shoulder. "Clod."

"Harlot."

LIX
THE GREAT LIE

The day the defeated Clthic army returned to camp was a disheartening one indeed. None of the golems walked alongside the few surviving Tethspeakers and K'relvic Nuns. S'teinel no longer blotted out the sky. Franco was nowhere to be seen…but Servius had survived. Half a dozen arrows were jutting out from several gaps in his plate armour, but he walked with his head held high. Mother Xalt'n did not share his optimism. Even from her place in the middle of the crowd, Fiammetta could feel the anguish in the Matriarch's soul. Sensing such defeat in Xalt'n's perfect form brought the former lady-in-waiting to anger. She did not deserve disappointment.

The process of breaking camp was done hurriedly. People became blurs as they secured supplies, folded up the tents, and saddled their steeds. Despite the clamour, Fiammetta could not join them. She did not belong with the rabble, collecting water, cooking meals, and tidying the camp. In her dreams, she saw the look of terror in Shaun Carver's eyes. She heard the frantic, desperate screams of those people she had set alight. It all made her tremble with excitement. She knew that she had a higher calling…and it was that calling which brought her to the heart of the Witch Den, where the Baptism tent was being dismantled.

Several commonfolk were loading wagons with demonic tools loaded in smooth grey boxes as Fiammetta approached. Commanding their efforts was H'vrsh, who seemed more concerned with the safety of the artefacts than the wellbeing of the workers. He did not even notice Fiammetta; he was too busy eyeing his couriers like a hawk. "Dread Priest, might I have a moment of your time?"

H'vrsh gave her one passing glance, then turned his focus away. "I am afraid not. Unless you wish for the Churchsworn to swarm upon us, I suggest that you assist us in making ready to depart."

Fiammetta straightened her posture and clasped her hands together. "I wish to be Baptised."

That bold claim was enough to snatch H'vrsh's full attention. His wolf skull face had its pulsing eyes transfixed on her. "I beg your pardon?"

“I have proven myself a devoted servant. I wish to help bolster the dwindling number of witches by–”

“You have proven *nothing*,” spat H’rvsh with a rare mild outburst of emotion. Fiammetta’s neck tensed and her face twitched. “To make such a demand is sacrilegious. I shall ignore this transgression and allow you to leave unpunished.”

Fiammetta’s eyes drilled into H’rvsh’s skull. “Why?”

“Do you think me a fool? You are driven by passion!” He spat the words like viscous poison that splattered across Fiammetta’s face, making her jolt and reel back. “You did not smite those apostates in the name of your faith! It was an excuse. You *craved* their deaths. That is why you are unworthy.”

Her eyelids fluttered. It wasn’t true. She…believed. Didn’t she? She fought hard to get herself to see the truth, but all she felt was the tingling that travelled down her neck when she straddled that helpless man and sliced his throat open. He was helpless before her…the way *she* had been helpless her entire life. She wanted to feel it again. The Dread Priest crept forward and leaned in so that his breath washed against Fiammetta’s ear. “I see how you defile the Matriarch with your gaze. Not only do you lust for her…you envy her. You both long to touch her…and wish to be her. This vain depravity makes you as ill-suited for the Baptism as any of those twisted vampires.”

Fiammetta bit her lip and felt her arms tremble. Where she expected to feel irrepressible fury, she instead felt overwhelming intoxication and anticipation. Xalt’n’s purity…her confidence…her strength… In the Matriarch’s presence, Fiammetta felt valuable. Insurmountable. She wanted to belong to her…and share in her beauty. There was only one person standing in her way. And so, without rage and instead with a feverish excitement, Fiammetta reached into her belt, removed a solid iron mace, then swung it at H’vrsh’s head.

The screams of the commoners were muted as Fiammetta watched the pieces of H’vrsh’s skull separate into hundreds of tiny shards. They drifted through the air, twirling like dancers. When his body hit the ground, the rest of the skull had shattered against the dirt. His brain, eyes, and throat were scattered there amongst the field of bone. His fingers twitched and his legs jerked back and forth. Fiammetta’s heart thrummed faster and faster as she absorbed the laboured death throes. She clutched the hem of her dress as her shallow breathing turned into laboured panting.

Fiammetta slipped out of her dress, tossed it aside, then lowered herself by the remains of H'vrsh's head. She tenderly ran a hand along his still whirring brain with one hand, and lifted the arcane pendant from his neck with the other. As she slung it around her own neck, she bit her lower lip and slammed H'vrsh's brain against the ground until it became a bent, crumpled mess.

Mother Xalt'n braced her hands on the table and closed her eyes. She took a deep breath as her affirmations cycled through her mind once more. *This 'anger' is not real. It is an illusion. This 'sadness' is not real. It is an illusion.* She expelled a gravelly breath, then repeated the process. For the Clthic Synod's first true failure to be such a catastrophic one had caused a relapse of the Great Lie in her mind. If she still had a human face, it would have been warped in a permanent scowl. Three golems, the great dragon S'teinel, Marshal Franco, and almost ten-thousand soldiers. All squandered.

The Clthic Matriarch stood up and straightened her posture. She would have to quench the false feelings that tempted her. She was but an unfeeling instrument through which the Devil's truth would be funnelled. All that mattered was that the Synod had to continue forward despite the setback.

"I shall return to my coven and ensure their cooperation," Servius said sternly. "As soon as they learn of Viktoria's demise, they will be at each other's throats in a mad scamper to take her place as our leader." Xalt'n turned and saw the vampire knight with his arms crossed, leaning against one of the shelter's wooden supports. If Servius had been a lesser man, he would have either died or ran for his life. Instead, he helped ensure that the entire army was not lost. Of the fourteen-thousand that set out for Wyrmsmouth, five-thousand had returned.

Xalt'n balled her hands into fists. "Have you ever heard of any mere mortals killing an elder vampire, Servius?"

He shook his head.

"I have a suspicion…and it is rousing the Great Lie within me," she admitted shakily. "Perhaps the one called Madsen was never a demon. Perhaps she is as the Churchsworn say. An angel."

Servius scoffed. "But your faith would have us believe that God and the Heavens are but a fabrication to keep us fearful and under heel."

"Yes. Because we had not been presented proof of their existence. Now, we have seen *three* golems, a dragon, and an elder vampire all killed in unison. Madsen must be responsible. She *did* resist when you found her in the Pale Spire, did she not?"

The vampire sighed. "She had been worryingly ignorant of your teachings, but I had thought it to be the influence of that Godslave."

Xalt'n's eyes scoured the ground. "The Father has seen our uprising and he is seeking to quell it. We cannot permit him to succeed."

Servius walked over to her, his armour clacking as he did. "You have my loyalty. In my one thousand years of life, I have seen that this world is nothing but a ceaseless, repeating cycle of death, destruction and despair. The sooner we return to the direct control of the Devil, the better. For all of us."

"I was concerned that you were a non-believer, Servius. But this loss has reminded me that as much as we strive to erase emotion from our minds, it is a sickness not easily treated. We all shall have our moments of weakness."

Servius took one last look at Xalt'n over his shoulder before he left. "Until next we meet, Mother Xalt'n."

The structure Xalt'n stood in was a simple wooden shelter; a roof suspended on a series of wooden struts and open on every side. She watched through the heavy rain as camp was broken and the Clthic Synod prepared to regroup. Xalt'n did not think it necessary before, but the loss at Wyrmsmouth made it clear. Using the Infernal Forge to simply spread Enlightenment was not enough. She was going to have to make pilgrimage to it…and take advantage of its full potential.

Footfalls garnered Xalt'n's attention. The sight that awaited her there in the rain made her quake. Fiammetta walked through the downpour. The only thing on her body was one of the sacred pendants, the kind that Xalt'n herself had entrusted only to her Tethspeakers. Their magic could be funnelled into the faithful to shed the chains of pain, allowing them to survive the ascetic flaying that would otherwise kill them. While Xalt'n watched the rain break against Fiammetta's uncovered form, she realised that she did not shiver out there in the cold. She did not even blink as the beads of water trickled over her face. The false sensations had been cast off…because she had used the pendant on herself. With that single act of defiance, she had broken the sacred covenant of the witch cults and undermined Xalt'n's entire doctrine. It was heresy of the highest order. So why did Xalt'n suddenly find her so much more intoxicating?

Xalt'n had to remind herself that she was just an object; a tool. But even for her, there was no denying the desire that she felt in her veins. Her eyes were pulled down the length of Fiammetta's half-burned body and she felt a vicious buzzing work its way through her.

Fiammetta's face was blank as she came to a halt inches from Xalt'n. She held a dagger out in front of her chest…then pressed it into her flesh. She did not break eye contact as she drew it down past her breasts, along her abdomen, and into her groin. Xalt'n failed to keep a shaky exhale from echoing out, and it seemed to make Fiammetta even more eager. With a massive incision stretching from her collarbone down to her genitals, Fiammetta cocked her head and playfully fondled the lips of the freshly sliced skin with a single finger. Blood flowed down her body to her groin, and slowly yet steadily dripped beads onto the ground. The gentle tapping of the droplets was muted by the heavy rainfall.

Xalt'n reached out, grabbed the edges of the massive gash…and ripped it open. The wet and almost deafening sounds of tearing and squelching made Fiammetta widen her eyes and gasp. With the false skin peeled open, the Matriarch laid eyes upon Fiammetta's exposed and glistening musculature. With every movement Fiammetta made, the bands of tendon twitched and flexed. Like they were beckoning her. Begging for her.

Like a poised snake, Xalt'n lashed forward and buried her teeth into the naked sinew on Fiammetta's chest. She could taste the blood and feel each individual strand of muscle as she caressed them with her tongue. Her teeth sank deeper and deeper into the tissue. All the while, she relished Fiammetta's sharp yelp of shock. As Xalt'n reared her head away, she made sure to do so at a tantalisingly slow pace. The meat in her mouth stretched, stretched, and stretched off of Fiammetta's body…until it began to string itself apart. She screamed with excitement. Xalt'n, with her shoulders rising and falling with each shallow breath she took, stared into Fiammetta's eyes with indescribable thirst. She turned her head and spat the piece of flesh onto the floor before snatching the knife from Fiammetta's hand.

For an hour, Mother Xalt'n furiously sawed and carved the skin from Fiammetta's quivering body. The pleasure she saw in the aspirant's face only fed her own enjoyment. By the time the ritual was complete, the peeled and chopped skin sat in a sloppy pile at Xalt'n's side. Fiammetta looked down at herself and ran the fingers of both hands along her sternum. Her face had been left unscathed for the time being…for Xalt'n still wanted to make use of it. Fiammetta smiled and panted as her tongue drew itself across her lips. The ecstasy…the arousal in her eyes… Xalt'n could contain herself no longer. She lunged forward and seized Fiammetta's head by the sides. "You are a blight upon me. You tempt me…you force me to feel these accursed things. I had banished the Great Lie from my mind…and then *you* arrived." The Matriarch unfurled her tongue, pressed it against the burnt side of Fiammetta's face, and dragged it upward. She tasted sweat, blood, and dirt on her disciple's face. When she drew back, she saw Fiammetta's eyes shimmering with delight. "I can no longer ignore you. And neither can *they*."

www.ingramcontent.com/pod-product-compliance
Lightning Source LLC
LaVergne TN
LVHW050911080826
845145LV00001B/47

* 9 7 8 1 7 6 3 7 5 3 6 8 6 *